"A gorgeously written b___ ___ ___ ___ beyond doubt. Come for the prose, and stay for the murders."
—*USA Today*

"A classic page-turner that would make a fine companion to a towel and beach chair, but also delves deeper into modern paranoia regarding money, class, and sexuality."
—*Newsday*

"Bollen keeps you guessing until the end of this intriguing, fatalistic novel."
—*Miami Herald*

"Christopher Bollen's *Orient* might well be this summer's most ambitious thriller or this summer's most thrilling work of literary fiction. There's a smorgasbord of delights in *Orient*, from its murderous plot to the cheeky fun Bollen has at the expense of the art world. And there is ample room in this expansive novel for surprisingly soulful descriptions of everything from the intricacies of beekeeping to the beauty of deer hunting. Most impressive is how Bollen's book is rich in literary diversions, moments of keen sociological and emotional insight—often into personal isolation—that transcend the conventions of its story."
—*Los Angeles Times*

"Engrossing. . . . The characters are drawn in vivid detail, and the atmosphere is thickly enveloping."
—*New York Times*

"This is beach reading that's as intelligent as it is absorbing."
—*People*

"The test of a thriller is arguably in the resolution, and *Orient*'s is satisfyingly tense. The guessing game takes in the whole community, all well-drawn, and all with motives to kill."
—*Financial Times*

"*The Great Gatsby* meets Donna Tartt. Suspenseful, beautifully written, and wonderfully atmospheric, *Orient* is that rare treat that is both a page-turner and a book you will want to savor."
—Philipp Meyer

"A book of real intelligence and line-by-line dexterity."
—*Chicago Tribune*

"Bollen takes a real place—the North Folk of Long Island—and weaves a mesmerizing fictional web of characters and mysteries into a story that is as viscerally thrilling as it is intellectually precise."
—*BookPage*

"Thrilling and suspenseful with subtle shots of hijinks hilarity, this book will have you feeling like you can't possibly turn the pages fast enough."
—Elle.com

"The quaint seaside village of Orient is not as pleasant as it seems, and Christopher Bollen will hold you spellbound as he reveals its secrets. A truly well-crafted and literate murder mystery that recalls the worlds of both P. D. James and *Twin Peaks*."
—Nelson DeMille

"The writer keeps us guessing about the perpetrator(s) behind the murders until the last chapter, but it is the placement of the story in such a well-detailed, realistic environment that separates *Orient* from most other books in the genre."
—CT News

"*Orient* is a taut and elegant suspense novel about strangers and strangeness, suspicion and forgiveness, reinvention and confession."
—Joshua Ferris, author of *To Rise Again at a Decent Hour*

"*Orient* is a compelling novel of tragic suspense. Bollen has a gift for tightly drawn characters and an ominous sense of place."
—A. M. Homes

ORIENT

ALSO BY CHRISTOPHER BOLLEN

Lightning People

ORIENT

A NOVEL

CHRISTOPHER BOLLEN

HARPER PERENNIAL

NEW YORK • LONDON • TORONTO • SYDNEY • NEW DELHI • AUCKLAND

HARPER ⬤ PERENNIAL

A hardcover edition of this book was published in 2015 by HarperCollins Publishers.

P.S.™ is a trademark of HarperCollins Publishers.

FIRST HARPER PERENNIAL EDITION PUBLISHED 2016.

Designed by Renato Stanisic

Map by Nick Springer, Springer Cartographics, LLC

Library of Congress Cataloging-in-Publication Data has been applied for.

ISBN 978-0-06-232996-7 (pbk.)

16 17 18 19 20   OV/RRD   10 9 8 7 6 5 4 3 2 1

FOR GEORGE

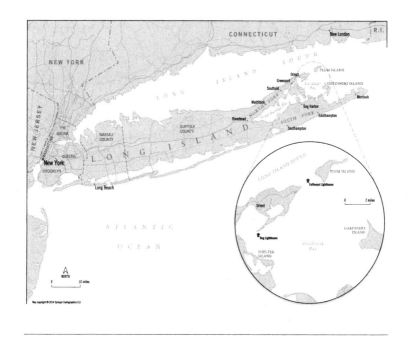

*Long Island (showing Orient, Plum Island, and Gardiners Island)
and inset map of Orient*

The invention of the ship was also the invention of the shipwreck.

—Paul Virilio

Prologue

This is how I first saw you, Long Island, on a map in the front seat of Paul Benchley's car. Like the body of a woman floating in New York harbor. It still amazes me that no one else sees the shape of a woman in that island sprawled along the coastline, her legs the two beach-lined forks that jut out to sea when the land splits, her hips and breasts the rocky inlets of oyster coves, her skull broken in the boroughs of New York City. Even now, when I close my eyes and try to picture the place where all the trouble happened, I see her drifting there in the waters of the east.

When people try to picture me, they undoubtedly recall only the last time they saw me, just before I went missing. There's been a lot of speculation about the night I left the far North Fork of Long Island—how a nineteen-year-old wanted for questioning in a string of murders managed to elude police and vigilant local drivers, both parties hurrying too slow through the pale marsh frost and winter Sound winds that turn the coast beds into grisly scrap yards of ice. That part is simple: I ran. What seems lost, in the growing storm of blame, is how I got there in the first place.

I don't expect you to believe the goodness of my intentions. I have learned too late a lesson about life in the better parts of America—that it takes merciless, distrusting, miserly acts in order to live an ordinary life. I came to Orient at tail end of summer, and I went by the name Mills Chevern. I arrived mostly innocent. Do you remember seeing me on those last warm days?

The air-conditioning in Paul's car spewed balmy tunnel exhaust as I traced my finger over the island on the map. Obviously, I didn't mention that it looked like a body to Paul; he might wonder if I'd lost my mind, and at that point Paul Benchley had few clues about the working of my mind to go on. Instead I kept my mouth shut and studied the halting traffic of the Midtown Tunnel. The truth is, I'd never known that land existed out in the Atlantic beyond the city. As a native of the West, I'd dreamed of the East since childhood, and I'd always imagined the country ending right there among the skyscrapers. But there is land, a hundred miles of it, beyond.

It was Paul who decided we should get out of town early that morning. "Weekend traffic," he said, with the special fatigue reserved for the topic. "Weekends keep getting longer just to account for it." We cleared the tunnel and the tollbooth and fought the sun that greased the windshield. Soon enough we were out in its stretch, a straight shot of expressway through warm and ravaged Long Island. One mall was alive and blinking, but the next was a ghost town of discount mausoleums, as if all the life-forms here had withered into asphalt. I pictured the ghosts of prudent shoppers haunting those silent, lacquered halls. The island's main harvest was parking lots; they grew thick around the off-ramps, thick as the trees that guided the highway and gave riders a sense of the wilderness that must once have covered the island from shoulder to foot.

Still, even today it is not entirely tame. We passed Wall Street traders in Budweiser-red Porsches and swerving out-of-state minivans, and I felt the heavy bass of radios in my teeth. We wove so quickly along those four eastbound lanes, opting mostly for the HOV, that I didn't bother to tell Paul how hungry I was, and every turnoff blurred by us as an afterthought. As the signs reading AT-TRACTIONS grew sparser and emptier, the sunlight picked through the dense Atlantic clouds, and, for a few minutes on those last speeding turns, we glowed. We took the Long Island Expressway to its last exits, and while most of the cars threaded south at the splitting, off to the Hamptons, we went north to Orient.

Paul had taken me out of the city to save me—those were his words. And I'll admit I needed saving. I had hitchhiked all the way from California locked in cars with strangers, but now in Paul's Mercedes I was anxious. His knuckles skimmed my knee as he maneuvered the stick, and I kept a lookout for train stations in case my nerves got the better of me.

On a thin, red artery of a county road, the last footprints of city life disappeared. Tiny private gas stations were already shuttered for the off-season. Apple orchards and vineyards blanketed the fields; between them, blue pines rolled their coats in the wind. I counted telephone poles—later, they would be decorated with my picture— and worried how many more there would be, leading us through vacant farmland. Paul licked his lips and smiled. "Peaceful, isn't it?" he said. I put my fingers on the door handle and looked back at the road, one long, black carpet to New York being yanked from under our wheels, and for the first time I could remember I was frightened to be traveling east.

I had lived in Manhattan for five months, first on the couches of friends I had known back west, then on the floors of acquaintances whose bad habits began at midnight and who threw blankets over their windows at the first tremors of dawn. I can still remember the panic on those mornings when the muscular lights of the city bleached into the mineral blue of the sky, and all the promises I had told myself at 1:00 and 2:00 and 5:00 A.M. tasted bitter and stale in my throat.

On the day Paul finally intervened, I was barely forming sentences, slumped in the hallway of his Chinatown apartment building. He lived next door to an acquaintance of mine, and we had exchanged small talk several times in the foyer of his building. I was new enough to New York to include a bit of recent history with my hellos, and Paul was old enough in New York to understand why a kid wearing the same dirty T-shirt would come banging on his neighbor's door so often. On that day, when Paul practically stumbled over me on his third-floor landing, he hardly recognized the grime-streaked teenager crouching like a gargoyle at his door.

He let me into his apartment, poured me lemony water, and offered me his phone, though I waved it off. "I'm not really like this," I kept repeating, but for a while I refused to say what I was like. Paul turned his sofa into a sickbed, and I stayed there until I shook out my shakes and my constant sweat soaked his cushions. I made sure to fall asleep before he could find subtle excuses to kick me out. In the morning, I showered, washed his dishes, and scoured the top of his stove. "You didn't have to," he said, squinting in disbelief to find both me and his apartment cleaner than he'd left us. "Yeah, I did. I'm good at helping." That's when I told Paul what I was like: mixed up in drugs, at bad ends, for sure, but someone who could straighten out if he managed to find his footing. Someone, I told him, who could be all right. After a long talk, he suggested that I get some distance from the city and come with him to help fix up his weekend house.

I repeat: it was not my idea to come this far east. But east sounded right, and I agreed. *Orient.* It still sounds beautiful, or would if I didn't know any better.

We gutted through the low, mud pastures. Roadkill bloodied the pavement, squirrels or maybe even family dogs that now served as meat for hawks that spiraled away at the approach of our car. Paul glided us through country bends as if they were as familiar as the curves of his signature. His face was kind-looking even in profile, with distinguished wrinkles and a brown mustache eaten gray at the edges. And he was generous in filling the lulls in conversation. He babbled on about the great native tribes that once roamed these fields, their gods all forgotten by now; from the looks of the empty A-frame churches we passed, tagged in weeds and crumpling under aluminum steeples, it seemed we'd done a decent job of forgetting our own.

I could taste the salt in the air before I saw the sea. After twenty minutes of wineries and cow barns, the boarded-up motels gradually gave way to open hotels with vacancies. Strip malls narrowed the view. Then suburban homes made their claim until they lost their lawns, and it all dropped off, so suddenly it almost hurt, into water.

We drove over the causeway. Each window was flooded with the reflection of water, so white I was scared when Paul let go of the steering wheel. Grabbing the map, he pointed to the sliver of road between the Long Island Sound and Gardiners Bay, and tapped the isolated landmass.

"That's Orient," he said.

"It looks like a bird," I replied, noticing how the land fattened out and then thinned to a beak. Not a predatory bird, like those road hawks. More like a small grouse or sparrow trying to lift off to fly east into the sky of the light blue Atlantic.

"Most of us think it looks like a flame," Paul said. "That's probably because of the lighthouse at the tip that the historical board is so proud of. I'll take you there. If you want to see it, that is."

"It's a bird," I repeated. Paul didn't know, I suppose, that I was something of an expert on Rorschach tests. All foster kids are. He didn't know much about my background—who I came from; why my family made their home in California; the eyes or mistakes of my mother and father—and for that matter, neither did I. I was never burdened with that information. But now you understand why I went with Paul so easily. I have always been up for adoption. I like to think I saved many California homes from foreclosure in my childhood due to the monthly checks the owners pooled in to shelter me.

The car slowed into a thicket of trees beyond the causeway. Lawns reappeared, along with two-story clapboard houses and faded porches with faded children's Big Wheels. Day care at a nearby elementary school let out, sending a swarm of tiny, rain-slickered bodies wandering across the street. They were the only things moving, besides the branches overhead. Even the sailboats docked in driveways were as still as held breath. As Paul stopped and waved at the crossing guard, I stared out the window at Orient.

It frightened me, this kind of raw innocence so close to the city, like the feeling of the temperature falling too fast.

It is hard for me to picture those first days without seeing the madness that was to follow. I realize now that the deaths in Orient would have happened whether I had made my way east or not. They were like matchsticks in a book waiting neatly to be ripped and burned. They remind me of something I'd heard years ago from one of my foster-care buddies, a twelve-year-old pyromaniac. "Everything burns," his girlish voice sang. "So you might as well learn how to handle it."

If I had stayed in New York City, I might have committed all sorts of unspeakable crimes. Instead I came to Orient and left two months later guilty of nothing more than trying to save myself. What else can I tell you that you won't believe? That I saw the killer's face the night I left? I did. I held a flare into the darkness and saw a face so familiar that anyone might pass it on the sidewalk and not blink an eye. They might even say hello.

I know it doesn't matter who I accuse. You have already decided who is responsible. You know by now that Mills Chevern isn't my real name. I picked it up on my way east and took it as my own. I will leave that name here with you now. I've cut and dyed my hair and removed my earring. The only feature I can't change is my gray front tooth, but I don't expect to be smiling much. Where am I going? Back into the nowhere of America, and I'll be there soon.

Like all things that run, I don't want to die. That's what a man is when he's running—not dying, refusing to. Still, the threat of being caught is always there, and I must keep going, as quietly as planes overhead, something moving at a terrible speed out of the corner of your eye and gone by the time you look again.

PART 1

The Year-Rounders

When news spread that Paul Benchley was bringing a foster-care kid to stay with him rent-free at his house on Youngs Road, many of his neighbors were understandably concerned. They had seen, all too recently, what outsiders were capable of. Not three months ago, during the Sycamore High senior picnic, a row of car windows had been smashed along Main Road. Some assumed it was a disgruntled student who'd failed out of Sycamore and was seeking revenge. But many more were sure it was the work of a delinquent, an unknown intruder pillaging the village for purses and electronics as Orient's proud graduating class danced on the nearby football field to bittersweet pop songs and the sex-and-gun ballads of hip-hop.

Pam Muldoon, whose daughter Lisa's car was looted in the robbery, was particularly enraged—so much so that even Orient year-rounders wondered if Pam was coming slightly unhinged. By graduation, most had forgotten about the whole episode. Lisa Muldoon herself could be found jogging on the beach by Bug Lighthouse, the iPod she'd lost in the incident replaced by a newer, lighter one clipped to her shorts.

Pam, on the other hand, couldn't let it go. Within days she announced that she'd started her own fund for the victims, pointing out that several kids didn't have the insurance to cover the damages. Throughout those grueling summer evenings, during the most dangerous season for Lyme disease contraction, Pam Muldoon went door to door with a small brown bag in her hand, disturbing her neighbors' dinners to ask for donations. Not a few residents winced as they scrounged around for a folded Alexander Hamilton after spotting her beelining up their steps. Her path might have seemed erratic—she canvassed three houses, then bypassed the next two, far fancier homes, with their pristine lawns and expensive cars ticking in the driveways like beds of fertile locusts—but Pam knew every house in Orient, and she chose only the year-rounders to bother with her missionary work.

To draw a map of Pam Muldoon's hopscotch course on those early summer evenings would be to chart Orient's changing demographics. It occurred to Pam that even five years ago she would have stopped at nearly every house, but so many city dwellers had descended upon the village in recent years that the tight-knit community had seemed to unravel, shedding countless native families who couldn't resist cashing in on the spiraling market value of their plots, despite the shoddy brick two-stories that often graced them. It was as if some noxious spell had blown across the bay from the south, transforming ordinary houses into exotic weekend getaways for the city's idle rich. Pam could remember a time when a bright coat of paint or a new backyard pool served as a point of communal pride. Now it meant something different: another empty set of chairs at the monthly council meeting, another late-night party spilling a scuttle of beer cans into the gutter, another pair of pale, spidery Manhattanites eyeing her grove of Spanish roses while frantically cell-phoning friends to describe the guts and bones of a potential easy-pick investment—perhaps even the Muldoons' house.

She stopped in front of what had once been the house of Frank and Elizabeth Daltwater. Elizabeth had babysat her as a child, and Pam had returned the favor by watching over the Daltwater girl for two winters. The Daltwaters had moved last year to a retirement village in Stony Brook, thanks to the two-million-dollar windfall that came when they sold their house. Now, Pam noticed, there were untreated cane swings swaying on the porch, oh-so-preciously decorated with Indonesian batik pillows; through the house's ancient handblown parlor windows, a horrendous neon-light art installation blinked two words: GET, then OFF. She kept walking.

The city people brought their decorators and landscapers and imported Japanese plum trees, but with them came city problems—not least of all, an uptick in crime. It wasn't just the window-smashing incident: last month, the brass placard had been stolen from the United Church of Christ, and vandals marred the Civil War obelisk on Village Lane with spray paint. A weekender's intoxicated guest tripped the alarm on the historic Old Point School-house at three in the morning, claiming he was looking for a place to take a leak. Some year-rounders wondered why Pam took these outsider invasions so personally. But what wasn't personal about safety issues in her own neighborhood? Lisa might be heading off to college, but she had two boys to look out for. To Pam, the threat of city encroachment was real and visceral; she actually pictured Orient as a kind of tapestry, its land shaped like a flame, unraveling at every weft and edge, leaving only a few remaining threads to hold the illusion of an unspoiled image. A kid like Bobby Murphy, he doesn't have wealthy parents, he can't do much more than go into the military and fight for this country. How was he supposed to pay for the damage to his car? And what would be next: smashed house windows? Didn't her neighbors realize she was trying to save what they had left?

So went Pam Muldoon into the June of a summer heat wave.

Pam finally abandoned her fund-raising campaign in August, just as Lisa was getting ready to leave home early for SUNY Buffalo's freshman jumpstart program. When Pam heard the news of Paul Benchley's new boarder, she was preparing for the Muldoons' annual end-of-summer picnic. The presence of another unknown intruder during another picnic set off alarms, reviving the low-grade anxiety she had only just begun to shrug off. Pam, already wounded by her daughter's eagerness to flee to college the first chance she got, felt a restless itch, a mounting irritation at the prospect that trouble was about to move in next door.

Paul Benchley's family had never called their house a mansion. They didn't have to; most of Orient did that for them. But it wasn't a mansion in the traditional sense. In other eastern enclaves studded with extravagant baronial estates, the Benchley house would have looked more like a sprawling servants' quarters marooned on a large parcel of grass. It wasn't particularly ornate or even well constructed. The only thing grand about the white clapboard farmhouse was the sheer space it contained, as if its early-nineteenth-century builders had taken perverse delight in adding small, impractical rooms that served only to cause future owners grief about walls too cramped for couches and ceilings too low for tall men. Still, it had sharp, ivy-framed eaves and a wraparound porch, and it managed to make the Muldoons' residence, just forty feet away, seem both dull and like it was trying too hard. (Pam's husband, Bryan, was color-blind when it came to house paint.)

Paul Benchley had grown up in that house. He had moved away for boarding school and college, and then settled in New York, but he still returned for holidays and summer weekends. He had spent a month in Orient last spring when his mother, a callous, overbearing woman smoothed of her harsher personality traits by dementia, was dying of cancer. Technically Paul Benchley was the weekender type that Pam despised, but he was a native Orient son. He hadn't sold the mansion when it was passed down to him and, to his credit, he didn't fix up his house to show it off. Best of all for the Muldoons, he stayed away for long periods; this allowed them to adopt his backyard as an extension of their own, strolling down to his tract of marshland on the Sound to watch the gulls swoop for crab at dusk. And Paul Benchley was nice. Still unmarried at forty-six, which was a little strange, but he was an ideal neighbor, invisible but dependable, a bird that found its way home at the right time of year.

Paul had called Bryan himself the evening before the picnic, explaining that he was bringing a teenager from the city to stay with him. Pam's husband responded with neighborly restraint, asking only a few minor questions. When Pam interrogated Bryan about the conversation at dinner, all he could muster was "Some kind of foster kid he met in New York who's having a hard time. Paul thinks Orient will be good for him." Pam believed in charity; she considered herself a firm practitioner of "live and let live." But such beliefs evaporated when it came to the stability of her own neighborhood. "What kind of hard time?" she asked her husband. "What do you think that could mean?" Bryan retreated to the basement after dinner to do twenty minutes on his rowing machine, but Pam's anxious brain refused to turn off. If Paul liked children so much, why hadn't he had his own or ever once offered to babysit? And how could he board a minor in a house he visited only two or three weekends a month? And, more to the point, what kind of "hard time" was this city kid bringing to the house next door?

Of course, Paul was nice. Pam couldn't deny that. But now Pam wondered if his outward friendliness was perhaps a little too friendly, a convenient smoke screen hiding a man she only assumed she knew. All she really knew for certain about Paul Benchley was that he had a successful career as an architect and a reputation as a decent amateur seascape painter on the North Fork. Some year-rounders occasionally murmured questions about Paul's sexuality, but Pam had never felt it was her business, not until news of this wayward teenager came to light.

Concerned that the pressures of the picnic might be unfairly darkening her judgment, she texted her friend Sarakit Herrig for reassurance. "Am I overreacting?" Within two minutes, Sarakit wrote back: "You have every right to be unnerved. It's called being a vigilant mother!" Pam took an extra sleeping pill that night, but her worries continued to mount.

The next morning, Pam spread linen tablecloths over the long cherry-wood table that occupied a permanent spot beneath the oak tree and the three smaller plastic tables her boys had assembled before disappearing to their bedrooms. A curling wind blew from the Sound that morning, carrying a wet, creasing chill, more beginning-of-fall than end-of-summer. Pam had pushed back the date of the picnic twice, hoping to entice Lisa down from college for the occasion, but all her overtures had been met with reluctant maybes. Earlier that morning, Lisa had called to say she wouldn't be waiting at the train station in Greenport.

The wind gathered force, stripping the plastic liners from the tables. Pam used coffee mugs and fistfuls of silverware to paperweight the corners. There was potato salad in the mixer, three-bean chili on the stove, and in just two short hours the Muldoon yard would be swarming with guests. Pam pushed her fingers through her coarse brown hair to give it more body and considered a bit of lipstick to enliven the pewter pallor of her skin. She had put on as many pounds as Lisa had lost over the summer with her manic pre-college exercise regimen. The breeze caught a tablecloth and yanked it tumbling across the lawn. As Pam ran after it, a mug in each hand, she glanced at her watch and realized she wouldn't have time to change before the guests started arriving. She would have to greet them in her madras shirt and gray gingham slacks; this was the outfit that would appear in the family's photo album and Facebook page for the Orient End of Summer Picnic.

An hour later, a few neighbors arrived to help with the final preparations. The Muldoon house opened at every sliding and screen door, and food, balloons, and folding chairs appeared as if a benign hurricane had come in through the windows and spilled the contents of the living room onto the lawn. One of the helpers was Karen Norgen, whom Pam spotted padding slowly across the grass in her rain slicker.

Karen was a retired nurse in the silver-haired halo of her midsixties. She was Christmas bulb–shaped and forever out of breath, but she had sharp eyes and nimble hands that were always quick to intercede without waiting to be asked. Karen carried a crystal punch bowl filled with slapping red liquid, and over this glass heirloom she gave Pam the latest update: the "kid" Paul Benchley was bringing to Orient was no child at all. He was eighteen or nineteen, an adult by any standard—and, worse, he wasn't even from New York, neither the city nor the state. "Terra incognita," Karen mused. "A total stranger. Go figure."

Pam took the heavy bowl from Karen's hands. She looked over at the Benchleys' mansion with fresh resentment. "Who did you hear that from?"

Karen had heard it directly from old Jeff Trader, a dependable source. Jeff was the never-out-of-work drunk who served as caretaker for dozens of year-rounder and weekender houses in Orient—including the Muldoons. He kept a jar of keys in his truck, making routine visits from house to house, ensuring that windows were locked, pipes drained of water in winter, smoke detectors stocked with fresh batteries, and that the food in refrigerators was eaten before it rotted. Jeff looked after Paul Benchley's house when he was away, and Paul had called him yesterday to ask him to air out the second bedroom.

"Paul told Bryan that this young man had been having a hard time," Pam confided.

"Well, if that's not a euphemism for drugs or crime, I'm not sure what is," Karen said, searching the table for a spoon.

Pam shook her head and let out a moan. Pam had been throwing this picnic for fourteen years, but she was not a hostess by nature. Just e-mailing out the invitations, let alone all the orchestrated prep work she had to finish before mustering the cheery exhilaration required for a successful event, put her in an aggravated mood. She channeled her worries into a chorus of rapid-fire questions for Karen, posed without pause or upturn. "If I started taking in stray teenagers no one knows, don't you think I'd have the decency to ask my neighbors first? Why does Paul Benchley feel the need to bring his goings-on in the city here? Wouldn't his Manhattan apartment be a more convenient place to house a stranger with problems?

When did Orient decide that it was okay to turn the house next-door to mine into a youth hostel?"

"Just what we need," Karen said, shaking her head as she stirred the punch. "More incidents."

Holly Drake, who owned an upscale textile shop on Little Bay Road, stopped tying balloons to the branch of an oak and turned toward Pam. Holly, although not born or raised in Orient, had lived in these parts since her marriage seven years ago and prided herself on being the voice of liberal reason whenever close-mindedness threatened to choke the village off from the twenty-first century. Holly bragged about her political causes, but Pam hadn't forgotten that she had refused to contribute to her car-window fund-raiser that summer.

"Pam," she said lightly, "don't you think you're overreacting? Paul's not adopting a kid. He's bringing a guest to stay at his house. What's wrong with that? He doesn't need permission. It's his private property. I don't think having this kid here will be an inconvenience to you—will it?"

"He's not a kid," Pam stammered, dredging a palm down her cheek. "I'm sorry, but there's a reason I don't live in the city. I like to know my neighbors. And you don't have children, Holly. Easy for you to say when trouble isn't lurking forty feet from their bedrooms."

Holly continued to inflict her calm, sensible smile through the gray noon light; red and purple balloons bobbed behind her, their strings tangling around the Plexiglas bird feeder. Holly believed in giving hysteria plenty of breathing space until it echoed back cheap and frantic to testify against itself. She waited a full fifteen seconds before responding.

"We all love you, Pam, for this wonderful picnic. But, honestly, if someone hadn't first described him as a 'foster kid,' would you really be that concerned? He's just a friend of Paul's who happens to be Lisa's age. Maybe we should wait to meet him before we call the police."

Pam Muldoon, realizing she was losing the argument, feigned a glance at her watch and headed across the yard toward her house. She had never really liked Holly Drake anyway, with her gaudy Middle Eastern fabrics and her self-righteous Obama stickers plastered on every ground-floor window. Pam shifted the dispute inward, fought inside her mind against a less amiable version of Holly Drake. And she kept it up, her silent battle, all through the beginning of the picnic, a one-sided war of brilliant moral volleys that Pam felt certain she had won.

The weather could not make up its mind. White sunlight etched a motif of leaves across the picnic tables and the grass. The sky managed a deep, summer blue, and mosquitoes skimmed across surfaces and ears as the season's totem insect. But silver clouds banded in the west, imposing the threat of rain. The wind carried droplets of salt water off the Sound, dampening faces and clinging to arms. The smell of algae mixed with the scent of Pam's dying roses and the earthy mulch piles the boys had raked.

The sun didn't produce much heat or haze, but there was enough summer left in the air to justify an end-of-summer celebration. Everything was clear that afternoon, every color its own, and there were so many colors, a dense scrum of neighbors eating and laughing and struggling out of their jackets to shake hands or dab potato salad on their plates. Even without Lisa and her high school friends, there were more guests on the Muldoon lawn than ever before: the familiar and the unfamiliar, the regulars and the intermittents; ancient Magdalena Kiefer, with her aluminum walking canes and Hispanic nurse; Ted and Sarakit Herrig; the handsome gay artist couple who had recently bought the old Raleigh home (and transformed an eyesore into a charming English cottage, even Pam had to admit); Adam Pruitt, with his volunteer fire department buddies; the Griffins, and the Morgensens, and Ina Jenkins tripping over her kennel of French bulldogs-slash-hoarding problem. They were all there and more, even several of the weekenders who had not received personal invitations, and Pam felt her bitterness ebb as she watched them eat from her plates and drink from her mugs. She labored to make them feel welcome, talking about her daughter and how sad Lisa was that she couldn't be here to join the fun. *This is the true spirit of Orient, you weekenders*, she thought. *Taste it, butter it, scoop it from the copper-plated bowl, enjoy it while it lasts.*

"So where's the boy?" Ina Jenkins asked her.

"Mine, you mean?"

"No." Ina tipped her head toward the Benchleys' mansion. "The foster kid."

Pam stopped petting the bulldog in Ina's arms.

"Oh, Ina, not today. Can we not mention that business at my party?"

"Paul took such care of his mother before she died. It's like he caught the care bug. Now he thinks he can help anyone." Ina jiggled the tiny, tapioca-colored dog against her breasts. "He just seems lonely to me. You know, I never cared much for his mother. Always such a snob about her family and their stature in the community. But Paul donated a bunch of art supplies to the elementary school last winter. And here he is, helping another needy kid."

"Please," Pam whispered. "Enough."

And then it occurred to her, like a wave of stomach sickness, that so many locals had crowded her lawn partly out of curiosity about the new arrival. She glanced around and noticed Bryan near the log pile, leaning close to Holly Drake, two glasses of white wine between them. Bryan, with his graying rake of hair and his robin's egg shirtsleeves rolled to the elbows, laughed nervously at whatever Huffington Post blog Holly was reciting by heart. His years of flirting with younger women hadn't eased, no matter how many times she called him on it, how many civilized barbecues ended in hushed fights while they loaded the dishwasher in hostile synchronicity. But now, as she watched him, she felt no flare of jealousy, only sympathy. How sad her husband looked as he chatted up that red-haired speck of a woman. Bryan had gotten old over the summer, his muscular chest sagging, his whole body seeming to shrink into the rack of his vertebrae, his blue eyes glassier, increments of age revealing themselves as she watched him stumble every morning from bed to bathroom, as if he had lost his balance.

Poor Bryan. It must mean something to him to have this moment with Holly, to stay in the game even when there was no chance at victory, and she opted not to intervene, to let him have it. Instead she scanned the lawn for Tommy, her eldest son. She felt the tremendous urge to hug him, to drape her arms around his collarbone and draw him into her, as if to reunite him briefly with her umbilical cord. And there he was, coming around the house in a black T-shirt and jeans, his Converses caked in mud, his short, wheat-colored hair causing the hollows of his eyes to stand out, so handsome that it took all her reserve not to call to him "my baby."

"Tommy," Pam yelled. "Come here for a minute, sweetheart."

His eyes rolled, but he walked toward her, wincing as she squeezed his shoulders.

"Ina, you know that Tommy has started his senior year at Sycamore," she said proudly.

"She doesn't care, Mom," Tommy mumbled.

"Of course she cares." Pam leaned over and kissed the back of his head, smelling the sweat of dank, unbathed boyhood and refusing to acknowledge a hint of what could be marijuana smoke. "Ina taught you in third grade. Of course she wants to know how you're progressing." Pam turned to Ina with a conspiratorial wink. "Can you believe he'll be off to college next year, just like Lisa?"

Ina played along. It was a teacher's burden to feign interest in the futures of every child who passed through her classroom. The two women traded opinions about colleges until Theo, Pam's youngest, appeared from around the oak tree. Theo squealed through a smear of chocolate syrup. His hands were cupped together, hiding and flaunting a valuable treasure.

"What have you got?" Tommy asked, pulling away from his mother.

Theo opened his filthy nine-year-old hands to expose a baby bird lying on his palm. It was gray-skinned and insect-eyed, its mechanical heart beating as it shivered featherless in the sun.

"Oh, honey, put it back where you found it," Pam ordered. "Its parents won't claim it if it smells like you. Put it where the cats can't get to it."

"It'll just die anyway," Tommy said. "Too late in the year for a baby. How weird that it even hatched. It must be a mutant."

"I found it on the ground," Theo whined, as if anything on the ground was fair game for whatever torture methods he had in mind.

Beth Shepherd crossed the lawn on her way back from the bathroom. She had her arm pressed against her stomach, and her face looked so pale that Pam worried she was sick. Beth had grown up in Orient, popular and outgoing, leaving a trail of village boys lovestruck behind her. She had left for college and an art career in the city, but five months ago she had returned, presumably for good, presumably to start a family with her new, foreign husband. Pam found Beth stoically beautiful. She wondered if Tommy found her beautiful too.

Beth staggered toward them, attracted by the quivering bird in Theo's hands. "Ohhh," she said as she stepped closer to examine it, sweeping her blond hair behind her ear. Theo closed his hand over the bird, either to shelter it from the wind or to reclaim it as his own.

That's when Paul Benchley's dented blue Mercedes appeared in the distance, driving slowly up the street. Pam saw it first, squinting in the sunlight as she steadied herself on Tommy's shoulder. As if to confirm Pam's worst suspicions, the other guests stopped talking, stopped eating, as the car eased into the gravel driveway that traced the border between Paul's property and the Muldoons'. It came to a halt, and the engine died. The guests waited patiently for the passenger-side door to open, and Pam realized, with sudden horror, what her annual picnic would look like: a welcome party for

Paul's foster kid, complete with balloons and punch and the entire Orient community assembled on her lawn to greet him. She stood and watched, dazed by the reflection of her oak tree on the passenger window.

Paul got out first and waved over the roof of his car. His glasses glinted white in the sun, his brown mustache offsetting a smile. As he walked around the car, the passenger door opened and two black sneakers touched the ground. A pair of worn blue jeans pivoted at the knee, and up rose a nest of black hair—of course his hair was black—followed by a thin white face with chapped lips and brown eyes, greasy-haired and pharmaceutical-eyed, skinny and agile and drained of expression, like a kid accustomed to emerging from the backseat of patrol cars.

"I want you to meet Mills," Paul called out, patting the young man on the back to lead him toward the picnic. "He's coming out to help me with the house for a few weeks."

"Ouch," Tommy cried, twisting out from under his mother's grasp. "Jesus, Mom."

Pam reached for her son, but Mills misinterpreted her gesture, lurching forward to shake her outstretched hand.

"Nice to meet you," Pam said flatly. The young man smiled, and she noticed his right front tooth was a lifeless shade of gray, the color of a dead bulb in her upstairs vanity mirror.

Pam turned away in defeat. "Well, everyone back to the picnic," she said. Only Paul and Theo followed her.

The two teenagers stood on the edge of the lawn, regarding each other. All was silent for a moment until Bryan opened a bottle of Prosecco and the party regained its nearsighted enthusiasm, circling the food on the tables and chewing over the latest local controversies: the government's imminent closure of Plum Island, the apocryphal sighting of an oil rig off the coast of Mastic Beach, the curse of the Sycamore girls' varsity soccer team. Theo laid his baby bird on a quilt Magdalena Kiefer had left on a chair;

it died there, undiscovered, until Magdalena's nurse picked off its sticky remains.

Pam Muldoon took refuge in the midst of her neighbors, throwing furious, unnoticed glances at Paul Benchley. Tommy and the foster kid continued to stand on the far perimeter, away from parental ears. When it came time to take pictures, the evening light had waned and a defect in the Muldoons' digital camera caused orbs of light to appear as snow falling across every image.

Most of the guests would catch glimpses of Pam, or Bryan, or one of the boys the next day or the next week, but some would not. A few would remember the end-of-summer picnic as the last time the Muldoons were seen together and alive.

CHAPTER 2

Beth Shepherd woke on the morning of the picnic with two hearts beating inside her. She climbed out of bed, releasing the sheets knotted around her ankles, and stood in front of her full-length mirror. Behind her she saw the white, lunar walls that had once been her parents' bedroom. Even with three applications of paint, a faint haze of rose chiffon exuded from the nacreous coats of Cosmic Ricotta that Beth had specifically chosen to excise all trace of her mother's favorite color. The pinkish glow served as an unwelcome reminder of two recent failures: her fizzled career as a painter in New York and her inability to eliminate Gail Sheely Shepherd Kendrick Laurito from her daily life in Orient. In fact, the chain saw drone of coffee beans being ground in the kitchen downstairs might well be the handiwork of Gail Sheely Shepherd Kendrick Laurito, slumped over the counter, trying to rouse her daughter out of bed with the most excusable assault available to a woman who had been told that the upstairs was no longer in her jurisdiction.

Beth glanced out the bedroom window and saw her husband, Gavril, marching across the backyard toward his studio, confirming that the sounds coming from the kitchen must be from her mother. She waited resignedly for what she knew would soon come wafting through the air vents, and, yep, there it was: *My life has been a tapestry . . .* at cloying, soft-rock, white-divorcée volume.

Beth lifted her T-shirt and stared at the oval doughnut of her stomach, the skin downy with fine blond hairs, the indent between her abdominal muscles showing no swelling, not yet. She spread her palm over her belly button, feeling for internal tremors. Her eyes ascended to her breasts, two small suction cups, and up to her face, still puffy and railroad-tracked with the imprint of a pillow seam, unsmiling. She should be happy. The pregnancy test she took secretly last night in the bathroom promised 90 percent accuracy. She had succeeded in her one sworn goal for moving out of the city and back into the house where she'd grown up. But the fact that Beth had to remind herself that she should be happy seemed to verify the self-diagnosis she'd reached while conducting research on the Internet last week in lieu of looking up pool covers. "Neurasthenia," the WebMD entry read, "a psycho-pathological term to denote a condition with symptoms of fatigue, anxiety, headache, neuralgia, and depressed mood." Check, check, check, check, and with the help of an online dictionary to define *neuralgia*, check. At the bottom of the entry, a dooming footnote: "Americans were said to be particularly prone to neurasthenia, which resulted in the nickname 'Americanitis.'"

Throughout her childhood in Orient, Beth had always believed herself to be *special*. She was an eager artist, a patient listener, an aggressive adolescent feminist in her Sycamore classroom; she excelled at math and sports, and was highly attuned to the emotional states of adults who hovered over her like the trees on Village Lane. Popularity just came to her, like sweaty palms or twenty-twenty vision. The Orient love fest around Beth had been so convincing that it propelled her to move to Manhattan, flush with confidence, to start college and a career in the arts. And now, after thirteen years in the city, she had returned to her hometown, replacing the futile dream of artist with the more realistic one of mother and wife of an artist. And it was here, in the very house where she'd begun, that she had come to understand herself as a lowly sufferer of a disease called Americanitis. What does an Americanitis survivor look like? Surely not Beth Shepherd, in the pink glimmer of her mother's bedroom, testing her urine for signs of new human life, hoping it might help her make sense of her own.

Beth scooped up her long blond hair and twisted it over her shoulder. She practiced rubbing her stomach in concentric circles, a habit she noticed expectant women performing, warming their hands on their own fecundity. She forced an exaggerated smile, the kind that at age thirty-two still came without a hint of the wrinkles her mother paid ungodly sums of money to remove from her own face. Every time Beth visited Orient over the last few years, her mother appeared less like the woman she had known since birth and more like a coquettish alien, a Mylar-balloon rendition whose trick for eternal youth was to confuse people so thoroughly about which parts of her face were real that they gave up guessing her age in frustration (it was fifty-eight). Beth found her mother's surgery addiction unhealthy and had told her so, swearing that she would allow herself to age naturally, proud of her laugh lines and serrated forehead. Gail had listened to her daughter's rant, rolling her eyes in signature fashion. "You'll see," Gail had laughed almost giddily. "You'll wake up one day and realize it's easier to ignore a few nasty comments than it is to watch your face fail before your eyes. Enjoy it while you have it, dear." Gail was like a broken machine that wouldn't stop dispensing advice.

When Beth moved back to Orient last April, she had promised to be nicer to her mother. After all, Gail had graciously offered Beth and Gavril the house, deciding it had become too difficult, after three marriages, to maintain alone. "Either you take it over or I sell it," Gail told her, announcing that she'd put a down payment on a condominium in Southold. That would put her twenty minutes away by car, and Beth had mistakenly hoped that was far enough to ensure that she'd call before visiting. Plus, after years in the city, Beth had forgotten how much the presence of her mother weighed on her nerves. It was easier to forgive a parent's shortfalls when the relationship was conducted primarily by phone.

Beth's father, an insurance salesman, had died in a car accident on the New Jersey Turnpike eleven years ago. After two months of mourning, Gail had surprised her daughter by transforming into a woman completely different from the quiet, cautious one who had raised her. She channeled her energy into her appearance, and then proceeded to turn marriage into a late-seeded form of social climbing through the Suffolk County ranks. Gail Sheely Shepherd became a Kendrick in a two-year union with a local real estate attorney who had handled the infamous sale of an old neighborhood mansion to a celebrity couple. Gail took her newfound cash reserves and funneled them into the Shepherd house, launching the first of two stunning renovations, adding a sunroom and remodeling the detached garage into a remote-controlled, soundproof "fun den." The Kendrick romance faded, but the divorce money went toward the first of two face-lifts, and soon she was presenting her reengineered façade to Mario Laurito, an Italian chef who had opened a tragically hip Italian bistro in Greenport. That marriage lasted long enough for a saltwater pool and a hot tub to replace her father's lavender garden. After that, Gail had soured on the house, complaining to Beth that it held too many ghosts, and began a subtle campaign to convince Beth and Gavril to see it as the perfect backdrop for whatever their lives had in store. Only after they moved in did Beth realize that the neighborhood had soured on Gail. Ten years of construction work had turned the widely admired Gail Sheely Shepherd into the widely reviled Gail Kendrick Laurito. In Beth's suspicious moments, she wondered if her mother's eagerness in having them take over the house was merely an attempt to restore the Shepherd name in Orient while managing to hold on to the escalating property value.

Beth pulled her shirt down. She walked into the bathroom, carefully testing the wetness of the floor with her toe before stepping on the tiles. Wasn't that the role of the soon-to-be mother, for the next seven months (assuming she was two months pregnant, assuming she was pregnant at all), to treat her body as delicately as if she were made of eggshells, a delivery system for fragile cargo? Another mirror awaited her on the medicine cabinet, but Beth opened its door to avoid catching her reflection. Why wasn't she spinning around in prepartum mania? She wanted to feel different, inside and out. There were two heartbeats within her now, a new body leaching nutrients from her blood, oxygenating with each inhaled breath, growing, gulping, solidifying.

Beth had failed as an artist. Her single gallery show, a series of portraits, had garnered nasty reviews from influential critics and anonymous bloggers alike—"Alice Neel on horse tranquilizers"; "Elizabeth Shepherd's brushstrokes lack confidence, like she's aiming to please rather than revolt against the institutional deadlock of genre painting. Her talent is evident but her passion is not"—and the portraits, returned unsold, haunted her East Village apartment for months like disappointed relatives.

In a fit of rage one whiskey-fueled evening, Beth had taken a kitchen knife and stabbed holes through the canvases. When Gavril returned home drunk from a dinner, he saw the scary violence that she had executed on her work and commended her on the improvement. "Ahh, Beth, they look so strong with wounds in them," he slurred. "You should take them back to the gallery and hang them again, like your own critique on the critique given to you." She knew it was only his wine-purpled attempt to be supportive. Was it true that she'd lost her confidence, that at some point in the city her passion had run dry? Maybe, but Beth couldn't help sensing another force at work: there was an ironic calculus that increasingly seemed to drive the art world, the game where one-upping or undermining every sincere gesture was the only pathway to artistic credibility. The secret she dared not admit in Gavril's intellectual art circles was this: she loved the beauty of paint applied by brush. Beauty was her embarrassing motivation that refused to mock itself. Beth remembered one Saturday afternoon, just before she decided to give up on New York, when she bumped into one of Gavril's artist friends after a day spent touring the Chelsea galleries. Luz Wilson, who now owned a huge weekend house on the tip of Orient, asked Beth what shows she had seen. With each new exhibit she mentioned,

Luz asked Beth if she liked it. Each time, Beth responded, "Yes, very much." Luz finally threw her hands up in despair. "My God, Beth, is there anything you don't like?"

After her career-killing show, the city seemed different to her, drained of color somehow, phony and cynical and very young. Beth had not been raised particularly religious—lapsed Presbyterian on both sides—but she could believe in a hell that involved getting *this close* to success, only to have her passion dismissed as second-rate. The ironic calculus that Beth couldn't apply to art suddenly seemed weirdly relevant to her life: Why not be exactly what you said you would never be? Why not embrace the idea of motherhood, move back to the country and concentrate on what was really important?

Gavril, a Romanian five years in America and unable to attend any dinner without drinking his weight in alcohol, loved the idea. Specifically, he loved the idea of having a child. And so did she. Yes, motherhood was a creative act too, she thought, pushing her hips against the sink's cold porcelain, more vital and affirming than anything she could fashion from paint. Why had she always assumed wanting a baby to be a mark of weakness? Why had she joked in her twenties about sending "get well" cards to girlfriends who had just announced their pregnancies? She scraped sleep from her eyelids with a tissue. Tossing it into the wastebasket, she noticed a corner of the pregnancy-test box peeking out from the trash where she had buried it last night. She pushed it back under the tissues, reluctant to give Gavril any false hope until she knew for certain. Today she would make an appointment with her doctor.

Beth had driven to Greenport yesterday to buy the test at Dooley's Pharmacy, the same place where she had bought her first pregnancy test at fifteen, naively charging the kit to the family account without realizing that her parents received a monthly itemized list of expenses. Her mother had knocked on her door, receipt in hand, to demand an explanation, a month—which felt like a lifetime— after the results had read negative. Her mother was still her mother then, clumsy with her words, anticipatorily wounded. Beth had lied.

She told her mother that it was for her best friend, Alison, that it had just been a scare, and she'd bought the test for her as a friend. Beth had spent the next three years of high school dealing with the aftermath, noting her mother's anxious silence every time she went for a sleepover at Alison's, as if Beth had stuffed her backpack with coat hangers and was going over to her friend's house to perform an abortion.

As she brushed her teeth, Beth considered the fact that she could have an abortion now—that even if she were 100 percent pregnant, she didn't have to have this child, this undetected heartbeat below her rib cage. At twenty-four, Beth had gotten an abortion at the clinic on Bleecker Street, and she was so overcome with gratitude for her constitutional rights over her own body that she donated one hundred dollars to Planned Parenthood every year at Christmas. All these years later, she could make an excuse, take the car into the city on Monday, and have the procedure again without Gavril ever knowing. But their entire idea in moving out to Orient had been to start a family. That's what Beth said she wanted. That's what Gavril said he wanted. He had agreed to transport his whole studio operation out into the backyard garage at the height of his success, turning the den, with its imported terrazzo floors, into a home for his erratic junk pile of multimedia art supplies. No, it would be self-ish of her not to want this baby now.

As she swung the mirror back to its original position, it occurred to her that her recent bout of depression was just as self-centered as her mother's chemical peels and five-hundred-dollar Botox treatments. Beth knew what was causing her Americanitis. She missed Manhattan. It took her five months away from the city to admit that. She had blamed Manhattan for her failures, not realizing that living there had become one of her defining characteristics.

Beth descended the staircase slowly, like a scuba diver leaving the warm sunlight of the second floor for the darkness underneath. Be nice to Gail, she told herself. Set the relationship on a new and brighter course.

Smackwater Jack, he bought a shotgun . . .

Beth walked into the kitchen and went straight to the CD player on the counter, pressing stop on Carole King. Her mother sat at the table in a sleeveless yellow dress, her fingers ribbed around a coffee mug. Her hair, once an auburn gray, now managed a copper shine not unlike the hair on young male swimmers who didn't wash the chlorine out. Instinctively, Beth searched the table for evidence of liquor that Gail might have added to her coffee, but when she bent over to kiss her mother's cheek, she purposely held her breath to avoid smelling any hint of alcohol.

"You slept late," her mother said, accepting the peck without returning one. "What's wrong? Are you not feeling well?"

It was no secret that Gail, obsessed though she was with defying the aging process, wanted a grandchild. Beth caught herself rolling her eyes, but forced herself to stop. That tic belonged to her mother.

"I always sleep late when the mornings get colder. I guess summer is finally over." She reached for a mug in the cabinet but wondered if she would have to stop drinking coffee now. She filled the cup under the faucet and watered the houseplants that Gavril kept adding to the kitchen: a fern, a rubber tree, a dinosaur cactus. It was a New York apartment trick that made no sense with an entire arboretum right outside the back door. "So, Mom, tell me. Why the early visit?"

"It's nearly ten," her mother said, shaking her arm to bring her watch face flat against her wrist. "And summer's not over. Look." She pointed to the window above the sink. Beth peered outside, where swabs of gray clouds hid the sunlight. Below the clouds was their pool, foregrounded against the slate blue Sound and the long gray stalks of wild grass.

"It's too cold for swimming," Beth said. "Do we drain the pool or just cover it over for the winter? Gavril is going to miss his afternoon laps."

Her mother was still staring at the window. "No, look," she said. "Not out the window, *inside* it. See that? A bee trapped in the glass." Beth refocused her eyes and noticed the tiny insect between two panes, crawling and falling, searching for a way out. "Summer can't be over if bees are still around. It's probably one of Magdalena's specimens. Of course I was too nice to ever complain about her hives. But you don't have to be."

Gail smiled triumphantly, glints of bleached, celestial teeth. The bee clung to the glass and wiped its antennae. She could see the circular plates of its abdomen curled like pencil shavings. The bee probably did belong to Magdalena Kiefer, the Shepherds' nearest neighbor. Magdalena had owned the cottage next door for as long as Beth had been alive; she had been a radical lesbian (and, rumor had it, a splinter member of the Weather Underground) long before Beth had come to know her as plump, arthritic Lena, cloaked in yarn throws. Whatever passion Magdalena once had to change the forecast of American society was now reserved for the rearing of bees. Her summer apiary consisted of three buzzing boxes on her lawn, which she dragged into her garage just before the autumn frost. It was not uncommon on hot August days to find Magdalena bent over in her backyard, supported by her nurse, both women covered neck to toe in white jumpsuits, wearing giant mesh helmets, as if they were residents of a retirement home on the moon.

Gail couldn't stand Magdalena. She had been one of the principal figures in the local junta against Gail's decade-long transformation of the Shepherd house. When Beth moved in, she had expected to inherit Magdalena's hostility, but the eighty-three-year-old spinster had been nothing but kind, sending over a jar of honey with a handwritten card that read "It's nice to have you back."

"I don't mind the bees," Beth said, trying to figure out a method of freeing the insect without opening the pane that would let it into the house.

"Is that so?" Gail replied. She spread her hands across the table, hands that did belong to a woman of fifty-eight, with purple veins constricting around bone. As long as plastic surgeons weren't out there pushing hand rejuvenation surgery, Beth knew that some reassuring presence of her mother remained intact.

Beth poured a cup of coffee and drank it down before she could reconsider. Gavril's art notebook lay open on the counter. "What-ever you say I am, I will be that for you, over and over," he'd written in his looping hand. Beth decided not to attempt decoding what it meant. Like the stock market ticker at the bottom of the news, her husband's scribblings served as ciphers to a system she didn't understand or trust. But suddenly she *was* feeling slightly sick. She lurched toward the table and pulled out a chair.

"You didn't tell me why you're here."

"Can't I visit?" her mother wheezed. "Am I violating your per-sonal space in my own house? Is it so wrong that I stop by for an hour to see my daughter and ask if she needs anything from town?"

"Of course not," Beth said with a sigh. "It's just that I'm trying to create some kind of routine here. I wanted to set up a painting studio in the second bedroom and bring in my old desk from—"

"I thought you'd given that up." Gail reached over to tuck a strand of hair behind Beth's ear. "Honey, you do look a little sick. Are you taking the supplements I brought you? You know they're good for"—Gail clawed at her sternum, like she was describing how to clear an obstructing object from her windpipe—"raising your hormone levels. For *fertility*"—her clawing hand rotated into an open-palm stop sign—"and not just that, for general health. You take one every morning and one again at night. They're not over-the-counter, Beth. A Chinese holistic doctor prescribed them, a friend of mine. They're *medical*, so they work."

On her way down the stairs, Beth had steeled her nerves, decid-ing on this supposedly blessed first morning of pregnancy to start a brand-new coalition with her mother, a temperate confederacy marked by patience and warmth. But two minutes into Gail's visit, Beth had already regressed into the moody, matricidal teenager, sit-ting here in the same toffee-colored kitchen with the same crooked shelves her father had never gotten around to fixing before he died. Right then and there, she decided not to share the results of the pregnancy test with her mother. Some leftover teenage piece of her was even tempted to deliver the baby before ever telling her mother she was pregnant. "There, I did it without you," she could say. "I didn't need your help." But that was a fantasy for faraway Manhattan; it could never work on the incredibly shrinking North Fork. Beth felt ashamed by her sudden anger even as she toyed with it.

"Sweet potatoes are good for irregular menstrual cycles, and plenty of peas. Misty O'Donnell is not only an interior decorator but she also found the time to be trained as a doula. That on top of having six grandkids! She says orgasms last a little longer in pregnant women because the uterus—"

"Please, Mom. Stop talking."

". . . gets engorged with blood. Misty says that now doctors can even run scans in the first trimester to check for Down syndrome or other chromosomal disorders, and—"

"Mom, enough."

". . . there are exercises, these stretches and yoga positions, that actually help take pressure off the cervix. They also help prevent obesity and allow the body to adjust to the shock of—"

"*I'm not pregnant!*" Beth shouted, rising from the table. "And I may never be. So please shut up."

It was the destiny of Gail's face to look most like her old self—most like the woman she didn't want to be—when she was hurt. Her eyes welled, her bottom lip distended, and she avoided Beth's gaze, cordoning her vision to the floor. Beth bent over her in guilt, collecting her mother's hand from the table and rubbing it in her own.

"I'm sorry," she said. "I just don't want to be bullied into anything. It will happen when it's time and until then I'd rather not talk about it."

"I just want you to be happy," her mother said with a show of perplexity that required her to remove her hand from Beth's palms and wave it through the air. "Why should I have to defend myself against that? I think I've been pretty lenient in my demands on you. You want this house, I give you this house. You want me not to go upstairs, I sit alone in the kitchen until you feel like coming down. You tell me you're ready to have a baby, I go out of my way to ask my own friends for advice that might . . ."

Magdalena, Beth thought. That could be a pretty name if the baby were a girl.

She hadn't gotten too far into the thought when Gavril appeared at the screened window of the back door, staring in like he needed permission to enter.

"Everything all right?" he asked. Gavril hadn't shaved in days. The pattern of the screen against his face deepened the crosshatch of black whiskers over his cheeks. He opened the door reluctantly, as if he were barging in on a private matter, as if Gavril didn't know that his presence was the only antidote to the brawls between mother and daughter. Gail adored him. Her shoulders relaxed, and her eyes widened in joy.

"Yes, yes," Gail assured him. "We were just discussing the picnic."

"What picnic?" Gavril asked.

"The Muldoons'," she replied, glancing over at Beth with a wink, as if to say, *don't worry, I'm covering for you, we won't tell Gavril what you were raving on about.* "The one they throw every year. Beth didn't tell you about it?"

Beth knew the picnic her mother was referring to. She had gone her last two years of high school and had heard that it had continued on as some punitive local tradition. Who knew why? The Muldoons weren't the friendliest of neighbors, just the most visible. And Beth knew one thing: they also hated her mother.

"A picnic," Gavril repeated with a smile. Beth could see his mind working, doubtlessly entranced with the kind of clichéd Americana that fascinated him. He had dragged Beth to the Fourth of July parade in Greenport, marveling at the flimsy pomp of the baton twirlers and marching bands. "I love this country—so medieval," he said over and over as the procession of Vietnam and Iraq veterans passed, until Beth finally told him to be quiet.

"Oh, but not the Muldoons," he howled now.

"Yes," her mother said, laughing.

"Then I can't go. They don't like artists."

"I'm sure they'd like you if they met you," Beth said, though she knew Gavril was right. Apparently Pam had gotten it into her head that artists were to blame for the recent wave of New Yorkers buying up local property to turn into weekend retreats. Pam perceived artists the way poor minority groups in the outer boroughs perceived artists: as garish, warning canaries sent down defenseless mine shafts, paving the way for gentrification, displacing families and prepping abandoned storefronts for coffeehouses and Swedish design boutiques. Last June, when an enterprising ceramist tried to turn the old fishing-tackle store on Village Lane into an art gallery, Pam ran to the historical board—her husband, Bryan, was a key member—and created so much red tape that the woman gave up in aggravation. All this time later, the storefront still stood empty and black, to Pam's enormous satisfaction.

"They don't like me either," Gail confided. "Bryan and Pam were so nice once, so . . ." She struggled for the word. "*Simple*. But I'll never forgive them for the way they treated me after Beth's father died. This town isn't a museum. What's the matter with doing a little renovation on a house that's a hundred and twenty years old?"

"It's a free country, right?" Gavril said, laughing.

"So I've been told."

Gavril and Gail had bonded over the summer, not exactly against Beth's wishes but despite her complaints that Gail needed to learn to give them space. If Beth were honest with herself, she might admit an annoyance with how much her mother liked Gavril, the very opposite in body and temperament from her cautious, yardstick-thin father. The way Gail expressed her affection—hugging, touching, giggling—felt like a betrayal to the memory of the man who had taken Beth out on the Sound on weekends to fish, who coaxed her into memorizing every country on every continent and the moons and planets circling the sun.

Truth be told, there might have been some lingering rebellion in

Beth's choice of mate. Gail wasn't supposed to swoon over a bulky Eastern European artist who ate his breakfast in his underwear. On their first date, two years ago, Gavril had made her watch a video of the 1989 execution of Nicolae Ceaușescu, the Romanian president, and his wife, Elena. He played the grainy, yellowed footage on his laptop. Sitting knee to knee on his bed, they watched the elderly couple bundled in thick wool coats argue as soldiers bound their hands and led them out to a concrete wall. After rounds of gunfire and a cloud of cement dust, the screen glimpsed the dead, bloodied bodies of a couple who could have passed for two mildly irritated immigrant grandparents on a winter walk in Queens.

Only this wasn't just any couple, not to Gavril. They were the reason that Gavril's early childhood memories involved lining up for hours for flour and milk or pawning ancestral silverware for Duracell batteries, ham radios, or even just ham. They were the leaders who forced Gavril's parents, two soap factory workers, to perform ridiculous (although admittedly beautiful) choreographed dance routines in colorful unitards for nationalistic amusement. Beth didn't know a single thing about Romania other than the prune-colored gymnasts she had watched during summer Olympic broadcasts in her childhood. After the execution footage ended, Gavril slapped down his computer top with pride. "That is how we deal with dictators in my country," he boasted. "This is what a people's revolution looks like."

It might not have been very promising, as first dates go, but Gavril Catargi proved shockingly earnest, so quick to profess his love for her and so soft with his large, meaty hands. She couldn't believe that a man who had survived the starvations of communism, and who was already being hailed in the art world for his macho destructive tendencies—marble statues smashed with a baseball bat on gallery floors; paint poured over expensive furniture; mounds of dirt and lead pipes excavated from walls and left for collectors to walk around admiringly in their once pristine penthouses—could be capable of sobbing in her arms when she finally answered his "I love you" with her own.

Beth had been seduced by Gavril's early art stardom, yes, but she fell in love with him because of his sensitivity; his constant need to touch and kiss her, as if she might vanish if his fondness ebbed in the slightest; his hunger to learn her favorite movies and novels; and, best of all, his sincere attention when she was upset about her paintings or her day job copyediting for a science periodical. At NYU, she'd been trained to distrust capitalistic America abstractly while appreciating its concrete comforts. But Gavril seriously loved this country, in theory and in practice. Unlike most artists, he didn't recoil from commercial success, and he was quick, whenever a conversation drifted toward socialism, to expound on the horrors of having nothing under the banner of sharing. "Don't complain about having food in your refrigerator," he griped. "Or lights that don't just work for two hours each day, or the fact that one out of every five of your neighbors isn't an informer being paid by the state to rat you out."

Gavril had violet, translucent skin. A small purple birthmark the shape of the Hawaiian islands stained his left cheek, as if battery acid had scalded him as a boy. His armpits were ripe Balkan forests. His fingernails were bruised mesa sunsets. His eyes were the color of bullet-scarred housing projects with deep, sunless interiors. His sweat smelled like burnt sage, the source of which she couldn't locate no matter how often she ransacked his thighs and chest. They ransacked each other quite a bit by the time they married in a small civil ceremony last year held in the rented library of the Swiss embassy (a spot Beth had chosen not for its political neutrality, but because the library offered a baby grand piano). In New York, the bed served as their preferred weekend destination, the sex lasting longer than the movies they put on to drown out their moans.

In their first months in Orient, though, Beth had noticed a change in Gavril. Most evident was the shift in their sex life, now driven by a galvanizing sense of purpose. Gavril's softness dissipated into a rougher, mechanical approach, often lasting only a few, frantic minutes; Beth sometimes left her own body midway through the act and imagined herself as some industrial material on which Gavril was unloading his surge of creativity. It was as though, having deserted her own painting career, now she was abandoning her own self, becoming merely a conduit for Gavril's ever-accruing list of *things he was making.* The bed became an arena, where he was the star performer. She knew she was being unreasonable, judging him too harshly, but she found it impossible to prevent the misgivings of the bedroom from infecting the rest of the house.

Gavril's honeymoon with the United States had also undergone a noticeable shift outside of Manhattan. Now that he was a naturalized citizen, he had started dropping peevish comments about America, "land of the free." He had received a citation in June for openly drinking beer on the beach at Orient State Park. He nearly doubled over in apoplexy when he was told he couldn't remove the fence around the swimming pool because it was required by law. When two gay friends explained to him that their marriage in the state of New York would be considered invalid when they crossed over to New Jersey, Gavril hugged them both as if they would soon be rounded up in a pogrom. The phrase "It's a free country, right?" became a staple of his Romanian-accented vernacular. Mindful that the Fourth of July parade might have reminded her husband a bit too much of Romanian dance spectaculars, she steered clear of the Labor Day fireworks on Shelter Island.

As the summer wore on, though, she noticed that Gavril started keeping an inventory of worrying anticapitalistic tactics in his art notebook. 1. "Don't make anything that can be sold." (Beth fretted about the future expenses of raising a child.) 2. "Undermine my own signature by claiming others have made my work." (A recent Catargi tar smear had just sold for $400,000 at auction.) 3. "Destroy the notion of objects created for market by turning life into art." (Beth was frightened by Gavril's new, single-minded gusto in bed.) 4. "When an artist can no longer make, he must unmake, he must kill, neuter, destroy." *(Umm . . .)* 5. "Pretend to live the ultimate suburban American dream with wife and child and only on deathbed reveal it had all been a charade." (*I could deal with that,* she surprised herself by thinking.) Beth knew she had no business reading Gavril's journal, even when he left it out on the kitchen counter. They were notes about his art, not about what they meant to each other.

She stared at him now, his thick body dark against the sunlight of the windows, and he stared back at her with lips pinched in a smile. She still loved him so much, her vain, sloppy husband with his underwear climbing out of his pants. He had trusted her enough to leave New York and move out here to be with her in this strange, new region of America. It was her turn to comfort him, to make him feel safe.

Beth was stepping forward to do just that, to kiss her husband on the Maui of his birthmark, when Gail slid from her chair and wrapped her arm around Gavril's chest. "Then none of us will go," Gail said happily. "We'll protest their bad behavior by refusing our company." (Had she been reading his notebook too?) "I hope it rains."

"Gavril," Beth said. "It might be nice. Why don't we go together? I'd like to spend the day out of the house, and there are still some neighbors you haven't met." Beth wrapped her arms around her own stomach, holding it protectively, and tried to reach Gavril with her eyes.

"Paul Benchley's bringing some young man out to live with him," her mother said. "A con artist from the city. That's what I heard. I'd like to see Pam's face when she meets her new neighbor."

"It's a free country, right?"

The mention of a New Yorker coming to live in Orient roused Beth's curiosity. Ironically, it was Gavril, not Beth, who had accumulated dozens of friends in their time here. His had all been imported—fellow artist expats on the North Fork with whom he got drunk, traded gossip about New York galleries, and hatched elaborate plots to turn Orient into a bohemian art colony. All of Beth's childhood friends had moved away or settled deeply into their families. Once so well liked, Beth now felt herself being sidestepped to home in on the prize of her more famous husband. She was desperate for a friend from the city—anyone, even a con artist.

"I don't believe all the talk about Paul being gay anyway," Gail went on. "When he was young, he used to date a lot of the girls out here. I guess people do change in the city. Although I'm sure Pam started that rumor just so she could brag about how tolerant she is."

"Well, we're going. Right, Gavril? You love picnics. There'll probably be a barbecue and a lot of American flags."

Gavril shook his head, even as he kept his loving smile.

"I'm sorry, Beth. But they don't welcome me. And I have too much work to do today."

"Traitor," she whispered and went upstairs to change.

Beth drove the five minutes to the Muldoons' house by herself. Parked cars lined the curb, and she decided, as a newly pregnant woman, that it was her right to block the driveway of the empty, for-sale Tudor five houses down. Maybe the first person to hear the news of her pregnancy would be a ticketing police officer.

The afternoon had grown cold as she approached the lawn, already busy and white with guests. She knew many of them, had known, had gone to school with or taken sailing lessons with them or seen them last at her father's funeral. But there was really no one with whom she could sustain a conversation, no one to play that essential life-support role a friend fills at a party. Beth occupied herself spooning single servings of potato salad on a plastic plate, eating it, and helping herself to more. She chatted with her old third grade teacher, Ina Jenkins, and with Adam Pruitt, a guy two years older who had nearly taken her virginity one summer night in the late 1990s and still carried the traces of his childhood good looks on a slender face falling to ruin with cigarettes and beer. But they spoke only of the past, twenty years behind them, and when the memories failed to find a foothold in the present she excused herself. If Gavril had come along, at least he could have lent the scene a sense of currency. Beth was relieved when Magdalena Kiefer, nestled beneath a shawl in a lawn chair, beckoned her over with a wave.

"How are the bees?" Beth asked as she knelt at the old woman's side.

Magdalena's short, white hair and splotched cheeks gave her a wise, matronly aura, that of a woman who had braced hard winds and, with squinted, cataract-blighted eyes, braced them still. She was like a season that was trying to hold on as fresher weather swept in to erase her. She placed a fingertip against Beth's cheek, as if she were feeling for familiarity.

"They come back now, better, not dying like they were a few seasons ago from that mysterious disease. It's a strong colony this year. I'll have to bring them into the garage this week. The queens are angry . . . September frost."

"One was caught in my kitchen window today," Beth said. Magdalena's filmy eyes brightened, and Beth remembered that she'd forgotten to free it by opening the outside pane. "I let it go," she lied.

"Must have been attracted to fruit," she whispered. Beth cupped her ears to hear her better, over the sound of Pam Muldoon shouting across the lawn for her son. "I'm so glad you and your husband are living next door. It's a breath of fresh air . . . because your mother's swimming pool and the terrible construction."

Beth laughed to indicate that she'd heard Magdalena, when in truth she'd caught only snippets of her speech, faint shapes of fish beneath the surface of the ocean. Kneeling there on the grass, she was distracted by the sudden churn of her stomach. She stood up quickly and swept her hand along the arm of the chair.

"Well, I'll have to stop by for a visit."

Magdalena caught her hand and grasped it as hard as her muscles allowed.

"I'd like you to come by," she said. "Tell you what might happen." Beth was back on her feet now and had an even harder time hearing her. "Could happen. And they are planning it . . ." Her mouth moved silently, as if air and voice were logjammed in her throat. Beth caught another few words: " . . . to be afraid. How could it be like that?"

"Okay," Beth said, turning the stillness of their hands into a departing shake. "This week. I'll knock on your door."

Beth hurried across the lawn toward the Muldoons' house and entered through a sliding door into the laundry room. Bicycles and skateboards were piled there erratically; a clothes dryer quaked against the concrete floor, its windowed stomach swirling with red socks and flesh-toned towels. Pressing her palm against her mouth, she sprinted into the kitchen. She tried the first closed door she could locate—mercifully, it was the bathroom. In a single motion, she managed to close the door with one hand, lift the toilet lid with the other, and vomit a surge of yellow liquid into the bowl. Was it the potato salad? Was it the baby? Beth had no idea.

After the heaving subsided, she hung her head over the toilet a minute longer, staring at a dish of dried rose petals on top of the tank. Then she flushed the toilet, ran the tap, and splashed cold water into her mouth. In the gray light of the bathroom, she studied her face, skeletal, cheekbones protruding like a child's kneecaps. The boyish indent of her chin fit Gavril's pinkie finger. It had been their little love gesture in Manhattan: Gavril stretching out his pinkie and pressing it into the divot like key to lock. She took a few deep breaths and smoothed her white dress. Someone knocked at the door, and when she opened it, Adam Pruitt stood in front of her grinning, as if it wasn't the bathroom he'd been looking for but her. But he was seventeen years too late to take her virginity, and she swept by him into the kitchen. The oven reeked of gas.

Outside, the ground warped below her, and Beth found herself looping far wide of the oak tree rather than walking toward it. She saw Pam's youngest son, Theo, his hands dished together, in his palms a baby bird. The poor creature was shivering, desperate, all bulging eyes, and the sight of it released another bout of queasiness. Beth feigned curiosity, hoping to liberate the bird from his clutches and at least let it die in peace in the crook of a tree. *It should be illegal for boys under fourteen to touch an animal that doesn't have teeth*, she thought.

"Ohhh," she cooed as she bent forward, pushing her hair behind her ear, preparing to snatch it up if she had to. Theo must have sensed her intentions, because he scooped one hand over the other and blocked access with his back. Pam stood three feet away, face pale and lips agitated, clearly in no mood to tolerate outside parenting. Beth quickly gave up on the mission. *Maybe some organisms are born to withstand torture*, she thought as she walked toward the drinks table. *Some things are meant to bear the pain and die.* She searched for something carbonated to calm her stomach.

Beth knew she should leave the picnic in case her sickness worsened. But returning home too early would only have confirmed what Gavril and her mother believed: that they weren't missing anything by skipping a party they weren't invited to in the first place. She forced herself to linger at the drinks table, scooping ice from the bucket to hydrate her tongue. As the sun sank over the rooftops and silvered the Sound through the oak branches, she realized that she'd forgotten to call her doctor to schedule an appointment. The office must already be closed. She would have to wait for days now for confirmation. When Paul Benchley tapped her on the shoulder, Beth wasn't sure how long she had been standing there, holding a cube of ice against her lip.

"Were you stung?" Paul asked. "Is your lip okay?"

"No. Yes. No." She threw the cube on the ground. "I was just in a daze."

Paul's face softened, and his mustache grew like an accordion under his wire-rimmed glasses. Beth liked Paul Benchley, as much as she knew him. She remembered him as a teenager when she was a child, being put to work by his tyrannical parents, taking out customers on the fishing excursions his father advertised from his Greenport bait shop, fixing every window and board of the Benchleys' dilapidated mansion—they even forced Paul to spend his summers running the old inn on the tip, which had been in his mother's family for generations. Paul had earned an Ivy League degree in architecture, and, as his career took off and his parents grew older, he paid their bills so they could remain in the mansion until their deaths. Beth remembered Paul's mother distinctly, a heavyset woman with speed-walking legs who ambled the coast in the afternoons, ignoring all property markers. Paul was long gone by then, working away in the city. A few years ago Gail had tried to hire Paul to oversee the latest remodeling of her house, hoping a local architect might alleviate the growing rancor, but he had gently declined. Beth realized now that her mother must have taken his refusal as just another snub against her.

Beth peered around Paul, looking for the so-called con artist he'd brought with him. Paul followed her gaze, then waved toward a young man lingering near the driveway. "Over here," he shouted. "Have you met Beth?"

So this was the con artist. His lips flickered the semblance of a smile, but he remained frozen on the driveway, digging his foot into the gravel. He looked younger than she had expected and lonelier than someone from New York, too unsure of himself to last long in that state of teenage indecision. His black hair swooped around his forehead, much like Gavril's when he didn't comb it before it dried. His face was angular and his skin newt white, his features so sharp they seemed engineered to cut through wind. In a few years, she thought, when his shoulders filled out he would be rather handsome. He didn't seem capable of a con.

"He's from New York?" she said.

"Only briefly. I've asked him to come out here to help me on the house. The truth is, he ran into a little trouble in Manhattan. Nothing criminal," Paul quickly clarified. "He's really a sweet kid that just got a bit misdirected in the city. I thought Orient might give him some stability."

"I get it. Instead of scaring him straight, you're hoping to bore him straight." It wasn't funny, and even Beth didn't try to save the joke by laughing. "Well, let me know if he needs anything. Even if you want someone to show him around for an afternoon—I'd be happy for the distraction."

"Would you?" Paul grabbed at the offer, as if she might retract it. "That would be very kind of you. I'm sure he'd love that."

"Of course," she said, smiling.

"By the way, congratulations. I hear you're married. Your husband's also an artist—did I get that right?"

"Yes." She laughed. "Another goddamned city artist, I'm sure some of the neighbors are thinking."

Paul just nodded, as if to convey, *That's how these Orient people are.*

"You know," Beth said, "the couple that bought your mother's old inn—they're friends of mine. Friends of my husband's really. Luz Wilson and Nathan Crimp. They're artists too."

"Well, they've got their work cut out for them," Paul said, shaking his head. "I heard it was bought, but I haven't been there in years. I don't know if the previous owners managed to make much headway, but that old shell was one bad hurricane from falling into the sea."

Beth decided not to tell him that Luz and Nathan had gutted the place, knocking down every wall and bulldozing every inch of lawn. The old inn was buffered by enough acres of land that their renovations hadn't caught the wrath of neighbors, the way her mother's had. Even though Paul was a city person, Beth saw no reason to sway the local tide against her friends. Luz and Nathan were such volatile personalities, they'd have no trouble doing that on their own.

Paul's guest was still standing on the sidelines. "So if you want to meet Mills, it looks like we're going to have to go to him."

Beth turned to collect her purse from the table as Paul headed off toward the driveway. Suddenly Pam Muldoon cut in front of her, breathing hard.

"Do you want to take plates home?" she asked Beth.

"Plates?"

Pam blinked in confusion. "Plates of food for your husband. We can wrap up some of the burgers. It's such a shame he couldn't join you. Don't you think he'd like that?" Pam nodded yes to her own question. "Come with me to the kitchen and I'll make a nice spread for . . . Gavin, isn't it? We've got too much to finish ourselves."

Pam tugged at her wrist, leading her toward the house. Beth wanted to flag down Paul but he was already too far away, disappearing across the yard. She tried to explain that food wasn't necessary, that her husband had probably already eaten, that his name was Gavril, that it would all go to waste in her refrigerator just as fast.

Fifteen minutes later, she carried a grocery bag of scraps out the front door. Night had settled on the lawn and cleared most of the picnic. Paul and the young man were gone. Sarakit Herrig was wrapping her three children in coats. Adam Pruitt winked at her, and she continued walking down the slope of the grass toward her car. She looked for a garbage can where she could toss Pam's food, but a Pearl Farms Realty sign was the only thing in sight.

Beth threw the bag in the backseat and started the ignition. She turned on the heat and felt safe inside the cramped cavern of the Nissan. It hummed, it moved at her command, it played her favorite songs and smelled of her perfume. The car was one of the few exotic pleasures of non-Manhattan life—indeed, it was a kind of proxy Manhattan, a compact space with everything in easy reach.

She drove down Youngs Road until she reached Main, one way east, the other west. One way offered a promise of family life with Gavril at her house, the other the charades of the city: a quiet studio apartment with jars of paint waiting to be used, windows with a view of the Brooklyn Bridge and beetle-black cars sliding across it, meaningless bathroom fucks with men not so different from Adam Pruitt. Which way would she go? Why did she even have to pick a direction? She tried to merge both arrows into one in her mind, but they bounced back into place as if on springs.

She turned onto Main Road, trying to picture not the arrows but herself, a pregnant woman in her early thirties. Beth had once painted faces so carefully that every fold and fissure of skin was scarred onto the canvas. All she could muster now of her own face was a faint white circle awaiting definition. Beth had no vision of herself. If she'd been forced to describe herself to a police sketch artist, the result would be a drawing of her at twenty different ages, none of them today, none of them right.

As she swiveled the rearview mirror to catch a glimpse of herself, a streak of light appeared out of the corner of her eye. She slammed on the brake, rocking forward against the steering wheel. Her head-lights homed in on a fluorescent orange square retreating into the night, with black shapes around it rotating, vibrating—a floating, fleeing danger sign. Beth stepped on the gas and passed a woman in a reflector vest running on the side of the road. Her shoes crunched the blond tufts of moonlit grass, her eyes staring forward in numb determination. House lights shined against the water, the top floors burning as night drew residents to higher ground.

On the road, the joggers were out. And somewhere in the darkness, so were the hunters.

CHAPTER 3

As Paul searched his pockets for his keys, he told Mills to "be prepared." The warning might have alarmed most first-time houseguests, but Mills had been prepared for the last two hours. He was sick of standing still.

The art of hitchhiking relied on constant motion. That meant not only walking along the road while trying to flag a ride, but also moving through towns and cities, never sleeping anywhere twice. It had taken Mills seventeen days to get from California to New York, and in that time he never once overstayed his welcome—whether at a diner or on a park bench or in the stone-scrubbed bus terminals where all the pay phones had lost their receivers. In theory hitchhiking seemed dangerous, but in reality the rhythm of hours and loose small talk fit his sense of purpose: jump in, cover some distance, and thank them for their kindness. He had encountered no nightmare scenarios, no serial killers scouring the desert, no meth labs burning holes in the atmosphere, no crooked cops or grandfathers with tampered passenger-door locks or gas-station ex-cons with makeshift dungeons. America, for Mills, had almost been one long, amicable disappointment. He hadn't stopped moving until he reached Manhattan.

The drive from the city with Paul had brought back the memory of travel. And once they arrived in Orient, Mills found the stillness difficult to take. As he loitered near the picnic, never quite joining in, Mills could tell already that the squint-mouthed hostess, Pam

Muldoon, didn't like him. Paul seemed oblivious, beckoning him over: "Come here. Have you met Beth?" Soon Pam called Tommy away on the excuse of needing paper towels ("Tommy, can you get some paper towels out of the kitchen cupboard?" "Tommy, the paper towels!"), and Mills lingered in the driveway, pushing his shoes through the gravel. It was Paul's house that interested him, anyway.

Mills had agreed to help Paul fix up his house without under-standing exactly what that meant. He'd pictured pipes bursting, tiles popping from bathroom walls, glinting figurines in need of a polish. Mills told Paul straight out that he wouldn't stay in Orient only out of Paul's sympathy. Sympathy was a necessary tool for hitchhiking, but Mills couldn't stand it beyond a one-hour window. "Are you sure you have something for me to do?" he had asked. Paul nodded in assurance, his Adam's apple bobbing under whiskered skin, his hands raised in oath. "Believe me, there's plenty," he said.

As the picnic wore on, Mills studied the white clapboard farm-house with its manicured bushes and paint-scabbed porch, search-ing for clues to the disorder that awaited him inside. Thanks to the foster homes of his childhood, Mills had developed a keen eye for predicting what state of emergency existed inside a house by the travesty of its front yard: mud plots resistant to grass but wild with Coors Light cans; duct-taped satellite dishes spiking off storm drains; plastic lounge chairs compressed by the weight of their owners, set facing the street like California thrones. Judged on these terms, Paul Benchley's house was peculiarly vacant of character. Maybe in the East, homes were too old and worn by years of salt water to bear the imprint of their owners. Except, that is, for the Muldoons', where the yanked-open screen doors and an upstairs window emblazoned with anarchy stickers carried the mark of fleeing children.

In the darkness of the porch, Paul stooped to locate the keyhole. For Mills, nights along the California beaches had possessed a feeling of limitlessness, the deep Pacific waters and glass-blown horizon a perfect dreamer's landscape. In Orient, the thick salt air closed in with the night like a pillow held over the dreamer's face. Paul unlocked the door, and Mills followed him into a small tin-ceilinged vestibule. He slid his hands over a radiator that was cold and sharp with rust. The night air was already tracing their breath in contrails.

As Paul fidgeted with the inner door, Mills focused on Paul's thinning bald spot. Mills wondered if Paul knew he was balding. Was it his duty as a friend to tell him? Or would it be taken as an insult? *Paul, I'm sorry. I feel like someone should tell you. It's the size of a quarter on the back of your head and there's probably still a chance you could stop it with some kind of over-the-counter lotion.* Instinctively, Mills touched the back of his own head, comforted by the clench of curls rooted to his scalp. He had no way of knowing the tide line of his own father's hair, or his mother's father's.

The door finally gave, and they both fell forward into warmer blackness. Mills hunted his brain for a compliment to compensate for his standoffish behavior at the picnic. "Your place, Paul," he said, stumbling. "It's beautiful."

"You haven't seen it yet," Paul replied, laughing. He flipped a light switch, and Mills did see it.

The front rooms were spare and neat to the point of compulsion, with little evidence of needing much more than a vacuum. But then Paul was an architect; naturally his parlor and dining room would reflect a man who drew clean lines for a living. Mills dropped his duffel bag by the door. As exhausted as he was by the drive and the unexpected hiatus of the picnic, he was also familiar with the clumsy negotiations of first nights in strange houses. "So here I am." "So this is my bed." "So I'll just lie down now and you can continue watching television like I was always here or never was." Many of his foster parents had existed primarily as hunched, aromatic shadows moving from bedroom to toilet. But Paul didn't lead Mills up the staircase or dismiss him with a spare set of towels. Instead he busied himself turning on more lights.

Mills rubbed the front of his jeans—a nervous habit, as if he were coaxing two resistant ponies out of a barn—and followed Paul into the parlor. A brown tweed sofa sat under lace-curtained windows;

a glass coffee table held a stack of *Architectural Digest*s. In the adjacent dining room, a long table cut across a sweep of whitewashed floorboards, slender chrome legs holding a heavy marble slab, deep midnight blue with foamy white fissures.

"It's like a flowing river," Mills said, running his fingers along the cold surface.

Paul smiled, impressed. His glasses glittered under the ceiling fixture.

"It was from a river in Africa," Paul said. "I've had it for five years and it's still ice cold on your arms when you lean on it. It's kept the coldness of the river and the earth. Don't you love a material that refuses to surrender its properties? We expect everything to behave like plastic, but this marble—the memory of its origin is stored in its core."

Mills returned the smile but removed his fingers, realizing that the table was one of many objects in the room that seemed to ask not to be touched. Some of Paul's possessions sat under glass jars on the mantel—a pair of antique binoculars, a taxidermied oriole, a miniature silver lighthouse with a red jewel fitted in its beacon. The only other contents of the front rooms were the shelves of books, their spines calling out the wonders of architecture, art, historic homes, and historic families. Paul must have spent all of his free time reading, or perhaps collecting books was so time-consuming that there weren't any hours left to read. Mills felt tired just surveying their titles.

As he scanned them, a sliver of panic rose in his throat. What was he doing, coming to stay here, a hundred miles away from the safety of Manhattan? This house was so pristine, it clearly needed no repair work. Mills suddenly wondered if Paul had brought him out here for reasons that weren't entirely benign. Mills hadn't done drugs, not heroin or even cocaine, in four days—four fingers and tomorrow would be five, an open hand—but the effects of his last weeks in New York still left him headachy and dehydrated, dulling his judgment and blunting his instincts. Only now in the quiet of

Paul's dining room, against the blackness of the windows and the wind jittering their casings, did Mills feel vulnerable, out of screaming distance, down to one of two very different men separated by a piece of excavated stone.

"Paul," he started. "I don't think you need me in this house."

Paul stared at him, his pupils so wide the blues of his eyes were reduced to coronas. But they didn't skirt his body or calculate his distance from the door. They remained on Mills's face, as if worried that his guest had found his home unsatisfactory, not as warm and welcoming as its owner.

"You're probably exhausted. Of course you are. Your bedroom's upstairs, but first let me show you what I had in mind."

Paul was not a man Mills would describe as handsome. He was short, with bristled, brown hair that reddened and silvered under ceiling bulbs. His complexion was as white as liquid soap, but he had a strong jaw and a broom-shaped mustache, the head of a lion whose mane had been shaved, and, Mills guessed, underneath his wool sweater, a gourdlike body of muscles and chest hair. Take a decade off Paul Benchley, and he would have been a man of harder substance. He had thick wrists, a neck etched with skin lines, and the beginning of a lump at his waist. If Paul's eyes were closed, he would have appeared old, a taker of too much space. Peering through his wire-rimmed glasses, though, his eyes were alert and pensive and mostly unwilling to see the worst. They had not seen the worst in Mills, and it was because of those eyes that Mills followed him down the hallway into the recesses of the house.

Mills had been duped before. Even two of his foster dads had seen something to like in him and tried to get what they could. They had sprung on him in his sleep, groping with reckless hands, probably not meaning to be so brutal, but then going slowly, attempting a seductive line of attack, might have triggered the standstill of fear, the same way a moment's hesitation can stop a person from running full throttle into the ocean. Mills had thrown the right amount of punches to protect himself.

The truth was, most of his "parents" had been rather uninterested in his growing body, obsessed more by how to clean the stains he left on their blankets than by how those stains got there in the first place. Mills understood that his preferred method of masturbation—and at nineteen he had only recently felt able to control that all-consuming urge—was embarrassingly infantile. He would lie on a bed or on the floor with a blanket wedged against his erection, rubbing against the bundled fabric, effectively humping the ground, until he came, usually on the blanket or across the carpet, no matter how strategically he had placed a wad of tissue. He'd never learned the art of self-gratification while seated on a toilet. It seemed one of the many lessons that had eluded him as he passed into adulthood—like shaving or using the correct fork or catching a football with the crutch of his shoulder. Thoughts of masturbation felt unnecessary to the point of derangement right here in Paul Benchley's house, but nevertheless the worry was there, triggering his anxiety the way thoughts of cigarettes provoke chain-smokers.

Paul turned around before opening the door at the end of the hall. "I don't want you to feel uncomfortable about being here," he said, placing his hand lightly on Mills's shoulder, as if he didn't want to trouble it with weight. "You've had a hard time in New York, and you should be focusing on getting away from that. So if this seems too much for you, we don't have to start tomorrow. Little by little. Whatever you're okay with. Just promise me one thing. No drugs find their way into this house."

"I promise," he said.

Even though Paul had seen him at his absolute lowest, scrounging his last dollars for the tiniest tinfoil of powder to snort, Mills didn't consider himself an addict. He would prove to Paul that he could accomplish any task asked of him, to pay him back for saving him. Mills could still be living another future in New York right now, slumped in a hallway, begging for change on the street, entering the apartments of strange men to perform his embarrassing floor ritual in front of them for fifty bucks. One of his first friends in the city had bragged about earning fifty bucks sampling the food of a senile cosmetics mogul who believed that his stepchildren were poisoning him. Those were junkie jobs, requiring little more skill than basic human functioning, and they were often lucrative. His friend, a Kentucky runaway fattened on grass-fed veal and stewed plums, always told him, "There's an economy for everything in New York. Someone will pay to cut your toenails if you're smart enough to find them." His friend could have been lying, covering up a darker cash source. He also could have been telling the truth.

"So what's back there?" Mills asked. "What am I in for?"

Paul opened the door. Room by room, light switch by light switch, through pleated lamp shades and ceiling bowls that doubled as insect morgues, the messy maze of the Benchley house slowly revealed itself. The shock of the number of rooms that forked and followed in never-ending architectural freefall was tempered only by the astounding amount of junk that was piled up within them. No wonder Paul kept his hallway door shut: something had to prevent the clutter from infecting the monastery of his parlor and dining room. The first rooms, at least, were navigable, though pocked with magazines in weedy, dog-eared piles, shoe boxes of opened and unopened envelopes, shoes with misplaced sole cushions, broken easels and replacement easels with dried canvases leaning against them ("these are my very amateur paintings," Paul said, picking up a seaside landscape bathed in yellow), canoe paddles, a portable grill asphyxiated by a long black cord, rolls of architectural blueprints, and an infestation of batteries that had crawled into wood crevices and died quietly on their expiration dates.

These first rooms, however, served only as recent storage. The deeper they went, the more they retreated into history—not Paul's history, but a history of dead people, his parents and doubtless others before them. At each new room, and through the haze of each porcelain lamp, the two went forward into a stewy sea of costume jewelry, Suffolk County phone books, landline telephones, air-conditioning units, a ceramic arms-out Jesus missing his back support and floating like a shipwreck victim awaiting rescue. Blackened picture frames held crooked family photographs. Paul had to shuffle sideways to carve a path, and Mills jumped to keep up, triggering clouds of dust as albums fell in his wake.

In another life, with all of his heroic pointing, Paul Benchley could have been a valiant sea captain. In this life, at this hour of night, he was just a beleaguered home owner standing knee-deep in waste. "None of this has been settled," Paul said tiredly. To Mills, some of it looked as settled as bedrock. Still, Paul kept pointing, kept opening doors, until finally history became garbage, literal garbage, the last room a tar pit of bloated black trash bags. "This is what I've already managed to throw out," he said. "I told you to be prepared."

What could Mills say? "Jesus, you weren't kidding." Yet he was strangely relieved by the junk—Paul really did need help, and no overnight job either, no afternoon sawing branches or sweeping a porch. They trudged back into the epicenter of the back rooms, where floral paper peeled from the walls, and broken plaster exposed buttery swabs of insulation. The cold here was finger numbing, and Mills fought back a shiver.

"Is this your mom and dad's stuff?" Mills asked, glancing around for one of the picture frames, a way to put faces to belongings.

Paul nodded. "And believe me, I'm not a pack rat. I just never got around to dealing with their things. My father died seven years ago and my mother went in June. I pushed it all back into these rooms, and since I only come up on weekends I never found the time. Well, now you've seen the worst of it." Guessing what Mills was looking for, he grabbed a stack of photographs from an open drawer, sifted quickly through them, and handed one over.

They looked happy, this old couple, engineers of their own stake in the twentieth-century suburban own-everything dream. His mother sat in a wooden foldout chair, her curly hair a premature gray, her hand poised on her shoulder to cup her husband's fingers. The husband stood behind her, belt around his kidneys, a captain's hat shadowing his eyes. His father was skinny, skin sunken but very tan, his smile coming less naturally than that of his wife. All this stuff had been theirs: the *Birds of Long Island* guides, the laundry basket of beige bras and silk dresses, three wise men and a donkey placed on a sheet of antacid medication. It was the fate of most household items to linger on after their owners, offering acciden-tal clues to their hopes and distractions. Paul's parents, it seemed, had been perfectly normal: they liked birds and religious tokens and wore unisex snow boots and battled indigestion. And now they were dead, survived by a legacy of by-product, an avalanche of junk that never stopped rolling.

Paul took the photograph from Mills's hands and returned it to the stack. "Honestly, I almost feel like I should burn these," he said. "I think that might be the kindest form of death for family pho-tographs. I've never seen anything more depressing than a box of old photos for sale in a Salvation Army. Those were all people who mattered. I guess that's the advantage of our digital age. You can just press delete at the end of your life and no one can touch you." Paul wiped his forehead. Sweat clouded his glasses.

"Do you miss them?" Mills asked. "Your parents, I mean."

Paul blinked at the question.

"Yes. They were very good people. Orient people. My father owned a bait shop in Greenport, owned a few boats too, rented them out for bluefish season. And my mother ran a hotel for a while. Well, a bed-and-breakfast–type place on the tip that had been in her family for almost a century. It wasn't very successful. Tourists stopped coming to Orient once the Hamptons took off. She had to let go of it to pay for my schooling, which was just as well. As a kid, I was put to work nights and weekends to keep up those rooms, which no one ever rented." Paul blew a channel of air; it whitened before it faded. He dropped the stack of pictures in the drawer and jiggled it shut.

"What about this house?" Mills asked. "How long has it been in your family?"

Paul glanced up at the ceiling's low, splintered crossbeams.

"My mother's family had it for generations. If you walk outside, all the property as far as you can see along the Sound belonged to them. My grandfather was forced to sell most of it when he got married, parceled it up, and that was the end of the potato farms. But my parents stayed on here, making ends meet. I suppose that's why I kept it when they died. I just can't bring myself to let go of something that's been in my family for so long. As you can see." Paul nodded to the junk piles and laughed feebly. Mills noticed a mouse darting behind the phone books. Animals had made their homes back here.

"I don't know," Paul said. "Maybe I'll just feel lonelier in this house after we clean all this out, with all these empty rooms. I think my parents always thought they'd have more kids . . ." He waved his arms like a Realtor, as if trying to fill the dead rooms with a flurry of life.

"Were you with your parents when they died? Did you"—Mills tried to find subtle roads—"take care of them?" Now that he'd seen their picture, he was curious to know how they had died. Why was a person's exact cause of death so often more fascinating than what they did with their life? Because it explained how they suffered, Mills thought, because it was a reminder that everyone suffers in the end.

"I was with my mom. I came up for her last month. Cancer got her. And the treatments got her worse, so she stopped attending the chemo sessions I set up. I did all the stupid things a child does when a parent is on her deathbed."

Mills didn't know what all those stupid things were. "Like?" he risked asking.

Paul cleared his throat. "Like I bought a digital camera to record her recollections. I thought it would be a kind of show of respect, to have those Benchley stories chronicled on film. She was so sick, all I managed to get was a dying woman repeating my questions back to me and then going quiet, staring up at the ceiling like the answers to the past were all written there. She had dementia in the end."

"You should have showed her the old photos. That might have helped remind her."

Paul dipped his head. He wasn't crying; Mills would have been able to see the tears behind his lenses. Grown men crying were like deep-water fish against aquarium glass, their mouths curved downward, drifting away from the light.

"I did try that," Paul admitted. "I carted in the albums, spread them on her lap. Finally, and this was one thing I did get on camera, she brought her arm up and knocked the albums off the bed. 'I'm sick of those times,' she said. 'Get them out of here and give me peace.'" Paul winced and forced a smile. "I realized how selfish it was, asking her to spend her last days entertaining me with memories. It's hard to lose a parent—especially losing them that way, before they die, till they have nothing left to say to you even while they still can." He paused. "Maybe the past stopped mattering to her. Maybe she was giving me permission to throw it all out." His eyes looked vacant now, like a newborn's, sliding around without absorbing details. Mills got the sense that Paul didn't bring him out here only for his extra set of hands. He didn't seem to have anyone else to talk to. Paul snapped awake, his cheeks flushed. "I'm sorry. I didn't mean to go on like that. About parents."

Mills lifted his hands to reassure him. It didn't bother him to talk about other people's parents, to know that children liked and sometimes missed their own.

Paul pinched his lips before he spoke. "You know nothing about your parents? Who they were, what happened before they gave you up? I mean, you must have some idea, right?"

"No, nothing—not a name or a reason," Mills replied. "And I never asked, either." The truth was, Mills had asked. For several years, on his birthday, he had gone to his caseworker and his counselor to ask for information, but they'd always shrugged while examining his file, UNKNOWN being their only response. He had tried other routes, with more enlightening results, but Mills liked Paul too much to burden this first night with sad stories. "I'm not a wounded kid, you know," he said. "It could have been worse. I learned how to tie my shoes same as everybody. If you don't know it, you don't miss it. And I had love around me most of the time." That was the second lie he'd told Paul Benchley in the past two minutes.

Paul nodded, as if he understood. "Well," he said, and let that be the final word. They drifted toward the front rooms, Paul extinguishing each light behind them, and Mills felt the impulse to wipe his feet when he reached the hallway, as if his shoes were soaked in a past he didn't want to track through the rest of the house. Paul placed his hand on the banister leading upstairs.

"I forgot about the picnic," he said as Mills lifted his duffel bag over his shoulder. "I hope that wasn't awkward for you. Meeting all of those neighbors in one fell swoop."

"I don't think your neighbor likes me. The mom," Mills said.

"Oh." Paul touched his shoulder delicately. "Pam's harmless. And I called ahead to let them know you were coming. Some people out here think the world ends at the causeway and anyone who manages to drive over it is trying to steal their souls. Or better yet, their views of the Sound. But most Orient people are pretty nice—if you answer enough of their questions and don't give them too much to gossip about."

"I won't tell them about your back rooms," Mills promised.

Paul laughed, clapping his hands together. "That's not what I was thinking of. But thanks."

They climbed the dark staircase—perhaps there was no switch on the ground floor, or perhaps Paul preferred the blue trail of moonlight that poured across the upstairs landing—to the colder second floor. Mills could feel the wooden beams shift under his sneakers, the house adjusting to his unfamiliar weight. Paul navigated the hall with quieter footsteps, walking past closed doors and less amateur seascapes framed in gold, limping slightly, as if reminded of a knee injury that was still healing.

Paul opened the last door and led him into a small bedroom. A different slant of moonlight, watery and white, spilled from the single window. The room's ceiling slumped downward, and cobwebs grazed Mills's forehead. He dropped his bag on the mattress, stiff from disuse, maybe never used. Maybe Mills was Paul's first guest. He noticed a small door and opened it, expecting a closet until he looked inside and realized it was bigger than that, though too small for a bed. It was a room with no obvious purpose, and with almost nothing inside—not a lamp or a desk or a bookshelf. The only decoration on the wall was a poster of a lighthouse, a squat, doom-windowed structure blistered by a sunset of pinks and grays. He called to Paul, who had taken a folded green towel out of the closet and set it on the dresser, placing a plastic-wrapped toothbrush on top of it.

"Weird room," Mills said, stepping farther into the tiny chamber. He felt his left foot give way, dropping into a bowl-shaped recess in the floor.

"Isn't it?" Paul leaned against the doorframe, hands shoved into his armpits. "It's a birthing room."

"A what?" Mills jumped from the hole, as if the basin might still hold amniotic remains.

"A birthing room. Women used to deliver babies here."

Mills shivered, he didn't know why, some childish spook about a room where long-dead babies had been pulled from long-dead mothers. They didn't have birthing rooms in California.

"Jesus—is this where *you* were born?"

"No, of course not." Paul's crossed arms suddenly read as a sign of rebuke. "But these were quite common in nineteenth-century homes. Whole lives would begin and end in one house. The purpose of a parlor, for example, was for the viewing of a dead body, for relatives to gather for their final visitation. It was only when entrepreneurs realized they could make money on death as well as life that the function of the home parlor was outsourced to the business of the funeral parlor. In fact, when death finally left the home parlor, the name of the room was changed to—"

"A living room," Mills guessed. "I never thought of that."

"I know that might sound like progress, but from an architect's perspective, I think it's pretty sad. No one is born or dies at home anymore. Now we just live in temporary units, made of shitty drywall as interchangeable as renters who tape up a few pictures and call a place home. There's nothing real about living anymore, is there? Every decade less and less." Paul wiped his mouth, and Mills stepped back into the bedroom. He was too tired for more architectural wisdom, another lecture on the wonders of doorknobs, the majesty of the hinge. There'd be time to hear them tomorrow. "Don't worry," Paul said smiling as Mills snaked by him. "It's not haunted."

"Oh, I don't believe in ghosts."

Paul nodded. "You're all set then? Have everything you need?" He retreated into the hall, saying good night as he shut the door.

Mills pulled off his shirt and slid out of his jeans, peeling off his white socks and tucking them into the cups of his shoes. In his underwear, his skin was blue, his nipples black as the moles that dotted his stomach. He slipped into the sharp bedsheets and stared out the window at the branches of an oak tree whisking against the glass. In just one day, he had gotten so far from New York. If he held his breath he could hear the water slapping against the shore. He wasn't sure if coming to Orient had been the right move. Part of him wanted to hitchhike back across the body of the woman on the map, racing toward her head to crawl through her eyes and return to those acquaintances whose nights were just beginning and wouldn't end until he awoke. Those places without birthing rooms or jungles of dead people's possessions—that seemed more like living to him, no matter what Paul said, maybe more so for all their drywall and borrowed furniture, so that the living stood out. He thought of his friend Marcella with her chubby scorched fingers and *mmmmm*-ing breaths, his friend Lucas with his unbuttoned shirts and hamster-cage ribs rocking over his knees.

An erection jabbed in his underwear. Out of habit, Mills rotated on his stomach and balled the sheet against it. His penis was darker than the rest of his skin, as if permanently stained in ink. He had been circumcised at birth, not sloppily like some men he had seen, but expertly cut, as smooth and round as a bicycle helmet. Why had he been circumcised? Had his parents requested it, out of religion or hygiene or tradition? Or was it because a doctor asked and they were too stunned or indifferent to care? It was the only clue his body carried of his birth, which, for all he knew, had taken place in a room as empty as the one ten feet from his bed.

He pushed his hips slowly against the sheet, wondering about Tommy next door. Was he circumcised? Here was a secret Mills kept: at nineteen, he was still a virgin. Only technically, and only concerning the opposite sex. He had been with men, and that's what he preferred; he'd been certain of it for years and more so every day, with every erection pointing like a compass needle on its own magnetic pull. He pictured Tommy next door, maybe gay, likely not, exotic to him for being so unexotic, his short blond hair only a few shades deeper than his skin, his eyes dark and sunken and blue.

Before his mother had called him away, Tommy had asked him a zillion questions about New York—did he live downtown, had he gone to clubs, was he a skateboarder, a gutter punk, some sort of artist, did he smoke pot, was it true that people still flinched every time they heard a loud noise, expecting an explosion—the whole time standing confidently on his parents' property, with the toughness of every spoiled suburban kid who imagined himself a gangster in his own front yard. Tommy had also asked about his earring— did it hurt—nodding to the stud in Mills's right lobe with its small, gold cross. Tommy seemed so intrigued by the pain it must have caused that Mills didn't have the heart to tell him he'd gotten it after a five-minute wait at a Sacramento strip mall, that eleven-year-old girls bore the puncture without much more than an *oh*. Did it hurt? Yes, and that's why he did it. Tommy was tall and wide-hipped, but Mills couldn't tell what kind of body lay underneath the black

T-shirt and jeans, what kind of person, what kind of smell or ability to reach over in the dark. There were certain things a person could only learn by touching someone else.

The bed started to creak against the floor, and Mills forced himself to flip onto his back. No wonder men learned to use their hands. Mills didn't know how far away Paul's bedroom was, so he pulled his underwear over his waist and collapsed his arms on his chest. He stared out the window and tried not to think about Manhattan. Maybe curiosity about Tommy was reason enough to stay in Orient, although Mills assumed teenagers with extremely normal existences were probably hopelessly disappointing in that respect. No, he would stay in Orient for himself. He smoothed his fingers over his chest and shut his eyes. Mills was still young enough to believe that his body, with so much of it uncharted, was the only home he would ever need.

CHAPTER 4

Gentle rocking, a splash in the water.

He came awake, drunk. Cold water choked him, salt guttering through his mouth and nose. He treaded, swimming, his hands clawing black liquid like a cat climbing a curtain just to keep his head above the surface. He felt the slapping waves of the bay against his cheeks and his heavy pant pockets weighing him down.

A boat groaned nearby, as a body pulled itself out of the water and slumped into its hold. He remembered sitting in the boat with a bottle of gin wedged between his thighs, as they steered into the harbor. Beefeater, too expensive not to drink. He must have blacked out. They must have capsized. "Hey," he shouted. "I'm still out here." He lifted his arms into the night air, but a second without treading brought him under. He gulped salt and paddled his hands to bring him back to the surface. Something was wrong with his legs. They weren't kicking right. "Hey," he called again. Nearby, waves lapped against the boat's hull. Stars melted around him, little broken shimmers. Water plugged his ears.

"Wait," he screamed, panicked now. "Get me the fuck out of here, would you?" He tried to bend his knees, but the motion jerked him under. He shut his eyes and squirmed his fingers down his uncooperative legs. He felt rope knotted around his calves, slippery as seaweed, too tight to unpick. Must have gotten tangled when they overturned. He tried to kick the rope clear. His ankles scraped together but wouldn't liberate. *Liberation, babies, paddy fields so orange they were kindling on a bonfire, all that air, all that oxygen burning up.* It was an old memory, too old for longing or repentance and not a good one either.

He shot his arms through the surface and pulled oxygen into his lungs. He saw the causeway one hundred feet to the west, strung like a tree branch in white glowing lights. He tried swimming toward it. The rope tightened and wrenched him into the black. He swam in the opposite direction, toward the deeper bay, but the rope yanked him back for another mouthful. He was caught in the eye of a clock and made rounds to all the numbers but couldn't break through them, couldn't go anywhere but straight up. He was punching the water at his neck now, the sleeves of his sweater weighted with what he punched. And, through the headache of sea and gin, he sensed the first fatigue of his muscles.

He heard an oar slip into the water. "Help," he yelled. He could hear himself as loud as day. "For fuck's sake, I'm stuck. Help me." A shadow rose from the boat's bow, alerted to his calls. The beam of a flashlight flooded his face. "Thank god," he sputtered, squinting through the shine. He paddled toward the light, which beaconed a few feet beyond his leash. "Thought I lost you. Got my legs wrapped in a rack rope. Gimme a knife or your keys or something. Hurry."

The light from the flashlight was tender, almost warm, and he saw the motion of an arm reach over the side. But the arm launched a streak of glass, and the bottle struck him on the forehead, knocking him under with a blunt jolt. He floated downward, stunned by the blow. When he swam to the surface, coughing and spitting, the light returned to his face, a light that took him a minute to realize was receding, fading like a sunset clocking out. "Wait," he shouted, "you can't do this. You can't leave me here." The light clicked off, and the boat careened away.

The gin bottle bobbed just beyond his reach. It went south with the tide. He dove under the water, tugging frantically on the rope, the only thing he could hold on to, the only thing that wouldn't give him up. For a second, he laughed, still drunk, *this is a bad dream,* and when it wasn't, exhausted from pulling, he tipped his head back on the water's surface, the wind on his nose blowing from ocean to land. *I won't pick a last memory*, he reasoned. *If I don't, I'll stay here until somebody finds me. I'll wait all night if I have to for the sun. They need me. They'll notice I'm gone and come looking.* Fish slithered around him. The stars moved in and out. He would remember how they moved, closer and then farther back, pushing at planets, wiping his coldness away, as his head dipped forward, and the night came in.

CHAPTER 5

At 5:58 A.M., the mist rolled off the water and into the tall brown grasses like steam off a gutted animal. There was the smell of life in it, the algae and the wheat, and the sun was low and waxy in the sky, rolling the mist white and not yet strong enough to burn it clear. Bryan Muldoon crouched in the scrub alongside Ted Herrig, both of them camouflaged in faded tan jackets, mint green cargo pants, and black rubber boots. Chip and Alistair crouched a ways behind them, the tops of their hats poking above the grass blades. Bryan had his prize in sight, a white-tailed doe eating the sweeter grasses thirty feet away, her mouth chewing lazily while her neck lifted by the urgency of her eyes, searching for anything that would cause her to run. She dipped her head down, content. Bryan drew his hand up and pointed at her to signal *Mine!*, but it was still 5:58 on his wristwatch and the legal state hunting hours began at six o'clock.

Bryan was a man of principle, an adherent to the minute details of regulations most other, lesser men breached. If he weren't here, even Ted would have rounded 5:58 to the hour, pulled the bow-string to his ear, the whole weapon wired like a mosquito hungry for blood, and taken the shot. But shave two minutes, and soon it's twenty, then an hour, and then the rules don't matter anymore, nothing but empty vessels tossing in the waves. The idea of floating out there in a sea of meaningless rules, where latitudinal and longitudinal lines tangled like seaweed, made him queasy.

His friend Ted was the geography teacher at Sycamore High, a man, like Bryan, who had a wife and three children, although his wife, Sarakit, was of Thai descent, and his children had been adopted from China, Vietnam, and Cambodia. Ted and Bryan served together on the Orient Historical Board, and they had hunted side by side for more than twenty years. Long ago, they had made a pact that if anything bad were to happen, each would look out for the other's children. As a result, Bryan was always auditioning Ted for the role of surrogate father, and he didn't necessarily approve of his friend's laid-back approach to life. Weren't Asian kids supposed to be the hope for America's future? Ted's children were blithe and style-conscious and destined for careers in fashion or TV, the kind of junk that blighted the Muldoons' living room during Theo's Saturday morning cartoon binge.

"Go on," Ted whispered. "She's there for you." The doe craned up, her ragged ears turning 280 degrees to pick up predatory vibrations. Bryan wrenched his eyes at Ted, code for silence. The 8 on his watch changed to 9. Ted's watch already read 6:01, but Ted didn't set his watch to International Atomic Time like Bryan did every morning before a hunt. International Atomic Time was based on the readings of three hundred atomic clocks located in sixty laboratories around the world; Bryan took comfort in the idea of those clocks, buried in disaster-proof orbs all over the globe, army-guarded and ticking to the same precise heartbeat. Time was the single asset that every country, every market, depended on. Bryan so admired those atomic clocks that for his eldest son's last four birthdays he had given him books about time and state-of-the-art GPS watches. His son had long stopped feigning gratitude, throwing the gift boxes on the sofa in defeat, his face as blank as a watch face without hands. It was an expression all parents understood in the vicinity of unwrapped, unwanted presents: *You don't get me, do you?* it said.

Another venture that held no interest for his son was hunting. Bryan had taught him the basics of the longbow, but on their single father-son hunting expedition two years ago, Tommy had brought along his iPhone and yawned each time he aimed and released an arrow, without enough velocity to puncture a balloon. Bryan assumed he would come around, but that window was rapidly closing, shutting them off from each other, a glass divider through which they could still see each other but not speak or touch. Had he failed as a father? Lisa and Theo loved him dearly, he was sure of that. But Tommy was a remote province in the Muldoon kingdom, accepting orders, attending the necessary functions, but without any of the patriotism that united them as a clan. Sometimes, late at night, Bryan peered in at Tommy asleep in his bed, and his eyes would water at the sight of his son, not because he loved him so much but because he knew him so little. He found himself getting emotional over Tommy far more often than he ever did over Lisa's stack of college brochures or the buttery swirls on the back of Theo's head. If only he could have a chance to try it all again with his son, to shake Tommy awake and show him what they were missing, what little time they had left.

His watch read 5:59. He locked the bow in the shaft and waited.

The joints in his knee tingled. The weight of crouching caused the arthritic pain in his ankles to shoot through his calves. He was getting too old for the squatting posture required for hunting. He'd soon have to give up the longbow for the easier January muzzle-loader gun season, or take up the minimal torture of fishing in the bay. Bluefish instead of venison steaks on the grill. That would be the first outward sign of old age, which so far had been contained to his body. His wife had noticed it before he had, in the sinewy droop of his arms and legs. And so had Holly Drake in that embarrassing finale of their six-month affair, when he couldn't manage an erection in the motel bed, when his penis bobbed, expanded an inch, shyly refused to venture farther, and finally deflated against his testicles as if in spite.

That was two weeks ago, and even though he'd offered to meet Holly again at the motel when her husband was at work, and even though she had accepted, he feared a repeat performance. Don't listen to women who swear that men age gracefully. They're simply conditioned to judge their own kind more harshly. Age broke the confidence of most men, desiccated their primordial jungles of self-esteem. Bryan looked over at Ted, his chapped face covered in freckles, fainter than the freckles that enveloped every inch of Holly's skin. When they had sex, Holly's freckles vanished into a volcanic blush—and there it went, bulging in his pants as he looked at Ted and thought of Holly, that stupid instrument in his own body, the one he'd relied on his whole life, growing confidently in his underwear when he least needed it. His watch read :00. The deer chewed its last mouthful. It was time.

Bryan rose in the grass. He positioned the bow at arm's length and pulled the arrow back with his fingers against the fletching. The pulleys of the compound bow turned silently to gain maximum mechanical advantage, tightening the nylon string. Bryan squinted as he aimed at the white fleck of her chest. He had to shoot for her body, her boiler room of internal organs—heart, liver, stomach—and not her head. He'd seen too many inexperienced bow hunters try to kill a deer with an arrow to the cranium, watching in horror as the arrow punctured the jaw and the deer skipped away with a wound that would take a week to prove fatal.

But Bryan also needed to consider his own hunting impediment: his spatial disorientation, triggered by a collision with a deer, which compromised his sense of distance and relation, so when his eye read a mark he was nearly a foot off. Bryan made the correction, aiming at her flank to account for his faulty internal compass. He drew the string to his shoulder and, in a move as quick as slitting his own throat, Adam's apple to ear, let the arrow fly.

Bryan's most legendary deer kill had not involved a bow. It took place on Sound Avenue, just across the street from McGovern Vineyards, and the weapon in question was his 2006 burgundy Range Rover. It was a rainy February afternoon four years ago, in the prime of the second rut. Long Island's uncontrolled deer population had long been a driver's worst nightmare, and that nightmare arrived for Bryan as he drove home from a security job in Riverhead, glancing at the road while listening to basketball scores on the radio. He couldn't separate his own memory of the accident from the newspaper report in the following day's paper, front page in the *Suffolk Times*, headline reading DEER, VEHICLE DESTROY ONE ANOTHER, and below it a color photograph of Bryan standing on the road drenched in blood. The photo was taken by a passing motorist, who managed to snap the gruesome portrait in the seconds before Bryan lost consciousness. He had struck a doe that was scrambling to its feet after being hit by another eastbound vehicle. The deer had rolled over the hood and crashed through his windshield, its hoof striking him in the face as his car continued forward and the deer back. The glass disgorged the animal, emptying its thoracic cavity as it soaked the front seats, the backseats, the rear compartment, burgundying the burgundy, before hurtling through the rear window and coming to rest in a bone pile on the concrete.

Bryan didn't remember the initial impact of the deer, nor did he remember its graceless exit through the back window, nor did he remember his Range Rover continuing on for forty feet before gliding into an embankment. He did not remember climbing out of the car or posing for a photograph. All he remembered was the single microsecond the deer had been there in the car with him, the punch to his face before the ache arrived, the deer's mammoth, mud-odor body blurring by him, and, worst of all, the sound the deer made. He didn't know if it came from its mouth or from its rupturing organs or even its contact on the leather upholstery, but it was the sound of fleshy fingers sliding on glass or the bubbling contractions of a watercooler when a drink was dispensed, but louder and deeper and less human than either of those sounds, a *blump ump ump* that caught in his inner ear and brought him to vomit when he regained consciousness in the intensive care unit of Eastern Long Island Hospital.

He was, as all people are everywhere, lucky to be alive. His family cried in relief at his bedside, even inaccessible Tommy. His

Range Rover had been taken to the place crashed cars go when their owners can't bear to look at them. Ted and Chip framed the *Suffolk Times* front page for him with an engraved plaque reading "Bryan Muldoon will do anything to tag a deer." Bryan later learned that there were 65,000 automobile collisions with deer in New York State every year, few of them fatal, yet he still felt special and lucky. But he wasn't special or lucky. Ever since the accident, he experienced momentary spells of disorientation, where he told his feet to go one way and they went another, where he aimed his arrow at a mark and it sailed a foot off course. And that sound, *blump ump ump*, revived by tires bouncing over potholes or draining Pam's water bottle into the bathroom sink, caused his head to go dizzy and his vision to star. He never told his doctor about it, because he feared the results of the tests. He never told Ted or Alistair or Chip, because he knew they'd tell him it was unsafe for him to hunt. *Blump ump ump*: it just stayed there in his head, locked behind imaginary doors in the mental room he created specifically for horrible things.

This morning, the doe saw it coming, maybe a microsecond before he released the bow. Her front legs kicked, and her haunches dipped to spring her forward. Now it was a race between the arrow and her speed. The black dart shot toward her, a thin wavering line, and her tail fanned out white. She started to run as the arrow cleaved the air, racing for her heart, flying faster than any bird, but she was galloping and her gray fur prickled. The arrow swung wide, just missing the mark; it would have hit its target if Bryan hadn't overcorrected in the first place. In another second she was cutting through the tall grasses and into a clutch of birch trees. Two other doe Bryan hadn't seen streamed behind her, scattering out as they reached the impenetrable safety of the woods.

"Shit," he said, standing up.

Chip and Alistair popped up from their grass trench. "Why the hell did you wait so long?" they said, though they knew why.

"Maybe the wind shifted, and she smelled us," Alistair offered, shaking his legs to circulate the blood.

They walked forward, these fathers without their sons, through the scrub and marsh to reclaim the arrow. Chip unscrewed a bottle of water and lifted it above his mouth, guzzling. *Ump, ump, ump.* Bryan bundled his finger around the bow and conjured up a network of doors—massive wooden gates, steel bank vaults, pressurized submarine doors—to block the horrible sound. He clenched his teeth but forced his lips into a smile, anxious to hide his panic.

"She was too old anyway," he said. "Her meat's already wormed. Wouldn't be worth the trouble to dress her."

"Slice and dice," Alistair chanted, unsnapping the sheath clipped to his belt and wielding his knife in the sign of the cross. They were all impatient for a kill. They wanted to fill their noses with the hot, acrid death that issued from a deer's carcass minutes after it drew its last breath, the smell that allowed them, as men, to tremble momentarily with the sensation of life, its heat and quiet. Chip let some of the bottled water pour on his face and unzipped his camouflaged jumpsuit, gutting himself open to the chilly air, his fat stomach spilling out and his white undershirt butterflied in sweat. Chip walked through his days the same way he walked around cars in his mechanic's shop in East Marion, sluggishly, like he knew there were deeper problems that a younger man might have the energy to fix but he'd settle for a few minor tweaks to keep the transmission running. Bryan did not consider it a betrayal that he took his own car to Greenport to get serviced. He liked Chip, but after his accident he didn't trust him to ensure the reliability of his vehicle.

The men stomped through the carpet of leaves that had fallen overnight in the state park, as if autumn had waited for Pam's end-of-summer picnic to begin its molting. Some patches were red and yellow, a few still green, but most of the leaves were cardboard brown, crumbling under their waterproof boots. Bryan paused a minute to enjoy the way he and his friends blended into the environment, their camel tans and drab greens mixing into the muddy scenery the same way his mother, in her floral blouses, disappeared into their living room curtains when he was a child. Bryan felt at ease in a world where no one stuck out, where living well meant meeting the world halfway. As he walked, he thought of Tommy in his predictable black T-shirts and jeans, his son in silhouette, as if he had purposely cut himself out of the happy family photograph. Oh, Tommy. What had Bryan done wrong? How could the boy slouch around without even a watch?

Over to his left, Ted whistled as he shook a cigarette from a crumpled pack of Camel Lights. It was Ted's outdoors-only indulgence, another strike against him in the potential-future-surrogate-father department. Bryan looked around and realized that his feet were leading him far right when he had asked them to head straight. He corrected his movement and returned to the group.

Alistair had grabbed hold of Chip's stomach, clawing it like a bowling ball. "If we want meat today, it's all right here," he said, shaking Chip's lard.

Chip smacked the hand away, then overcompensated with a tilt of his chin. "Go on, take a good handful," he said. "That's what a man feels like. None of this waxing and dieting and *an-oh-rectum nerv-oh-sa* that killed off the dinosaurs and the Indians. I'll tell you what will ruin white men. Not greenhouse gases or warming oceans or cigarettes. It's vanity, plain and simple. It's weakening you, Alistair. Those eyebrows of yours sure are getting thin. I could swear they used to meet above your nose, didn't they?"

Alistair fingered the space between his eyebrows, and looked to Bryan for support. "Well, then your wife will make it through the next Ice Age A-OK," he said after a pause. "What a relief when the next superior beings find Barbara squatting on an ice floe, and all of their books will show what white women once looked like, a bit like you but meaner and with a hairier back."

"Yep, sounds like white women to me," Ted agreed, relishing the fact that he didn't belong to one. He carefully snuffed the half-smoked cigarette on his boot and collected the butt in his pocket.

"Bryan, did you see Beth Shepherd at your picnic?" Alistair asked him. "I'd give a deer to spend a minute between those tits. I could see her nipples poking through her dress."

"Like she'd let you," Chip replied. "She's got an Armenian ogre for a husband."

"He's an artist," Alistair said, dangling a limp wrist.

Bryan laughed along with the barbs, but he resisted trading any himself. He never spoke ill of a family member, never swapped sexual fantasies about local women like Beth Shepherd, and never commented on people's weight or money troubles. That was the greasy talk of feeble men. Bryan was proud of the fact that he took care of his own body, twenty minutes on his basement rowing machine every night to make up for Pam's indulgent use of butter. Unlike Ted or Alistair or Chip, he also had a real secret life that wasn't the stuff of backslapping fantasy. He had cheated on Pam with three different women since the car crash four years ago, although cheating after twenty years of marriage and one near-death experience seemed like the wrong description for those tidy, dispassionate rendezvous. They were testing grounds for his own virility, a simple compromise a man made in an otherwise successful career as husband and father.

To Bryan, these dalliances hardly seemed like cheating because there was no love involved. Bryan would do anything for Pam: risk his life for her, hold her at night when she cried, anything. But the truth of what a person needed in order to feel human wasn't always something you could discover by asking the people who knew him best. The answer was in the moments he went missing from his life, the quiet corners in the day that were his alone; because they were secret, because those precious seconds were so carefully counted and stored, they were his.

Still, the muscles in his neck tightened at times, flares from Bryan's conscience causing him to wonder if he was really any better than his hunting partners after all. Maybe he was worse.

Alistair pointed to a herd of deer clipping through the marsh grasses, shooting single-file over the hillcrest that sloped down to the beach. Five doe were running as if spooked, each one a feasting prize if brought to earth.

"Why are they bolting?" Ted wondered.

"It's not rut yet. They can't be fleeing a buck," Chip said as he followed them with his finger. The deer scrambled through the state park grounds and into the flatter grasses of private property, where licensed hunting was not allowed.

"Let's follow them," Alistair suggested.

Bryan shook his head. Tagging a doe on private property was illegal. And there was another reason he didn't want to be seen on that property: he and Ted, as senior members of the historical board, were quietly negotiating to purchase it in hopes of preserving it from development, protecting it from an invasion of condos or golf-course greens. Looking past the ridge where the deer had come, beyond the tall grasses and planks where osprey built their branching nests, he could see the churning blue waters of the Sound, the swirling currents of Plum Gut, and, beyond the water, the faint coastline of Plum Island.

If he squinted, he could make out the white buildings on the island, the restricted government laboratories that were home to the U.S. Animal Disease Center. It was inside this distant compound, heavily protected by Homeland Security, that government scientists conducted research on animal pathogens. Plum Island hung off the coast of Orient in the vaporous haze of a mirage, but by the standards of local legend it was very real. There, government scientists conducted clandestine biological warfare experiments on live animals. For decades, stories had circulated that killing agents like anthrax were being cultivated there. It was widely believed by the residents of Orient that Lyme disease had been invented in those laboratories, created by the government to inflict on future enemies, and that the disease had been carried by wildlife across the water to the North Fork and the neighboring feeding grounds of Connecticut. It was biological warfare turned on its own citizens as they enjoyed their summer picnics and trips to the beach. When do the defense measures of a paranoid country become their own agents of self-destruction?

By some hardwired collective desire on the part of the year-rounders, the threat of living so close to such a dangerous landmark had been neutralized, dismissed as the lunatic talk of conspiracy theorists, fringe-literature writers, and fishermen with too much time to kill. Whenever the moon-eyed, antigovernment sort appeared by the carload in Orient wearing their WE WANT ANSWERS T-shirts, the locals dismissed their questions with a wave of their hands. "It's all perfectly safe," they insisted, until it was more like "IT'S ALL PERFECTLY SAFE!" An Orient year-rounder who openly questioned such home truths about Plum Island received cold shoulders and suspicious eyes.

Unlike most of the residents, Bryan had actually been to Plum Island. A few years ago, his security company had been awarded a short-term government contract to set motion detectors along its dock. He had taken the ferry over and was given a tour by armed officials of the management offices and the neighboring grounds. He had watched the deer amble through the grasses, the terrain of Plum Island so much like Orient but wilder, weed strewn and vacant of homes or service roads. "You let the deer run free?" he asked the official leading the tour, a man wearing a hard hat that made Bryan wonder what could fall on him out in the open. "We shoot them on sight," the man replied, although the deer he saw were not taken down.

Bryan had signed a confidentiality agreement as thick as an almanac, and when he got back he said only, "Yeah, I went out there," and placed his finger to his lips. He hadn't seen the labs, or their notoriously efficient waste-management system, or even the ammunition room they purportedly maintained in case of terrorist attack. But the memory of those deer—which ran free on the island throughout the two weeks it took to rig the dock—troubled him when he returned home, a mile and a drip of salt water away from the facility. After that, he started using gloves when field-dressing his game and cooked his steaks until they were practically bricks of charcoal.

In theory, an island is a paradise of protection, guarded from human encroachment by its own geography. But any hunter knows that an island has pores too small for humans to slip through but large enough for animals to exploit. Deer swam. So did coyotes. They could paddle through the turbulent Plum Gut to hunt or graze on the island, collecting any mutant germ-warfare strain they came across, and carry it back to the mainland on the smallest follicle of skin. Birds flew easily from Orient to Plum. So did bats. Bryan couldn't watch deer crowd his backyard, staring from his sliding door, without thinking of their fur as disease carriers, their heads and legs as warning skulls and crossbones. It would take only one of them, wet from the water, fat from Plum, to wipe away all life as he knew it.

He kneeled down to retrieve the arrow in the grass. His right hand missed by a foot, scooping up nothing. He concentrated on bringing his fingers over to where the arrow lay. A black dot lifted up from the island, as if it were an asteroid falling in reverse, but as it rose it tilted and became an army helicopter transporting government officials. It sped toward them over the Sound, and Bryan could hear its rotor blades ticking in the morning air. The sound of a helicopter overhead was the worst *blump ump ump* sound of all. He squeezed his eyes shut as the reverb invaded his ears, and stayed there, heart on knee, until the helicopter banked and drifted off.

"Is that Adam?" Alistair asked. Bryan hadn't noticed the truck parked on the road just outside of the parkland. It was rusted and red and had FIRE DEPT painted in yellow across its side. A rack of antlers protruded from the open back. Bryan stood up and watched as Adam and two hunting partners emerged through the grasses, their faces painted in paisley smears of green and black. They all had infrared night-vision specs hanging around their necks, and one of them had an air horn hooked on his belt. The group had clearly been hunting for most of the night, right through the prohibited hours. They rested their crossbows on their shoulders. Even under the face paint, they looked tired and hungover. Bryan put his hands on hips and shook his head. He had half a mind to report Adam to park patrol.

"You know night hunting's not allowed," he yelled.

The whites of Adam Pruitt's eyes bulged defiantly. "I don't want to hear it," he shouted. "There's enough deer for all of us." Adam and his two friends, who Bryan couldn't identify underneath their makeup, marched toward them. They were a younger, thinner, more menacing version of Bryan's heavyset, middle-aged posse, just a decade or so older than their own sons. Bryan had already given Adam this lecture twice this season.

"I'm serious, Adam. This isn't a national park. You go hunting at night, scaring the deer out with your air horns, shooting at whatever moves. There are homes all around here. With children in them. One day you're going to shoot a kid with one of your crossbows—which also aren't legal, by the way—and you're going to wonder why you didn't listen to me."

"Listen, Bryan." Adam slid right up into the older man's face. His skin smelled of liquor and his eyes were veined from lack of sleep. "When you get to be sheriff of Suffolk County I might be interested in your instructions. In the meantime, mind your own business."

The truth was, Bryan didn't hate Adam Pruitt. Adam was the head of Orient's volunteer fire department, an empty title at best, since no house had burned in Orient since Bryan could remember, but he appreciated Adam's commitment to the community. The real reason for the anger was only known to Bryan and Adam and lost on the other men. Three months ago, Adam had started planning to open his own local home-security business, a direct competitor to Bryan's time-trusted company. They were now business rivals forced to act like neighbors.

"And I think you're drunk on top of it," Bryan managed, although he took a step back to defuse the encounter. It was an instinctive retreat that he regretted as soon as his feet regained their stillness. He was glad Tommy wasn't here to watch his father bow before a younger man.

Bryan wiped the back of his hand over his lip in a tough, masculine motion, but one that also shielded his face in case Adam decided to throw a punch. He searched out the faces of his comrades, the ones not painted green and black against the soft blue dome of the sky. Ted, Alistair, and Chip stood by staring, scared and sympathetic, all of them looking like old men in their embarrassing camouflage suits. Bryan's fingernails shook against the buttons of his jacket. He was an old man too, or getting there.

"This is bullshit. Tell him," one of Adam's buddies murmured as he relieved his shoulder of the crossbow. "What we found over there."

Adam bobbed his head and, in a surprising show of civility, extended his hand. Bryan didn't want to shake it, but he had little choice.

"We can agree to disagree," Adam said, then lifted his finger and pointed to the hillcrest, inviting Bryan and the others to follow.

They trudged through the phragmites, thick and squirreling as the blades brushed against their faces, lethal with ticks. As they descended the slope to the wet, rocky sand of the beach, gnats and flies clouded the air. An odor of decay struck Bryan's nose, and he pressed his hand over his mouth.

Lying on the beach, bubbling as the tide pulled back like a sheet, was something dead. At least it looked dead, if *dead* meant *once alive*. Larger than a dog, the size of a deer but with shorter, pudgier legs, the shape of a man but with the spinal crouch of an animal that moved on all fours, the thing sprawled on the shore. Its skin was hairless, icicle blue, and sand-caked, home to a colony of flies. Bryan saw it first and crinkled his lips. But the blast radius of its presence spread outward, and soon Chip and Alistair stiffened behind him, their noses and shoulders recoiling.

"What the hell is that?" Chip wailed.

"Whatever it is, it washed in with the tide." Adam pointed to the Sound. Already an armada of sailboats rocked in the deeper channels. The water rolled in, slapping against the monster's hide and wetting their boots.

"But what is it?" Chip repeated.

"What *isn't* it?" one of Adam's friends replied.

At first Bryan took one of its bloated hooves for a head, but when he looked more closely he noticed a snoutlike protrusion at its far tip, a mouth open like a rabid raccoon, with spiky yellow teeth growing out of spit-white gums. The thing looked like one of Theo's childhood picture books that split in three panels, where each panel exhibited a different animal part. The game was either to get all the parts to fit a familiar image or to get them wildly wrong. The snout suggested a wild boar, the teeth a dog, its front claw reaching out, as if to pull itself back into the ocean, a badger. It looked like a creature from Bryan's nightmares, and it wasn't much of a leap to tilt his eyes from the cadaver, through the jagged band of the Sound, past the white ornament of the lighthouse, and reach the specter of an island where animals were tested for their mutant possibilities. When Bryan looked around, every man on the beach was gazing at the island.

"You think it came from Plum?" Adam asked, kicking the animal on its rump. The body took the blow with the smallest rigor-mortal quiver. The flies flinched and repositioned themselves.

"Let's not jump to conclusions," Bryan cautioned.

"Hell if I *won't* jump to conclusions," Chip screamed. "Where else did it come from? That's what they do to animals in those labs. Genetically reengineering them. Messing with their chromosomes. I don't care if it's not kosher to talk about. That fucking island is a disaster area waiting to break loose. There's nothing natural about it."

Adam located a stick of driftwood and started prying the mouth open. Water and seaweed poured from its jaw.

Bryan raised his hand. "You better leave it," he said. "We have to notify the park rangers."

"But I found it," Adam whined in a way that reminded Bryan of his youngest son. "I mean, we did. Not you. If there's reward money, I want to make sure we get that fact straight."

"It could be anything," Alistair said, a surprising voice of reason. "A few weeks floating in the water, even you might look like that."

But even he couldn't look away from the island in the distance, its hazardous labs the same white of the lighthouse. "Still, I'll be happy when they shut Plum down. Where did they say they were moving it?" There had been increasing talk of relocating the facility.

"Somewhere in Kansas," Ted said.

"Manhattan, Kansas," Bryan clarified. It struck him as ironic that the government had chosen a town by that name to relocate operations, as if they couldn't separate their most covert biowarfare experiments from some lingering link to New York. Bryan pictured the shape of Manhattan scored into Kansan cornfields like the alien crop circles he'd seen on TV. Maybe that pattern would extend so far that it took in all five boroughs, and then the outstretched arm of Long Island, and finally Orient itself. *Another Manhattan*, he thought. Another New York in the center of the country. Maybe all of New York's problems could be dumped there too, leaving them alone and safe. "I'll be glad when it's gone," he said aloud.

They stood on the beach for another minute, bodies black and green and white and mud brown, a motley group of bow hunters straddling the coast, staring into the sea. Their fear of the creature seemed to lift, and they caught each other's eyes, stunned and eager and a little bit giddy at what they had discovered. The real reward of hunting was not the kill but the story of the kill, not the antlers above the fireplace but the tale of how the antlers got there, and now each of them had a story. They hiked back into the park, searching for someone to tell.

CHAPTER 6

His hand was bleeding. Mills had dropped the black trash bag to place the last wedge of an orange in his mouth. When he reached down to reclaim the bag on Paul's driveway, a nail poking from the plastic sliced his palm. It wasn't a deep cut, but he couldn't retract the scream once it cleared his throat.

The sound echoed against neighboring garage doors, stirring starlings from the trees. Morning church bells droned through the rainless autumn air. A few curtains in nearby houses drew back, and Tommy, seated on his family's picnic table, plucked the headphones from his ears. As Mills's palm pooled with blood, Tommy jumped from his lonely downhill-skier crouch and walked across the lawn.

Mills hadn't been looking to draw attention. In fact he would have preferred to finish his morning chore without a single run-in with the Muldoons. But at Tommy's approach, he didn't exactly downgrade the emergency to a minor scrape. Mills was experienced enough to understand what gay men were often forced to be in this world: romantic opportunists. It was one of the many exotic boons to being a newcomer in Manhattan to assume that most guys passing on the street might be potential conquests. Like the manicured elms that lined the blocks, every young resident of that city seemed capable of being climbed. Walking had become Mills's chief pastime. On the sidewalks of New York, the eyes of pedestrians shifted like bulls in pens. Some charged the gate, beating toward their target with ferocious interest, while others remained in their enclosures, swatting sweat. The trick of eye contact was an urban sport. Now, a hundred miles east of Manhattan, in the quiet, wind-blown village of Orient, POW flags replaced the city's ubiquitous rainbow streamers, and Mills knew no rules for the game of meaningful stares.

Still, it was Tommy's eyes that interested him. They were a sunless sky blue, wide and blank like a sky where the weather never changed. And like such a sky, they were interrupted only briefly by anything that migrated across them. Right now that thing was Mills's left hand. Tommy squinted as he grabbed it, let the blood trickle through the fingers he opened, and inspected the cut.

"You don't need stitches," Tommy concluded, pressing Mills's fingers over the wound and squeezing them to stanch the blood. He lifted his head and smirked, almost as if he enjoyed inflicting some small degree of pain under the guise of helping him. "But we should bandage it."

"It doesn't hurt," Mills replied coolly. His voice dipped two octaves. He kicked the trash bag for added effect. Mills still possessed the childhood tic of punishing inanimate objects for their abuses. "Paul must have a first aid kit. He isn't here though."

Tommy nodded and tilted his head toward his family's house. Mills scanned the area for any sign of Tommy's mother, expecting to find her cross-armed in one of the doorways. Pam Muldoon was nowhere to be seen.

Tommy raised his hand in the air. Sunlight drifted between his bloodied fingers. "We've got Band-Aids. Come on."

Mills had woken late that morning, unsure, for a few grasping seconds, of where on the planet he was. He loved that ten-second feeling of not knowing where or who or how, the brain failing to locate itself with certainty anywhere in the universe. Mills always felt those fleeting seconds upon waking were the closest anyone got to the pure substance of being—before walls closed in and the mind raced to reassemble a specific day and room. But soon he noticed the towel on the dresser, the toothbrush still wrapped in cellophane, and the squawking discord of birds out the window like the sound of wire hangers shuffled on a rack. Mills tried to hold on to that bodily sense of lightness, the feeling of life with no sickly residue of drugs in his system. He had forgotten the joy of waking without an impending sense of collapse.

By the time he showered and changed in the upstairs bathroom, Paul had already disappeared, leaving a car-shaped gravel patch in the driveway and a note on the kitchen table next to a plate of co-agulated eggs. "M, gone into town for groceries. I'm afraid I'm an early riser. If you want to get a start, drag the trash bags to the curb for tomorrow's collection. P."

Mills forked the eggs down the sink's rubber-throated drain and helped himself to one of the oranges on top of the refrigerator. He peeled its thick, tumorous skin, collecting the rinds in his pocket as he placed a triangle of fruit between his teeth. The bitter taste of the orange reminded him of California. A family of Mexican women had sold oranges by the crate at a stand across the street from his primary school in Modesto. They were probably still lingering on that road, those beetle brown women with their dusty melons penned in the world outside of his school's wire-netted windows. Mills chewed the seeds and took the unsupervised opportunity to creep back upstairs to explore Paul's bedroom. It sat on the opposite end of the hallway, a safe, soundproof distance from the one he occupied. It was sparse and chilly and floated with spectral dust. Leaves outside the window were turning cinnamon, and neighboring rooftops had already collected many of the fallen in their gutters.

The sheets on Paul's bed were monastically tucked and folded, as if by an architect's ruler, and Mills resisted the urge to dent the pillows just to see if Paul would notice. His eyes traveled the room. Fragments of a personality decorated the rosewood bureau: a ceramic bowl of one-dollar coins, ticket stubs to summer orchestra recitals, a framed photograph of Paul as a squirrel-haired teenager in a gray boarding-school uniform, a mug from a college honorary society bragging "we are the superior beings" in a Gothic font. Also on the bureau was a vial of medication: "Vicodin, to take at the onset of extreme pain," dated from earlier in the summer. Mills wondered what kind of extreme pain brought Paul to get the prescription—perhaps the same pain that caused his limp in the hallway last night. He debated pocketing two of the pills for later enjoyment—taking Vicodin was like leaning into the curves on a highway—but he decided to leave the medication alone.

The suitcase Paul had brought from the city was stowed by the closet. On the inside closet door, where most people hung a mirror, were two framed diplomas, one from Columbia and the other from Cornell, as if those certificates were the truer reflection of the man Paul Benchley wanted to see when he dressed.

Mills had never loved a home, never felt tied or obligated to one, at least not a home made of mortar, wood, and cinder blocks. If any of the houses that defined his childhood were ever demolished, he wouldn't feel a thing. When he thought of California, his mind tracked oceanic deserts, thickets of woods with trees like unbent staples, strip-mall parking lots, and courthouse steps, places no one really owned, and thus always safely his. In his last years in Modesto, so many new homes were still half-built, their foundations dug and cemented and left to collect rainwater when the mortgage crisis cleared away the construction workers. It was in these open-sky basements that Mills had tried his first cigarettes, learned bicycle tricks like wheelies and endos, and kissed a boy his age. He hoped those houses were never built, magnificent California ruins destroyed only if they were ever conceived.

He paused before a map of grouse-shaped Orient, which hung on the wall across from Paul's bed. It was an old map of property lines with large sections penciled in red, before the land was divided and the potato fields replanted with seedling grass, before Paul's grandfather parceled his plot across the Sound and triggered the spreading patchwork of Suffolk County suburbs. Mills located the Benchley house on the map, pressing his finger on the black, cross-hatched square. The picture frame jiggled at his touch, as if something kept it from falling flush with the wall.

He placed his half-eaten orange on the bureau and lifted the map from its hook. A green matchbook was wedged in the frame's metal bracket. He pulled it from its lodging. A swordfish curled over a militia of slim black letters that spelled out SEAVIEW RESORTS MOTEL. He opened the book flap and found the name "Eleanor," and a ten-digit number written in purple ink. So Paul did have a secret still worth hiding from the ghosts of his parents.

And now Mills had a possible answer to his own unasked question. He had assumed Paul was gay, and he was surprised at the wave of disappointment he felt upon discovering a woman's name scrawled on a matchbook advertising "cheap room rates." Paul was not like him. He was an ally, yes, but not a sharer of similar roads. To discover someone was ordinary always struck Mills as a kind of betrayal. Whenever a man Mills presumed was gay turned out to be straight, the aura about him crumbled, the clues reassembling into the most indistinctive brand of human being—normal, hiding nothing, a mind like a weather vane that moved with the prevailing winds. Mills returned the matchbook to the bracket and steadied the frame against the wall. The loneliness that engulfed him on his way to take out the trash was the loneliness of a clear-cut world.

The Muldoons' screen door slammed against his shoulder. Reluctant to get blood on the hallway carpeting, he lifted his arm to his chest and shoved his foot out to catch a drop of blood that fell from his thumb. Tommy laughed at the sight of him, pinned in the doorway, using his own shoe to prevent a cleaning nightmare. Tommy grabbed a towel off the end table and tossed it. Mills caught it with his wounded hand, staining its decorative fall-leaf stitching, marring Pam Muldoon's seasonal accessory. He wrapped it around his palm and applied his fingers to the cut.

"Who's with you?" a little boy shouted, the contours of his head haloed against the ultraviolet glow of a flat-screen television. Tommy's brother was having a difficult time maneuvering the character of his video game. The man on the screen kept moving, his legs and arms repeating a walking rhythm, but he was thwarted by the obvious barrier of a wall.

"This is Theo," Tommy said as he watched his brother from behind the striped sofa. "And he's doing it wrong. Theo, you have to use the B button when you move left or right."

"I am using the B button," the little boy screamed. "Dad showed me last night. But I can't get through the door."

"Dad," Tommy hissed. He climbed over the sofa, knocked his brother aside with his knee, and mutinied the controller. "Dad can't walk through a door in this world successfully. How the hell do you expect him to do it in a game?"

Mills glanced around the darkened den. Boat wheels hung on floral wallpaper. Circular armies of family photographs gathered on circular tabletops. Teak baskets cradled magazines and remote controls. Throw pillows softened the sharp ligaments of armchairs. Children's board games towered in a corner under a pile of college catalogs. High above the television set, the head of a deer stared tenderly down at the suburban mire, its stomach the flat screen where an animated man now accomplished the act of walking through a door.

"Stop," Theo wailed, his hands reaching for the controller. Tommy let him have it and watched as Theo immediately drove the man into the nearest wall. Tommy waved his hands in resignation. Theo quit the game and loaded a new one, clearly a favorite he'd already mastered, where laser beams anatomically violated the random materialization of a criminal caste—aliens, black men, crying white babies with automatic rifles.

Mills stepped backward into the sunlight by the front door. On the hallway table, a copy of the SUNY Buffalo freshman orientation calendar caught his eye, yellow highlighter circled three times around "November 2–4, Parents Weekend!!!" Tommy seemed to have forgotten the reason for Mills's visit. He stood in front of the television and helped himself to a bowl of popcorn. Mills unwrapped the towel to examine the wound. Bits of towel fluff stuck to the drying blood.

"I think I just need a Band-Aid and I'm good to go."

"Sorry," Tommy said, hopping over the sofa and beckoning him toward the stairs. Mills followed him up the carpeted steps, half-barricaded by laundry baskets. The wall along the stairs had been painted lime green in that antic 1990s decor trick of supplying a splash of invigorating color—probably the last time the Muldoons had found the time or energy to consider their interior something more than a utility container for children. Upstairs, Tommy guided Mills toward his bedroom door.

If Mills had expected to discover the vulnerable heart of Tommy Muldoon by entering his most personal space, he was sadly disappointed. Tommy's bedroom contained a sagging twin mattress and a few laminated shelves, crammed with science-fiction books and rocks collected from a beach. "Hold on a minute," Tommy said before retreating into the hallway to gather the first aid supplies. The tart aroma of unwashed clothes and inexpensive cologne permeated the room, admittedly a striking revolt against a house that otherwise reeked of lemon disinfectant.

Two of Tommy's four walls were painted black. The other two were plastered with posters of black hip-hop artists, black NBA players, and black Corvettes, each degree of blackness yellowed from rounds of sunlight through the window. As Mills suspected, it was Tommy's window that was emblazoned with decals of circled As, small cries of anarchy reaching any seat-belted minivan driver whose eye happened to drift to the second floor. The bedroom aligned so faithfully with the cosmology of white male teenagers' bedrooms everywhere that Mills was encouraged by the one staple it lacked: pictures of bikini-clad women. Maybe Tommy Muldoon would yet prove an unordinary creature hiding in the decorative fog of the Orient suburbs.

"Let's pour alcohol on it," Tommy proposed, more in the tone of science experimenter than nurse. He carried in a bottle of rubbing alcohol and a box of bandages. Mills took a seat on the bed and felt the soft corrugation of an eggshell foam pad beneath the galaxy-patterned sheet, as if suggesting a more delicate being than the boy who thumbtacked ghettos over his walls. Mills rested his elbow on his knee and allowed Tommy to hold the underside of his hand.

"This might sting," Tommy warned as he lifted the bottle over the cut.

"Shouldn't we do this over the sink?"

"I don't care if we make a little mess." It did sting as the alcohol ran over his palm, and drops of blood leaked onto the carpet. Blood on Pam Muldoon's towel downstairs, blood on the beige carpet in her son's bedroom—Mills felt like a wounded animal secretly taken in. "Don't worry. I like the smell of chemicals," Tommy said. "Do you think if you sniffed this you'd get high?"

Mills decided not to say yes. "Are your parents home?"

Tommy shook his head. "My dad's out hunting, and my mom's at one of her charity meetings. You'll hear if she comes in. She sets the alarm whenever she enters. She's lucky my dad owns a security business. She's obsessed with an alarm on every window and door lately. I have to unset it every time I want to go outside. I keep telling her, no one wants your painted egg collection. No one wants Aunt Tilda's wedding china." Tommy wrinkled his nose at the idiocy of home safety precautions. "But she says, 'It's not the china I'm protecting, it's you.' Me." He pointed to his chest, as if inviting Mills to imagine a burglar stealing him. Mills started to worry that he'd soon hear the beeps of an alarm being set, locking him into the house and into another encounter with Pam Muldoon.

Tommy screwed the lid back on and reached up to place the bottle on the highest shelf. As he stretched, the bottom of his sweatshirt lifted, and Mills glimpsed the pale, white-pimpled skin of his waist, a blond zipper of hair tracking up from the elastic of his underwear, two blue artery veins swelling against his pelvic bone. Mills averted his eyes before Tommy could notice.

Tommy picked the largest bandage in the box, stretching its adhesive strips over Mills's palm. He pressed the cotton square on the cut and looked up with a smile of accomplishment.

"So is he gay or isn't he?" Tommy asked, as if intuiting the very question circling Mills's mind. Mills swallowed and remained breathing.

"Who is?"

"Paul Benchley. Is he gay or not?"

"He's not," Mills blurted with a brusqueness that surprised even him. Was he overcompensating to protect his own identity? Yes. Or perhaps he simply didn't want Tommy to misinterpret his arrangement with Paul. "I think he has some woman he's quiet about. Eleanor's her name. Do you know her?"

"Nope." Tommy sat on the bed next to him. He leaned back, bolstered on his elbows, spreading his torso and legs out, almost offering the flat thoroughfare of his body for inspection. Tommy dropped his neck back and smiled, revealing a slight overlap of his front teeth that wasn't evident when Mills looked at him directly. Hairs almost white from the window light fuzzed around his chin.

Tommy must have known he was handsome. He was two years past the age when men first get a glimpse of how their features take hold in the world. He must have understood how every line of his face conspired to lead a looker toward the depth of his eyes. His forehead sloped down to his blond brows. His beaklike nose ascended toward the inner arcs of his sockets. Even a small, white scar on his upper lip, curled like a fishhook, pointed upward. And once the looker found himself in those ice-blue cul-de-sacs, there wasn't so much as a flicker of engagement. Tommy's eyes were blank and withdrawn, disloyal custodians to the welcoming smile spread under them.

"Eleanor, huh. That surprises me," Tommy said. "I thought I had Paul Benchley pegged. I thought he had nobody. It's pretty easy to peg everyone out here. They all have secrets, you know. Some worse than others, although the worst ones are my specialty. You must have discovered something interesting about Paul. I won't use it against him if you tell me."

Mills didn't want to admit how little he knew of Paul. Nor did he want to betray his host simply to score a few points with Tommy Muldoon. Sensing that Tommy was just testing his ability to keep a secret, he shook his head and opened his bandaged hand.

"Sorry."

"Paul hit a tree in his car last June," Tommy said with a smile that didn't fit the information he was disclosing. Tommy clearly liked accidents, what they did to people, the sounds they made. "Just a few blocks from here on Main Road. The police were called. I think he had to go to the hospital."

That explained Paul's limp and the pain medication on his bureau. Paul seemed like such a cautious driver on their way out from the city; perhaps he was overcautious, aware of what it meant to lose control.

"Yeah, he limps a bit. That's probably why he has me out here, to carry the heavier stuff to the trash. He's got five broken microwaves but not a single television set. Isn't that weird?"

Tommy didn't seem to be listening. He tipped forward with his left arm extended, his thumb and pointer nearing Mills's face. Mills felt two fingertips pinch his earlobe, and his blood quickened only to stall in his cheeks. Tommy pressed on the earring, pushing the lobe against the metal clasp.

"Do you feel that in your ear all the time?" he asked with a grin that was either flirtatious or malicious, Mills couldn't tell which. Perhaps it was just another of Tommy's psychological tests. He had nothing to lose with a stranger like Mills; he could assume any personality at his whim, and what he offered could be snatched away at the first hint of reciprocation. Mills had played this game too many times in his youth to come up on the losing end, but his inability to read Tommy irritated him. He jerked his head to the side to free his ear from Tommy's fingers.

"I was just looking at it," he said, laughing. "I've been thinking about getting one. Why are you blushing?"

Draw a line between youth and maturity however you want. But for Mills that line was a rope in the water, swaying back and forth in the tides, a frail cord that, at nineteen, he could swim under and back as he wished. Right now, he had to remind himself that he was the older one, two years older, not a high-school student like Tommy, and by that slight advantage he should feel less intimidated in his company. Only Mills's brain didn't seem to understand the merits of seniority, just as his body couldn't register the KEEP OUT signs of Tommy's eyes.

Mills's hand trembled a few inches from the nylon belt around Tommy's waist, which fastened in the center with a plastic clip. What if he reached over and unclipped the belt? What if he settled his fingers on that hair-lined stomach for a split second? What if something he wanted could actually happen on the starched galaxy sheets of Tommy's bed? His resolve faded like radioactive fallout across the six-inch gulf between them. The problem was that Mills had never played the seducer before. He was pitifully incapable of making a move that wasn't reactive. In desperation, he jumped off the bed and spun around to land in Tommy's mesh-upholstered desk chair. Tommy remained leaning on his elbow with a humorous look on his face.

"So tell me some of the secrets you know," Mills said to change the topic.

Tommy rose slowly, pulling himself up with his stomach muscles, and leaned down toward a small black safe on the floor. An orange label on its side marked it as fire resistant. A bumper sticker on its door notified visitors that THE DAYS OF OPTIMISM ARE OVER. Tommy spun the combination lock and opened its iron door.

"My dad gave me this safe from his company. I keep all of my secrets in here. Do you want a cigarette?" He pulled out a pack of Marlboros. "A shot of whiskey?" Out came a silver hip flask and a decorative Giants shot glass. "How about some weed? My friend got it for me from a dealer in Riverhead. When I visit my sister at college this winter, I'm going to buy some more. Lisa promised she'd take me partying." Tommy said "partying" the way his mother probably said "Christmas" and the way Mills had once said "New York." A plastic Baggie of green, leafy powder flashed in Tommy's hand. Mills couldn't resist a pitying smile for the teenager, forced to conceal his contraband in a fireproof security safe as if his secrets were rare and combustible, in danger of confiscation by anyone other than his mom. The days of Pam Muldoon's optimism about her son may have been numbered, but Tommy's days weren't. Those were just beginning.

"So you want a hit or what?"

Mills did want weed, just enough to kill the pain in his hand, but he shook his head, remembering his promise to Paul. No drugs. Tommy carefully pinched some of the marijuana from the Baggie, packed it into the tip of an already hollowed-out Marlboro, and opened the anarchy window.

"Those are your secrets?" Mills couldn't resist a tone of disappointment. But he did resist saying, *You realize I've sat in rooms with people our age with belts tourniqueted around their arms and you're worried about smoking a Marlboro Light mixed with a little potent oregano out the window of your childhood bedroom?* The rush of experience finally put him on even ground.

Tommy lit the cigarette and took a deep drag. He feigned contemplation as he volcanoed smoke from his lips.

"Those are *my* secrets. I have others," he said as he tapped the safe with his foot. "But you don't know any of the people in Orient, so they wouldn't interest you. They're mostly about money."

"Money?"

"Yeah. Or love too, I guess. What people own and how desperate they are to get more of it. It always comes down to that, you know. It's all a fucking trap, owning things, places, people. The way I see it, we don't own things. We get owned. Even the new people who moved out here from New York—they're just as bad as the ones who've been in Orient for eternity. They're just losers with cooler cars."

"What's the worst you've got on somebody?" Mills asked.

Tommy shook his head. Mills rubbed the bandage on his palm. The pain throbbed into his wrist; just one lungful of pot would have helped to relieve it. "What about your parents then? What do you have on them?"

Tommy squinted, as if gauging whether Mills could be trusted. Tendrils of smoke grew around him, flowering in the window light like time-lapse film of blossoming plants.

"My parents," he whispered hoarsely. "What an advertisement for marriage. Is that what marriage is, to be lonely with someone at the end of your life?"

Mills could offer no wisdom on the subject of marriage. Still, some bit of reassurance seemed in order. "I'm sure it's not so bad," he said. "They're probably just used to each other. No one walks around holding hands forever. Why? Is their marriage in trouble?"

Tommy stared at his bedroom door, as if a portal to a different dimension began to swirl there, a stoner portal where time ticked backward. "I feel sorry for my father. Fucking hypocrite, trying to teach me the value of family and treasuring every second together." Tommy broke from his reverie. "Oh, never mind," he groaned. Clearly he wasn't going to tell Mills any specifics. Tommy must have learned that sharing secrets jeopardized their value. He was a collector, not a giver. "It's fine. What do you expect from a man who parades around the house naked? He's one of those dads who feels no obligation to wear a towel on his way to the shower. I mean, he's obviously hungry for attention, right?" Mills didn't realize those kinds of dads existed. He imagined the houses in Orient hiding naked, sagging fathers who strutted past their storm windows to the horror of their families. "Can you picture mothers doing that? God, that'd be fucking hilarious." Tommy licked his fingers and rolled the tip of the cigarette. "Lisa would always yell at him about it before she left for college. She said she couldn't invite friends over because she never knew when Dad would be walking around with his penis dangling out. I love how scandalized Lisa gets. She's my hero. But I get it. Dad's just getting old. He wants someone to appreciate his body. Anybody. Even his own family. How pathetic is that?"

"People are lonely."

"Yeah, *lone-ly.* A lot of people are lonely out here. That's one thing you'll learn. You'd be surprised how lonely some of these upstanding neighbors get. You ever heard of the Seaview Motel?"

"Yes," Mills said. He imagined voluptuous, easily placated Eleanor waiting by a curtained window for Paul's Mercedes to roll into the lot.

"That's loneliness right there on the side of the road. I'm never getting married. I can promise you that."

Tommy's eyelids were leaden, and his lips smacked loosely together. He sat amid thick, driftless smoke as if a shotgun had been fired under his legs. But his eyes fixed intently on Mills, just then, for the first time that morning.

"Have you ever done anything for money?"

Mills flinched. "What do you mean?"

"I don't know. Anything."

"No." The question shouldn't have hurt him but it did. Tommy had taken him for some kind of street hustler, with his earring and his city background and his trip out here under the charitable wing of an upstanding neighbor like Paul Benchley. It wasn't just the embarrassment of the question. It was the embarrassment of knowing that it wasn't such an illogical conclusion to draw. He shifted angrily in his seat.

"I didn't mean to suggest you had," Tommy said, his eyes almost sincere as they watered from a drag. "I haven't either. But I would. I would do almost anything for money. Try anything. I'm serious. One day, when I get out of here, I just might."

Was there anything as innocent as willful self-destruction? Mills wondered if, when Tommy did finally get out of Orient, he'd lose his brutal act, if there would be a short window in his life when his coldness subsided and he'd be capable of opening and softening for someone else, before it all slammed shut and Tommy Muldoon became the hard, reckless man he seemed intent to become. Mills felt sorry for the person who climbed through that window in Tommy's future and hoped that person managed to climb back out before getting trapped in there alone.

"So what do you want out of your life then?" Tommy asked, his hand gripping the air.

Mills decided to answer honestly. "To be happy, I guess."

"Happy?" Tommy's lips cringed. "Jesus, that's a horrible answer. That's the reason stupid people stay out here. You know what I want?" He didn't wait for Mills to say yes. "To try everything. All sorts of trials and errors. Do as much as any person can. I don't care if I fail. Failing is just as good as succeeding half the time. A few scars, some demons to run away from, blood on the highway—" Mills assumed that last bit came from some song lyric. "That means you've really lived." It was the kind of existential monologue only recited by the eagerly stoned, and Mills endured it with his hands clutching the armrests. He had shifted into that other role gay men were expected to perform in this world: patient listeners. "I want to sleep with people, steal, get run out of town, leave my fingerprints on every scene. We have a name for it, our generation. It's our Baghdad."

"Your what?"

"My Baghdad," Tommy said laughing, knowing it was dumb, savoring the dumbness, and maybe also its truth. "The situation you get into knowing it's fucked-up but you keep doing it anyway, making it an even bigger disaster. Everyone gets one, but that's how you learn. It builds character, makes you dirty and real. You know you're a superpower when you can lose every war and still be a superpower. Maybe you're a superpower because you can *afford* to lose them. Same here. There should be a Web site that records all the risks a person has taken, all the famous people they've met, all their gnarly trips and bad decisions. Like a Web site that ranks who's lived the most."

"Isn't that called Facebook?" Mills asked. He had briefly, in high school, created a Facebook profile on the library computer; it must still exist somewhere on a random server, gathering unwanted friendship requests from people he had encountered by accident. People like Tommy Muldoon.

"Not Facebook. That's for my parents," Tommy wheezed. His left eye squinted, as if settling on a mark. "Sometimes when I use Google maps and zoom in on my house, I wish I'd known the exact moment the satellite was taking the picture so I could have climbed up on the roof wearing my father's orange hunting vest. That way it could have recorded me and shown that I was here, a bright dot scorched on the earth. What good is the Internet if you can't become something bigger than you started? We can be like saints with our own status updates. Who else will be trusted to record the miracles?" Tommy was beyond reason now, and Mills realized how similarly ridiculous he must have sounded when he was high all of those nights in the city, talking about life like he was living it rather than fleeing it with every hour he spent folded up on a stranger's couch.

"You said at the picnic you were an orphan."

"No, I didn't."

"Well, *somebody* told me that," Tommy rasped. "Anyway, you should feel lucky you don't have parents. It's families that stop people. All they're good for is guilt. But I'm not going to let my parents stop me. I've already got my plans. And it isn't college. It's so much more than that. Lisa understands. She made her escape one way and I'll make mine another. All I need is some cash."

"I thought the days of optimism were over," Mills said, nodding to the bumper sticker.

Tommy laughed. "For some they are. For some they were over the first day they started. Not me. But everyone becomes an example of something that's gone wrong."

The sound of beeping woke Tommy from his future. Startled, he extinguished his cigarette on the window ledge and bent down to repack his safe. "Pass me a tissue," he ordered, gesturing to the box of Kleenex on his desk. Tommy bundled the butt in the tissue and buried it in his trash can. Mills heard Pam Muldoon downstairs, her faint voice through the floorboards asking Theo where Tommy was. "Merrily, merrily, merrily, merrily . . ." Theo started singing, his voice like swarming bees.

A thin column of smoke rose from the trash can. The smell of burning tissue mixed with expired cologne.

"Your trash is on fire," Mills said.

"Shit." Tommy searched the room for liquid and grabbed the bottle of rubbing alcohol.

"Not that," Mills whispered. "You'll set the whole room on fire."

"Good thinking," Tommy agreed, stomping his foot into the plastic bin. "Merrily, merrily, merrily, merrily . . ." Now both Theo and Pam were singing the nursery rhyme together, their voices competing in rounds. A louder beeping started to echo through the bedroom. Mills scanned the ceiling for a fire alarm, but Tommy hobbled to his desk to ransack the books and papers, his foot stuck in the trash can.

"It's not the alarm," he said. "It's these stupid watches my dad can't stop buying me for presents. They keep going off." He found a high-tech watch with its bands still encased in plastic and smashed it against the desk until the beeping stopped. "Why does he buy me a watch every year? I have a clock on my cell phone." Mills noticed a picture frame on Tommy's desk that held a photograph of him and his older sister, their arms wrapped around each other against blue water that might be a pool or an ocean. "Merrily, merrily,

merrily . . ." A phone rang downstairs, and booming steps ran to answer it. "Mom?"

"I like talking to you." Tommy's face was only a few inches from his own. Tommy rested his hand on the tip of Mills's shoulder. "I feel like I can be honest with you. I can't do that with most of my friends. And now that Lisa's gone, not with anyone really."

Mills returned the smile. Mills hadn't revealed anything about himself during their one-sided conversation, but Tommy had probably told him more in the last fifteen minutes than he'd told anyone else in a long time. Maybe Mills had mistaken loneliness for maliciousness, two teenage diseases that shared the same symptoms. "I wanted to ask," Tommy said, the arrogance in his voice gone. "How did you get your tooth like that? Why is it gray?"

"It's been like that since I can remember," Mills said, putting his thumb to it. "The root's dead. I can't feel a thing."

The bedroom door began to bang.

"Go away," Tommy yelled.

"Open up," the little boy screamed. "Mom says to come down right now."

Tommy dropped his hand from Mills's shoulder. He lifted his leg from the trash can and stood at the door.

"What is it? We're busy."

"They found a body," Theo screamed with delight.

Mills stared out the window, only half there, trying to remember the next line of the nursery rhyme Theo and his mother had been singing.

"What? An animal? Not another one of your birds."

"No," Theo swore. "Not an animal. A person. He's drowned and he's floating in the bay."

CHAPTER 7

From the causeway, the body looked like a bobbing tire.

Fishermen often used a tire to mark the location of a shellfish rack in the harbor, the makeshift buoys flossing the deeper channels while serving as perches for gulls bathing in the autumn light. Had it not been for the kayakers, the body might have gone undiscovered for days.

The kayakers had paddled into Orient Harbor to escape the chop of Gardiners Bay. They careened into the calmer water, nearing the cars that slid like wet pearls across the causeway. When they saw the floating object, the kayakers sailed close enough to make out two swollen arms and the back of a head submerged to its ears. The men quickly rowed to the beach to flag down a passing motorist. By the time they called 911, other cars had stopped on the shoulder. As they waited for the police to arrive, several Orient neighbors crowded along the beach, staring and pointing and shielding their eyes from the glint of the morning haze.

"What's happening there?" Gavril asked, glancing through the windshield from the passenger seat. "Should we see?" Beth pulled over to the side of the causeway, coming bumper to bumper with a silver station wagon. As they walked toward the shoreline, Beth noticed Sarakit Herrig eyeing her with a bitten lip.

"It's floating wrong," Karen Norgen said, using her cell phone as a visor. "It's too still, and it's not moving with the current. All this fuss, and I'm sure it's nothing. It's probably just a lobster crate."

"Beth, you just bumped my car," Sarakit said civilly. "And my kids are inside."

"Oh, I'm sorry, Mrs. Herrig." Beth looked over her shoulder and waved apologetically at the three pale faces haunting the station wagon's windows. "I didn't even notice."

"Well, next time *try* to notice." Sarakit turned her attention to Gavril, the latest foreign newcomer to marry into the Orient community. With his melanin-deficient skin and un-epicanthic eye folds, he would doubtlessly suffer a far shorter probationary period than Sarakit had. Twenty years ago, when Sarakit first moved to Orient with Ted, Beth remembered neighbors watching her with equal doses of fascination and bewilderment—fascination over the alien beauty of her salamander skin and long black hair; bewilderment at her sharp-sawed, staccato accent, which left them straining to comprehend the most rudimentary sentences. Even after she perfected her English, older Orient residents sometimes treated Sarakit Charoenthammawat Herrig like a bizarre Bangkok curio recently cleared by customs control. But Beth found her impressively determined, starting her own travel agency, Pearl Explorations, in Greenport and using her striking appearance as a customized billboard for foreign travel. When the Internet leached away the travel business, Sarakit refused to fold. Instead she expanded, opening Pearl Farms Realty, entering the far more lucrative and less exotic field of real estate. Beth admired the woman's resourcefulness and didn't understand why she treated her so coldly in return. Beth tried to disarm her with a smile. Sarakit stared past her at the station wagon.

"If it's true what the kayakers said, I don't want my children to see," Sarakit murmured. "I don't want their memories scarred."

"See what?" Gavril asked. "What's the matter?"

"Those kayakers over there think they found a body," Sarakit said.

"In the water?" Beth asked in disbelief. "A person, you mean?"

"But they're wrong," Karen declared. "At least I pray they are. Maybe they've been drinking and think it's funny. They're from

Cutchogue." Karen seemed to believe the nearby village of Cut-chogue was known for its drunken liars.

Beth stared out across the water and saw an object drifting a hundred feet from shore. The kayakers had taken their boat out again, not bothering to wait for the police, who always took an eternity to dispatch a cruiser from Southold. As they paddled toward the floating tire—at least that's what it looked like to Beth—she searched the beach, trying to read the faces of the onlookers. Over by the edge of the causeway, she saw Paul's teenage guest climb down toward the water with Tommy Muldoon. Pam was behind them, trying to order her son back to the house.

All eyes were on the kayakers as they reached the object. One of the men pushed it with his paddle, and the tire hardly budged.

"See," Karen said. "Nothing to be worried about. I was about to have a heart attack. It could have been someone we know."

The kayakers didn't seem as relieved. When one of them leaned over the vessel, what he lifted up had the distinct outline of a human arm.

A collective gasp was heard across the beach like air through a tunnel. The kayakers shouted toward the shore, but it was far, and the words reached the beach flat and undecipherable.

"We can't hear you," George Morgensen, an Orient retiree, yelled between his palms.

The kayakers called again. Those who were closest, standing with their bare feet in the water, heard *ife, life*—no, *knife*. He needed a knife.

George dug a Swiss Army knife out of his pocket. "He can have it, but I'm not swimming out there. It's a matter for the police."

Before Beth could stop him, Gavril grabbed the knife from George's hand. Tommy Muldoon jogged over, and without so much as a nod between them, the two men started walking toward the water.

"Gavril," Beth said, stepping forward. "What are you doing?"

He glanced at her with solemn eyes. Then he lifted his shirt over his head and unbuckled his pants. Tommy stripped as well, two very different body types exposed to the licking wind that pulled fast off the water and rinsed them with its chill—one young and hairless, with each goose bump amplified on his star-white skin, the other hunched and hair-patched and turning a chafing red. Beth was relieved that Gavril had worn boxer shorts and not his skimpy briefs with their broken elastic. Suddenly, her throat tensed and she couldn't swallow. She felt frightened. Not because of the distance—Gavril was a strong swimmer from all of his summer laps in the pool. And not out of any fear of law enforcement—thanks to their marriage, no xenophobic investigator could threaten to deport him. No, she was frightened because she loved him, and watching his almost naked body take quick, storklike steps in the first contractions of waves made him appear vulnerable to her, something that could be taken away.

Tommy and Gavril dove into the water and swam with synchronized arm strokes against the stalling current. Pam Muldoon nearly twisted her ankle as she stumbled onto the sand.

"What does he think he's doing?" she wailed. She turned to Beth. "What does your husband think he's doing with my son?" Beth stared back, her jaw fallen open.

Sarakit intervened. "Pam, he's trying to help."

Pam brought her hand to her mouth, as if to call her son back, but no words came. Like everyone else, she would have to watch as they made their slow progress toward the dark shape in the harbor.

Beth glanced back at the road, hoping to see a police cruiser. She spotted Paul's foster kid standing near one of the guardrail poles, pinching his lower lip, looking reluctant to get involved. To Beth he looked like one of those ragged, sand-caked kids more common in southern beach towns, emerging through the dunes and plastic-tangled weeds to eke out a living on the boardwalk, then retreating to their scraped-together lives in the lots behind the tourist billboards. Orient was not that kind of beach town, but some flint in the young man's face caused Beth to keep her eyes on him. He looked over at her, and they held each other's stare; when she wiped her eyes, he didn't turn away.

The small diamond of her wedding ring sparkled just as the sea sparkled, blades of sun glittering sharper and clearer in the water than in the real sun overhead. Somewhere in all that fractured light, her husband swam. She stood helplessly by, turning her ring with her thumb, as he took stroke after stroke. Why had she waited to tell him she was pregnant? Would he have been so quick to dive into the water if he'd known he was going to be a father—that his responsibilities lay with her onshore?

Soon she heard a siren blaring in the west. A flash of red light came through the trees of East Marion, and finally a police car pulled up against the guardrail. A young officer climbed out with a radio at his mouth. Behind it came Magdalena's rusted Volvo, by-passing the cruiser and parking in front of Sarakit's station wagon.

"What's going on out there?" the officer asked, nodding toward the harbor. For a second no one on the shoreline spoke.

"There *might* be a body," George Morgensen finally bristled, perhaps overcompensating for his earlier lack of courage.

"They went to pull it in," Sarakit told the officer as she clenched her keys and hurried to her car. "I'm sorry, but my kids," she said before slamming the door. The officer consulted a voice on the other end of his radio.

"Beth," Magdalena called. She had lowered her passenger-side window a crack and craned her mouth toward the opening. Her nurse sat in the shadow of the driver's seat. "Did they say there was a body?"

Beth walked over and placed her hand against the glass. "We don't know yet," she said. "Gavril went out to help."

Magdalena stared up at her in concern. "I don't believe that. I can't remember the last time anyone drowned out here."

Beth couldn't remember either. She turned around to locate Gavril, fear and love turning the ground into water and making the harbor seem like the only solid object. The two swimmers had made it to the body.

She could see Tommy yanking at the arms, but he couldn't seem to move them. The kayakers pointed their fingers under the surface, and Gavril lifted up, collecting air, and vanished. The body began to twist and finally broke loose, rotating counterclockwise in the current.

"Oh god, it *is* a body," Karen said with fingers trembling against her mouth. "It really is."

"It must have been caught on a net or something," George told the officer. "Why else would they need my knife?"

"But who is it?" Karen gasped. "And where's their boat?"

"Who is it?" Magdalena repeated. Others around Beth did too— *who? who?*—and then the question died as Gavril and Tommy started swimming back to shore, holding the body at each armpit. The kayakers paddled behind them in an unhurried procession. The officer hopped in the water up to his knees and waited with his arm extended. As the body drew closer, she could see a patch of black hair, and then two arms covered in a tattered brown sweater, but still no clue to the identity of the victim. The bystanders on the beach waited, hands folded or strapped over mouths or silently ticking off neighbors they prayed it wouldn't become.

In the shallows, Tommy let go of the body and climbed tiredly toward the beach, scaling the bank with wobbly legs. The officer treaded out with swatting arms to finish the job of bringing it to shore.

Pam gathered her son's clothes and covered his shoulders with his pants, furiously swabbing him dry.

"For god's sake, who is it?" Karen begged.

Tommy took four heavy breaths and swallowed a final bite of air to bring his voice up. "I don't know for sure," he said, panting. "But it looks like Jeff Trader."

"Jeff?" George asked and looked at the body for confirmation. Gavril and the officer dragged him onto the sand and turned him over. The face was bloated with skin so blue it looked swathed in refrigerator frost, like a man who had died not by drowning but from prolonged exposure to the cold. The deep, unshaven creases of the cheeks and the fingernails bruised black from years of repair work and the dark, ratty mustache curled over his upper lip confirmed that it was Jeff, the drunk, pink-eyed caretaker of Orient homes.

"What happened to him?" Karen cried. "Oh, poor man."

George Morgensen bent down to examine the rope knotted around the legs. "Poor old Jeff. Must have fallen in and got tangled up. Might have been drinking as he did." He reached his palm out for Gavril to return the knife.

"Who did they say it was?" Magdalena pleaded from the crack in the window. She had a clear view of the body ten feet from her car, but her eyes were too damaged to see.

"It's the caretaker," she said. "It's Jeff."

Her scream was really only a whimper, but onlookers glanced at the Volvo to locate its source.

"Are you okay?" Beth asked. Magdalena gripped the collar of her shirt and rolled up her window with a jerking motion. As the nurse pulled onto the causeway, Beth saw her own handprint on the glass, a purple smudge where her neighbor's face had been.

Gavril sat down on one of the boulders and slipped his shirt over his head. Beth found his shoes and carried them over. Karen Norgen was turning in circles on the beach, as if looking for someone she couldn't find.

"I was scared," Beth said as she dropped the shoes at her husband's feet. "I know what you did was right, but it scared me." Gavril grabbed her arm to pull her next to him on the rock. "There's something you should know," she said, but the fear had gone from her and the timing was wrong.

"That man did not get stuck on a rope, he was tied to it," Gavril said, wiping water from his nose. He shook his head and shoved his feet through his pant legs.

"What do you mean?" she asked, wrapping her arm around him. Gavril spit salt water and shook his head again.

The officer jogged to his car to retrieve a blanket. Before he covered the body, a red truck shot over the causeway from Orient. It pulled up to the beach with rock music blasting, its hood shining with spotlights under the sickly noon sun. Adam Pruitt didn't wait to turn off the engine before climbing out of the front seat.

"You people aren't going to believe what we found over in the park," he shouted. He stopped in his tracks, his eyes bulging, just as an officer swept a blanket over what was left of Jeff Trader.

"Let's go home," Gavril said.

When Beth searched the remaining faces on the beach for the young man she had promised to show around Orient, she couldn't find him. All she heard was the rustle of weeds.

It was the unfortunate fate of Jeff Trader to die on the same day the creature was discovered. The vision of his body, bobbing like a cork off Gardiners Bay, merged in the local imagination with the mutant animal washed up on the state beach in sight of Plum Island. At first, the talk around Orient granted Jeff the advantage, and dinner tables and fishing docks were ripe with recollections: how they'd miss the daily sight of his white truck driving from one house to another to fix windows or clear storm drains or restock toilet paper, always with his pickle jar of house keys on the dashboard. How he never had a nasty word for anybody—not the year-rounders he helped with sudden, inconvenient chores, nor the weekenders who relied on him to watch their properties when they weren't around. How Jeff really had only one love, alcohol, and his truck was often found idling in front of Indian Liquors on State Route 25, where he bought minibottles of bourbon and gin that fit into his overall pockets. How his double-wide trailer at the end of Beach Lane had been so lovingly bolstered with a stable for sheep that even his oldest neighbors had forgotten it was a mobile home, or remembered a time when it wasn't there. "Just this afternoon," Ina Jenkins said somberly to her neighbor, "I couldn't get the pilot light on my oven to catch and I dialed Jeff on my phone by reflex. This was three hours after I heard he was dead." The loss of Jeff Trader was marked not in terms of who he was but for what he did, and the list of small chores he performed was so long that no one would have been surprised if all the houses collapsed in his absence.

But Jeff Trader's death was ultimately supplanted, in the common conversation, by news of the strange creature—thanks in part to the three unmarked vans of military personnel that breezed into Orient State Park on Sunday afternoon to document and remove the cadaver. A fleeting evening news report on Channel 11, and two write-ups in the following day's *Suffolk Times*, stoked the bizarre finding into a possible laboratory cover-up, even a federal conspiracy. The fact that Jeff Trader had also been found in the water—and that his body had, for a time, been splayed on a nearby stretch of beach—so distorted the news of his death that before long August Floyd, who ran the outdoor organic vegetable stand, found himself wondering aloud, "What did Jeff Trader have to do with Plum? How did he get himself caught up with that mess?"

Most residents in Orient dismissed such ideas, assuming that Jeff had either fallen into the water drunk on a predawn fishing trip or drunkenly got himself tangled on the line of a shellfish rack. The Southold police opened a case, but the investigation never considered using the word *homicide*. (Southold had not opened a case that used the word *homicide* in nearly ten years.) The autopsy proved that Jeff had died of drowning, with enough alcohol in his blood to qualify as acutely intoxicated at time of death. Jeff Trader had no relatives to call for a deeper investigation, nor could anyone name an enemy who would want to do him in. "He was harmless," Karen Norgen swore. "It harmed us to lose him." The sheriff's department agreed to leave the case open-ended, and Reverend Ann Whitlen found it in her Christian heart to waive the church rental fee and perform a Wednesday morning funeral at United Church of Christ as long as it didn't impinge on the eleven-thirty Ecumenical Ministries Meeting. Everyone was doing what they could to honor the lonely man who had been as ever-present as evergreens in the village.

Still, the coincidence of the two bodies discovered in Orient on the very same morning created an impulsive association. For many residents, the mere mention of Jeff Trader's death sparked memories of the newspaper photo of the creature, or of Adam Pruitt's poetic description to anyone who would listen. Jeff Trader, in their minds, became something rotting, diseased, mutated; many believed that he too had washed ashore, naked, with green, decomposing flesh, because of the well water pumped into his mobile unit or through a virus he had contracted from insect bites or exposure to livestock. Jeff was another reminder of how much safer it would be when operations on Plum closed down.

Very few showed up at his funeral. Two men dispatched by the Veterans League of Long Island, sporting silver toupees and silver medals, placed a folded flag on the coffin to honor his service in the Vietnam War. The property owners he had devotedly served— some for decades, others for months—sent flowery wreaths, all of them signed by the hand of the same Greenport florist. Orient's love for Jeff Trader filled the church's vestibule with roses and left most of the pews empty. But one person was there—one who had spent hours talking to him through the years, sharing stories, finding out what truth there was to learn about a man.

Magdalena Kiefer sat in the last pew throughout the liturgy, aluminum canes at her side. She did not believe in god but she had her suspicions.

t was a black, vibrating smudge. Only when the doctor traced his finger over the monitor and said "head" and "arm buds" and "tail" could Beth discern some form of life. It was seven weeks old, the doctor told her, and it was already the size of a chestnut. To Beth it looked like a turtle removed from its shell.

When the doctor gazed down at her on the hydraulic memory-foam chair, she responded with the kind of smile she supposed other pregnant women gave at the first sight of their fetus on a sonogram. An open smile, scrunched shoulders, head tilted back in rapture or relief. The gynecologist nodded and told her that the baby looked healthy. It wouldn't be a he or a she for another few weeks. All of that was being determined at this very moment inside the gender war room of her uterus. He asked her if she wanted a printout of the image to take home. A printout, like a receipt or a copy of her resume, something to update her files.

On the Wednesday morning of Jeff Trader's funeral, Beth confirmed her pregnancy. She walked back to her car, her 90 percent likelihood giving way to 100 percent certainty. Two steps ahead of her in the Greenport parking lot, another expectant mother in a green dress two sizes too big—a blimp of happiness—furiously tapped on her cell phone, sending a screen grab of her own fetus to a dozen numbers on her contact list. Her baby was already circulating in the bloodstream of global satellite communications. Beth folded her black-and-white printout and placed it in her purse.

"Is there anything I need to do now?" she had asked the doctor.

He laughed without blinking. "Not a thing. You're already doing it. Millions of years of evolution have proven much more effective than anything I could prescribe. Just relax, be patient, stay healthy, and schedule your next appointment in three weeks."

Relax. Be patient. Not a thing. There is an art to killing time. Beth had become a master of that murder. After the moving boxes had been unpacked, the furniture arranged, and the accounts updated with the new billing address, Beth had learned the black art of time consumption—wasting hours loitering at windows, inspecting glassware for chips, reading old copies of the *New Yorker*, looking up *New Yorker* words she didn't know, like *peristyle*, entirely aware even as she ran her eyes over the definition ("an open space enclosed by a colonnade"), that tomorrow she would remember neither the definitions nor the words themselves.

At first her lack of industry came as a blow. She almost missed her freelance days, restyling inert technical copy into overexcited prose in the windowless midtown publishing offices of the *Scientific Frontier*. At least then her time had been worth something in nonexistential, market terms: eighteen dollars an hour. In Orient, Beth had finally been blessed with the rare, invaluable gift of time, and with so much of it on her hands, all she could do with it was panic. *I could have made $174.58 today*, she thought. *Instead I made Gavril a sandwich.*

Gavril was the definition of industry. He woke at dawn, disappeared into the backyard studio, and returned to the house at night exhausted. In New York too they had seen each other only at night, but in the city their separation starved them, making them crave contact with one among eight million. Out here, they ran out of conversation before Beth lit the dinner candles. Beth blamed it on her lack of a vocation. If only she could start painting again, she thought. If only she had the courage to face an empty canvas and apply one stroke of color. The city had offered the constant distraction of danger. Orient offered the far more dangerous distraction of peace—restless peace invading each window in the morning, with the same view of the blue pines and wild grasses tipping in the wind.

But soon Beth learned the trick. To kill time successfully, she must take delight in watching it die. She must retrain herself not to think that every action needed a purpose, that a purpose robbed an act of its joy. So she tried to appreciate the miracle of the lopsided floorboards on her bare feet, or the heat of the sun on her hands when she washed them under the kitchen faucet. She tried to believe that life was experienced more fully when each breath wasn't accounted for. Days went by. Hours evaporated as she examined the peeling paint above the rafters over the fallow tomato garden without thinking of how to tend to the paint or the garden. The seasons changed in front of her. She didn't feel guilty when the Greenport attendant pumped gas into her tank and she used that expensive fuel to drive aimlessly around the back roads of Orient. She was no longer embarrassed to tell Gavril that her plan for each day was "nothing." Each swallow of water chilled by cubes of prismatic ice became its own moment of transcendence. Leisure opened like a sinkhole at her feet.

But she couldn't go on this way for long. Beth was too workaday American for the peaceful transcendence of eastern religions (*feel the vibration of the dishwasher on your hip, saith the Buddha*). She was driving herself crazy with this unarmed showdown with the abyss. So, on that Wednesday morning, she should have been happy to discover that she hadn't spent the last seven weeks doing *nothing*. In fact, her body had been an epicenter of activity. "We hoped, we prayed, and now it's here," she said as she drove purposefully over the causeway toward home. So why wasn't Beth happier? Why had she felt the need to perform the role of blissful mother in front of the gynecologist? Why hadn't she said what came to her while her legs were splayed in his chair: "I'm not sure. I don't know. How much time do I have to think it over?"

"You wanted this," she said harshly, looking at herself in the rearview mirror. "You wanted this, you told Gavril you wanted this, and now you've gotten exactly what you deserve."

She pulled into the driveway, heartened at least by the absence of her mother's car. She searched her purse for her keys as she walked toward the porch, noticing a lime green pamphlet wedged in the doorframe. Beth pulled it out and examined its black lettering:

The Orient Monster
What biohazard experiments are being conducted on Plum without the public's knowledge?

A muddy Xeroxed photograph of the mutant animal appeared below the title. On the inside page, a paragraph was devoted to Aafia Siddiqui, a Pakistani doctor ("and suspected al-Qaeda operative") who had been arrested in 2008 carrying plans to induce a mass casualty attack on Plum Island Animal Disease Center. Beth glanced at the houses across the street and saw the same lime green flyers decorating the doors. She shoved the pamphlet in her purse and fit her key into the lock.

Today she would tell him. She washed her hands under the kitchen faucet without appreciating the warming sun. She would prepare lunch for Gavril and carry it out to the studio with a glass of whiskey and tell him to lift it for a toast. Then she would unfold the printout and let him see the evidence for himself. As she collected the ingredients for a sandwich, a smile broke across her face for the first time that day, an unforced smile that matched her mood. That was all she needed to do, tell Gavril, and all her doubts and fears about motherhood would be released or at least forgotten in the eight-month marathon of soon-to-be parents preparing for the birth.

She cut the sandwich diagonally, poured the whiskey, and gathered the folded printout from her purse. She crossed the grass and heard rock music blast through the renovated garage. Beth opened the studio door, surprised by her own excitement. Gavril did not like being disturbed in the middle of the day, and even the promise of the momentary annoyance that would flash across his face excited her because she knew another emotion would soon overtake it, the rapture or relief of fatherhood. A thunderstorm giving way to sun.

Two pints of ice cream sat on a metal cart by the door, the ice cream melted into a chocolate-vanilla soup. He had already eaten. Drums blasted from the rafter's speakers and echoed through the cavernous space. Due to some trick of insulation, the studio remained mausoleum-cold year-round, and she shivered as she set the plate down on the cart. Gavril was on all fours in the middle of the garage, stirring a black puddle of tar with a wooden stick on the terrazzo floor. She wondered if even Gail could really forgive her son-in-law for the damage he was inflicting on her property.

"I'm working," he said gruffly when he saw her. He leaned back on his knees and wiped his nose with his sweatshirt sleeve. "I thought you would be out all day."

"I was out," she said, anticipating this reaction, almost teasing his irritation in order to heighten the surprise of the coming news. "And now I'm back and I brought you a sandwich. And some whiskey." Beth dangled the glass in front of her. That's when she noticed strands of blond hair stuck in the tar puddle at Gavril's knees. "Is that my hair?" she asked.

Gavril sighed. He did not enjoy explaining his work.

"Beth, I cannot be interrupted," he said, almost yelling as the music abruptly ended. He climbed to his feet and reached out to accept the whiskey. She walked over to him and gave him the glass. He nodded at the tar. There were bones in it, chicken bones, and what looked like fingernail clippings, and long blond strands that caused her to gather her hair protectively in her fist.

"Gavril, where did you get my hair?" she demanded.

Gavril winced at the sting of the alcohol. "I took it from brush," he admitted. He squinted and grabbed her wrist to keep her from stomping off. "I did not think you would mind. I am doing experiment." Gavril's English grew conveniently broken anytime he sensed that Beth was growing angry. Unfortunately, that only made her angrier, as if articles and contractions were somehow beneath him.

"You could have asked first."

"Ahh, Beth, I am trying to make something. I don't want to ask every time an idea comes. This is why it's better not to interrupt me. Not to come back here. I have already been bothered once today."

"Fine, I won't bother you," she said defensively. "I'll keep to the house, but then you don't bother me in there without knocking first."

"What is the problem? It's just like how you made that painting on our floor in New York." Gavril had proposed to Beth in the kitchen of their East Village apartment at precisely 2:13 P.M. on the microwave clock. Their kitchen window faced west, toward a view of graffiti-scrawled tenement rooftops, and Beth had surprised Gavril by painting the four squares of light that shone through the window onto the kitchen floor at precisely 2:13 P.M. on the microwave clock—a romantic gesture that she hoped would remind them both of their love whenever the sunlight aligned with the white painted shapes. This tar puddle of human remains—*her* human remains—was nothing like her kitchen installation, and Beth glared at him to advertise her response.

"Don't be mad," he said. "I've had this vision stuck in my head ever since I saw that body in the harbor. That black speck of death floating in the sea. It was like a shadow of the worst possible fear. Like an oil slick in the ocean, killing all life that swims into it. Only I *did* swim to it and touched it and brought it back." He stared at her with a pained expression, and Beth queasily realized how much the description matched the very image she had seen on the monitor in the doctor's office. "A black human stain just floating there. I can't stop thinking about it. How awful it was and pure, like a computer bleep or a fly, destroying just because it is there. So I wanted to re-create it, to make that smudge right here. It is supposed to look disgusting." As he squinted, the Hawaiian Islands stretched across his cheek.

Beth stepped back. She tried not to connect this puddle of tar stuck with bones and fingernail clippings and her own blond hair with the fetal smudge on the printout in her hand. But as she stared down, all she could think of was the pulsing shape on the monitor.

"It will grow," he said. "It will keep eating away all the clean space. That will be my next work. A landscape, or the death that hides in a landscape because it is always there." He finished his whiskey. Beth was too dazed to open the printout now, too afraid the screen shot would match the puddle at her feet and rob them both of the joy. She felt dizzy from the tar fumes and noticed that the lime green leaflet on the mutant animal had gotten tucked in the fold of the paper. She shoved the printout under her arm and, without another word, walked to the door.

"I almost forgot," Gavril said as she touched the knob. "That nurse stopped by while you were out, the one from next door. She said Magdalena would like you to drop by today. She probably wants to complain about me making noise. Don't listen to her. I'll see you at dinner, okay?"

The fresh air revived her. The tips of sailboats rocked in the Sound over the pink-tinted trees, the color of autumn turning colder, the color of baby balloons and crib liners and blankets all ready to descend on her in the coming months. Gavril's new piece had shaken her, but she told herself she was acting stupid. It was just art. It had nothing to do with her, with them. She stopped on the lawn and tried to think rationally, but nothing came. Just the cold breeze blowing sidelong, scattering leaves.

Beth made her visit in the late afternoon. Magdalena's nurse, Alvara, answered the door. She was tall and lanky, with aristocratic cheekbones and yellow dish gloves stretched to her elbows. "She will be so glad you come. Messus Kiefer very anxious." Alvara led Beth through a blue-carpeted living room furnished with a rosewood armoire and an ancient, ticking grandfather clock. They passed through a cramped galley kitchen and entered a screened-in sunroom fitted with wicker chairs and raffia stools draped in orange cushions. The screen that shut the sunroom off from the backyard was sagged and warped, distorting the green grass into gauzy waves. In the far corner, Magdalena sat with one foot propped on a stool, the table by her side covered in newspapers, medicine bottles, and a small plastic terrarium.

The frail old woman stared blindly, deer-eyed, at the approaching figure. Only at five feet did she recognize Beth. She swatted her blistered fingers, beckoning her closer. Beth swept forward and allowed those coarse, disfigured stubs to cup her chin.

"Take the newspapers off, sit," she said warmly, pointing to a stool. "Thank you for coming. So good of you." Against the wicker halo of her chair, Magdalena appeared almost stately with her shorn white hair. Her voice had also gained traction, her words sharp and forceful instead of sailing faintly from her throat. The last time Beth had seen her, on the beach when they found Jeff Trader, she had looked so close to death. Now Magdalena leaned forward to glance through an interior window and whispered, "Let's wait until Alvara leaves. She scolds me for holding any opinions that aren't about bed, bathroom, or bees."

"I was just admiring your beautiful furniture on my way in here," she said. "The armoire and the clock. I keep telling my husband that we need to invest in some quality furniture if we decide to stay for good."

"Oh, that old stuff," Magdalena said. "They've been here as long as I have. They belonged to Molly." Molly was Magdalena's longtime girlfriend, who had died of breast cancer a few years before Beth was born. From what Beth heard, they had been a loving couple, holding hands while they strolled the country fields. Even Orient's most closed-minded citizens had accepted the two women as lovers without debate. Beth assumed that was because Magdalena had never asked for their acceptance, and thus never gave them the option of turning her away.

Beth noticed the terrarium on the table flurrying with honeybees. A few crawled restlessly up its sides.

"How are the bees?" she asked. It was the single topic she knew her neighbor to appreciate—the way a child who expresses a passing interest in horses finds that every family gift or conversation for years thereafter revolves around horses, until the simple pastime has turned into an unsettling obsession. "Did you bring the hives in yet for autumn?"

"I will this week," Magdalena replied. She grabbed the terrarium and opened the lid. Beth wanted to caution her, but before she could, Magdalena dipped her hand inside and drew out one of the insects, holding it pinched between her fingertips. "These are the males," she said. Beth leaned in to examine it. "Any stimulation," Magdalena said, and finished the thought by gently rubbing her fingers together. The bee's hoary tail split open, and a thin, stamenlike organ shot out and curled. "Like all males, harmless and easily aroused." She laughed. "It's the females you have to be careful about."

Magdalena took such pleasure in her bees that for a moment Beth envied the hobby. The cataracts in the woman's eyes seemed to clear as she stared at the insect, which crawled slowly along the notch of her finger.

"The Greeks used to say that gods and animals were born whole. It is only humans who need to develop, that they become complete only with the help of a community. It's the state of that community that can turn a human into a god or a beast." She dropped the bee into the terrarium and returned it slowly to the table. "Maybe that's bullshit. I happen to like the beasts. But I didn't ask you to visit just so I could bore you. I do have a point."

"You aren't boring me."

Alvara dipped her head into the sunroom, her hands clenching her purse strap, a tattered windbreaker covering her white uniform.

"Ma'am," she said to announce her presence.

"Oh, yes, Alvara, you can go for the night. Thank you." Alvara nodded and withdrew. Magdalena's hands reached for Beth's arm. "If I had known at your age that I'd be taking advantage of immigrant labor . . . If I had known I would become a *ma'am* to a Mexican woman who crossed the border so she could cook my meals and wash my back." She paused briefly. "Well, if I don't hire her she's in a far worse situation, isn't she? So here I am at eighty-three, caught in an ethical trap set by a system I used to fight. All your convictions come back to mock you when you reach a certain age."

"I'm not sure I ever had any convictions," Beth replied. She felt able to be honest with Magdalena, here in her sunroom that smelled of honey and tiger balm. "Isn't that awful to admit?"

"Yes, *your* generation," Magdalena said with a shaking head. "We fought all the battles thinking you would continue our work. Only you never did. They call today the age of individuality. My god, what were we before? Maybe we made it all too comfortable for you. But the war's not over, Beth. It's just harder to perceive."

"Where does Alvara live?" Talking with the elderly meant constantly changing the subject to prevent the conversation from falling into despair.

"On the rough side of Greenport. In the shacks where the potato pickers used to live. Her husband and son work the vineyards, tending to the grapes. Oh, it's a pretty idea to have wines from the North Fork. All the vineyards cropping up around us make us feel very sophisticated, like a little French tableau. But it's still field labor for illegal Mexicans we treat like slaves. You think about that the next time you drive the back roads to Riverhead and see all of those wineries. Look closely. Who's out in the fields collecting the harvest?" Magdalena mimed spitting into her lap. "Wine tastings. They don't even drink it. They spit it right out."

Beth smiled wanly. She wondered if all people, given eighty years, eventually turned on the world. Maybe it was their way of leaving it behind. But she did wonder whether Magdalena might have ended up less bitter if she had had children of her own, if she'd had grandchildren coming to listen to her instead of Beth. Or were children just a consolation for those who hadn't produced anything meaningful with their minds? Beth closed her eyes to vanquish the thought.

"How is that husband of yours?" Magdalena asked.

"Gavril? He's fine. He's hard at work on his next art piece."

"Work," Magdalena repeated dismissively. "He's always in that garage making noise, going in and out. I've watched him. Or Alvara has, and she reports back to me. Bringing friends in, drinking, playing around by the pool." Magdalena touched Beth's wrist. "I don't mean to pry. But you're so lovely, ever since you were a child. I just want to make sure he's good to you, that he cares about you and your . . ."

Beth smiled, a polite way of signaling a change in subject.

"He does," she said. "Now did you want me to do something for you?"

Magdalena gathered herself in her chair. "Today I came from Jeff Trader's funeral."

"Yes." Beth sighed. "I didn't know you two were friends. I hardly knew him myself."

"I suppose you know that the police consider it a suicide."

"Something like that."

"Something like that indeed," she replied. "Only it wasn't a suicide. I'll tell you what it was." She shot Beth a warning look and craned her neck. "It was murder."

Magdalena let the word settle over the room for a minute. But it would take Beth more than a minute to make sense of it. Was Magdalena crazy, senile, or so lonely she couldn't accept the loss of the local caretaker without blaming society?

"I can't believe it would be—" Beth began.

The old woman exhaled deeply, a drone of disappointment. She reached for her aluminum canes and rearranged them against the arm of her chair. "It was murder," she said again, louder. "I know what you're thinking. Poor Miss Kiefer. She's finally ready for the retirement home. But I'm certain I'm right. I knew Jeff well. He wouldn't have taken his own life. I admit he might have been drunk when he died. But what was he doing out in the harbor on a Sunday morning?"

Beth blinked in ignorance.

"If he went there by himself, where was his truck? I had Alvara drive by his house on Beach Lane. It's still there, parked in the driveway. He certainly didn't walk the four miles. Someone drove him there. Someone took him out on the water. I'm guessing in a boat. Someone got him into the water and tied that rope around his legs, knotted it"—Magdalena clenched the folds of her pants—"knowing that he couldn't keep his head above water for long, knowing eventually he'd drown. A person or persons. Someone killed him. Someone left him out there to die."

"But," Beth said, coming to sanity's defense, until she was stopped by Magdalena's wagging finger.

"Anyone who knew Jeff, really knew him, knew he didn't like to swim. He didn't fish either. And I'll be damned if he decided to jump into the water on a Sunday morning and start fiddling around with a shellfish rack. Those racks are private property, and anyone who's lived in Orient long enough knows that fishermen are willing to shoot a person who messes around with their livelihood. It's nonsense," she hissed. A small white bubble formed on her lips; she wiped it away with a shaky knuckle. "The whole idea is preposterous. You'd think anyone in Orient would see that immediately. But instead . . ." Magdalena dug through the newspapers on the table and located the same lime green pamphlet that had appeared on Beth's door. "Instead, this is what concerns them. This drivel, this fear of science. We don't care about a man who spent his entire life serving this village, but we're willing to take to the streets over some sad animal that washed up on the shore. They're scared all right, scared of the wrong thing."

Magdalena hesitated long enough for Beth to ask a question.

"But who would want to kill Jeff Trader? Why on earth would someone—" She almost said "bother" but caught herself.

Magdalena shifted in her chair. Her eyes blinked slowly, as if to clear the fogs of cataract or memory, and her voice grew weak from the exertion of talking.

"We split them last spring," she said, nodding toward the three hives spaced out on her backyard lawn. "You take a young queen and you separate her with a batch of drones, and, after a while, they accept her as their new queen or they don't. Jeff helped me. We did everything right, but the drones wouldn't take. The queen died, but I kept the box out there anyway, because I didn't want Jeff to know we had failed. You can't always build a new colony. The bees have minds of their own." It took Beth a minute of staring into Magdalena's eyes to realize she was crying. Beth reached for a tissue, but the old woman shook her head. "It wasn't a likely friendship," she said quietly. "A man who fought in a war and a woman who fought against it. But we both suffered wounds from those years, and those wounds begin to look the same after a while. I never served him a drink in my house. That was my only stipulation. But I pretended to turn away when he added a little gin to his coffee. You don't punish someone for figuring out how to survive."

"He was a kind man," Beth said reassuringly, although she had no idea if that was accurate.

Magdalena stared at her like she had missed her point.

"Jeff had keys to every home in Orient. He knew things—secrets. Secrets people leave out on their tables. After a few coffees, he'd brag that he had so much dirt on most of our neighbors, he could live off blackmail for the rest of his life. I'm not saying he was blackmailing anybody. I don't believe he was that kind of man. He never told me what he knew. But in the last few months, he started to act differently. Nervous. He said something bad was going on. He said it scared him and he didn't know if he should leave it alone or not. But he did tell me he was keeping records. He had a book, a brown leather journal, the kind sailors use to note their navigation. He hid it behind some cereal, I think, in the kitchen of his mobile home."

Beth could see where Magdalena's thoughts were heading, and she wondered if she went to the bathroom and waited long enough before coming back, whether Magdalena would be sleeping when she returned.

"I want you to go to his house and find that book for me," she said. "I want you to bring that book back along with the jar of keys he kept in his truck. Will you do that for me, please?"

"Oh," Beth said quickly. "I'm not sure I can. It's trespassing. I bet the police have already sealed his house off."

Magdalena's lips puckered. She closed her eyes and opened them again, clearing them slightly.

"It's your town," she stammered. "It's more your town than it is mine at this point. I don't see this as a favor." Magdalena started to rise from her chair but fell back against the cushions, her arms and legs showing deep patches of purple and blue that reminded Beth of the shades of skin in her unsellable portraits. Beth bent forward to help her, which amounted to holding her shoulders steady against the wicker.

"Don't— But you must. You have to," Magdalena sputtered, kicking her legs.

Without thinking, because Beth did have a decent heart and that made it hard to refuse the elderly, she said, "Okay, all right. If it means that much to you."

"It's your town," she repeated. "It's you who must decide what kind of place this is for your family. It's not just a given. I hope you realize that."

Beth didn't. Not really. But Magdalena was speaking with such force that she could only nod in consent. "I'll stop by tomorrow," Beth said. "I can look. I can't promise I'll find anything." Those words seemed to soothe her more than Beth's awkward clamp on her collarbone. "But if you really believe it was murder, don't you think you should talk to the police?"

Magdalena snorted. "You think they would listen to what I have to say? If Alvara doesn't believe me, why should they? You'll find when you get old just how much people care to listen. I'd go myself, but I can barely walk. Something bad is happening, and I think it has to do with Orient."

"With Orient?"

"The last time I saw Jeff, he showed up unexpectedly and just stood there," she said, pointing across the room at the door. "He was so upset he refused to sit down. Something wasn't right. He wasn't himself. He said to me, 'The historical board is up to something, disguising itself as good.' He said he was worried that something bad was going to happen. Of course, I thought he was drunk. He was slurring his words, and I could smell the liquor. He was in an awful state. I told him to sit until he calmed down, but he ignored me. He left in such a hurry. Now I think he came here because he was scared."

"But aren't you on the historical board?" Beth asked. "What could he have meant?"

Magdalena swatted her away. "Please just bring me the book. That's all I ask. I wouldn't want to involve a pregnant woman in anything dangerous."

Beth let go of Magdalena's shoulders. She stood to her full height and roped her arms over her stomach.

"Why do you think I'm pregnant?"

Magdalena smirked. "My dear, I'm not completely blind. I see you right in front of me. You have that glow of extra blood. It's what makes pregnant women look so happy. Tell me I'm not wrong."

In the silence that followed, Beth heard the water groaning in the pipes and the beams of the house shift and settle. Through the trees in Magdalena's backyard, she saw the lights in Gavril's studio, yellow and spidery against the dying sun.

CHAPTER 9

B eth didn't drive to Jeff Trader's home the following day. Gavril borrowed her car for a meeting in the city with his gallerist, Samuel Veiseler, so she stayed indoors, guiltily avoiding the windows that looked out onto Magdalena's property. She sat at her laptop, browsing baby accessories on Web sites that were as cute and convivial as New Age cults ("every safe-n-snug baby needs the Safety First Alpha Omega Elite Convertible Car Seat with a 'Munchkin on the Move' decal at no added delivery"). On a search engine, she typed in "when do pregnant" and the engine predicted the rest of her thought: "women start showing." Most pregnancies became physically apparent within twelve to sixteen weeks, when the top of the uterus grew out of the pelvic cavity, which, according to Beth's calculations and despite her sudden anatomical horror, meant she had just over a month to make some sort of announcement or decision. She didn't intend to wait that long to tell Gavril the news, but the blank October grid on the kitchen calendar budding with opportunities and delays consoled her. She typed in "what are other signs of pregnancy."

If the Internet were planet Earth, the amount of space devoted to pregnancies, motherhood, infants, and toddlers would surely fill a continent. Of course, the Internet had an enormous investment in the subject: those future babies would be its next generation of users. Beth's computer froze twice during these searches, as clicked-on Web sites disappeared into an unclicked-on landslide of pop-up windows offering coupons, discounts, mommy membership sign-up forms, vitamin supplements, and directories of local pediatricians. The third time it froze, she closed both the laptop and her eyes, trying to feel the limits of her own body, its mass and shape, its devotion to being Elizabeth Shepherd, here and now, in the first days of October on the fingerlike peninsula of the North Fork.

The next day, she didn't go to Jeff Trader's house either. She watched from the kitchen window as a green Subaru pulled into Magdalena's driveway, and Cole Drake, holding his briefcase to his chest, rushed up to the cottage porch. Beth wondered if the old woman had grown impatient of waiting and enlisted the local lawyer to scout for Jeff Trader's journal. That seemed unlikely. Beth had gone to high school with Cole Drake, and even then he'd had the makings of the cold, limp-eyed contract drafter he eventually became. He had the same haircut as he did in school, short on the sides, longer on top, the style of a man two months out of the military. Beth couldn't grasp what his pretty wife, Holly, had seen in him. She imagined Cole naked, his pasty, hairless body, the bony nodes of his sternum an extension of his pronounced Adam's apple, and quickly dressed him again. Gail honked twice from the road, attention-getting full-second drones, and Beth hurried out the back door with her purse. Gavril waved through the glare of the garage window, smiling, it seemed to her, at the promise of an afternoon safe from interruptions.

Her mother had arranged a shopping excursion in Riverhead, had phoned her twice that morning to say how much she was looking forward to it, what fun they were going to have, gilding the day so thoroughly that it could only end in disappointment. Beth spent much of the day sitting with husbands outside dressing rooms as Gail appeared in different silk dresses, leaning against the doorframes in sultry poses, one leg overlapping the other, as if she were navigating the walkway of a phantom yacht. Beth spent their lunch break giving her mother a tutorial on her brand-new iPhone. That's what children eventually were for their aging parents: custodians of technology, free personal IT departments keeping them from disappearing forever from the universal cloud. Gail asked Beth to take her picture with the phone. After Beth clicked five shots of her mother in the watery light of the diner, Gail insisted that she add the prettiest one to a number of dating apps. "Upload me," she begged from across the table. It sounded more like "Unload me."

On the third day, Beth found herself out of viable excuses for avoiding Jeff Trader's house, although she still had plenty of rational ones. Magdalena had lost her mind in suspecting Jeff Trader was murdered in one of the safest, crime-proof zip codes on the eastern seaboard. Beth had no business tracking through the house of a recently deceased stranger on the hunt for some apocryphal book. Moreover, assuming there was any truth to what Magdalena said, she didn't feel safe entering the house of a murder victim alone. The idea frightened her, the way crypts in graveyards frightened her, or freshly emptied and Lysoled rooms in retirement homes. She considered lying to Magdalena, telling her she'd gone over and found nothing, but she worried that the old woman would ask questions about Jeff Trader's house that she had no way of answering convincingly. So, on the third day, Beth steeled her courage and headed to her car. Almost as an afterthought, she remembered a promise she'd made to a neighbor, and realized it was the perfect solution: she could pick up Paul's foster kid, bring him with her to Jeff's house, and be done with two obligations in a matter of hours.

The Benchley mansion bordered the Sound just as her own house did, six streets west on Main Road, a five-minute drive if the Connecticut ferry didn't clog the streets with its procession of commuters. She parked behind the blue Mercedes in the driveway and climbed the porch. Lights burned in the front windows. She rang the chrome bell and heard the hum reverberate through the hallway. After a minute, she rang again, and when no one answered, she walked around the house, following a curve of box hedges that had probably been pruned last by Jeff Trader.

The oak trees between the Benchley and Muldoon lawns shook, as if something invisible were alive in the branches, causing leaves to shudder to the ground. The day was silent and growing colder as the sun rose toward noon. The box hedges ended, and black trash bags filled their place. Tied and twisted garbage piled against Paul's basement windows. One side of the back door was reserved for a heap of metal—two bicycles, five broken folding chairs, fan blades, fishing poles, a blender. Beth was about to knock on the door, but her eye caught a splotch of red through the wild grasses and cat briars that separated the Benchley lawn from the shoreline. She descended the trail of beaten weeds and found Paul sitting on a lawn chair in a red cable-knit sweater. An easel stood between him and the water, and he dabbed his brush into a palette of paint.

"I don't mean to interrupt," Beth said as she approached. She examined the painting, a scenic landscape of the Sound and, in its far corner, a frail, faint suggestion of Bug Lighthouse, not yet fleshed out in the creams and crimsons on Paul's board. For Beth, watching someone else paint was like being a fallen nun watching someone else pray: she felt a combination of jealousy and judgment, along with an awareness of how misplaced those emotions were. Paul wasn't a bad painter, only conventional, re-creating a postcard, marvelously untroubled by critiques of the neo-Marxist, cyber-capitalist, post-human Manhattan variety. Gavril knew all those critiques so well that he might even turn them back on themselves and pronounce Paul's landscapes ingenious. Outsider art was big that year. So was insider art. Her own paintings had fallen, unwelcome, somewhere in between.

Paul spun around, the tip of his mustache flecked with white paint. He smiled and placed his palette and brush in the grass by his shoe.

"Please don't look," he said, cringing. "You and your husband are real artists. I'd hate to hear all the things I'm doing wrong."

Beth shook her head. "No. You're doing a wonderful job. You're capturing the light perfectly." She put her hand on Paul's shoulder and leaned in to breathe the paint's stringent polyurethane. "I miss that smell," she said. "I haven't picked up a brush in so long. I'm afraid I've lost the nerve. And if you're worried about Gavril, here's a little secret. He can't draw to save his life. He tried to sketch me once on a bar napkin. He might as well have used a pool stick."

"I can't keep up with contemporary art," Paul replied, swatting off the compliment as he rose from his chair. "Painting is just a meditative practice for me. A way to take in the beauty of the scenery while it's still here. I put a few finished works in the local craft show. Maybe I end up decorating some bathrooms if I'm lucky. But with all the real artists moving out here lately, I might even lose that distinction. How much is Gavril's work going for these days?" It had become increasingly acceptable to merge the topic of art with sales prices in everyday conversation, as if the general public finally understood art's value: as a form of currency that could be cashed in like poker chips.

"I've been sworn to secrecy." She clasped her hips and stared out at the Sound, where a white duplex ferry lumbered in the water, taking its hourly crossing from New London, Connecticut, to the landing on the tip next to the restricted Plum terminal. Something about the landscape captured in Paul's painting was disturbing her orientation, her innate sense of geography, and only when she looked for the lighthouse that Paul had sketched on the canvas did she realize the obvious discrepancy. The lighthouse was too far east, on the bay side instead of the Sound, hidden by miles of rocky outlooks and thick, lashing reeds.

"You're cheating," she said. "There's no lighthouse from here. Not even Coffeepot. And certainly not Bug."

Paul took in the view, untroubled by the observation.

"You know, I helped consult on the rebuilding of Bug Light back in 1990," he said. Beth did know that. The original Bug Lighthouse was burned down by arsonists in 1963, and she remembered the long summer of Orient celebrations when the historical board raised the money to build an exact replica, sailing in the new lighthouse on a tugboat and installing it on the same crown of rock. "I did it gratis, of course," Paul went on. "I had just graduated from architecture school and was still fresh to the field. I swear, I still worry that it'll collapse into the sea, given how green I was. But the board didn't like their landscape robbed of that fixture. It's funny—back then, they thought it would help bring in tourism. Now new people are the last thing the historical board wants to encourage." He turned to her. "So what do you think? Did the board do the right thing? Or is the lighthouse just a big Disney lie, a ruse to make us feel connected to some maritime past?"

"If it still prevents boats from crashing at night," she said. "And looks good in your paintings."

"A very functional lie," Paul agreed. "Functional and pretty. So there you have it. I guess I feel the liberty to rearrange the landscape a little bit. We natives have that license."

"I've never been out to Bug Light," she said. "Is it falling down?"

"The county's always threatening to sell it. Who'd want to buy it, though? And I hear Arthur Cleaver donates a nice chunk of money every year to keep it running." Arthur Cleaver was one of the resident boat fanatics, a millionaire from Manhattan who served as counsel for the historical board.

"That's nice of him," she said. "I'd hate to see it gone."

They took the trail up to the lawn. Beth spotted her future car companion carrying a radiator out of the house. He tossed it on the metal heap and returned inside, dusting gloved hands.

"I hope this purge doesn't mean you're planning on selling," she said.

Paul rubbed his chin. A gust of wind picked through his hair to upset its careful part. "No, I'm not selling. Not yet, anyway. I'd like to keep the house for as long as I can afford it. The older I get the more I appreciate Orient when I'm in the city."

"That's odd, because the longer I'm out here the more I miss the city," she said, pausing at an elder bush to pick one of its white, weedy flowers. She twisted its stem and plucked its wet petals as she walked. It occurred to her that she and Paul had similar histories: both were Orient children who had fled to New York for careers and had recently returned to take possession of their family houses. Their migration patterns were consistent; the success of that migration probably wasn't. "I thought you worked in Manhattan," she said. "How do you manage to get the time off like this during the week?"

Paul bunched the sleeves of his sweater. His glasses were white with the reflection of the mansion shining off of them.

"I took a leave of absence. My firm had me on a project that fell through and I decided I'd finally fix this place up instead of jump in to help with another corporate-park development. So I'm doing a little work from here on my computer, trying to unlearn how to be an obsessive round-the-clock architect. It's been years since I've spent the fall at home, and Mills is turning out to be good company. That said, he's probably regretting his decision to come right about now. I might have overestimated a teenager's need for a little peace and tranquility."

"Oh, he'll get used to it," Beth replied, thinking the opposite.

"He's been so quick to jump in. It would have taken me weeks to clear out what he's managed in just a few days. You don't realize how old you've become until someone young comes around to remind you. Maybe the only way to stay young is by staying away from the young."

"Tell that to my mother," she muttered, thinking of Gail's surgery addiction. She regretted the comment as soon as it left her lips; it was unfair to attack Gail in a village that had already turned against her.

"How is your mother?" Paul asked. "I hope Magdalena isn't giving you a hard time about her. Lena's a real sweetheart when you—"

"I just saw Magdalena, actually." She turned to Paul. "She's pretty shaken up about Jeff Trader."

"That's a blow," he said, taking off his glasses and wiping the lenses with his sweater. "I talked to him a few days before he died. I keep trying to remember if he sounded any different. I told him I needed the second bedroom aired out and he asked why. I said I had a guest coming in from the city, a kid who was going to help around the house. You know what he said to me? 'Seems like there are a few people in Orient who shouldn't be.' I let it pass—honestly, it seemed like he was drunk, and I thought he was upset that I was giving away his job. I had to reassure him the situation was only temporary. But I keep thinking about it, and for the life of me I can't figure out what he meant. Losing Jeff was bad enough, but I feel terrible that Mills saw the body. He was on the beach when they pulled him in."

"So was I. Gavril swam out and got him." Beth dropped the flower on the grass. "But that's why I'm here." Paul stared at her in confusion. "For Mills, I mean. You remember I said I'd take him on a drive, so if you want to give him a few hours off to—"

There was a scraping sound at the back door, and Beth watched as Mills strained to maintain his grip on an outdated microwave. He finally managed to toss it on the discards pile, went inside, and returned a minute later with his arms full of plant basins, cracked buckets, and a red gas canister.

"Mills," Paul called. "Why don't you take a break? You remember Beth from the picnic?" He left Beth on the lawn and jogged over to take the containers from Mills. The two men spoke for a moment by the house. The teenager eyed her as he took off his gloves. She smiled and then stopped smiling, reluctant to seem like an approved babysitter. She wondered if she looked more like someone from Paul's generation than from his.

Paul and Mills headed toward her. The young man was dressed like a scarecrow, in an ill-fitting checkered shirt and denim pants that were too bulky and grease stained to belong to someone his age. She settled on his face to spare him embarrassment, and her eye lighted on his gray front tooth, the color of the clouds overhead.

Mills held out his hand. "We met before, sort of."

"At the picnic," she said, taking his grip. His fingernails were black with grit.

"No, the beach." He had watched her cry on the side of the causeway.

She nodded. "Do you want to go for a drive? I can show you a few of the local attractions if you don't mind stopping off with me at a house for an errand."

Paul thanked Beth with his eyes, and promised a lunch of oysters on their return.

"Let me change first," Mills said, tapping his shirt buttons. "Unless you also have plans to put me to work." A boy's irreverent smile broke through his lips. "But Paul might not be okay with that. He has me on retainer."

"Don't take him to the slave cemetery," Paul joked.

Guilt made for an exceptionally spirited tour. Beth was so mortified about bringing Mills to a dead man's house that she stalled for an hour before taking the turn down Beach Lane, filling the time with side trips to places she'd half-forgotten about, historical landmarks of such minor interest to anyone but the historical board that their muddy knolls were untouched by human tracks. On Bird's Eye Lane, right by Karen Norgen's home, was the settlers' graveyard of 1690, a small gully of crabgrass shaped like the base of a mouth. Black stone teeth grew unevenly from the ground, tilted at odd angles toward the sky. Beth pointed to the few semilegible stones: HERE LIES AGNES VAILS, D. 172 and ALFRED BROWN PAS 1753. Moss invaded each stone in bright yellow spills, covering dates and crosses. Agnes Vails's marker was crowned by a carving of Mary holding the infant Christ; the mother's face had eroded into a concave puncture, but the baby had survived the centuries. The mother was holding the baby out, as if trying to give it away.

They climbed back in the car, and Beth navigated the lumbering dirt road with its homemade sign, PRIVATE—UNAUTHORIZED CARS KICK UP DUST, to ward off unwanted traffic. A hundred yards from the onyx chess pieces and pink-marble bread loaves of Old Oysterponds Cemetery, down a winding gravel pass, sat the Orient slave cemetery, wreathed by tall brown grasses. The cemetery was heart shaped and buzzed with cicadas. Beth read aloud from the historical board's bronze plaque: "Slavery persisted in Oysterponds until about 1830. Here were buried some twenty slaves. Here also lie the remains of Dr. Seth H. Tuthill, proprietor of 'Hog Pond Farm,' and those of his wife, Maria. It was their wish that they be buried with their former servants." Eighteen baseball-size rocks lay buried in the dirt, absent of engravings, and at the front were upright marble slabs for Seth and Maria, decorated with fresh daisies by Tuthill descendants who still owned land in Orient. The smell of wet mud made the graves seem almost fresh.

"That was sad," Mills said when they returned to the car. He zipped his hoodie up his chest and squirreled his hands in his sleeves. Beth turned on the heat but didn't ask him to roll up his window.

"Yeah, those poor people couldn't even escape their masters in death." Beth made a U-turn and proceeded down the street, where desolate-looking new houses huddled against freshly planted hedges.

"Orient's got a lot of cemeteries," Mills said. "Is that all your historical board does, keep these old plots going?"

"Among other things," she said.

Mills picked his teeth with his fingernail. "Dead people are easy to love." He looked out at an unremarkable stretch of grass, identified by a plaque as the former site of an Indian village. "What about that cemetery we went by before? The one with all the marble."

"Oh, Oysterponds," Beth said. "That's not interesting. It's normal." She hesitated before adding, "It's where my father's buried."

He glanced at her, but she kept her eyes straight ahead.

"Do you want to visit him?" Beth hadn't visited the grave once in all the months she had been back in Orient. She pictured its smooth red marble, with two thin crosses etched on either side of his name.

When she looked over, Mills was staring at her. The gold cross of his earring glinted in the sunlight.

"I like your earring," she said. "Were you raised religious?"

"No," he replied, touching it with his finger. "It's just a reminder of someone I lost. Like the crosses families stick on the side of the road where a loved one died in an accident." Beth had never visited the section of the New Jersey Turnpike where her father died. It had never occurred to her to place a cross at the scene of his accident; she was never really certain whether people left them as memorials or as warnings of sharp turns, anyway.

"A reminder," Beth repeated, strangely flattered that he had confided in her. Mills was like a refractory water pump: it took immense effort to get a flow going, but when a few drops dribbled from the spout, they felt precious, like something to drink. "Was it a friend?"

"More like a stranger," he said quietly. He stretched his arms and rubbed his scalp on the headrest. "Why don't you show me a place *without* a plaque," he said, laughing. "You're from around here, right? There's got to be something that's just yours."

Beth steered the Nissan down Village Lane. The street followed the shoreline of the bay, past the long dock of the Orient Yacht Club with its moored sailboats blanketed in blue tarps. Newer houses competed for bay views, purposely built to emulate New England fishing cottages. She wanted him to witness the beauty of the water, its waves beating toward the tip in the pull of the current to open sea. It was beautiful, this stretch of Orient, wild with tawny sword grass that hushed in the wind and with seagulls rotating in the air. Like any resident forced to play tour guide, Beth turned tourist herself, taken aback by the beauty of the village, its monastic quiet interrupted by birds and frozen light. Why had it come alive for her only when Mills sat beside her? Why couldn't she appreciate the view on her own?

Two deer sprinted through the fields, flowing like a stream. She let the car idle on the road. From this vantage point, Bug Light projected from a mound of rocks one hundred yards out in the water, two floors of pristine lighthouse white over a brown cement base, like a fat woman lifting her skirt to pee. Behind it, the faint haze of Gardiners Island hung like a band of locusts.

"Is this the bay or the Sound?" Mills asked. "I'm usually good with directions, but out here I keep getting turned around."

"It's the bay." She grabbed Mills's hand and drew a flame shape on his palm. "You and I are in houses on the Sound," she explained, pressing her fingers to his skin. "That's north. In fact, if you walked the shoreline from Paul's house, you'd be in my backyard in twenty minutes. And in another half hour you'd make it to the tip."

"Paul said his mom used to own a hotel out that way."

"That's right," she nodded. Paul's mother had sold the farmhouse decades ago, and three or four Orient families had lived there before Luz Wilson and Nathan Crimp, Gavril's artist friends, bought it at auction for an egregious price last May. The farmhouse wasn't far from Jeff Trader's mobile home. She seized the opportunity. "Do you want to see it?"

"Maybe later," he said. "I like it here."

They sat in silence, watching sailboats nod in the distance, and the silence remained with them as Beth finally shifted into drive and stepped on the gas. She didn't ask Mills a single question about his background, not ancient or recent. She knew he was an orphan, and Paul mentioned that he had met some trouble in the city; drugs, she guessed. With so many topics off-limits, Beth fell back on the weather. "In winter, this all turns to ice," she told him, pointing at the coves of water gnarled with marsh branches. "Sometimes, when a hard storm comes, it even cuts the causeway off from the mainland. Then you're really stuck out here. You can go crazy waiting for the sun."

"All we had in Modesto was sun," Mills said. "It was constant there. And all the plants and dirt and skin were so brown that it seemed like the sun was still burning even when it was overcast."

"That's like Orient but with fish," she said, laughing. "Have you noticed how everyone's skin around here is as gray as striped bass?" Mills reached his hand out the window to catch the wet salt air as it wove through his fingers.

"Not you," he said.

She liked him, even without the compliment. She liked his frank way of talking and his even franker way of saying nothing for ten-minute stretches. She had cultivated the Manhattan tendency to admire those who felt no need to fill the silence.

Two impulses Beth had long thought extinct competed for her attention as she drove from the bay. One was to mother him, to buy him lunch or simply press her palms to his forehead. The other was to paint him. Beth found herself examining Mills's pale skin as it roped into shadow in the crooks of his neck and the wiry hairs of his sideburns creeping up into the liquid ink of black, loose curls. She thought of colors—ochers, emeralds, and blues—from paint tubes she hadn't considered for nearly a year. It had been so long since she'd felt this way—*inspired*. She sped east on Main Road, racing toward the tip, afraid at any minute that she'd lose the sensation, this happiness for the company of a stranger who reminded her why she'd once enjoyed painting strangers in the first place. To love them, to—that terrible technological term now ruined for all time—*connect*.

What Beth did not want to do was drive to Jeff Trader's property. Strangled by a sense of duty, she finally forced the car to take the turnoff through the barren fields near the Point. On a corner lawn, an orange sign bowed in the wind. PLUM ISLAND HORRORS: DEMAND ANSWERS FROM OUR BOARD AT THE MONDAY MEETING.

"I have a favor to ask," she said, staring ahead at the road. "The guy you saw dead on the beach? We have to go to his house"—she purposely did not use the words *break in*—"to retrieve a book for my neighbor. She's an old lady, probably crazy, but she was a close friend of his. I promised."

Mills tapped his feet on the floor and wiped his hands along his thighs.

"So you have me stealing for you."

"*With* me, not for me," she corrected. "I was scared to go alone."

"You were scared?" he asked, straightening up. "Okay. But in case we're caught, it was your idea."

As the waters of the Atlantic gathered in the horizon, signs of personal ownership grew rare. Fields stretched in fallow creams and purples, blistered after a long summer by the sudden cold, and roads ended for no apparent reason, as if the developers had run out of ideas miles before the land reached the sea. After a series of labyrinthine turns, Beth pulled onto Beach Lane, a squalid, ramshackle foothold of civilization at the tip. She counted the houses that led toward the three acres of land on the Sound that belonged to Jeff Trader. A handful of disheveled single-story units appeared, built from wood and aluminum and oxidized gray from years of conflict with ocean squalls. Of no consequence to local history, they'd been allowed to steep in the salt air, littered with rusted lawn mowers and splintered plastic baby pools and broken, netted porches. Here and there some recent, richer settlers had made a bit of headway, erecting bland suburban two-stories so fresh that trees had not yet been planted in their designated mulch beds. Slowing down to look for Jeff's driveway, she noticed a young woman leaping off the front steps of a red, aluminum-sided bungalow.

The woman looked familiar to her, vaguely, but Beth couldn't pinpoint where or how. Her brown hair was twisted back in a French braid. She wore a pair of unseasonably tight turquoise shorts over tan, slender legs. A sweatshirt covered her chest, its Coca-Cola-lettered logo asking, WHY DON'T WE SAIL FIRST? As Beth slowed in front of the house, the young woman gazed nervously at the car, as if suddenly conscious of traffic. She pulled the sweatshirt hood over her head, turned around, and darted back into the darkness of the porch.

"Who's that?" Mills asked as he rotated to catch sight of her.

"No idea," Beth replied. "It's the off-season—probably a girl from Greenport hiding from her parents."

"Finally, some trouble," Mills said approvingly.

"Oh, so a dead body and a break-in aren't enough for you?"

She pulled into Jeff Trader's driveway. The lid of his mailbox hung open on the post, its mouth jammed with withered memorial carnations. Just as Magdalena had said, Jeff's white truck was parked at the end of the driveway, though Beth was surprised not to see yellow police tape on the front door. The mobile home had sunk so deeply in the earth that wheat grew around its cement blocks. A jerry-rigged front deck hung with tools and empty plant basins. The windows were shut and curtained, a few starred with masking tape to prevent shattering in hurricane winds. Beth took a breath, reminded Mills what they were looking for—a leather notebook of some kind, probably hidden behind cereal boxes in a kitchen cabinet—and got out of the car. "Let's be quick. Then we're done, and neither of us gets arrested."

They climbed the oak steps, eaten soft with mildew, and tested the locked doorknob.

"Let's try around the back," she said. The temperature had dipped, and their breaths left their mouths like smoke from separate campfires. The cement walkway, slippery with moss, disappeared into firmer grass patched with dandelions. The last monarchs, migrating south, clung to the trunks of cedar trees. Three cats, two gray and one marbled yellow, ran from a crevice under the mobile home and wove around their ankles. Mills squatted to pet the smallest one, but it deflected his hand, scurrying between Beth's legs. It bowed its yellow back against her calves.

"They must be starving," he said. "And there are more. Listen."

Beth heard low groans that intensified as she and Mills rounded the unit, a chorus of neglect. A wooden barn had been built against the back of the house, reeking of hay and the sweat of livestock and manure. "Baap-*meh*," "baap-*meh*," came the moans as they entered the darkness of the barn. She could sense things moving in the blackness. She saw flashes of eyes as the animals drove their bodies against the stable gate.

"Have they even been fed?" Mills asked, leaning over the pen to see five bleating sheep, as dirty and thin as old pillows. "Jesus, has anyone bothered to feed them since he died? They don't even have water." Mills's eyes adjusted to the darkness faster than Beth's did. He located a garbage can full of feed and dispensed five shovel scoops into their trough. He filled a metal bucket with water from a spigot next to a lassoed hose.

"He didn't have children," Beth said, "or any other relatives. I don't know who owns this place now. The village, maybe. There was no one to come."

"No one to come?" Mills repeated. "*Someone* should have known to. You don't just leave things to die if you don't own them."

Beth proceeded blindly toward the house, groping along the wall, her knuckles knocking against tools, until she found the back door and turned the knob. She entered the stale, dank camper. The windows were covered with shades that drew faint outlines of light. In that minute, there was only the ticking of clocks, out of sync, their heavy tin beats resonating against the thin metal walls. When her eyes acclimated, she found herself in a room that looked as if it had been picked up and shaken. Books were scattered on the floor, papers strewn across the table; a painting that must have hung over the sleeper couch had been slashed, its frame in splinters on the carpet. Jeff Trader's home appeared to have been ransacked, by probing police detectives or by vandals who had heard of a local's death or maybe by someone else. Beth stiffened. Was that person still here? There was no other car in the driveway.

"Hey," she called. "Can you come in here with me?"

She tried to swallow her fear. The clocks weren't helping—each stroke invading the room, each perfect tick out of place in the home of a dead man. Clocks needed people the way longitudinal lines needed latitudinal lines to cross them, or an hour hand needed a minute hand to counter it. Without Jeff Trader, the clocks weren't calibrating anything but eternity. Beth felt sick in Jeff

Trader's house the way she hadn't in any of the graveyards they had visited, because here life had not been put to rest. It just continued on without the living, in credit card statements and phone numbers tacked to particleboard and a candy bar left half eaten on the coffee table.

Beth leaned against the grooved metal wall, where a row of clocks hung: a waxy grandfather etched with angels, an alpine cuckoo with a pinecone pendulum, two chrome-plated tide clocks reading the six and twelve of high and low water, a boat-wheel clock registering the phases of the moon. Sea people relied on these clocks. The sea was a clock too. Her father had always told her that. Just like the sun. And so was the fetus inside her, counting down or up. A thought that made no sense crept over her, and there was nothing she could do with it once it arrived: *I'm scared of what happens to me when I die.*

Mills touched her shoulder and must have noticed her seasick face. He stopped the grandfather and the cuckoo with a still finger.

"What went on in here?" he asked, taking in the mess. "Did the guy live like this, or was it searched?"

"I don't know," she said.

Jajajajaja. Beth heard the sound and clenched Mills's arm. The door that led into a connecting room, shut tight, jittered against its lock. But it kept jittering, jostled by air traveling through the unit. Mills laughed as he unclamped her fingers.

"Stop it," he said. "Are you trying to freak me out?"

"Sorry." Beth hadn't told Mills about Magdalena's idea that Jeff Trader was murdered, for fear he would have refused to come. Gathering her courage, she crossed the room and quickly swept the door open. Gnats spiraled through the kitchen, following a congested flight path above a bowl of molding fruit. The cabinet doors hung open on their hinges. Her feet kicked cans of tuna fish as she moved around the kitchen table. The sweet odor of a dead mouse wafted from under the sink. A minifridge hummed in the corner, its door open, watery ice trays on its racks. What would happen to all of this stuff without a relative to claim it? Beth wondered. Was there a special county task force allocated to clear out the homes of the unloved?

"Nice neighborhood," Mills grumbled, picking up the lime green pamphlet from the table. "You're all worried about some dead mutant animal that washes up, but no one cares about the animals dying of starvation out back."

"It's because of Plum," she said as she glanced into the cabinets. "The animal disease lab. Orient has always been obsessed with the idea that the government is screwing with its wildlife. Or obsessed with not talking about it." For a second time that day, Beth felt a wave of disorientation, not with space, not due to a lighthouse sketched in the wrong place in Paul's painting. This was disorientation with time. It took her a moment to pinpoint the cause. She stared at the pamphlet in Mills's hand.

"Jeff died on the morning they discovered that creature."

"So?" Mills stepped into the pantry, pushing brooms and mops aside.

"So," she said. "How did that pamphlet find its way into the kitchen? He'd already been dead by the time those were put on everyone's door."

"Oh," Mills responded. "Someone must have taken it from the door and tossed it on the table."

"Exactly. That means someone has been here. The same person who tore this place apart." She sifted through the contents of the cabinets. Magdalena said that the book was hidden behind boxes of cereal. One shelf above the sink was devoted to cereal—expired granolas and sweeter, candied loops. She pushed the boxes aside and swept her hands into the depths of the cabinet, all the way to the wood, scooping at corners. She shook each box of cereal. "I can't find it. Maybe someone else already found it. Shit. Magdalena will never forgive me."

Mills crouched below the sink and rifled through the lower

cabinets of tools, extension cords, and fluorescent cleaning bottles. "It's not here," he said.

"It's brown leather," she explained. "Like a navigational book."

He stared up at her quizzically. "I meant the cat food." He slammed the doors and left her to look in the barn. Beth groped under the table in case Jeff taped the book to its base. She slid her fingers through the silverware. There was hardly any point in continuing her search. Whoever had been here before her had done an expert job ripping the kitchen apart. The book was gone, and she'd have to face Magdalena empty-handed three days after the old woman asked her to perform one simple favor.

Mills returned to the kitchen carrying a brown paper sack. "I found it out by the stable. Not your book. The food for the cats." He knocked the bowl of fruit to the floor as he settled the bag on the table, then took three plastic dishes from the sink.

"I don't think we should touch anything else," she said. "I think we should leave."

"I need to feed them," he said, glancing up at her. "If we don't . . ."

"Fine, all right."

Beth was touched by his concern. Maybe he felt a special compassion for the orphaned animals. If her doubts about motherhood grew, if they became too hard and suicidal, maybe she could give the baby up for adoption and it would end up like the young man in front of her—not a victim of abandonment, not scarred by the mistakes of his parents, perhaps better off for not having grown up with such parents. But of course it was an absurd thought: Gavril would never let her give the child away. As soon as she told him about her pregnancy, there would be no way back.

Mills looked up at her and smiled. "Guess what?" he said, pulling a brown leather book from the bag. It was dusted in kibble. COORDINATES was embossed on the cover.

"No way. In the cat food. Not *his* cereal."

"See," Mills replied, "and you thought I wasn't being helpful."

She reached across the table to take the journal. As Mills passed it to her, a piece of paper fell from the pages and landed faceup on the linoleum. It was a snapshot of a woman, her face vandalized by black ink, with devil horns drawn on her forehead and a beard on her chin. Her eyes were scratched out.

"One more thing," Beth said over the hood of her car. "The keys. They're in a jar in his truck. We're supposed to take those too." Mills hurried to the truck, opened the driver-side door, and crawled across the cushions. She watched him search the cabin, tossing newspapers and shirts. He ducked his head out.

"Not here. No jar. No keys."

"Are you sure?" she called.

"There's nowhere for a jar of keys to hide."

He shut the truck and jogged back to her car. At least they had the book. She would not return to Magdalena entirely empty-handed. But Beth wondered if the same person who ransacked the trailer had also made off with the keys to so many Orient houses. She backed out of the driveway, thankful to have Jeff Trader's mobile home in her rearview mirror. She remembered the advice of her doctor: *relax, take it easy, just rest.*

She drove west on Main Road, passing the expansive estate that belonged to Arthur Cleaver—a grandiose monument to Greco-Roman architecture circa 1983, one of the few atrocious luxury mansions that had been built in Orient before the historical board cracked down on such extravagances. Its pink stucco façade glimmered between a militant file of sapling sugar maples, their skinny trunks painted white like the legs of racehorses. She passed cornfields, barren but for a few patches of fall flowers, that were still owned and farmed by Orient's oldest families. A mile of deer forest blurred by them, yellow but for the occasional black real estate sign—FOR SALE, FOR LEASE, FOR FARMING ONLY. Trees the shape and color of fireworks hung over the road. She passed Sycamore

High School and Old Oysterponds Cemetery and Orient's single gas station, now shuttered for winter. The farther she drove from the tip, the saner she felt.

"What's so special about this book anyway?" Mills asked, flipping through its coffee-stained pages.

"I'm not sure. What does it say?"

She looked across the front seat at the pages. Each one listed a local address, and divided into columns marked LATITUDE and LONGITUDE, printed tightly in black pen, were records of duties Jeff Trader had performed. Mills read aloud from a few random entries: "mow lawn," "drain pipes," "two tabs disinfectant in water well," "scrub boiler," "reboot alarm." A dull inventory of caretaker tasks: it hardly seemed worth the trouble. Mills closed the book and concentrated on the snapshot, defaced with such force that Beth could see score marks on the other side of the paper.

"Do you know her?" he asked as he held the photo up.

Beth took the snapshot and tried to study it as she stole glances at the road. The woman's face was too obscured, though a sweep of red hair showed between the devil horns.

"It could be anyone. It could be my mother," she said with a laugh and studied it more carefully. "It really could be my mother." The hair was similar to her mother's before she began dyeing it. The woman wore a yellow tracksuit and stood in front of a yard of shorn Bermuda grass and out-of-focus rosebushes. The Shepherds had never grown roses in their yard, and Beth was relieved by the discrepancy. "What did this woman do to piss Jeff Trader off so much?"

"Maybe she was his girlfriend," Mills said. Beth wasn't sure Jeff even had teeth under his rat mustache. "She dumped him, and he spent his nights haunted by her. Maybe that's why he killed himself."

"Do you have a girlfriend?" Beth asked, concentrating on the road. "Have you ever done that to the picture of a girl who dumped you?"

Mills rubbed his thighs and stared out the window. He seemed to be examining his face in the side mirror.

"Do you think I'd have a girlfriend?" he asked matter-of-factly.

"Sure. You're a handsome guy."

He swiveled his neck and brought his cheek against the headrest. "You really think I'm handsome?"

She stopped for a red light and took the opportunity to study his face. His jawline dipped faintly and disappeared into his neck as if it had not yet decided how sharp his chin would split. His lips were smooth and pinkish brown, like the wet undersides of shoreline pebbles. Maybe on their next outing she would find the courage to ask him if she could paint him.

"Yes," she said. She had no way of evaluating the beauty of someone so young. All young people looked beautiful to her now. "But what are you, nineteen? Wait a few more years. When you're twenty-two or twenty-three, you'll be at peak handsomeness. Then no girl will be able to resist you."

"You're wrong," he said. He scooped hair into a knot above his forehead. "People have always said that to me. 'Oh, when you were younger you must have been so cute.' Or, 'In a few years, you'll really be good-looking.' But I wasn't cute when I was younger, and I won't be more anything in a few years. I've always looked like this—in between. Is there ever an age when a person looks exactly like themselves?"

She turned onto Browns Hill and headed toward the Kiefer house.

"Magdalena will be able to tell us who the woman is," she said, setting the photo on the dash.

As they drove down Beth's street, flashing red lights swept through the trees and across the windows of the houses. She slowed down. Two patrol cars were parked in front of Magdalena's house. In the driveway, an ambulance sat with its back doors open, serving as a makeshift bench for a few EMT workers. Hope was an ambulance in transit—not a parked ambulance serving as a communal bench. As they drove closer, Beth saw Magdalena's garage door raised and fragments of gold littered across the blacktop.

"What's going on?" Mills leaned forward against the strap of his seat belt.

Beth drove past the patrol cars and parked in her driveway. Unhooking her belt, she wrestled out of the car. Mills was already scurrying around the hood with the book in his hand, and together they proceeded through the melee of concerned neighbors and EMT personnel. Beth waited for someone to stop her—a police officer gathering her in his chest for consolation or crowd control—but no one did. Her feet crunched the golden specks on the driveway. She entered the garage and was blinded with flashes by a man squatting with a camera over his face. Beyond a barricade of buckets, two coarse, rash-purple legs lay on the ground, outstretched, as if running sideways. A light-blue housedress was lifted to her thighs. The rest of the body was hidden behind three white bee boxes.

"Ma'am," the photographer yelled. A police officer tried to grab her arm, but she pushed his hand away. She stepped forward to glance over the boxes and saw Magdalena's face, red and bloated, her cheek resting near a drain, her ruined blue eyes staring at nothing, her hands knotted at her breasts. Her whole body was nothing, a hunk of fat and tissue dressed in clothes. The drain had more air moving in and out of it than her open mouth.

Now it was the police officer's turn to call her ma'am. "Ma'am, please step back. Are you a relative?" He touched her arm firmly, and when she turned around, she recognized him: Mike Gilburn. She hadn't seen him since high school. She'd gone on a few dates with Mike junior year—mostly out of guilt, since Mike Gilburn was ruthlessly nice, even when she threw him over. She heard he'd become a detective with the Southold Township Police Department, had married and divorced. In the last fifteen years, he had grown old and bearded, with wrinkles like withered rose petals around his eyes.

"Beth?" Mike said in disbelief. "My god, it's you."

Her hands were shaking. They shook at her chest as he led her out of the garage. Her voice shook as well. "Mike, I'm her neighbor."

But there were other worried neighbors there too, lingering at a respectful distance on the curb. "And her friend."

"I'm sorry about that. It's probably best you return to your house and let us finish up in here." He tapped the Southold Township badge pinned to his shirt pocket. "I didn't know you were back on the North Fork."

"What happened?" she demanded. She looked up at him, and he glanced down at his notebook, as if he'd already written down the answer to her question. The page was blank.

"She's dead," he said. "Her nurse found her about an hour ago. She must have been tending to her bees and suffered some kind of attack."

"Attack?" She was having trouble processing simple words.

"Heart seems likely. There are bee stings down her arms. Looks like she got stung pretty badly and suffered some sort of cardiac event. We don't know exactly, but she had heart problems. She was old. Are you staying at your mother's place? I haven't seen you since—"

Beth stared at him in confusion. Mike noticed her distorted face, and his smile became a seagull slowly shrinking into the distance. She started to ramble, trying to explain that it might not be an accident, that Magdalena believed in murderers, as if believing in murderers could somehow make you more likely to become a murder victim.

"Murder?" Mike repeated. His neck shot back and his voice tightened. "There's no indication that this is a murder scene. Wait a minute, Beth. Why would you suspect foul play?"

"Because, Mike, Magdalena told me just the other day that she thought someone had murdered her friend."

"What friend?" Mike was holding her by her elbows.

"Jeff Trader."

The young officer who Beth had seen on the beach stepped forward.

"The old man who drowned himself out in Gardiners," he informed the detective.

"I know who Jeff Trader is," Mike said gruffly. He looked at Beth. "You mean, Jeff's suicide."

"No, Mike," she screamed. She kept repeating Mike's name to remind him that she wasn't crazy, that they'd been friends once, that he owed it to her to hear her out. But all the *Mike*ing wasn't helping. "Not a suicide. He was murdered too. Someone knotted the rope around his legs."

"Beth." He moaned. "What are you talking about? Are you all right?"

"It was murder. Jeff was murdered and now maybe Magdalena was. Please just listen."

Mike winced—as if he was recalling those five dates they'd had almost two decades ago, as if he'd been the one to break it off because of some disturbing character trait that was now revealing itself at full force. He let go of her elbows and reached into his pocket. Beth looked around. The neighbors were staring at her now, people she'd known since she was a toddler, who had bought Girl Scout cookies from her, who'd complained to her parents about her reckless driving and sent her congratulatory cards with five or ten dollars on her graduation day. Neighbors she'd hardly spoken to since she'd returned to Orient. They watched her now with stunned expressions. Choking back her tears, she chose the off-ramp to self-preservation and said no more.

Mike handed her his business card.

"You're upset and you need to go home and calm down," he leaned in and whispered. "You're creating a scene. When you calm down and your thinking is clearer, you can call me. But your friend was eighty, and there are no signs of a break-in. No signs of suspicious death. Beth, think carefully before you start making accusations. You know what people out here are like. You know how that kind of talk can work everyone into a panic." Mike clapped her shoulder. "Kurt," he told the young officer, "can you escort—"

"I can make it home on my own."

Beth ignored the stares of neighbors as she headed down the

driveway. The golden specks sprinkled on the asphalt, she saw now, were the carcasses of honeybees, killed by the cold as they fled the garage. As she passed the ambulance, she heard a voice call her name.

"Lizbeth." Magdalena's nurse, Alvara, was sitting on the truck's bumper, a police blanket draped over her shoulders. Beth hugged her, and the nurse cupped her hands. "She dead when I come. She just lie there. Stung. Poor Messus Kiefer." Alvara crossed herself.

"What was she doing in the garage alone?" Beth asked quietly.

Alvara shrugged. "She never go to the hives without wearing protection. She was too smart for that." Alvara's eyes fidgeted nervously, and her fingers gripped Beth's hands. "Lizbeth," the nurse murmured. "It is a crime."

"I know it is," Beth said. She was thankful that someone else had reached the same conclusion. "I think you're right."

"It is a crime for me to be here. I not legal. I afraid I be deported. And my family, all of us, sent back. They tell me stay for more questions. I must walk off now. Please do not tell them my real name."

Beth stared at Alvara in devastation. But out of duty she brought her arm around the nurse's shoulder.

"Let's walk off together," she said. "It will look okay if you're with me." Beth collected Alvara against her chest. The young police officer trailed behind them.

"Ma'am, she needs to stay in case we have more questions."

"This woman is cold," she snapped. "I'm taking her where it's warm, if you don't mind." Without a superior to guide him, the officer stepped back, looking in vain to Mike Gilburn for instruction. Beth led Alvara onto the Shepherd lawn. She glanced back to make sure Mike and Kurt weren't running to detain them and saw Mills standing across the street. He waved the journal in his hand. "Ma'am, ma'am," Kurt called. Adding Mills to the situation would only complicate matters. Beth gestured toward Paul's house, signaling for him to go.

"Ma'am." They kept walking, shoulders huddled in the wind. Gavril stood on the front porch with his arms folded, watching their progress through the bed of ivy. The police lights stained Gavril's face. He held the front door open for the two women and, ten minutes later, held the back door open for Alvara as she escaped into the safety of Long Island.

CHAPTER 10

Paul said it was disrespectful, in light of Magdalena's passing, to order pizza. "I don't want to spend the night a friend died waiting for Domino's to pull into my driveway." He leveled his eyes at Mills, then let out a subdued laugh. It was the first time Paul had laughed since Mills had brought him the news.

What was appropriate to eat on the night one of Orient's local stalwarts took her last breath? The homemade honey Magdalena had given the Benchleys each Christmas—ten years of unopened amber jars, taking up an entire shelf in the kitchen? Frozen pizzas, or peanut-butter sandwiches, or the locally caught oysters Paul had forgotten to buy at the farm stand for lunch? What do the living eat on a day of death?

Paul's refrigerator contained scant provisions: a sliced loaf of whole wheat bread, a carton of eggs, a frosted jar of peanut butter, ten potatoes sprouting floral outgrowths. The Domino's Pizza in Greenport, its building shaped like a pizza box exploding with astral light, as if heaven itself were among the twenty-three menu toppings, was the only restaurant willing to deliver beyond the causeway. Mills wanted pizza—Magdalena would have wanted them to eat, wouldn't she, not starve?—but as a newcomer he had no standing to argue, and besides Paul had spent the majority of the afternoon in the cellar, preferring to be alone.

. . . .

Mills had walked the two miles home from Beth's house. He watched the news of Magdalena's death travel through the village, almost as if his own presence carried the message. Front doors opened and residents stumbled down their walks with their hands on their hips, staring toward the house they couldn't see, staring at him because they could. As he approached Paul's steps, he caught a shadow moving behind the glass in the front door.

"Paul?" he called, climbing to the porch. The door flew wide and a thin black woman stepped onto the welcome mat, the smoke from a cigarette circling the diamonds on her fingers. Her short hair was slippery and knotted close to the scalp. Her eyes were long and heavy-lidded; though she wore an ordinary black polo, its collar flipped up around her jaw, he smelled the expensive, churchlike scent of her perfume. She stood so confidently on the welcome mat, this strange young black woman in the middle of whitewashed Long Island, that for a moment Mills wondered if he'd wandered back to the wrong address. Mills hadn't seen a single black person during his stay in Orient. He thought of the slaves buried in the Tuthill cemetery; maybe they too had descendants in the area.

"Yo," she said, waving her cigarette.

"Can I help you?" He hid Jeff Trader's book in his back pocket.

"Doubtful," she replied. "I'm looking for Paul Benchley. He seems to be out." She didn't mention the fact that she had already invited herself in.

"He's painting," Mills said. "This is *his* house."

She nodded to express, *Yeah, dumbass, I already know that.* "Which is why I'm here." She tapped ash on the porch. "I'm a painter too. Well, not Benchley's kind." She grunted like she found the comparison amusing. "He does seascapes, right? Anyway, I have a house out here now and I'm doing a series of portraits of some of the locals. I heard Paul's family has been out here forever, so I thought he might be willing to sit for me." She took a drag and waited, as if she expected him to hurry up with her lunch order. "I'm Luz," she said with a smile. *Luz* like *fuzz, buzz.* She took so long to bestow a smile that when it arrived it felt like a reward.

"Mills," he said.

"Yeah, I heard about you. Heard you were staying here." She glanced at him as if assessing a bad reputation. Mills felt not for the first time that his body communicated a message that was lost on him but clear to others. "You know the doorbells in these prehistoric homes—they barely burp. The door was unlocked, so I went inside to see if he was around. You can do that out here, make yourself welcome, unlike in Manhattan." She shrugged and guttered smoke through her teeth. "Screw it." She jumped down the steps and headed for the street with graceless, stomping feet. He quickly descended after her, shepherding her off the property like a small mutt herding an uncaring game bird. She flicked her cigarette, a speeding bullet, into the curb.

"Do you want me to tell him you stopped by?"

She eyed him over the roof of her black sports coupe. "No. Better not to. I'll come by another time." He watched her drive toward Main Road, in the direction of the death that brought the neighbors to stand on their porches, oblivious, car windows rattling with the bass of her speakers.

Mills rounded the house and found Paul carting his wet landscape across the lawn. "I lost track of time," Paul yelled. "I need to get our groceries before the market closes. Otherwise, it's pizza night."

When Mills told him the news of Magdalena Kiefer, Paul dropped the canvas, leaving a smudge of the sea on the grass. It was clear that Paul didn't want to cry in front of him. He made an excuse about stowing his paint supplies in the cellar, and Mills watched him open the bulkhead doors and climb down the back steps.

Mills went up to his bedroom, sitting against the sill and flipping through the pages of Jeff Trader's journal. There had to be something of interest in those pages. Each address had its list of tedious tasks—as if it were a warning to Mills not to get too comfortable in the role of Paul's housecleaner. Eventually he would have to find a skill, something he was good at, something dependable—and hopefully not just a minimum-wage job where time was a tract of land parceled off until there was no acreage left. What did Mills want from his future—anything more specific than a city? For so long New York had been his only direction.

He glanced across the lawn at the Muldoons' house, as he had many times in the last week, hoping to catch sight of Tommy (coming home from school, taking out the garbage, flicking cigarette butts into his backyard at night). Mills had told Tommy that what he wanted out of his future was to be happy, as if happiness were a shell game no one had much chance of winning. Tommy wanted to blow the world up and be the last man standing—was that a skill that could be applied to anything but pain? Mills envisioned Tommy at his future job, a Wall Street one-percenter or cult leader or research scientist who tested brand-name products on laboratory animals. Heroic practitioners of other people's pain. Mills also envisioned Tommy naked in the shower. He couldn't help it. Scrubbing, dripping, water swirling, a drain with the perfect view.

Finding the Muldoons' windows lacking in glimpses of nudity—even the constantly naked father—Mills returned his attention to the book. Since he couldn't identify the addresses, he had no idea what certain notes referred to. But at some point in each entry, the boring inventory of jobs shifted in tone—"unpaid," "overdue," "last statement," "calls to PF Real," "cheating with Holly," "B. & Y. at Seaview." Cheating, at least, seemed promising, a hint of discord beneath the mundane happiness of all the well-maintained homes. Mills remembered what Beth had said to the detective in Magdalena's driveway—"murder," a word she hadn't used once during their drive. Was this book worth murder? Had the old woman been killed before she could read it? Had Jeff Trader been another victim?

As a child, Mills had imagined that his biological parents had been murdered, Manson-like, or gunned down in a botched carjacking, or pushed to their deaths from the cliffs of Big Sur. Murdered parents seemed preferable to living ones who never showed up to reclaim him. He never wanted to imagine his real parents happy. It was better for him to be happy by imagining them dead. At least until he discovered that one of them was very much alive, not seventy miles from Modesto.

At the bottom of every page, Jeff Trader had scrawled one of three simple words—*yes, maybe,* or *no. Yes, yes, no, maybe, yes, no, no, yes, yes.* The last page was devoted to a list of numbers, $200, $150, $500, and the last, $2,000, circled four times in black pen. The price of maintaining happiness, Mills supposed. As the sun set, he placed the book in his duffel bag for safekeeping and finally gave in to his appetite.

"Peanut butter sandwiches will have to do," Paul said, sighing. Mills found him standing at the open refrigerator for what might have been minutes or hours. Paul quickly reactivated, shutting the door and removing two plates from the cabinet. "I'll go into town tomorrow. I promise to be a better cook. I feel bad feeding you such awful meals after you've been working hard."

Mills *had* been working hard. In the past week, he had managed to clear out an entire room of Benchley junk. At first Paul was devoutly unsentimental—out go the canoe paddles, the phone books, the 1980s Toshiba microwave, the buckets and canisters and tattered guides to deep-sea fishing. But as the room emptied out, Paul stepped away from his laptop at the dining room table and gazed somberly at his mother's box of toiletries and his childhood croquet set. "Maybe we don't throw it all out," he said meekly. "No, never mind. I keep thinking I might still have children one day, but what kind of child would want this stuff? Children aren't old women. Pitch it. Don't let me interrupt." In the end, the only things Paul insisted on keeping were photo albums and Orient-related bric-a-brac. When Mills discovered a rolled-up map of Orient, much like the smaller map in his bedroom, Paul pronounced it a rare specimen. "Maybe I'll donate it to the historical museum, which I still haven't taken you to yet. Fair warning: we were royalists in the American Revolution. That doesn't get a lot of play during the winter fund-raisers, but it's a fact."

As they sat in the flickering light of the dining room, Mills pressed his wrists against the cold African marble and considered mentioning the prospect of a murderer to Paul. Paul chewed on his triangle of sandwich, washing it down with chilled red wine from an East Marion vineyard. Pieces of damp, tugged hair jutted around his forehead like rough waves. The fireplace crackled lit balls of newspaper. Paul smiled at Mills, his teeth yellowed by the flames.

"I'm glad Beth drove you around today," he said gently. "You just needed a change of scenery. Soon all that business in New York will be like a bad dream."

"Beth took me to a bunch of cemeteries," Mills told him. "Which one are your parents buried in?"

Paul looked at him over the rims of his glasses.

"Oysterponds. Did she take you there?" Mills shook his head. "That's where my mom and dad are buried, their ashes anyway. And that's where Magdalena will go. I suppose I should call about helping with the arrangements. Lena was so kind when my mother was dying, stopping by to check on us. Lena was always going out of her way, not just for me, for everybody. I can't imagine Orient without her. I wonder if she left her money to the historical society. She was a longtime board member."

"Is that where you're leaving your money?" Mills asked. "If you don't have children, I mean." Mills was embarrassed to find himself imagining a future in which Paul was childless save for one adopted son he had brought to Orient to help with his house, leaving all his money and property to the closest thing to a relative he had. It was a passing daydream, one of a dozen futures that turned to dust before it set. But Mills enjoyed pacing through the back rooms, picturing what he would do with them if they were his.

Paul breathed heavily through his nose. "I haven't really decided on that. I hope I don't have to for some time." He winked. "And where'd you get the idea I had any money?"

Mills had found a shoe box of bank statements, the accounts an asteroid shower of zeroes. He couldn't decipher how much was company money and how much personal, but Paul clearly worked in high figures. He'd been successful as an architect, but also, Mills thought, a slave to that success. Even out here on his Orient sabbatical, Paul tinkered on his computer blueprints—"I just have to send this draft by tomorrow's deadline"—like a kid chained to a video game.

"Nowhere," Mills lied. He struggled to find an excuse for the question. "You just mentioned a few days ago that you wanted to donate some of your Orient stuff to the museum. It made me think—you're throwing out junk you don't expect your own children will want, but you're certain future generations will want to preserve those old maps. What if they just stop caring? At some point there's going to be too much history for anyone to keep up with it all." All that history, Mills thought. All that junk. It seemed so much easier to throw it away.

If their dinner had required silverware, Paul would have set down his knife and fork. Instead he picked up his wineglass and swilled the liquid.

"You never know, I guess. But don't you think it's important to preserve some traces of the past?" Paul tongued his cheek. "I agree that history isn't worth much if it's just a bunch of artifacts to look at. But there's a reason people hold on to their ancestors. There has to be something in our survival instinct that compels us to remember what happened and use that information as a guide." The point was alien to Mills. He had no ancestors. People in Modesto looked at you funny if you tried to tell them about last week. When he was younger and an arcade on H Street with a superior pinball machine suddenly closed, he went to the gas station across the road to ask if it had moved. The cashier lifted her tired, mascaraed eyes and muttered, "Never heard of it."

"I guess you're right," Mills said.

Paul slapped his napkin on the table and left his chair, disappearing down the hallway with heavy, receding steps. Mills hadn't thought it would be so easy to upset Paul. In the past week, no subject had seemed off-limits between them, except for love and sex, two topics Mills had learned to avoid like a tightrope walker over the Niagara Falls of messy, personal conversations. He was thankful when Paul returned with the rolled-up, camel-colored map. He spread it across the table and pointed to the tip.

"What I always thought was telling about Orient was the two islands just off the coast." Paul's finger traced two competing circles of land just beyond the bird beak. "One is Plum, owned by the government, a laboratory presumably for the common good. The other is Gardiners Island, owned privately—in fact, one of the largest privately owned islands in the United States. It was bought from the Indians in the seventeenth century by an English soldier and granted by the king. Lion Gardiner's descendants still own it, three hundred years later." Paul took a sip of wine to let the history lesson settle over his student. "So there you have it, two opposing forces, side by side, hanging just off our coast: public-controlled property and a private estate, the rights of the individual versus the betterment of the community. If that isn't a split personality in geographic form, I don't know what is."

"A family can own a whole island?" Mills couldn't let go of the most sensational aspect. "That same family has been around since the seventeenth century? Out there? Eating dinner right now?" Mills glanced out the window. "I wonder what they're eating."

"All families have been around since the seventeenth century," Paul said, laughing.

"I mean, in one place."

"Yeah. You've got to hand it to the Gardiner descendants—they know how to hang on to their land." Paul cleared his throat. "But what I'm trying to say is, those two islands are just like the minds of most people in Orient. They want conservancy, they want to preserve the natural land, they want to hold on to the history and keep Orient untouched by private development. But they also distrust the government. They don't like laws cracking down on them, deciding what they can and can't do with their property. Why else is every house getting swamped with these green leaflets on the horrors of mutant animals? It's meant to scare us, to make us think the government is creating trouble behind our backs." Paul braided his fingers together in front of his stomach. "Gardiner versus Plum, private versus public, wrestling over which will win."

Paul twittered his thumbs for ten seconds, and Mills actually watched to see if one thumb would pin the other. The match was called off, and Paul returned to his seat to finish his sandwich.

"Sorry. I get pedantic after a few glasses of wine." He stared across the table to gauge whether his sole audience member was bored.

"Which side are you on?"

Paul laughed and clenched his teeth. "I plead the Fifth. You know how you stay popular in Orient? You keep your mouth shut when some of these deep-rooted families get to choosing sides. That's what's good about doing a painting of the lighthouse. Everyone can agree on how pretty it is." Paul took a bite and chewed. Five chews gave him time to contemplate. "Thing is, Plum is going to lose that animal disease lab soon. And the Gardiner survivors can't afford the upkeep on their grounds much longer. Those islands are about to change, and I bet there'll be a fight over who gets them." Paul's tongue churned through peanut butter, a ship in a lagoon.

Paul should have children, Mills thought. He had never wished children on anyone, but suddenly he hoped that one day Paul would marry Eleanor or another woman whose number might be lurking on a matchbook somewhere in this house. He should populate Orient and watch his children take sides in the conflict.

"But you're an architect," Mills said. "You develop property too, right?"

"Yes, I believe in buildings. Just not crappy ones. Not the kind you see popping up like birdhouses for the elderly the closer you get to the city. And, I'm afraid, I'm still a full-time architect. I thought I was going to have time to get this place fixed up. I've hardly even helped you throw out all that junk."

Paul reached over and patted the table, a substitution for Mills's hand. Paul had many tiny teeth inside his smile. Mills had begun to appreciate the moments it flared in his direction. Paul seemed less lonely then, grateful for the company, not just a walking encyclopedia stiff from being so rarely opened.

"I'm sorry you saw what you did today," Paul said. "I'm sorry for what you saw last week. I promise we don't usually have this much dying out here. I hope you'll stay and finish up the house with me." He returned his hand to his plate.

Mills decided not to mention Beth by name. He liked her too much—needed her too much, her company and car—to have her darkened in the mind of his host.

"I heard some talk that Magdalena was murdered."

Paul dropped his crust on the plate and shook his head.

"Who said that?"

"Some people, a neighbor on the street. Just one person. I didn't know them."

"Can't they even let an old woman die in peace? Can't they not turn everything into a conspiracy? Can't they—"

Mills regretted his next sentence as soon as he spoke it. But it was too enticing not to imagine that he had entered the house of a homicide victim, too lurid not to at least verbalize the possibility. What was the point of a confidant if not to speak outlandishly about the dead?

"And Jeff Trader too. One after the other. By the same killer."

Paul reached for the bottle and poured a small dose of wine. He sipped thirstily.

"Whoever is saying that is just trying to upset everyone. The year-rounders might claim to hate the summer people, but I think they've grown used to them—they get a little lonely in the fall when it's just the regulars. The carnival's gone."

"So you don't believe it could be murder?"

"No." Paul set his glass down and stared at Mills, as if his verdict had not been heard. "Not a chance. There's no one out here like that. And there's no reason to kill them."

A noise broke from the foyer, sending Mills and Paul into separate jolts. Paul's arm knocked his glass, and red wine spilled into the grooves of the marble. Mills rescued the map, rolling it up to keep his fingers occupied. The doorbell rang again. Polite knocking followed. Paul rose and hurried to the door.

Mills heard two unfamiliar voices on the porch. He crept through the living room and lingered in the shadows of the doorway to catch sight of the visitors.

A couple in their midforties wearing matching canvas jackets stood in front of Paul. The man had wavy orange hair, thinning to a bald island of freckles at the crown. Next to him was an Asian woman with a strikingly small nose and mouth, as if forfeiting space for her eyes. Long black lashes curled from their rims. Her hair was gathered in a top bun, almost ridiculing her partner's lack in its endless twists and tucks. They gesticulated like professional politicians, fists clenched, palms stretched out, hearts tapped.

"So it's essential to get home owners there," the Asian woman was saying when Mills moved close enough to hear. "To galvanize as much support as possible. Especially from those like you, Paul, with such roots. We need to take matters into our own hands."

"Yes," the man spoke up, belched up, missing a cue or two and trying to overcompensate. "Bryan wants to express that as well. He'd really like to see you there. He told me so."

"Because we can't leave it up to Southold. Not the way things are going. Not after the water-main debacle."

"Well, I'll think about it," Paul replied, his hands balled in his pant pockets.

Another heart tap from the woman, and Mills thought he saw her wink. With those lashes it was difficult to tell.

"Monday at seven. Same as always. Poquatuck Hall. Magdalena would have wanted us to continue her fight. We're dedicating the proposal to her. The Kiefer Nondevelopment Advocacy Initiative. After all, the plan was her idea."

"That's awfully nice." Paul nodded and kicked the corner of his welcome mat. The woman winked again. No, it wasn't a wink. It was a blink, as her eyes peered around Paul and froze on Mills, half-hidden behind the doorframe. Paul followed her stare.

"Have you two met Mills?" He glanced back and beckoned him onto the porch, apologizing to him with his eyes.

"Mills, this is Ted and Sarakit Herrig. They're neighbors from over on—"

Sarakit gripped his hand, keeping his fingers buried between her smooth palms. "I've heard so much about you," she said. "I was wondering when we'd meet. It's nice to have visitors in the colder months. It's so gorgeous out here in autumn, and most people don't stay to appreciate it."

Ted extended a hand, giving Mills an excuse to pull away from his wife.

"Ted and Sarakit are on the Orient Historical Board," Paul said. "I was just giving Mills a lecture in local politics."

"I hope you said nice things," Sarakit said. She dipped her head. "You should come too," she told Mills. "It's important to get the youth involved. Like Obama." She smiled at Mills as if she'd just mentioned a pop star that bridged generations. "Fang is coming. That's our oldest. He's almost getting to be your age."

"Sarakit, he's only fourteen," Ted said.

"I know how old our son is," she sang from the side of her mouth. She returned her attention to Paul. "So we'll see you. We'll count on your being there."

They backed down the porch, lost in the night before they reached the sidewalk. Paul closed the door and found his empty wineglass, shaking his head as he poured a last sip and drank it back.

"Not everyone in Orient has two minds. The historical board certainly doesn't." He gathered the plates, twittering his thumbs on the china. "Magdalena's not dead a day, and they're already out lobbying. Don't let the quiet of this town fool you. It's all just—"

Mills had stopped listening. He was looking at a pale face in the dining room window. Tommy blew a perfect smoke ring against the storm glass.

Mills feigned exhaustion and went up early to his bedroom. He waited until he heard Paul turn on the shower at the end of the hall, then put Jeff Trader's book in his back pocket and closed his bedroom door behind him. Thinking he could impress Tommy, or at least seize a minute's focus in the screaming playground of his mind, he told himself that he wasn't betraying Beth by showing him the journal—that Tommy, the self-declared keeper of Orient secrets, might be able to shed some light on its contents. He tiptoed down the stairs, slipped quietly through the first and second door, and stepped out into the cold. House lights beamed onto driveways and porches across the street, safety lights that Mills hadn't noticed on previous nights. He should have brought a jacket. The wind ripped through his shirt, sticking the fabric to his skin.

Tommy, bundled in a bulky Sycamore Bucks sweatshirt, stood by the hedges. He flicked his lighter and placed the flame under his chin to jack-o'-lantern his face.

"What took you so long?" he huffed. "It's fucking freezing. And it's not like I'm waiting out here to get laid." Mills smiled in disappointment. "You really need to get a cell phone. Pray for the teenager without a cell phone. I don't think you realize how unarmed you are for the vicissitudes of the future."

"Vicissitudes?" Mills repeated.

Tommy rubbed his chest, as if to assess any spontaneous muscular development. "You're so lucky you never had to study for the SAT. My dad's forcing me to take an SAT prep class an hour before school starts, just when the girls' cross-country team is showering in the locker room. There I am, in the same building with all those naked girls, and I'm stuck memorizing a bunch of twenty-syllable words. *Rebarbative. Pusillanimous.*" Tommy paused to imagine the melee of locker-room crocuses, or, at least, he seemed to want Mills to think he was.

"Let's go down to the beach." Tommy walked fast, but Mills had learned the geography of Paul's backyard in the past week, and he managed to avoid tripping over the lawn sprinklers or stepping into the marsh weeds. Tommy brandished his silver flask, took a gulp, and offered it to Mills. "It'll keep you warm," he said. "Lisa left a bottle of Jägermeister in her room, knowing I'd find it."

Mills took a small pull. It tasted like cough syrup, or like syrup to induce coughing.

"Crazy shit today, huh? With Ms. Kiefer dying like that. I mean, granted, she was ancient. And not even a week after Jeff Trader. You know I swam out into the harbor to get him, right?"

"Yeah." Was Tommy so self-absorbed that he'd forgotten that Mills had gone with him to the beach that afternoon? The question answered itself.

"Thank god I was stoned or I wouldn't have had the courage. Man, he was heavy. Like a bag of potatoes soaked in water. Skin like potatoes too." In the moonlight, Tommy's cheeks were the color of blueberries; the rest of his skin and hair was ghost white. "It's a shame no one bothered to take a picture. That was a heroic scene. A thing of legend. And where were the reporters? You don't see an act of courage in Orient very often. Why are there always cameras around when some kindergartener at a craft fair has her face painted like a cat and the *Suffolk Times* runs that huge on the front page? But when a local high school student, Thomas Muldoon, seventeen, bravely strips to his underwear and reels in a dead man, there's not a reporter in sight. I mean, I didn't do it for congratulations, but it still would have been nice. You didn't take a picture, did you? Oh, right, no phone."

"I'm sure there'll be a next time," Mills joked. Either Tommy didn't get the joke or he didn't find it funny. It hung awkwardly in the air, exposing fragile hope.

Tommy took another sip from the flask. He leaped over the rocks that descended to the pebbled shoreline, stopping just short of the black shallows. Mills followed slowly, careful of the cavities between the rocks. The far-off house lights of Connecticut sparkled, fog-stunted, across the Sound. Tommy had his hands tucked in his front pouch pocket, pulling the sweatshirt's deer-head emblem flush against his chest. Odd, Mills thought—the high school mascot was also the area's most-hunted animal.

"Wanna go for a swim?" Tommy asked with a grin. Mills studied the water. It must be freezing. As much as he'd like to swim into the Sound with Tommy, shivering in close circles, he didn't have the willpower to endure the cold past his knees. Tommy steadied himself on Mills's shoulder and started kicking off his shoes.

"I can't go in there."

"Oh, come on. Don't be a pussy."

Mills pushed Tommy's hand off his shoulder.

"No way."

Tommy nodded, laughing. "I was only kidding. It's below zero." He pinched his pants at the knees and walked a few feet into the water. "Freezing," he reported, jumping as he returned to the beach. Bright water dripped like coins from his ankles. They found a boulder ten yards down and sat on it, side by side.

"You think it was just a coincidence," Mills asked, "that Jeff Trader and Magdalena died within a week of each other?" He was trying to propose the possibility of murder to Tommy. That could be the secret they shared, the fantasy of a psychopath running around Orient; that mutual belief could bring them closer together, perhaps close enough to convince Tommy, so willing to try anything, to try something new with him. It was using the idea of murder in the service of lust.

"What? You mean you think they were taken out or something?" Tommy considered it for a minute. The tide raced in and receded. "That hadn't occurred to me. You know, Jeff Trader was pretty stuck on that rope. I didn't cut him loose. Beth's husband did that. I didn't go under to see how he was caught. But the first thing my mom said when we got back to the house was, 'Jeff Trader has a set of our keys.' "

"I know something about those keys."

"What?" Tommy grabbed Mills's wrist. "Tell me. Come on."

Savoring the moment—Tommy at full attention with his hand on his wrist—Mills finally conceded a few secrets. He told Tommy about Beth taking him to Jeff's property, about the book she'd been looking for and the jar of keys they hadn't found in his truck. "Then we went back, and Magdalena was dead."

"Fuck," Tommy yelled. "You're kidding me. I don't know, though. To kill an old man for his keys and then an old woman for wanting them. That's pretty desperate just to gain access to some of the most boring houses on Long Island." Tommy was speaking so loudly that Mills hushed him. "No one can hear us out here," Tommy said, quietly now. "It's just us."

Just them. And with Tommy's fingers still pressed against his wrist. Mills wished for the confidence to wrap his hand around Tommy's neck and make a move that wouldn't result in a punch. Instead he sat there shivering. Their bodies were practically the same age, covered in the same smooth material, running with the same blue substance, fast and cold as Canadian rivers. They were separate ecosystems coming into near contact, hosts to separate microorganisms and shaped by separate storms.

Tommy let go of Mills's wrist, jammed his hands into his sweatshirt pouch, and pulled his flask out for another sip.

"Not likely," he said with stinging breath.

"Maybe he was killed for this book." Mills took the journal from his pocket and waved it. "Jeff was writing down secrets, I think."

Tommy grabbed the book before Mills could pull it away.

"Holy shit. Addresses," he said, holding the flame of his lighter against the pages. He slumped forward, trying to decipher the tiny black print. "What kind of secrets was he into?"

"You can't have it," Mills said, reaching to recover it.

Tommy blocked his arm. "Why not? You don't know the people here. What difference does it make to you? You're a stranger. These are my neighbors."

"I need to give it back to Beth."

"Screw Beth." When Mills reached for it again, Tommy pushed him in the chest, harder than either anticipated, and Mills fell backward, slipping off the rock and slamming his shoulder against the beach. The fall hadn't hurt, hadn't destroyed much more than one-sided romance, but Tommy stared down worryingly, as if the reason for the shove had entirely escaped him.

"I'm sorry," he said, reaching out to pull him up. "Just let me borrow it. I'll give it back to you tomorrow."

Mills shook his head. He sat on the rock again, a few inches away.

"Look, I promise," Tommy bargained. "There could be things about my family in here. Jeff Trader fixed our porch last month."

"I thought you said there was nothing wrong in your family."

The Sound spread against the pebbles. Tommy's face whitened in the water's reflection as he watched its flow and retreat.

"You'd need to have had a family to understand," Tommy mumbled, his voice a broken chord. "Like my father. Nothing but a cheater. Cheats all the time. I don't blame Lisa for going to college way upstate just to get the hell away from him. I'll do the same thing when I'm done with school. As far as I can, with whatever money I can find. There are more fucked-up creatures in this town than the one that washed up from Plum."

Mills wanted to put his arm around Tommy simply to comfort him.

"You're not the only one with problems," Mills said. "I wouldn't be out here fixing up Paul's house if New York hadn't been filled with them."

"What did you do?" Tommy looked over with interest.

Mills knew he could impress Tommy simply by listing his missteps. He could so easily describe New York as a paradise of lurid dreams: drugs and all-night music and half-nude bodies twisted across couches, a version of the truth decorated into a brag. But Tommy might find that version a dream worth believing in, might see that mirage in the west and head toward it, arms and mouth open. No young person was ever enticed by the reality of a place, its mornings and not its nights.

"Drugs, the worst stuff," Mills said in the dullest voice he could muster. "It's not something I'm proud of. It was the easiest thing to fall into, and the weakest are the last to stop. I guess I didn't care anymore once I got to New York. Like I'd hit the end of the country and wanted to keep moving, however I could. At the end, it didn't feel like moving. It felt like dying slowly on someone's floor. To be honest, experience isn't always such a good thing." There went his chances of seducing Tommy on the endless upsides of new experiences.

Tommy pressed his knuckles on Mills's leg. Maybe he was just part of a generation that always needed to do something with their hands.

"I caught that about you," he said softly, so unlike the Tommy Muldoon that Mills had come to know. "I figured as much. You know, you really aren't that hard to read. I think I know what you're about." Tommy turned to him with shivering teeth.

Branches broke. Frozen grass snapped under foot in the black shrubbery behind them. Mills spun around. Tommy searched for his shoes.

"Someone's out there," Mills whispered. "Behind us."

They concentrated on the silence, trying to pick up loose sounds in it.

"Tommy," a woman's voice called. "Are you out there? You need to come in this instant. You've got school tomorrow." A dark shape shifted near the trail leading to the beach.

"It's my mother. I've gotta go." Tommy shoved his feet into his shoes and raced up the trail. He had left his silver flask on the rock, but not the book. Mills wanted to call him back for it, but he was afraid Pam Muldoon would recognize his voice and ban him from ever seeing her son again. He waited for five minutes, angry for losing the book, worried that Beth would stop by tomorrow and demand its return.

He climbed the rocks, shoving the flask in his back pocket as he crossed the lawn. The light in Tommy's window blinked on and off like a boat signal in the ocean. He reached the porch and opened the front door.

Beeping invaded the foyer. A box above the light switch in the parlor flashed red. Paul sprinted down the steps in a T-shirt and sweatpants, his shoulders bunched and his hands in clumsy fists until he caught sight of the intruder. He went directly to the box and punched in the code. His eyes were fluttering like canaries in a shaken cage.

"Why did you turn the alarm on?" Mills asked.

"For security. I thought you'd gone to bed."

"I thought you weren't scared. I thought you said there wasn't anyone dangerous out here."

Paul turned around and feigned a calm smile.

"It was you who put that in my mind," he wheezed. "And anyway I was just testing that the damn thing still worked." Paul balanced his hand on the wall and filled his lungs with air. "Okay, I admit you frightened me."

Mills apologized, tugging on Paul's shoulders as they climbed the steps. Mills put the flask in the bowl of the birthing room for safe-keeping. Out the window, the light in Tommy's room was on, a kid catching up on his reading. Maybe Pam Muldoon had been right to worry about Mills's influence on her children. Mills couldn't shake the ominous feeling that he'd just introduced Tommy to the kind of book that would destroy him.

CHAPTER 11

Naked and wet from the shower, she walked assertively through the darkened bungalow. Too assertively, Adam Pruitt thought, as if she'd only recently come to understand the dynamics of her body. He was naked as well, lying on his bed, arms splayed across the sheets and his legs forming the number 4. Tattoos decorated his ribs: on his left an orange tiger, on his right a black treble clef. They trembled as he breathed. He watched as she slid her hand under the chair cushion, located her cell phone, scrolled through missed calls and texts, and returned the phone to its soundproof hiding place. She climbed onto the bed, weightlessly mounted him with corrugated knees on either side of his shoulders, and spidered her fingers against the wall.

"You want some?" she asked. "Go on."

He liked hearing her talk like that because he knew it was foreign to her. The fact that he wasn't actually in the mood might have put a damper on the situation, but Adam did not consider himself a selfish sex partner. He stuck out his tongue.

"You want me to lick it?" He looked up, beyond the smooth white vase of her stomach, between the two rounded cones of her tits, up to a throat that gulped and a bottom lip that trailed white from scraping teeth.

"Yes," she said.

He rooted his tongue between the entry doors, drawn together like the dorsal wings of a beetle. His tongue chafed against trimmed hair and hit a pocket of emptiness, which gave him a hard-on because now he was inside of her, so inside there was no barrier. His nose snailed against her pubic hair. He expected her to moan in pleasure but she remained silent, and Adam quickly broke from his time-tested approach and burrowed his face in, sloppily licking. Neither of them made pleasure moans, and Adam wondered if he was doing this only for her benefit and she was letting him only for his, the usual sex paradox. His hands climbed her body and found her arms. He yanked her down until she lay next to him, and he flipped on top of her.

"Condom," she said. He grabbed a gold square off his nightstand, tore it open, and milked the rubber down his shaft. These were awkward seconds for a man, no matter how attractive the woman under him appeared—legs open, breasts resting on the rib cage—because a man has to stay hard while the woman watches in some negative quiet where irrevocable judgments are formed. She did the right thing, pinching his left nipple, not painfully but enough to give him an electric prod. He had a difficult time putting it in her, but finally her body accepted him. That's all it took: he jiggled it, not in and out but clockwise, and the tension of her muscles made him come almost instantly. When he realized he was coming, really coming, running home instead of to first base, he started thrusting in and out, determined not to leave her unsatisfied.

"Oh," she said.

"Fuck," he said through clenched teeth.

"That's right. Okay."

"Fu-u-*uck*."

He spent, and their lips met when he fell against her. He rolled over. His skin was wet from perspiration and from the shower water she hadn't toweled off. Her hair was almost black when it was wet, though in a matter of minutes it would dry light brown. Adam waited until it was light brown to tell her she shouldn't be here.

"I know I shouldn't," she agreed. "Wasn't that the whole point?"

"What I mean is, you should be back at the motel. Why did we go to the trouble of getting you that room if you're going to camp out at my place?" He resolved to leave the bed, sat up, and picked up his underwear from the floor with his toes. "I've got work to do."

In a belated demonstration of modesty, she wrapped the sheet around her breasts. "I don't see why you need to crash that stupid meeting," she said. "I know you don't really believe that stuff."

"I believe it." He stood up and located his jeans. He was usually a neat person, but since she'd arrived at his bungalow, his clothes were constantly in balls on the floor. What point was there in folding laundry and stowing it in his dresser if he was just going to act like a pig whenever he had company? He was thirty-four, damn it. Adam was the kind of man who kept reminding himself how old he was.

"Bullshit," she said. She snaked across the mattress, reached over to the stack of lime green paper in the corner—losing for a moment her makeshift top—and took a pamphlet. She unfolded it and began to read the text, which Adam had meticulously crafted with the help of Wikipedia: "A mutant animal washes up in Orient, discovered by local hunters, and is immediately confiscated by government agents who have yet to produce any explanation or reassurance for a concerned public. A public who shares the water with a level-three biological-warfare and animal-disease laboratory that has been conducting clanstine—I think you meant *clandestine*—genetic experiments since 1954 without—"

"—once opening the site to private inspectors to determine its health risks on area wildlife and population." He stopped quoting. "I know what it says, I wrote it."

"This poor woman," she said, tapping the section about the terrorist doctor who had her terrorist sights on Plum. "What kind of woman keeps mass-annihilation plans in her purse on the way to the airport?"

Adam dressed in a hurried manner, hoping to indicate that he had somewhere important to be. He found his wristwatch next to a box of tampons, which should be in her motel room and not at his house.

"Anyway, didn't they already announce that Plum Island is closing down in a couple of years?"

"So?" he said. "Don't you think it's better to find out the truth before the government packs up and decides it's no longer their problem? Out of sight, out of responsibility. Too bad, folks. Lyme disease? It's all in your head. And Lyme might be the least of it. There could be far worse viruses out there."

"Adam," she said meaningfully. He threw her bra on the bed. "You really need to focus on building your own business, not trying to drum up paranoia."

He took a second to appreciate how seamlessly women's breasts were stowed in cells of elastic and lace.

"Security *is* my business," he stammered. "At least it will be. And when I come to be seen as the man who was brave enough to ask the hard questions and get answers, people on the North Fork will start coming to me for their security needs."

She smiled, unconvinced, and returned the pamphlet to the stack.

"I don't understand why that's so hard for you to understand," he whined. "I'm not some outdated alarm company, like Muldoon Security, singular. I'm offering a whole new variety of services, plural—water testing, soil graphs, toxic air readings, the security of *this* century. The security that you aren't being poisoned in your own home."

Until recently, Adam had been having trouble raising the seed money to start Pruitt Securities, even after selling off his father's six Sound-front acres to a neighbor. He thought about his father for a moment, the bulk and sweaty weight of him, a man who had died of mesothelioma after forty years of working as a construction worker laying asbestos-lined pipe for the township, until those toxic materials finally delivered the cancer to his lungs. In his last days, his father took in air like a man drowning, straining every muscle for one precious lungful. Sometimes it seemed like the whole point of life was not to die the same death as your father.

"I'm so tired of hearing about security," she moaned.

"Security," he said tauntingly as he placed a Marlboro between his lips and lit the tip.

"I don't see how you're paying for this." She stood up and kicked the box of posters he'd made at the Kinko's in Riverhead. "If you can afford all this, why can't you take me out to dinner?"

"You can't go out to dinner." He let smoke drift from his tongue, a beating wick. "You aren't supposed to *be* in Orient, remember?"

She dressed lazily, pulling on her jeans and stretching a sweatshirt over her head, the belated question WHY DON'T WE SAIL FIRST? emblazoned across it. He was relieved that she wouldn't be there when he and his friends barged into Poquatuck Hall. They'd wave the posters printed with his photos of the mutant creature; it looked to him like a toxic monster villain in a comic book, like Geryon in his dead mother's illustrated copy of Dante. Except it was Orient's very own genetic nightmare come to life.

She watched him smoke as if she were smoking, lips puckered, pupils widening at intake. She clucked her tongue.

"It wasn't even real, was it? That creature on the shore."

She was starting to annoy him. She'd been annoying him for the past two weeks. There was an expiration date on all relationships, and he suspected they were nearing theirs. Adam had never been good at ending things. He ended them by thinking of them as ended and moving on.

"Don't be stupid," he told her. His lips were still covered in her juice. It sopped the filter of his cigarette.

"Fine. I just don't want to go back to Seaview. It's fucking boring."

"It was your decision."

"How was I to know?" she said. "I'm not from around here anymore."

"Sure you're not."

She gave him the finger, then used the finger to draw a heart in the fog on the bathroom mirror.

. . . .

Bryan Muldoon brought his posters to Poquatuck alone. Theo had complained at dinner that his cheeks felt warm, "like microwave cheeks," and Pam decided to skip the crucial town meeting to keep their youngest in bed with an armada of cold water bottles.

Ted was uncharacteristically prompt, waiting for Bryan at precisely 6:30 by the glass announcement board outside Poquatuck Hall, and together they entered the gray-shingled building on the corner of Village Lane. Poquatuck was built in 1874 by the same architect who had constructed the bridge between Orient and East Marion. Both structures were designed to foster connection—one by geography, the other through community—and all roads in Orient eventually led to one or the other. Bryan and Ted assembled a row of folding chairs across the stage, set Bryan's four posters on stands, and propped an out-of-focus photograph of their departed fellow board member Magdalena Kiefer against the stage, her frail, expressionless face blown up and glued sloppily onto a sheet of cardboard. Ted set two pots of poinsettias at the corners to hold it in place.

"It could look a little more professional," Bryan said, comparing Ted's work to his own: four sleek posters—pie charts and graphs—printed on expensive backing.

Ted offered an apologetic smile. "It's the sentiment. And we can't scrap it. Her name's on the initiative." He stepped back. "From a distance, you don't even notice the glue."

Bryan turned to lock eyes with Ted. "I'm worried about those Plum Island agitators. Those signs out by the tip: 'Demand answers.' Don't they understand we're fighting for the same thing? To preserve the land, to keep it safe." Ted nodded, familiar with Bryan's stump speech.

"This is something I can never tell my students, but do you know what geography really is?" Ted asked. "It's not the shapes of countries or a list of trade routes. Geography is a snapshot of war, plain and simple. It's a record of the state of hostile powers at a moment of suspended animation." Ted spread his hands, suddenly transported in a way that rarely came over him in his high school classroom with its nicotine-colored pull-down maps. "There's always going to be a fight for land. And it's never going to stay put without some muscle to defend it." Ted gestured toward the room of empty tables and chairs. "You sell the initiative tonight and we'll save it. Remember how well we did with the water-main debacle."

Bryan did take solace in that. Two years ago, seemingly out of nowhere, the county had submitted a proposal to extend a three-mile water main from East Marion to Orient, bringing the first public water service to a village whose residents had been relying on their own private wells since its settlement. But the proposal met with so much hostility that locals took to calling it "the water-main debacle" or "the main debacle" or, eventually, just "the debacle." It was the closest Orient ever got to declaring civil war on the rest of Long Island.

It wasn't just that the project would have created a construction nightmare on the two-lane causeway. The key chairs of the Orient Historical Board foresaw far more dangerous stakes in the Suffolk County Water Authority's overzealous proposal. What was at stake was the power to keep Orient out of the easy reaches of developers. As long as underground wells were the town's only source of water, no high-rise condominium complexes could blight the coastline. No cavernous Walmarts or shoe box Radissons or grease-windowed restaurant chains could clear precious farmland and set up shop. Without public water, even ten toilets flushing successively would paralyze the plumbing. When SCWA, buoyed by federal stimulus money, announced its intentions, they touted the benefits of cleaner water and the freedom from having to maintain antiquated tanks. But what the historical board saw was the ghost of Orient's future: the concrete, suburban sprawl that had already enveloped the rest of Long Island, one industrial pressure-flush toilet at a time. The entire fate of Orient rested on a matter of pipes.

Bryan Muldoon and his eight fellow board members were not elected or county-approved. Their membership was self-selected, based on family status and a commitment to community affairs. The Orient Historical Board, or OHB, had been formed casually four decades ago to aid in the preservation of several Federal-style settlement buildings—the old nineteenth-century boardinghouse, the older eighteenth-century schoolhouse—that stood opposite Poquatuck Hall on Village Lane. But as time went on the board expanded its mission, beyond preserving the past, to preserving the present. The Orient Historical Board held no official power in Suffolk County, but unofficially it held the power of influence and outrage. In the last decade alone, the board had pressured the county into passing zoning laws on Orient real estate (ten-acre, five-acre, and two-acre plots could not be easily subdivided; commercial development was strictly forbidden). In return, OHB lent its support to the county superintendent during election years. The cycle of reciprocal altruism had harmoniously persisted until two years ago, when SCWA went AWOL on OHB.

Bryan led the effort against the water main. He organized petitions, went door to door to collect signatures, artistically Photoshopped images of midwestern supermalls onto Orient farms, called for the impeachment of the superintendent, and brought supporters to flood the monthly council meeting in Southold with fevered complaints—the unifying message being, "when water comes, development follows." When the water company's CEO insisted that the main would supply only twenty-four homes on Browns Hill with water, the answer was, No sir, that's just the beginning. When environmental agents revealed that a test of private wells in Orient turned up troubling amounts of gasoline by-product, Bryan and his allies made a public show of guzzling the tap water with unbelievable thirst. When certain previously faithful residents admitted that they might actually like their toilet waste to disappear in a single flush or their sprinkler systems to sprinkle continuously, the reprisals were subtle but swift: longstanding neighborhood cookouts were canceled, birthdays no longer acknowledged, even a few car tires deflated overnight. Finally, after months of negotiations, the proposal was shelved, "until we fix a few internal problems with the water map." But the CEO insisted to Bryan, during their final, tense encounter, that their retreat was only temporary. "You can't fight progress forever. Modernization has a way of happening."

After the debacle, OHB no longer felt safe leaving Orient's future up to Suffolk County. Tonight, at seven o'clock, Bryan Muldoon would go on the offensive. As he ran through his talking points, he noticed a journalist from the *Suffolk Times* lingering near the front door with a young, safari-capped photographer. The first year-rounders were drifting into the hall, grabbing a flyer and helping themselves to the brownies Karen Norgen had baked.

The photograph of Magdalena brought a needed solemnity to the proceedings. The initiative they were here to debate—a non-development trust—had been Magdalena's brainchild, an embryo that Bryan instantly surrogate-fathered, calling in favors from environmental liaisons and spending his nights studying how similar conservation easements had preserved Montana's cattle fields and wild trout fisheries. Magdalena's untimely death was the first obstacle they'd encountered. Bryan could preach the statistics supporting voluntary conservation, but it was Lena's elderly graciousness, and her long relationship with the local farmers, that Bryan had been counting on to drive the message from brain to heart.

Sarakit Herrig climbed the steps to the stage. She offered a curt hello before rearranging the stands for a more dramatic display. George Morgensen appeared, dressed in his retirement uniform of mismatched golf pastels. The other four members of the board were the elderly offspring of ancestral families—Max Griffin, Helen Floyd, Kelley Flanner, Archie Young—whose combined ownership of Orient counted in the hundreds of acres. Each had the chapped faces and invisible chins of early North Fork pioneers (now on view in sepia photographs in the museum's "Pioneers of Peace" gallery). Arthur Cleaver had driven out from the city to fulfill his role as the board's legal counsel. Bryan knew that Arthur, a distinguished attorney with iron hair who seemed to perspire duty-free cologne, had no passion for the trust, but his volunteer work kept him abreast of local controversies. Bryan took Arthur as the kind of man who enjoyed the thrill of watching disasters from a distance.

The members took their seats as attendees flooded the hall; the meeting's autumn date conveniently tipped the scales away from the summer weekenders. Bryan noticed his hunting buddy Alistair Swallow, Mitch Tabach with his aluminum legs and brand-new hip, Paul Benchley with his morose foster-care ward, the Stillpasses, Ina Jenkins, Reverend Ann Whitlen, and even Roe diCorcia, a corn farmer and obdurate enemy of OHB, who had supported the water-main proposal because it would have aided in the irrigation of his crops. Everyone spoke in whispers of Magdalena, and Bryan heard Karen Norgen use the word *murder* twice, the second time within the same breath as "Beth Shepherd." Beth's mother, Gail, slipped in a little after seven—a surprise, since most assumed she had been driven back over the causeway to Southold for good.

"Let's get started," Bryan said, standing on the stage with the microphone to his lips. "First I'd like to take a moment of silence for our recently departed board member, Magdalena Kiefer. Magdalena, who passed away this weekend, would have appreciated the strong turnout tonight, bringing us together for this important cause."

What was the acceptable increment of time for a moment of silence? Two seconds? Five? Eight? Bryan realized he'd forgotten to mention that Magdalena's funeral was tomorrow. Should he do it now? No, he must stick to his script.

"Magdalena was adamant about the initiative that I am going to spell out for you this evening, and we can only hope to honor her years of hard preservation work by naming it after her. She will be buried tomorrow." He had stumbled into the ad lib to his own irritation. "At her funeral. Tomorrow. And naturally in our next meeting we will be electing a new board member to replace her." He winced. "Not that we *can* replace her. But the funeral, it's tomorrow. Now back to the reason we're here."

The bright overhead lights created a metallic shine on the white faces staring up at him. Friendly faces, but ugly here inside Poquatuck, with its acrylic cream walls. How ugly humans could be when jammed together in one room, all the color of cereal sitting too long in milk. Bryan felt a bead of sweat on his brow. He wished someone would open a window to bring some cold air into the hall.

"Do they know what Magdalena died of?" a voice called out from the circular tables, a man's voice, but Bryan couldn't locate the questioner. Whispers spread on the floor. Bryan heard the phrase "Plum monster."

"I believe she had a heart attack," Bryan replied. The photographer snapped a picture. The reporter wrote on her pad. "I saw Magdalena a few days before she died," he said, awkwardly, as if he were admitting a secret, "and she was adamant about this initiative." He was stumbling again, and he looked to history to bolster his confidence. "All of you remember how successfully we halted the water main two years ago. We have each other to thank for that victory." Roe diCorcia raised his hand, but Bryan ignored it. He had finally found his rhythm. "But the work's not over, folks. Not by a long shot. That was a wake-up call to OHB that we need to take the preservation of Orient into our own hands."

Bryan walked over to the first poster. "Today, I want to share our plan for conservancy. We have fended off encroachment with zoning regulations, but we all know the powers that be in Southold are not to be trusted in enforcing those conditions." The poster bore the headline THE KIEFER NONDEVELOPMENT ADVOCACY INITIATIVE, over a shot of phragmites and the sun-dappled waves of the Sound. He tapped the cardboard. "Today OHB takes one step further. We have filed for nonprofit status as a conservancy trust. This will give us the community power to control what gets built in our own backyards. But we need your help and agreement. Friends, the decision is with you. The Kiefer Nondevelopment Advocacy Initiative promises to protect nature and wildlife in Orient—and it comes with a financial benefit to all.

"Simply put, the trust is asking to buy the development rights on your land—to keep it out of the reaches of commercial development forever."

There was a stir in the room: more whispering, a few indignant grunts. The eight figures on stage smiled through the reaction, and Bryan stepped carefully over to his next poster, an aerial shot of Orient divided by property lines.

"Now, the trust owning your development rights has nothing to do with owning your land. That still belongs to you in every way. What we own is the promise that nothing commercial will ever be built on it. It takes only one developer to get his hands on a sizeable plot"—he purposely pointed to the diCorcia farm—"a loophole in the zoning laws, and a little cash stuffed in the right Southold pocket, to turn that land into a condominium community. You can already hear the sales pitch: 'rustic living for city buyers with premium ocean views and a soon-to-be-opened multiplex, fitness center, and Whole Foods, all just steps from your door.' That could happen, *will* happen, unless the trust steps in to preserve its sanctity—not for five years, not for ten, but forever. We don't want to become another Hamptons. The Orient we love today should be the same Orient your grandkids will enjoy when they start their families." For one minute, Bryan stood silent on the stage, hoping the vision was taking shape in their minds.

In the back corner, Roe diCorcia cleared his throat and stood up, all six foot four inches of him, rising out of the audience in tan overalls like a cancerous cornstalk.

"It's a rotten deal," Roe complained. "You might not be buying the land, but you're buying control over what I can do with it. You're deciding what I can build and how I can carve it up. And, meanwhile, you're destroying my property values. You've gotta be kidding me. When we go to sell, who's going to pay what the land is worth when there's a lead anchor like that attached?"

Bryan stepped over to the third poster, full of rainbow-colored pie charts and graphs; he'd designed it to advertise the financial windfall in such an agreement, but now, onstage, it all looked so convoluted. Sarakit's smile began to tighten.

George stepped in. "Roe, the trust is planning to ask a fair price. That's money straight up. Plus, in the long run, if neighbors also sell their development rights, that could actually increase the value of the land, because the buyer is protected from a condominium subdivision built right next door."

"And it *is* a fair price," Sarakit intoned.

Cole Drake stood up from his table. He stared with an intensity of a man who had discovered that his wife had been cheating on him. Bryan couldn't decide if Holly's absence from the meeting proved or disproved that fear. He quickly tried to wipe his palms on his pants, but in doing so he dropped the microphone, sending a clumsy reverberation blasting from the speakers: *Blump ump, blump ump, ump, ump.* Bryan closed his eyes, waiting for the speakers to clear the horrible echo.

"Where is the trust getting all the cash to buy these rights, anyway?" Cole demanded. "It sounds like a protection racket."

Bryan knew that the answers were on the final poster, the one that listed possible revenue streams: tax-free donations, willed legacy gifts, fund-raisers, environmental grants, the selling off of certain properties it owned in East Marion that were of no conservational import. But he walked in the wrong direction, right instead of left, and found himself back at the first poster, as if Orient's revenue questions could be found in the romantic, soft-focus picture of Orient.

"Other side," Ted whispered. Bryan looked at him dazed, a look Ted only matched in return. Ted turned to the crowd.

"This is only an introduction. The point of this meeting is to familiarize you with the initiative. Obviously there are a number of legal and ethical questions that we'll be happy to discuss with each resident individually. The point is that we have found a way to preserve our home. No property is too small to sell its development rights. Sarakit and I have pledged to sell the rights on our three acres when OHB receives nonprofit-trust status. And Archie has agreed to sell the rights to his ninety acres. It will be owned by all of us—by the community, under the trust."

"So you're basically selling your own land back to yourself and making a profit?" someone shouted.

"What we will own isn't freedom *to*, it's freedom *from*," Ted explained. "Geography isn't something that just happens. As the teacher to many of your—"

Bryan finally got his bearings, stepping across the stage to the final poster. Before he got there, though, he spotted a band of dark shapes moving across the Poquatuck windows—dark human shapes, which passed the three windows on their way to the front door.

"Please, someone," Bryan said urgently into the microphone, "lock the door."

But they were already through it, black shapes even under the bright overhead fixtures. Five young men in head-to-toe hunting outfits held lime green posters of the creature on the beach. Adam Pruitt was their leader, a man every audience member knew as much for his current position as the head of the volunteer fire department as for his thirty-four years of low ambition and sporadic employment. Some looked offended by his intrusion; others seemed thankful for the entertainment. Adam carried a sign reading MUTANT PLUM in leaky, bloodred marker. His disruption had all the finesse of a high school theater production.

"We wouldn't be interrupting if this weren't important," he shouted.

"This is unacceptable, son," Bryan said into the microphone, hoping to gain the upper hand with a show of patronizing civility. "We are having a conservancy meeting here. You can schedule your conspiracy meeting for another time."

Adam faced the audience. The *Suffolk Times* photographer crouched to snap pictures like he imagined himself in a war zone.

"Conservancy is our issue," Adam said. "Conserving water, animals, air, and soil from a fun house of genetic-testing horrors that has been violating nature for a half-century right off our coast."

Adam pointed out the window. "For as long as I can remember, we've put up with it, accepting the lab without ever asking a single question about how it might be affecting our health and homes. Ever since I was a boy." Bryan hoped the year-rounders would remember Adam as a boy—as the school bully, the Greenport shoplifter with a face full of acne and free-floating rage. How many remembered when all the village stop signs were stolen—then found in the trunk of Adam's Chevy Malibu? "If this is a town meeting, I think that merits a town discussion."

To Bryan's disappointment, many in the crowd nodded. Roe di-Corcia clapped. Two of the intruders climbed up to put their own posters on the stands, causing Helen Floyd and Kelley Flanner to vacate the stage.

"Adam, you're just scaring people," Bryan said into the microphone. "That's not a discussion."

Adam turned to him.

"You saw that monster on the beach, same as we did. It was a mutant, stewing right there in our water. I thought security was important to you. I thought that was how you made a living. How can you stand here and tell us we shouldn't be scared?"

Bryan felt obliged to respond but his microphone had been unplugged.

"We all saw what happened to Jeff Trader," Adam shouted. "How much longer are we expected to drink the water, eat the local fish, find mosquito bites on our arms, watch the deer graze, and not wonder what that level-three animal-disease lab is doing every day right on our horizon? They're not out there worrying about our safety. They're developing disease agents. Foot-and-mouth, Ebola, polio, Lyme, cholera, swine fever, West Nile, duck plague—we *know* those are out there on Plum, and who knows how many others besides. It's not natural."

Mitch Tabach, with his prosthetic hip, seemed to agree. Reverend Ann Whitlen nodded along: it *wasn't* natural. Bryan had already ruled Ann out as a supporter, due to the fact that she believed in the Rapture and wouldn't care what happened to the land after God sky-vacuumed his followers away.

The Stillpasses left their table. Paul Benchley and his teenage delinquent hurried to the door. But Cole Drake shouted, "Go on," and the Michelsons started perusing Adam's brochures. Bryan wondered when Adam would start handing out refrigerator magnets for Pruitt Securities and his ludicrous environmental tests.

"My advice," Adam said, "is not to trust others to take care of you. Just because they say 'everything's going to be fine,' doesn't mean it *is* fine. We haven't heard a single word from the government on what that mutant was. Don't we as citizens deserve the truth? We need to stand up and demand answers."

Bryan was tired of standing. As he hopped off the stage, his pant cuff caught on the corner of Magdalena's photograph and tipped it forward over the red poinsettia leaves. "This doesn't help us," Bryan yelled. "Adam, you have no idea how important it is that we save Orient from the *actual* threat it's facing. What we need is a plan for the future, how to protect our village from development, starting today."

Adam had seen this one coming, and he grinned as he responded. "Bryan, has it ever occurred to you that no one is going to *want* to buy the land out here if it's polluted? You're so scared of developers. Hell, if it's a biohazard, we'll be praying for them. You're the one who's missing the point."

"I *see* your point," Bryan muttered. Adam called for volunteers to join him in protesting at the next council meeting in Southold. Behind him was the gluey, tilted picture of Magdalena, a woman who had spent the last years of her life fighting to preserve the ecosystem of Orient. She had been so beloved in the community for her dedication that it seemed incidental, maybe even disrespectful, to mention that she'd been killed by wild animals, stung at least partially to death by indigenous bees.

CHAPTER **12**

One of the stranger things Beth learned about her husband after they moved to Orient was his fear of the dark. After sunset, darkness settled so thick in the house that walking to the bathroom or climbing the stairs felt like donning a blindfold. Despite all of Gail's hysterical remodeling, she had never bothered to update the electrical wiring. Sensible light switches near doorways were rare. Most of the rooms were lit by ceiling lamps with long beaded chains, forcing the light-seeker to swat the air in hopes of catching the phantom string.

In New York, Beth had detected no hint of Gavril's nyctophobia. Their East Village apartment glimmered yellow at all hours, thanks to the constant light from the street. In Orient, however, Gavril complained that he felt drowned by the blackness, like a child adrift in the ocean. During their first weeks there, Beth often woke to find him calling out to her from the hallway, needing her voice to lead him back to bed. "I'm embarrassed," he admitted one morning, eyes swollen from lack of sleep. "In the night, I had to go to the bathroom, but I was so scared I waited until dawn to pee. I almost went out the window."

"You almost jumped out the window, or you almost peed out the window?"

"Both."

Beth had always been comfortable with darkness; she had never thought that an otherwise highly functioning adult could envision strange, serial-murdering horrors awaiting him on a simple ten-yard trip to the toilet. She bought Gavril a flashlight to keep on his side of the bed, but for weeks thereafter, Beth would be startled awake by an intense spotlight on her face.

"Just making sure it's still you," he said before climbing under the blankets.

"Who else would it be? Oh, just get under the covers. I'll hold you."

Before she knew she was pregnant, Gavril had been her child. "The darkness is as heavy as soup. I can't even see my hand," Gavril said in bed, presumably holding up a hand neither of them could see.

Now, finally, Gavril had learned to sleep soundly, moving his arms in dreams. After Magdalena's death, it was Beth who stayed awake, marginally terrified. Was that the sound of a key turning in the kitchen door? Was that creak someone's foot on the creaky third stair? Had the person who killed Jeff and Magdalena heard her tell Mike Gilburn it was murder, and decided she too must be silenced?

Beth had to go to the bathroom. Lately she had to go all the time, but she couldn't bring herself to go out into the hall, where a killer could stab her or snap her neck with ease. If she was attacked, would she scream for help? And would that wake up Gavril, making him the second victim? Would she love him enough to stay silent while she was being murdered, just so he could live?

She shifted in the sheets, wishing women could urinate out windows. She distracted herself by imagining a dildolike contraption that women could strap on to urinate with masculine precision. But the fear soon returned, settling back into her like stirred sand returning to the sea floor. It was fear that made a person feel most alone—even a married woman in the safety of her childhood home next to her two-hundred-pound husband.

In the two days since Magdalena's death, Beth had tried to convince herself that she'd behaved irrationally, a slave to her raging hormones, as if her own body had sacrificed her sanity to support the new life within her. That new life was in her right now, growing, dividing, mimicking her heartbeat. It could be gotten rid of. A trip into the city for an appointment at the clinic was all it would take. And they could try again later, when she was ready. She willed herself not to think of the fetus as a baby. It was a *mass*, and she would think of it that way until she decided if she would keep it.

Gavril shifted next to her, slamming his elbow against her ribs, and she rolled onto her side to keep their skin from touching. She listened to the clock tick. She had thought of driving over to Paul Benchley's to collect Jeff Trader's book from Mills that evening, but she'd decided against it, reluctant to give more free rein to her insanity. Mike Gilburn's incredulous reaction to her had left her feeling ashamed. Her outburst to the detective—*he was murdered, she was murdered*—now sounded to her like the ranting of a delusional mind.

Yet no matter how often in the past two days Beth admonished herself for acting irrationally, her mind kept leading her back to the evidence. Magdalena had told her that someone had murdered Jeff Trader. The caretaker himself had pointed the blame at the OHB when he spoke to Magdalena just before he died. Only days later, Magdalena herself was dead. How was murder an irrational conclusion to draw? The problem was, Beth had been the only person to hear Magdalena's suspicions. She couldn't shake the sense that it was her duty to pursue that possibility. It was, at least, a distraction from sitting around in indecision about the mass. Tomorrow she would call Mike Gilburn to ask for a deeper investigation. Tomorrow she would retrieve the book from Mills. Tomorrow, after Magdalena's funeral, she would try to work out what possible gain there was in two loosely connected deaths.

A shuffling sound came from the walkway outside the kitchen door. Hinges yawned. Wood slapped. Beth quickly sat up and shook Gavril's shoulder. She was never certain he was awake until she saw his eyes.

"*Ce este?*" he groaned. "What?"

"Gavril," she whispered. She couldn't make out the contours of his face. Only the liquid cowry-shell eyes, already shrinking closed again. "I think there's someone downstairs."

"Go back to sleep," he mumbled, roping his arm around her.

"No." She gouged a finger in his armpit, causing him to flinch. "I really think I heard something."

"I don't hear anything." He was alert now, listening, or at least pretending to listen. He pushed his chest against her and began to rub his groin against her hip. She shoved him back by the shoulder. "Don't."

"Come on." He tried again, slipping his fingers under the elastic of her underwear. She squeezed his hand to stop it from foraging deeper. "What's wrong with you?" Gavril withdrew his hand. "We have not had sex in almost a month. Why can't I?"

"I don't want to." She had to match his wounded tone to affect a stalemate. "I'm not in the mood."

"Never in the mood lately," he said gruffly. "How can we have a baby when we don't—"

"Maybe I don't want a baby right now." She said it more calmly than she had intended. He grabbed for her breast, and she knocked his hand away. Gavril crouched on his knees, wide awake with rejection.

"Why are you acting this way to me?" His eyes and lips were wet; the tips of his shoulders gathered a trace of moonlight. "We used to do it every night. Now you don't let me touch you. What have I done?"

"Nothing," she whined. She hated that whine, that last bit of girl in her.

"You don't want a child anymore?"

"Someone is downstairs!" She no longer thought anyone was downstairs, but she hadn't worked out a map for this convoluted midnight conversation. Beth wasn't exactly lying when she said: "And I told you, and you didn't listen, that our next-door neighbor might have been murdered."

"Murdered." He laughed. "American obsession. You're too smart for that. Why are you acting crazy lately?"

"And you're still not listening to me. I heard something. But, sure let's fuck while there's a burglar in our kitchen." Beth pulled her underwear down to her knees to drive the insanity home. She lay there, exposed to the cold, arms crossed against her stomach.

"Now maybe I'm not in the mood." Gavril grabbed his pillow and hugged it against his stomach. "You've been—"

Glass shattered. A chair toppled over in the kitchen. The sounds Beth had only invented became real sounds, the last sounds of vulnerable sleepers before they were killed. For a minute they lay frozen, two people living every second except this one, a second that felt like it couldn't possibly be theirs to live. People were murdered so easily because they didn't believe they could be.

Gavril jumped from the bed and located his flashlight. "Someone is downstairs," he whispered. "We push the bed against the door. We take the bed apart and use the metal for bats. We go out the window."

A broom whisking across linoleum. Glass shards dumped into a soft, yielding substance.

Beth pulled her underwear up. She climbed off the mattress and placed her palms against the bedroom door.

"Is someone there?" she screamed.

"Don't, Beth," Gavril pleaded. But her act emboldened him, and he gently pushed her aside to turn the knob. "You stay here. I go." In her nightmare, she died in the hallway, Gavril after her in the bed, not vice versa. Best to die first, not second. What had seemed to her an act of bravery, she now understood as the easier sequence. "*Çine esti tu?*" Gavril yelled. "*Lasati!*"

Footsteps. Loud, clunky footsteps.

"Gavie, it's Mom," Gail called from the bottom of the steps. "Sorry. Broke a glass. A little tipsy. Couldn't drive home so I used my keys. Don't worry about me. I'll curl up on the couch. Don't you worry about Mom."

"You scared us half to death," Beth shouted into the darkness. "Don't ever do that again." She placed her forehead against Gavril's shoulder. They were both moonlit with sweat.

. . . .

For once, Beth got out of bed first. She went downstairs to a living room of long morning shadows and small dark furniture. A quilt was folded on the couch, one of its cushions still dented against the arm. Gail stood in the kitchen brewing coffee, her skirt rumpled, her feet webbed in beige panty hose. Outside, branches swayed in the rain. A fly crawled across the window over the sink. Gail's high heels were stowed by the plant pots.

"I'm going to kill you," Beth said flatly. "I mean it. I'm actually going to kill you right now."

Gail turned with an exaggerated smile. Gail was an expert turner. She must practice turning with a grand expression on her face in front of her condo mirror.

"My lord, what a fuss you're making." She chose a mug from the shelf for her daughter. "I'm sorry I didn't call first. I figured it best not to wake you. And it would have been fine if you hadn't left a glass on the counter for anyone to knock over. I hope it wasn't a favorite. I think I managed to get all of the slivers." Gail diligently inspected the floor for sharp, bright slivers.

"Never again, okay? Unless you want to give us both a heart attack. What were you doing in Orient last night anyway? Drunk."

"I was *drinking*, not drunk," her mother said. "I had a few glasses of wine at Ina Jenkins's house after the town meeting at Poquatuck. Have you seen your third grade teacher lately? Homely as ever, I'm afraid. And all those dogs. Just because they're purebreds doesn't mean they should be allowed on a table." Gail shook her head. "But Ina did have a little gossip. Apparently Sycamore is terminating Ted Herrig after the semester. Cutting back on the entire geography department. And good riddance, as far as I'm concerned. Who needs a teacher to show someone how to look at a map? But I feel for his family. He and Sarakit were there last night, lecturing." Gail started recounting the story of the town hall meeting. When she mentioned Magdalena, Beth glanced at the microwave clock.

"Are you going to her funeral today?" Beth asked.

"Why would I? I'm the last person she'd want there. I believe in respecting the wishes of the dead."

"I'm going," Beth replied.

Gail gave her a thin smile. "That's sweet of you. I raised you right." Her mother poured twin coffees. "Is Gavril going with you?"

"No. He refuses to set foot in a church. He thinks religion is humanity's way of trying to be as immortal as a cockroach. Anyway, he hardly knew her. But I knew her. And you did too."

Gail shrugged and opened the refrigerator. "I'm convinced soy milk is detrimental to fertility. Oh, thank god, you have two percent!"

"Has it occurred to you that Magdalena might have been murdered?"

Gail clasped her hands together and stared out the window at her old nemesis's cottage. "Are you accusing me? I wouldn't blame you if you did. That woman was a bully. She actually bullied me. Still, that's a little far-fetched. Murdered at that age? In that ramshackle house? You've been in the city too long." Gail dropped into a chair with the heavy resignation of a commuter settling in for a long train ride. "New York City, where no one knows a single thing about the people living right next door. Am I right? You could share a wall with someone for twenty years and never learn their first name. I can just see the real estate ads: 'You will never be invited to a neighborhood barbecue. No one will make eye contact in the elevator.' That sounds like heaven." She took a sip and burned her tongue, wincing in pain.

"If that's what you want, why would you go to a town hall meeting?"

"Honey, I own this house and the two and a half acres it sits on. When the board starts talking about new zoning restrictions, I damn well better pay attention. I'm invested. Bryan Muldoon really shamed himself last night. It was a delight to watch." Gail held her head up by the temple.

Beth sat down across from her. "Did Jeff Trader ever do repairs for you?"

"Yes. Here and there. Who do you think was going to clean the gutters? Mario? I would have paid to see that. Jeff even installed our boiler." Gail looked around the kitchen, as if she could gauge the air temperature by sight. "Do you have the heat on? That thing has a warranty. Why is it so cold in here?"

"So he had keys? Keys to this house?"

"Let me think." Gail ruminated, counting on her fingers either husbands or the number of times she'd been forced to change the locks. "Yeah, he probably does. Did. Not that it matters." She nodded toward the windows. "None of the latches actually work. The historical board wouldn't let me do all the improvements I wanted. They insisted that the façade couldn't be touched. *The original fingerprint needs to be preserved*, they said. *For who?* I said. What about those of us who are living inside the fingerprint? How about wanting to keep warm in a fingerprint?"

"It's called a footprint, not a fingerprint," Beth corrected. But her mother was right: the house was one big open door. Beth had been breaking into the Shepherd house since she'd started dating as a teenager, and now her distant memories of jiggling open windows or climbing up the trestle at 2:00 A.M. came back as frightening reminders of the defenselessness of its current occupants.

"If you're thinking about getting an alarm system," Gail said, "I hear Adam Pruitt has started his own security company. Do me the courtesy of not going with Bryan." Beth looked at her mother. Her hair was in need of a touch-up; a thin, gray cloud bank was showing beneath the chemical copper. Beth thought of the photograph of the red-haired woman found in Jeff's book.

"Did you and Jeff Trader get along? Was there ever a fight between you two?"

Gail looked taken aback.

"Why are you asking me so many questions? What you should be asking me is how I can help with your project." She eyed the area of the table that hid Beth's stomach. "How's it going? Don't tell Gavril, but I was talking to him the other day and he—"

"Mother, did you and Jeff Trader not get along?"

"What?" A housefly landed on the lip of Gail's mug and she shooed it away. Her fingernails were chipped. Beth had never questioned her mother's finances, but she wondered if this evident cosmetic decline meant that Gail was hurting for money. "I never really thought of Jeff as someone to get along with. So I guess that means we did. We certainly never fought. Why are you constantly changing the subject?"

Beth got up, opened the back door, and walked around the house to her car. The mailman was in the driveway, shielded from the rain in a layer of transparent plastic, like a newspaper. He waved at her and said, "Congratulations."

Confused, she ignored him and glanced at the windshield of her car. The snapshot of the woman was visible on the dashboard for anyone to see. Beth opened the car door and grabbed it. She carried it back into the kitchen and held it up in front of her mother, who was downing the dregs in her mug.

"Is this you?" Beth pointed to the red-haired woman with horns, a goatee, and scratched-out eyes standing by a rosebush. Gail looked up at her, horrified. Did her mother think she was making a joke about her plastic surgery? Did she think Beth had drawn the horns herself?

"No, that's not me. What an insensitive thing to say. After how giving I've been."

"I didn't mean—"

Her mother stood up to reclaim her shoes.

"I'm not interested in being insulted."

"Mom."

"Something's come over you lately. And I don't like it. You've become a different person. You're selfish. And you're mean." Gail brought her arms out for balance as she shoved each foot into its appropriate heel.

Gavril stumbled into the kitchen, one hand scratching his facial hair, the other holding a pile of mail he'd collected from the floor of the foyer. He tossed the mail on the table and smiled at his mother-in-law.

"Rough night?" he asked.

"Rough morning," she replied. "Your wife is becoming intolerable. She needs to be reminded of the importance of the family she has left."

Gavril was used to humoring the long-standing feud of the Shepherd women, trying as much as possible not to take either side. Suddenly, his smile morphed into a grimace. "That fly," he said. "Do you hear it? That buzz." The housefly zigzagged through the air, its drone increasing and falling away, cruising slowly then speeding up for turns. "That awful sound. It's exactly like the bugs back in Bucharest." Gavril picked up a flyer from the mail and chased the insect around the kitchen. "Those little black listening devices," he said. "In my childhood we called them bugs, just as you do. The Securitate put them in the walls of our homes. When they went bad, they sounded just like a bug, like a fly." He swatted and missed. "For days we would hear it buzzing. 'The flies are back,' we would say, because that is all we could say. If we wanted to talk we would say, 'Dad wants to go outside for a smoke.' Then the police would come, pretending to be janitors, and it would be fixed, silent again. The bug, an insect listening." The fly froze on the wall, and Gavril swung and smashed it. He threw the flyer on the table, the juicy insect smeared across its postage square. "They killed thousands of my people with their little bugs. To this day, when I see an insect, I think it is spying on me."

"See," Gail said, gathering her purse as she looked at her daughter. "Your life could be a lot worse. You should be thankful for how easy you have it."

"Oh, she's not so bad." Gavril pinched Beth's waist and commandeered her coffee cup. "This weekend we're throwing a party."

"A party?" Beth hadn't agreed to that. She had a moment of déjà vu. *Haven't I been here before? Haven't I had this exact conversation in the kitchen with Gavril and Gail? Haven't I already lived this once?* To live in a small town was to accept déjà vu as a daily sensation. "I'm not sure it's the right time for a party."

"Too late." Gavril smiled. "I already invited the friends we have out here. You know, Gail, the North Fork has become very *chic* for artists. And my gallerist is coming from the city. And Luz and Nathan, and Isaiah. A last party before I finish the work for my next show."

"Look at her. She's worried I'll come," Gail said coldly. "She's really awful to me. I'm sure she'll yell at you the minute I leave for mentioning the party in front of me. Beth, I'm not going to come, for God's sake."

But it wasn't the prospect of her mother's attendance that caused Beth to turn pale. It was the dead-insect flyer, and three others in the stack of mail Gavril had brought from the foyer. *Now that you're pregnant, the real sales begin,* read one in bloated marshmallow letters. *Baby cribs! Baby mobiles! Baby blankets! Baby everything!!!* Demanding, jubilant, openmouthed infants infested the flyers, promising freebies, discounts, and a dancing chorus of pink-and-blue dollar signs. Each one was addressed in computer type to Elizabeth Shepherd. How did they find her? Just because she'd spent a few hours searching baby sites on her computer? She'd been careful not to fill out a single form. Had her gynecologist sold her address?

As nonchalantly as possible, Beth gathered up the flyers before her husband or mother could notice their common theme. "I have to get ready," she said as she left the kitchen. She had saved herself for today, but there would be mail tomorrow, and the day after, endless opportunities for an onslaught of baby announcements to fall into the hands of those she wanted to keep her secret from the most. Who could she call to stop the delivery? Ripping the flyers to pieces, Beth hurried upstairs to dress for a funeral.

CHAPTER 13

Most of Orient braved the rain to bid good-bye to Magdalena. Beth arrived at the church late and had to settle for a seat in the last pew, far from the altar decorated in white roses and yellow four-o'clocks. It hardly mattered. All funerals followed the same sluggish formula. The same prayers, from the Twenty-third Psalm; the same lumbering notes of the organ; the same wallet-size cards listing the vital stats of the deceased; the same poly-blend black blazers and black knit sweaters and midnight-blue stockings; the same coughers coughing; the same loving words recited about the dead.

Beth had no objection: funerals had been spared the culture's otherwise relentless carnival need to entertain. Still, sitting in the last pew of the Orient United Church of Christ, Beth thought back to how practically everyone with whom she'd smoked pot pledged that they wanted their ashes sprinkled on Mount Kilimanjaro, or wanted the guests to wear leis and build a bonfire on the beach, or wanted a giant party thrown at Dizmo's Tavern in their honor. Surely her generation wasn't the first to hope for some touch of the personal to dignify their commemorations. Surely, this bray-ing organ solo and rote floral spray wasn't what Magdalena Kiefer would have wanted. Even in the age of individuality, death remained on the side of the masses. Perhaps dependability was the chief com-fort of a funeral, as dependable as banisters for mourners to lean on. Who can lean on Kilimanjaro?

Beth watched her neighbors concentrate on sitting still. They sat quietly, pained but not crying, for an old woman who had lingered in death's sunroom for years. The organist sang "Here I Am Lord," off-key and distractedly, as if she were singing to herself. "*Is it I, Lord? I have heard you calling in the night.*" Karen Norgen turned in her pew to glance at Beth while placing a chalky tablet on her tongue, a mint or an aspirin. Four high school students, released from third period, carried the casket to the hearse.

On the church's rain-soaked steps, black umbrellas bloomed. Beth declined Arthur Cleaver's offer to share his umbrella. He held it over her anyway, and she was forced to lean into him, smelling chemical gardenias.

"I'm not going to the cemetery," she told him. "I'm just walking to my car."

"Yes," he said, drawing out the word. "I wanted to ask you a question. I noticed your mother at the town meeting last night. I hope this doesn't sound inappropriate, but do you own your house now, or does it still belong to your mother?"

"She owns it," Beth replied. She was walking quickly up the sidewalk, and either out of courtesy or the need to glean more information, the thin, older man in gray cashmere kept pace with her.

"I only asked because OHB wanted to know who to speak to about selling the development rights. Your property is a sizeable lot on the Sound, and they're hoping to ensure its protection." He held up his hand. "I'm merely an ambassador here. As you know, your mother doesn't get along with certain members of the board. They were wary of approaching her directly."

"She doesn't have plans to turn it into an art gallery, if that's what the board is afraid of."

Cleaver smiled. "They feel they never know with your mother. It would be money up front for her, and, of course, she'd still own the land." He cleared his throat. "Personally, it doesn't matter to me. I only serve as their counsel, and they asked me to approach you about it."

Beth smirked. Orient's entire population counted somewhere in the seven hundreds, and yet her neighbors were trying to negotiate with her through an attorney.

"I have an inappropriate question for you, then," Beth said, jumping a puddle, which Arthur took the time to sidestep. "Did Magdalena leave her land to OHB? I mean, since she didn't have any relatives."

"Unfortunate thing, that," he said, stopping. They had bypassed his red Lexus. Cleaver's courtesy extended only as far as his car. "She was going to wait until the board set itself up as a trust. She wanted to guarantee that her property would be preserved as part of the conservancy. I guess we all thought she'd live a few more years. Who could have expected a heart attack over bees?"

"I see," Beth said. The rain slicked her cheeks. She thought of Jeff Trader's warning that something wasn't right with OHB. "You don't know of any reason Magdalena might have grown doubtful of the board, do you? That maybe there was some cause for her to second-guess its motives?"

Cleaver shook his head. "Magdalena's name is on the conservancy initiative. She was a highly dedicated member of OHB."

"So what happens to her estate?"

"Estate," he repeated drolly. "You'd have to ask Cole Drake. He's that kind of local lawyer. I wouldn't know what to advise a woman like Ms. Kiefer. I deal in corporations, not individuals. I try to steer clear of messy emotional decisions. And that's how most people make decisions, isn't it? Emotionally." Cleaver took a step back, the umbrella no longer even pretending to shelter her.

Beth wondered if Arthur Cleaver ever cried. His face was perfectly engineered for it, with carved aqueducts from eyes to jaw to dispense tears efficiently. The only real passion she knew Cleaver to possess was for paddle wheel steamboats, the kind that used to travel from Manhattan to Orient a hundred years ago to transport vacationers to the beaches and hunting fields. For the past five years, he had been building an exact replica of a wrecked 1902 Baltimore steamer on the lawn behind his neoclassical mansion, importing tropical hardwoods to reconstruct the antique vessel right on his rolling escarpment above the Sound. Most Orient residents had never actually seen the boat up close. It was referred to locally as Arthur's Ark, and some joked that the first sign of the end of the world would be Cleaver's steamer floating off to sea, loaded with his treasures and none of his neighbors.

"How's the steamboat going?" she asked him.

Cleaver sighed. His right eye twitched. "It's nearly complete. To be honest, I'm thinking of moving to another part of Long Island. Somewhere quieter. With so many of you young people moving here lately, I'm not certain the peace will continue. Perhaps my ark, as they call it, will be seaworthy after all."

Beth remembered what Paul had told her about Cleaver donating money for the preservation of Bug Light. "That would be a shame. I hear you're the man responsible for keeping the lighthouse up."

"That's an idea," Cleaver said with brightening eyes. "Maybe I'll just buy that and make my home on an island, out in the blue and away from all encroachment."

Arthur shut his umbrella and climbed into his car, the gray suede upholstery hyena-spotted with flecks of rain. He waited for the hearse to pass on Main Road before heading off in the direction of the causeway.

Beth hurried along the sidewalk, passing the fire department and its open garage doors. She decided to try calling the post office on her cell, but the automated prompts only led her in a circle back to the introductory main menu. She tried one of the 800 numbers she remembered from the flyers and entered a similar labyrinth: "Press one for cribs, two for clothing, three for . . ." She pressed zero. Another option menu. Zero. Another. Zero. Zero. Zero. Main menu.

Finally, she found Mike Gilburn's card in her purse and dialed his number. His live, hoarse voice grumbled "Gilburn" on the other end. How satisfying to call a number and find a human being on the other end.

"Hi, Mike, it's Beth." The silence of incomprehension followed. "Beth Shepherd. From high school. From Magdalena Kiefer's driveway."

"Oh, Beth," he said in a lighter tone. "Sorry. I'm drowning in paperwork here. Hey, I heard you've moved back to the old neighborhood. Have you seen your friend, Alison—what's her married name now, Eschmeyer?"

"No, I haven't," she said quickly. "Look, I wanted to apologize for my behavior the other day. I know I probably seemed a little unhinged."

"No need to apologize. Don't wor—" She didn't let Mike get too far in his pardon. She was calling to reset the alarm.

"You told me to call if I still believed her death wasn't an accident. I mean"—what was the correct term for a normal death?— "natural." She tried again. "You told me to call you if I still had doubts."

"Yes, I guess I did," he said slowly, his sinuses thick with disappointment. He sounded younger over the phone. If she didn't know him, she'd think Detective Gilburn was in his twenties. "I thought I made it clear that we weren't treating this case as a homicide."

"That's why I'm calling. I wanted to follow up. I wondered if any further evidence came to light. For instance, an autopsy."

"We'd have to exhume her in order to perform one. The coroner consulted with her physician. Beth, she was eighty-three."

"I'm aware of that. But, Mike, Magdalena invited me to her house a few days before she died for the sole purpose of telling me that she suspected someone had killed Jeff Trader. She was certain of it. And she was frightened."

"And all I can say, again, is that she was eighty-three. Old people suffer delusions. I wouldn't be surprised if that stress contributed to her heart attack, or at least her decision to play around with her beehives." Mike exhaled into the receiver. She knew he was trying to summon his patience for a woman he'd known since puberty. She heard him shuffling papers on his desk and wondered if Mike had a special app on his phone that produced the sound, just to help shorten irritating calls. "I'll be blunt with you. We have no reason, none at all, to assume there was any foul play. And the Southold Police Department doesn't have the manpower to follow up on every suspicious whim of a neighbor, even if that neighbor is a friend of mine. We don't have a special homicide unit. I'm homicide. I'm felonies. I'm fender benders. Hell, I'm lost pets." He laughed in frustration. "I've had all of that under my jurisdiction for a year now. And I'm afraid I have you to thank for the six other phone calls I've gotten about the Kiefer case."

"So others have called?" Beth stopped in front of the Tabachs' white Cape Cod. The brown heads of hydrangeas were bobbing like workhorses in the rain.

"Yes, and two of them mentioned you as the reason they were concerned."

"I haven't said a thing."

"They must have heard you screaming at the scene. Six calls about an elderly woman's death. And more than thirty calls related to that creature that washed to shore. My phone's been ringing around the clock. 'Test my water, it doesn't look right.' 'Is it safe to eat local produce?' Don't be offended, but maybe being isolated out in Orient has gotten to you a little bit. All this quiet after you've been in the city for so long."

Beth offered no defense.

"And now I'm getting calls about suspicious persons in the vicinity. Outsiders with criminal backgrounds. It's not the job of the police to vet every character that passes through the North Fork." Mike eased out of his tirade, as if he'd worn himself out. "Give me your number. If anything does turn up I'll contact you."

She recited ten digits, wondering whether he was even writing them down.

"If I happen to get my hands on proof, will you listen then?" she asked. Did Jeff Trader's journal actually count as proof? At least it was something she could hold in her hand, something that couldn't be dismissed as a hysterical invention.

"It would be a pleasure to see you if you have anything tangible to show to me. But, Beth, I'm going to be straight with you. It didn't do either of us any favors that the single witness to Magdalena Kiefer's death, one Stephanie Smith, was seen leaving the scene under your supervision. I'll bet her name was Stephanie. She sure looked like a Stephanie. Stephanies are known for their Mexican accents. It's a good thing we aren't investigating because my superiors would drill me for not charging you with hampering a police investigation. Just so we're clear."

Again she offered no defense.

Mike paused. When she heard his voice again it sounded more weathered, as if it had aged ten years.

"I guess you heard about my divorce."

"Yes. I'm sorry."

"Jill's gone. Been gone a few months, and I don't blame her. After three years, we couldn't wear down the parts of each other that didn't fit. I'm just thankful we didn't have children. Although maybe kids would have been one way to wear us down." He went silent, expecting Beth to fill the dead space. Mike was a guard dog that was suddenly rolling over to expose his vulnerable underside. She didn't pet him. She needed him to stay on the job, a guard dog with a nose and teeth. "All right," he said with a sigh. "You tell your neighbors to check the paper this week. There's an official report on the Plum creature coming out. That should put an end to some of these calls."

Beth unlocked her car and wiped her face with a tissue. She turned the windshield wipers to high as she drove east on Main Road, slowing them as the downpour receded. Beth tried turning them off altogether, but they continued to whisk across the glass in skidding bursts. By the time she pulled into the Drakes' driveway on Little Bay Road, a cold sun simmered in the sky and the wipers still wouldn't shut off.

The Drakes' house was surrounded by a white picket fence, suggesting not so much exclusion as invitation. ORIENT TAPESTRIES, BY APPOINTMENT read the sign that hung from a chain on the porch below a sweep of floral woodwork. A glance through the window revealed a motley of batiks, saris, woven rugs, and embroidered linens artfully arranged on the window seat, advertising Holly Drake's incongruously down-home far-east imported textile business. Beth rang the bell. When Holly answered, her freckled skin looked dewy from the shower, her hair wrapped in a yellow towel.

"What a surprise," Holly said. "I just saw you at the funeral. Are you here to look at some fabrics?"

"I was actually hoping for a word with your husband," Beth replied.

"Oh, Cole's in the den watching the game. I was just changing. Come in." Holly opened the door wider, and Beth noticed Holly's fingernails, chewed down to the cuticles. Like any house accustomed to hosting strangers, the front rooms were organized to emphasize routine happiness. A photo of the young couple hung above a vase of orchids. A shot from their wedding leaned on a polished table, with Holly guiding her husband's cake-clenched fingers toward her open mouth. One of Holly's saris was tacked like a gigantic butterfly on the wall. The lacquered pinewood floorboards allowed no dust to rupture their oily crescents and hand-carved pegs.

Holly led Beth into a room outfitted in rugs and gold-leaf textiles, FedEx boxes and packing material. The bulk of Holly's business was mail order, and a humming desktop computer displayed a slide show of draped fabrics that were shot on the window seat on the opposite side of the room. The sound of televised crowds and sports announcers echoed from the darkness of the den. Holly pushed the sliding doors open, cautioning Beth to be careful of the sunken step. Cole was slumped on the couch, staring at the flat screen. He pulled a remote control from between his legs and pressed the mute button as Beth took a chair across from him.

"It's an antique," Holly warned her. "I wouldn't move around too much. But you're so light." Where was Holly from originally? Chicago? Sarasota? Swampscott? Beth couldn't remember. Her accent seemed sculpted by cable news executives.

Cole looked at his wife with a blank expression, and Holly excused herself to finish changing.

Beth had known Cole Drake most of her life. He'd been two years ahead of her in high school, and his presence was like a long list of negatives: too lean and injury-prone for organized sports, too morose and handsome for marching band. Cole was never friendly; Beth, quite popular at Sycamore, always thought he looked like the kind of kid who should grow up in one of the huge western states where land put a natural barrier between people. Even now, he eyed Beth like he was still hostile toward her likeable teenage self. Beth could have done without visiting Cole altogether, but he'd been the only other visitor to Magdalena's house she'd seen in the days before her death.

"I spoke with Arthur Cleaver today," Beth said. "I asked who handled Magdalena's will. He said you did." Cole glanced at the television for a moment, waiting for the score, then brought his brown eyes silently back and waited for her to continue. "I'm not sure I'm even allowed to ask this, but I was her friend, so I wondered what you two talked about when you visited her the day before she died. I saw you out my window."

"Come to collect, huh?" If he had punctuated that sentence with a laugh it might have broken the tension.

"No, of course not," she said. "I wouldn't expect to receive anything. It's more—well, I also spoke with Magdalena a few days before she died, and she seemed worried about something. She was really broken up about Jeff Trader's death. Did she mention him to you?"

"He died *intestate*. No will and no inheritors. His property will go to the state to settle." Cole checked the score and scowled. Whatever vague clue Beth had been hoping to glean, this trip hardly seemed worth the gas it took to drive here. What would Cole know about a woman like Magdalena Kiefer, anyway? The only virtue she probably appreciated in him was his efficiency.

Beth narrowed her approach. "She didn't say anything strange to you on that visit? Maybe she mentioned someone she distrusted? Or anyone she was worried about?"

Cole crossed his arms over his lap and wedged his tongue against his cheek. He held his emotions the way men were forced to hold their wife's purse: close to the chest with their jaw muscles clenched in embarrassment. Gavril never minded holding Beth's purse.

"Magdalena distrusted a lot of people," he said. "For good reasons or for no reasons at all. She distrusted me, for one. Your mother, for another. I never cared for her in particular." Beth assumed Cole was still referring to Magdalena, not Gail. "But, no, she didn't say anything to me that day. And if she had, I would have assumed it was a symptom of her age. Those hippie types get a little lost in the head when the years start adding up. She wanted to leave everything to her nurse. Not the house, but all of the stuff in it. Most of her money will go to that woman's son, although it's going to be a headache for me to send her small savings to some kid's address in Mexico when he actually lives ten miles down the interstate."

Holly tiptoed through the room in a yellow velour tracksuit, her curly red hair falling over her shoulders. "Don't mind me, don't mind me," she whispered as she passed the couch and opened the glass door to escape into the backyard. Beth shifted on the wobbly chair and leaned in to focus Cole's attention.

"So that's why you went over to her house. She wanted you to change her will."

Cole had the lawyer's trait of speaking each sentence in the same dreary monotone.

"That's right. And you'll be happy to know that she left you a few things. An armoire and a grandfather clock." Beth remembered admiring those pieces on her visit. "You clean up pretty well, actually. Not that a couple of beat-up antiques really amount to a motive for killing her, do they?" Cole smiled, at last, though without a hint of warmth.

"So you also think Magdalena was murdered?"

"Did I say that?" He grunted. A last-minute field goal leveled the score. Beth was competing with a stadium of twenty thousand. "It's no secret you think she was. I've heard more than one person tell me you've been swearing murder up and down. I'd be careful if I were you. Holly's been locking all our windows at night. She's hounding me about getting an alarm put in."

"I *have not* been saying that."

Cole didn't like loud noises. The fluctuation in her voice unnerved him. He propped the pillows against his ribs.

"But I'll tell you something, since you've come all this way. There *was* something peculiar. You may know that I'm not fond of the board and all their benevolent plans to save us, so you can take what I say or don't. But Magdalena demanded that I come see her that day so she could alter the key beneficiary in her will. She was going to leave her house and acreage to OHB, but out of nowhere she wanted that struck. Had me run over to sign a new will without that condition. You can say, as some do, that she was waiting for the trust to be set up, shifting around her assets before the big announcement, but that's not what it seemed like to me. Seemed to me like she changed her mind altogether. She wouldn't tell me why, and it wasn't my place to ask. But my guess is, she didn't want the historical board to have it. Didn't want to put it all in Bryan Muldoon's pocket. Problem is, without any relatives, the land goes to the state to settle. Same as Jeff Trader, in case you're in the market."

"Does the historical board know she changed her will?"

"Bryan, George, and Sarakit all phoned me separately the day after she died. They weren't exactly pleased by the news."

Cole leaned back on his sofa, unmuted the game with his remote, and called an end to the conversation. Beth stood up and thanked him. As she began to leave she heard his voice through the televised screams.

"Funny, you moving back here."

She turned. His attention was on the screen.

"Excuse me?"

"You moving back here. In high school, you were always going on about New York and all the fancy things you were going to do out there. And now you're back here with the rest of us. Just funny, that's all. How it ends up."

Beth struggled to take the insult up the sunken stair, one foot in front of the other. She could not remember a single incident involving Cole Drake that would have caused him to resent her for fifteen years. Was he alone in his view of her, or were there others—adults now, stretched and swollen versions of the kids she'd known—watching her from their windows with the kind of raw hate that only comes from youthful resentment? She passed through the makeshift showroom and opened the front door with unsteady hands.

Beth was halfway toward the gate when Holly rounded the house, wearing gardening gloves with her yellow tracksuit, a pair of pruning shears in her gloved fingers.

"Did you get what you came for?" she asked, using the glove to shade her eyes. She read Beth's puzzled expression. "Don't mind Cole. You know husbands. Never interrupt them during a game." Holly squinted as she smiled. Beth felt another flash of déjà vu, not for a moment lived twice, but for a moment repeated from a photograph—the one she'd found in Jeff Trader's journal. Holly's red hair was bright against the lawn of dead Bermuda grass, which would grow alien green in summer. Behind her, thorny bushes would blossom with summer rosebuds.

CHAPTER **14**

At the Floyd Organic Farm Stand, on a gravel crescent off Main Road, Paul selected autumn vegetables. Even in the rain he was fastidious, palming Jerusalem artichokes, squeezing zucchinis, inspecting kale for wilted leaves. August Floyd, manning the family-owned stand, watched with the bleary enthusiasm of a farmer who had survived a decade of near-death alcoholism and another decade of near-death redundancy, thanks to competition from the Greenport supermarkets. His slackened face only blinked when the wind swept the rain against his broken nose.

If darker times had left their scars, his customers' more recent prosperity cushioned them. August Floyd was zippered into a brand-name fleece jacket. His hands guarded a money box teeming with tens and twenties. The stand promised vegetables grown from something called heritage seeds, and this promise brought cars to idle on the gravel as shoppers from as far away as Mattituck pilfered the once-cheap, now high-priced inventory. The shoppers were young and assertive, their hair cropped and disheveled by Manhattan salons, their cars new and gleaming against the downpour. Their bumpers were decorated in Obama stickers. August Floyd's mud-caked Chevy still preferred Romney. The shoppers tried to barter. August tapped the price signs. The shoppers relented. They wanted lavender. August told them it was out of season.

A few Orient natives burrowed through the vegetable bins, feeling no need to step aside for the over-the-causeway customers. Karen

Norgen, her skin as gray-green as algae, her hair still whipped into silver curls from the funeral, was midway through a rant aimed at August's ears. "I've been picking blackberries from those bushes ever since I was a child. I always used the Tabor lawn to access the beach. My parents used that lawn. And this woman who calls herself an *art advisor*—god knows what that means—moves in last year, shows up one time all season, and now she tells me I'm trespassing! On a lawn my parents have been crossing since they were children. Art advisor. You can make money saying shit is gold, and I can't walk across a lawn. . . ."

A German shepherd and a scrawny collie mix sniffed the car grilles for bird carcasses. Mills watched the German shepherd mount the smaller dog, humping her as he glanced dully around. After a few too many nervous giggles from shoppers, August clapped his hands. "Spark, get off her." He hurled an apple, hitting the dog on its side. The shepherd climbed off its mate, his purple tongue lolling, but when he tried to trot away, the collie was pulled behind him. They were still joined, hind to hind, the shepherd's penis stuck in the collie's opening.

"She was eating a canapé," Karen wailed. "On a Tuesday afternoon. By herself! While she was telling me I was no longer allowed to pick blackberries!"

Paul asked for a dozen oysters from one of the Igloo ice coolers.

"Have you ever tried an oyster?" he asked Mills. "It's like eating the sneeze of the sea. I mean that in a good way."

Mills couldn't take his eyes off the dogs. They were scampering around the cars, stuck together, trying to run in opposite directions like conjoined twins desperate to separate. They looked embarrassed, as if confused by an instinct that had betrayed them.

"I think they're in pain," Mills said.

"Just came out of the bay this morning," August told Paul as he scooped twelve oysters into a plastic bag and double-knotted the end.

"Do you think that blackberry bush will be there next spring? I don't. That woman is building a Japanese rock garden." Karen shook her head in bewilderment. "I don't know what we're in for with these new people," she huffed. "I was thinking I'd throw in my name to fill Magdalena's seat on the board. Just to help out where I can. August, Paul, what do you think?" Karen only glanced at Mills when she thought he wasn't looking.

Paul smiled at Karen and nodded. He quickly turned to Mills. "I've got to find my steel shucking gloves. Have you seen those gloves in the kitchen? They look like Michael Jackson gloves. Opens them right up."

The dogs whined as they ran diagonally, trying to break apart, and whined viciously when they couldn't. They spun in circles, slamming against the fender of a Jeep, then running back to back in a yanking sidestep toward Main Road. The shepherd's eyes were white with fear, his penis bent painfully back, causing a twinge of sympathy in Mills's groin. The collie swiveled around to bite her mate. She yelped and tried to roll on the ground to dislodge him. The shepherd dug his paws in the gravel and dragged her up. He sniffed the thrown apple, as if a second of distraction would clear up the crisis.

"They're getting too close to the road," Mills said to August Floyd.

"They're animals. They know what they're doing." But August noticed his dogs were indeed a few feet from the whipping traffic. "It's forty total," he told Paul, then jogged over to the dogs. August kicked them back with his boot and kept kicking until they drifted over the gravel, not as two dogs but as a single flinching, double-headed organism. They disappeared into the thick marsh grasses, growling and snapping but still fused end to end. The grass shook as shoppers continued their excavation of the vegetable bins. When Mills looked up, Karen was studying him, her mouth forming a reluctant smile. August counted his money.

Paul and Mills returned to the Mercedes, loading six pumpkins onto the backseat.

"I wish we could make sure those dogs got free okay," Mills said as he climbed into the car. He watched the grass, hoping to see one of the dogs lope out alone.

"I'm sure they'll work it out." Paul pressed his foot on the clutch and let out a moan. He rubbed his knee. "It flares up when it rains," he said through his teeth, as if tasting sour meat.

"We can go home," Mills said. "We don't need to go to the tip today."

Paul waved a dismissive hand. "I'll be fine."

Yesterday, Mills had found an old sign in one of the back rooms, tucked between a carton of empty bicentennial 7-Up cans and a bundle of synthetic neckties. At first he'd mistaken it for a flag, covered in twenty years of velvet dust. As his fingers wiped the dirt from the surface, red letters appeared: TERPO. He rubbed until OYSTERPONDS INN ran across the wooden board. He carried it into the dining room, and Paul held it up admiringly as if it were a family photograph.

The sign had belonged to Paul's mother. It had hung on the porch of the inn her family had owned for three generations. Paul decided he would pick Mills up after Magdalena's funeral and they could drive to the inn to deliver it as a gift to the young couple who'd recently bought the place. "Beth told me they were artists. They can put it in their kitchen," Paul said, "or maybe hang it right on the porch if the hooks are still there. People like that, a touch of history." Mills decided not to destroy the neighborly fantasy by voicing his own opinion: *People don't like that. People don't enjoy former owners showing up at their houses, inviting themselves in, and turning their rooms into photo albums in which their own faces do not appear.* But, behind the gesture, Mills sensed a secret motivation at work. Paul was curious to see what the new residents had done to his mother's farmhouse. Scrubbed and de-splintered, the sign was now lying in Paul's backseat with the pumpkins.

As they drove east, Paul shook his sore leg to improve his circulation.

"How did you hurt it?" Mills asked. He knew the answer, but he decided not to mention the car accident Tommy had told him about. Paul had made it clear how much he abhorred Orient gossip, and Mills understood why: it seemed like every house in Orient had an electric fan of gossip blowing the curtains in their windows. Paul preferred the stagnant air of his own separate world.

"I had an accident last June. Wasn't watching the road as I was coming in from the causeway and hit a tree." He pulled at his tie with two fingers. "No big deal. But every so often my knee shoots with needles. My doctor says I need physical therapy, but do I really want to pay someone to watch me bend my leg for an hour? It's getting better, little by little." He patted his left knee through his black wool pants.

At least Mills wasn't also wearing a black suit. His jeans and long-sleeved T-shirt would prevent them from being mistaken for a pair of father-son Christian missionaries when they showed up at the old inn. Mills stared at the water-flecked fields they passed, remembering the scenery from his drive with Beth to Jeff Trader's house. He almost asked Paul if they could check on the cats and sheep, but that would have been another admission of sticking his nose in places it didn't belong. How could Mills explain rummaging around the home of a dead man?

Every so often, pictures of the Plum monster appeared on passing lawns—PROTECT YOUR HOME FROM CONTAGIONS. PROTECT YOUR FUTURE WITH THE STATE-OF-THE-ART. CALL PRUITT SECURITIES— mixed in among the PEARL FARMS DREAM HOME for-sale signs. It wasn't much of a leap to make a connection between the monster's decaying shape and the real estate markers in close proximity, linking them together by cause and effect. "Adam's signs aren't doing wonders for property values, I'll tell you that much," Paul said.

Mills pitied the creature. Even if it was a mutant, designed in a lab in some twisted experiment to merge the ugliest features of the animal kingdom, it had still been alive at one point, and somewhere in its brain pan had possessed the desire to live. Mills imagined it escaping from its cage in the night, clawing its way through barbed wire, its paws touching earth for the first time in the short history of its species, and diving into the water, thinking it could swim. It must have enjoyed that minute before drowning, snorting the clean night air, contemplating the comfort of heat and blood and the rough tug of jimsonweed on its skin.

"If it were cute it wouldn't look like such a threat," Mills said.

"A panda crossed with a Yorkshire terrier and the slightest dose of sloth?"

Mills had relied on adorability for much of his childhood. He fixed his eyes on the clouds that stretched skeletally over the bay.

"Well, even if it started out under a microscope, it should have some rights, shouldn't it?"

"If you say so," Paul said, nodding. He steered the car around the deeper puddles, his knee stronger. "We have rights too, if you say so. That's all rights are—just values that enough people agree that they share."

"I am saying so," Mills replied. He wasn't in the mood for one of Paul's fatherly lessons on relativism. *Fine*, he thought, *bring it into existence, stick needles into it, and exterminate it as soon as it gets out of hand.* Welcome to the life cycle of the twenty-first century. The dogs at the farm stand combined in his mind with the creature on Adam Pruitt's ads until it all felt slightly sickening, like the earth itself was a giant petri dish for the growth of horrible organisms. He tried to picture the creature in its cage in a basement laboratory at Plum, prodded and tortured by white-suited needle-wielders with sharp, lucid eyes. Often, Mills found himself despising the human species, praying for its inevitable extinction, even as he was enjoying a slice of pizza or taking the bus. He had come to view hating human beings abstractly as the most convenient way of living with a conscience in the world.

Paul glanced over at him, gauging his agitation, and dropped his smile. "I'm not trying to argue with you," he said. "I think this whole mutant thing is a bunch of bullshit."

"It's not bullshit," Mills snapped. "If it's the future, it's something to consider."

Paul rubbed his mustache, his eyes shifting from amused to meditative. The tires of approaching cars created small tidal bores that crashed against the side of the Mercedes.

"Here's what I think," Paul said after a minute. "Pruitt's signs don't mean *protect your future*. They mean *protect yourself from it*. Why is it that when everyone thinks of the future these days they're always bringing up visions of the apocalypse? It's a fear that anything new must signal the end of days. I find it pretty sad that a whole generation has become terrified of what's to come. When I was a kid, we were so optimistic. We were cheering for more men on the moon."

"You can't be that old," he replied. For Mills, dreams of traveling to the moon appeared in the same grainy, black-and-white footage as the first televised landing—a program that had already been canceled before he had been born. The dream could barely withstand the advancement of color. "And you don't even own a television set."

Paul straightened his glasses.

"I'm afraid I am old now." He laughed, as if his birth year were a punch line that kept getting funnier every time he remembered it. "How long before kids look at me the way I once looked at people born in the nineteenth century?"

Mills rested his temple against the window. He couldn't imagine anyone born in the nineteenth century.

"Do you think one day those kinds of mutant creatures will be normal?" he asked. The car slowed, waiting for a clear turn onto a dirt road. "Like a regular feature in zoos?"

Paul thought about it. "Probably." He rotated the wheel. "Can you think of one scientific breakthrough that was ever stopped? It all becomes a reality eventually. Best not to waste your strength trying to fight the future. It's like trying to punch the Internet. But if you're asking about that Plum monster, I doubt it was real."

Oak branches tangled above them, a canopy of wicker. Whatever Paul had imagined by way of renovations to his mother's farmhouse inn did not prepare him for what he found crowning the bluff a mile north of Main Road. As the car approached the house, air leaked from his lips. "At least it's the same shape," he rasped.

The main floor of the house was grand, almost as large as the Benchley mansion, with a smaller second story stacked like a captain's cabin at its peak, an elevated roost to watch storms rolling on the sea. They pulled into the driveway, parking behind a black sports coupe. Even from this distance, the house had a blurry patina, an out-of-focus sea mirage that gleamed with leathery plastic. Mills couldn't blink it clear. Twenty feet to the side, a backhoe leaned its yellow claw into the dirt. Mud mounds made a maze on the lawn. Paul lugged the wooden sign from the backseat, staring piteously at the mud trenches.

"Can't fight the future, right?" Mills couldn't resist saying as he unfastened his seat belt. Paul winced, forcing the kind of smile that came over those who had been justly punched. They followed a trail of white paving stones up to what must have once been the porch. A U of grassless dirt indicated its former site. If they drove to a landfill fifty miles away, Paul could have surely found the rotting beams and hung his sign on its original pegs. Instead, he pretended to set it swinging in midair.

"Well, they have the right, after what they paid," Paul said with a sigh, his eyes squinting under his glasses. "The door is still here, so they didn't scrap everything." He pointed to the slab of ocher wood with a brass eyehole staring from between two pillars. The door was there, but the walls around it weren't. The entire house was wrapped in plastic tarps, like a contamination site; Mills expected men in Hazmat suits to emerge, warning them to keep away. The wind jittered the plastic seams, revealing flashes of the interior: glimpses of sharp, minimalist furniture, a fur coat slung over an ivory end table, a Persian carpet that swept under a liquor cabinet stocked with vast bleached bottles. Mills pushed his face between the tarp edges and noticed a roll of twenties lying within reach, amid a pile of keys and matchbooks. Everything inside the house winked with an odorless prosperity, a headachy shine engineered to reflect the current owners.

"These poor people," Paul said, "having to live in a construction site."

"These rich people, you mean," Mills whispered.

Paul tapped softly on the front door, as if he feared he might knock it over. "They have to be rich," he said. "This house and its forty acres cost well over six million. It was quite a controversy to see an old house like this go so far beyond the asking price." Paul waited patiently at the door, but no wealthy artist opened it to greet him.

"No one's home," Mills said. "Who did you say these artists were?" Paul stepped back to take in the upper floor, searching for signs of life.

"They're from the city. Beth said the man's name is Nathan. And his wife is Liz or Luz or something like that." Mills turned from the tarps and stared at him. The sports car in the driveway belonged to the black woman who had visited Paul's house on the day Magdalena died.

"She came around to see you," Mills told him. "But you were out. She said she wanted to paint your portrait."

"Paint me?" Paul's lips tightened in confusion. "Why would she want to do that? I've never met either of them. But they should have told me they were doing this kind of construction. I could have dug up the floor plans and saved them on the contractor bill."

Mills walked to the front door and tried the handle. Paul grabbed his arm.

"We can't just walk in."

"She invited herself into your house. So we get to do the same." The handle didn't budge. Mills could have easily stepped through a gap in the tarps and unlocked the door from the inside, but that seemed a more sinister form of intrusion, as if even invisible walls were not allowed to be breached. For a minute they both stood awkwardly in front of the only obstacle that prevented Paul from his trip through memory's bed-and-breakfast.

"Oh, well," Paul said in resignation, as if to bluff the house into opening its door to him. "I can at least show you the grounds." He pointed toward the Sound, then followed his own finger, a divining rod to locate the past. The blue water curved around giant, jagged rocks, pushed against the coastline in the last Ice Age. Any farther push would have saved them the burden of the trip. Gulls skimmed the water like descending planes. The black-and-white thimble of a lighthouse rose from an island of stones. "Coffeepot," Paul told him. "There used to be lounge chairs just on the edge of this cliff. And over there a gazebo that slid onto the beach during the hurricane of '71." They hiked across the lawn, Mills snaking his arms around his stomach to keep warm. Seven half-dug rectangles were engraved in the grass, as if the backhoe had furiously attacked the earth and now stood shamefully on the perimeter, deflecting blame. Paul shook his head and rubbed the back of his neck, agitated the way any previous homeowner is who disapproves of their successor's renovations. Mills could see that all of the construction work rattled him, like a memory being ripped apart. He let Paul walk a few feet across the lawn by himself.

"Why all of the digging?" Mills asked.

Paul spun around and attempted a weak smile. "I think they're trying to build a pool. Or several pools. Or maybe they keep changing their mind about where they want to put it." He pushed his heel into the frozen dirt. "They should have asked a local for advice first. This land used to be a salt farm before my mother's family took it over. It was flooded with water from the Sound and baked by the sun into salt crystals. My family had to build up the cliff and harden the ground with clay to keep it stable. It's too risky and expensive to dig a pool here. The previous residents knew that." Paul finally threw his hand up, releasing himself of blame. "Well, it's not my problem. Anyway, they'll have to wait for spring now to continue. The ground's frozen."

"Maybe you should write them a note."

Paul grunted. "I'm already giving them a hotel sign. And I guess we *are* technically trespassing. They really are making the place their own, aren't they?" He scanned the perimeter of the lawn, his eyes stopping on a patch of overgrown weeds not far from a row of tree stumps. He headed toward it, and Mills jogged to catch up.

"Right here was the first building I ever built." Paul tucked the board under his arm and used both hands to push aside a clump of yellow briars. A large circular slab of crumbling concrete, swathed in moss and bird shit, protruded an inch from the ground. A wreath of uncut grass covered its sides. To Mills it didn't seem a very impressive start for a career in architecture.

"You built this?"

"No," Paul said, laughing. "This was just the base. I must have been six or seven. It was long after the first Bug Light burned down. But Bug was my mom's favorite lighthouse, and she missed it so much that my father and I poured this slab of cement and assembled our own model out of wood and mesh. It was eight feet high, a cheap little replica, but it withstood the wind and snow before my mother sold the place. We used to light the top with candles, and at night I'd pretend to be a boat, guiding toward it, the whole horizon black but for that little star of yellow. There were so few guests, we spent our evenings here without anyone else around."

"You were an architect even as a kid," Mills said. He felt as long as Paul didn't look back at the obliterated house he could drift in recollections without being reminded of their expiration date. The sea was still the sea, a blue field swirling with foaming tongues.

"Yeah, I think that little lighthouse started my interest in architecture." Paul gazed at him with a sorrow so clean it seemed inviting.

"Do you wish your mom hadn't sold this place?"

"No," he replied, letting the weeds fall back over the slab. "It was a money trap, a dust hotel, and we couldn't afford to keep it up. Houses are for people to live in, and these new owners are at least taking the trouble to remodel it. They could have torn it down." Paul examined the old inn again, rattling like a plastic bag caught on a rock. "Part of the reason my mother sold it was to pay for the last years of my boarding school. St. Peter's, all-boys, in Westchester. From the age of seven on, I only came home during the summer, when they put me to work here or on my father's fishing boats. I spent most of the summer out at sea as a kid." He pointed far out in the water. "Jesus, I got sunburned."

"Why didn't you just go to school here?" Mills asked.

"My mom worried I might flounder in the local school system and end up a fisherman like my father, a deckhand with the stink of brine on my neck. Some of the people in Orient thought she was a snob for that, but she saw it as an investment. Worth more to her than this place. And it *was* an investment. Because, in the end, she couldn't have kept the house on Youngs Road without the checks I wrote to pay for it. But that's what they expected of me, and it was my turn to give back." Paul stared at him, gathering a speech about the sterling benefits of a top-notch education, but he let the subject drift. It occurred to Mills that children were retirement packages for their parents, a way to ensure their own survival. The Benchleys had raised their son like a racehorse, betting their livelihoods on a winning pedigree. Now his success was all he had. Paul might not have ended up such a smart, lonely man if his parents hadn't sent him away so young. Of course, Mills realized, the same could be said of him.

"It's a good thing the historical board never came out here." Paul nodded at the house. "I'm surprised they haven't raised a stink about the renovations. Maybe they couldn't see it from the road. Or, at this point, maybe they're just glad it wasn't sold to a development company. I bet Bryan will be paying a visit about selling their development rights. He should. I'd hate to see this land parceled up."

Over the ridge, Mills noticed a wooden dock stretching into the water. A blue speedboat was tied to the end, snapping in the current against its taut ropes.

"Did you have a boat like that?" Mills asked.

Paul shook his head, hardly glancing at the craft. He was still envisioning his tiny ersatz lighthouse on the lawn, as if it were guiding him back to his parents, blinking moth-winged, lit with candles, far away even close up.

"No. The dock must have been another addition after we left. A boat like that can get you around Orient much faster than the roads. That's one way to beat traffic." Paul shook his head and started toward the house. He pulled the wood sign from under his arm. "I'll leave this at the door. Let them figure out if they want to keep it or not."

On their walk to the car, Mills looked back at the house. One of the tarps had come unfastened, curling in the air like hardened smoke, exposing a collection of paint supplies, canisters, and canvases. In the upstairs window, Mills saw the faint, dark face of a woman in the glass, watching their departure. Before he could smile at her, two white arms wrapped around her and pulled her into the shadows.

Paul drove home carefully, his hands gripping the steering wheel at ten and two o'clock. "Orient sure is changing," he said. They didn't speak any more about the future. For Paul, it had already arrived.

Paul's porch steps had a wobbly second beam. It didn't wobble for him, but it did for every less-accustomed foot. Mills performed a jumping sidestep to avoid it, knowing that if Paul heard the creak he'd be the one to spend the afternoon trying to fix it with a hammer. The leaves in the front lawn were already looking like a postparty cleanup job—a joy to watch falling, a backache once they reached the ground. Paul carried the farm-stand bags into the kitchen, promising a lunch of oysters if he could find his special gloves. Mills, having lost his appetite somewhere between the dogs and the Pruitt signs of the creature, resigned himself to his duties in handling the vanishing empire of Benchley belongings.

They had established an unthinking rhythm in the past weeks, coming together for occasional sparks of conversation between their exiles in separate parts of the house, as if days were vast, placid lakes in which their boats occasionally met. Often Mills had to remind himself that the house wasn't his and would never be, no matter how much effort he put into its upkeep. But he couldn't help feeling he was discovering the secret routine of adult life, a bargain with time and space, a way to squeeze through its compressions with the least amount of resistance. Homes all over America must be riddled with the same quiet acts of cabinet opening and garbage dragging, the silent human orchestra of getting by. So different from Manhattan, Mills thought, with its loud acoustics of getting on and ahead.

He walked through the back rooms, taking a moment to appreciate the results of his work. A majority of the rooms were navigable now. Couches had regained their legs and arms; they were no longer couch-shaped piles of magazines and festering winter coats. Books were stacked against the walls, photo albums and frames arranged in keepsake piles.

In the first days of cleaning, no item had seemed worth more consideration than the time it took to put it in a trash bag. But as the junk diminished, objects began to take on added dimension. They told stories of the people who owned them: the arms on a pair of red sunglasses, bent to adjust to uneven ears. The sleep button on an alarm clock, worn more deeply than the other buttons. A brass horse head ashtray, property of a smoker who extinguished butts only on the stallion's ears. Paul's parents might have been gone, but they lasted, in the ground and throughout these rooms. Mills wondered what future archaeologists could learn about him by examining his belongings. He'd been alive for nineteen years, but he worried he would forever remain an incidental set of fingerprints in the lives of others.

There was once a family called the Fosters. That was the first line of a joke Mills and his foster-care friends often told while waiting in the blue bowl seats of the social services offices. The Fosters decided to take in a foster kid, even though they had two children of their own. The father got caught up in some shady dealings with a criminal organization. One night, when the foster kid was out, a hit man came to the Foster home and murdered the entire family in retaliation. Shot the father and the mother and the two children on the spot. Just as the hit man was about to leave, the foster kid walked through the door. The hit man pointed his gun and yelled, "Are you a Foster kid?" The foster kid looked around, appraising the family's television set and video game console and snack cabinet and, after a moment, said, "Maybe. But before I go with you, how big is your TV?" For a long time that was the only joke Mills knew by heart.

He sat on his knees and started sorting through a stack of shoe boxes, taking his time. In a few weeks, he'd be finished clearing the rooms, and when that job ended, the need for him would end as well. Would Paul ask him to stay on, taking him in like an adopted son? Or would he drive him back to the city, dropping him off in Chinatown with a few dollars in his pocket and a grateful, stay-in-touch wave? And when he got to the city, would the same old vices be there to welcome him back? As long as Mills remained with Paul, dry and quiet in Orient, he felt that he was safe.

He tossed a shoe box lid on the floor and leafed through a sheaf of mildewed papers. A copper bullet rolled against the cardboard; Mills shook it out and set it on the floor. He found a copy of Paul's birth certificate inside an envelope: Paul Andrew Benchley, born at Eastern Long Island Hospital, on November 3, 1966. Mills made a note of the birthday, less than two weeks away. Maybe he'd surprise Paul with a cake. Beth could drive him to a bakery in Greenport and he could have Paul's name inscribed on the frosting. But just as Mills imagined adding candles and darkening the lights in the dining room, an uninvited question interrupted the festivities. Was the cake an honest gesture? Or was it a means of worming his way deeper into Paul Benchley's heart?

No foster kid was naïve to the art of manipulation. There was an art to Polaroid day at social services, rehearsed by children and encouraged by the counselors. A blank face. Eyes wide and vaguely watery. An open smile, with the least amount of twist at the creases. Chin up and eyes staring down. Never chin down and eyes up—that was the face of trouble, and no foster parent wanted trouble sleeping in the bedroom down the hall. On starving black kids in Africa, that expression read as defenseless, wronged, a plea to please send money. On unwanted white kids in America, it read as purse raider, fire starter, mutilator of pets. Even now, when Mills posed for a photograph, he tilted his chin up and dropped his eyes into brimming sunsets. At nineteen, his entire life had been recorded in that same pose, over and over, and collected in his case file.

A small batch of photos was stuck to the bottom of the shoe box. Mills carefully peeled them from the cardboard. One was a shot of Paul at his prom, next to a bony date with streaked and feathered hair. HAPPY ORIENT BUCKS read the taxonomic banner over their heads. Paul looked thinner and more vulnerable, with an eruption of pimples on his chin. His date was waxy and romantically sun-damaged. It was the only evidence of Paul's romantic life that Mills had discovered in his weeks in Orient, besides the Eleanor matchbook. It had surprised Mills how few pictures of Paul as an adult had turned up in his parents' possessions. There were plenty of photos of him as a child, working out at sea on his father's boats. But after the age of thirty, there were only four or five pictures to mark his years. It seemed as if he had spent the past two decades avoiding his parents' camera, or their camera avoiding him, perhaps for his inability to bring home a decent date. Parents did not like to take pictures of their children, year after year, standing alone.

There were three other photographs at the bottom of the box, black-and-white portraits of two dark-haired boys sitting on the porch of the farmhouse inn. The squat boy in overalls with a strong chin and an easy smile was clearly Paul. He was the center of each photograph. On the sidelines was another boy, scrawny, with crooked arms. Paul looked like the picture of health by comparison. The other boy's lip was split with a cleft, and he had morose, empty eyes that suggested mental impairment.

Mills opened a second shoe box and discovered a supply of safety flares. He considered taking one, in case he and Tommy ever made another walk to the beach at night. He noticed a glimmer of black metal at the bottom of the box and reached in to pull it out. He found a gun, an old service revolver that must have belonged to Paul's father. The bullet on the floor must match it. Mills had never held a gun before. His fingers gripped the handle like a confident handshake. Guns were designed to feel natural in the hand, as if the gun were reaching out to greet the open palm. But once gripped, it possessed the dead weight of its purpose, heavy, blunt, and compact. Mills checked that the gun was unloaded and aimed it at the wall. He pulled the trigger, and the cylinder clicked.

Footsteps moved through the back rooms. Mills dropped the gun and bullet into the box of flares and shut the lid. He gathered the photos from the floor.

"Mills?" Paul called as he neared the tiny room, five rooms from the front door and four rooms from the back. It was the appendix of the house, useless except for its need to take up space.

Paul leaned against the doorframe, his hands wedged into his armpits. A smile cut across his face, and it was that smile—unadorned with a mustache—that caused Paul to look naked and strange.

"It's gone," Mills said, lifting up from his crouch. "You shaved it." Mills had never seen Paul without his mustache, and it struck him how different a man could look with one minor revision. Absent his facial hair, Paul was younger, more handsome, more immediate, his round face offering no branch for the eye to settle, no shelter for his expression to hide. Paul had dimples lurking around his mouth, bent shyly at his lips like the legs of a fawn.

"I told you I was old. And it was starting to go gray. I only grew it to look older in the first place. And now that the rest of me caught up, it really wasn't doing me any favors. I decided after our talk in the car. Do I look like a different person? Less nineteenth century? More twenty-first?"

"Completely," Mills said. "And you're right. You do look younger."

"Don't worry, that's the only change. Although I knew a colleague who shaved his beard off and two months later he divorced his wife and started climbing every mountain in Tibet. He blamed his unhappiness on his facial hair. Said it was holding him back, like a muzzle on a dog." Paul noticed the photographs in Mills's hand and nodded at them. "What are those, more photos? They never end, do they? They're like weeds back here."

Mills considered making an excuse to avoid handing them over. The visit to the inn had been enough of a trip into the past, and too many memories in too short a time could turn a little wayward water into a flood zone. Mills couldn't think of a way to hide the photos without drawing more attention to them, so he held up one of the snapshots of the two boys. Paul's face whitened except for the razor marks above his lip.

"My god," he said as he reached for it. "Where did you find this?" He took the picture and studied it. "Patrick. My brother. I didn't know any of these survived."

"You have a brother?"

Paul took off his glasses and used his wrist to wipe his eyes. His fingers trembled as he returned the frames to his nose.

"*Had.* One year younger. He died when I was six. He was very sickly, right from the start. Scoliosis, anemia, you name it. And he was born with a blockage in his intestines. Surgeries couldn't fix it. He threw up everything he ate. And that was the end of him, starving and weak, no matter how much food my parents pushed down his throat." Paul took the other photos and kept shuffling through them, as if there were more than three. "His death destroyed my parents. It got to where they couldn't bear to see a picture of him. Every time they did, it broke their hearts. I thought they'd thrown them all away. I can't believe you found these." Paul stared at him, his teeth making crunching noises in his mouth. "It's like seeing a ghost."

Mills placed his hand on Paul's shoulder.

"Sorry," Paul said, trying to blink away his tears. "I don't know why it's hit me like it has."

"I'll leave you—"

"No. No need for that. It was so long ago." Paul closed his eyes and tipped his head back. "I haven't seen a picture of Patrick in more than thirty years." Paul stacked the photos in his palm. "Life would have been less lonely if he had lived. I used to carry him onto the porch just so he could be out in the sun. He was such a sweet kid. I sometimes think that if he had survived, the burden on me would have been lighter, you know? Like there would have been someone else to share the family with." Mills handed Paul the snapshot of him at his prom.

"This isn't a joke," Paul said, laughing. He seemed relieved for the change of subject. "This is a crime against my better judgment. Look at that tuxedo. All those ruffles. Fashion's supposed to make you feel good but, looking back, it just makes you feel stupid. I came back from boarding school just to go to her prom." He sighed. "We've all been too many different people in our lives."

"We were bound to find a few sad reminders back here. Maybe I should have put them in a box and—"

"No," Paul said. He loosened his shoulders by rowing them back. "It's just been quite a day. This is why I used to keep my visits to Orient short. You never know when the past is hiding behind a bush, waiting to jump out and bite. No, I'm glad you found them. And I can handle whatever else is back here. It would be a disappointment if it were all so easy to throw away." He held his stomach and leaned against the wall.

Mills slung his arm around Paul's shoulder and hugged him, pressing his chin into the pillow of Paul's neck. Paul stiffened before relaxing in the embrace. "I'm going to finish getting the stuff out of the car," Mills whispered. He left the room before Paul could call him back.

Mills jumped down the porch steps and scanned the Muldoons' lawn for traces of Tommy. Tommy had promised to return Jeff Trader's journal, but in the past few days every attempt to corner him had been met with annoying evasion, like trying to get a mosquito to return some blood. Mills had thrown pebbles at Tommy's window, only to watch the light turn off. He had tried to wave down Tommy's car in the morning, only to see it speed away. Mills had considered ringing the doorbell, but the sight of Pam Muldoon in the front windows stopped him short. Maybe Tommy had found Jeff Trader's secrets too enticing to return. Maybe he'd discovered the key to the book's value, the reason Magdalena Kiefer had been so insistent on obtaining it. Mills tried not to imagine what reckless uses Tommy might be envisioning for this fresh cache of secrets. He dreaded the moment Beth would stop by, today or tomorrow or any moment now, to pick it up.

He opened the back door of the Mercedes and started collecting the small, lopsided pumpkins in the crook of his arm. As he glanced through the back window he saw the rain-blurred silhouette of a young man walking up the street. A ghostly shape marched defiantly through the gray afternoon. He let go of the pumpkins and ducked out of the car.

Tommy strode toward him, his shoulder blades scrunched, his eyes cellophane-white and leaking across his cheeks. Was there anything more beautiful than a young man crying? Anything as rare? His knuckles slashed at his tears.

"I'm done with it," Tommy said, staring directly at him. "Done trusting people. Done believing in them and acting good for everyone else. Staying in my place. Always in my fucking place," he sputtered. "Where does it get you? What the fuck difference does it make?"

Mills had no idea what Tommy was talking about, but the knuckles hadn't stopped the tears. "What's the matter?" Mills shut the car door and met him halfway down the drive.

"There's no point if they just disappoint you," Tommy said through chokes. "What a liar. So pathetic. Nothing ever changes. People turn out to be the worst things you could ever think of them. God. What a fucking embarrassment. I'm not going to end up like that, I'll tell you that much."

"What's wrong?" Mills asked again, reaching his hand out but afraid to make contact with Tommy's black windbreaker. He held his palm open an inch from Tommy's arm, as if asking for permission to land. Tommy's eyes narrowed and he sucked snot into his throat.

"Nothing," he snapped. "None of it matters anyway." Tommy's fingers grabbed at his own windbreaker. "Jesus, all I want to do is get out of here." *Here* could have been Orient—or, by the way his fingers were grabbing at his chest, his own body. "To not be stuck like this."

Tommy's upper lip was shaped like the wheel well of a speeding car, his jawbone pivoting and clenching. Mills felt there was a violence to such beauty, the way it disturbed the air like a rogue frequency scrambling the airwaves. The rest of the world faded around it, dull and overcast and easily forgotten. All of Mills's vital organs seemed to deactivate in Tommy's presence. *Say you want to mug me, I will go with you. Tell me to lie down in the middle of the street, I will lie down.* It was torture not to touch it, a bird at sea unable to find a place to land, but he knew that the torture grew worse after beauty departed, leaving the dull stillness of the landscape without its only beacon.

"I need to get that book back from you," Mills said, his brain still mildly operable. "I promised Beth."

Tommy spit yellow phlegm on Paul's dead blueberry bush. "You want to come to my room. That's what you want. Fine. Let's go, then."

Mills followed Tommy through the front door and up the carpeted steps. He heard someone in the laundry room, pressing buttons to bring the dryer to its coughing tumble. That was the order of the world downstairs, and now he and Tommy were on top of that order, quiet as thieves in the second-floor hallway. They reached his bedroom, and Tommy closed the door behind them. Mills saw his own dried blood spots by the foot of the bed. The star-constellation sheets had been removed, replaced by a constellation of NBA logos.

Posters of successful black men—glistening basketball players; hooded, gold-chained rappers—covered the walls. Tommy leaned down and worked the combination on his safe. He took out a room-temperature beer and opened it, gulping down half the can. He pulled his windbreaker off and threw it on the bed.

"You have my flask, don't you?" he said without turning around.

"Yeah. It's in my room."

"It's not your room. It's Paul Benchley's room. You're just a visitor here. No one knows who you are." Tommy seemed to make that distinction for his own peace of mind. That fact was worth more to him than it was to Mills.

"So where's the book?" was all he could think to say.

"Is that what you want?" Tommy turned around and snapped off the can's metal tab. He pressed his thumb against the broken ring. His face was red from crying, but the tears had stopped. The blood under his skin brought out the yellow of his hair, a cartoonish yellow, a crayon's idea of blond. Tommy's eyes fixed on him, their blues as shallow as they had always been but deep enough to accommodate an unspent sorrow. "I know what you want. What you've been waiting around for. Mills milling around for scraps. Is that why they named you that? Whoever named you did a good job." Tommy was too untethered for the insult to sting. He leaned against his desk, curling his fingers behind him on the edge of the wood, as if he were bracing himself against an impending acceleration of the Earth. Mills swore he could feel its rotation shift. He thought of astronauts in retirement jumping around their Florida living rooms, trying to free themselves from gravity again.

"What happened? Was it something you found out about in that book?"

"Don't pretend you care." Tommy smiled coldly. "I know why you're up here."

"Why am I up here?" Mills knew why he was up here. Or he thought he did. His reasons had changed, a motivational shuffle in his heart and underwear.

"How long are you going to stay in Orient?"

"Not long," Mills lied. He planned to stay for as long as Paul would let him, but it was unwise right now to give Tommy an indeterminate timetable.

"Good. I figured." Tommy widened the stance and took a teeth-filtered breath. "So it doesn't matter, right?" His lip snarled. "Go on. If this is what you want, fine. I dare you." Even desperate to perform an act that he couldn't undo, Tommy stuck to the jingoisms of adolescence.

"Dare me?"

"Are you just going to stand there and repeat everything I say?" His voice was slick with momentum, though his body seemed frozen in place. Tommy waited with the tense posture of a man who had climbed into a lion's pen. Mills froze in the center of the room, presumably the lion that didn't know what to make of the unusual food source. Tommy's voice erupted. "What? You too scared? You're a pussy, Mills. You know that. Go on. You have my permission. There won't be another time."

"I don't think I—" Mills stalled.

"Yes, you do. It's them that don't want you to."

"Are you asking me—"

"Just shut up before I change my mind."

Mills stepped forward. Tommy swiveled his chin, as if rejecting a kiss before it was even offered. The refusal broke Mills's sympathy, and absent of sympathy, he found the courage to shove his hand against the zipper of Tommy's pants. He felt the spongy bulge of delicate instruments. Blood rushed to his head, his vision numb and starry as if it were on some sort of time delay from reality. When he unsnapped the top button, he was shocked by how easily it opened. He consulted Tommy's face one last time. Tommy squinted, took a breath, flicked his tongue across his overlapping front teeth, and brought his head to rest against the shelf above his desk. Mills dropped to his knees and unzipped Tommy's pants.

Missing kids. Mills didn't know why, as he leaned on his knees and hooked his fingers over the waistline of Tommy's jeans, he thought of missing children. Kids missing for years, for decades; kids who went out on bike rides or on walks to the store and never returned. Kids on milk cartons and on billboard posters in the last picture taken of them, "Have you seen this child?" though the picture was ten years old and the kid, if alive, wouldn't look like that now. All their parents had left was a description: "Last seen wearing gray sweatpants, a green T-shirt, blue size nine Air Jordans, white socks," as if the clothes were what the parents wanted back because they couldn't have their child. Tommy wore blue jeans, a yellow T-shirt, black Converses, brown socks, and even as Mills lowered Tommy's jeans he could not imagine the body underneath them.

Mills pulled the pants to Tommy's kneecaps. Hair flurried around the bone and disappeared up his thighs. The skin turned from tan to white, like the sand on a beach when the tide went out. He lifted Tommy's shirt to find a matching trail of hair swirling around his stomach. Mills tugged the underwear down until it fit into the valley of his jeans. Tommy's penis bobbed like an animal that had been exposed from under a rock, moving clumsily without the protection of its hiding place. His pubic hair was a gnarled yellow, like the burnt edge of a fried egg. His penis shot upward, uncircumcised. Mills opened his mouth.

Not a missing kid at all, but a young man right in front of him, alive and well. Mills slowly rocked his head, acclimating his tongue and teeth. Tommy took over the task of holding up his shirt, the expression of his face strangely neutral, almost scientific, as he stared down. He whimpered and timidly pressed his hand on the back of Mills's head. This is what Tommy wanted. And what Mills had wanted. He kept reminding himself of that as he dredged his glands for spit. *This is what I wanted, since that first day on the lawn.* But it was hard work, his neck muscles straining, his knees fatigued from the weight of holding himself up, his tongue feeling a slight uncertainty, which caused him to draw his lips tighter and quicken his rhythm. Mills's foot kicked the desk chair. Sunlight found its way across the carpet. A car alarm bleated down the block. It was hard work. It was what he wanted.

Tommy lifted his shirt over his head, until it stretched around the back of his neck but still sleeved his arms. His chest contracted with thin blue veins. Mills could taste brine mixing with his saliva, like the taste of expired Mountain Dew, and, with each breath through his nose, he smelled tinny sweat and soap. Maybe in all of the labored breathing he didn't hear the footstep on the stairs, but Tommy did. Tommy suddenly shoved him on the shoulders, and Mills fell backward on his knees. From his seventeen years inhabiting the house, Tommy instinctively calibrated the exact amount of time between foot on stair and hand at door. He wrestled his shirt over his head, and waddled, jean-shackled, to the window, making safe distance. He stood next to the open safe, motioning Mills to get to his feet while he yanked his underwear back up around his hips.

As Mills rose, he saw Jeff Trader's journal lying in the safe. His blood, which had traveled in so many directions in the last ten minutes, stalled in his throat.

"Can you at least give me—"

"Definitions," Tommy hissed. "That didn't mean—"

The bedroom door swung open, rearranging the shadows across the floor. Mills had assumed Tommy had locked the door. How could he not? A teenager who kept such minor secrets in a safe and a big secret out in the open in an unlocked room. Pam Muldoon gazed in, asking, "What is going on in here?" She looked directly at her son. His underwear was on, his T-shirt tucked into the elastic, but his jeans were still balled around his knees. Pam looked around, confused, and then saw Mills on the other side of the room. "What are you doing in my house? You are forbidden to be in my house!"

Tommy glared at him. Mills's lips hurt when he tried to move them. He stood in the gray light of the bedroom, unsure of his place.

"Mom, calm down," Tommy said, lifting his pants and struggling with the button. "Nothing's going on. Jesus, can you knock first?"

"Oh, something is going on!" she shouted, her voice trembling. She stared at Mills almost hopefully, as if he might provide an answer, as if he could protect her. "What are you doing in here? What made you think you could come up here?"

"Stop it," Tommy whined.

"I will not stop it." Her fingers squeezed her forearms so tightly they yellowed. No, she wasn't looking at him like he could help her. She was looking at him like someone had left a gate open at a house in California and he had run two thousand miles across the country to come sniffing around her family. "I'm thinking about your future," she said to her son. "And this kid doesn't have one."

"Shut up," Tommy screamed.

Mills was too stunned to ask for the journal now. The situation had moved past any chance of getting what he'd come for. He would be lucky to get out of the house without being hit.

"For God's sake, why were your pants down?"

Mills knocked against Pam's elbow as he raced out of the room. He rounded the hall and skidded down the steps, his left shoulder sliding along the lime green wall. He opened the front door, triggering the blare of an alarm, and broke into a headlong sprint. He didn't look back, afraid he'd discover that Pam Muldoon was chasing behind him as if trying to get her son back.

He ran into Paul's house, up the steps, and into his bedroom. He stripped off his clothes and fell against the beams of the floor. The wood took the beats of his heart, and the cement took the beats of the wood, and the soil took the beats of the cement. Kids in the world went missing every day and so did parents. Mills knew that no one was looking for him. No one was waiting for a phone call with news about where he was. So he delivered the news to himself. *I'm here. I'm alive.* He gave his excitement to the floor.

CHAPTER 15

W hen the rain stopped, the seagulls stalked the road. They flapped their black-tipped wings on the cement and left the trees to inland birds. Mills kneeled on the sofa cushions, staring out the parlor window. He wasn't there to bird-watch. He was scanning the front lawn for angry Muldoons to appear and pronounce their hatred of him, the violator of their blameless son. He half expected Pam or Bryan to ring the doorbell to have it out with Paul. Mills would be given fifteen minutes to pack his bag before being put on the first train back to New York. An hour passed, and then another. Paul worked on his laptop in the dining room, oblivious to the coming threat.

Paul asked him more than once why he was looking out the window. "Are you waiting for a delivery? Are there birds falling from the sky?" Paul left his chair to examine the view himself. "Seriously, Mills, enough. You're making me nervous. There's nothing out there."

Mills had never told a foster parent about his sexuality. The secret swam inside of him like a great white shark that couldn't escape the channel of his windpipe. It wasn't that he was ashamed of being gay; in fact, it was one of the few dependable shelters he knew in the chaos of temporary homes, like a prayer he could recite every night in any unfamiliar bedroom or over any badly cooked meal. It simply made no sense to come out multiple times to multiple sets of foster families, each overcrowded kitchen falling silent at the news, each eye staring interminably into the distance where other people's messes began to undermine their own sense of order. So, early on, Mills toughened the parts of him that were weak, the weakest parts being the quickest to callus. He acquired the grunts and skirting eyes of secret-keepers. His plan since childhood had always been to move east to the city where no one cared what men did with each other.

He had now overshot that city by one hundred miles, and Paul stood in the center of his living room, waiting for an answer.

"I was over at Tommy's," he started.

"Tommy's," Paul said.

"Yeah, and I don't know. His parents don't like me."

"I told you not to worry about the Muldoons."

"Just for the time I've spent with their son. Like it's my fault he gets into things they don't approve of. I'm not sure there's such thing as a bad influence, not if you want the same things."

Mills glanced at Paul with a painful smile, and he was sure Paul knew, understood, right then. Paul let out a whistle and started clearing the dishes from lunch. Twelve oyster shells circled the plate. Paul had eaten six of them, but Mills had lost his appetite for quivering mucus.

"We're not talking about drugs here, are we?" Paul asked. His face was an unreliable barometer.

"No, not drugs, of course not," Mills replied. "I told you, I'm done with that." How clean did he have to come? Should he tell Paul about the hand job he gave to a thirty-eight-year-old truck driver on a highway in Arizona? About the young, handsome hitchhiker with low-lidded eyes from Fort Bragg, California, a guy about his own age named Millford Chevern, who took his virginity in a cornfield near the Nebraska border? It was a little late for confessions, and explicit details only confused the point. Mills sat on the sofa, cupping his mouth in his hand. "I hope you know I wouldn't consciously do anything to upset you. Or ruin your standing with your neighbors. You've been so kind to me."

Paul didn't hesitate. He rested the plate on the coffee table and leaned over the couch. "There's no trouble with me. Got that?" he said. "There's nothing you could do that would make you unwelcome here. So please, for the love of God, get away from the window. I'm willing to buy a television right now if you promise not to go near that window for the rest of the night."

For a second, their eyes locked, as if they were test-driving each other for a future they were both too old to share: son to father and father to son. Paul held the stare until Mills broke it. If other details about himself had been a lie, this truth went deeper than the fact of his real name. Paul carried the dishes into the kitchen, and Mills got up to stack kindling into the fireplace. The fire ate the logs.

It was the sound of Beth's car in the driveway that brought Mills racing back to the window. She slammed her car door and proceeded up the porch steps. Her clothes were rumpled and her skin was iridescent, glossy as porcelain left out in the rain. Still, Beth had the confident walk of someone beautiful, the stride of someone who had been told she was attractive early in life: even if the beauty eventually faded, the confidence remained. Mills opened the front door before Beth had time to ring the bell.

She gave him a tired smile. "Sorry it took me so long to come back for you," she said. He returned the smile, aggressively festive, fearing at any moment that she'd ask for the book.

"No problem. I wasn't just waiting around. Paul's kept me busy. Do you want to go for another drive?"

"A drive? Where?" she asked. The sun had descended behind the roof, darkening the houses across the street.

"I was thinking Jeff Trader's." Mills felt the need to get far away from Youngs Road for an hour. "I want to make sure those animals have been fed."

"I'm not sure we should go back there."

"Please," he whispered.

She nodded reluctantly and told him to bring a raincoat. "And the book," she said. "I want to take it to the police. For what it's worth."

"There's a problem," he mumbled. "I don't have it right now." He fidgeted his foot on the welcome mat. "I'll explain in the car."

Beth's jaw hung open, so wide that he could see three silver fillings. "What do you mean you don't have it? I gave it to you to keep safe. That's why I'm here. Mills, I need that book."

"It's not far from here, and I'll get it back. Please let me explain in the car."

She turned in irritation and headed down the porch. He studied the Muldoons' home as he followed her, searching its windows for internal developments. A silver station wagon careened up the street, slowing in front of Paul's driveway and stopping a few feet beyond it. The late afternoon breeze carried droplets from the Sound, cold and side-winding and unbraiding the leafless branches. Beth and Mills had almost made it to her Nissan when he heard the yawn of a screen door, and even before he lifted his head, he knew he'd find her marching toward him across her lawn.

Pam Muldoon had changed her clothes in the hours since he last saw her. Her brown hair was tied back, and she wore an Orient sweatshirt emblazoned with beach chairs and a candy-cane umbrella, the kind that must be sold in Greenport gift shops for tourists who never crossed the causeway to fact-check their purchases. Her mouth was etched with wrinkles. She pointed her finger as she advanced.

"You," Pam Muldoon said. Beth stopped cold, and Mills knocked into her. "Don't you walk away. I want to make things perfectly clear."

"Hello, Mrs. Muldoon," Beth called, trying to lighten the mood or merely resorting to the tone used to dispatch neighbors with an economy of words.

"Hello, Beth," Pam responded, losing her mark for a moment to offer a dismissive nod. "This isn't about you. This is about him."

"About Mills?"

"Let's get into your car," he said.

"Oh, no you don't," Pam spat, halting a foot from the driveway. "I don't know what you were doing up there. But *you*. Are *not allowed*. *Anywhere* near my house. Or my children. Is that understood?"

Heat coursed through him. His body was standing still, but in his mind he was running away at high speed, going somewhere up above him, into the sky. The station wagon idled by the sidewalk. Mills turned to see Paul stepping onto the porch.

"That's a little harsh," Beth said, wrinkling her nose. "We aren't going anywhere near your house. I'm taking him to my car."

"Beth, I'll ask you to keep out of this. Where is Paul? I want to talk to him about this abuse of my property and the endangerment of my children."

"Ma'am, I think you're overreacting," Mills said, staring directly at her even as he drifted behind Beth's elbow. "I'm sorry if you got the wrong idea."

A simple apology, however halfhearted, was the worst offense. A cable snapped in the bridge of Pam Muldoon's composure; then another cable broke, and the bridge began to crumble. She jammed her foot on the gravel, pointing her finger at his nose. Beth raised her hand and knocked Pam's wrist aside, a gesture of protection that surprised Pam as much as it did Mills.

"There's no need to point your finger at him," Beth stammered, clearly also surprised by her own reaction. "He's an adult. He doesn't need to be treated like a child."

"That's precisely my point," Pam cried. "He's an adult, freeloading in the house next door to mine, and he's a danger to my son. He's a danger, and I'm not going to sit by while Tommy is victimized by some hooligan who was never given permission, not by me and not by Bryan—"

"Wait, what exactly happened?" Beth asked.

"Oh, plenty," Pam wheezed. "Or plenty if I hadn't been there to stop it."

Paul's feet lumbered down the porch. His shoulders were pitched back, a wider, taller Paul than Mills had ever witnessed, his freshly shaven lip pursed, his eyes blinded by lenses the color of frost.

"Good, there you are. Paul, I have been a very patient neighbor, but this is too much even for me."

"I think we all need to calm down," Paul said, placing his hand in front of Mills's chest. Mills didn't move a muscle. Under those muscles, rebellion was breaking loose. He felt suffocated by the mother in front of him and embarrassed by Paul's display of protection. Was this the kind of a desperate family scenario he had avoided in his years as a foster kid—a child to talk over, a pawn at the mercy of squabbling grown-ups? "I think you need to stop yelling at my guest," Paul said.

"Guest," Pam repeated. Her anger was free-floating, a molecular rage collecting all of them in her storm. "I am not asking you, I'm telling you. This kid, this *adult*, has been in my home, up in the bedroom of my son, and I won't stand for it."

The screen door yawned again. Tommy darted from the house, striding halfway across the lawn before stopping with his arms crossed.

"Mom, stop it," he whined, already bored by the subject, worn out by the fatigue of managing hostile forces. Mills had found him so beautiful earlier that afternoon, a rare specimen he had wanted so much that he would have given his pinkie for what they had done in his bedroom. Where had that beauty gone? Tommy was wearing the same yellow T-shirt and the same jeans that Mills had gently unbuttoned, camouflaged by the shadows of the oak trees and the gritty brick of his family's ugly, turquoise-trimmed house. He looked like any young man haunting his own front yard, reckless in his pastime, kind when convenient, living beyond his emotional means, doomed to a life of crossed arms in the safety of his property. Mills smiled at him, trying to find the young man from before. Tommy looked at him coldly. "Mom, I was changing! Upstairs, I was changing! That's all!"

"That's what you might have *thought* you were doing, but I know what this kid was thinking."

"That's enough," Paul said. "You have no right to come out here—"

"I have every right," Pam shouted. "I have every right in the world. And I will call the police next time before I have to come over here again. You don't let your *guest* get anywhere near my house or my children. Am I making myself clear?"

The doors of the silver station wagon opened. Sarakit Herrig climbed out, squinting up at the driveway as her two youngest children, pretty and fragile with plump lips and boneless cheeks, got out of the backseat. They were wearing fluorescent sweat suits, hot pinks and four-alarm oranges, hugging bright green backpacks. Their black hair was cut in the shape of cereal bowls. The smaller boy was crying. "I want to go to the mall! I don't want to play with Theo. Please please please."

"We will go to the mall this weekend," Sarakit promised, pulling her youngest by the arm. Her attention was caught by the four figures huddled against the side of the yard.

"You're on my property," Paul whispered to Pam. "Please don't come onto my property. Not if you're going to behave like this."

Pam's face melted, a tight ball of newsprint slowly losing its shape.

"I'm a mother," she said in anguish. "I have three children that I've raised in this house next to yours for twenty years. I helped your mother as much as I could when she was sick. This isn't Manhattan, Paul. You've lived in the city too long to realize what this neighborhood means. He can do whatever he wants in the rest of the world. I have no problem with that. I don't interfere with the goings-on of strangers somewhere else. But not on my property. Not with my son. Do you even know where he comes from?"

Paul responded in a voice that could have been asking for a stick of butter. "I'm sorry you feel that way. You've said your piece. Now please step off my property."

Theo ran from the screen door, bypassing by his older brother as he charged his play dates with a stick. Sarakit's two boys shrunk from the impending blows. Pam lifted her hands up, realized that Sarakit was watching, then stepped theatrically across the division of gravel and grass. In that moment, Mills understood the meaning of private property: this side is mine and that side is yours. On this side, he was protected; on the Muldoons' side he could be arrested or shot. It was as if all his rights evaporated as soon as the gravel ended and the grass began.

As Pam retreated she assumed the posture of a harried mother. She approached Sarakit and the three children on the sidewalk and palmed Theo's head for stability. Tommy had disappeared.

"That didn't go well," Paul said, shaken. He looked at Beth. "I'm sorry about that. I suppose she'll be asking for background checks on anyone I invite into my house in the future."

Beth shrugged. "The Muldoons were like that with my mom too. Once they decided they didn't like her, they just went after her until she moved."

Mills no longer wanted to drive to Jeff Trader's house. He no longer wanted to stay in Orient. Maybe the best solution was a train ticket back to New York.

"She'll come to her senses," Paul said, clapping Mills's shoulder. "But maybe it's best if you keep off their yard for a while. Were you two going somewhere?"

"Just for a drive," Beth said. She looked at Mills. "Are you coming?"

Beth didn't say a word as she drove toward Main Road. She waited until she made the left turn before hazarding the obvious question.

"What did you do to get her going like that?"

Mills decided Beth could handle the answer. He decided he could handle speaking it.

"I gave her son a blow job."

Beth doubled over against the steering wheel, laughing through the bends in the road. "Well, no wonder. And here I was defending you." She let a minute of driving cushion the conversation. "Why didn't you tell me you liked guys?"

"Why would you think I didn't?"

"No reason. But I could have told you that you picked the wrong guy to get hung up on. The Muldoons aren't nice people."

"I'm not hung up on him," he grumbled. "And why shouldn't I do what I want? Don't you?" She didn't reply, and Mills took her silence for judgment. He hated the idea that she might feel sorry for him, like he needed her to protect him from the nastier truths of the world. "Maybe I'm not nice. Maybe I don't have to be."

The car sped across the empty farmland. Beth at least had driving to keep her busy. Mills picked at the rubber of the window frame. When the quiet grew too uncomfortable, he turned on the radio and searched the stations.

"We're having a party on Friday night," Beth said. "My husband is, actually. But you're welcome to come. It might be good for you to see some other young people—youngish, anyway. My age. Orient has other types than just the Muldoons. There are plenty of livelier, more progressive people out here if you dig deep enough."

"You mean gay? Just say the word if that's what you mean." It was the first time he'd said the word aloud to refer to himself. He took a slow breath. Miles from Youngs Road, he felt the anger leaking out of him and regretted attacking Beth when all she had been trying to do was help.

"Yes, gay people too," she said. "What, you think that makes you special?"

"Kind of."

"Well, you should come anyway. If you don't like it, it's not a long walk home. Now, where's Jeff Trader's book?"

"You aren't going to be happy when I tell you. Tommy took it. It's locked in his bedroom safe. Which wouldn't be a huge problem if I weren't forbidden from entering their house ever again."

"You have to get it back," she demanded.

"I will."

"I mean it. I don't care how you figure it out, but you have to." She glanced at him. "You have to do it for me. I need that book."

"You really think it matters? That it has something to do with those deaths?"

She stayed silent for a minute, staring ahead. The dark sky was pocked with coast lights.

"You know what I found out?" she said. "That photo we found in the book. It's of a woman named Holly Drake. I was at her house today and saw her standing in front of her rosebushes. Red hair, yellow tracksuit."

"Did you ask her about it?"

"No. What was I supposed to say?"

"Why did Jeff Trader consider you the devil? Were you responsible for drowning a caretaker who no one seemed to care about?"

Beth was too aggravated to use her turn signal.

"You didn't know Magdalena. So I can understand if you think I'm being ridiculous. All I'm asking is that you get that book back. She begged me to find it, and I need to respect that wish. She was killed because of something she knew about Jeff. It's my duty to give that book to the police. Without it, I have nothing."

Mills decided to help her, or, at the very least, to humor her. There was no harm in pushing her suspicions a little farther into the darkness. He rubbed his legs as he told her what he had already discovered on Jeff Trader's pages. "It seems like he was writing down secrets—or upsetting things, anyway—about the homeowners he served. Maybe he was killed because of something he found out. Maybe there's a secret in there that one of your neighbors didn't want to get out."

"You've got to get that book back," she said.

A love song came on the radio, and Beth changed the station. A weather report predicted a nor'easter moving up the eastern coast, consolidating squalls. The forecaster estimated a 70 percent chance of snow on the eastern end of Long Island within the next five days.

"I've never seen snow fall," Mills said as he watched the silver fields dissolve in the dusk.

"It can get bad out here. When it snows in Orient, it's the quietest place on earth."

"Are you happy living out here? Happy with your husband, with your—" He did not say *life*, because life seemed too fixed a word to describe as happy or not. Life was more like the houses they passed than the bodies inside of them.

Beth dug her nails into the steering wheel. "I moved out here thinking it would bring us closer together. Or me closer to myself. But I don't think either of those things happened." She quickly touched his knee. "I'm not trying to make you feel sorry for me. I guess I'd just forgotten how settled everything is outside of the city. You can see the sun rise on the bay and set on the Sound, and that's the whole day, there it is, and another and another. I wasn't prepared to be so settled."

Mills hadn't grown up in a settled place. Modesto was the coin-return cup of America, valley of the spare-change people, all nickels and dimes who had tumbled like leftovers out of a country that had no use for them, with their hacking desert coughs and dirt from other places shoved under their nails. They were spinning around in the heat, waiting to be collected and counted up. Into what, he didn't know. But Beth was right. There were no people like that in Orient.

"Are you going to start a family here? That's what you do when you're married at your age out here. That's the point of it all, right?"

Beth turned to him, half-startled, and stared at his face, not unlike drivers who picked him up as a hitchhiker and proceeded to guess his worst intentions for the first few miles.

"I don't think so," she said.

They drove down Beach Lane in the dark and pulled into Jeff Trader's driveway. A real estate sign hung by the curb, swinging in the wind. Beth waited in the car as Mills crept around the mobile home to the barn. The sheep were no longer in the stables. The bowls he had left for the cats had been cleared from the step and thrown away.

PART 2

The New People

Winter makes alterations. It shrinks windows in their frames, freezes water to stress the pipes, and attacks the joints with arthritic compression. It clears the fields of autumn buds and the houses of lingering guests. Lights shine palely in windows through the reflection of frost, and smoke issues from chimneys, blown sideways like steam from moving trains. Storm windows are latched by hook and nail over openings that once let in flies and sun.

In the village of Orient, the unsettled settle, and the deer hunters, bright as bloodstains in their jumpsuits, tag and field-dress their prizes with the speed of emergency surgery. Winter turns the sea first copper and then black, and, before the ice silences it, an anxious blue as it rubs against the shoreline. Smaller trawls and fishing boats are rare. Sails can't hold the wind, and motors smoke from the strain of the current. The dirt is concrete, and the houses are liquid, white hides over shifting animals. Not-too-distant Greenport becomes cosmopolitan, and "out there" means over the causeway, where the lawns and beaches lie barren. Winter runs like a streak of fire, brightening all of the houses before they go dark.

It used to be that if a house wasn't sold by October, it would sit empty until March. It used to be that in these months, Orient was most like itself, a prudent clapboard village capable of weathering ocean storms, having weathered them countless times before. It used to be that everything had already happened here; now it seemed like very little had. An early winter storm front was headed from the south, due north toward the eastern fingers. The new people didn't follow the weather, and so they changed what Orient was.

Gavril Catargi wouldn't listen to the forecast and refused to cancel the party on account of snow. Gavril became practically Ceauşescuan on the matter of party preparations. Beth had known about this eccentricity ever since planning the reception of their wedding, which she assumed had been under her jurisdiction until Gavril pushed her aside, redrew the menu, and moved the entire event from a friend's loft in Chelsea to a private garden in Sutton Place. Beth had let him take the reins, having grown so tired of parties by the time of their wedding that she barely worked up the energy to attend her own. It seemed to her that there was nothing so debilitating to productivity in New York as all the birthday parties alone. *It's my birthday; Here are the plans for my Kubrick–themed birthday on Central Park West; MY BIRTHDAY midnight to 4:00 A.M. at the Mop Cellar, open bar until 3:00 A.M.!!!!*—the invitations flooded her e-mail like some cyber virus bent on crashing her sanity. Attending a birthday party in New York was a gauge of friendship, never mind that she only saw most of those friends once a year on their birthdays. Orient had offered a welcome break, a paradise of uncelebrated days; only because Gavril had yet to throw a party, in all of their months here, did she feel she owed him one now.

They had spent all of Friday cleaning the house. Sweeping, sponging, pulling out dead flowers from the mulch beds, color co-ordinating the bookshelves, prepping her husband's special dish of *jumari*, which looked like mutant doughnuts and tasted like mildewed pig. Gavril would have made a marvelous labor-camp leader: *Scrub harder, Beth*, and *No, no, no, if the toilet water is coming up bubbles there is too much soap residue in the bowl*, and *Not the brown quilt, the blue one, to match the blinds and the Elizabeth Peyton*. The experience gave Beth a newfound respect for Gavril's art assistants in the city. At noon, Gavril drove into Greenport to pick up the alcohol. His absence gave Beth a chance to confront the mailman.

"You want to stop all your mail?" He had a closely trimmed beard and teeth the yellow of a stamp's underside.

"No," she said. "Just the ones about babies." She shuffled through the stack and pulled out a waxy circular for No-Bumpy-Baby Car Seats. "I didn't sign up for these. I don't want them."

"Well, miss, it's not illegal for merchants to send coupons."

"I know it isn't *illegal*," she said. "But it's harassing."

"Miss. It's also not illegal to throw them out."

"Yes, but you see, I really, *really* don't want them."

"Want them?" The notion confused him. "I'm not sure anyone *wants* most mail. But I have to say, commercial bulk mail is what keeps the post office in business. Without it, in this day and age, the mail system wouldn't exist."

"But if all I'm getting is bulk mail I don't want, what's the point?" His brow furrowed.

"I suppose the point is that you might get some letters or packages mixed in that you *do* want, or didn't know you were going to receive. Miss, my advice is to stop giving out your address."

"I didn't give out my address," she stammered. "These companies have targeted me without my permission. You see, I don't have a baby. But all this baby stuff keeps arriving. Some of it even says I'm pregnant. It's upsetting."

"I'm a carrier. My job is to deliver, not to determine what you do or don't want. As long as it's sent, I have to bring it."

"But can't I block certain senders?"

"If everyone could block junk mail, there'd be no mail at all. For god's sake, some people appreciate my job."

He trudged off with his bloated shoulder bag; neither rain nor snow nor heat nor sense could stop him. Beth rested her forehead against the door, worn out by the existentialism of the postal service. She sifted through the mail, pulling all the baby reminders and putting them in a garbage bag, which she hid carefully in the hall closet behind bulky coats and unused rain boots.

When Gavril returned with the crates of liquor, he went around the ground floor, hanging artwork he had received as gifts from fellow artists. He was certain they would expect to find their works featured prominently on the walls. "We can take them down tomorrow," he said. Out they came, paintings and collages and grim sculptural assemblages of feathers, metal, and glue, like photos of unloved relatives displayed for the duration of a family reunion.

As Beth was arranging the bottles in the kitchen, Gavril rushed in, hurtling like a trapped sparrow around the room. He held a letter in his hand, one she had left under a candle on the first night they had moved in last April. She had written it while standing amid their unpacked boxes. It had been a warm night. The windows had let in the smell of magnolias and grass, and they had built a fire in the fireplace because it seemed a waste to wait until winter.

"Do you remember when you wrote this?" Gavril asked, waving the folded paper. His brown eyes had softened, as if that small memory from April meant more to him than all of those he had brought from Romania. "You thought lighting the candle would bring us luck."

She took the letter. It was in her neat handwriting of six months ago, more sprightly in its cursive than she was capable of writing now.

On the first night in our new house (and my old one) I hope this fresh start brings us happiness and peace. I hope we can start a family here, and that our child (the first of two, Gavril says five) will be as lucky as I was to grow up in a safe, warm pocket of the world with every direction open to her or him (Gavril says him). We are fortunate people. We need only this roof and each other. The rest can be sold or stolen or lost.

Who was this woman from six months ago? Beth didn't recognize her, not even as the husband she wrote about was breathing into her ear. The letter was written by a different person altogether. And the letter only spoke of what had been lost between the sending and receiving. The woman who wrote it had not lived in Orient since high school, and had not yet lived in Orient through this past summer and fall. That woman had not telephoned Planned Parenthood, as Beth had done this morning, to schedule an appointment.

Gavril slipped his arms around her waist. As always before a shower, he smelled of sage, the herb burned in new houses to clear out ghosts. He kissed her neck from ear to collarbone. If she could write the letter now, she thought, it would read differently: *Sell it off, give it away, just go west to the city and stay there—it was a mistake to come back. There is no fresh start. All there is here is doubt.*

"Read it to me," Gavril said.

"I don't want to. It sounds stupid."

"It's not stupid. It's perfect."

"I sound like a child. It would have been better luck to burn it."

"The best things are said in simple words."

Gavril was hugging what he didn't know they already had, and he would never know because she wasn't going to keep it. She struggled to turn around in his arms. He pressed his palms against her back to bring her closer.

"Should we relight the candle tonight? And keep the letter there during the party?" He didn't seem bothered when she didn't answer. "I will be so busy soon, making the new work for my show. You will have to remind me about making a baby. But don't let me forget. I need to be successful for him. I don't want him to think his father is a lazy man who lived for free in his mother-in-law's house." Beth moved from his arms, picking up two vodka bottles so he couldn't pin her against the counter.

"Ah, at least you can drink tonight. No drinking when you're pregnant. And no driving around all day on the ice." She thought of what a prison he would make this house if her stomach expanded beyond her waist. "Should we prepare the guest bedroom for Nathan? By midnight he'll be too drunk to drive." His birthmark relaxed to the neutrality of Hawaii. "What's the matter? You're giving me your unhappy look."

"I don't mean to," she said.

"All is okay with us, yes? We're good?"

"We're good," she said, returning the bottles to the table. "Everything's fine. I'll make up the room. We might have a few overnight guests tonight if the storm is as bad as they're predicting."

Beth wore a dress she had inherited from her mother, a white cotton shift with eyelet lace around the hem in the shape of wildflowers. There were a few water stains on the back that the dry cleaner hadn't been able to remove, but the front had remained unsoiled since the 1970s, and its shape concealed whatever weight she had gained in the last months. None of the guests would think to study her body for signs of pregnancy, except of course for Luz Wilson, a professional observer of other people's weaknesses.

The name Luz was originally pronounced *looz*, but its bearer had changed it to *luhz* at the age of eighteen, when she moved into the city from Trenton, New Jersey. During her first semester at Columbia, the school had experienced a blight of *luz* graffiti tags around campus. All these years later, Luz Wilson was a successful portrait painter whose personality and opinions were as confrontational as her work. She had championed Beth's paintings, an unsolicited endorsement for which Beth was grateful, though it came only after the negative reviews in New York had rendered her work noncompetitive. Not that there were many similarities: where Beth's paintings were careful and precise, as if to let their subjects speak for themselves, Luz's portraits—of prison guards, accused rapists, smug dewy children of the obscenely rich—were executed in the angry hand of their maker, as if each sitter had been soaked in formaldehyde. Luz's *opinions* were infamous even among Gavril's opinionated artist crowd, generally colored by whatever academic theorist she was reading at the time; Beth knew how quickly Luz could turn even a simple cotton dress into an object lesson in Lacan, Žižek, Badiou, Butler, Althusser, or her trusted fallback, Foucault.

Beth spent a moment at the full-length mirror manufacturing the Luzian dialogue that was sure to rain down on her by the end of the night: *You've worn your mother's dress to repeat her sins, not to emulate her, but to destroy her by regulating her sins as common values in the hegemony of feminine virtue. You discredit by redeeming. You parrot her to ensure her silence. The dress isn't an inheritance, it's warfare against the woman who gave birth to you.* The very exercise gave Beth a headache.

There was little question as to why Luz Wilson, a child of factory workers—"a screw factory and, yes, all connotations apply"—had achieved such prominence in the art world. It wasn't simply the camera-ready beauty of her African-Chinese heritage (cheekbones like onions, eyelids like envelopes, skin like unsweetened iced tea, black hair worn short and wrenched into cornrows that made the eye water just to look at them). Luz had serious talent, and she also possessed the ability to antagonize. Even the press releases on her shows read like grad school dissertations. She posed nude, but for construction boots, in her husband's art photographs. She boycotted museum shows that didn't include an equal representation of women, but boycotted women-only survey shows, finding them sanctimonious. In New York, Luz hosted parties in her loft that included famous hip-hop artists, whom she alone called by their Christian names. And she seemed fluent in a wide variety of languages—among them, to Beth's annoyance, Berlitz Romanian.

Luz's husband, the artist Nathan Crimp, was a handsome, chalk-thin New Englander born not so much from parents as mated bank accounts. (His grandfather had invented the polymer seal for the shoelace aglet.) Nathan feigned a savant's naïveté ("I think my favorite color really is purple," he'd say feelingly. "It's sad and also cheerful"), but beneath the childlike guile he was just as ambitious as Luz. They seemed happy as a couple, their temperaments balancing each other, their hands often reaching out silently at parties, always taken instantly by the other.

Luz and Nathan were Gavril's friends; to Beth they were neighbors. A month after she and Gavril moved to Orient, Luz and Nathan purchased the old farmhouse inn, with its prismatic views of the Sound and a private dock equipped with a Stingray speedboat. The purchase had one-upped Gavril, but Nathan hastened to defend himself against complaints of ostentation. "Richard Serra's had a house in Orient for years. You aren't the first one out here, my friend. And now we can visit each other constantly and get drunk." They did get drunk that summer, Gavril and Nathan, usually in the shallow end of the backyard pool, planning art manifestos that gave Beth ulcers to overhear. One July afternoon, Luz even tried to spark a female version of their husbands' male bonding, phoning Beth to ask if she'd like to sit for a portrait. "I thought you did portraits of people you hated," Beth replied. "I never said that. Who said that? You're projecting. So are you in?" Beth was not.

Luz Wilson exploited Orient the way all new settlers do, making it hers by reframing its past to her liking. She tracked down surviving descendants of old Orient families who no longer owned their estates—field farmers, mostly, and a few roughnecks who vivisected fish on the Greenport docks—and paid them one dollar more than minimum wage to come to her studio at the farmhouse to pose for her. "Don't you love it? A child of a slave and a Commie immigrant painting the master class in one of their dispossessed ancestral houses." Beth did not love it. Her family had been part of that master class.

Gavril and Nathan got wasted every Tuesday afternoon that summer, tanning themselves crimson in her mother's pool. The Orient year-rounders viewed them as savages, trying to steal the land from those to whom it properly belonged. And they looked like savages—Gavril, Nathan, Luz, the others, all of them that summer. They drank top-shelf and drove erratically and wore expensive clothes and did money dances around glittering pools whose slate basins were vacuumed by roving drones. They slicked their hair back, spread themselves across lounge chairs, and flung watermelon rinds on magazines.

And as they sat back, enjoying themselves, their reputations grew. Among Nathan Crimp's notable recent artworks:

"The Boiler Spoiler" (2011). A white canvas boiler jumpsuit, on which Crimp stenciled plot summaries revealing the endings of popular books, films, and TV shows such as "Harry Potter does not die" and "The creepy Martin son is the killer in *Dragon Tattoo*." Crimp described the work as "cultural anthrax" in a society "satisfied with controlled narratives." After wearing the jumpsuit around New York, he was repeatedly assaulted by passersby for ruining the plots. (ref. *Artforum*, December 2011).

"I'll Help You Get Your Green Card" (2012). Since green card candidates are forced to accumulate "press" to prove their value in the United States, Crimp created a monthly newspaper called "I'll Help You Get Your Green Card," profiling New York–area immigrants complete with hyperbolic texts on their acute societal importance ("The country will turn to anarchy without chef Sven Laggerholm's meatballs"), which they could then use in their citizenship applications. (Gavril Catargi was one of thirty participants.) (ref. *Art in America*, May 2012).

"This Sentence Is Negative" (2013). Using a mold of an AK-47 assault weapon, Crimp created a series of sculptures—some of them made of 14-karat gold, some of worthless pyrite. Collectors would not be told whether they were buying a work of massive monetary value or of fool's gold. "Bad taste or bad collecting strategy?" (ref. *The New York Times*, Roberta Smith, April 13, 2013).

"Dreams from My Grandfather" (2013–ongoing). In this performative work, Crimp trips over his own untied shoelaces at gallery openings and files a police report against the gallery for negligence. Lawsuits pending. "Are the supposedly free bastions of art galleries obliged to follow strict city zoning and fire codes? Can someone be made rich by the accident of a shoelace?" (ref. *New York* online, Jerry Saltz).

Luz and Nathan had used the money they made on their art to float the initial $4.1 million asking price of the old farmhouse inn and its forty-one untouched acres. Only when a second bidder emerged, tipping the price toward six million, did Nathan's family subsidize the difference. They paid for the property in cash.

"That's a nice dress," Luz said to Beth, cracking open a bottle of vodka at the kitchen counter. Beth waited, bracing herself for a follow-up lecture that didn't come. Luz, in a loose, blue, over-the-shoulder sweater, her lips painted orange, took a drag from her cigarette and acknowledged her painting that Gavril had hung an hour ago on the kitchen wall. "You put mine up, finally," she said with a knowing smile. "What about your work? You been painting?"

"No," Beth replied. She held out an empty glass toward the bottle. "Not too much, though. Just a sip."

"Just a sip," Luz repeated, laughing. "We don't have to compensate for the overconsumption of our husbands. I see Gavril turned the hot tub on. Is that an invitation to see me in my underwear?" She didn't wait for a response. "Tell me, how cold does it get out here in the winter?"

"Freezing," Beth said. "And it's only mid-October. Are you and Nathan planning on spending the entire winter in Orient?"

"It's an experiment we're conducting. Can we survive together in the middle of nowhere without delivery or a decent grocery store—or, in Nathan's case, a decent drug dealer—and find we're alive come spring?" She breathed out smoke and took a sip, pivoting an ice cube between her teeth. "Although I heard there was a murder out here. That caretaker. I guess it's not the peaceful dream community we were conned into believing it was when we bought the place."

"It might not have been murder," Beth said, trying to distance herself from the rumor.

"Poor man. Poor white men are the saddest. The burden of no excuses."

"You knew him?"

"Yeah." Luz crunched the ice cube and swallowed. "He came over and fixed things. You want something done, you hire local. Quite a talker, Jeff was. On and on and on."

"Really? You spoke to him?" Beth was flummoxed: in Luz's brief exposure to Orient, she had already made first-name headway into a community, *Beth's* community, that had so far resisted Beth Shepherd at every turn. "What about?"

"We made a deal that he'd drive to Riverhead to pick up paints for me. I lost five hundred dollars on his death. Never showed with the goods. And I wasn't the only artist he had that kind of arrangement with. Maybe someone robbed him. Or killed him for pocketing our hard-earned money." She took another gulp. "So why aren't you painting?"

"I'm not ready."

"Who's ready?" Her orange lips contorted. "Come on, what are you going to do with yourself if you don't get back to work? What will you end up being, Gavril's wife? *Tsk tsk tsk.*" She shook her head and stared at the bottom of her glass. "You're too smart for that. A waste of talent. Wasted talent is a woman standing behind a husband thinking she's his rock when all she really is is his step."

"I've been busy, Luz. And I've got all winter."

"Hmm. You've got hobbies, then?"

Beth thought about it. She had no hobbies. Before she quit her job copyediting for *Scientific Frontier*, she'd considered applying for an open position as a junior editor—until she saw all the résumés that had piled up, hundreds and hundreds, from ambitious recent college graduates with journalism degrees that were as useful in the current job market as Japanese fighting swords. On many résumés, there was a line at the bottom of the page reserved for hobbies: "golf, opera, meditation, maze topiary, Sudoku, YouTube movie spoofs." What were Beth's hobbies? Sitting still, reading the first paragraphs in the newspaper's art section, wasting gas. To call any of those activities hobbies was to turn the marrow of life into a pastime—which, she realized, was Luz's point.

"Nope, uh-uh. They aren't allowed. Tell her, Beth." Luz crooked a finger over her glass, a paint-scabbed nail as sharp as a switch-blade. "This is a party for adults. You have to leave immediately. Good-bye, Shelley. Lovely to see you." Beth turned to find Shelley Bass with her two-month-old infant nestled against her chest in a tie-dye sling. She'd traveled all the way from her rental in Peconic to be unwelcomed in the Shepherd kitchen. Shelley was a mixed-media artist of middling talent, her graying hair wrapped in a matching tie-dye scarf. She endured Luz's attack with a distressed smile: like the others, she was used to Luz's theatrics and suffered her with only mild impatience.

Beth greeted Shelley with a kiss on the cheek.

"I'm sorry I had to bring the baby. I won't stay long. Brent had business in the city, and I couldn't find a sitter."

"It's not a problem," Beth assured her. She performed the requi-site ten-second examination of the infant, cooing over how cute he was. Shelley's five-year-old daughter ran from behind her mother's legs, hoisting an iPad over her head.

"Look what I drew!" the little girl shouted.

Luz reached for the vodka to refresh her drink. "If I'd known it was going to be this kind of party I would have stayed home."

"I drew a person," the girl said proudly. Every drawing was a miracle at that age. She raised the iPad to reveal a blotch of beige skin with black dots for the orifices and digital lines streaming from its crown.

"I see the art world's bad influence is trickling down to the younger generation," Luz said. "It looks like one of Isaiah's canvases, tortured for no good reason. Lord, I pity the generation raised on post-abstract art."

"Don't tell her that. Come here, honey." Shelley reached out for her daughter's hand. "Go sit in the corner and draw more people for us. Mommy will find you a snack." The girl scampered off, her tie-dye socks slipping across the wood.

"And you all match," Luz said.

Beth and Shelley exchanged agonized glances. Shelley picked up the orange juice carton and used the mixer as her refreshment.

"You're awful," Shelley said, glancing at Luz as she jiggled the bundle at her chest. "It's not exactly easy to raise two children. I haven't had a single moment to myself since Kiki was born. No time for my work. Up at five-thirty every morning. It's all I can do to bathe myself. I've learned to nap while pushing a swing. Everyone expects you to be able to live your own life *and* give everything to two needy kids. On the drive here I decided I've been having a nervous breakdown for the past five years, only I haven't had the time to do anything about it." Shelley rubbed her forehead and glanced around the kitchen, as if looking for sharp pieces of metal to protect her children from or use to slit her wrists.

"Hey, you know what?" Luz asked, crossing her ankles as she leaned against the counter. "I work hard *not* to have a child. Where I come from, you're expected to be knocked up by fifteen. I've worked my ass off to be barren. And I don't even mean contraception. I mean the social pressure not to turn my body into a human factory. And guess what? We knew from *Go*, there ain't no break room in that factory. So spare me the agony of motherhood. You could have been a conscientious objector, but you chose to go to war in a time without a draft. So you'll forgive me if I'm slow to salute you."

"Luz," Beth said. "Enough."

Luz reached into her pocket and drew out a small Baggie of yellow-and-black pills. She shook two out in her palm. "Here,

Shelley, take these. Bumblebees will calm you right down. They'll put some color back into your world."

"No thanks," Shelley replied. The infant started to wail, and the mother instinctively pushed her scoop-neck collar down to offer a long, thin nipple, chewed up like the end of a teenager's soda straw. Luz slipped a pill into her mouth and gulped it back. "Do you know the Aristotelian model? I think it should be applied to mothers who bring their babies onto airplanes—"

Luz was interrupted midsentence by the arrival of Isaiah Goodman and his boyfriend, Vince Donnelly. Isaiah was an artist, and Vince was an environmentally conscious small-time literary publisher. A former catalog model, Vince had taken his ability to wear the preppy vestments of the leisure class to heart and brought the heretofore goth Isaiah into the jersey-cotton, equestrian-accented, whale-boned-belt fold. If they hadn't been gay, they would have looked like assholes. And if they hadn't been priced out of the Hamptons, they would never have made Orient their second home.

Isaiah and Vince had moved into the old Raleigh cottage, about a mile east on the Sound. They took to the soil surprisingly quickly, raising an enviable tomato garden, which they called a trial run before locating a surrogate and filling their garden with babies. At least that was Vince's plan. Isaiah was more resistant, shaking his head behind his boyfriend's shoulder when Vince started describing the process of double-sperm in vitro fertilization, which would prevent them from knowing which one of them was the biological father. Luz had the same patience for gay men wanting babies as she had for women wanting babies, but they had the good sense not to bring the subject up while she was in the room. Instead Vince mentioned the Orient monster.

"Did you guys read the paper today?" he asked. "They said it was all a hoax."

"Made of stitched-together animal parts," Isaiah reported. "So the Home Security press release said. Imagine being the PR flack for that organization. What makes a good press launch for biowarfare agents? What's the party like?"

"They're probably lying," Vince replied. "What else are they going to say? That it *was* an escaped mutant? At least that monster made everyone stop and wonder about pollutants." Vince had used his fledgling publishing house to reprint a number of 1970s back-to-the-land essays on the fragility of Mother Earth. No one bothered to read them, and even his friends grew distracted when he started blathering on about fracking or the melting ice shelf. "Think of all the viruses draining off that island."

"Don't tell Nathan that creature was a fake," Luz warned them. "He'll be jealous he didn't think of it himself. He's been looking for a project out here to inflict on the locals."

"Oh, good luck," Vince said, whisking his blond bangs back and selecting a bottle of tequila. "My dream is to fill the empty chair on the Orient Historical Board. But they hate us, because we're new or because we drive nicer cars or because we can't tell stories about a record-breaking fish that was caught in 1983."

"Right," Isaiah added. "Whose dick do you have to suck in the backseat of a Subaru to even get a meeting with those people?" Vince rolled his eyes. "I'm joking," Isaiah said.

Vince had something of the owner of a vicious dog in him. He seemed to like when Isaiah misbehaved so he could demonstrate his ability to put him in his place. Isaiah hadn't fallen as deeply in love with Orient as his boyfriend had. When they bought their house four months ago, Isaiah had mistakenly taken the bay as an extension of the Atlantic Ocean, and quickly realized on his first swim out that it offered none of the tumbling, surfer-dotted waves that crashed thirty miles south on the beaches of Montauk. He referred to Orient seawater as "the used bathwater of the East End." His resentment hadn't eased over time. "I could sit in a lawn chair anywhere," he suddenly said to Vince, continuing an argument they must have started on the drive over. "Luz, I will ask you one more time. Can I please borrow your speedboat?"

"No," she said.

Gavril's art dealer, Samuel Veiseler, entered the kitchen through the back door, still miming the act of wiping his feet on the mat. His suit was wrinkled from the two-hour drive from the city, and his red eyes were strained from handling the icy turnoffs after sundown. Beth shook his hand and offered him a drink. Luz heard his order—gin and Coke—and went about preparing one. It was no secret that Nathan Crimp wanted to leave his own gallery and join Gavril at Veiseler Projects. For all of her conspicuous rebellion, Luz recognized this as an opportunity to play the dutiful wife, and to Beth it seemed like she even managed to intensify her beauty, as if she could turn on her attractiveness with a switch—eyes wider, lips parted, her sweater slipping down just enough to present the contour of a breast. Beth stepped out of her way.

Nathan and Gavril emerged from the living room, bringing its loud voices with them. Gavril was holding a plate of figs dolloped with crab and sprigs of thyme. "I'm honored you could come," he said to Samuel as he stumbled forward with his platter. "I'll take you to the studio later and you can see what I've been working on. I'm still in the early stages, so we both have to use our imaginations."

"I'll come too," Nathan interrupted. Only Beth caught the flinch in Gavril's shoulders.

Nathan yanked at his tie, trying to unleash himself. Luz proceeded to straighten the knot. He kissed her forehead, and she pinched his sides. They somehow made even a simple display of affection seem holy in its intimacy and the rest of the world smaller for a moment than they were. Beth noticed that she and Nathan had the same light hair and skin color, that of a mildewed paperback novel. They were about the same height too, with the same thin bones that flared at the knuckles and joints (although Nathan suffered the lingering injuries of the rich: a bad back from horses, a bad stomach from too much foreign meat, a jittery nervous system from never having to wait in a line). For no conceivable reason, Beth imagined what her children would have looked like if Nathan had been their father: small, nonspecific humans not unlike the drawing Shelley's daughter had created on her iPad, beige slabs of human material with openings and hair in all the right places. Finishing her vodka, Beth forced herself to leave the kitchen to tend to the fire.

She used her father's steel poker to flip the logs. Anthony Shepherd had known the art of keeping a fire going: Keep the logs moving. Use newsprint and kindling only at the base. Let the flames find their own way in. As she started crumpling a piece of newspaper, she discovered the *Suffolk Times* article on the Orient monster: ". . . elaborate hoax conducted against Plum Island, timed to its impending closure. Investigators believe the prank was orchestrated by area teenagers or environmental advocacy groups angry over the impact of the controversial animal disease center on soil, water, and wildlife." She balled the page, along with news from farther away, which she discovered only as she prepared to burn it. *Spaceship on Mars, Chinese drilling in Angola, a new species of grasshopper discovered in Laos*—all of it so quick to light. There would be more tomorrow.

Isaiah passed her en route from the bathroom, saying hello to a few of the artists lounging on the sofa or clumped around the windowsills. The downstairs toilet was already groaning under the stress of too many flushes. Beth touched Isaiah's arm.

"I have to ask a favor," she said. "I have a friend coming who's staying out here. He's a kid."

"Like how old?" Isaiah asked suspiciously, as if she had confused him for a willing babysitter.

"Like almost twenty. That's still a kid to me."

"The foster kid at what's his name's place?"

"Yes. At Paul Benchley's. Can you just do me a favor and be nice to him? Not everyone here always is."

"Vince and I heard about him from our neighbors," Isaiah said. His dark hair was messily parted, as if by fingers instead of a comb. "We drove by the house he's staying at and saw him dragging out bags of trash. He's cute."

"I'm just asking for you to be kind. He's young, and I don't want—"

"Luz to lay into him?" Isaiah nodded. "Of course I'll be nice. When am I ever not? But Carson is coming, and I'm sure he's bringing his own boy gang, so he won't be the only kid. And honestly, Beth, have you taken a good look at—"

"Mills."

"He looks like the type that can handle himself. Oh, and you may want to tell Gavril that I don't mind seeing my collage above the toilet, but it's going to fall apart if anyone showers in there. Paper is extremely sensitive to moisture."

"I'm sure he'll move it tomorrow."

"Yeah." Isaiah smirked. "We all live the lie for each other. Better you don't leave it up. Last month our cleaning lady spent an hour Windexing one of Anne Shore's Plexiglas paintings. 'Meester Isaiah, I finally clean dirt off glass.' And sure enough, she did. How do you fire someone for doing their job?"

Carson Fore preferred entering a house by the front door, even though Gavril had taken pains to install battery-operated lawn lights leading around to the back to emphasize the view of his studio. Carson rang the doorbell. It was his nature to make a grand entrance. After Beth opened the door, he scurried into the foyer with a skullcap over his balding head, thick black glasses perched on his nose, a moth-holed coat already swirling off his shoulders, and rubber boots tracking frozen dirt on the runner.

"Hello, dear," he said, hugging Beth. Carson was an urban landscape photographer beloved in the New York art community, a keeper of art world memories in more lurid, less prosperous times, and while he had no money to speak of, he did have friends, and he made himself a guest in their homes, sweeping in and overstaying and rearranging their bookcases and mementos, bringing a Victorian spirit more fitting to the houses than to their current occupants. (Even his complexion was a shade of yellow-green that recalled the row houses in certain parts of London.) At present, he was overstaying at the house of a successful art adviser on Tabor Road, whom Gavril refused to invite for fear she'd pass out business cards.

"It's practically Antarctic out there," Carson said. "I thought we should all wear sleigh bells, and I worried I'd have to throw a few of the boys to the wolves like that wonderful bridal-party scene in *My Ántonia.*" The boys were behind him, crew cut acolytes in tight jackets who used Carson like a passport to enter the homes of artists they admired. There were four of them, and even though Carson listed their names as they entered, hovering an unsteady Parkinson's hand over each of their heads, she hadn't caught a single one. They were young and gay and the femininity of their teenage years had only recently hardened into the muscle of a competitive sexual economy. Their muscles met the demands of the city, and the city met the demands of their muscles.

Behind them appeared another visitor: Mills Chevern, holding a bottle of wine Paul must have given him. He was skinnier than Carson's boys, less sculpted, but, for Beth, he was the first guest she was relieved to see all night.

"Wait, I don't recognize this one," Carson said, staring at him. "Maybe the wolves spit him back out."

"He's with me," Beth said. Mills handed the bottle to her and nodded his head, lifting his chin as if to speak, but no words drifted from his lips.

"Okay, I'm shutting the door. Down the hallway," she ordered. "Carson, please eat some of Gavril's *jumari*. No one has touched it."

"Can you blame them? I'm trying to stay alive, not give myself dysentery." His voice traveled through the hallway and boomed in the living room. "God, Isaiah, you and your *lifetime companion* were supposed to pick us up. We ran here with wolves at our heels while you two were lip-synching to NPR."

She turned to Mills, who was standing against the wall, a wool hat bunched over his heart. "I'm glad you decided to come," she said.

"I said I would."

"Well, there are a lot of new people here for you to meet. Don't be scared. Come on." She swept her arm around his shoulders and led him toward the noise.

After her second sip of vodka, Beth decided it was unwise for guests to use the hot tub. She worried about finding towels for them, about their level of intoxication near the warm water, about the body fluids that might swirl in the jets come morning. Gavril hushed her, smoking a crumbling joint between his thumb and chubby pointer.

"When did you start smoking pot again?" she asked.

"Samuel rolled it. I couldn't refuse," he said, inhaling and straining to keep the smoke from escaping his lips. "Why don't you join them in hot tub? Put on your swimsuit."

She shook her head. Shelley's daughter raced from under the kitchen table, a lighter in her hand. The little girl ran into the living room, offering to light people's cigarettes. Finally, Luz took her up on the service, bending down to catch the thin blue flame. Luz walked into the kitchen and touched Beth on the shoulder. She took a drag and ashed in the sink.

"Shelley's stoned and she's breast-feeding like crazy," she said. "Or maybe I'm stoned, and watching Shelley breast-feed is crazy. Are we going in or not?" She looked at them. "The hot tub."

Gavril told her that he had to show Samuel his studio first and to go ahead without him.

"Do you want to borrow a swimsuit?" Beth asked her.

"No need," Luz said. "Everyone here has seen me naked. After that, modesty is just a construct. Where's Nathan?"

Nathan tapped the kitchen window with his wedding band and circled around to the door. He opened it halfway, beckoning them outside. His cheeks were red from the cold, and the skin around his eyebrows was as white as clay. As Beth stepped out onto the porch, the wind ripped through her dress, kiting it to the side.

The temperature must have dipped near zero by now. The hot tub steamed at full boil, and several bodies jumped and resettled in the mist.

"That house," Nathan said, pointing across the lawn toward Magdalena's cottage. "That little house with the little old dead woman inside."

"I see it," Luz said. "It's adorable."

Isaiah joined them, toweling off as he walked across the patio, his footsteps creating ice prints across the concrete. The hair on his arms swirled like the grain in split wood. He followed their gaze across the property line. "Whose place is that?" he asked. "There are no lights on."

"It's the woman you were talking about," Nathan said to his wife. "The one who keeled over into her bees."

"I didn't know her," Luz replied. "I've never been in there before." She rubbed her arms and threw them around Beth for warmth, her forearm pressing against Beth's breasts. Beth felt a surprise sensation at Luz's touch, a stirring of blood like a lamp in a cave. If things had been different, if they were younger or still unmarried, she wondered if they might have been lovers. Maybe it would have been Luz she fell in love with, like Magdalena and her girlfriend, Molly. For a single freezing moment Beth wished she were still young enough to experiment, that she still possessed the capacity to explore. They shivered against each other, and Beth placed her hand on Luz's fingers to keep her close.

"Is that house for sale?" Luz asked.

"Beth, you know more than me," Gavril said. "Is it on the market?"

"I'm not sure."

"Oh, Nathan, we should buy it."

Nathan frowned. "We just bought a house. We already have more land than we need. Our backyard is full of holes. We spent millions of dollars to live in a construction site. We literally don't have walls."

"I could use it as my studio," Luz said, squeezing Beth tightly, as if to enlist her support. "I'd paint it black. I'm sure we could afford it. It's just a speck of a place. How much could it really go for?"

"That's not the point," Nathan said, shaking his head in a rare show of restraint.

Luz grunted. "The privileged must be circumspect when it comes to money because they're conditioned to consider affluence a measure of their intelligence. People like me, people from nothing, we don't have that hang-up. We just like to spend. There's nothing I love more than when someone poor wins the lottery and five years later they've run through it and have to go back to waiting tables. Why does that shock anyone? That's exactly what we were told to do—to treat money as something we weren't meant to have."

"Luz considers bankruptcy an aspiration. But let's ask her when she gets there," Nathan replied.

"I'll never be bankrupt as long as I have you," Luz sang deviously.

"Maybe we should buy it," Gavril ventured.

"Gavril," Beth snapped. "We don't need it either."

"What? It is next to our property. It is a smart investment to add to our land."

Beth didn't mention the faulty logic in Gavril's premise—that the house they lived in didn't belong to them. It belonged to Gail. This was her mother's property, and she and Gavril were living on it, rent free, only temporarily. Did he actually think this house and its Sound-front acres were going to end up in his name? Even if they did stay out here permanently, it would be decades before Beth inherited the place.

"If you guys aren't interested, I have a friend who's been looking for a house just about that size." Isaiah stepped onto the lawn with his cell phone to take a photograph. Beth felt a wave of protection for Magdalena's tiny home, which had resisted as much as a fresh coat of paint for as long as she could remember. She fought the urge to grab Isaiah's phone before it flashed. "The bigger houses are so overvalued this year. Vince and I had to bid way over price just to get ours."

"We did too. Practically broke us," Nathan said, as if it were a secret that his family bankrolled whatever he couldn't afford on his own.

"This one's perfect, because it looks like nothing," Isaiah said.

"I want it," Luz insisted.

"Are you drunk?" Nathan asked her.

"Maybe we all buy it together," Gavril said, "and add it to our colony."

The dark shape of an animal wavered across Magdalena's porch, a cat or possum. The wind whistled in the gutters. These artists had fought so hard to leave the bland sinkholes of their beginnings, throwing their childhoods away to escape to the city, and now here they were, desperate to return to the suburbs, paying obscene amounts for the kinds of houses and neighborhoods that had trapped them in their youths. Beth imagined a perverse nightmare future: artists pushing lawn mowers, clogging supermarket aisles, running PTA bake-offs, bullying their boys and girls for lowbatting-averages in Little League, attending church, singing in the choir. It was as if the whole system had finally caved in on itself, a picture inside a picture of what was supposed to be the way out.

Luz slipped her arms down Beth's stomach, then let go with a start, as if she'd touched a burning pot.

"What?" Beth asked.

"Nothing," Luz said. "Never mind."

"I'm going in. Don't any of you get near that house," Beth said, hurrying with a blushed face to escape the cold.

In the kitchen, at midnight, Mills stood by the doorway, watching as Beth told Gavril to shut up.

"I only ask," he said, sitting on the counter.

"Can I get you a drink?" she asked Mills. He shook his head.

"In Bucharest, so many orphans. So many dirty children huffing paint. They beg for change to sniff it"—Gavril mimed a bag over his mouth and inhaled. "Paint covers their mouths in subway stations. They sleep on the ground with paint like silver drool running down their chins. All unwanted. This is why I ask, because I don't understand it in America. Ceaușescu outlawed abortion"—Beth's ears reddened and her molasses feet knocked into a chair leg—"because he wanted to supply more workers for the factories. He wanted a bigger population of slaves. But here in America, you already have bad unemployment, and you have no factories in need of more bodies. Instead you let your government be filled with religious fanatics saying the same thing as my dictator. No abortion. No contraception. But the same party complains about the poor. Too many of them. Too useless. A weight on the system. I do not understand this."

"We have iced tea," Beth said to Mills, with an apologetic smile.

"So I only ask your friend if he thinks his parents were religious."

"I don't know who they were," Mills said, rubbing his legs and glancing into the living room. He looked everywhere but at Gavril, crouched on the counter, kicking his heels against the cabinet door, creating a drumbeat of metronomic bangs.

"He said he doesn't know, so stop asking," Beth said, pouring a last sip of vodka. The microwave clock read 12:06. Out the window, snow flurries danced in the wind. "Mills didn't come over to be interrogated."

"It's okay," Mills said. "I'm not offended. I just don't know the answer." His eyes finally made their way to Gavril. "Sorry." Beth clutched Mills's arm.

When Mills left the kitchen, Beth put her hands on her hips. "Jesus," she said. "Show some respect."

"I am respecting," Gavril said lightly. "I show interest by asking questions. He is not a child. He can ask me anything he likes, I wouldn't be upset. Why are you so sensitive tonight?"

"Yes, I'm being sensitive. I wish you could be the same."

Gavril jumped from the counter. He whispered something in Romanian as he opened the refrigerator door.

"What did you say?" she asked. Gavril busied himself adding a lemon to his cup of tequila, pretending not to hear her. "What did you just call me?"

Gavril tried to reach for her but she stepped back, a retaliation that registered in her husband's eyes.

"You coddle that kid, and you don't let me touch you. It is you who is acting wrong tonight." Beth sipped her drink to give her mouth both a task and a blockade. "Can you be nice to the man you married? It's an important night, and these are my colleagues. I do everything to make a nice party and you walk around like my personal censor, telling me everything I say is wrong."

"What if everything you're saying *is* wrong? That bullshit about buying Magdalena's house."

"Ah, of course you will be the sober villain. It is just fun. You take everything too seriously. You hate before you love. What will you do when we have a child? He will not be a dark fool like that one."

"Yes, Gavril, every word you say is wrong—"

Samuel Veiseler walked into the kitchen, pausing at the doorway as if to test whether he had interrupted a domestic dispute or a moment of marital bliss. Beth gathered the empty paper plates off the counter and shoved them into the trash.

"I have to go soon," Samuel announced. "The roads are getting bad and I have to get back to Manhattan. It's too uncertain out here. Shall we?"

"Yes, yes," Gavril said. "Wait until you see my new studio, best flooring and soundproof. Perfect conditions for work." He led him out the back door as Shelley called to Beth from the living room.

"I can't find my coat." Beth went to retrieve Shelley's coat from the closet. Orange vomit clung to Shelley's shoulder, the baby's or her own.

A half hour later, Beth searched for Mills on the ground floor, where lingering guests swayed and mined the toppings of Gavril's hors d'oeuvres. Their cups were clutched as if they contained the best chance of happiness. Frivolity had reached its moment of paranoia: would the liquor outlast the remaining guests? It was after midnight, and a storm was coming, but the electricity could last forever, and only the old and the obligated felt the burden of the hour. Gavril's art assistants kissed by the front door. It was pretty to watch two young people kiss, their mouths elastic, their histories briefer and needier of consequences. Luz Wilson's clothes hung on the railing.

Beth climbed the steps. If it hadn't been her house, if the door hadn't led to her childhood bedroom, she might have knocked. When she opened it, smoke rolled through the trapped air. She waved a hand through the haze, which hung like thread, obscuring several bodies seated in a circle, as if warming themselves at an indoor campfire: Carson, his boys, and Mills, off in the corner.

"When we finally left the bedroom at seven in the morning," she heard Carson telling his band of young men, "the rest of the apartment had been robbed. They took the furniture, all my camera equipment, they even took Cookie's clothes. The only thing they left was the cat, which they had brushed and fed." Noticing Beth at the door, Carson asked belatedly if they could smoke inside.

She smiled at him, and then at Mills, who quickly stood up, clambered over the other young men, and shuffled into the hallway. Before Beth closed the door, she smelled a sweetness to the burning, a substance more acrid than tobacco in the smoke.

"Don't worry, I didn't partake," he said. "I wanted to. But I didn't."

She was glad to hear it. She'd forgotten about his problems in the city and didn't want to be responsible for his time beyond Paul Benchley's watch.

"You haven't gotten the full tour," she said, leading him down the hall and opening the door of the master bedroom. When she pulled the chain to the ceiling light, she was relieved to find the room empty. Moths rippled toward the overhead fixture. Mills scanned the pinkish walls. He walked toward a painting that Gavril had hung earlier, a canvas with bedsprings stapled on its stretched linen. Mills pressed his finger on a spring and let it pop back out.

"Did you make this?" he asked.

"Oh, God, no," she said, sitting on the corner of the bed. "It's really ugly, isn't it? No, I did figurative paintings. Portraits. In fact, some of them are packed up in the bedroom you were just in. If they haven't already gone yellow, Carson's lungs will finish the job."

"*Did*?" Mills asked, nervously toying with his earring. "You don't paint anymore?"

"No," she said. "I mean, I might start again. I just haven't found much inspiration. But I want to, I hope to. Oh, who knows?" A vein was constricting at her right temple. The pain went away when she closed her eye.

"I can't believe all your friends make a living on this stuff." He pressed another spring and watched it bob. "What is something like this worth?"

She considered it, a muddled logarithm of prominence versus prospect versus previous sales versus popularity of medium. "I don't know. That's by a pretty successful artist. Maybe fifty or sixty grand at auction."

"No way," Mills wailed. "Sixty thousand dollars for this? You've got to be kidding." He quickly stopped the spring. "Who would be that, that—"

"Insane?" She smiled, leaning back on the mattress. "There's a market out there."

Beth smoothed her dress against her stomach. She had no clue what Luz had felt around her belly, a slight cushion of fat at most. She couldn't have sensed any movement. Beth prayed that she'd misunderstood Luz's reaction and considered asking Mills to touch her stomach to tell her if he noticed anything out of place. *Out of place*—yes, that's all it was, a body that had become disorganized, a scrambled body she was forced to hide under an inherited dress.

"But it's hideous," Mills said. "I don't mean to disrespect what your friends do, but I'm confused how these pieces of art could be worth that much. And you have a hundred of them all over your house. Face it, Beth, you're a millionaire. What an arrangement all your friends have. You can mint each other thousands of dollars. *Here, I made this in twenty minutes. Now you're rich!*"

She laughed, and so, finally, did he. It was as if the real Mills, a softer set of eyes, were suddenly visible through the weeds where he hid himself. She wanted very much to touch him.

"Maybe I should start making art," he said, almost seriously. "I know I sound dumb, but what does it do for people? If I knew that, maybe I could make it too."

"Well," she said. She once had a speech reserved for this occasion: a benediction against philistinism, a well-oiled sales pitch in favor of taste. It had been a long time since anyone had asked her the question. These days, everyone seemed like an expert. Mills stepped closer to the painting, standing on tiptoe in his sneakers. His finger twisted a curl of his hair.

"I mean, it's ugly but it's hardly shocking. It's easy to make, so it doesn't require a special skill. It isn't nice to look at. At best, it's a creepy sort of decoration. Like a deer head over a fireplace, but one that doesn't match the rest of the room."

"That's more like it."

"So?" He watched her intently, expecting an answer.

"It's internal," she said, flailing her hands. Her manifesto had escaped her. Why *was* it worth so much? Instead, another truth came rushing in to fill its place. "It's an internal economy, with its own forms of regulation. It starts with the work and the hype that surrounds it. Those two things move through the system. And as they do, the product gathers value, through interest and attention and critique and speculation. But at all times the work itself must remain"—she thought of the precise word—"ineffable, indeterminate, between. It doesn't point this way or that way, or it points different places depending upon where you are."

"Like a compass," Mills offered.

"No, a compass has a function. The work cannot have a function." She drew herself up, intent on expressing this clearly, as if her own sanity rested on the answer. "It doesn't make any sense. None of it does. It's just a bubble that won't burst. I used to understand it, but I don't anymore. Now I just accept it and play along, and as long as I play along it keeps expanding. Maybe that's what it is, a place for the world to put its confusion." Her eyes stung. "Now maybe you understand why I can't paint. I've lost the point of it. Frankly, I can't stand all of the intellectual doubletalk. I mean, you're right. It's a bunch of springs on fabric." She wiped her eyes. "I shouldn't say this, but when I met Gavril and he showed me his work, I knew it was good because it looked so wrong. It looked like the ruins of something right. And I knew when I saw it that he'd be brilliant. And I was right. I've been right. Gavril is a brilliant man."

Why were her eyes watering? Why was the color draining from the room, making all the furniture—the dresser, the bed, the full-length mirror in which she looked every morning to find herself sleeping next to her husband—seem as demented as the springs on the painting? She blamed the vodka for her tears, for an already weakened body that was convulsing and driving her hands against her face, for her failure to make sense of any of it—the art, this house, Gavril and his gallerist standing over a puddle of tar, the man who brought mail to her door. "I guess it's an education."

Mills sat down next to her, placing his hand on her back. He didn't tell her to stop crying. He simply held her back and let her finish.

"God, I'm just like my mother," she said, "crying on the corner of the bed over nothing. I like to think she did that only after my father died, but it started before. She always left the door open so I would come in when I heard her sobbing, or so she could stop when she heard me coming. I never knew which."

He touched her knee. His eyes weren't absent when she looked at him. His lips moved together, building warmth. She might have kissed him if she hadn't known better. She might kiss him anyway.

"Maybe it's just a different way for people to see," he said. "Maybe it doesn't have to answer anything. It's perfect that some things can be just like you said—confusion. There needs to be a place for that."

"Does there?" she asked. "Is that really what we need more of? Isn't there enough?"

"It puts food on the table. And it gives all of your friends nice lives. So it does do something. Maybe you're just expecting too much."

"Maybe," she said. Somehow, for the last six months, she'd thought she hadn't been expecting enough. She rounded her shoulders. "I'm sorry Gavril gave you such a hard time. Part of that brilliant-artist trip is the license to ask a lot of stupid questions, thinking he can be honest where others are afraid."

He stared at the floor. She thought she could see the lights within him disappearing one by one. If she did paint again, she'd want to start with his face, if only to stoke that light, to free the fire and open it to the air.

"It didn't bother me," he said. "I told him I didn't know anything about my parents, but that's not true. I found my mother, saw her just as I see you."

"Oh, man, that must have been hard," she said. "Did you spend any time with her?"

"Not much. We spoke. Not like you and I are talking, though. Like we were strangers trying to sell each other things."

She waited, but he didn't continue. She didn't press him. She had no right to push him further. But she no longer felt like she was talking to a child. They sat together on the edge of the bed, staring forward, as if they were traveling in the front seat of her car.

The sound of glass, shattering, came through the window from the back porch. Beth heard feet slapping on the pavement, followed by a sharp, aborted scream. "I better make sure no one's hurt," she said. She hurried down the steps and moved through the deserted living room. She heard engines revving in the driveway and saw headlights passing through the windows before disappearing down the road. Luz rushed through the back door, her breasts shaking as she reached for a towel. Her dark skin was wet and glinting, her white underwear tracing a shell of hair.

"Our husbands are at it, fighting," she said, covering her chest with the towel. "Those men are idiots, wrestling like dogs."

"About what?"

"Whatever it's about, it's over each other." Luz managed to compose a smile for Mills as she scooted by him to locate her clothes. "Hi. We've met before."

"Get out here, Luz, we're leaving," Nathan yelled from outside. Beth watched him walk past the living room window, a trickle of blood running from his lip. Gavril slammed the kitchen door, holding his bleeding hand by the wrist.

"He cut you?" Beth reached for the towel, but Luz had already taken it.

"No," Gavril said, running the gash under the sink. "I was picking up glass."

"What happened? What were you fighting—"

"Nothing. Jealousy, no talent, trying to steal my career from me, making up lies." His face contorted. Beth kneeled down to get the first aid kit from the cabinet. "Get out," Gavril yelled after Nathan. "Leave and do not come back."

Beth glanced over her shoulder. At the end of the hallway, Luz was pulling on her pants, her sweater hanging from her sinewy arms. In profile, bent at her waist, she almost looked like she was smiling, a caught shark hanging from a fishing dock. Mills stood against the wall.

"Maybe you should go," she said to him. He nodded and grabbed his coat from the corner. "And don't forget, you need to get that *thing* back for me."

"Yes, no more party. Everyone out." Gavril held his hand out for Beth to dress the wound. Mills stepped around them, glanced back at Beth, then left as wordlessly as he had come.

Outside, Nathan honked his horn.

"Is he okay?" Luz asked in the doorway, clutching her jacket.

"I'm okay," Gavril answered. The anger had died, and, with it, his spirit.

"It was a lovely party," she said, winking at Beth. "And to think we almost made it through without remembering who the real stars of the night are. When you two make up tomorrow, please don't give the rest of us a second thought." She moved to kiss them, thought better of it, and made her way to the door.

They stood in the kitchen a few degrees apart. It was so quiet Beth could hear the hush of falling snow. There was a moment after a party when desolation crept over rooms that once were filled with noise. Beth knew she should try to cheer Gavril up with a memory or a kiss, but she didn't. She left the kitchen as her husband flexed his injured hand and went outside to pick up the glass.

Beth fell asleep before Gavril came to bed. When she woke at five in the morning, he wasn't lying next to her. Snow covered the backyard. The lights in the garage were off, but from the window she saw his faint footprints leading to its door.

CHAPTER 17

The nor'easter came to Orient like a night parade, whistling and trumpeting and waking residents from their sleep. What it left was quieter than sleep: two feet of snow and lakes of ice that glittered like sheet metal. The streets were empty except for a few bundled figures setting their marks on the white. In winter, that urge to leave the first footprint was as human as crying at death. Cars were locked in snowdrifts, and the air was gritty with the smell of burning wood.

After a winter storm, Orient hung so motionless that it was easy to forget the village was surrounded by water. The first reminder was the voice of a radio announcer broadcasting news of the condition of the causeway. The water had breached the road, icing it over and cutting the village off from the mainland. Until the county plows and salt trucks cleared a lane, no one could get in or out.

Paul carried in logs from the woodpile and arranged them in the fireplace. Mills rummaged through the downstairs closets for boots, gloves, a wool cap, and a nylon snowsuit, which zippered so tightly across his chest he could barely breathe. Paul stood watching with an incredulous smirk as Mills dressed, missing the significance of the occasion. For a westerner, snow was a special occasion; being absent from Mills's life, it had rubbed itself into his dreams. Mills jumped at the chance to meet the snow in full uniform, like an Alaskan donning flippers and a snorkel mask in the Caribbean.

"It's really not that cold," Paul said. "You're going to overheat in two minutes."

"Then I'll come back in in two minutes."

Mills lasted twenty. He slipped on ice patches and fell on his padded side. His thighs whisked as he ran in circles, and he wore himself out trying to keep upright. He took lunar strides across the lawn, his lungs hoarse from the cold, sweat prickling against his woolen cap. It seemed to him that he'd finally found his reason for coming to Orient: overnight the town looked less menacing and far lonelier, able to cling to the smallest bead of life like a faucet holding a drip of water.

It was the presence of the Muldoons that finally drove him back inside. Theo sprinted from his house with a sled. Tommy stumbled out in a sweatshirt and jeans, his sneakers kicking up flurries. The father, Bryan, stood at the door, trying to talk Tommy into taking a shovel. Mills hurried up the porch steps. He didn't even stop to shake off the snow on the welcome mat, in case he looked over and found Tommy returning his gaze. Mills no longer wanted anything to do with the teenager next door. He was a casualty of another season, a warm current that had gone cold.

Winter exposed the weaknesses of the Benchley mansion. Chilly air leaked through the floorboards, the pipes shook out gluey streams of water, and the dishes trembled in the kitchen cabinets with every step. Mills learned the reason for all the books in the living room: they were distractions for Paul in his breaks from the computer. Mills went up to his room and sat by the window. Through the frosted glass, he saw Tommy and his brother rolling a large ball of snow across their yard, one ball and then another, until four globes formed a row by the curb. Tommy issued directions and Theo followed them, scurrying over the balls like a spider tending its eggs. The late morning sun hit the bedroom window, blinding the glass with yellow frost.

Mills thought of the sun in California, and the hard, white light beating down on his mother as she walked along the street. Perhaps the memory came to him because he had spoken of her to Beth the night before. He had stood on a corner in Sacramento, almost eight months ago, in the merciless heat of that stone-white capital. He had learned that his mother lived here, a mere hour-and-a-half bus ride from Modesto. For his whole life, she had been an hour-and-a-half bus ride away: a twenty-dollar bus ticket, seventy miles up the I-5 through the green vacuum of the central valley, six blocks west of the depot where Mexicans sold scoops of flavored ice for fifty cents. Anyone with twenty dollars could take that trip. But finding her had cost five hundred and twenty dollars, a sum he had earned mowing lawns on weekends.

The records on his birth were sealed, but the county's attempt to digitize its records had left a hole in its security walls that foster kids had learned to exploit. There was a small-time hacker in Stockton who charged five hundred bucks to break into the county database, and a second hack matched the name of the parent to a current place of employment. Mills knew several friends who had used the service; some had confronted their parents and returned with money, or pictures of siblings, or black eyes and quiet voices. Mills sent the money in cash, and the response had brought him to that corner in downtown Sacramento, across the street from a jewelry store.

Under a flapping green awning, a neon sign in the shop's window read CENTRAL GOLD WE BUY WE SELL. BUY blinked blue and SELL flatlined red. He stood across the street for an hour, the sun pressing on his skin, his stomach swirling, the sweat of his legs speckling his only pair of dress pants. Every time he worked up the courage to cross the street, the traffic swelled and his resolve seemed to blow away with the exhaust. Finally, he saw her walking toward the store: a thin middle-aged woman in a leopard-print dress, with dark, wavy hair that collected on her shoulders, black sunglasses that hid her eyes, and a nose that was dented at the tip like the seam in a peach. He knew it was his mother, knew it from the stillness of her lips, anchor shaped and uneasily moved. He felt a strange, misplaced pride when a businessman looked over his shoulder to study the movement of her hips. She stopped at the door of the jewelry store, gathering her hair at her neck the way a person in a rainier city stopped to gather the folds of an umbrella. It was so bright she seemed to melt into the glass. The door gave in, and she disappeared into the darkness of Central Gold.

Mills was startled out of the memory by the sound of Pam calling to her boys. Tommy and Theo had built four snowmen—one for each member of the family, except their absent sister. Their bodies were arranged facing the street in invitation, with black batteries for eyes, leaves for mouths, sticks for arms, and scarves wrapped around their necks, tight as nooses. Tommy fit a Giants cap on his snowman and placed pinecone eyebrows over his mother's Duracell eyes. Pam had come out to see their work, and she paced around the family portrait and hugged her sons, face tight with joy. For once, Tommy seemed to welcome his mother's company, receiving her hug and keeping his arm around her shoulder. Mills was happy to see that the incident in his bedroom hadn't left any noticeable hostility. Perhaps the four snowmen were a kind of peace offering, a return of the happy Muldoons, arms stretched wide to embrace all of Orient. At night, Mills thought, the lawn lights would make them look like a family of smiling ghosts.

While Pam kneeled in the snow and took photos of the snowmen, Tommy stood to the side, awkward even among the snow family. When Theo and Pam ran back to the house, Tommy did something strange: he removed the eyes from the father and placed the two batteries, like buckshot, into the snow where its heart would be.

Tommy squinted up at the bedroom window. Mills stepped back. When he looked out again, Tommy was gone.

The snow melted quickly—first to sludge, and then altogether, uncovering the brittle grass, retreating into islands of white. The Muldoon snowmen withstood the thaw, grinning crookedly, as if they were certain another storm would preserve them through the winter.

Mills was sorry to see the snow disappear. He had enjoyed the two days marooned in the house, sitting by the fire. As Paul worked away on his laptop, Mills played rounds of solitaire and flipped through art books, trying to figure out the trick that earned Beth's artist friends so much attention and money.

Beth phoned on Sunday afternoon, telling him she'd take him for a drive when the roads were better. He knew she'd expect him to have Jeff Trader's book by then. Before Beth could mention it, Mills started whispering to her about a plan he'd been hatching to surprise Paul with a birthday cake. Would she take him to the bakery in Greenport?

"Okay," she said, but she wouldn't be diverted from her purpose. "Did you manage to get the book?"

"No, but I will."

"You have to," she insisted. Then she told him that Isaiah Goodman, one of the artists at her party, wanted to invite him over for dinner next week. "He'll pick you up," she said. "He and his boyfriend are very nice. It'll be good for you." Mills realized that Beth had probably coerced Isaiah into extending the invitation, but he was grateful for the kindness. Beth recited Isaiah's number, which he jotted down on a scrap of paper. And just like that, as one season changed into another, he felt that Orient was opening itself up to him.

When he returned to the parlor, Paul was picking up a lime green pamphlet that had been slipped under the front door. The same picture of the creature decorated the front flap, but this time with a new message: WHAT ELSE DO YOU EXPECT THE GOVERNMENT TO SAY? A SKEPTICAL ORIENT IS A SAFE ORIENT. The pamphlet listed the date of the next council meeting in Southold, asking residents to confront the board about environmental concerns related to five decades of exposure to Plum.

"He's still at it?" Paul groaned, tossing the pamphlet in the kindling stack.

"Maybe he really believes that the lab has messed up the land," Mills said.

"What Adam is trying to do is jump-start his security company with all of his newfangled environmental tests, and he feels like people won't shell out money unless they're scared. What he doesn't understand is, the more new people come out and buy up the land, the more they'll want security to protect their houses. But with all those posters of mutant corpses all over town, who's going to want to move to Orient in the first place?"

Mills sat on the floor, flipping through an art book. "But like he said in that meeting, if the land turns out to be toxic, no one's going to buy it."

"Exactly," Paul snorted. "So maybe it's in his best interest not to ask those kinds of questions. But you tell folks out here how to run a business, they'll do the exact opposite just to prove they're not city-minded." Paul shook his head, and Mills thought of the mug on the bureau in his bedroom: *We are the superior beings.* As Mills watched Paul hovering at his laptop, he considered how lonely superior beings must be in this world, so superior they didn't even need the confusion of love or sex to distract them. Then again, maybe superior beings made ideal foster parents: they took over for those who couldn't deal with the burden of what love or sex had brought them.

Mills picked up his deck of cards. "Should we play a game of hearts?"

Paul checked his watch. "I have to go to Greenport to get groceries. The causeway should be clear by now. You want to come?"

Mills chose to stay by the fire. By the time Paul pulled out of the driveway, the sun had already set. Mills walked through the backrooms and out the door, hopping over the last islands of snow. A few boats swayed in the distance, near the Connecticut side of the Sound. He hoped Tommy might see him from his bedroom window and come down—not for another replay of that mistaken moment between them, but to return the book and shake hands in peace.

The bushes rustled. The presence of a deer was no longer a remarkable sight to Mills, but the doe walked out into the open accompanied by a snow-flecked fawn. Their purple hides bristled and their noses smoked. The mother watched Mills as she strode across the grass. The fawn trembled, almost as if he were a reflection of himself in water, taking shy steps. A strip of yellow plastic wound around his neck, loose as a dog collar. If the plastic didn't fall off, Mills thought, it would strangle the fawn as it grew. There was nothing he could do about it; another step and the deer would bolt. He could only hope the plastic broke free before it became a noose.

He went inside and lay down on the tweed sofa. He slept so deeply that he didn't hear Paul when he returned with the groceries. He slept until a few minutes after midnight, when he was awakened by sounds like loud thunder and crashing waves. He opened his eyes and saw the glass coffee table reflecting orange. Mills heard screaming, and, beyond the screams, the sirens.

Bryan Muldoon had gone to bed angry. He had tried to sit down with his son to have "the talk"—a compilation of specific talks bundled together in an after-dinner father-son summit. The topic was "What the hell is the matter with you, Tommy?" It had gone as badly as Bryan had predicted. Bryan wished he could put his arms around his eldest son, half shaking him, half hugging him, a shake-hug of love and correction. Instead Tommy just sat on the kitchen chair with his hands braced on the seat, looking like he might bolt at any moment.

Pam had supplied a working script for Bryan to follow: mediocre grades, a lapsed interest in the extracurriculars in which he once excelled, a disrespect toward his parents' rules for peaceful cohabitation, a sullen quiet that seemed to permeate his entire being in his last year at home before college. Pam had provided Bryan with a stack of state university catalogs, should the conversation take an aspirational turn.

Bryan started with the extracurriculars ("Are we done?"), jumped to a SUNY Purchase catalog ("If I take the catalog upstairs, are we done?") and then freestyled a passionate speech about his own work with OHB and how important it was to preserve the community. Bryan's fingers massaged the kitchen table, as if he were smoothing Orient's fields for future grandchildren. Pointing to the admissions requirements in the SUNY catalog, he suggested that Tommy could pitch in and help him with the Kiefer Nondevelopment Advocacy Initiative. "How good will that look on your application?" he encouraged. What he really meant was, *How good will that feel to help your father with something he cares about. How good will that be for us, Tommy, spending time together on the streets where I used to carry you on my shoulders and race you along the beaches until my lungs hurt but I wouldn't show you that I was tired because I wanted you to think I was strong?*

Tommy let go of the seat, slumping into its upholstery.

"I might take a year off before going to college," he mumbled into his palm.

Bryan controlled himself. He spoke slowly, serenely, in the measured tone he used to convince older couples to install a security camera at their front door without scaring them about who they might find at night on their bedroom monitor.

"Taking time off—that might seem exciting right now, but I swear to you, a college degree will take you all those places you're imagining a whole lot faster. When we all go up to visit Lisa for Parents' Orientation Weekend, you'll see how exciting campus life can be."

Tommy laughed and hid a smile in his palm. Bryan hoped it was the first crack in his son's tough exterior. "You don't have much time left in this house," he continued, "with your mom and me. I know you're bored of it, but one day you'll wish you'd treasured every last minute."

Tommy took a breath and stared at the table. "If I move into the city, would you pay for an apartment?"

"Tommy . . ."

"Just the amount you give Lisa for her dorm."

"Tommy, please . . ."

"Or the money you spend on the rooms you rent for your own enjoyment."

Bryan's hands shot off the table, shrinking into fists. His heart sent blood coursing through his chest, and when that blood reached his face it was very hot. SUNY Purchase suddenly seemed like an opportunity to send his son away rather than a means of keeping him close.

"I work hard, every day—" Bryan didn't know where he was going with this sentence. It didn't have a direction; it was the language of covering the quiet, throwing carpets over floors, twisting radio knobs, tapping nails. "And business is getting tough, now with this added competition, and I can't promise there will be money for Theo when it's time for college, or Lisa if she decides to go to law school, and your mother wants to help her parents move to Florida. All of this pressure on me to make sure you're provided for, and I work every single day . . ." This was Bryan's oblique way of begging Tommy not to speak another word about what he might know, or maybe it was his attempt to explain himself. Either way, Bryan could no longer look his son in the eye.

"How did it go?" Pam asked afterward. She was lying in bed, knees bent under the coverlet. Her blue sleeping pills sat beside a glass of water like two small boats waiting to be set adrift on her tongue.

He unbuttoned his shirt and kicked off his loafers. He unfastened the leather strap of his watch and placed it on the bedside table. He sat down on his side of the mattress, his back to his wife, the white hair on his chest feathered against the droop of his muscles. "Not well. I don't know what's the matter with him. I don't know what to do with a son like that." *You don't have much time left in this house. You'll wish you'd treasured every last minute.* Before she took her sleeping pills, Pam did something that Bryan couldn't remember her doing in years. She rolled onto her side and stroked his back.

Bryan woke a few minutes after midnight to the sound of beeping. It roused him softly through his dreams. He had learned to love the perfect increments of those high-decibel beeps. They emitted seamlessly from machines that he had made his career installing:

for twenty years that sound of electronic crickets, which signaled security and peace of mind. Metal badge-shaped Muldoon Security signs were staked in front yards all across the North Fork. And after thirty seconds, if the correct four-digit code was not punched into the keypad, wailing sirens overtook the beeping with an automatic call to the police department in Southold. Sirens wailed around him, and a second beeping reverberated through the hallway, louder and foreign, like cicadas at close range. It was the fire alarm.

Bryan bolted awake. Smoke hung in the air, and something warm was spreading under the mattress, as if the cap on Pam's water bottle had been dislodged. He shot his legs over the bed as he realized that the alarms were coming from his own house. His feet burned when they touched the floor.

The house was on fire.

Pam. The boys. Theo and Tommy, not Lisa, she was safe upstate.

"Pam," he screamed to the body next to him. He tried to shake her out of her drugged sleep before he ran toward the hallway. "Get up, there's a fire!" The smoke thickened as he tried to hurry into the hallway, then left or right, one way Tommy, the other Theo. He'd go both ways—no, he'd go to one and then the other, first right to Theo, then left to Tommy, youngest first and then the oldest. But Bryan never made it out of the bedroom. His feet went left when he told them to go right, his body and mind disoriented in the smoke, and the door he opened led to the walk-in closet. He stumbled against a laundry basket, spilling clothes across the floor, and his legs gave out around the loose fabric. He struggled to get back on his feet, but by now he was choking. He tasted flint on his tongue and felt the wheezing in his lungs.

The sound of two competing alarms was so loud that he couldn't hear anything else—no sign that his kids were breaking windows, were jumping out, were falling to safety. Pam was still in the bed. Smoke curled above his head, creating a hundred crooked halos. And then there was light, all around him, starry and hot, and he tried one last time to stand, he had stood up so many times in his life, and he lurched over his knees but his breath was gone, and he wished he had the breath to say he was sorry, terribly sorry, for what exactly he did not know, and wouldn't, and those he wanted to tell were deep in the wailing, beyond his hands, somewhere in the lightness, which moved him without his having to move at all, which felt like standing up without ever reaching the end of that beautiful motion.

Eleven minutes after the emergency call went out, the Orient Volunteer Fire Department arrived on the scene. Neighbors had already gathered on the street, their cheeks dancing with yellow flames, unable to do anything, not even look away. The Denmeyers. The Griffins. The two elderly Merriband sisters. Karen Norgen. The bystanders wore blankets around their shoulders and hugged each other, as if those embraces could somehow be transferred to the Muldoons. At first the fire seemed to be confined to the windows, bright orange flags waving in each frame. But soon, as the fire spread, it flared so thick that it turned the night soft and the air loud with its moan. Black shapes appeared in the upper windows, and bystanders prayed at first that the shapes were human, one of the boys or Pam, then prayed the opposite as the shapes dissolved in flames.

The Muldoon house, which neighbors drove by every day and could sketch by memory on a napkin, had always seemed a small, featureless convention of wood and brick. But the fire opened it, showed off its many rooms, the glass side patio bursting with light, the living room a paper lantern with space to burn, even Pam's rose-bushes blossoming with flickers. The house was old and relented slowly, but the furniture inside was new and combustible, and the blaze ate through its meat and joints. Before the trucks arrived, the fire remained in the house, confined to its shape, but soon the house was in the fire, the way a setting sun holds a distant home within its disc. No living thing jumped from its edges.

The emergency call had gone out to the electronic pagers of all fifty-five members of the volunteer fire department. Thirty-one were awake and in range, and within seven minutes they had assembled at the station on Main Road, speed-dressing in their helmets and Kevlar reflector coats. Their lights and alarms swirled through the night frost as they drove the two engines and one heavy rescue pumper up the icy corridor of Youngs Road. The volunteers were a diverse group of Orient men: older farmers whose families had been given the first land grants from the king, religious and temperate and Republican with old tattoos and out-of-shape bodies; then there were the younger, drunker, high-fivers who were quicker to enter a burning house and more precise with their reflexes.

Adam Pruitt, as head of the department, steered the lead engine into the Muldoons' driveway and called out orders as he leaped from the cab. The men worked in tandem, each aware of his role from their monthly drills. They unleashed the hoses across the lawn and secured them to the tanks as other men opened the street's fire well, one of the underground water basins that served as the village hydrants. Adam radioed headquarters in Southold for backup, trucks from Greenport and Mattituck; they would be slow on the ice that was still barricading half the causeway. "Is anyone inside? Has anyone gotten out?" Adam shouted. The bystanders said nothing, their tongues broken in their mouths. Adam knew what that might mean: four bodies.

Bystanders stepped back as the heat swelled. Just to stand twenty feet from the house was to feel what the fire could do to a body, bringing the liquid to the surface, sucking oxygen from the lips and nose. Beams crackled and split; a stench of smoldering synthetics swept through the oaks; the whole house seemed to turn on its foundation, roaring as an eave dropped like paper on the lawn. "Just keep it moving," Adam yelled to his men. To stand still for a second was to risk becoming dazed by it, staring infatuated at the fire like an angry form of love.

They blasted water from the nozzles and drenched the roof and walls, beating back the highest flames. Hoses stretched from the well's opening as men suited up in respirators and masks, chancing the porch steps and axing the glass in the front windows. They sprayed the ceiling through the windows to break the thermal mass before the fresh air fed it. The fire was at 1400 degrees; no way this was electrical, no way this was a cigarette left burning or a gas stove catching a dish towel or a wire gone to rot in a socket. Adam knew by the color of the smoke and the smell it left in his nostrils. This was fire with intention.

The well water quieted the blaze, pacifying the wood to runny char, but under that char were embers ready to relight. Fire was patient too. The firefighters crawled through the front door on their knees, as debris flew above their helmets like summer birds. For a few optimistic minutes it seemed to be under control—the roof was still a roof, the walls were walls—but the hoses had emptied the nearest well, the spouts dribbled, and the fire took advantage, shooting higher, feeding from the inside out until it engulfed the second floor. The beams popped and the roof caved toward collapse. "Out, out, get the fuck out right now," Adam ordered.

They'd need to relay water from another well, a hundred yards down the road; if the Muldoon family hadn't gotten out already, they wouldn't get out now. Had Bryan Muldoon thought about those minutes when he blocked the county water-main proposal? That main would have brought hydrants to every street in Orient, an endless supply from the county water grid. Adam didn't have time to consider the irony of it. George Morgensen unbuckled his coat by the engine's rear step and started working the relay pump. Sirens sang from the causeway with the promise of water and fresh men.

The flames were shooting from the roof into the branches of the oaks, threatening to spread in any direction it wanted. But the hoses fattened again and the water flew into the trees, cascading along the Muldoons' roof until finally black smoke replaced the flames. The Greenport firefighters ran to relieve the Orient volunteers. They dropped to their knees below the smoke line, crawling through what was left of the downstairs. Adam Pruitt knew they'd need the coroner. And not just that, but the detectives, the arson squad, and the mandatory ambulance with its false sense of hope. What was left of the long-standing Muldoons drifted like steam into the night sky.

Eleven minutes from call to scene, thirty-six to extinguish the blaze. How quickly a house was erased.

Mills watched from the street with the other neighbors. He had run from the sofa as soon as he saw the reflection of orange spilling through the living room. Paul joined him two minutes later, holding a coat he hadn't put on, in slippers wet from the snow. Police detectives and friends created a brief gridlock of cars and sorrow on the street, grief-stricken bodies unable to walk, hurrying detectives with no time for grief. Firefighters dug through the rubble. The left side of the house gaped open from roof to basement. There was talk of survivors—no names were mentioned; to say Theo or Tommy or Pam or Bryan was to recall them in happier times—but no survivors were whisked into the idling ambulance. When a neighbor asked if the two brown Labradors were searching for the family, the officer shook his head. "Arson dogs to detect an accelerant." A team of paramedics carried stretchers into the house. Paul took Mills by the shoulders and told him they should go inside before the stretchers came out again.

Pam and Theo had been discovered in their beds. Bryan had been found in a fetal position on his bedroom-closet floor. Tommy's body was the only one not found in a bedroom. It was lying in the upstairs hallway. His window had been smashed from the inside out, suggesting that he might have considered jumping before moving into the hallway to try the stairs. Or perhaps he went into the hall to rescue his family. He should have been discovered first, but the ceiling had caved in on him; firefighters had trampled on the boards before noticing his blackened fist. The detectives tried to get in touch with Lisa Muldoon at her dormitory at SUNY Buffalo, but Pam's parents, reached at 2:00 A.M. at their condo in Islip, demanded that they be the ones to break the news.

Finally, the trucks and police cars pulled out of the driveway, backing up so noiselessly it was as if the Muldoons were still asleep. For a while darkness returned to the street, an unsettling quiet like a matchbook in a drawer.

At dawn, Mills put on a pair of Paul's mud boots and a blue winter coat. Certain that Paul had set the door alarm, he jimmied open a back window and climbed out. Mist from the Sound mixed with the steam from the rubble. The wind brought passing toxic squalls, making the low morning cloud bank smell artificial. He walked toward what was left of the house, darting around back in case a neighbor was staring out a window. He ducked under the police tape. There were pieces of the family everywhere—picture frames, an axed kitchen table, pots and pans and pillows charred and left in syrupy puddles, clothes strewn like fishing nets across the grass. Everything the Muldoons had collected in their home was spread across the lawn for all to see. Someone—a firefighter?—had placed a half-burned needlepoint sampler, "CONSERVE WATER, CONSERVE . . ." on the dislodged washing machine, pinned under a chunk of brick.

Mills picked up a fireplace poker and thrust its arrowed hook in the mud. He had come to say some last words to Tommy, to mourn or remember him somehow. Tommy's desk chair and garbage can lay under a sheet of corrugated metal. Whatever Tommy had been in life had died with him: a kid with so many escape plans, who had failed to escape the one house he pledged to leave. He and the house were gone now, and he would remain that kid in Orient who perished with his family, one of the tragic Muldoons, until even that recollection thinned to nothing. Mills wondered if a seventeen-year-old victim would be called a boy or a man in the newspaper. Probably a son, he thought.

He moved through the rubble, knocking chunks of wood apart with the poker. He saw the black safe with its flaming orange sticker poking from scrolls of carpeting. The DAYS OF OPTIMISM decal bubbled illegibly across its door. Mills wedged the tip of the poker against the hinge and steadied his boot on the safe. He put all his weight on the poker until the metal door snapped, and pieces of a shot glass fell out on the dirt. Mills knelt down and removed Jeff Trader's journal along with the rest of Tommy's secret stash—a slip of paper and a computerized watch, the kind Tommy said his father kept giving him as gifts. Mills pressed its on button to see if it worked. The large, rectangular screen turned blue and told the time, and at the bottom was an icon marked NOTES.

Mills picked through the safe, unsure of what to do with most of the stuff he found. Should he remove the Baggie of pot to save Tommy from being remembered as a druggie? He shoved it in his coat pocket. What about the cherry-flavored condoms? The pack of cigarettes? The framed photograph of Tommy and his sister, which Mills had last seen propped on his desk? He left those in the safe.

Mindful that what he was doing constituted tampering with evidence, he quickly ducked back under the police tape, the journal and watch in his hand. He escaped just in time. A green-and-white taxi pulled in front of the driveway, and a young woman, only slightly older than Tommy, climbed out. She ran toward her house, past the four snowmen that still stood at a safe distance by the curb. Then she turned away, looking up and down the street, as if her childhood house could be found somewhere else, anywhere but in the blackened structure at the end of the walk. The cabdriver waited, turning off the engine and, after a moment, the meter. There was no house for Lisa Muldoon to enter, so she stood in front of its remains, whimpering wordless sounds. She had Pam's sharp chin, Mills saw, and her father's pointed nose, and her oldest brother's deep-set eyes. Finally, she looked at the snowmen—four members of her family with their arms extended, faces slick and melting—and fell to her knees. The thin Indian driver helped her into the taxi, and they vanished green-and-white down the tree-lined street.

CHAPTER 18

When Beth was nine years old, her father decided that her dog needed to be put to sleep. "Sane things can't live with insane things," Anthony Shepherd had said to her as she hugged Moonshine, a pit-bull mutt they had adopted from the North Shore Animal League. The shelter's vet had estimated Moonshine's age at four, but his hair was so paper-clip gray—the parts of him that still grew hair—that he looked much older. He smelled and walked older too, taking a solid minute to get to his feet when a squirrel dotted the lawn. The only thing Moonshine did quickly was bite. He bit her father when he reached under the table at dinner. He bit mailmen and neighbors and other dogs and any animal that was too slow to escape.

The only person Moonshine didn't bite was Beth. She could kiss his black lips, or jump on him when he slept, or pull food from his dish, and he wouldn't so much as growl. But after two years and twelve substantial bites, her father decided he had to be put down. Beth remembered the dog's sour breath on her face—some of the last breaths Moonshine ever took—as she swore to her father that she'd never love another animal again. And she remembered her father's words, even now as she stared out the front window—*sane things can't live with insane things*—two days after the fire.

Across the street, the Aug family was in the process of bringing home a gray pit bull mix from the pound. To announce the arrival of the intimidating pet, they hung a BEWARE OF DOG sign on their fence, where their old PERMANENTLY GONE FISHING sign used to be. Next door to the Augs, a green van marked PRUITT SECURITIES was parked in the Stillpasses' driveway. Two of Adam's workers spent the afternoon there, running wires through the ground-floor windows. Beth considered reversing her childhood promise never to own another animal. She was suddenly open to discussing the possibility of getting a vicious dog, or an alarm system, or any other desperate home-security precaution. The problem was, ever since the party, Gavril had retreated into his work and the two of them had barely spoken.

The house was cold, but Beth didn't build a fire. Even staring into the fireplace reminded her of the Muldoons. After Beth heard the news, she spent hours pacing through the house, frightened and anxious, fearful of hearing the follow-up report that the fire wasn't accidental. Jeff Trader had warned Magdalena about the historical board, and now he and two of its key members, Magdalena and Bryan Muldoon, were dead. If someone had killed Jeff, and then murdered Magdalena for what she suspected about Jeff's death, had that same person burned the Muldoons' house down?

Normally she would have looked to Gavril to tell her she was overreacting, but he'd been locked in his studio for four nights straight, working past midnight and sleeping on the cot. Each morning, he entered the kitchen with bags under his eyes, muttering a halfhearted apology: "I didn't mean to, I just dozed off." She couldn't argue. His excuse was valid, repellent to guilt trips: now that he confirmed a show at Veiseler Projects scheduled for the spring, he was under immense pressure to produce new work. But his long exile in the garage felt like he'd pressed pause on their marriage. Beth was left to the silence of the house, a half-empty bed, and a mind still troubled by her failure to convince the police to investigate the first two deaths before anything worse could happen.

In the wake of the storm, she had canceled her appointment at Planned Parenthood. Now, after the fire, she remained homebound, afraid to venture into the village in case her worst fears were articulated: *the fire wasn't accidental.* The two houses across the street were her only clues to the village consensus, and new alarm systems and guard dogs were not positive signs. Her mother hadn't phoned or visited since the fire, which was unlike her. Gail had hated Pam and Bryan, but she could have applied a theatrical solemnity to the occasion to demonstrate her compassion. It was unlike her to stay away from other people's disasters.

Beth finally decided to call her. "Hi, Mom," she said when Gail picked up.

"Yes, dear," her mother whispered. "I'm sorry I haven't phoned. I've been having some work done on the condo. You know, improving it to increase its value."

Beth tried to control a wave of panic. "You're not planning on selling it?" she asked. With Magdalena and the Muldoons gone, it wouldn't be beyond her mother to plan a spectacular return to Orient. "We just moved in. We're not ready to leave yet."

Her mother sighed. "I'm upgrading the bathroom. For heaven's sake, honey, be reasonable. How is everything there? Tragic, just tragic, what happened to that family. I hear it wasn't electrical."

"What have you heard?"

Over the sound of hammering, Gail told her. "The police are investigating. I imagine they'll have quite a job on their hands. Where do you start on a list of people who didn't like the Muldoons? You'd be better off making a list of those who did."

"Well, you didn't like them. That's one name."

Beth was met with a minute of hostile silence. "Honey, that's not funny," Gail said. "Children were killed. It breaks my heart to think of two kids killed along with those parents. Just chilling, that whole family dying at home, after they were so indignant about everyone else not making any upgrades. Karma is such a nasty thing. Your father always said that, and I agree." It was difficult to believe that Anthony Shepherd, an insurance salesman, believed in karma—unplanned events were his specialty—but Gail routinely projected any convenient creed on her first husband.

"I'm surprised you haven't visited, that's all," Beth said.

"Well, this is new. For once my daughter is asking me to visit. What's the matter? Do you have news for me? That might bring some cheer to Orient."

Beth's hand went to her stomach. She could tell Gail right now that she was pregnant and those simple words would change every step of her future. All of her decisions could be placed in the hands of others.

"I haven't even seen Gavril. He's locked in his studio working."

"You've got to let him make money," Gail said. "I'm telling you this while you're young. There are only a few opportunities for the money to come in, and when you're older you'll be desperate for every dollar you've managed to put away. It's a shame young people don't realize that. All I have is this condo and the house. You better be taking good care of it. Tell Gavril to be careful about those floors in the garage. They're terrazzo. Worth their weight—*No, no, watch the carpeting.* Honey, I've got to go. But do me a favor, will you? Clean out some of the closets in the house for me?"

"Why?"

"Because there's no point in having all that junk lying around. It's a firetrap. Beth, I've really got to run. They're scratching the porcelain. You can't trust these workers. I think they're used to talking to women through a divider of Plexiglas."

Gavril's journal lay open on the counter. He had etched a box in black pen across the page, and below it he had written "*gloves.*" The rest of the page was filled with indecipherable Romanian, spaced like a shopping list. Beth turned the page and saw other notes. "*The house is a lie.*" "*Creative theft.*" "*Ask lawyer about ownership.*" Glued to the pages were newspaper photographs of oil spills, birds and deer twisted like broken umbrellas in black pools of tar.

She poured a glass of whiskey and decided to carry it out to the studio for Gavril. She needed to touch him, to feel the weight of his arms and to press her forehead against his neck. If she hadn't been pregnant, if Gavril didn't have his show, she'd beg him to spend whatever money they had on a vacation: Hawaii like his birthmark,

Bucharest to visit his parents, New York City to re-create their first days again, anywhere where the neighbors weren't securing themselves against a potential murderer. She crossed the lawn and opened the garage door, looking for Gavril's hunched shape in the studio. They were still a couple. Nothing was lost, not yet.

Luz stood on the plastic tarp that covered the floor of the garage, gripping her hips, rocking on her red high-tops. She wore tight jeans and a long blue sweater, her cornrows loosened into soft brown fuzz. She was staring at the clumps of tar Gavril had shaped into grisly two-foot mounds.

Beth heard Gavril's voice echo through the garage. "It just isn't good. It feels empty. Too conventional. No thrust."

"I don't think so," Luz replied. "But do what you want. It's you who has to live with the consequences. Maybe I'm just not getting what you're after."

"You have to give me time on that. I'm not sure yet what I mean. It is not my job to know what it means, is it? I stop when it is the right time to stop."

"That's what I love about us, we don't have to be accountable," Luz said. She noticed Beth standing at the door, drew the sleeve of her sweater to her mouth, and straightened her back. "Beth, I was going to come and knock on your door after I finished visiting Gavril."

Seeing Luz was like being handed a lavish bouquet of flowers in the hospital: a gift of beauty that seemed like an unwanted intrusion from the outer world. Gavril crawled from around a blackened mound, a white surgical mask hanging around his neck.

"I brought you a drink," Beth said, brandishing the glass. "What are you two doing?"

"Luz was just giving me her opinion."

"I'm afraid I haven't been much help." Luz chewed on her sweater sleeve. "My advice to most artists is not to ask me for advice. But Gavril's having such a hard time. That's what we were talking about. He's threatening to cancel his show." Gavril glared up at her, as if to hush her. She rubbed her sleeve against her teeth. "Just keep going. You've got time to change your mind. It's a free country." Luz laughed at her own imitation of Gavril.

A bag of oysters sat on the cart by the door, tied with a pink ribbon and taped with a piece of stationery. "That's from Nathan," Luz said, walking over to the bag and handing it to Beth. "It's his way of apologizing for his behavior at the party. He really feels awful about the fight, which means he hardly remembers it. Nathan tends to black out, which is great for him but messy for those who still have to deal with the aftermath."

Beth unfolded the note. The stationery bore the personalized heading NATHAN CRIMP, printed in a clean blue font beneath the outline of an oyster shell. "To the Catargis, I come in peace. Love, N."

Luz plunked the oysters down on the cart. "Gavril can enjoy them. You can't eat seafood, right?" Luz asked, with a knowing, threatening Luzian smile.

Beth's throat tightened. "Why would you say that?"

"I just thought— Well, I don't know about those things." She touched Beth's arm. "What do you think about that fire? Horrible. Makes you feel lucky . . ."

"To be alive," Beth said, grateful for the change in subject.

"No. Not to be from around here, where someone might want you dead. Didn't you hear? Word is it was arson. My God, Beth, this is your neighborhood. Don't you keep up with what's going on?" Luz shook her head. "Well, I have my own work to do. I just hope my sitters don't cancel with all that's going on. You two should come by for dinner this week. And if you don't mind, save the oyster shells for me. I've been thinking of incorporating them into my work. Maybe I'll tape pornographic pictures to them and hand them out as Christmas gifts." She spun around, her neck swelling with thin cables.

"*Le revedere*," she sang in Romanian.

"*Sarut*," Beth's husband said.

Luz slipped out the door, a hint of lilac perfume lingering behind to mix with the odor of tar. Beth picked up Gavril's drink and crossed the studio to where he knelt, scraping tar on a black mound that was littered with branches and bones and old photographs. Beth averted her eyes from the photos, afraid to see pictures of them from happier times. When your own hairbrush isn't safe, how can you protect photo albums? The tar mounds looked, to her, like the worst sculptures Gavril had ever produced, not just ugly but inert. He gazed up at her, his eyelids swollen from lack of sleep.

"I didn't think you liked hearing anyone's opinions on your work?"

Gavril leaned back on his knees, sighing. "She just came in to give us that present. Besides, maybe it's good to ask a second opinion."

"You've never asked for my opinion."

He looked up at her, then dropped his scraper on the tarp. "Don't nag me about this. Luz is artist. She came in by surprise, so I asked her."

"I am an artist. *Was*, anyway." Beth heard the whine in her voice and recognized a person she didn't want to be: a woman begging for attention, a wife threatened by the opinions of other women, the kind of woman who turns other women into enemies simply because they're more confident. Beth was becoming the kind of woman she and Gavril used to make fun of on their walks home from dinner in New York. Could their marriage be saved if she and Gavril bonded over how much they disliked the new Beth?

"Please, don't make me feel guilty. I am having a hard time. These pieces just look dead. No life to them. I cannot get them to work. In New York I could, but here . . ." He waved his hands. Beth studied the disasters. It had started with a puddle of tar, a stain in the water, and that stain had evolved into budding lumps, like some primordial soup generating mass before it crawled out to begin a new species. At least Beth guessed that was Gavril's intention, when really the mounds looked more like the kind of scorched furniture that must be spread across the Muldoons' lawn. Some of the lumps were decorated with golden marbles, glimmering like bees, and the photos, perhaps collected from a thrift store, were of long-dead people laughing, vacations neither of them had taken, times that looked more sincere because they happened before either of them was born. "I try to build up the death—to make it alive, real, my own Orient landscape—but it doesn't work. Just dead. And the more it builds, the worse it becomes. What you see may be the end of my career. One bad show, Beth, and I end up an art teacher at a small college on Long Island. One bad show and everything before is worth nothing. People only remember the last thing you've made."

She bent down to put her arms around him, ignoring the tar from his overalls that smeared across her sweatshirt, trying to bring her lips to his. He heaved a sigh and slowly pushed her away. She fought him, digging her fingers into his back, trying to wear him down with affection. She slipped her hand toward his crotch, but he grabbed her wrist. She stopped.

"Why don't we take a vacation?" she said. "Why don't we leave for a week or two? Somewhere romantic. That fire scared me, Gavril. Couldn't we?" She begged him again. "Just the two of us. Only a week or two. Maybe it will give you some distance to think. You'll still have the rest of the winter to finish the work."

Gavril stood up, stepping over the wet vats of tar heated by small blue flames. Animal bones that Gavril must have bought from the butcher sat in a queasy pile, rib cages and humerus bones, some with their blue meat still attached. She thought she saw a sheep's skull under a hoof. Bags of oyster shells and animal fur spilled across the tarp. These were the materials her chosen mate preferred. Gavril placed the white mask over his mouth and pointed at it. "*Ou houldn't ee in here, reathing the umes.*"

Beth pulled the mask from his mouth. His lips were tight beneath it.

"We could buy tickets online and leave tonight," she said. "Wouldn't it be wonderful? Just us. To get out of Orient for a while. To forget what's happening out here."

His eyes hollowed.

"How do we pay for a trip?" he said angrily. "I work. This is what I do for money. And now that I need to work, you want to run off and spend what we don't have. This is all we have, Beth. I have not asked you to contribute. I know you've had a hard time and I know you needed to take a break. But don't ask me to throw away my career because you're tired or bored or scared of your own house that I agreed to live in because that is what you wanted. To come here. To give up New York to be with you. You asked for this, remember?" He stared at her with his dirty teeth moving, his brown eyes staring directly into hers. "What more do you want from me?"

She snapped the mask against his mouth and walked toward the door. Gavril didn't run after her. He must have pulled the mask down because she heard him say "I love you," clearly. Then he said, "But you need to leave me alone."

On her way back to the house, Beth saw a gray sedan parked in the driveway, its metal doors corroded by snow and salt. As she opened the back door, she heard the doorbell ring. She hurried through the house and unlocked the dead bolts on the front door. By the time she got it open, Mike Gilburn was already retreating down the walk.

He turned in surprise and headed back toward her, scratching his beard. Even though they were about the same age, gray strands had already woven their way through his patchy brown hair. "The last time I came to your door like this I was picking you up," he said, smiling. "Did I bring roses?"

"Carnations, I think," Beth said, although she couldn't remember any flowers, couldn't remember one solid detail in the mental photo album of teenage dates that hadn't resulted in heartbreak or sex. She thought she recalled a horror movie, maybe a few beers over a pinball machine.

"I wish I could say that's why I'm here." His sentence brought him to shuffle his heels. His face reddened. "Not to take you out. I hear you're married. What I meant was, I wish this was a social call."

When she'd called the detective on the day of Magdalena's funeral, he had made her feel like the local busybody. How old did you have to be before you qualified for that title? At thirty-two, Beth might be the youngest busybody ever.

"It's funny," Mike said, tipping back on his heels. "Just last month I was thinking about giving up my place in Southold and moving back out here to a little Orient fixer-upper. I found one for sale not far from here. Sarakit Herrig was the agent for the house and she told me not to even bother bidding. Too many interested parties willing to go sky-high for a property on the Sound, she said. She told me I ought to hold on to what I have." Mike seemed proud of his meager paycheck, buoyant in his hybrid sneaker/dress shoes. "That's quite a business strategy Sarakit's got going. Cut everyone out but the rich. I wanted to remind her that her husband taught me geography in school."

"Things have changed out here," Beth replied.

"Well, I just drove by it and it's still sitting vacant. Maybe those sky-highers had second thoughts. Maybe now she'd accept money from a guy like me."

Beth smiled impatiently. She was still bruised by the fact that he hadn't listened to her. "What can I do for you, Mike?"

"I'm sorry I didn't take your call as seriously as I should have." His voice was the Long Island-ese of her childhood, clipped consonants, a saxophone of vowels. Bad for apologies. "You can't blame me. The deceased you were worried about was very old, and we still have no reason to assume her death was suspicious."

"I don't blame you," she said slowly, intentionally unhysterical. "I just wish you had listened. I think of you as a friend."

"Of course," Mike said in relief. He scratched his beard again. His white shirt was stained yellow under the armpits, hardened by washing and dark with fresh sweat. She wondered if he'd decided not to wear a coat so she'd be more likely to invite him in. Or maybe he simply wanted to appear less official, an acquaintance instead of a police detective. He kept looking over her shoulder, as if to catch sight of her phantom husband in the hallway. His left hand gripped a notebook ceremonially. He had no pen. "I'm glad you think of me as a friend. I was hoping you would." He paused. "You heard about the fire." He cast his eyes past Magdalena's lawn, toward the Muldoons' home farther west along the Sound.

"It was arson, wasn't it?"

He nodded. "We detected an accelerant poured through the ground floor."

"Who would do that?"

Mike scratched his beard again, a tic so persistent she wanted to suggest he shave it off. "That's what we're trying to determine. We don't have any strong leads yet. It's a fresh case. Seems everyone in Orient has their own opinions about who could have been responsible. And then there's the insurance company's opinion. They'd like to pin it on the eldest son. He seemed to have some problems with his family—normal teenage stuff, but he wasn't found in his room like the rest of them. If a family member started the fire, the insurance company could fight the claim."

Beth didn't know much about Tommy Muldoon other than what she'd gleaned seeing him walking down Main Road after school. He was the sort of remote, maladjusted kid who would have attracted her in high school. She didn't know much about his personality other than the fact that he and Mills had been friends, or more than friends—a more-ness that had sent Pam out on her motherly warpath the last time Beth saw her alive.

"I can't believe a kid would turn on his family like that," she said. Mike nodded, scratched.

"Yeah, have you been watching the local news? All those pictures of the Muldoons they keep showing, like the perfect family, arms around each other, so many picnics. I didn't know a family could throw so many picnics. It would be hard, in that light, to press a case for the fire being started by the son. These cases get played out in the court of public opinion too. Of course, we want to solve the case whether the community's bringing any pressure or not."

"I haven't been watching the news," she told him as she leaned against the doorframe. "And, to be honest, I haven't left my house in days, so I don't know what's going on."

"I'm not solving this alone," Mike said, jerking the conversation forward, impatiently guiding it toward his purpose. "The fire marshal's involved too, and he's threatening to bring in some bigwigs from the city to take over. I've only had this position for a year, and they keep trying to back burner me. They don't think a Southold detective has the experience to investigate such a vicious case. I keep telling them that a local detective's going to know the people who can help get to the bottom of it." He tapped his notebook. "I came here because I remembered what you said about Magdalena. I know you've only been back for a few months, but I got the feeling you've been paying attention to things. So I just stopped by to ask you, as a friend, if you had any observations that might help me. Anything strange or connected."

"Connected?"

"Just anything that could shed some light." Mike Gilburn's lips twitched. For Beth, it was a glimpse of how desperate he was. Mike was still trying to get a cat out of a tree, and there were four bodies in the Southold morgue that, for once, he couldn't dismiss as natural deaths. "People out here are scared. And more than one of them has brought up your name, because they've heard you believe Magdalena Kiefer was murdered."

Beth closed her eyes. She had meant to come back to Orient to start a new life. Now death was greeting her on the front porch.

"Tell me again why you thought your neighbor was killed."

"First of all, I'm not involved with any of this. I don't really enjoy being thought of as the woman in Orient brewing crazy stories about murder. Six months ago, I was living in Manhattan." She tossed her fingers, a cultivated gesture of urban anomie. "I pretty much keep to myself."

"I understand that."

"Just so you do," she said. "As for Magdalena, it all goes back to Jeff Trader. Magdalena thought he knew something, something bad happening out here—and before you ask, I don't know what it was. She told me that Jeff had changed in recent months, gotten nervous and fearful. Apparently he came to see her right before he died, drunk and rambling on about the historical board. Magdalena was convinced he was killed out in the harbor. Not suicide or an accident, but murdered over something he had found out. Maybe it involved the historical board, or maybe it was unrelated, a secret someone else didn't want discovered. All I know is, a few days later, Magdalena was also dead. That's what I was trying to tell you in her driveway." Mike raised a defensive hand, but Beth kept talking. "Maybe Magdalena was killed because of what she suspected. Maybe someone silenced her before she could speak."

Mike looked down at his blank notebook in frustration. "You said on the phone that you might have evidence."

Beth didn't know whether Mills had managed to retrieve Jeff's journal before the fire. It might already be destroyed, lying amid the char of Tommy's former bedroom. But a whimper escaped her throat as she realized that Tommy had been the last person to have the book. Now Tommy was dead, as if the book itself had brought on each crime.

"Are you okay?" Mike asked, cocking his head.

"I had a journal that belonged to Jeff Trader. Magdalena gave it to me to hold on to." She wasn't going to admit to trespassing.

"Can I see it?"

"I'm not sure where it is," she stalled. "I'll have to look for it." Mike's expression quickly changed, and he grunted almost skeptically. He didn't believe her. But she refused to implicate Mills, not until she had spoken with him. "I've been having a hard time lately," she improvised. "I'm sorry. My husband and I, we've been trying to have a baby, but it doesn't look like that's going to happen."

Mike nodded apologetically. She remembered his recent divorce and the loneliness in his voice when he talked about the children he and his wife didn't get around to having. "When you find the book, can you please call me?" He slipped a business card from his shirt pocket.

"I already have your number."

He gave it to her anyway. "Right now I'm not treating either of those deaths as related. But I'd like to see that book. I'd consider it a favor if you took the time to look for it. One last question, Beth, and then I promise I'll let you get back to your day." He touched his fingers to her arm. He had small, sensitive hands, un-cop-like hands, better for consoling victims than for cuffing perpetrators. "Do you know anyone who had a problem with the Muldoons? Anyone who was in a fight with them? Any reason at all that someone might wish them harm?"

She was glad she hadn't mentioned Mills. Even a small-time cop like Mike Gilburn was bound to learn of the argument between Mills and Pam before long. She wanted desperately to protect him, to fake an alibi if he needed one, to cast suspicion anywhere but in the direction of Paul's unknown foster kid. There was no stopping suspicion once it settled on a person. When one bird found a boulder rising from the water, other birds followed until they built a colony, squabbling over every inch.

"No," she said. "I mean, I know there was a lot of disagreement about Bryan's plans for conservancy, but nothing that would lead to murder."

"I thought you said the historical board might have been the reason that Jeff Trader was killed."

"He warned Magdalena about the board. But she sat on that board too. She did change her will just before she died. She decided not to leave her house to OHB, so that could be important."

Mike smiled at his first moment of insight. "Then they wouldn't have had much to gain by killing her, would they?"

"God, I don't know." She groaned. "Are you sure the fire wasn't accidental? How do you know that an accelerant was poured intentionally through the house? Couldn't there be other explanations? Who knows what happens behind closed doors?"

Mike scratched his beard. She noticed that he still wore his wedding ring. Why would a man keep wearing his wedding ring months after signing his divorce papers? It was like chastening the hand for what it could no longer reach for in support.

"There's a reason we can't pin it on Tommy," he said. "The front door of the Muldoons' house had been opened. Not broken in by the firefighters, but opened. The alarm system had gone off. Why would a kid who meant to burn his house down allow the alarm system to go off before he lit the match? And where did he put the canister? Tommy died in the upstairs hallway. We didn't find any sort of gas can at the scene. Whoever started the fire must have taken the canister with him. Out the front door, the same way he came in."

She closed her eyes and gripped the doorknob. Mike thanked her. "Call me when you find the book. Or if anything else occurs to you. Even if you just want to talk."

Beth stepped into the hall. "Mike," she said as he proceeded down the walk. "How's the daughter? Is Lisa Muldoon holding up okay?"

Mike froze and turned his head.

"She's as bad as you could expect. Came down from college in Buffalo and arrived the next morning. We've got her staying at the Seaview. Someone should pray for that poor girl."

Beth closed the door and walked up the stairs. She took her clothes off, stepped into the shower, and leaned into the warm jet that rinsed her face. Her stomach was beginning to bowl out just below her navel, as firm as muscle. She hugged herself under the nozzle and thought of Mills and the argument with Pam in Paul's front yard, right out in the open where anyone could see. She felt she had to do something to help him, and waiting around wasn't it. Beth tied a towel around her waist and entered the bedroom. Pulling open the drawer of her end table, she took out Jeff Trader's pen-ravaged photograph of Holly Drake. "What about you?" she said.

CHAPTER 19

I n a matter of days, Pruitt Securities signs popped up on the front lawns of Orient like late-blooming flowers. Beth saw that the Drakes had one staked in their lawn. Through the wavy glass of the front windows, beyond the elaborate display of jacquard swatches and lotus motifs, she saw Holly sitting alone in a leather chair, bent forward like the arm of a desk lamp. Holly was sobbing, her shoulders and long red hair shaking, a tissue bunched in her fingers. Her silks were spread around her on the carpet, like sunning lizards in a terrarium. Beth stepped back and rang the bell. It took two minutes for Holly to compose herself.

When the door opened, Holly stared out from the shadows. Her freckled skin was blotched red, and her nose was running.

"Oh, I'm sorry," Beth said, feigning surprise. "Is this a bad time? Of course it is. It's a bad time in general out here. I can come back."

Holly shook her head and sniveled. "If you want to see Cole again, he's at his office. You can try him there."

"No, I'm actually here for your fabrics," she said, pointing to a gaudy turquoise batik through the window. "I wanted to buy one for a birthday present. But honestly if this isn't—"

"No, no, it's fine. Please." Holly swept her fingers through her hair and straightened herself into the role of saleswoman. Beth knew that Holly couldn't afford, even in sorrow, to turn away a customer—especially a customer who had fashionable Manhattan friends with conspicuous bank accounts, not when her home textile emporium had languished so long out of sync with the regional tastes of Eastern Long Island. She ushered Beth into the showroom parlor, messier than it had been on her first visit, with fabrics and papers strewn across the desk and floor. A tuna sandwich lay abandoned on a plate after a single bite. Holly balanced herself on the edge of the desk, her black sweater brightening her long, red hair.

A marbled cat wound between the desk legs and made a run for the hallway, but not fast enough for Holly, who scooped it up and brought its neck to her cheek. "Pearl, behave."

"I didn't know you had a cat." Beth reached out in its general direction but had no intention of petting it. Do not approach cats when trying to affect a general sense of harmony and compassion. Cats are mutinous betrayers; never count on them for cooperation.

"She was a stray. Showed up a week ago and wouldn't leave the back door. Her cries broke my heart. I have to keep her in the basement when Cole's home—he doesn't like them. He doesn't realize they just need someone to give them a little affection." Holly sneezed and the cat sprang from her chest, jumping across the Persian carpet and scampering up the steps. Beth wondered if it was one of the cats Mills had fed at Jeff Trader's house. Holly dabbed at her nose with the tissue.

"Maybe you're allergic," Beth said.

Holly waved off the idea, gliding through her showroom. Her fair, freckled skin was rash red and blotchy, a barometer of her suffering. It was the kind of skin that made for a terrible liar.

"What are you looking for exactly?" Holly asked, wearily. "I have some gorgeous pillowcases from Iran that have just arrived. Or some South Indian napkins, beaded by local women. Ten cents on every dollar fights sex slavery."

Beth walked to the window seat, her fingers flipping through swatches of soft embroidery, feigning admiration. They were beautiful, though overpriced for a market that had yet to settle on the North Fork. But Beth respected Holly's commitment to the exotic wares, which seemed to contradict the plain suburban man she had married. Could anyone be less exotic than Cole Drake? She had always liked Holly, the way she liked any woman who used bumper stickers to declare her right to choose and the injustices of the death penalty—two very un–Cole Drake opinions. Perhaps if she hadn't come here to interrogate Holly, they might have become friends, sharing lunches and books and protesting the protestors outside the Hauppauge Planned Parenthood clinic.

Holly vanished down the sunken step to the den but soon rematerialized, wearing a pair of velvet house slippers. "I have some saris coming in a shipment this week. They're over sixty years old, too delicate to wear, but they're gold-threaded and make for wonderful wall décor. I don't know who you're shopping for. A loved one maybe? Or a friend?" Beth had presumed that getting Holly to talk in her grief would be easy, but Holly checked her tears, biting down on the pain. She was tougher than Beth had expected.

"Holly, are you okay? Maybe we should sit down?" Beth asked, touching her shoulder, a surprise attack of compassion.

"No," Holly said coolly, stepping backward in alarm, as if Beth had asked if she needed to go to the hospital. "I mean, why?"

Beth tried again. There seemed to be some specific implication in Holly's grief, something about the death of the Muldoons that had struck her particularly hard.

"I know what it's like to be alone out here," Beth said. "I don't have many people to talk to either. The quiet can get to you." Beth grabbed Holly's wrist. When she didn't withdraw it, she led her toward the couch. Beth sat first, leaving Holly no option but to do the same.

"I'm sorry," Holly managed. "I'm just so broken up about the fire, about Bryan and his family killed like that. How could that happen to such sweet people? Bryan was doing so much good in the village, or trying to. Why would anyone do that to him?"

Beth was surprised by the way Holly spoke about the tragedy. She thought she'd been closer to Pam, but it was Bryan's name that brought tears to her eyes.

"How's everything with Cole? Are you two doing okay?"

Holly lifted her chin in a manner implying that the labor of chin-lifting was noble under the circumstances. "You're right," she said weakly. "It does get lonely out here, and friends haven't come easily. Orient has always been Cole's home, not mine. I've tried to make the most of it. I opened this shop. This useless, stupid shop where I make no money except for what I sell online. I don't even need this show-room. I could sell my textiles from anywhere. You know, this wasn't exactly my plan. I was in medical school at Syracuse when I met Cole. He was getting his law degree. One summer I went to Karachi as a volunteer nurse, and the women in those NGO camps were so impressive, so inspiring to me, that when I came back I started work-ing in textiles made by the women there. I quit school and married Cole, and for a while I was happy. But now, I'd give anything to go back and finish my degree. I used to hate those cold dissections, but I'd love to do them now. Love to feel like I was getting my fingers under the skin, touching something real."

Holly examined the pink undersides of her hands, scalloped and cracked from the dry winter air.

"It was my mistake," she said somberly. "Quitting and moving out here, I mean. It wasn't Cole's fault. You asked how we're doing. I don't know. And now with the fire, and poor Bryan and his family dead, and this living room full of colors from a world away . . ."

Holly was trembling now.

"Can I tell you something?" Beth asked. Holly gazed at her be-wilderedly, as if she could barely imagine that anyone else had re-grets. "My husband and I came out here to start a family. He moved out here for me, the same way you did for Cole. And now I feel selfish, because I don't think I want a family anymore. I'd rather not have a kid. How do you go back on something you promised? But I realize that it's not selfish to change your mind. You have to make concessions. You don't have to be held hostage by the person you once thought yourself to be."

Holly slid her hand over her stomach. "I've made concessions," she whimpered. "I've done things I didn't intend. Children. There won't be any. Cole doesn't want them."

Beth took her chance.

"You were very close to Bryan Muldoon, weren't you?"

The allegation woke Holly. "Who told you that?" She stiffened her shoulders. "Who said so? Did Bryan tell you that? He couldn't have."

Beth massaged Holly's knee. "No one told me," she said softly. "But I could see it between you two even at the picnic. I'm not going to say a word. I would never break your confidence like that. I want you to know that I understand." Beth had just wanted to gain Holly's trust, but now she felt that she'd hold true to her promise of confidence. Perhaps they could be friends after all.

"Are you sure Bryan didn't tell you?" Holly dropped the tissue on the floor. "Look, I liked Pam. And I want to respect the memory of that family, even if they're gone and I'm the one who's left, having to live with it all by myself." She breathed into the room, eyes dulled by the fabrics embroidered by hundreds of faceless women that spilled around her feet. "I didn't expect it to go further than what it was. What it was for me was a break in time, a minute outside of my life. Two married people with obligations and nowhere to go but a motel room once a week. Jesus, that sounds cheap. But it wasn't cheap. I used to stay in that rented room at the Seaview for the rest of the afternoon once Bryan left. I'd sit on the bed and look out at the Sound and convince myself that I was happy. Do you know how much convincing that takes?" Tears ran down her freckled cheeks. She purposely didn't look at Beth. "Did Bryan say anything about me? If he told you, I'd like to hear what he said. It would mean something to me."

"He didn't," Beth admitted. "I don't know if he told anyone. I'm sure you would have heard if Pam had found out."

Holly collected herself on the couch. Her bitten fingernails dug into the armrest. "She didn't know. Absolutely not. Anyway, Bryan and I stopped about a month ago." She glanced sidelong at Beth, and her voice deepened. "Pam *did not* find out. There was no split, no scene. It just ended. The affair was casual. We were intelligent adults. Until I heard about the fire, it hadn't even occurred to me that I had come to depend on it." Beth nodded but swept her eyes to the floor too quickly. Holly yanked her forearm and squeezed. "Don't look away like that. I said, there was no scene. I wasn't interested in breaking up his family and I wasn't going to destroy it if I couldn't have Bryan all to myself." Holly laughed hoarsely. "I didn't set that house on fire, if that's what you're thinking. My god, I would never."

"I don't think that," Beth said.

"And I wasn't the first. Bryan had been with other women, women he took to the Seaview before I ever came along. That evil bitch, Eleanor, who runs the motel always made these snide little comments. 'A new one, mister. Hope you don't mind the same room. Getting to be your room, isn't it? Number thirty-one.' So I swear, if you're thinking I could have done that, poured gasoline around his house and lit a match like some heartbroken harridan, you're wrong. I didn't care about those other women. I don't expect anyone to be a saint. I'm not. I'm sure Pam wasn't. Maybe only Cole is. Maybe that's my punishment, having to share my life with a saint."

"What about Cole? Did he find out?" As soon as the words left her mouth, Beth regretted them. She should have allowed a minute to pass before asking that. She had overstepped, moving too swiftly beyond the temporary shelter she had built in their conversation. Holly stood up, retreating to the sliding door near the den, creating hostile space between them.

"Why are you asking?"

"I was just concerned," she faltered.

"He was in the city for business that night. Is that why you're asking, because he wasn't here with me?" Her thoughts seemed to fly across her face as she spoke, each one redder than the last. "Did you even come here to buy a present? Cole's office has a branch in Manhattan, for Christ's sake. He commutes there for meetings all the time. I drove him to the train station myself." The words came angrily, as if Holly had already realized the inconvenience of her husband's absence on the night of the fire, which denied either of them an alibi. Holly's eyes narrowed. "Whose birthday is it? Don't lie to me."

Before Holly could push any further, Beth fished through her purse and pulled out the photograph. When she held it out, Holly squinted at it, her brain erasing the devil horns and the scratched-out eyes and the goatee, to see herself smiling on her own summer lawn. She snatched the photo from Beth's fingers.

"What is this? Why did you do this to me?" Holly stared at her as if she suddenly thought Beth herself might be capable of taking a match to an Orient house. "This is my picture. Cole took this of me two summers ago. I can tell by the roses. It should be in our picture drawer."

"I found it in a book belonging to Jeff Trader. I wondered why Jeff would do this to a photo of you. That's why I'm here, to ask you about it."

"Jeff Trader," Holly said furiously, relishing the bitter memory with a flicking tongue. "He didn't like me. But so what? I didn't like him either. He did odd jobs for us for a few years. Cole insisted. Give the local drunk his due. I guess Cole saw that disgusting man as some sort of village mascot. But he wasn't harmless. He stood around asking me all kinds of personal questions. Were we planning to have children? If we did, were we going to move into a bigger home or build onto the back of this one? Did Cole like his job? Was I happily married?" She snorted after the last question. "It's not innocent to ask those kind of questions, even when you do reek of liquor at ten in the morning. Finally, I caught him searching through the drawers of my desk—looking for I don't know what, cash most likely—and I fired him on the spot. I told him I was going to call the police and warn other families out here. Isn't that what a good neighbor is supposed to do when the man who takes care of all the houses in Orient turns out to be a thief?"

Beth smiled wanly and leaned forward to reclaim the photograph, but Holly held it to her chest. "No, I'm keeping this. It belongs to me. I don't know who you think you are, but you have no right to enter my house and ask me to justify what I've done when all I'm guilty of is unhappiness. Infidelity, sure, but that's unhappiness by another means. I was only trying to do what any human being would do." Holly attacked her own sweater with groping hands.

"I'm not asking—"

"You tricked me. And I've defended you in this community time and time again when there were nasty words spoken about you. And, believe me, there have been plenty." Holly pulled on a red rivulet of hair by its tip. "What an arrogant snob you are. Cold and judgmental, condescending, just like your mother. I guess I didn't see the resemblance until now." Beth gathered her purse, and Holly pointed toward the hallway. "Get out."

But both women froze at the oncoming roar of a motor. They watched through the glass as a green Subaru pulled into the driveway. Cole climbed out, carrying his briefcase, warped and embryonic through each adjoining pane. Holly blew deep breaths, warning Beth with her eyes. She picked up a batik swirling with peacocks and jagged striations, stretching the fabric between her arms, and started extolling its virtues before the key turned in the lock.

"It's block printed by little girls in Malaysia with natural inks. The peacock is a common symbol in the east for holiness and purity and the virtue of friendship because it shows its true colors." The front door opened, and a shadow passed into the foyer. "Not to mention the eye of the feather, always watching. The silver unblinking eye of god. If you look closely, the background pattern is fire. When you move the fabric, it looks like it's burning. And the eyes are all over it, watching, resistant to flames."

Cole stepped into the room, his skinny body barely filling his suit. The sharp folds of his necktie matched the sharp side part in his hair. He glanced at the two women entranced by the batik under the showroom lights. When Beth looked over her shoulder, he fixed his stare on her and passed through the parlor toward the den.

"Sweetie, you're back early. It's only two o'clock." Cole clenched and unclenched his hand like it had been wounded. "Beth's just buying a birthday present. Your friend is going to love this. And what a steal, just two hundred dollars. Cash only. A percentage goes to the Malaysian orphan fund. Shall I wrap it in tissue?" Beth had only $130 in her wallet, but Holly took it without counting. She bagged the batik without wrapping it in tissue.

"That armoire and grandfather clock are sitting in Magdalena's house waiting for you to collect them," Cole said, almost numb, as he set his briefcase down by the step. There were certain houses where the air was so crowded with disappointments they were as claustrophobic as an elevator between floors. "I can't promise they'll be there after her house gets sold. You can take them whenever you want. Your choice."

Beth wanted to ask if the Kiefer property was for sale, but Cole vanished into the den. Holly led her to the door. The marbled cat tried to flee the house, making a desperate low-crawling dash at freedom, but Holly stopped it with her slipper.

"Don't come back," Holly said as she waved.

CHAPTER 20

Mills sat on his bed, scrolling through Tommy's computer watch. Besides a clock, a compass, a weather forecast, and a game devoted to brick building, the only other feature on the high-tech watch was a file reserved for notes. Tommy recorded his secrets in a jumpy list, interspersed with rambling cultural observations time-stamped over the course of the past year. "What would 9/11 have been like if the people trapped in the towers had Facebook and Instagram and smartphones? The world would have tracked the fall of the towers through constant Twitter updates." "Wilt Chamberlain slept with 20,000 women; Fidel Castro 35,000. Communists and basketball players believe in quantity. But wouldn't better sex dudes have their scores handicapped by repeats?" "SAT vocab reminder: Even using the word grandiloquent is grandiloquent." "Jack Kerouac slept with men. Jesse Arnez keeps wearing a Jack Kerouac T-shirt to school. Jesse Arnez must be willing to try things." "Where does all our garbage go? Our world would be a moonscape of trash without garbage men. Why is there no national garbage men day? Because we'd have to treat them like men and not like garbage."

Mills was impressed with Tommy's private thoughts. Mills had an airtight room in his mind for his own desires, but Tommy had built this room in his phone for his musings, never meant for outside eyes, and in reading them Mills found the sorrow for the young man's death that he hadn't managed to summon while standing in the burned remains on the lawn. You can't will ghosts to haunt you. They elude when prompted; like weather, they must come on their own. One entry, from August, even included a salacious personal entry: "7.25 inches, ¼ inch bigger than last year." Women had cup sizes to track their development. Men had a ruler and hope.

But there were other entries on the watch, less personal, that suggested why Tommy felt he needed to hide it in a locked safe. "Dad loaned 10k to Ted Herrig; can't pay it back? Mom doesn't know." "Parties on Arthur's Ark always include Gardiner descendants. WTF? Island?" "Rm. 31 Seaview motel. 3 dif women, all married!" "Karen N. closeted lesbian." "Rev. Whitlen, 2013 C-Class Mercedes. Church funds?" "Roe diC, three screaming messages on dad's answering machine." "Why is old Raleigh house so hard to buy?" "Orient Monster, bodies of animals: raccoon, dog, pig, deer, badger, sheep. All local wildlife." "Big artist = total fraud."

The parade of local gossip went on in digital type. Mills recalled Tommy standing in his boy-smelling bedroom, bragging about how he'd escape Orient once he found the money to get away. Mills wondered if he'd been saving up these Orient secrets in hopes of one day using them as blackmail. And he also wondered if the darker secrets in Jeff Trader's journal had sped that plan along, spurring Tommy to blackmail someone. Could that someone have resorted to arson to keep him silent? Fire was a good way to destroy both the evidence and the kid who clumsily wielded it.

The last entry was written on the day Mills had found Tommy walking up the street in a rage. "She's a liar. Seaview room for one. Should I turn her in?" Her not *him*—not Bryan Muldoon, but a woman. What could Tommy have turned her in for? Had he found a woman's name in Jeff Trader's book and matched it to one of his father's affairs? Along with Jeff's journal, Mills had found a piece of paper in the safe, engraved with a drawing of an oyster shell in profile, the circle of a pearl lodged in its crevice. On it Tommy had scrawled, "Orient's real threat is its trust." Mills didn't know what to make of the note. As a sensationally normal seventeen-year-old,

Tommy was susceptible to sensationalism. By "trust," did he mean the trust set up for the Kiefer Nondevelopment Initiative? Or was he warning against trust in general—the kind applied to neighbors that they'd always look out for one other?

The fire had spooked Mills, burning nightmares into his dreams. He had stayed indoors for the past two days. Paul was even more disturbed by his neighbors' deaths. Mills heard him making choking sounds as he stared out of the parlor window, like a hand drill hushed by a bed pillow: *Umph, erg, oh, errr*—as if he were registering the fact of the fire over and over again. *They're dead. The Muldoons are dead. The people next door are gone.* Paul set the alarm system every night and darted around the house placing fresh batteries in the smoke detectors. He even brought a rope ladder up from the cellar and told Mills, as casually as anyone could when discussing home-safety precautions, that he'd leave it in the upstairs closet in case they had to climb out of a second-floor window.

"Who do you think set the fire?" Mills had asked him bluntly.

"Let's wait to hear the final verdict from the police before we start pointing fingers," Paul said, feigning calm. To Mills he seemed New York naïve, suffering under the same delusional mentality he'd witnessed in every other affluent white resident of that metropolis. From the safe haven of their urban fortress of coffee shops and yoga studios and flower-lined delis, they had all convinced themselves that New York City was still the most dangerous city in America. New Yorkers should spend a week in Modesto, Mills thought, where carjackings and desert shotgun assaults were as constant as quinceañera parties in the public gardens.

The morning after the fire, three officers had knocked on Paul's door. A bearded plainclothes detective and two uniformed cops stood on the porch and asked questions while Mills listened from the shadows of the foyer. Had Paul seen anyone suspicious the day of the fire, creeping around the Muldoons' house? Had he noticed any erratic behavior in the family members? Had Paul been home all night? The questions were "just procedure," Detective Gilburn promised, scratching his beard as he flipped through his notebook, nodding along to Paul's answers. "We'll be coming back, if we need to, for a thorough statement," the detective said as he shook Paul's hand. "Again, just procedure. And it will give you a little time to remember if anything comes to mind."

Erratic behavior. Creeping around the house. Mills tried to let the questions pass through him without sharpening them into hooks.

Paul had asked him, over lunch that afternoon, if he had woken on the couch before or after the fire started. Mills told him after, that he had heard the noise of the blaze or the sirens or maybe the neighbors collecting on the sidewalk. What he recalled most vividly was the orange light spilling across the coffee table.

"I saw you asleep before I went upstairs to bed," Paul said. "If the police come back, I just don't want—" He stopped, his fists balled against his plate.

"What?"

"Nothing." Paul's foot stamped the floor, as if applying a car brake. A labored smile intercepted his thoughts. "It will be fine. It's just that in all the years I've lived here, I've never witnessed something like this. The whole village is going to be in hysterics. I pray they find a defective electrical socket before the funeral. It's awful that every time I step outside, the remains of that house are right beside us." There was a sharp tug in his voice, like Christmas lights yanked from a tree. "I was about thirteen when Bryan and Pam moved in. They were this young, happy couple. My mother took a liking to Pam. Helped her with her garden and when she was pregnant with Lisa." Mills had a hard time imagining Pam and Bryan just starting out; they seemed to him as fixed and severe as military statues. "And they were so good to me when my mother was sick. I just can't wrap my head around it. Theo was nine. Tommy, seventeen. Kids in their own home." Paul shut all the curtains on the left side of the house to blind them from the rubble. Mills peered through them, watching a team of red-vested investigators sift through the debris. One of the pieces of evidence they carted away was Tommy's safe. It must have seemed more valuable once the bumper sticker was obliterated from its door.

Paul tried to get back to work on his laptop—"Just putting some finishing touches on this corporate headquarters my firm's present-ing for an international food distributor. It'll never get built. All I do is design corporate buildings that never end up getting built." Mills sat on the parlor floor, sorting ancient VHS tapes and a summer's worth of news clippings from the rededication of Bug Light in 1990, when the ersatz lighthouse was feted with fireworks and a marching band. He blew the dust off of Paul's digital video camera and added it to the keepsake box.

Neither of them made much headway with their work. Paul had hardly eaten, and he drank an entire bottle of a North Fork Cab-ernet, pacing nervously at the front windows, as if expecting the police to return, or some kind of village mob. The sidewalk slowly filled with bouquets, teddy bears, and farewell signs—"we will not forget you Tommy. ♥, Sycamore Senior Class"—before a series of rain squalls reduced them to mulch.

When Paul decided to hose the ash off the side of the house, he told Mills that he'd do it alone. "Just stay inside. You don't need to do every repair," he said while putting on his mud boots. Mills under-stood that Paul was trying to protect him by keeping him out of sight.

Mills could have left, but leaving now would look suspicious. *The kid next door, disappearing for no reason days after the fire.* But more than that, Mills felt like he possessed the keys to the crime—Tommy's notes and Jeff's journal, two pieces of evidence that must hold some answer. If the fire turned out to be connected to Jeff Trader and Magdalena Kiefer, Mills was already deep in the mix, standing on the median with cars speeding past him both ways. Just a little while longer, he thought, as he left his duffel bag unzipped and kept his clothes in the guest room's dresser drawers.When a car pulled in the driveway and Paul knocked on his bedroom door, he yelled "Just a second" and hid Tommy's watch and Jeff's book in the birthing room bowl. "Come in."

Paul smiled like a benign jailer. "Beth is here. She thought you might want to take a drive to Greenport."

"Oh, thanks. Tell her I'll be right down." He shoved the book and the items from Tommy's safe into a plastic bag and carried it downstairs. Beth stood in the foyer, her eyes following his descent. Outside, the air was cold with low, whipping winds. The sun was blocked by sea clouds, spilling light like a waterlogged dishrag.

"We're going to Greenport?" he asked her.

"Maybe farther," she said as she opened the car door. "Depends on what we're looking for."

In the cramped cavern of the Nissan, over the five-years-out-of-date rock music that formed Beth's five-years-out-of-date CD collection (CDs! ancient windmills of technology), they both agreed that it might be wise to drive to the Seaview Resorts Motel. Beth spent the drive recounting her semidisastrous visit to Holly Drake.

"If Jeff hated Holly because she fired him and threatened to tell his other customers that he was a thief, that might explain the devil horns," Mills said. "Maybe he *was* a thief. And maybe he found something he wasn't supposed to see."

"That's what I was thinking," she said. "Holly has no alibi for the night of the fire. Neither does her husband. He was supposedly in the city on business."

Near the corner of Village Lane, they drove past a memorial portrait of the Muldoons taped to a telephone pole, amid the garage sale announcements and rain-faded PROTECT YOUR FUTURE Pruitt Securities ads.

"Is Cole Drake the kind of man who would burn down the house of the guy who was sleeping with his wife?"

Beth shrugged. "There's a lot of pent-up anger in that man. He's also Magdalena's lawyer, however that fits in. Besides her nurse, he was the last person I know of to speak with her before she died.

Maybe Cole did find out about the affair. But Holly told me she wasn't the first woman Bryan had snuck off to the Seaview with. So, if Cole's not an option, another husband could be. Or another woman. I think we should just go down and look at the motel. It doesn't hurt."

"Bryan had at least three affairs," Mills confirmed. He told Beth about the watch in Tommy's safe, pulled it out of the bag, and started reading Tommy's notes on local misconduct.

"Ted Herrig is so nice! He taught me geography."

"Roe diCorcia is a tough farmer. I wouldn't cross him. His family goes back at least a century. And when farming has been in your family for a hundred years you're not exactly tolerant when it comes to threatening your crop yield."

"Karen Norgen—gay? She used to put on these horrendous puppet shows at Poquatuck Hall when I was a kid. Every station of the cross was a felt marionette carrying a wood coffee stirrer on its shoulder. I wonder if Magdalena knew."

Mills read the last entry, about a woman checking in alone at the Seaview.

"You didn't see Tommy that day," he said. "Something upset him. A *her*."

Beth watched the road. "I don't know if it was a good idea to tamper with that safe. What if someone saw you?"

"No one saw me." He reached into the bag and pulled out Jeff Trader's book. "And I got this back."

Beth eyed it. "Thank god. I told the detective I had it. If he asks, you never saw it, okay?"

"Okay," he said, returning it to the bag.

"I'm not joking," she said. "You never touched it." Mills caught the same protective tone in her voice that he heard in Paul's when he offered to help hose off the house. He lowered the volume on the radio.

"Why are you going to the Seaview?" he asked. "Why are you determined to get involved in this whole thing?"

Beth checked her speed as they whipped across the causeway toward the trees of East Marion, where snow still clung to the branches.

"I feel like I didn't help Magdalena like I promised. I should have taken her more seriously," she said. Then she tapped his knee, as if to induct him too into her list of obligations. "I'm sorry about Tommy," she said. "I know you two were close."

"We weren't that close," he replied. "But still I feel bad for him. I think there was something in him that could have been good if he'd been given the chance. . . . I don't know. He didn't deserve to die like that."

Sincerity put Mills in an irritated mood, so he turned away and concentrated on the scenery. He hadn't come this far west in more than a month. The world flew by faster with each mile they burned. Houses gave up their clapboard exteriors for more ornate suburban mash-ups. Window shutters became merely decorative. Convenience stores and gas stations lined the road, aged to the color of traffic exhaust. Five cars waited for a clear turn onto a street marked with an arrow toward Greenport. Beth drove by it, in the direction of Manhattan, and Mills resisted the urge to tell her to keep driving until the wasted tract houses of Queens appeared and beyond it the needle tips of the faraway island. They were running up the woman's leg on the map. The air already seemed warmer. He shifted in the upholstery, his body gluier than he imagined muscles to be, as if some homing device in his brain had caught a signal that faded beyond the causeway.

"The way I see it, there are three parts," Beth said, spreading her fingers on the steering wheel. "There's Magdalena and Jeff, there's the historical board, and there's the death of the Muldoons. I just can't figure out how they're related. *If* they're related."

"Will the historical board be able to continue without Bryan?" Mills asked.

"Nothing will stop them," Beth replied. She slowed at the presence of merging cars. "My mother lives out this way."

"If Jeff died because of something he found out, then maybe the Muldoons were killed because Tommy had uncovered the answer in Jeff's book. Maybe it was blackmail. I think Tommy may have been capable of that. If it's all about hiding an affair, then we're back to Holly Drake. It could be that simple. Although I don't know how OHB fits in, except for the fact that Cole helped Magdalena change her will. But that's what lawyers do."

Beth glided the car onto a gravel cutout. "Let's just check this place out."

On a metal sign overhead, a curving swordfish jumped in midair. Under it, the words SEAVIEW RESORTS MOTEL were stamped in slender, aristocratic letters. Set off of Route 48, the motel was a long, single-story accordion of pink stucco, its 1950s flair overlaid with a 1970s grittiness. A 1990s renovation had resulted in a stainless-steel bubble in the center that served as the check-in entrance. There were fifty rooms running from end to end, each with brass number plates and peepholes corroded green on the doors. It was the kind of motel that might look charming in a Web site thumbnail, but in person it evoked hypochondriac fantasies about scabies, lice, bedbugs, and microbes multiplying on torn condom wrappers. Mills suddenly missed the invisible fear of mutant diseases in Orient. Were bedbugs designed on Plum Island? Chlamydia? Beth stopped the car in front of the door marked 18.

"Bryan used room thirty-one," he said.

She pulled the emergency brake. "I thought we'd try to be subtle."

What the Seaview did have was its spectacular namesake. Beyond the motel, Mills could hear the slapping surf of Long Island Sound. The air was damp with sea vapor. Gulls crapped fish remains onto the motel's tin roof.

"This place is notorious," Beth said. "If you want to have an affair on the North Fork, this is where you come. Like all things out here, if you want to be secretive, you end up going to the most obvious place." She opened the door and climbed out. "We have to look for the owner. I think Holly said her name was Eleanor."

Mills's hand froze on the door handle. Eleanor, the name on Paul's matchbook. So she wasn't some secret afternoon lover after all, waiting there for Paul's blue Mercedes. Yet Paul had hidden the proprietor's name behind his framed picture of Orient. Mills didn't know what to make of it, except to wonder all over again about Paul's sexuality. He'd have to see Eleanor before he could rule her out as a love interest.

The Seaview had seemed like some sort of key to the deaths, but as Beth and Mills stood there in its pebbled parking lot, it looked more like a giant pink dead bolt. Perhaps they'd both just needed an excuse to stretch their legs somewhere inland where no one would recognize them. He followed Beth through the swinging door. A sign hung on the window: CHECK IN ANYTIME. CHECK OUT THE SAME.

Animal prints were supposed to be sexy, but the accumulation of patterns at the Seaview's welcome desk/piano bar/restaurant lounge spoke a language of camouflaged despair. Instead of pheromones, Lysol and gin oozed from the darkened interior. The carpet was zebra striped, the velvet wallpaper leopard spotted, the eight stool cushions at the bar a mangy jaguar, which no drinker occupied, and the counter's gray leather trim had the cracked epidermis of a rhinoceros. Peacock feathers in golden vases fluttered what air they could. A short, bald man in a tuxedo jacket played at the baby grand, winking first to them and then to his fishbowl tip jar. *Sail away, sail away, sail away*, he Enya-ed. Beth glanced at Mills, eyes warning *Do not laugh*. He was one kitschy cue away from misbehaving. How could anyone who snuck off here take their affairs seriously? But the piano player switched to Elton John midsong—*Oh ohhh, change is gonna do me good*—and Mills felt himself betraying his first impressions. He liked the Seaview and its peccable tastes.

Beth walked to the bar, tended by a woman—at least she must have been a woman once, twenty years ago, in the prime of her seventies—with skin the texture of redwood bark. She shook a silver shaker with a sound that reproduced small bones breaking. Her eyes were as black as hair-clogged drains, and a firework of wrinkles shot out at her temples from years of squinting in the dark. She wore a peach dress with its sleeves sawed off. The dress's right breast was covered in political pins: Romney, McCain, Bush, Dole, Bush, Reagan, Nixon, Goldwater. At some point, by accident or aversion, Gerald Ford had fallen out of sainthood.

"Hi," Beth said, palming the rhino skin.

"Ya here for lanch?" the old woman asked. "Outta season so outside deck is cloused. But take any table in the dinin rum and we'll serve ya." She spoke the language of the east, the tongue of the lost tribe of Eastern Long Island, a tuneless birdcall not unlike a dropped metal lid revolving on a floor. When exactly had that accent faded from the local speech? Could younger Long Islanders even understand her? Mills raced to comprehend each sentence as it faded.

"No, we just stopped in—"

"Ya wanna rum then? Not too many bookins since it's winta. We'll fit ya."

"No, no." Beth sat on a deflating stool. Mills took the one next to her. "Just a drink. Scotch if you have it. Straight."

The old woman smiled. She had managed to keep three teeth in her gums—sharp and black, like Wall Street buildings after hours. "That's what I drink. But not til fivah. It's only one thuty. People who drink this early arh bored with themselves. They hate theyr own company." She had earned the nonagenarian's right to insult her customers. Perhaps that was her most endearing quality.

"What can I say?" Beth replied. "I'm bored with myself."

She appreciated Beth's response. "And who's this?" She eyed Mills. "Sorry, sweets, I can barely see ya. I got no eyesyt left. Lou, wherah my glasses."

The piano player sang, "In your basket, Eleanor." Then he sang "Ain't We Got Fun." *"Every morning, every evening, ain't we got fun? Not much money, oh, but honey, ain't we got fun?"*

So this was Eleanor. Paul had no love life.

"I'll have water," Mills said. Eleanor hated to hear someone order water more than she hated scotch at one-thirty. She sneered. Smaller fireworks flared from her lip. "A Guinness then," he said.

"Fancy. You from New Yok City? Folks from New Yok City tip good. Unless theyr black." She shook her head and disappeared behind the counter to reappear with a wicker basket. Storm-window-thick lenses in a clear plastic frame were held up in front of her eyes, their arms still crossed over the glass. She peered through them, as if looking through a mail slot. "No, ya ain't black. But ya do look young. No need to ID ya." She reserved a look of disapproval for Beth, presumably for robbing the cradle. "I tell ya, every year we get more of them black folk coming out heyr. Not tipping is like stealin, which is what they do best." Beth and Mills laughed hollowly. Because Eleanor was uneducated, because she was old, because she was born early in the last century, and because they needed her for information, they forgave her racism. And yet because they forgave her, they both felt guilty, as if her racism were now their burden, a contagion they had inhaled. They both briefly dipped their heads in shame. On the bar, Eleanor placed two drinks between their empty white hands.

"In the winter, in the summer, don't we have fun? Times are bum and getting bummer, still we have fun."

"I'm from Orient," Beth told the old woman, leading her away from the subject of race. It worked. Eleanor's face softened from redwood to oak.

"I love Orient. Love the ospreys. We get our oystahs for the restaurant out theyr. From August Floyd. But the prices! And all the gays! The gays arh goin out theyr like crazy. No wondah it costs so much." Mills pursed his lips. Eleanor dropped her glasses in the basket. "Gays have money because they don't have kids. Soon ya wont need Sycamore High anymorh and the place will be turned into a gym. What's theyr to be proud of? Stop rubbin my nose in yah pride and go back to New Yok."

Beth dipped her head alone.

"There's nothing sure, the rich get rich and the poor get poor. In the meantime, in between time, ain't we got fun?"

"It must be crowded in summer here," Mills offered.

"We can't run this place forevah. Gonna be too expensive to keep up. Then they'll miss me. Where else arh people gonna go for theyr good tyme?"

"That would be a shame," Beth said. "I know lots of people in Orient who love to come here. I tell everyone, no better hotel than the Seaview." No closer hotel, at least.

"Damn right. Hear that, Lou?" Lou winked. Mills scrounged his pockets for a dollar and left his stool to drop it in the fishbowl. Lou tried to thank him, but Eleanor overheard. "Lou, no talkin. Just singin. Ya ain't given free rent to chit-chat."

When Mills returned to his stool, Eleanor smiled with the certainty of being the bar's main attraction. "Gets hardah and hardah," she said. "Heyr's a joke. How do ya tell if a Polish man has been cheatin on ya with ya sistah? If you wake up at night and yahr dad's not in ya bed." Faint laughter massaged the air. Eleanor leaned over the bar, directly in front of Beth's face. The Bush pins clamored on the wood. "Speakin of people from Orient, got the daughter of that family kelled in the fire stayin heyr. *Been* heyr. And her grandparents come and see her. So sad. She's been eatin by herself in the dinin rum. I give her some extra food to be kind. I wish she'd have more visitahs, her boyfriend or someone." Beth nodded at the sadness.

"Yes, her father was a friend of mine," Beth said. Eleanor found that surprising. She remained leaning over the bar to study Beth's face.

"Really? Nevah seen ya before, if ya know what I mean." She laughed.

"I didn't come here with him, but a friend of mine did." Beth cleared her throat. "She's shaken up about the fire. Probably because she came here so often with Bryan. This was their special place. Room thirty-one."

Eleanor seemed to be eating something invisible. Her teeth rolled around. "I knew her fathah pretty well, but obviously I couldn't tell the poor girl that. Wouldn't be fair to her or to her dad. I respect the privacy of my patrons. But he used Seaview quite a bit. Didn't he, Lou?" Lou galloped on the keys into a fast-tempo version of "Nobody Does It Better." "It's not all sleeze heyr. People come to have fun. And so they should. Not my bizeness. The whole place ain't gonna be my bizeness for long."

"Do you remember the women he came with?" Beth asked. "I know there was a redhead named Holly. But were there others that you could describe? I think it would help my friend to talk to them." Beth's cheeks flushed at the question, though her modesty seemed misplaced; Mills felt sure she could tell Eleanor that she'd just had a gangbang with ten men in one of the guest rooms and she wouldn't blink, as long as there weren't any blacks, Polish men, or gays among them.

"Talk? Now that would be quite a convahsashion."

Beth pulled her wallet from her purse and placed it on the bar. Eleanor noticed it. "Well, theyr were a few, including the redhead. But I can't name them of couse." Eleanor brought two meaty fingers to her eyes and pushed on her eyelids to indicate near-blindness. "I can only see so much. The doc says operation, but I ain't all blind. It was Bryan who usually got the keys and paid in cash. I take cash. Wives and husbands, they look at credit cahd bills. I understand for my patrons. I don't judge. It's not the fuckin Waldorf. I gotta pay my bills, same as you." But then Eleanor seemed to pause a moment, as if to recall an itching detail. She gummed her teeth, sucking them clean, and raised a finger, swatting it in a circle, like a woman tuning her ears to a song.

Eleanor dug through her wicker basket. A pincushion, a child's pacifier, spiderwebs of cell phone chargers, cuff links the shape of whales, an asthma inhaler, a scrunchie with black hairs still stuck to its elastic, an inside-out golf glove—an inventory of forgotten items, overlooked by harried, dressing lovers in midregret. Near the bottom, she finally discovered her prize: a silver pendant, its chain knotted up in a bundle of charger cords. She worked as patiently as a seamstress to undo the tangles.

"Heyr it is." She breathed in satisfaction, a triumph of memory over time. She dangled the pendant in front of their eyes. "The woman left this one tyme in rum thuty-one. The woman nevah came back for it." The pendant consisted of two silver ligaments, the cursive shape of the letter *L*. She dropped it in the basket. "I don't steal," she spat as if they had accused her of it. "Lou, didn't I return that mahvelous ten-carat ruby ring once."

"Sure you did. If you say so," the piano player sang.

"The setting at least." She laughed.

A light-skinned Mexican man carried a stack of plates through the bar, struggling as he slid open the mahogany door to the dining room. Light from the Sound-front windows invaded the bar, revealing the dust they'd been breathing. The dining room was surprisingly refined, with glass tabletops over salmon cloth and napkins shaped like nurse caps over spotless china settings. The water of the Sound danced in the gray sunlight, a hypnotic rocking that made the motel seem boatlike, lost at sea, far enough away from land to convince adulterers that they had escaped their juiceless lives. It was a stunning view, with a faint trail of Connecticut cutting through the haze; it must have been even more beautiful at sunset, filling the bar and its fifty rooms with otherworldly pinks. The Seaview earned the distinction of its name. When Eleanor died, Mills thought, maybe the ghosts of remorseful intercourse would leave with her, and the view of the Sound would remain. At the end of a long wood dock, a corroded green motorboat battled the waves, SEAVIEW painted across its side.

The waiter tripped on a chair leg and the crash of dinner plates followed. "Chico!" Eleanor screamed. That was one potential advantage in working for a racist: Mills doubted she'd be able to identify the waiter, a navy of nicknamed Chicos fulfilling captain's orders in a language she couldn't comprehend. In the strong light, Eleanor seemed even blinder, using her arms to guide herself around the perimeter of the bar. Beth took the opportunity to grab the pendant from the wicker basket, bundling the necklace into her palm. She stood up and took her wallet, placing two twenties under her untouched scotch.

Lou thundered out a chorus of "Smooth Operator" as they fled.

"I feel like I just learned why old people need to die in order for the world to progress," Mills said as they stepped into the parking lot. "Still, I kind of liked her."

"You don't see that kind much anymore," Beth said. "When I was little, you still came across a lot of old people like that out here. My mother always called them the Generation Before the Greatest Generation. I think she meant they weren't prudes."

They both stopped halfway toward the car. In the parking lot, near the single-digit motel rooms, Lisa Muldoon stood sobbing. Her brown hair—the same chestnut as Pam's—was twisted into a braid. A gray sweatshirt covered her chest and tight acid-wash jeans tapered down to a pair of pebble-dusted flats. An older couple was trying to leave her, putting car doors between them as emotional buffers. The grandmother weakened, slammed her door, and ran back to hug her. Lisa fell apart, succumbing to gravity, wiggling in the woman's arms.

"Poor girl," Beth said. Lisa spotted them over her grandmother's shoulder, stared, and then buried her eyes in her grandmother's collarbone.

They pulled out of the parking lot and headed east toward Orient. Beth tossed the necklace into Mills's lap.

"What is it? An *L*?" she asked.

He held it carefully between his fingers.

"Could be. Or a fancy *C*? No, it's an *L*. But the clamp is weird, so it hangs like a crooked *L*. Yeah, an *L*. Unless it's a crooked *A*, missing its crossbar."

"An *L*," Beth said as she glanced at it. She repeated *L* five times, thinking of names in Orient that began with the initial. "Obviously, it can't be Lisa."

"No. Eleanor said it came from Bryan's room. Number thirty-one. Even if it was Lisa's, Eleanor could have just given it back to her."

"Mills, the woman is clearly blind."

"So are you thinking it might have been some other woman who caused the fire? Or another woman's jealous husband? That fits with Magdalena and Jeff Trader, if they happened to find out."

Beth swerved to avoid a squirrel that skittered across the road, its body a Morse code of long dashes and dots.

"I don't know what I'm thinking," Beth said. "It could have been someone who had nothing to do with Bryan's love life. I don't know what we expected to find there. It was your idea to visit the Seaview." Mills didn't remind her that they'd agreed on the Seaview together. "I just keep thinking about poor Lisa, crying her heart out back there. Can you imagine? If she'd been home visiting from college, or one year younger and still in high school, she might be dead too. I wouldn't want to stay in Orient either. All the remainders. I mean, reminders."

The causeway wavered between two bodies of water. The shoreline bubbled with sand and weeds at low tide. Seagulls grazed on insects, burying their beaks in the sludge. An old abandoned rowboat was marooned in the mud on the bay side, awaiting the water's return to lift it and give it purpose. A metal chain attached it to a wood post. Twice a day, Mills thought, that rowboat must float and beach. He looked out to where Jeff's body had bobbed; the sun glinted there.

"Did you ever notice the shape of Long Island?" Mills said, staring at the waves. "It looks like a woman."

"Yes!" Beth gasped, her voice nearly breaking. "I've always thought that. No one else sees it. With her head turned toward New Jersey and her hair streaming along the coast of Connecticut like a bride wearing a long veil." Mills didn't tell Beth that he saw the woman's head as bashed in by the anvil of Manhattan, not a bride but a murder victim. "I've thought that since I was little," she said as they sped across the causeway. "And no one understood what the hell I was talking about. I used to trace the outline of that woman on a map and fill her in with crayons. That might have been my first portrait. Virgin bride floating in the sea."

Mills pictured the map in Paul's car with its foldout grid of New York. "Where did Lisa Muldoon go to college anyway?"

"Upstate," Beth replied. "SUNY Buffalo, I think. It's about an eight-hour drive from here. She came down as soon as she heard. I guess she'll stay at least until the funeral." Mills tried not to think about Tommy's uneven shoulders and wavy yellow hair under a sheet in the county morgue. He was probably already at the funeral home, stowed in tufted cotton. "I wonder what she'll do now that her family's gone," she said. The causeway opened into trees. "There's no reason for her to come back to Orient after the funeral except to visit the graves. And then one day you just stop visiting the cemetery altogether, like I did. There comes a point when they're not there anymore. It's just ground."

Mills watched the familiar Orient geography return, the homing device of the city no longer detectable. Beth eased onto Youngs Road. As they neared Paul's house, they saw a dirty gray sedan blocking the driveway. Beth looked over at him.

"That's Mike Gilburn's car," she said. "The detective. Leave Jeff's book with me. Don't mention anything about it."

Mills nodded and handed her the bag. "Be careful," she said. "Be careful, with what you tell the detective. And we'll see each other tomorrow, okay?"

Beth's car disappeared down the street, and Mills was left there with no other ride in sight. In his hand he held the silver pendant, which he'd forgotten to give to Beth. He slipped it in his pocket with Tommy's watch and gazed straight ahead to prevent looking toward the Muldoons' property. The reek of burning furniture was starting to fade.

CHAPTER 21

Paul was perched on the edge of the sofa, his left knee galloping. The two officers had moved Paul's modernist chairs into a
more convivial circle. One was wearing rumpled plainclothes,
the other a uniform. Mills walked softly into the parlor, lifting his
chin, offering his most innocent expression. Paul rose slightly when
he saw him, extending his arm. "Here he is." The two heads turned
simultaneously. "Mills, this is Detective Michael Gilburn and, I'm
sorry . . ."

"Deputy Kurt Parker," the younger officer stated. Gilburn stood
and shook Mills's hand. Paul sat down, his knee a racehorse on the
final stretch. Then it stopped.

"Paul was just filling us in on your stay in Orient," Gilburn said,
scratching his beard. He didn't need to point to the unoccupied seat
next to Paul on the sofa. It seemed apparent that Mills was expected
to fill it. Mills tried to make the act of sitting so close to Paul a
natural, daily event, as if they often shared the tweed sofa, sitting
just inches apart, studying the marble dining table and the rack of
wineglasses hanging upside down like luminous bats.

"Yes, I've been out here for about month and a half," Mills said
cheerfully. "I love Orient, a really nice community. I mean, before
the fire."

Deputy Parker watched his superior the way a new hire studied
an experienced waiter. Mills found himself studying Parker's boyish
face for his candid reactions.

"And Paul says you two are friends from New York."

"That's right." Mills nodded. "We met in his building. I knew someone who lives on his floor. We became friends, and when Paul offered to let me come out here and help with repairs to his house, I was eager to spend some time outside the city. I wanted to see the beautiful countryside." As a foster kid, Mills had been schooled on hyperbolizing the truth—to authorities, to prospective parents, to caseworkers who'd heard every sad story before, and yet somehow yielded to each new troubled face. Mills knew how to repackage the darker details into a sympathetic account. At least he hoped still he did. Gilburn's warm grin invited confidence. Gilburn was just doing his job. Gilburn had a few questions that his superiors were forcing him to ask. Gilburn happened to love strange, ear-pierced teenagers, recently relocated from the city, who lived forty feet from a crime scene.

"I'm glad you like our neck of the sea. We're pretty proud of it too. That fire must have been a shock to you. It was a shock to us. We don't have incidents like that too often out here. So you can probably understand why this town isn't sitting as pretty as it was last week."

"Awful," Mills intoned. "Tragic. They were a nice family. Very kind to me."

Paul leaned forward. "Mills didn't get to see much of the village. I've unfortunately had him cleaning out all the junk in here, thick as the walls. He hasn't gotten to meet many of the neighbors. It's my fault. I should learn to throw things away."

"Jill and I did a spring clean last April," Gilburn confided. "We tossed three years in five days. And then Jill kept tossing. She tossed all her stuff into her car, and soon that left too. You pull out one brick and the rest start to fall." Only Paul laughed. Gilburn looked out the front window, his face pale. Parker bit his lip. "But you did make a few friends out here." Gilburn's eyes strayed back to Mills. "Someone just dropped you off."

"Yeah, the few that I've met have been so friendly. They keep wanting to show me the beaches and lighthouses."

Gilburn cleared his throat. Deputy Parker finally brought his eyes to Mills.

"Were you friendly with Thomas Muldoon?"

Mills's mouth went desert dry. He pushed his tongue against his bottom teeth. "Yeah. I liked Tommy. We were about the same age. We talked once or twice when we happened to catch each other out front. He was a senior in high school, wasn't he?"

"So you were friends," Gilburn said.

Mills half-nodded.

"Close?"

"No."

"But close enough?"

Close enough for what? Mills decided to snip the hair that Gilburn was trying to split. "I wouldn't say we knew each other very well. We were friendly. We talked about music and sports, the usual stuff." Mills wondered if he could name a single athlete or rapper tacked to Tommy's bedroom walls.

"What about the mother, Pam?"

"I didn't really speak to her much."

Gilburn watched him carefully. His hand stiffened on his chin. "You never went into their home?"

"Once. I cut my hand pulling garbage to the curb and Tommy let me use their first aid kit." He opened his palm to reveal no lasting scar. "He bandaged it for me."

"Only once?" Now the memory of the blow job in Tommy's bedroom started to seem like a perversion of the dead, the moans of a young man who couldn't moan anymore. Mills couldn't tell Gilburn what he and Tommy had been to each other. He didn't even know himself. But he could see the detective looking at him through Pam's eyes: a juvenile delinquent with an appetite for trouble, an outsider with a penchant for criminality, for stealing car stereos and maybe impressionable teenagers away from their families. Gilburn liked what he saw: a possibility. If Mills had been female, he would never have been asked such questions. If he had been a lot of things, he would never have been asked such questions.

"I think I was in their house just once."

Gilburn pushed himself back in the leather recliner, demonstrating an innate discomfort with modern design. He sprung forward again, kicking his feet to regain a sense of the floor.

"I'm sorry to ask you all these questions. I know it may seem invasive, but it's just us following protocol. You see, we have reason to believe that the fire might have been arson, so you can understand that we have to rule out all options, even unlikely ones." Mills nodded amicably and rubbed his legs. But Gilburn wasn't finished. He examined his notebook. He passed time reading from its pages. "Someone mentioned that they saw you and Pam in a dispute a few days before the fire, right on the driveway. Do you mind telling me what that was about?"

Mills gulped while trying not to show his throat muscles straining. Paul crouched so far forward he was no longer actually using the sofa as a seat.

"Mike, I told you that was just a misunderstanding." Gilburn's hand silenced Paul. Mills noticed a small *J* tattooed on the detective's palm. The *J* probably stood for the ex-wife he mentioned. The tattoo made him seem tougher and weaker at the same time.

"Let the boy speak. I understand that neighbors have little fracases."

Who had told the detective about the argument? Sarakit Herrig, who'd come by with her two sons for a playdate that afternoon? A neighbor across the street who happened to glance out the window? If it was Sarakit, Pam might have told her all about their fight, might have confessed over coffee that she'd found Tommy and Mills in a semicompromising position in her house just hours before. But Mills doubted she would have confided that in a neighbor. It would have reflected badly on Tommy, which would have reflected badly on Pam—and Pam held herself out to Orient like a washed and polished mirror, bouncing sunlight back into their eyes. She would never have shared a story in which Tommy had a fondness for male strangers.

"Mrs. Muldoon was worried about Tommy," Mills said with his hand on his chest. "He wasn't getting the grades he needed for college, so she didn't want him spending time on anything that wasn't homework." He was hoping to make the whole episode sound as suburban as cutting the grass. Gilburn scratched his beard. "She didn't seem to want me hanging around to distract him. I tried to tell her that was fine by me, but she kept arguing about it. I think Mrs. Muldoon was under a lot of stress. She didn't seem happy. Honestly, I didn't take the fight personally. As I told you, Tommy and I weren't that close."

"Just as I said," Paul drawled. "It was a stupid misunderstanding. The week before, Pam and I argued about garbage pickup. It wasn't a big deal."

Gilburn nodded like he understood. He tapped Kurt Parker's knee, as if he'd caught his deputy napping. "Yeah, we've determined there was some friction in the family. It might have been that. Thank you for answering my questions." He slapped his notebook on his leg but didn't quite stand up. "One more thing. Again, just procedure. Where were you on the night of the fire?"

"Mills and I were sitting together, right here," Paul said. "We were sitting in this room, just as we are now. I remember I had gone to the bathroom upstairs and heard Mills call up to me, saying he saw flames through the window. He went outside, and I ran to get my coat. We stood on the curb with the other neighbors, watching helplessly. I'm sure the neighbors told you we were there?"

Mills nodded along with the lie. "That's right. We were sitting right here."

"And you never heard or saw anything peculiar in the hour before the fire? A car drive up or a fight or footsteps? Anything, no matter how trivial?"

"I wish I had," Mills said. "I'd like to help you find the person responsible. If it turns out it was arson. I might not have been Pam

Muldoon's favorite human being, but no one should die like that. I just don't know the people out here, so I can't think who would want to do that."

"Okay," Gilburn chirped. "Thank you for your cooperation." He sighed like he hadn't found what he was looking for, like the ten-minute interrogation had been a waste of precious police time. Gilburn and Parker headed to the door, and Paul followed behind, shepherding them with his arms. Halfway toward the foyer, the detective spun around. He pulled a pen from his jacket pocket and foisted it, along with his notebook, toward Mills.

"If you could write down your full name and the city where you were born, it would be a big help in terms of background checks. Just procedure. Might not even need to bother." The pen weighed in his hand, an unwieldy bayonet. Mills wrote "Millford Chevern, Fort Bragg, California," on the pad, praying that the real Millford Chevern was still on the road, sending postcards to distant sisters, out of trouble and out of jail. He prayed that his driver's license photo would be bad enough to render identification inconclusive. He prayed that Millford Chevern had lived a model life, that he'd never had his fingerprints memorialized in the ink-spotted paperwork of city records. To admit his real name, now, would be tantamount to confession.

"Thanks," Gilburn said. "Millford is a cool name. I had a cousin named Mildon."

The deputy stood on the porch, inspecting the charred remains of the house next door. Gilburn clapped Paul's shoulder on their way to the door. "Thanks again, Paul. You both let me know if either of you plan on leaving Orient soon. Just in case we have follow-up."

"Yes, you can trust me," Paul said. "We're not going anywhere."

"I mean it. Promise me that." Gilburn hesitated on the brass doorsill, hovering an inch before the welcome mat, letting a sweep of cold air blow in. "So you'll be at the funeral tomorrow?"

"They were my closest neighbors for more than thirty years," Paul howled. At the last possible second, he had finally lost his composure. "Of course I'm going to their funeral. Mike, just *ask me* if Mills and I killed the Muldoons. Just ask and we'll tell you. We didn't."

"Oh, gosh, Paul, I never meant to imply that."

Gilburn stepped outside, his arms waving in apology. Paul shut the door and breathed against its frame. He returned to the parlor with a muddled head that no amount of shaking could fix. He waited until the sedan shot headlights through the windows and reversed into the street.

"They think I did it?" Mills asked, looking up at him, worried he'd find even the slightest twitch of suspicion on Paul's face. He considered confessing the truth about his name right then. What was left but confession—confess, confess, confess, until every stone inside of him had been turned over? He didn't even know what was under half those stones anymore. He hadn't uttered his real name in almost a year.

"They're desperate to catch whoever did, that's all," Paul said. "No, they don't think you did it. They're asking everybody, house to house. I watched them make the rounds all afternoon." Paul squeezed Mills's shoulder. "You've got nothing to worry about, okay?"

He tried to believe Paul. He believed him so much he could almost will himself to believe that they'd been sitting in the living room together on the night of the fire, providing each other with alibis.

"What about that lie you told them? That we were sitting here together that night?"

Paul sat down next to him, as if they did actually sit side by side on the couch in the evening, staring emptily into the dining room.

"I know," Paul said tiredly. "But I had to."

"Why?"

"I just did," he spat, rubbing his head. "So what if we were sleeping? Every single person in Orient was asleep when that fire started. So what if you were on the sofa and I was upstairs? It's just to clear you from their minds."

Mills realized what both Paul and Beth had recognized in the situation, that he was a likely suspect.

"So we clear each other in case they suspect me." Mills paused. "Or you."

Paul laughed. His eyes rolled behind his lids and he gave a pained smile. "Or me, right. Think of it as helping me out. Maybe they do think I did it. Angry that the Muldoons were using my backyard to access the Sound without my permission, I was provoked into a rage that caused me to pour gasoline around their house." Under the glaze of his glasses, Paul's eyes were like missing pieces in a jigsaw puzzle. It was a relief to see Paul scared, like Mills wasn't alone in the fear. "Are you asking me if I did it?" Paul said. "Because you're right. I guess I don't have an alibi."

"No."

"We were lucky the fire didn't spread to this house. In a way, we were spared. But maybe I am a suspect in Mike's notebook. I do live next to them. We did have that fight. They drilled me with questions before you arrived. Mike had the audacity to ask if I had fire insurance, like I was hoping for the flames to spread just so I could cash in. Then he asked if I had any ambitions to fill Bryan's seat on the historical board. I told him I wouldn't do it if they paid me." Paul's voice drifted off. He pinched the back of his neck. "There's got to be someone—a business associate, a jilted neighbor, someone with a motive. We just have to let the police find that person. Let them follow the lead to another door. They will eventually. There's too much public outcry for them not to discover the truth."

"I could leave tonight," Mills said quietly. "I could take the train in and disappear. Then you wouldn't have to deal with it in case they suspect—"

Paul swatted off his glasses and wiped his face. Mills knew how bad that would look, after Paul had given the detective his word. And there were plenty of other potential suspects: he and Beth had already uncovered a number of leads, almost without trying. Surely Gilburn had drummed up more suspects than they had.

"I don't think that would be a good idea," Paul muttered. "It would draw attention to you if you tried to leave right now. It would look like guilt." A thread of air escaped his lips. "Although I can't force you to stay. I'm not your father. You need to do what's best for you. If you think getting out—"

"I won't leave," Mills interrupted. "But you know I didn't do it, right? You know I had nothing to do with that fire. I want to make that clear. Because if you have any doubts—"

"You don't have to tell me that." Paul collected Mills's hands on the cushion, rubbing his knuckles with his thumbs. Paul looked tired without his glasses, like a man forced to row a boat at sea with a spoon. He picked his words carefully, moving his lips in halting jerks. "I want to tell you something. Maybe it's a reason why I told the detective what I did. I lied to you when you found that picture of my brother. Patrick was my brother, but not by blood."

"He was adopted?"

Paul shook his head. His skin was ashen.

"No. My parents took him in as a foster kid when he was a toddler. His family had abandoned him right here on the North Fork—if a teen mother and a drunk dockworker who both hightailed it to Florida count as family. Patrick drifted around in temporary homes for a while, but no one kept him for long. He was already so sick by then. That's when my mom and dad brought him to stay here. He could barely leave the house, with all his illnesses, so I did all the chores, so that my mother could take care of him. But I didn't mind, because I wanted a brother, and Patrick was the sweetest kid I ever met. He loved lighthouses. That's what he and my mother shared. That's part of the reason my father and I built that little replica out at the inn—so my mom could see it and remember him after he died. He had operations that we paid for, because the state wouldn't pay for his medical bills. Elective surgery," Paul hissed. "It's not elective if it saves your life. But they had already given him up as lost. We used to tell him he was a descendent of the Gardiners, just so he felt valuable. But Patrick *was* valuable, to us."

Mills sat so close to Paul that he could smell him, earthy as mulch turned over in a garden. The veins in his wrists pulsed. Paul's voice was a drone of water in a pipe or rain behind a curtained window.

"My parents were working to adopt him, but he died of the blockage in his intestines before the process was finalized. We couldn't even bury Patrick ourselves, since he wasn't technically part of our family. They didn't allow us that last privilege. I'll never forget how much that hurt my mother. To her he was just like a son. It didn't matter that he wasn't blood."

Mills tried to picture the dark-haired boy in the photograph, tried to imagine the disease in his stomach that was already consuming him from the inside out when he sat for the camera with Paul on the porch. He tried to picture the homes the boy must have gone through before finding one that would take in a sick child. Most families would rather take in a sick dog than a sick kid. Paul squeezed his fingers. "I went away to boarding school right after he died. I think my mom couldn't handle the grief of losing him after she tried so hard. Our lives would have been so different if he had lived. When I came home in the summers, we never spoke about him, but something had changed. We became the kind of family that talks about nothing but work."

Paul waved his hand to clear away the memory.

"What I'm trying to say," he said, sputtering, "is that a part of me saw Patrick in you. And I've wanted you to feel at home here because you deserve that. To have some kind of base where you're more than a guest. Maybe that was stupid of me. You're an adult. You don't need to be adopted. But I thought, with all these extra rooms, that Orient would be a good place."

"I *do* like it here," Mills swore. He didn't dare make eye contact, as if his eyes would expose some failure in him, the larvae scored in the meat. "It's my fault that I got mixed up with the Muldoons." He wished he could take back his infatuation with Tommy. Or rather, he wished Tommy had protected his own secrets as carefully as the ones he kept hidden in his safe. He understood Tommy's need for a small black space he could lock at his command. What was the name Mills Chevern but a door that only he could access, as if the most honest things about a person were those kept out of sight?

"I guess I've been pretty lonely," Paul said, nodding along to his own diagnosis. "I guess I just thought this house was big enough."

The house was big enough. It accommodated possibilities that had seemed out of reach to Mills: future Thanksgivings, future Christmases, future boyfriends following him up the steps to meet a middle-aged man with a tender lion's head. Those were the possibilities being offered to him on the couch as evening darkened, a spare set of keys, and part of him did want that, vaguely, like wanting spring.

"I'd like to stay for a while," he said, his eyes trained on the cushion. "No promises for how long."

"As long as you want." Paul returned his glasses to his nose.

Mills pulled his knuckles from Paul's fingers. He didn't want Paul to be the first to break away. But, as he returned his hand to his lap, a switch flipped in his head, a doubt that undermined Paul's kindness just as it was being expressed. It was Mills's way of staving off future disappointment. Turn the kindness against itself, distrust it until it died. Without Mills, Paul had no alibi for the fire. Paul could have brought him out here and given him free run of his house simply to establish one. The entire last month might have been engineered for the meeting they just had with the police, Mills nodding along to Paul's lie, providing him with a cover story he would never have had if he lived alone.

It took imagination to superimpose a killer on the man hunched beside him, his eyes still shiny from his sad generosity, but it wasn't entirely impossible. Paul could be bribing him now with the promise of a home to prevent Mills from speaking the truth to the police. The idea ran through him hot and cold, like a fever changing direction. He remembered Eleanor's name on the Seaview matchbook hidden behind the frame.

"You know, Beth and I went to the Seaview today," Mills said, trying to gut-check Paul with his suspicions.

"The Seaview?" Paul cocked his head. He too seemed in need of a lighter subject, a man who had just offered his house and was met with a teenager's shrugging *maybe*. "Why would you two go there?"

"Oh, not like that." Mills blushed. "Beth had it in her mind that the motel had something to do with the Muldoons. We met Eleanor, the woman who runs the place."

Paul fell back on the sofa. "Oh, she's a beast!" he said, laughing. "The true North Fork monster. I've been dealing with her a bit recently." Paul looked over at the fireplace, a neutral zone. "I can trust you, right?" Paul didn't wait for him to confirm it. "I have a secret project that I work on when things are slow at the firm. An idea to buy that dumpy motel from Eleanor and rebuild it as a modern bed-and-breakfast. Like the one my mom ran at the farmhouse I took you to."

"A hotel?" Mills whispered, caught off guard. "You never told me you wanted to do that." He was surprised to hear a hint of betrayal in his own voice.

"It was a secret," Paul said, smiling. "I guess it's in the blood. Just a little place for visitors to the North Fork. Not as grand as Oysterponds Inn but also not a money trap."

"Why didn't you just buy back the farmhouse when it was up for sale last spring?"

"I said a *little* place," Paul stammered, getting to his feet. "That house was priced at several million even before the bidding started. We almost went bankrupt once over that place. I'm not interested in trying it again." Paul went to pick up his laptop from the dining room table and brought it back to the couch, typing in his password and clicking on a file titled SEA.pdf. "You've got to promise to keep it a secret. At least until it happens."

Mills nodded, and an architectural rendering of a building filled the screen. The bones of the current Seaview were hardly visible through its cosmetic upgrade: huge picture windows framing the blue waters, dining rooms and decks jutting above the rocks, a canopy of willows shading the long sweep of guest doors, a shell replacing a swordfish on a sign above the entrance. It looked as beautiful as any dream could that was rendered in straight lines. "Eleanor's got to give it up sometime, and if I don't get it before she dies, her grandchildren will sell it to the highest bidder. It'll end up as a strip mall if I can't convince her that I want to respect the history of the place. Getting her to sign, though, is like trying to marry the devil. As soon as you agree on a price, she thinks you're trying to steal from her."

Mills had never seen Paul so animated. In all his agonizing over his own future, he had never once asked Paul what he wanted out of his. It had been easier for him to imagine Paul as an possible murderer than as a middle-aged man with a modest dream.

"It's a great idea," Mills said encouragingly. "You already know how to build."

"Not just build, but conserve. Keep the history and the beauty of the view. It's not in Orient, but it's close enough, and it's a lot easier than getting around all of the zoning laws and squabbling neighbors out here. That's why I like it—because it's in-between."

"You should have kept the old Oysterponds sign."

"It's best to start fresh. This is my chance to break free from all those corporate parks and do something that's mine. No more onyx ogres with tinted conference-room windows. I hate that my biggest contribution to date has been perfecting the parking-lot grid."

"I hope you keep the bar inside. I could bartend." Paul's dream was contagious. "We could hang your landscapes in the guest rooms. And you could build another miniature Bug lighthouse on the rocks."

"Maybe." Paul snorted. "It's just a little dream for now." Paul closed the computer in embarrassment. His dream, once exposed, faced its own potential failure. "So what did you find there?" Paul asked. "What about the Muldoons?"

"Nothing," Mills said. "I guess we just went to stretch our legs."

They ate mackerel for dinner, scooping up pieces of fish around its open eye. Their conversation drifted away from the Muldoons and the police. But Mills prayed that the detective would solve the case, that the perpetrator would be a stranger, a luckless pyromaniac who happened through town. If Mills adopted Orient as his home, he'd need to have his name removed from Gilburn's list of suspects. Mills wondered if he was contracting the disease of the suburbs: the desire to be liked. After all, the Muldoons were the only ones who hadn't welcomed him.

When he went upstairs, he realized that he no longer felt afraid of the birthing room or the scraping oak branches in the wind. He'd been in Orient for almost two months, and maybe that was enough to claim it as his. *My bedroom. My dresser. My toothbrush, laid out on a green towel of the very same quality as the man who owns the house—no cheaper and no finer.* He went to bed thinking of Lisa Muldoon, who had lost a family in nearly the same instant that Mills had been offered one. He thought of her crying in the parking lot of the Seaview, shivering with small, lost steps. And he thought of himself, with each step more firmly planted in the Orient soil.

It was deep into the night when a bolt shot through him like a cramp of stomach sickness. He woke, reaching his arms out over the blanket, remembering something that had been bothering him earlier in the day. It was a revelation that caused him to think of the Muldoons as strangers, to each other and to the rest.

CHAPTER 22

A nerve pinched in Adam Pruitt's shoulder, trembling his hand whenever he grabbed a pen to write down a customer order. Now his hand shook as he tried to knot his tie in the mirror, dressing for a funeral he didn't have the time or interest to attend. He would be expected to pay his respects at the service for the Muldoons at the United Church of Christ, even though Bryan Muldoon had been his main business competitor, even though Adam had never darkened United Church of Christ with his prayers, even though Pruitt Securities was now trying to keep up with an influx of work that his five-man outfit could barely handle. He had the Muldoons to thank for the sudden windfall; that was one prayer that had been answered. Everyone on the North Fork suddenly wanted a security system, and no one wanted to hire Muldoon Security, since it was an intruder who'd apparently killed Bryan Muldoon and his family in their home. On paper, Pruitt Securities was thriving— more contracts in the last two weeks than he'd imagined possible for his first year in business. But Adam had not anticipated the immense amount of effort it would take to keep up with demand. If he faltered in accepting a single job, a bigger security company from Long Island would swoop in to plant its badge on an Orient lawn—and he knew how quickly weeds could spread on local soil.

Adam had hijacked Bryan's own suppliers, offering the exact same security equipment at a slightly cheaper rate, relying on the same Riverhead telecom service to direct satellite calls to emergency responders and process forgotten codes to harried homeowners trying to remember the answer to their secret password questions while alarms wailed into the receiver.

All of the special services Adam had promoted on their flyers had been put on hold. So far, his company wasn't offering anything beyond what Muldoon Security provided, for less money. Adam was still in negotiations with a New York City–based environmental lab to supply the soil and water testing he had advertised. Not even the richest new residents would spend two thousand dollars to test their wells and garden when contamination seemed like a county responsibility. How had Bryan managed to run his business day after day, pulled on all sides by installation appointments, late payments, and nervous clients? For one thing, he hadn't hired his out-of-work hunting buddies. Installations that should take one hour took four, when his so-called technicians showed up, if they showed up sober. Adam had leased a green van, but they forgot to lock its doors when they went crawling through bushes trying to secure wobbly Orient windows, leaving thousands of dollars' worth of equipment exposed. He needed to fire Dennis, and Josh had to be warned about lighting up on porches, and Toby needed a refresher on the basics of using a screwdriver. How had Bryan managed to turn this kind of business into a profitable enterprise that paid for a house, three children, and time to hunt on weekends—and still left him time to volunteer on the historical board? If Adam hadn't hated Bryan, he would have admired him. Now that he was dead, he did.

Adam pawed at his tie, but the knot dissolved as he tried to tighten it. A wave of laziness overtook him, a warm laziness that Adam used to enjoy, like slipping into a heated pool in his underwear. It was the kind of laziness that turned the simplest tasks into a concentrated effort: a fifteen-minute drive to Greenport to park the car and walk to the back of the IGA for two pints of milk and up to the front of the IGA to buy the milk and drive fifteen minutes back to his bungalow just to pour the milk over granola for breakfast. As a child, Adam had been a workhorse for his father. Clean the gutters, mow the lawn, wax the deck, tar the leak in the roof. He had worked and worked, so hard that by the age of eighteen he had come to view adulthood as a form of retirement.

Adam lit a cigarette, ignoring his ringing cell for fear that it was another customer or collection agency—or, worse, her. She wouldn't stop calling, crying, demanding that he see her, that he come right now. He hadn't seen her in days. The relationship he wanted with a woman was the kind he had with the four ferns he watered in his bungalow—the commitment of sticking his fingers in them once a week and giving them just enough to live on. But that wasn't what she wanted, what she *had been promised, what she had done to be with him.* His bed was tangled in blankets; it would be so easy to crawl under them and sleep until noon. Some days, Adam seemed almost to stop existing for whole minutes, his brain gone blank like a computer in sleep mode. He used to love that gift of nothing, of not being someone for a stretch of time, but now he had to fight to stay centered. The business owned him, and she thought she did too.

He hadn't been an extraordinary child. He knew that. Mediocre grades, the normal interests in football and guns, talents designed for hobbies instead of ways out. He was prized in Orient as a teenager because he hadn't been extraordinary. The extraordinary never stayed out here, they moved to the city as soon as they could, and so the year-rounders crowded around him and loved him with their hands and words, because they knew he would live here forever. They were patriotic about his disappointments. All he had done in the last few months was find a way to be extraordinary. Pruitt Securities was suddenly a booming business. Badge-shaped signs bearing his name were cropping up on every lawn. As the head of the Orient Volunteer Fire Department, he had bravely rushed to put out the biggest fire ever to scorch the village. But there were still steps to be taken, one this week when no one was looking. His cell phone rang again. Unidentified number. He let it go to voice mail and finished his cigarette.

He needed to hire a secretary, someone to field the calls. But that meant more money that he didn't have to spend, another employee who wanted five dollars more than minimum wage and health care and wasn't there a union that stipulated holidays and a 401K? Dennis had asked for a 401K—Dennis, a man who could barely find his shower in the morning, but who knew what he stood for, and would stand for it until he was replaced by the cheaper labor of the illegal Mexicans in Greenport. Adam couldn't hire a Mexican for a secretary. Security required an American accent.

Instead, he was spending the money he'd saved up for the '67 Maserati he already imagined rehabbing and driving around Orient to show off just how extraordinary he had become. But he froze in his cluttered bedroom, unable to move his hands to knot his tie. At his feet was a box of lime green flyers and another box of Pruitt Securities signs. He'd need to borrow more money. Maybe he could borrow money from her. There was so much money in Orient lately, green fields of it, guarded with security systems he'd installed but wasn't allowed to touch.

Yesterday he had gone to the old farmhouse inn to do a job estimate for an artist couple, a gorgeous black woman and her pale, whiny husband. They were bickering about furniture—eight thousand dollars for an anemic, understuffed couch, a couch the husband no longer deemed worthy to sit on. The husband sat in a leather chair with his shirt unbuttoned, holding a glass of whiskey, yelling about the couch and the bulldozed holes in the yard. The husband was the very sort of man Adam's father had despised, the kind who made money just by sitting around and letting his investments do his work, the kind who had married a gorgeous black woman to prove a point.

"I can't secure the house until you've finished construction," Adam tried explaining to her. "There's no way to rig a system when you've got plastic-covered holes for walls. I can't even install lasers in your yard because of all of the dirt mounds."

"We're excavating," the black woman replied. She stretched her arms over her head, cracked the bones in her back, and shut her eyes. "We may never finish construction," she said with a restless smile. "We may just keep adding and changing. We're like that." He hated her but very much wanted to take her to bed, to show her that he could do things to her that her husband couldn't.

"You've got a great face," she had told him. "I'd like to paint you if you're ever up for it. I've been doing a series on people out here." The husband winced and drank his whiskey. The husband tried to apologize with his eyes, but for what, a compliment? Because she was right, Adam did have a great face—muscular where the husband's was bland and formless, like a coin in a washing machine. He laughed at the compliment and examined her small breasts, as if trying to figure out how an intruder might get at them. Behind their house, beyond the half-dug holes, he saw a speedboat tied to their private dock. They had the money to be lazy, and Adam had a laziness that money would have loved. What could this couple have accomplished in their short lives to make them so rich?

He glanced around his cramped bungalow, its chipped wood and hairy corners. He had two Pruitt Securities signs in his front lawn—no security system yet, he'd been too busy, but the signs were what really mattered. He had that speech on repeat: "Intruders see this sign, they move on to the next house. This piece of metal is your best deterrent." If he wasn't in the security business, he realized, he might actually enjoy watching those rich weekenders, who were buying up Orient like it was one gigantic yard sale, get robbed of their obscenely expensive furniture, their ridiculous collections of art.

His father had collected only one thing in his life, and that was rifles. Even when he was dying of lung cancer, leashed by a long thin tube to an oxygen tank, he carried two rifles around his property just waiting for a chance to use them. On those last days, as Adam held his father's hand at his hospital bed, squeezing it to distract him from the morbid ICU soundtrack of game-show applause and ventilating machines, his father had told him, "You keep my property and you keep those rifles. Don't let anyone get to them." Adam sold the property and every rifle but one. He needed the money a little more than he needed his dead father's wishes met. But now he understood what his father had been trying to protect him from: when you let strangers in, Orient won't be yours anymore, and where will you go with your slim talent and low ambition when the more extraordinary make your home into theirs?

His cell phone rang. "Pruitt Securities, how can we protect you? . . . Yeah, I know. I know, don't worry, I'm on it. I'll be there. But we need to talk about money." As he hung up, he fought through another wave of laziness and pulled his arms through the sleeves of his jacket. He opened the front door and walked around the bungalow. It was a cold, sunless day that brought out the blackness of the branches, a perfect day for a funeral, for sunglasses to hide dry eyes.

Before he left, there was one more thing he had to do. He walked toward the shed in his backyard, catching the smell of the carcasses from the hunt even before he opened the padlocked door. His cell phone vibrated. It was her. The plant wanted water.

The water might be toxic, you never knew, thanks to Bryan Muldoon's success in blocking the county water main. Adam knew that, sooner or later, he would convince the wealthy, worried Orient homeowners to pay to have their wells and pools tested—the money that could make him extraordinary. He knew the one vulnerable spot in the fences of the rich: it was fear. Fear was viral, airborne, contagious. It opened doors for him. It allowed him to touch things that weren't his.

CHAPTER 23

Before the eleven o'clock funeral mass, Lisa Muldoon performed a private ceremony on her family's front lawn. Wearing a black wool dress and midnight blue stockings, she carried a bag of sunflower seeds up the driveway and stopped at a giant oak. The tree's highest branches were gnarled by the fire, but its lowest branch still supported a Plexiglas bird feeder shaped like a translucent lighthouse. Lisa unhooked the feeder and poured in the seeds. She returned the feeder to its chain and stepped back to watch it buoy in the morning light. Her grandparents stood behind her, clutching a blanket.

It didn't take long for the birds to find the food. Perhaps they remembered it from past winters, when Theo kept it stocked as part of his chores. The finches were first, pecking down the oak and flitting on the feeder's saucer perch. Female cardinals in their dreary roses and browns soon displaced them, until they too were frightened away by woodpeckers. On the ground, squirrels competed for fallen seeds, gnawing on the husks with their apelike fingers.

Lisa watched for half an hour as the feeder became a cluster of whirling feathers, the same way that flies clustered on roadkill, the same way that, an hour from now, mourners would cluster around Lisa on the steps of the church, trying to hug her or whisper sympathies in her ear. She curled the top of the bag and turned, her lips quivering, her eyes purposely avoiding the blackened carcass of the house. Her grandmother wrapped the blanket around her, and they proceeded down the driveway past four piles of snow. The snowmen had dissolved from a spike in temperature. The Muldoon house was two days away from demolition.

That morning, Beth sat at her kitchen table, performing her own remembrance of the dead. She flipped through Jeff Trader's journal, trying to discern the reason Magdalena had been so adamant about getting it back. Most of the entries started out the same: "check boiler, pilot light, garbage lids, window locks, fire alarms, drainpipes, sterilize well with tablet, mow lawn, replace pool cover, install storm windows . . ." Variations depended upon the wealth of the tenant and the size of the house: "spray wasp nest in shed," "let in Whirlpool repairman," "sponge redwood dining room floor with Du Mur Lubricated Polish." She scanned the first several lines and flicked to another page. Not for the first time, Beth missed the tenement apartments of Manhattan, how they crumbled around her in relentless decay, but as a renter it wasn't her problem. In contrast, the houses of Orient were hungry, crib-sick babies in constant need of attention. How much effort went into maintaining those dilapidated shells.

If Jeff had any dealings with the historical board, Beth couldn't find them in the pages. Why had he warned Magdalena about OHB on his last visit? Was it that bleak warning alone that had caused her to change her will? Mike Gilburn was right. OHB lost more than it gained in Magdalena's death. And now the head of that board was also dead, to be buried that afternoon under the eyes of its remaining members—Ted and Sarakit Herrig, George Morgensen, Max Griffin, Helen Floyd, Kelley Flanner, Archie Young. Since the death of the Muldoons, Beth had heard nothing further about the call for development rights. Talk of conservancy had disappeared like talk of mutant animals on Plum—a bigger storm had pushed those coastal clouds away.

Beth found the page that listed her own address. She read the tasks that Jeff had done for her mother. "Rake leaves, clean pool filters, unclog gutters, change front door lock, sweep chimney and flue"—the list was instructive. No wonder the old creaker had been slowly falling apart in the six months she and Gavril had moved in: they had done none of these basic chores. But suddenly midparagraph, the list morphed into a different entry, the kind that spoke of human failings in need of very different repair. "$80,000 in savings, second divorce finalized, car insurance defaulted, condo brochures, hated by all, dependence on prescription painkillers, cosmetic-surgery costs on long-term payment plan, collection agency calls unreturned, sells Laurito's sailboat." At the bottom of the page, Jeff Trader had written a single word: *yes.*

Beth jumped as she heard the mail drop through the slot and scatter in the hall. But her heart continued to skip as she reread the entry. Jeff Trader's depiction of her mother was as accurate as it was unkind. She flipped through the book again, and in the middle of each list, the information mutated from odd jobs to secrets, just as Mills had said. The Drake home: "H unhappy, little revenue in home business, C doesn't want children, C passed over as law partner, H + B affair, C football gambling addiction." Jeff Trader hadn't been snooping through Holly's drawers for money. He had been snooping for secrets to record in his journal. At the bottom of the Drake page was the word *yes.*

Beth located Magdalena's page—"install grip bar in bathroom, restock firewood, order netting for hives, 83 with heart trouble, fight with B over initiative, concerned about price of farmhouse sale, hides jewelry in armoire from nurse's son, suspicious of two city artists"— and at the bottom of her page was the damning word again: *yes.* She turned the pages haphazardly. She found the Floyds: "Five children, three live at home/help with farm work" and at the bottom *no.* The Muldoons: "B three affairs at Seaview, oldest son bad grades, daughter in college, paying full tuition, youngest takes pills for ADHD, P sees therapist, B's security contracts flagging" and then *no.* The Herrigs: "S travel business near bankruptcy, second mortgage on home, T yearly earning $53,000, three adopted children, five credit cards at limit, T sells second car, divorce papers sent but shredded, PFarms targeting city buyers as last-ditch effort," and at the bottom *no*. Luz Wilson and Nathan Crimp: "millionaires, pornography collection, no children, looking to buy more land, L writes $3000 checks to family in Trenton, N cashes $30,000 checks from family in Boston, no debt, drug problem, new speedboat," and the word *maybe*. Arthur Cleaver was a blank page except for the word *yes*. Isaiah Goodman and Vince Donnelly: "openly gay, openly everything, I wants to move to Hamptons, V environmental fanatic, money troubles," *yes*. Karen Norgen: "bitter about artists, low on money, cancerous lump benign, fight with Morgensen over bushes, passed over as board member," *maybe*. Roe diCorcia: "corn crop failed, two seasons, gov farm subsidy denied, oldest child mental illness, possible incest, fight with B over water main, private meeting with superintendent," and the word, as black as Jeff Trader's laugh: *yes*.

Beth went on reading, peering with Jeff through the doors of each home, where owners' secrets and sufferings were left out on counters or tucked quietly into drawers. Thanks to his pickle jar of keys, the caretaker had unlimited access to a world of hurt, and it would have hurt anyone he'd worked for if their secrets had been exposed. Beth felt certain that Jeff Trader had been killed over this cache of broken confidences. Had "yes" marked the people he had blackmailed? The people who could be blackmailed? The weakest and most desperate of Orient homeowners? Holly Drake had admitted having a final argument with Jeff Trader; perhaps he'd threatened her. How much had it been worth to Holly to keep her affair from her husband? And how many others had folded and given Jeff money in return for his silence? The last page of the book documented sums of money: $200, $150, $500, $2,000. Were those the prices of keeping quiet?

She pictured Jeff Trader drowning, realizing as his mouth slipped under the water that he'd mistaken the trust of a man or woman who had mistaken his trust first. She thought of Tommy Muldoon, also being buried that afternoon. Mills had said that Tommy might have had the reckless intentions of a blackmailer. Had he too been murdered for trying to exploit the book's contents? Or was his mere possession of the book a cause for arson? She pulled out a note tucked in the book, a piece of thick card stock decorated with a drawing of an oyster shell: "Orient's real threat is its trust."

The book was a matter for Mike Gilburn. Only Mills and Mike knew she had it. Even if she gave it to Mike, the killer might learn that she'd read it. How quickly would this house burn? She pictured a map of Orient marked by *yes*es and *no*s, each a flame consuming its wick, held from the wind by a tin-shaped house to keep it from spreading. In Manhattan, no one cared about a neighbor's missteps over love or money. In Orient, such sins were unforgivable, unforgotten. Better to move than to face a village that knew the exact make and color of shame.

A car pulled into the driveway. Beth watched as a slender figure passed the windows and opened the kitchen door.

"Don't look so surprised," Gail said as she let herself in. She wore silken burgundy, and her low-heeled pumps brought her down to her daughter's height. "I *did* know them forever. I feel like it's my duty to pay my respects." Her recently shoddy hair and nails had been restored to full chemical shine, befitting a woman preparing to bid farewell to her old Orient enemies. First Magdalena, now the Muldoons. Who was left but Beth and Gavril to stand between Gail and her native dominion?

There was only one problem: Beth was also wearing burgundy, a wool sweater and thick, twill pants, like a faded photograph of her mother in her prime.

"We'll look like stewardesses," Beth said as she poured Gail a cup of coffee.

"It's a good thing I stopped by, then. You still have time to change."

Beth set the cup on the counter and pulled the journal from the table. "I asked you once about Jeff Trader," Beth reminded her. Gail sighed and headed for the downstairs bathroom, where she busied herself straightening the hand towels. "I'm going to ask you a strange question and I'd appreciate an honest answer."

"I'm always honest," her mother called.

"Did Jeff Trader ever try to use anything against you?"

"Use anything? Against me?" The voice was an echo. "You mean like a weapon? Honey, I'm sure I wasn't his type."

"No, I mean, like blackmail. Did he ever try to extort money from you? Something he knew about that he could use against you?" The majority of Trader's list on her mother was harmless—cosmetic surgeries, divorce—but a pill dependency and financial ruin might have been worth some kind of payoff.

Gail returned to the kitchen, her china white nails ticking through the stack of mail. Beth lunged for it, grabbing the envelopes in her hands with such ferocity that Gail tightened her grip as if by reflex. They wrestled over it briefly before Beth finally overpowered her, flattening the mail against her chest.

"What's the matter?" Gail's mouth hung open like a stable door from which a horse had just stampeded. "I still get mail delivered to me here. I was just checking. Is that a letter from your doctor? What does it say?"

Gail was right: there was an envelope from her gynecologist, a thin piece of paper in its waxy window. She was lucky she'd snatched the bundle before her mother could slit the envelope with her nail.

"We're expecting some important papers for Gavril," Beth lied. "About his immigration." She waved a Citibank envelope addressed to her husband, a stiff new bank card evident through the paper. "Anyway," she said, "you didn't answer my question about Jeff Trader."

Gail brought the coffee cup to her lips. She sniffed it before sipping. "I don't know the first thing about extortion. Honey, Jeff Trader was so drunk most days that he could barely make it from his car to the door. Now get changed." She examined her wristwatch. "We have to be there in twenty minutes. Is Gavril coming?"

"No, he's working in his studio and asked me not to interrupt him."

"I'll just peek in and—"

"He doesn't want to be disturbed," she insisted. There were two ads for playpens in the mail. Knobby toddlers climbed inside the structures as if they came with the product.

Gail stared out the window and tapped her nail against the glass. "Now, would you look at that," she said.

Beth craned her neck and saw a woman in a purple pantsuit unlock the front door of Magdalena's cottage. "Must be a Realtor," Gail said. "They're going to try to sell that house. I wonder how much they'll ask for it. It's half the size of this one." Beth remembered the furniture she had yet to claim. Did she even want a grandfather clock that belonged to a murder victim, or the armoire where Magdalena had hid her jewelry from Alvara's son? "God, I pray I'll get some decent neighbors," her mother said. "City people are the only types who will buy out here now. They're the only ones who aren't worried about some maniac setting homes on fire. I don't think there's any way they'll get their asking price. Okay, hurry. We don't have all day."

"Did you know that Magdalena changed her will before she died?" Beth looked at her mother, the frosted makeup disguising the plain Long Island woman underneath. Had she truly seen her mother in the last ten years? Beth was horrified to realize that she didn't know exactly what Gail looked like even as she stood in front of her; all she had to go on was the failing memory of who she had been. Rouge was smeared across her face like brake lights on a wet road. Her poor mother, addicted to pain medication and still paying for the surgeries that had gotten her hooked. "She was going to leave her house to the Orient Historical Board," Beth said, "but suddenly had that clause expunged. Don't you find that odd?" It would have been odd to anyone who didn't know that Jeff Trader had warned Magdalena about the historical board on his last visit.

Gail shrugged. "Roe diCorcia said she would have been livid to see her name on that initiative. Didn't want anything to do with it. He told me that as we were leaving Poquatuck on the night of the town hall meeting. That was the last time I ever saw Bryan Muldoon. Oh, honey." Gail reached out and tucked a strand of hair behind Beth's ear. "You never know what life has in store. You better do everything you want now before your body fails and your dreams grow so moldy all they're good for is the trash. There isn't time and things never happen at a better moment. Your father wanted to wait to have you, but I put my foot down. If you had come any later, you would still have been a child when he died. I think, in some way, I knew that."

"Mom, Dad didn't have cancer. He died in an accident. That could have happened at any time."

"Your father waited. I know he did. He waited to die until after you were gone." Gail watched the woman in the purple pantsuit enter Magdalena's house. "I was going to wait until after the funeral to bring this up, but money is getting so tight. And as I said, there's never a right time."

"And?"

"*And,*" she trumpeted. "I need you and Gavril to *at least* pay the monthly property tax if you're going to stay here for another year."

"Of course," Beth replied, setting her mug in the sink. "I'm sorry I didn't offer sooner. But what if we decide to stay for more than a year?"

"Is that likely?" It was as if Gail had guessed her daughter's trouble in reassimilating into village life. And she was right: her closest friend in Orient was a teenage orphan who might leave any day. Gail steadied herself in her heels. "For a while I thought it was likely. I thought you were going to give me a grandchild here, and that's why I was willing to pay the taxes. But I've been holding on to too many dreams of my own." Gail's lipstick grin was rather noble in its defeat. It broke Beth's heart.

"I don't know what to tell you, Mom."

"I'm going to have to sell sometime. Not right now. I won't get what it's worth with all the madness going on. You'd have to be a fool to sell a house in Orient at this point, even though I've gotten calls. Sarakit said she'd help me when it comes time. I might have to take her up on that, one day, soon. . . ." Gail rolled her eyes, impatient with her own evasion. "Speaking of, honey, I might need to ask you and Gavril for a little help in terms of money. Just a loan, after how generous I've been. A few thousand to start."

Beth took her mother's hand, which was chilly in her fingers. She wasn't aware of how warm her own fingers were until they made contact with Gail's skin.

"Mom, are you in trouble?" Beth was also sick of evasion. "Are you taking pills? It's nothing to be embarrassed about." Gail smiled nervously, broad enough that Beth could see the veins in her gums. The rest of her face didn't move a muscle. "I'm being serious. Are you addicted? Do you need some help?"

"Never," she swore. "Never ever. Honestly, I've never had the addict's discipline. I don't know where you'd get an idea like that." They should Botox murder defendants on trial, Beth thought. Nothing in Gail's face gave her agony away. She was as convincing as statuary.

Beth opened the hall closet and dumped the baby announcements in the hidden plastic bag. As she climbed the stairs, she ripped open the envelope from her doctor, praying it said, "We regret to inform you that we were mistaken. Our ultrasound equipment was malfunctioning on the day we examined you. You aren't pregnant. Sorry for the inconvenience." Instead it was copying her on the bill that was sent to her insurance and reminding her to schedule her next checkup. Her mother was right. There was no time left for indecision. She changed from burgundy to gray.

By eleven o'clock that morning, the better half of Orient had gathered in the pews of United Church of Christ. So many residents had taken the morning off to mourn: those who had known the Muldoons for a lifetime, and those who had first met them as recently as their last end-of-summer picnic. The mourners included Bryan's employees, hunting partners, and fellow OHB members; Pam's friends and covolunteers on various North Fork projects (Save the Osprey, Heart & Hale Elderly Meal Drive, the Maritime Museum Fun-Raisers, the Orient Historical Society Docents); Tommy's entire senior class of Sycamore High, a somber, slouching teenage army bereft of the psychic comfort of their cell phones; and several small, unspeaking children in First Communion clothes who had playdated Theo.

Beth also counted Orient's most dependable residents: Holly Drake with her veil of freckles, Karen Norgen, George Morgensen, Arthur Cleaver. Even Roe diCorcia in the last pew, his camel hair jacket rigor mortis from years hanging in a dry-cleaning bag. Ted and Sarakit Herrig sat in the second pew behind Lisa and her grandparents. Adam Pruitt, in sunglasses, mouthed the words to the opening hymn, and Beth watched as Luz tiptoed down the side aisle to claim a seat by the electric candles. Beth couldn't fathom Luz's motivation for attending—maybe it was research for her portrait series. Mills and Paul sat on the opposite side. Beth waved at Mills, who had clearly borrowed a coat and tie from Paul. The coat sleeves gaped wide at his wrists, and the bulky shoulders gave him an awkward, overstated demeanor, like a new funeral home assistant unsure how much grief to add to the commemoration.

"Lisa fed the birds this morning," her mother whispered. "Heartbreaking."

Four caskets were spaced before the altar, flat mahogany boxes with sprays of yellow lilies dangling over the lids. The coffins were all the same size, with no indication of which Muldoon lay hidden in the velvet-lined beds. The display was too much for Lisa, who spent most of the service with her hands cupped over her mouth, red nose flared above her knuckles. How easily the dead were dispensed with, in mahogany boxes nailed shut and slipped in vaults to prevent the earth from penetrating bone. It was not the dead who watched over the living, as Reverend Ann Whitlen said at the pulpit, but the living who watched over the dead.

As Reverend Whitlen read the Twenty-third Psalm, Beth thought of the note Tommy had written: "Orient's real threat is its trust." She glanced around at the funeral's teary, warm-blooded faces. Every single person looked as if something sweet had broken in them, a bit of the trust that had held them together in this small suburban hamlet cut off from civilization, reassuring them that neighbors would always look out for neighbors, that no one would want any of them dead. Such trust was no longer a given in Orient.

Ted stepped from his pew, briefly pressing his hand on Lisa's shoulder, and walked to the pulpit with his head bowed. He sighed into the microphone. "I ask us all to take a moment to stop thinking of causes, or of who could have done such a brutal act to the kindest, most generous family Orient has ever known. I ask us to think, instead, about the four neighbors we have lost. Their love should not be stolen from us by the atrocity of their deaths."

As Ted recounted a few honeycombed Muldoon memories, even the driest eyes brimmed with sorrow. "As we all know, Bryan was a savior to Orient. He was the head of the historical board, which meant the world to him. I was honored to serve with him on OHB for twenty years. And I know"—Ted choked, as if being slowly consumed by gas fumes—"he would want us to continue the fight against development. The initiative is named for Magdalena Kiefer, but we will fight in Bryan's name to ensure a green future in Orient. At Lisa's request, Sarakit and I are manning a table outside of the church for anyone who wants to receive more information on the Nondevelopment Initiative and honor Bryan and his family by carrying on his battle to protect Orient, to which our dear friend committed his life. I cannot think of a better tribute. We can still realize his dream." Ted left the podium with his head high, certain the audience was on his side. There was nothing left to do but sing "Amazing Grace."

The crowd outside the church spilled onto the lawn, where Sarakit and Ted took their place behind a table borrowed from Karen Norgen, clipboards and brochures arranged before them. Most of the mourners moved around anxiously in the cold, lost in their individual cabins of thought. Amid them, Lisa's stillness had an unpiloted effect. She was hugged by friends and strangers, was told of virtues or an unselfish favor performed, was offered food or a seat at Thanksgiving dinner. She looked into each of their faces as if staring into a cavern from which human sounds echoed but never cohered into sense. The four caskets were wheeled past her like luggage organized for transport by a divine concierge.

Leaving her mother with Ina Jenkins, Beth searched the church grounds for Mills. Someone tapped her shoulder, and she turned to find Luz in a white shirt and a silk tuxedo jacket with black gloves buttoned at her wrists.

"Why are you wearing gloves?"

"You should see my hands." Luz smiled, holding up a hand and flexing leather fingers. "They're electric blue from painting. I thought it might be more respectful to wear these than to come to a funeral like I'd just fisted an alien." Luz's upper lip snarled and she quickly fit a cigarette into its crevice. "My skin color already freaks these people out. I bet half of those farmers"—she pointed her lighter toward Helen Floyd before flicking it—"think I was the Muldoons' cook. *Mastah's dead. What iz'a gonna do now?*" Luz grunted. "Persecution does wonders for personal integrity. Still, the looks I get."

"Did you know them?"

Luz bit the smoke and let it slide from the side of her mouth.

"Yes. I knew them. Not well. But Bryan was a nice guy. He came by to welcome Nathan and me when we moved in. Said he was glad to see one of the bigger houses in Orient going to a young couple. I think he expected toddlers to materialize around our legs. He told us about all of Orient's hidden treasures, the history of the buildings and lighthouses. Then he got all conservancy on us. But I liked him. I even showed him the paintings I was doing of his neighbors. He promised he'd take me hunting one weekend. He raved about the quality of the deer. He didn't seem to realize our bedroom has a prime view of Plum—I'd rather not eat bush meat somebody gunned down and seasoned with Ebola."

"You know they use bows out here more than guns."

"I might need a gun," Luz said. Beth imagined Pam Muldoon catching a black woman with a gun running around Orient and the weeks of racial insinuation that would have followed—with phrases like "that rich woman" or "that artist" standing in for "that black woman." Did those local gossips know that Luz supported her entire family in Trenton with her work? Of course not. Beth had learned that only by reading Jeff Trader's journal. Karen Norgen passed nearby, eyeing Beth strangely, wrapping herself protectively in a hand-crocheted scarf.

"I mean it. I'm frightened," Luz whispered. "Two nights ago I heard someone walking around our property. I heard footsteps and rustling in the grasses by the water. When I got up to look, I swear I saw a shadow near the dock. I almost had a heart attack. I went around making sure all the doors were locked." She laughed uneasily. A contrail of breath and cigarette smoke drifted from her lips. "The doors were just fine. The problem is, we don't have walls. We're about the least protected house out here. Maybe we should go back to the city for a while. Or maybe we should just sell and find a new house somewhere deeper in the woods. Nathan thinks the danger is good for his work. And he has a point—everyone loves a dead artist. It's the living ones that people can't tolerate." It occurred to Beth that the obscenely rich and the obscenely poor had one thing in common: neither really lived anywhere for long. One by choice, the other by necessity, they came and went as if the entire world were padding for their beds.

Luz wrapped her arms around Beth's shoulders. Many were hugging on the church's lawn just as they were. Holly was leaning on the church railing, her head turned toward the grotto so no one could see her face.

"How are you doing?" Luz asked. "Are you holding up okay? You know, if you ever want to talk to me, about anything, I'm here." Beth gently slipped from Luz's embrace. Luz exhaled. "Will you and Gavril at least come for dinner tomorrow night? There's no reason *we* can't get together and remember that our own lives have nothing to do with these local deaths."

Ted waved a clipboard at Roe diCorcia. The tall farmer took it, pressed an ungulate fist on its page, and dropped the board on the table with a clack.

"You people are still at it? Even after Bryan's death?" The farmer shook his head. His chin-length hair fell forward, curled from its time spent gathered in a ponytail.

"Now, Roe," Ted said.

"It ain't going to happen. Your little eco-friendly fairy tale ain't going to happen. This was farming land long before it was cute-house land." Roe cocked a finger at Ted's wind- and tear-streaked face. His voice was the relentless sound of car wheels stuck in a snowbank. "And I tell you what. That water-main proposal wasn't beaten. It was temp-o-rarily shelved. And I'm making it my mission to get it back on the table at the Water Authority. You can write that down on your clipboard. We need improvements, not pretty views. Did you ever think that if Bryan hadn't blocked the water main, we would've had hydrants that might've saved his wife and kids? Did you ever think about that, Ted? Someone should." Roe crossed himself, and with the last horizontal slash of his wrist, flicked his fingers to renounce the Herrigs.

"Don't be disrespectful," Sarakit shouted at the retreating farmer. "We are trying to save *your* land. You don't realize what they're going to build right next to your corn, Roe. One day you'll see and you'll apologize."

Roe stopped five feet from the table. "Lady, you and your Pearl Farms outfit are the ones selling the land to the folks who are going to build on it. Why don't you ask them if they want a water main?"

Sarakit spent a second blinking her eyes before responding, as if Roe's insult were a gnat caught in her sclera. "I will get every one of my customers on board with this initiative. We live here too. All of us do. We just care about each other more."

Sarakit rubbed her husband's back, consoling herself by

dispensing consolation. Had they been teetering on divorce, as Jeff Trader's journal suggested? If so, perhaps it was sharing their OHB duties that had brought the spark back to their marriage. With Magdalena and Bryan dead, their love must be a raging fireplace. The other board members hadn't bothered to help man the table, but it hardly mattered: it was obvious to Beth, after five minutes lingering near the stand, that most year-rounders had grown wary of the conservancy mission. Olivia Aug quickly scanned a brochure, then returned it to the stack. "Oh, I don't know. Without Bryan, it just seems like the energy is gone. Maybe in a month or two when all this passes. Then maybe I'll be able to think it over." Karen Norgen marched up to the table—as if it were her prize cedar heirloom, not the conservancy, that was being snubbed—and signed her name. Sarakit stacked the literature that no one took. *Thou preparest a table before me in the presence of mine enemies.* Psalm Twenty-three.

"I would invite your young friend to dinner, but it's art people only," Luz said. "Don't tell him I said so, but I think Gavril's a little jealous of Mills."

Beth turned. Luz was grinding her cigarette into the dirt with her shoe.

"If he is, I wouldn't know. These days he's barely even living in the house."

"Give him a break," she wheezed. "He's under huge pressure. Gavril talks a good game, but he's like the rest of us. A slave to his reputation. You've got family here. You've got history. You've got that baby you two have been planning. What does he have out here but his work?"

Did Luz know she was pregnant, or was she just fishing? Beth couldn't tell. Luz hated babies, but Beth suspected that she would secretly enjoy seeing Beth strapped to one—a fresh target of antagonism, a perfect object lesson in Luz's own superiority over the sins of fertility. Luz chewed on the seam of her glove.

"'An ambitious effort.' That's what *Newsday* called my last show. You spill your blood on the wall and that's all they have to say about it. You know how hard it is to actually touch the world? To make a mark on it? You die and they bury you in it."

"We'll come by for dinner tomorrow," Beth said and left her to walk across the grass. She caught sight of Mills and Paul, marooned on the lawn in Paul's suits, the white spike of the UCC steeple behind them. Mills nodded gratefully when he saw her, as if she could break the spell of emptiness that surrounded them. She noticed eyes—Karen Norgen's under light-blue eye shadow, Helen Floyd's tinted by red sunglasses—staring at Mills, talking in hushed tones, watching him the way deer watched a still intruder, uncertain whether it might attack. She was about to head over and rescue him when a hand gripped her arm.

It was Sarakit, with her tense, thin-lipped smile. She was an attractive woman, with smooth, marmoreal skin despite her middle age, though her taste for the Long Island camouflage of catalog fleeces and pilled crewneck sweaters robbed her beauty of its force.

"Hello, Beth," she said. A clipboard was wedged against her ribs.

"I told Mr. Cleaver already. I don't own the house. My mother does. If you want to talk about development rights, you'll have to speak with Gail. She's around here somewhere." Beth scanned the lawn for a woman in burgundy.

"It isn't about that," Sarakit blurted. A few tears clouded her eyes. "I want to hear from your mouth what that fight was about."

"What fight?"

Sarakit glared at her like she was being purposefully uncooperative.

"You know what fight," she said more loudly. "And on this day of all days, you should respect the question." The eyes of the year-rounders, once fixed on Mills, had turned to her. "I want to know what that young man over there was arguing with Pam about days before the fire."

"I don't know what you—"

"Yes you do." Sarakit's voice was burning. Her breath smoked. Ted got up from the table with the weary resignation of a Calvary bystander in one of the church's copper Stations of the Cross reliefs. "You were there. I saw you. Pam was angry about something that kid did, that foster kid of Paul's, and I want to know what it was." Paul heard his name and headed toward them; Mills stayed behind on the lawn, rubbing his legs.

"What's going on?" Paul asked.

"Sarakit is just upset," Ted said. In response, Sarakit slapped her husband in the stomach, dropping the clipboard on the ground.

"I *am* upset," she moaned in defense. "My friends were murdered, and no one has been arrested. I'm not saying he did it. All I'm asking for is an honest answer. What did that young man do to the Muldoons to make Pam so upset? Will someone please tell me? Why is no one speaking up? It happened just days before the fire. We're a community, aren't we?" Realizing she was making a scene, Sarakit pulled her wool collar to her neck. "You shouldn't be here," she said toward the young man alone on the lawn. "They weren't your friends."

Paul tried to apologize. "The police have already—" he whispered. Beth left Sarakit midhysteria and walked over to Mills, standing frozen in the Orient chill like a foam core target. In front of the remaining mourners of the UCC congregation, she took his hand. The mourners looked on, eyeing her cautiously. Their houses were not as safe as they had been a week ago. There was a murderer among them who hadn't been caught. After the quiet solemnity of the funeral, they spoke in clipped suspicions. "The arsonist wasn't a complete stranger to the family. Whoever it was had keys." "They were all alive when the fire started. The coroner found soot in their throats." "The motive wasn't robbery. Who brings gasoline to rob a house?"

Beth felt the neighbors' stares on her. Maybe taking Mills's hand wasn't as supportive as she had intended it to be. After all, she'd been the first one to cry murder, long before the Muldoons were killed, and now murder had come. Off in the distance, she saw Mike Gilburn leaning against his sedan in the parking lot. He nodded. She walked off with Mills in the direction of her house.

"I didn't want to come," Mills mumbled on the sidewalk. "I knew people would look at me weird. But Paul said I should for Tommy."

"I know," she said. "It will blow over. Sarakit's lost her mind."

The limousine carrying Lisa, the only surviving Muldoon, passed them by en route to the graveyard.

When they got to Beth's house, she opened the back door to the kitchen. Gavril had already eaten lunch; his plate was in the sink.

"I found the secrets in the journal," she told Mills as she poured him a glass of water.

"I found out something too," Mills said, removing his suit coat. "Well, I didn't find out, exactly. I remembered." The daylight silvered his face, and as he gazed at her with eyes eased by her company, she felt again the instinct to paint him. Maybe that had been the lesson of the morning: there was no more time to wait for approval from others—not strangers, nor Gavril, not even herself. A mark on the world was made that way, by pushing into it, by digging as deep as she could go.

"What did you remember?" Beth asked. She opened the refrigerator to search out the ingredients of a sandwich for him.

"Lisa Muldoon," he said, gripping the table. "She's the girl we saw that day we drove to Jeff Trader's place. The one leaving that red bungalow. She hasn't been away at college. She's been in Orient all along."

CHAPTER 24

Beth and Mills sat in the car, surveying the bungalow from which Lisa Muldoon had stumbled in her hooded sweatshirt only a few weeks ago, attempting to hide as they drove past. Plant leaves stuck against the frosted window. The lights inside were off, and the driveway was empty. Two Pruitt Securities badges marked the bungalow as protected. When Mills asked her who the place belonged to, she shrugged.

"The question is, why would she be here and not at her own house?" Beth tapped the steering wheel, her fingers turning white with cold.

"The Muldoons thought she was at college," Mills said. "Tommy did. He admired her so much for getting out of Orient. Lisa obviously didn't want her family to know she was back."

"Maybe it was just a weekend visit," Beth suggested, as if out of respect for the young woman she had watched bury her family that morning. "We don't know that she's been in Orient the whole time."

Mills grunted and turned to her. "What if she's been staying at the Seaview all these weeks? She's the *her* that Tommy discovered at the motel, the one he wondered if he should turn in to his parents. He must have caught her there when she was supposed to be away at college and he felt like she'd betrayed him by coming back."

Beth glanced down the block for oncoming cars. The bungalow was still quiet and empty. "Let's take a look," she said. "It's too cold to sit here all day."

She unhooked the chain-link gate, opening it for Mills and letting it swing in case they needed a quick retreat. In the shadows of the porch, it was even colder. She tapped her knuckles on the door.

"No one's home."

She opened the metal mailbox on the door but found only coupons and Pearl Farms flyers addressed to "resident." Mills cupped his hands against the window and peered in, and she copied him. Beyond the leaves of a few ferns, a mattress in the center of the room was strewn with blankets and sheets. On a plywood table, papers and hand tools suggested a squabble of white- and blue-collar work. A sailor's map of Orient, marking its precise tides and coves, lay unfolded on the floor.

"A man lives here," she said.

"Did you try the doorknob?" Mills asked.

"It's got an alarm," she said, pointing to the Pruitt signs in the yard. "And I think we should stop breaking into homes on Beach Lane."

"Look on the doorknob to the bathroom," he muttered into his palms. A white bra hung there by its strap. "Could be Lisa's. The man could be her boyfriend. But why wouldn't she just stay with him here? Why would she take a room at a motel?"

"Because the Seaview isn't in Orient," Beth said. "There's less of a chance of running into someone she knew. Unless she ran into her father there during one of his visits." In her mind, Muldoons suddenly swarmed the old motel like termites.

"The *L*," Mills said. "From the necklace."

Beth stepped back from the window. "I don't know Lisa. She was a little girl when I lived out here. But I will say she did look genuinely upset at the funeral. Would she murder her family just to prevent them from knowing that she dropped out of college? Or just because she caught her father having an affair? Maybe we should tell Detective Gilburn and let the police handle it."

Mills warmed his fists with his breath. Beth had lent him one of Gavril's down coats, and she grabbed its tails to zipper him into it.

"She lied about being away," Mills said. "Not just to her parents. To the police. Why?" Before she could stop him, he jumped from the porch and started walking around the house. She followed. The side of the house was dotted with plastic buckets full of rocks; the owner seemed to collect them the way others collect spare change in jars. The aluminum siding was sun-warped and encrusted in ice. The guts of a lawn mower lay in the grass, its motor sprouting dead summer weeds. An old bee box was similarly autopsied, its racks thrown in the dirt. The bungalow's back door had long since rusted shut, and there were no back windows, nothing to look through for a clue to the owner's identity. Beth noticed a woodshed half-hidden behind two overgrown spirea bushes and walked toward it as Mills circled the house. Five feet from its padlocked door, the odor of rot filled her nose. She gagged as she covered her mouth. Beyond the backyard fencing, she saw Jeff Trader's property, cleared of its mobile unit, dragged away by some machine that had left deep grooves in the mud. Beyond the barren field, the Sound sparkled its colorless mercury.

"Hey," screamed a voice behind her. "Get the fuck away from—"

She spun around: it was Adam Pruitt, storming toward her, his right hand brandishing a hammer.

They recognized each other simultaneously. Adam's scowl softened, though his grip didn't ease on the hammer. "Well, well," he said. "I didn't expect you to show up. What do I owe this privilege?" He stopped midlawn, forcing her to step away from the shed. He was still wearing his suit from the funeral. Behind him, the red fire department truck was parked in the drive.

"Is this your place?" she asked. "I mean, I was hoping it was."

"Yeah. I live here now. I sold my dad's house months ago." He sniffled and wiped snot on his sleeve. The hammer pivoted in his fingers. He licked his front teeth, as if grooming them for a smile. The smile didn't come. "Why are you here?"

"I tried to call first." She laughed dumbly, like the girl she'd been in high school, the one who went along with Adam and his friends when they stole motorboats and loaded them with beer and built bonfires on outlying islands. The guys got in trouble but never named her as a participant to the cops. Adam Pruitt was always in trouble; if he'd implicated her in half the mischief they'd gotten into, she might not have escaped Orient with an NYU scholarship and a sterling reputation. The mass inside her might have been a Pruitt instead of a Catargi.

"It's a start-up," he said.

"What is?"

"My company." The smile, when it arrived, was proud. She had seen arrogance in Adam's face before, and drunkenness and delinquency, but pride recast him as a more vulnerable man. "I don't have a secretary yet, but I need to hire one *a-sap*. As you probably know, business is booming. I tell you, if the government had respected the land, we wouldn't be in such a mess. Think of what we were exposed to as children out here, getting zapped by those poisons and microbes from Plum. We're lucky we turned out so good-looking, huh?"

"Congratulations," she said, her body in clumsy contrapposto. She allowed Adam to follow the curves of her hips and breasts, waiting for him to let go of the hammer.

"When do you want me to come over?" he asked. She stared at him, trying to imagine Lisa Muldoon in his bungalow, letting his hands root across her teenage body. Adam caught the uncertainty on her face. "To do an inspection. You're here for a security system, right?"

"We need one," she agreed, recovering quickly. "And for the garage. It's Gavril's studio now, my husband's. Lots of expensive artworks."

"Art works," he repeated, turning the second word into a verb. "I remember that your mom put in a pool. She might have been the first to go with that organic saltwater variety, with no chlorine to kill the bacteria. We can test the water. And I recommend a soil graph. I wouldn't eat a tomato in Orient without running a toxic spec. You're friends with that artist couple who bought the old farmhouse inn, right? I was over there yesterday. Man, they've got their work cut out for them."

"Yeah. Luz and Nathan."

"They're digging holes out there like mad. You fuck with the land that much, the house is going to slide right onto the beach. Everyone from around here knows that. I'd appreciate you putting a word in with them about running some environmental checks."

"I saw you at the funeral today," Beth said, pushing him toward the reason for her visit. "I feel so bad about what Lisa is going through."

Adam's mouth shifted, its hinges crooked like a broken suitcase. He reached his free hand into his coat pocket and pulled out a pack of cigarettes. He shook one out for her, but she shook her head. He dropped the hammer and lit one for himself.

"Yeah, for that to happen to such a sweet girl," he said. "Can't say I know her that well, but when I lost my parents it's like a chunk of my past went with them. When I cleaned the house out, I didn't know what the fuck to do with my old childhood drawings. I thought about keeping them, but why? I burned them in the fireplace. All those houses we painted in Mrs. Jenkins's class went up like we never should have bothered." He sighed. "But Dad would have been proud to know that his name was meaning something to the people in Orient. Security. Protection. Fighting those environmental cancers, the kind that ripped through his lungs like paint thinner. That's what you're here for, right? A system? You want you and your husband to be safe?" His eyes flitted between her and the shed. A doubt stumbled through him, she could tell, stumbled and fell and smacked its chin on the ground. She felt blood rushing to her tongue, but before she could say a word, Adam spotted another figure in the backyard, prompting him to lean down and reclaim the hammer.

"I'm coming," she called. She touched Adam's arm as she passed him. "I'll call you about an inspection," she said. "Maybe next week if you aren't too booked?"

Adam studied the young man trespassing on his property.

"Hey, kid," he yelled, pointing his cigarette at him. "You better think twice before walking around a stranger's house. I don't mind Beth, but you're not known to me. If you don't respect a fence, you're likely to be stopped by something worse."

"I'm sorry, Adam, we're leaving," she said over her shoulder. Mills did his best to appear unfazed. They jogged to the car, and she started the ignition.

"So Lisa Muldoon was with Adam Pruitt," Beth said. "He always did like them young."

"Wasn't Adam her father's main competitor?" Mills asked, buckling his seat belt. "Maybe they were in it together. She killed the family she hated and he killed the man whose business he wanted. Jeff Trader could have found out what they were planning. He might have seen Lisa. He lived next door."

Beth remembered something Paul had said to her the first day she had gone over to pick Mills up, when the air was still warm with autumn and Jeff Trader was still the only dead body in Orient. Jeff had told Paul that there were some people in Orient who shouldn't be there. He could have been referring to Lisa.

As she drove, Mills stoked the fire of his new theory. "Don't you see? It fits. Jeff Trader knew she was here, not away at college. They had to get rid of him before they went ahead with their plan. Maybe Jeff told Magdalena about Lisa being back. So she also had to be taken care of. Then it was only her family that was keeping them apart. No way they would have approved of Adam."

"So they did it for love?" she said skeptically. Was there some romantic failing inside of Beth that prevented her from seeing love as a motivation for murder?

"Haven't you ever heard of a kid killing her parents? And guess who knows how to set a fire that can't be extinguished?" Mills said. "A firefighter."

They trailed behind a mud-splattered Chevy on Main Road until it turned north up a dirt road. Beth followed the pickup as it rumbled up an incline, setting their teeth on edge.

"Where are you going?" Mills asked, steadying his hand on the dashboard as farmland slid past the windows, hot hay yellow in a frost-blistered field.

"I want to ask Roe diCorcia a question. Maybe this time, you wait in the car."

Half a mile off Main Road, past a miracle of farmland that grew soil-depleting corn one year and soil-replenishing soybeans the next, bordered by razor wire and patrolled by Rottweilers that gleamed yellow or green for most of their starving summers, stood a white pine farmhouse that belonged to the diCorcia family. Beth had grown up frightened of the diCorcias, as all good children were taught to be. The family was the marrow of Orient legend: bitter and creepy and proud owners of an arsenal of shotguns that made no exception for the local field stray. The diCorcias, when spotted around the village, seemed happy to confirm their own mystique with gruff words and tightly squeezed faces—as if they were forever stepping on a blister—and with the *rat-a-tat* backfire of their truck.

If reputations in Orient were built on a series of isolated social contests, the diCorcias had dropped out of the tournament alto-gether, preferring certain infamy to the constant scramble for status. Refusing to play, they opened themselves up to rumor. The note Jeff Trader had written in his journal—"possible incest"—had already circulated among Orient children for decades. Who did the diCorcias mate with if not each other? What self-respecting person would have them? *Them*, for the past twenty years, had meant Roe; his wife and adult daughter rarely stepped foot off their acres of cropland. DiCor-cia females were as hard to spot as bobwhite quails, and a rare sight-ing was regarded with vituperative awe: *Did you see what they were wearing? Dresses right out of the '70s—the 1870s. Do they even have running water? I'm not sure they ever learned to read.*

These memories came back to Beth as she bounced the Nissan toward an oasis of hilltop spruces. Under their branches, the farmhouse magnified. It was as big as the Benchley mansion and just as decrepit, not from lack of use but through the unbroken inhabitance of diCorcias dating back a hundred years. Roe's grandfather must have been more ostentatious—it was he who must have added the glint of colored Victorian glass to the diamond windows along the second floor, and planted grapevines that still climbed a wagonwheel trellis—but such indulgences had since been bred out of the bloodline. The widow's walk crowning the roof and the chains on the porch for a phantom swing were reminders of a time when independent corn farmers were viewed as more than soil grunts. Now their kind of poverty made for stunning scenery, the very sort of landscape the historical board hoped frantically to preserve. Roe diCorcia's only adornment to the house was a large satellite dish clamped to the widow's walk. The diCorcias were clinging to the twentieth century, not the nineteenth.

Roe got out of his Chevy. Beth lowered her window as she slowed behind it, raising her hand through the crack, palm open, a white flag of peace. Roe slammed his door and glared as he wiped his fingers on a rag.

"Stay put," she said to Mills. She climbed out, struck by a hilltop view of flat yellow fields so bountiful she could hardly believe such undeveloped acreage still existed in Orient. Behind the house, the Sound foamed and the distant ferry to Connecticut was a flyspeck on raw, blue meat. Deer fled into the fields, frightened by the cars, their white hinds dirtied with manure and leaves.

"What do you want?" Roe yelled. A denim coat hung over his camel hair jacket. A smear of dirt from the steering wheel striped his pants. Roe scooped up his hair and tied it back. "If you had something to say to me, you should have spoke your piece at the church. I don't like people coming up here uninvited." A stray lock of hair swayed between his eyes.

"I know," Beth replied. A gratuitous smile would have insulted him. If years of overgracious suburbanites hadn't tamed Roe's heart, her smile wasn't likely to convert him. She stared again at the view. The hay covering the soil winked with icicles. If she owned this much land, she thought, she might keep people off it too. Roe snapped his fingers to bring her attention back to him. An old Rottweiler with hair-patched skin lay near the porch, its whole body panting in dehydration. Roe followed her eyes to the dog.

"Been sick. Ate or drank something awful. All the dogs been sick lately. Could have been poisoned for all I know, by one of our upstanding neighbors."

"I just have a question for you, and then I'll go." This seemed to soften Roe a bit, enough that he leaned against the truck, chewing on his cheek.

"I'm listening. Elizabeth, right? You're Anthony's daughter. He wasn't a bad man. Not saying we was friends, but he knew how to keep to his business. He knew where everyone's lines were."

"Thank you," she said. "I wanted to ask you about Magdalena Kiefer."

Roe's face pitched back. A gulp traveled down his throat.

"I thought you were here about OHB." He laughed. "You eastern city people have your heads screwed on wrong. You keep walking forward but your eyes are facing back." His fingers braced the tailgate. "Eastern people talk about saving this place. They'll ruin it by trying to save it." Roe kept saying *eastern people* like he lived in the west, like the city was somewhere beyond his view of the Atlantic.

"Magdalena was part of OHB too."

"Yeah, she was," Roe admitted. "And Lena was the only decent thing about it. She didn't think helping preserve the land had anything to do with taking away my rights. I got a right to say what gets built on my property. I got a right to water my crops from the county grid. I pay my taxes. You eastern people and your postcard reality. It ain't a place if it's frozen in time. Well, you'll see. You'll see just what you get for stealing me of my means."

"Mr. diCorcia," Beth said pleasantly. "I was born here too. We aren't from different places. I'm not trying to steal anything from you."

Roe leaned farther back, his entire body weight held by his grip on the truck.

"You *used to* be from around here. You ain't no more. You left. And when you come back from a place like that, you're changed. That city over there is where you belong." He pointed his chin toward the Sound, another wrong direction. "I know what kind of friends you brought back with you. I see 'em, clear as day. They think because they have money they can turn Orient into a resort. But I live out here, at least, I do today. Maybe not much longer. I might have to parcel out a few of these prize acres you and your friends drive past like you're on vacation. Like I grow these crops for scenery so you can gaze at them from your speedboats and sports cars. No, young lady, you ain't from here. You may live here, and you may own it all soon. But this ain't your place."

"I get why you don't like OHB," she sputtered. "I get why you were angry at Bryan Muldoon for blocking the water main—"

"Angry?" Roe found her choice of words humorous. "That man ruined me for the past two seasons of corn. All I could grow was sorghum because I couldn't irrigate enough with my wells, even with the pumpers I had to pay out of my own pocket to haul in. Angry at Bryan? No, I wasn't angry. I was almost bankrupt. Angry doesn't begin to fix how I felt about that arrogant coward who blocked my lifeline."

"What about Miss Kiefer? Was she angry? You told my mother the night of the town meeting that Magdalena would have been upset to have her name on that new initiative. I was hoping you could tell me why."

"Lena understood that I work the land for a living. She valued those of us who are fighting to make ends meet. She would never have backed an initiative that offered a few farmers down on their luck some hush money to sell off their development rights just so they could eat for another year and the whole time be robbed of what their land is worth. First Bryan took away our water, and, when that broke us, he tried to give us money for our development rights. You take that away too, you're basically putting us out of business. You're saying no to infrastructure we need to stay afloat. Without that, all these fields will have to be broken up into little plots so you eastern city people can come in and build your dream chalets."

Roe let go of the truck and threw his hands up, as if he were lecturing an inner-city student. "You don't get it. Lena did. She would have fought that piece of shit scam, not put her name on it. Seems maybe someone got rid of her before she could. It embarrasses me that other farmers, like the Floyds, are sitting ducks on that board, blinded by a second in the spotlight. They ought to know better than to listen to Bryan. Guess who makes money if the land gets carved up and more rich folks like your friends move here? Small home owners like Bryan, that's who, 'cause their property value increases. A security company like Muldoon. It gets a wave of new business. Real estate agencies, like the one owned by that Oriental woman. She gets a commission on every sale. I tell you, OHB stinks like manure, 'cause that's what it is."

Jeff Trader had tried to warn Magdalena about OHB on his last visit. And now Roe was pointing blame at OHB too, hinting that the board had led to her death. Had Jeff Trader known that OHB was going to go behind Magdalena's back on the initiative? Was Jeff silenced before he could speak? If that's what happened, why kill Bryan? He was the initiative's main proponent. It occurred to Beth that there might be more than one murderer. Jeff and Magdalena might have been killed by someone connected to OHB, and Bryan might have been killed by a desperate farmer who needed to stop him before the trust got under way.

"Who do you think killed the Muldoons?" she asked bluntly.

Roe looked around, at the white-scabbed spruces, at the wagon-wheel trellis, at the brown American flag blowing over the porch steps and his dying dog.

"Could have been anyone with a conscience. You? Me? The land?" Roe's eyes were wide, his forehead a Sahara of rolling dunes.

"The land he thought he was saving? Maybe the community killed him before he could destroy it. Sometimes God works in not-so-mysterious ways, young lady. And remember, you reap what you sow. The Kingdom of God is like a mustard seed, which sown, grows up and becomes greater than all of the herbs, and puts out its branches, and is bigger than the man who planted it. And it will kill that man who is nothing but a speck under its shade if he don't respect it. You want to know who killed Bryan? Look around you. A man who is a thief in the night will be burnt by the sun come morning. Until then, I've got work to do—"

The farm door burst open, and a lean, big-boned woman ran from the darkness toward the cars. Her loose cornflower dress was splattered in grease, her bare feet red with rashes. Her eyes were set close at the bridge of her nose, like a pair of tightly wrapped cocoons, and her open mouth was a pink bucket of gums. It hung open naturally, as if in constant pain or joy. She ran in a distracted, faraway manner, a pair of binoculars swinging against her chest.

"Daddy," the woman screamed. Her hair was as blond as corn silk. An old woman with pinned silver hair, Roe's wife, peered out from the doorframe.

"Ray Ann," Roe drawled. "You get back inside. You need to put your shoes on. Shoes on." Ray Ann launched herself into her father's chest, and he put his arm around her to hold her in his warmth. The young woman was clearly disabled; Beth couldn't name the syndrome, but it seemed chromosomal, some genetic defect. Ray Ann might be Beth's age, born in Orient around the same time, and her disability was the reason she rarely left the farm in childhood—not because she couldn't make the trip, but because Beth and her friends would have shown her no mercy. Roe stared at Beth as he removed the binoculars from around his daughter's neck.

"Let me show you what you have brought me," he said. Roe tested the binoculars and rotated their lenses until they caught a vision to the east. He handed them to Beth and pointed. "Look over there. Right beyond that sap maple."

She took the binoculars. Through them, she saw a large farm-house covered in plastic tarps. Its lawn was trenched in giant mud holes, and through a clear sheet of plastic she saw Nathan Crimp in the nude, gyrating on a Persian rug, a bowl of red berries in his hands. An imported white man, with an impressive lack of body hair, eating imported fruit on an imported rug.

"Those are my new neighbors to the left. On the right I've got Arthur Cleaver and his Greek temple of sin, with a giant flat screen of stocks and a paddle wheel boat that don't do nothing but serve as a party favor. I'm being squeezed on both sides by people who can sell their development rights because they can move whenever they feel like it. What's it to them? There's a blight on this land, but it ain't from Plum. It's from a different island altogether, and I bet you lived there high and pretty. Now if you don't mind."

Beth returned to her car. Mills had been listening through a crack in the window. She put the Nissan in reverse and headed down the thin dirt trail. The white farmhouse disappeared in her rearview mirror, replaced by a wash of hay fields.

"Did you catch all that?" she asked.

"Most of it," Mills said. "But I still think we're right about Lisa and Adam. Why did you bother drilling him like that?"

"Because of what Jeff told Magdalena about OHB. Adam and Lisa aren't on the board. That part doesn't fit your theory. Jeff warned her for a reason. I wanted to see if Roe knew what that reason was."

"Jeff was a drunk," he replied. "Roe diCorcia has a motive to kill the Muldoons, and clearly it wouldn't be a strain on his conscience. But it doesn't change the fact that Lisa lied about being at college."

"I know it doesn't."

"So you're going to tell the detective?" Mills stared at her for a minute, as if he could override her brain with sheer hope. When had Mills decided that the police were a force of good, to be apprised at every turn?

"Why does it make such a difference to you?" she asked.

He rubbed his palms on his thighs. "I might stay here for a while," he said. "And it's best if the murders get cleared up quickly. So you'll tell the detective?"

"Yes," she promised. "But I'll respect Lisa enough not to make accusations on the day she buried her family. We can talk it over tomorrow when you come to my house."

His lips bent. "I'm coming over tomorrow?"

"I want to paint your portrait," she said.

Mills checked his face in the side mirror, as if to see how it would appear on a flat surface. "Okay. But I have a favor to ask in return."

"Name it."

"I need you to get that cake for me for Paul's birthday. I want to surprise him. Would you get one for me from the bakery in Greenport? If you pick it up tomorrow, I'll hide it in the back of our refrigerator."

"*Our* refrigerator?"

"Paul's." Mills blushed, and Beth was sorry that she had corrected him. "*His* refrigerator."

After Beth dropped Mills off, she allowed her mind to run with color, with oil paints that had long gone dry in her studio yet wettened instantly when she imagined the blank canvas. The thought of painting eased her fears, and the excitement of her one small decision emboldened her about other uncertainties: the mass inside her, her growing disconnection from Gavril. She had buried herself too long in the comfort of indecision. As she pulled into her driveway, she felt for the first time in many months like a woman with a direction. Standing still meant going nowhere. A place was made by moving toward it.

The lights were on in the garage, and the house itself was empty. She dropped her purse on the kitchen table and hurried up to the spare bedroom to open the boxes and set a fresh canvas on the easel.

As she dug through the dusty tins of paint tubes, a light pain shot through her stomach. Beth froze in place. Another tremor came, hot and thin as a wire. She waited for further activity. One final needle passed through her and sunk back into her organs like an unsuccessful mutiny. There was no more. Tomorrow she would call the doctor in Greenport, or maybe Planned Parenthood on Bleecker Street. She would make an appointment and keep to her decision, just as she would paint Mills tomorrow and see the work to completion, whether it was any good or not. As she stood there, she heard footsteps downstairs in the living room, then the hushed, cushioned sound of objects being moved. A door slammed.

"Gavril?" she called. "Are you there?"

She walked into the hallway and went down the steps. "Gavril?" No voice broke the silence. The sun was setting, and lurid pinks reflected on the painted walls. She reached the foyer and turned down the hall. "Is anyone there? Hello?"

The living room was a bruising blue as night began to settle. Its lingering smells of dead flowers and dried whiskey were more potent in the darkness. Then she noticed that the two armchairs in the living room had traded places, the leather low-back switched with the recliner, both pointing in an awkward formation away from the couch. She couldn't remember if they'd been that way fifteen minutes ago when she'd passed through the room to go upstairs. She blinked, as if her brain were suffering a bout of dyslexia that could be fixed by closing her eyes. She glanced at the front door and saw her purse hanging from the hall closet doorknob. "Gavril?" she called again. She headed down the foyer. Cold light bled from the bottom of the front door, meaning it was still ajar. She pushed her hand against it, and the bolt slipped into its lock.

Out the front window, the lawn was empty.

She grabbed her purse and looked through it as she stepped back into the living room. Nothing was missing, but she had left her purse in the kitchen. Beth stared at the chairs again, now certain that they hadn't been arranged that way when she went upstairs.

Nothing was actually wrong—the room was almost normal—but in that sliver of difference, that clock tick away from the correct time, panic started building in her hands and throat. Someone had been in here. Just a few minutes ago, while she was upstairs. Someone had broken into the house. She ran through the kitchen, certain that someone would reach out and grab her before she made it to the back door, to stab her or break her neck. She crossed the lawn, her arms thrashing, and opened the garage to a blast of rock music. Gavril was on his knees, a torch in his hand.

"Gavril," she said, panting. "Were you just in the house?"

"What?" He turned off the music. "In the house? No, I have been working. I'm very busy, Beth. The collectors are coming tomorrow for Luz's dinner."

"You weren't just in the house?"

"I told you I wasn't." He stretched the band of his mask around his neck.

"Someone was just in the house," she screamed. She stepped toward him on the plastic, and he put his hands out to catch her—no, not to catch her, to prevent her from coming any closer.

"Stop. The tar is not dry. You will ruin it."

The urgency of running had been replaced with the affront of being stopped in place.

"Gavril, someone was just in the house. You didn't move the chairs in the living room?" Her heart pulsed, and her mouth was dry. She wanted to step toward him, to take his hands in hers, but the barricade of glistening tar mounds separated them. "I'm telling you, someone moved the furniture around."

Gavril tried to process the information. "Someone broke into the house when you were home to move the chairs in the living room?"

Her fear was not so complete that there wasn't room for spite. "Don't make me sound crazy," she snapped. "Someone was in our house, changing things."

He stared at her with concern. Hawaii lost three islands.

"Beth, what you say makes no sense."

"It doesn't have to make sense. I'm telling you what happened. The chairs are in different positions. Someone broke in and moved them. And put my purse in the hall. Someone has keys that they got from Jeff Trader's jar. The same jar that held the keys to the Muldoons' home."

Gavril stood up and wiped his fingers on a rag, just as Roe diCorcia had done.

"What's wrong with you? You are not acting like yourself. No one is out here to hurt you. Maybe you only think the furniture has changed. Are you sure you didn't move them and forgot?"

"Yes, I'm sure."

"Why would someone break into a house to redecorate?" He waited for her answer with tolerant eyes, so patient that she wanted to punch them shut. "What do you tell police? Man redid my living room and left?"

She realized, right then, that in a span of two months they had lost each other. It should have come as a harder blow than it did, simple and clear and sad. Maybe Gavril had already detected it. Maybe it had happened so slowly, like age, that she hadn't noticed the damage. The changes had been so minor from day to day. How many moments could be removed from a marriage before it was no longer a marriage? How many nights could they spend apart until they were no longer a couple who shared the same bed? All she knew was that when she looked at her husband's unshaven face, with its scalding birthmark and heavy eyelids, she no longer felt drawn to come any closer.

"Did Luz tell you about her dinner tomorrow night with the collectors? She said you agreed to come at the funeral today. You cannot back out."

The lumps of tar, she saw now, had expanded into walls. Gavril's work was a dead house, blackened and scorched, and it was in this dead house that he'd chosen to live day and night away from her. This was his own landscape of Orient, and he had placed himself happily in its frame. Maybe their marriage was reparable. Maybe they would save it after Gavril's show when he had time to inspect the rubble. But right now Beth recognized that Gavril was not a person she could run to for support. One step forward and she would ruin what he had made.

"I'm going to have the locks changed," she said coldly. "Let me know if you want a set."

He called after her but she left the garage, slamming the door behind her. She returned to the living room and moved the chairs back to their correct positions. The house looked like it had never been touched. The intrusion had been so invasive it left no visible scar, only the subtlest readjustment, and because the house was peaceful, perfect, with not a single object broken, there was no use in calling the police. That was what frightened her most—the peace that the house took on, the violence of its many quiet rooms, darkening one by one as she went upstairs and pushed the dresser against the bedroom door.

CHAPTER 25

Mills's body rebelled the way most teenage bodies do right before an important day: two huge pimples lined his upper lip, bright as LED lights, as if a plane might pass safely between their craters. They sprouted in the night amid his soft whiskers. Like most teens, Mills saw nothing but TWO PIMPLES when he studied himself in the mirror. He went to work applying finger pressure to their fractious borders, compressing the sides until white oil erupted from their centers. Afterward, he bathed his face in hot water and took a razor to his chin to scrape the black moss. He was still a terrible shaver three years into the ritual, which was less an art than a form of flagellation: *Ouch, oww, Christ.*

Paul knocked on the bathroom door. "You all right in there?" Mills opened it, revealing a face full of gashes that seemed almost emergency room–worthy.

Paul tried to teach him the art of shaving. "Run against the grain of the hair," he said, mimicking a smooth arc with his finger up his neck. "It's more about the motion. The smoother and quicker, the less chance of getting cut." Mills tried for grace, but he caught the razor on his chin, sending a dribble of blood down his neck. Paul ripped bits of tissue to stanch it. He showed him how to pinch his nose to manage the hairs under the nostrils—another cut—and how to balance out the shaving cream at each sideburn to preserve their symmetry. When he was through, Mills's right sideburn was two centimeters shorter than the left. But the worst was shaving over the zits: the razor dragged the broken skin, sending small shocks around his mouth.

"I can't do it," he said, dropping the razor in the sink. "It fucking hurts."

Paul picked up the razor and returned it to his hands. "You have to finish. It's going to look worse if you don't."

Mills took a breath—he'd survived a month on the open road but could barely withstand a few seconds of grooming—and whisked the razor once, then twice, over the sores. He splashed water to remove the cream, and the face in the mirror looked like it had been tagged by subway vandals. Below the sores, his gray front tooth appeared particularly nefarious. When he closed his mouth, he hid the tooth but emphasized the sores. Paul handed him a towel. "Take a shower, and then we'll put a Band-Aid over it. We'll give it time to heal."

"I can't have a Band-Aid. Beth is painting my portrait today. I'm supposed to look like myself."

"Well, don't you?"

Paul clapped his shoulders, and they stood at the mirror, as if practicing for their own family portrait—two men of different ages with no physical likeness, yet bonded by a close, invisible connection. That was the beauty of America, Mills thought: everyone looked like they were from a different home planet.

Mills had finally grown accustomed to Paul's face without his mustache. Men had facial hair and women had makeup, which seemed a fair rationing of disguises. Mills had neither to hide the wounds on his face.

"I'm taking the day off to paint too," Paul said, stepping out of the bathroom when Mills took off his T-shirt. "I'm doing a winter scene of the Sound. Maybe Beth and I can put on an art show at Poquatuck together. Although I'm sure she'd never forgive me for suggesting that."

"She might."

"What? Forgive me? I'm afraid my idea of what constitutes art went out of style a few decades ago. What do they call the paintings I do? Craft? Therapy? A crime against good taste?"

"They'll look nice in the Seaview's hotel rooms," Mills said.

Paul glanced at him. "Motel art."

Mills considered telling Paul what he and Beth had learned the day before, about Lisa and Adam and the possibility that they might be responsible for the fire. But Mills knew that neither he nor Paul could deliver that news to the police. It would look too much like an attempt to deflect blame. Detective Gilburn would be more inclined to listen if the information came from an objective source. Nevertheless, after he showered, he went down to the kitchen and told Paul that Beth had discovered a lead.

"She thinks she's found a connection in all of the deaths," he said. "You know, the Muldoons and Magdalena and Jeff Trader." Paul was buttoning himself into Mills's favorite blue winter coat, one of several items he'd borrowed from Paul's closet and had begun to consider his. Paul gathered his canvas and paint box, standing with the stooped posture of a man embarking on a fishing trip. "It makes sense, doesn't it?" Mills said. "That all those deaths are related?"

Paul tapped the refrigerator with his boot, staring down. "It might not be my place to say, but Beth should be careful about what she says out loud. Especially if it turns out those deaths *are* related." He looked at Mills. "But what *is* my place is your involvement. I don't want you getting more mixed up in this. You get caught digging around for suspects, asking a bunch of questions, it's going to look like you're hunting for trouble. You saw what happened with Sarakit at the church yesterday. It's always too easy to blame the stranger. So for my sake, let's just leave it to the police."

Mills nodded, and Paul covered his bald spot with a cap. He noticed Mills's eyes on his coat. "We should get you a good winter coat like this, shouldn't we? I'm sure you're sick of wearing my hand-me-downs." Paul lumbered down the hall and headed out the back door.

When the morning light struck the parlor window, a yellow stain appeared on the glass. It was thicker and milkier than frost. Mills suspected a bird had flown into the glass in the night. When he opened the front door, he found broken shells sprinkled on the porch and another yellow splotch on the railing. He jumped down the steps and turned to the house. Six yellow yolk smears dotted the peeling façade. Paul's house had been egged in the night—a sure sign of unwelcome, doubtless meant for him, confirmation that others besides the police and Sarakit Herrig suspected him of the crimes. Mills quickly filled a bucket with water and began to wash the egg splatters. Paul must not have noticed the vandalism, and Mills didn't want him to find out, in case he withdrew his offer to let him stay indefinitely.

He scoured the yolk on the ground floor, frozen in its runny descent, then carted out a ladder to reach the highest stain, just to the right of Paul's bedroom window. Through the window, he saw the photographs he'd found in the box—Paul at prom; Paul and his dead brother, Patrick—stacked under the mug on the bureau, as if to flatten their curls. He wished he'd asked Beth to buy a picture frame to give as a birthday present. Mills glanced down the street, hoping the neighbors hadn't noticed the stains. One open display of hostility could be all it took to prod others to add their voices, a chorus running down Youngs Road toward Main and from there spreading throughout the entire village.

As he was returning the ladder to its storage space by the cellar doors, he heard a branch snap several yards away. When he looked up, he saw Lisa Muldoon stumbling across her lawn with a bag of birdseed at her chest. He watched as she filled the feeder and sat down on the single picnic bench that had been spared in the fire. Tomorrow the county demolition team would knock down the remains of her house.

He slipped quietly toward her, studying the plain origami of her face. Grief had dissolved her youth, hollowing her cheeks and sharpening her features. He could see Tommy in her eyes, their sockets deep enough to hold dollar coins. When her cell phone rang, Mills was only ten feet away from her, stepping lightly to prevent the frozen grass from crunching underfoot. She checked the number and put the phone to her ear.

"Why haven't you been calling me back?" Belligerence mixed with anguish, the lowest tremors of a violin. "Can we meet right now? . . . Tell them to meet you later. . . . You're just going to have to find the time. You don't think I'm busy? You don't think I'm worth a little rearrangement after what I've rearranged? . . . Fine, in an hour then. Noon . . . No, not your house. Somewhere easier. At the beach, right by the view of Bug Light . . . Why would that be an inconvenient spot? That's our place. . . . No, *you* don't be late. I don't want to be treated this way. I used to accept it but I don't anymore. . . . Say it. I want to hear you say it." She hung up.

Mills tried to reach the final oak tree on Paul's lawn, six feet from where she sat, but his shoe caught a stick and she turned around at the noise. She eyed him darkly and sniffled. He raised his hand and said, so quietly it sounded exactly like what it was, a testing call between two strangers, *hello.*

Lisa coughed. "The kid next door," she murmured. *The kid.* They were roughly the same age; he might even be a little older, and he was years beyond Lisa Muldoon in life experience, or had been until the fire.

"I'm Mills," he said, standing still. He was surprised by how childish the sentence sounded. No one gave their own name voluntarily. Lisa Muldoon, potential killer, fought long strands of hair blowing against her cheeks. A mole dotted her temple like a fly frozen on her skin. She sat staring across the invisible property line that separated her land from Paul's.

"I've heard about you," she said. "You're staying in Paul Benchley's house. I heard you were here on the night of the fire." Fire brought water, her blue eyes running, which she wiped with her sweatshirt sleeve. A cardinal pecked at the feeder, then flew off.

"I *was* here that night," he said, stepping toward her. She slid over so he could share the bench. He sat down, close to the edge so they wouldn't touch. Lisa bundled her baggy sweatshirt against her stomach and slid her knees away from him, public bench style. "By the time we saw the flames there was nothing we could do." He thought it smart to bury himself in *we*.

She nodded and raised her hand, flattening it in the air, opening her fingers to filter her view of the house. "They were in their bedrooms. Except for Tommy. The police said they found him on the landing. I keep thinking of him there. That's where he always stood. Yelling at Dad. Unwilling to go to bed or down for dinner. Listening when I was on the phone in my room. He stood on that landing the day I left for college, asking me with his eyes not to leave him. Even before it happened, I always pictured him standing there." Her chin quivered. "I've come here every day since I've been back. I try to think what the fire must have looked like from a distance. But I always end up seeing Tommy, standing on the landing, making his usual stance of protest. He was too young to know what he was even mad about."

She pushed her palm against her eyes and cried into it. The four members of her family were still real to her, so fresh they were not yet given to the ground. Mills realized he was having doubts about his own suspicions. There was no question that Lisa had lied to the police about being away at college, but did that necessarily mean she had murdered her entire family? He'd been so sure yesterday in Beth's car, in the adrenaline of fitting the pieces together. But right now on the bench, a ruler's worth of space between them, he worried that he'd jammed those pieces into place.

"I didn't know Tommy well," Mills said, "but we were friendly. He was funny. And quick. And he talked a lot about you." She wiped her nose and swayed like she had heard this song too many times.

"People always tell you that when your family dies. *They talked about you so much. They were so proud of you.* Like it's a consolation."

"But I mean it," he said gently. "I remember he kept a picture of you on the desk in his bedroom. He really loved you. Kind of idolized you, in fact."

She gave him a sidelong glance, her brown hair spilling around her mouth like rivulets of syrup.

"You were in his room?" she asked. "You went upstairs to his room?"

Mills tucked his lips against his teeth, a contrite sting of culpability. She wasn't asking that question lightly. But then he remembered: he'd already told the police he'd been in the house. He wasn't admitting to anything he hadn't already confessed.

"Yeah. When I hurt my hand. Tommy bandaged it." Her eyes continued to study him skeptically. He decided to test his own suspicions on her. "He told me he saw you. Maybe when you were visiting recently, about a week or two ago? I remember him coming back home, saying he'd seen his sister somewhere nearby." He watched her reaction. The intake of breath. The eyelids that opened and closed. The jaw reset by a lock of teeth.

"You're wrong," she said, preferring the sight of the bird feeder to his face. A squirrel climbed along the oak branch, steadying itself for a jump onto the feeder's perch. The squirrel couldn't build up the courage, jolting forward and shrinking back. "I've been away at school. I haven't seen my family since August. Otherwise I would have been here. *In my house. With them. In Oysterponds Cemetery now.*" She broke down again, coughing phlegm, her shoulders convulsing like she was being driven over potholes.

"I guess I'm wrong. I thought he mentioned the Seaview." She shifted, rising slightly, which tipped the bench, and Mills caught himself with his foot before he toppled to the ground. She returned to her seat, giving him the counterweight, but she pressed her knees together, shoving herself into the smallest quantity of space. "Anyway," Mills said casually, "I'm not from around here so I still get places and people mixed up. And as I said, I didn't know Tommy that well."

"Not many did. But I knew him. I loved my brother. Both of my brothers." She stared at the charred walls and the black furniture that spilled across the grass. "And they were stolen from me. Not taken. Stolen. By some lunatic who didn't think they deserved to live." She roped her arms around her stomach and bent into them, the safety bar on a roller coaster. "And all I have is their absence. Every day of my life, all I will ever have is them gone."

"You have memories," he said, the sentence ghostwritten by every movie he had seen. It seemed inadequate, and Lisa rolled her eyes in acknowledgment.

"The police only got a few items from the house that were salvageable. Just junk. Nothing valuable or personal, nothing theirs. It took one match and my entire life up to this point was stolen from me. My bedroom, their bedrooms, the den. One match. Where are the pictures of us? Where are the little scraps of who we were? That's why I fill the bird feeder every day. It's the one thing that survived."

As much as Mills had decided not to like Lisa Muldoon, as hopeful as he'd been that the key to the crime rested at the feet of the last surviving family member, in that moment she reached for his knee, and he only felt pity for her. Her body slumped into his, and he was forced to hold her up, jamming his foot into the dirt to keep the bench from tossing them both to the ground. Her neck smelled of cigarette smoke and peppermint. She dug her chin into his chest. With nothing left of her family, all she could hold on to was a stranger.

"I have something," he said. "Tommy left his flask one night down by the beach. He forgot it, and I meant to give it back to him. It's a silver—"

Lisa lifted her head, her eyebrows rising, her mouth opening in confusion—every feature forming a zero. "I know that flask," she blurted. "It belonged to my grandfather. It was given to Tommy when he died. You have it?"

"Yeah. I meant to see him again to give it back, but I never did. But if you want it—"

"Yes, I want it," she said. She pulled away and settled on the side of the bench. "Can you get it for me now?"

"Sure," he said. Lisa blinked impatiently, as if she couldn't accept a second's delay before he followed her orders. He almost wished he hadn't offered it to her. Mills stood up slowly, giving Lisa a chance to readjust her balance on the bench. He crossed the lawn and went into the house.

The flask was in the birthing room, hidden along with Tommy's watch and the necklace they'd taken from the motel. As he reached down to grab the flask, the poster of Bug Light caught his eye. The photo of the lighthouse must have been taken from the beach—the same spot where Lisa was headed next, according to the phone call he'd overheard. "Their place." He kneeled back down and gathered the necklace in his hand. If he could prove that it belonged to her, that she was the *L* of the pendant, it would mean that Lisa had seen her father at the Seaview—that she'd been staying there long before her supposed return the morning after the fire.

By the time he made it down to the porch, Lisa was standing on the walk, staring at the scrubbed egg stains. She had put on black knit gloves and was checking the time on her phone.

Mills held out the flask and she took it, examining its smooth gunmetal surface. She didn't need to thank him. Or she didn't feel the need to.

"I'm surprised he gave this to you," she said, looking up at him.

"He didn't. He left it by mistake."

"It was a gift from my grandfather," she repeated, as if he hadn't heard her the first time. "He brought it back from the war."

"He didn't mean to leave it. His mom, *your* mom, was calling and he was in a hurry. I think he filled it with some of the alcohol he found in your room."

She pursed her lips. Mills realized that every detail he had just mentioned—Tommy, Pam, her bedroom, the alcohol she hid in her closet—no longer existed.

"I'm glad you gave this to me," she said quietly. "I'm glad to have it."

He took his chance. His hands shook as he held the chain up, dangling the silver *L* in front of her.

"I also found this on the lawn, right by one of the oak trees. I thought it might belong to you." Lisa caught the pendant in her palm.

"No, I've never seen it before. It's not mine. My name doesn't begin with a *J*."

Mills realized it was backward. He flipped the pendant until it became an *L*.

"It's still the wrong initial."

"But your name is Lisa—"

"Short for Elizabeth," she said. "I'd use an *E* for any expensive jewelry. Anything I cared about. You know, for when I become an adult."

He nodded and pulled the pendant away before she could close her fingers over it. She paused, glancing at him hesitantly, as if unsure of what to make of this unfamiliar young man standing complacently on the street that had been hers since she was born. "So you live here now, huh?" Lisa's voice was almost flinty, like the sound of stones struck together, like her mother's pinched tone mixed with a sorority girl's laziness with vowels. Lisa had Pam's deliberate eyes, and now she seemed to turn them on Mills for the first time.

"I'm here for now," he told her. "I'm helping Paul."

She reached into her coat pocket and pulled out car keys along with a pack of peppermint gum. She would want fresh breath if she were going to meet Adam Pruitt on the beach at noon, as she'd said on the phone. "I'm staying at the Seaview now. Maybe that's why you were confused," she said, chewing the gum with her back teeth. "And I think I saw you there two days ago. Why would you go there with Beth Shepherd?"

Mills rubbed his mouth, accidentally breaking open one of his shaving scabs.

"Just for a drink and to enjoy the view," he said. "It has a nice bar."

Lisa dropped her head to study the flask. She held it the way a mother holds a diaper, pinched between her fingers. It still contained leftover Jägermeister that he and Tommy had shared. Mills thought of the blood from his cut hand, and the syrupy alcohol, and other liquids: his short involvement with Tommy had been filled with fluids, none of which his older sister would understand.

"My brother had strange tendencies," she said as she turned toward a white car parked on the curb. NORTH FORK RENTALS was emblazoned on the side door, bisected with speedy lines to indicate quick departures. Lisa slipped the flask into the empty birdseed bag. "He was too trusting, for one. And he liked people who didn't fit in. He wanted to experience too much, and it got him into trouble."

Mills steeled himself against her insinuations, standing deliberately still.

"I know he might have said mean things about my family, but if he did he was only trying to impress you. He loved them. I like to think he died trying to save them from whoever found their way in. That's why he was on the landing. Because he knew that person shouldn't be there."

Mills flexed his hand around the pendant. "I like to think he died without much pain," he said.

"Yeah?" Lisa rasped. "You like to think that? Well, go on and think that if it makes you feel better."

"It's too bad you weren't at the Seaview before. It's too bad you didn't get to see Tommy like I thought he said you did."

"Like I said, you're confused." Her eyes narrowed. "You don't know what you're talking about." She turned and walked to her car.

Mills didn't wave good-bye. He doubted Lisa bothered to look back as she pulled away. He hurried into the house to find a coat. Beth couldn't drive him to the beach: she was in Greenport, buying Paul's birthday cake, and he was supposed to meet her at two o'clock at her place. He had forty minutes to get to the beach across from Bug Light to catch Lisa with Adam—that would prove they were a couple. He couldn't ask Paul for a ride, either: he'd already warned Mills not to hunt for trouble. Instead he rummaged through the scrap paper by the kitchen telephone and found the only other number he could think of.

"Hi, Isaiah. It's Mills Chevern, Beth's friend. I was wondering if you could do me a favor."

Isaiah Goodman's old Saab was outfitted with new leather upholstery, but its original engine rattled when it backed out of Paul's driveway. Isaiah also had two punctures above his lip, the site of former piercings. Peeking out from under his shirt collar were the letters *RE*, in black calligraphy, the tail end of a tattoo that graced his neck. Mills tried to guess the remainder of the word: *Sabre, flare, lucre.* Despite the vestigial evidence of a younger and rougher Isaiah Goodman, the current Isaiah wore a crisp blue button-down, black corduroys, and boat shoes. Isaiah's dark hair was cut short before it could will itself into curls, and he had a sizable gap between his front teeth. A pinkie ring tapped along to the wailing Middle Eastern disco. He steered them onto Main Road, the car's surround-sound audio system blasting a soundtrack of Algerian flutes and drums.

Mills knew that Isaiah Goodman was (1) gay and (2) an artist, but he read as (1) straight and (2) the kind of corporate trader in Manhattan who bought up the rooftops of tenement buildings and erected Shinto shrines of one-way mirrored glass, marring the bleak romance of the skyline. Men who bought rooftops in the city tended to lack imagination and friends, dry-humping the residents below them with their real estate. *Sceptre, vulture, perjure, leisure.* Art must have kept Isaiah in shape, judging from his muscular wrists and the shirt buttons that squinted on his chest. Mills cupped his hand over his lips to hide his pimples. His feet kept slipping on the books that carpeted the passenger-side floor—*The Land Remembers, The Tyranny of the Food Profiteers, Our Metaphysical Soil,* all emblazoned with dated sunsets. "Don't worry about stepping on those." Isaiah laughed. "They belong to Vince."

Mills tapped his fingers absentmindedly on the window.

"You in a big rush to get to the beach?" Isaiah asked. The sky was black-blooded with clouds. Stray drips dotted the windshield, never thickening into rain.

"I want to see Bug Light," Mills said. That hardly sounded urgent, so he elaborated. "And I have to meet someone."

Isaiah nodded. "And they couldn't give you a lift? Must be an important meeting." He held the steering wheel with one hand between his legs. "Vince and I went out to Bug Light last June. The Maritime Museum was offering a special tour by boat. We took the trip out and climbed on the rocks, gulls and cormorants spinning around our heads, trying to gouge our eyes out. Jesus, you wouldn't believe how badly that lighthouse is constructed. Splintering wood, shattered windows, rickety stairs just to get inside—and then, once you're in it, it's just a mechanical light switch with a timer attached. Off, on, like a bomb." Mills didn't mention that Paul had helped reconstruct Bug Light in 1990, although he felt guilty for not defending it. "Vince actually asked the tour guide if it was for sale!" Isaiah found this immensely funny. The Saab swerved over the yellow lines as he laughed. "I said, no *eff-ing* way. We're already isolated enough in our cottage. I don't need to take a boat every time I want to reach civilization. But Vince has got a horrible romance addiction. When the other visitors weren't looking, he found a patch of dirt between the rocks, pulled a little garden trowel from his coat, dug a hole, and dropped in a Japanese maple seed. He put something else in the hole too, but he wouldn't tell me what. Last week he went to the beach with his binoculars and swears he saw a tiny green shoot out there, amid the snow and boulders. He calls it our tree. He likes that it will grow out in the open and no one will be able to do a thing about it."

Mills liked the gesture. Out there on the island, it might escape weeding. "That's sweet," he said.

"Yeah," Isaiah burred, irritated at having to agree. He tilted his neck: *ore.* "I guess it is. Another sun worshiper planting sedition among the year-rounders. At least until that millionaire Arthur

Cleaver pays to have it ripped out." When he and Vince had gone to buy their English cottage last June, he told Mills, they had both felt like unwanted squatters crashing a Republican convention. The cottage leaked water, holes punctured the floorboards, and mice had set up a free-love commune in the basement by the furnace. And still, every time they put in an offer beyond the asking price, they were instantly outbid. Vince soon got it into his photogenic head that Orient locals had banded together to buy the cottage just to keep yet another artist couple from Manhattan from getting their unfilthy hands on one of their precious Sound-front homes.

"They'd reached their quota on fussy urbanites," Isaiah said. "The other bidders were from here on the North Fork, so we felt they were biased against us." Isaiah was content to back off and let the year-rounders have the cottage if they wanted it so much. It was a smudge of a place, a dismal version of a vacation, and they still had time to find a summer rental in the Hamptons. But Vince took the affront personally. He cleared out his savings, negotiated a loan from the owner of his former modeling agency, and went eighty thousand dollars beyond the reigning bid. "Vince convinced me it was a smart investment," Isaiah wheezed, paying only mild attention to oncoming traffic. "Especially once Plum and Gardiners Islands go up for sale in the next few years. Then even the little houses in Orient will be worth a fortune." But Isaiah knew it was really a matter of pride. "Vince would not be defeated. I've never seen a man so dedicated to so little, this box of stapled-together walls on a mud patch."

And now here they were in the poverty of their winnings, tiling the floors and stuffing steel wool in the kitchen cracks all by themselves because they didn't have the money to hire a proper contractor. "Vince *still* thinks it was the right decision," Isaiah said. "He thinks he's won something. And now he wants to buy *more* land in Orient. He says he'll find the money. He's already got his eyes on other properties. Just like some of the other artists out here. Some of them think we should all go in on it together."

Isaiah looked over, checking his trapped audience's attention span, admiring his occidental profile.

"Do you have a boyfriend?" Isaiah asked suddenly. Mills hadn't told Isaiah that he was gay. "Sorry if that's a personal question. I'm not trying to corner you."

"No, it's cool," Mills replied. "I don't have a boyfriend. I'm single." It was the first time he had ever defined himself as single, which felt like defining himself as American in a foreign country. It sounded advanced and self-reliant and lonely.

"Wait," Isaiah moaned. "You aren't going out to the beach for a secret date, are you?"

"No," he said in quick defense.

Isaiah cracked his knuckles, using his thighs to steady the wheel.

"That's good, because you know they monitor the park with cameras, and they're not too cool around here with public hook-ups." Mills wasn't sure if Isaiah was joking or not, even when he ignored the road to present him with a pristine, gap-toothed grin, as if a glimpse of Isaiah's smile was worth a crash.

Mills checked the clock on the console. It was 11:58. Lisa Muldoon must already be parking her rental car, searching for Adam Pruitt along the beach. On Main Road there was traffic racing to the tip to catch the noon ferry to Connecticut. Ahead of them was a delivery truck with GREENPORT ARTISANAL FLORISTS written across its back doors in the same calligraphic script as Isaiah's neck tattoo. A hothouse of yellow lilies quivered in the windows.

"I'm impressed you're willing to spend so much time out here," Isaiah said. "When I was your age, I couldn't stand to be outside of New York for a minute, paranoid that I was going to miss something. God, those years were tiring. I was in a band." Isaiah pulled down the collar of his shirt and completed the word: *encore*. "That was the name of our group. We didn't do encores. Maybe that's why we weren't very popular. But I guess the city isn't as alive as it used to be. Now young people have the Internet and a zillion phone apps so you don't need an actual place to congregate. You can be everywhere, nowhere, a floating message-spewing entity. We used to rely on drugs to get that sensation. No matter how crowded the party is, after a while you're really only talking to yourself."

"I don't have a phone," Mills said. "Or a computer." They passed the turnoff to the diCorcia farm; the flower truck took the next left, disappearing up a thin dirt trail.

"Living in reality full-time is underappreciated. It's a dying art. I think that's why so many artists have moved out here."

"Totally," Mills replied, as if his reasons for being off the grid were philosophical, not financial. Isaiah drove into the park entrance, passing the unattended ranger shack. Gray wood planks grew out of the ponds, nesting grounds for breeding ospreys. A few abandoned nests still crowned the beacons.

Mills scanned the view. Sand and pebbles threaded through the grasses. Deep into the ash-blue sea sat the fat, sun-whitened lighthouse, a suburban clapboard marooned offshore. It looked defenseless there, one hundred yards out, an easy target for vandals like the ones who burned down the original in 1963. On the other hand, its impenetrable moat gave it a good claim to being the safest house in Orient. Mills imagined Isaiah and Vince living out there, standing under their maple tree. Maybe that's what Vince had seen in the lighthouse, an island of safety just for them.

"So you want me to take you to the end, or—"

"Here's fine." Mills unbuckled his seat belt. Isaiah let the car glide to a halt. He rotated in his seat and touched Mills on the knee.

"Hey, I was serious about you coming over for dinner. Vince is a decent cook, and the mice are gone, I swear. Whenever you want. Or even if you just need a place to crash. We're the little English cottage on Edwards Lane. We'd love to have you." Mills wasn't sure if Isaiah was intimating a more accommodating situation than dinner or a place to crash. He wondered if he and Vince were monogamous. He remembered seeing them on the night of Beth's party, kissing briefly against the refrigerator. It had seemed so normal to him, so easy; that was what had shocked him most. They seemed to have picked the lock on each other's secret doors. He tried to imagine the handsome couple by the refrigerator as two sweaty bodies in a bedroom, one on top of the other. Which did what to the other? Mills kept rotating the two men in his mind, which he never had to do when he imagined straight couples having sex. Their sex seemed more intimate for his not knowing. Then he complicated the arithmetic by trying to imagine himself between them, three bodies fusing, six arms, a train of heads facing the same direction. Mills shifted his leg away from Isaiah's fingers.

"Thanks for the ride. I'll call you about dinner." He climbed out of the car. Isaiah waved through the windshield as he drove in reverse down the park road. Mills wished he'd brought Paul's video camera to film Lisa and Adam reuniting at the beach by Bug Light.

The wind on the tip blew in circles, whipping around his shoulders. The sea's surface was zippered in foam, and a few old men shaped like lanterns in their thick coats stood on the rocks with their fishing poles. Vacant picnic tables lined the sandbar. A lone deer stumbled across the road and into the inland ponds. As Mills headed toward the picnic tables, he noticed Lisa's car parked in a side lot farther down the beach. He saw her in the distance, hugging herself as she stared at the lighthouse, its windows dark, its lamp unlit. Beyond Bug Light was the open Atlantic. Adam Pruitt hadn't yet joined her. Mills wasn't too late.

A black Jeep roared from the park's entrance. It slid by him and jerked to a stop ten feet ahead, then slowly reversed. The driver-side window rolled down in fits of manual unwinding, and a bearded man with flesh-colored teeth smiled at him. "That's him," the guy said. "That's the faggot who lit up the Muldoon house!" The insult was tossed out the window, dousing him like a cup of soda. Mills looked around for another car—for anyone besides the old fishermen, who were more like salt columns than sources of safety. As he backed off into the grass, one of the Jeep doors swung open. "I want to teach that little shit what it means to hurt someone from Orient."

Mills barreled through the tall grass, disappearing into its thick, unbending braid. He heard feet running on the pavement, and he twisted through the blades until he reached the rocks on the beach, swirling with jetties of seawater. He felt his breath abandon him, as if he'd already been punched in the stomach. His muscles tightened, but he ran as fast as he could along the rocks, jumping to keep his feet from getting stuck. Two of the men had fought through the phragmites and circled behind him on the beach. They were fatter and shorter than he was, but one held a crowbar as they hopscotched over the rocks. He could hear the Jeep driving along the road, lost behind the grass. He followed the water, gasping as he wove in the direction of Main Road, in the opposite direction of the lighthouse and Lisa.

Mills heard one of the men behind him fall, yelping as his ankle was pinioned between rocks, but the guy with the crowbar was still on his feet. A wire fence loomed ahead with a triangular orange sign across it: WARNING. FEDERALLY RESTRICTED AREA. DEPARTMENT OF HOMELAND SECURITY, which sounded both secure and hazardous. There was a gap between the fence and the grasses, and Mills hurtled through it, out of the park. Ahead was the ferry landing for Plum, beyond it the ferry to Connecticut.

He ran by the gates of Plum, tasting blood in his mouth, glancing over his shoulder as the guy with the crowbar leapt onto the concrete, giving him the speed of solid ground. Inside the restricted Plum terminal he saw men in business suits waiting for the ferry, but they were too far to hear a cry for help. The black Jeep had reached the park entrance but was stuck behind cars turning onto the feeder road to the ferry terminal. Mills finally made it to the ferry hub, snaking through the cars waiting in line, all of their windows sealed. A green sign welcomed new arrivals to the state of New York.

He considered running toward the ferry, but he didn't have a car or the price of a ticket, and the dilapidated restaurant on the pier looked as if it had been boarded up for winter. There were no police cars or officers or anyone besides a pair of white hands poking out from a toll booth. He passed the terminal and ran down a small dirt road until the beach returned, diminishing his traction. He kicked up stones as he followed the beach west; Beth and Paul both lived miles away, but other houses grew erratically along the coast. For a second, there was no sign of the Jeep or the man waving the crowbar. But as he climbed up a rocky slope, which began to waver into cliffs, he spotted all three men. They were thirty feet behind him, and they were red-faced and wheezing, but they weren't giving up their chase. They knew the geography better than he did. The bearded driver sprinted out of sight into a thicket of trees.

Mills roped between the beach and the manicured lawns of large, wax-windowed houses, high as cruise ships above the blue water, a stray pebble working its way into the heel of his shoe. He combed the houses above him for lights or open doors or people standing on their decks, potential rescuers. A thought came into his brain like a spot of blood beginning to clot: *I don't want to spend the five unbearable minutes it will take for them to inflict their pain. I wish I were already beaten up.*

Just as he was slowing down, knees aflame, the bearded driver burst from behind a nearby house in a flank attack, his speed increased by the descent of the lawn. "Little shit," he yelled. Mills fought through the melt of his muscles for whatever strength he had left, springing up a small incline as the man rounded behind him, four feet galloping together as if they were a single horse. Ahead he saw a speedboat tied to a dock and up the hill a farmhouse draped in tarps. He'd been there before: it was the old farmhouse inn, the rich artists' new remodeling project. If he climbed up to its deck he could crash through one of the tarps and beg them for help.

Phragmites bristled ahead, gluts of wind-tossed green, and the mud was wet under his feet from high tide. The driver tried to grab him, lunging, and Mills swiveled as he ducked through the tall weeds that swatted his face. He gave one last jump to escape, and the ground below him disappeared, no longer there to catch his fall. It dropped away into a gulley of sand. Mills fell, landing on something hard and reeking so badly of brine that he kept his eyes shut. He expected a fist or a foot or a crowbar to bash him in the ribs.

"Holy shit. No fucking way." The driver was looking down where he'd fallen, his mouth open. He looked scared, not like a predator anymore but huntable too. Reaching for a handhold beneath him, Mills touched bone and thick fur. Embedded in the sand, a few feet from the sea, was an animal, or some kind of hybrid of animals, split, fissured, lab-replicated, reorganized, dead. It had the skeletal head of a deer with its long purple tongue uncurled, the claws of a raccoon bunched up against its slick pig chest, its eyes pierced with the wings of insects, its back feet two hooves dragging seaweed from the surf. Mills thought he could make out two separate spinal cords in its back, but the second cord ended in a fist of meat, a pincushion of flies. Mills almost vomited as he scrambled off the monster, wiping his hands on his body. He jumped back to avoid the oncoming tide—as if the water itself were contaminated—and the driver, who'd been chasing him for the last ten minutes, reached out to lift him out of the pit.

His two friends stood overhead, dumbstruck by the creature, then lifted their eyes toward Plum. "Another one? It can't be. Holy shit. Wait until Adam hears."

"I told you that's why Pruitt Securities is fucking important," the driver panted. "There's something seriously wrong with the land out here."

"Just look at that thing," the crowbar-wielding guy said. He glanced at Mills and nodded like they were old friends, like the presence of the mutant had instantly reshuffled their loyalties. "It's got two backbones. It's more of a mutant than the first one."

A breeze came down from the house above, carrying a whiff of cigarette smoke. The four men looked up to see a black woman leaning over the farmhouse railing.

"*Yo.* You know this is private property, right?" Luz called down to them.

"Ma'am," the bearded driver yelled. "We don't mean any trouble. You'd better call the police."

CHAPTER 26

A isle three of Dooley's Pharmacy was reserved for feminine products. Actually, the aisle started near the cash register with condoms and lubricants, but the shelves quickly gave way to vaginal condoms and yeast-infection treatments, followed by pillowed bricks of maxi-pads, tampons, day liners, and douches, and somewhere midway along the aisle, a fleet of home-pregnancy tests with product shots of sticks floating in a white dimension outside of time or space. After the tests came the baby goods: pacifiers, diapers, rattles, nursing bottles, rash powders, dolls. At the far end of the aisle was the pharmacy's copy machine, an ungainly metal box that duplicated any material pressed to its stomach for twenty-five cents per page.

Beth had come to Dooley's Pharmacy in Greenport for replication. Before she handed over Jeff Trader's journal to Mike Gilburn, she wanted a copy for herself. She opened the lid, flattened the book, and pressed COPY to an astral burst of light. A page spit from the slot, still hot from its rotation through the machine.

Dooley's was the same pharmacy Beth had visited at fifteen for her first home-pregnancy test and again for her last test more than a month ago. She had made her first pilgrimage to the pharmacy at twelve, alone, terrified of aisle three, searching for her first box of tampons or perhaps a bottle of glue so she could seal her vagina and prevent it from ever leaking again during chemistry. She supposed that other women found happiness in places like aisle three. She pulled the last copy from the machine, then walked to aisle five and opened a bottle of aspirin.

The early winter weather had brought a leaden stillness to the streets of Greenport. The nicer restaurants and boating shops had switched to winter hours, weekends only. Even Mario Laurito's increasingly passé Italian restaurant read CHIUSO on its stainless-steel door. Pearl Farms/Pearl Explorations, Sarakit Herrig's corner real estate and travel agency, had a note taped to its glass. Underneath the agency's oyster-shell logo, the sign read WINTER HOURS BY APPOINTMENT. Sarakit's corporate mélange of exotic foreign travel and North Fork real estate had a schizophrenic appeal; Beth assumed that wealthy Manhattanites appreciated the mixed message, that the same agent could find you a Sound-front retreat or a trip to the Far East.

The pastel merry-go-round by the harbor was dark, its horses frozen. Even the teenagers smoking weed on the docks seemed sluggish and underwhelmed. Beth passed into the bakery, its windows flecked in snow, its display cakes yellowed and cracked, as if they'd been baked by chain-smokers. Christmas music jingled too early in the shop. Beth selected a cake decorated with a lighthouse, the icing a barbershop pole of red and white amid blue frosted waves. Most of the others were white and blank, like faces in hospital rooms.

"That one's chocolate mud. You want anything written on it?" the counterwoman asked. "It's two dollars a word." The same fee they paid writers per word at the *Scientific Frontier*. She tried to think of something clever, but settled on "Happy Birthday Paul."

Luz had been sending her clever texts all morning: "The Russians are coming!"—tonight was their dinner with the Russian collectors—and then, an hour later, "Remind me, have the Romanians forgiven the Soviets for abandoning them during the Cold War?" *Maybe I should have that iced onto a cake*, Beth thought, *and serve it as a surprise at dinner.* Beth was dreading the evening, especially since she and Gavril were still barely speaking. "Add an exclamation point," she told the woman frosting the cake.

Beth carried the cake box to the car. With time to kill before Mills came to sit for his portrait at two, she decided to stop by the Herrigs' on her way home. Sarakit's outburst at the funeral had unnerved her, and Beth felt that she herself had handled the situation badly. Sarakit had asked her a simple question—what had they been fighting about?—and while she couldn't have answered with the truth (a blow job! was there anything more inconsequential?), at least she could have tried to convince Sarakit that it had nothing to do with the fire. Beth thumbed through Jeff Trader's book to reread his secrets on the Herrigs: divorce papers sent but shredded, Sarakit's travel business failing. She remembered her mother saying that Ted was losing his job, and Tommy had made a note about a loan that now wouldn't need to be repaid.

Driving along the causeway, its sides still guard-railed with snow, she phoned the Greenport locksmith to ask if they could change her locks.

"We're backed up," the clerk replied. "It's a small outfit here, and we got a full clipboard of requests from you people in Orient. Won't be able to free up till next week. Everyone's spooked since the fire." She told him it was an emergency, that she'd pay double. "Everyone's willing to pay double. Used to be, Jeff Trader would take care of the locks for you. If you're in a pinch, you can try Pruitt Securities. They'll get it done—maybe upside down, but done." She made an appointment for next Tuesday.

The Herrigs lived in the old Traylor House on Diedricks Road, one turnoff past Youngs Road, sharing a backyard with the houses that faced the Muldoons. Theirs was a clapboard two-story of New England simplicity, the board-and-batten shutters on its dormer windows ornamented with hand-carved latches. Three nylon wind socks the shape of dragons whirled across the porch. Children's toys were strewn on the lawn—a roller skate, a hula hoop, a deserted army of action figures that circled a fluorescent machine gun. A Muldoon Security sign tilted in the breeze. As she approached the door, it was opened by a little boy with black, bowl-cut hair and slender eyelids: the Herrigs' youngest, adopted from Cambodia, wearing a plastic tiara. He aimed a yellow water pistol at her and pulled the trigger. The gun was empty.

"You're dead," he said. Beth feigned a bullet to her heart. Years of babysitting had taught her that kids gave up shooting you if you died right away.

"You got me," she said. The little boy tucked the barrel in the waistline of his pants. His miniature Nike Airs were pumped to full inflation. "I'm Nhean," he told her. If Beth hadn't known that Ted and Sarakit had adopted three boys, she wouldn't have been certain about his sex. He twirled on one foot and slammed into a side table, knocking a stack of business cards to the floor. Beth stepped into the foyer to help pick them up. She felt the thick card stock and saw the Pearl Farms logo, an open oyster in profile clenching a pearl—the same logo that Nathan Crimp used for his stationery, and Tommy Muldoon had used to jot down his warning about Orient's trust.

"Your mom wouldn't want you leaving a mess," she said as she gathered up the cards.

"I always wash my face after a hard day," Nhean exclaimed, his black eyes glistening. Beth heard cartoons echoing from the den.

"That's a good idea." She stacked the papers on the table.

"That's why I use Neutrogena Active. Because the last thing you want is an oily face." It took Beth longer than it should have to realize that the seven-year-old in front of her was quoting a commercial.

A taller, older boy shuffled into the hall. "Nhean, shut up." He rolled his eyes and smiled at Beth, holding a bag of Cheetos to his stomach. "I've seen you before, around the neighborhood. And that day when the man drowned in the harbor. I'm Ronald." He must be the middle child, adopted from Vietnam. "Are you here for my mom or my dad?" Ronald wore black pleather pants, a lime green belt, and a checkerboard sweater of pink and gray—a surprising display of fashion-consciousness, as Ted and Sarakit were both morbidly ordinary dressers.

"Either one," she said. "Maybe your mom."

"She's around." Ronald beckoned her to follow him down a hallway lined with framed posters of coastal cities: Cape Town, Bangkok, Jakarta, Shanghai, Manila, Honolulu. They ran in order from west to east, like clocks in banks showing different time zones. The décor made sense for the home of a travel agent and a geography teacher, and yet their three sons seemed to find their cultural roots at Riverhead Centre Mall.

Ronald reached a wood sliding door and pulled it open. Behind it was a lamp-lit room full of rotating objects: a black circulating fan, a purple fish swimming in a glass bowl, and, in the corner, Sarakit, in a gray sweatsuit, exercising on an elliptical machine. She stopped treading when she noticed Beth; a look of confusion crossed her face as she waited for the pedals to cease spinning. Beth glanced into the hallway. Ronald had gone back to his cartoons, leaving her to explain her sudden appearance in the house.

"I'm sorry to bother you," Beth said. "Nhean let me in."

Sarakit grabbed the towel from the elliptical console and wiped her neck. "Ny-han," she said.

"And Ronald brought me in here. I didn't know you were busy."

"Well." She panted as she climbed off the machine. "It's better if we talk in the kitchen." Sarakit's long hair was knotted back like a belt loop, and Beth followed its sheeny bounce through the hallway.

When Beth was young, Sarakit Herrig—new both to Orient and the United States—had been warm and friendly to her, if difficult to understand. These days, though, Sarakit seemed to treat her as just another nuisance, a younger version of her mother waiting for the opportunity to inflict more turmoil on the village. Maybe she thought Beth would last only a few months before Gail returned, reprising her role as the archenemy of the historical board.

Beth entered the kitchen, searching for some decorative detail or home improvement to compliment Sarakit on. Unfortunately, the kitchen was an American landslide of easy-grabs and hard-to-throw-outs. The peeling yellow laminate counters were cluttered with Solo cups, Hefty sandwich bags, loose batteries, Pottery Barn catalogs, and crayons. It was the kind of headache that might induce the aspirin of divorce. Sarakit went to the faucet and poured a glass of water.

"Nhean and Ronald were both sick this morning, so I let them stay home from school. They seem to have magically gotten better." Sarakit checked the clock on the oven. "Ted should be home any minute. He always comes home on his lunch period."

"I'm actually here to see you," she said. Uninvited into any particular corner of the kitchen, Beth leaned neutrally against the counter. "I was in Greenport this morning and I saw your sign for winter hours."

"I still work even though I'm home," Sarakit said matter-of-factly.

"It amazes me that you can balance travel *and* real estate. You'd think one would be a full-time job."

"Both *are* full-time jobs," she said, shrugging, as if hard work were merely a condition of life. "The travel business has mostly gone online. I finally broke down and got my Realtor license in the spring. Someone has to pay the bills." Sarakit rested the glass on her stomach and watched Beth the way an older woman with kids watches a younger one without any, with a mix of curiosity and vindication. "I don't have it as easy as you do. You've got a husband making a lot of money. I've dealt with my share of artists from the city looking for weekend homes out here. I know what they're making these days. I suppose you've heard about Ted."

Beth blinked. Sarakit did not. "They've decided to terminate his position at Sycamore at the end of the year. How's that for twenty years of teaching in our community school system?" She gulped her water and turned to refill the glass. "How's that for committing your life to educating the children of Orient? And you know what gets me? They don't cut art or music. They cut *geography*." Sarakit practically bit the water. "So I'd say it's a good time to transition.

Who's going to travel to Thailand when they don't even know how to find it on a map? The escalating land values out here are the only thing helping us keep this house, and it's better that I do it than some agent from the Hamptons who doesn't know the first thing about this side of the bay."

Beth nodded, although she wanted to point out that her own children seemed like they might want to make their futures in art or music.

"Nhean, get in here this instant!" The little boy skidded down the hall in his socks. He had removed his sneakers, but not his tiara. At least Sarakit didn't seem to have any problem about her son's choice of accessories. Beth decided that allowance was reason enough to like her. "Did you leave the bread out? How many times do I have to ask you to keep it in the fridge? It attracts ants."

Nhean danced toward the loaf on the counter and threw it in the refrigerator. Sarakit smeared a wet kitchen rag over his mouth. "Remember, Fang has soccer practice tonight," she said to Nhean, although she looked at Beth. "Fang is our oldest. He's almost fifteen."

Fang was adopted from China, Beth remembered. She wondered why Sarakit and Ted had decided to adopt: Was she unable to have children? Had she purposely decided only to adopt boys from her region of the world?

"Did you find the adoption process difficult?" she asked.

Sarakit stared at her apoplectically, as if Beth had just suggested they try on each other's underwear. "Nhean, go watch television. Where's that cold that kept you up all night?" Nhean sprinted toward his cartoons. "Please don't mention adoption in front of the kids."

"Oh, I'm sorry," Beth gasped, springing from the counter. "I thought they knew."

"They do know, but they don't need to be reminded that everyone else does," Sarakit said. "To answer your question, I took children from overcrowded orphanages that counted every rice grain in a bowl. It wasn't difficult. It was a duty. And no matter how they've been treated in Orient, by other families who only want to see reflections of themselves in their kids, all my boys have run circles around their classmates in grades and talent." She drank her water down, and in those five seconds Beth wished she could withdraw the adoption question. Luckily, she didn't have to. "I'm very busy, Beth. I've got a showing today at three. And as you can imagine, with everything that's been going on lately, no one in their right mind wants to buy a house in Orient. I've got more calls in the last week from people who want to sell than I've had in the whole six months since I started Pearl Farms. You wouldn't believe what some of your neighbors think their houses are worth."

"Mike Gilburn's looking," Beth ventured. "He told me he tried to buy a fixer-upper on the Sound from you a few months back."

Sarakit winced at the reminder of a lost sale. "That was before I knew we'd need a police presence in the village. It looks like I can kiss those city buyers good-bye." She shook her head futilely. "First the travel business goes bust, now it's real estate. That mutant on the beach was poison enough. But now, with the fire . . ."

"Are you the one selling Magdalena's house?" Beth wondered if the pant-suited woman she'd seen opening her neighbor's cottage was a Pearl Farms agent.

Sarakit closed her eyes, and for a moment her features lost their pinched severity. Beth had inherited her mother's annoying habit of applying imaginary makeup to women's faces, painting them up and pushing them back out into the world, as if a fascist cosmetics counter existed deep in the department store of her mind. But Sarakit Herrig was beautiful without a drop of makeup.

"Pearl Farms is handling that property, yes," Sarakit said patiently.

"Magdalena willed me her armoire and grandfather clock. I promise to come get them before you start showing the place. Cole Drake told me they're still in there."

Sarakit looked genuinely surprised. She tapped her nails on the counter, then swept a few crumbs into her palm.

"Well, that's Lena's right. Personally, whatever's in that will I take with a grain of salt." Beth leaned forward over a box of Hefty CinchSaks, imploring Sarakit to explain. "Cole Drake tricked her into removing the transfer of her property to OHB in her will. He convinced her that it would be easier taxwise if she waited until the trust received full nonprofit status. And she listened to him. In her last days, she listened to him. Outrageous." Sarakit's lips jutted. "A complete lie manufactured by a greedy lawyer who's making a profit on the sale. Cole's always hated the board because it has an ethic beyond the bottom line. And because we chose Arthur Cleaver for our counsel instead of him. Pure spite. Magdalena would have wanted that property preserved. Everyone knows that."

"So Cole Drake is an enemy of the board?"

"Uh, yeah," Sarakit said. She opened a drawer and started sorting silverware, seizing a chore to validate the time-suck of a conversation.

"Was Jeff Trader an enemy of the board, too? He and Magdalena were friends. I always thought it was strange they died right after each other." Beth let the point settle in for a second. Sarakit scraped a bit of residue off a fork tine. "You know, Jeff warned Magdalena about OHB. She told me that a few days before she died. Maybe that's why she changed her will."

"Warned her? Jeff Trader?" Sarakit laughed as she dropped the fork in the drawer. "Jeff was probably saying that to distract her while he robbed her purse. He used to do repairs for us. He'd stand in this kitchen and ask me all kinds of ridiculous questions. But, yeah, he wasn't on OHB's side. Which is a shame, because we would have given him money for the development rights to his land. Think of all the alcohol he could have bought." With that, she slammed the drawer with her hip.

The front door opened and Nhean and Ronald rushed to greet their father, rattling off a list of toys they'd just seen on TV. Ted carried a nylon briefcase into the kitchen, dropping it into one of the chairs. His orange hair was an unruly spray of hen wings. The skin around his eyes was blotchy, as if he'd taken the five-minute drive from the school to cry for the Muldoons, or for his early retirement, or for his wife, who might divorce a husband who was no longer providing a stable paycheck. He smiled at Beth, straightening his hair with his freckled fingers.

"To what do we owe this visit?" he asked. "Did Sarakit offer you tea?"

"I was about to," Sarakit said as she took the loaf of bread out of the refrigerator. Tea would require five minutes to boil the water, thirty seconds to find the bag and unwrap it, and ten minutes for Beth to sip it. Tea was not forthcoming.

"No need," Beth replied. "I'm actually here because you asked me a question at the funeral, and I want to apologize for not answering." For the first time, Sarakit looked at her with interest. She stopped untying the bread bag. "You were right, Mrs. Herrig, I was standing with Pam and Mills on their front lawn that afternoon." Sarakit glanced at Ted when she mentioned Mills's name. "And, yes, Pam was upset. Tommy and Mills had become friends, and Pam didn't approve because she thought Tommy was too impressionable to hang out with a kid from the city. She got it into her head that he was some sort of juvenile delinquent. But I've become close with Mills, and I can tell you he isn't like that. He's very honest, and thoughtful, and—"

"Drugs," Ted interrupted. "We heard from others that he was a drug addict."

Beth shook her head. "Not the case. He came to a party at my house, and he wouldn't even touch the liquor."

"You invited a minor to a party serving liquor?" Sarakit shot a look at Ted. *See. I told you. Just like her mother.*

"All I want to say is that, with everything going on, it would be easy to get the wrong impression. The three of us know what Orient can be like. And once one person wrongly accuses an innocent kid of something as awful as arson"—she looked at Sarakit—"his reputation is basically ruined. Soon everyone suspects him, and then there's no end to it."

Ted waited out the speech like a teacher enduring a student's botched recitation of history, nodding thoughtfully, raising a finger only when she finished.

"Beth," he said, "I made a vow to Bryan that I'd take care of his children if anything were to happen." His eyes grew starry under the track lighting. "And I can't even do that now, because the two boys who would have needed us were killed. But I do know that Pam was a wonderful mother. And if she had a problem with your young friend, it wasn't for nothing. I'm not saying he had anything to do with the fire. But it's something the police should consider. Just as they're considering everyone else who knew the Muldoons. That's fair, isn't it?"

That was fair. Sort of. But Beth knew the flaw in that logic. Mills wouldn't be considered the same way she would be considered, or Ted, or Sarakit.

"He didn't do it," she said. "I'm telling you, Mills had nothing to do with the fire."

Sarakit took a step toward her. "Those detectives came into *our* house," she wailed, "and had the audacity to ask us where *we* were the night of the fire." She tapped her chest. "We, who have been close friends of the Muldoons for twenty years. And we were forced to tell Mike Gilburn that we were in bed when we heard the sirens, and I reached over and held Ted's hand and told him it was *nothing*. Nothing, because I could never have imagined, I could never have known—" She turned to the sink, her fists bracing the counter. "And if we have to be asked those kinds of questions, I don't see why *he* shouldn't have to be."

Ted walked over to his wife and hugged her from behind.

"We couldn't have known," he whispered. "And we couldn't have done anything, even if we had rushed over." He glanced at Beth. "We won't set foot on Youngs Road. Neither of us can handle seeing the remains of that house. It's too much. I was supposed to take care of Tommy and Theo, as well as Lisa."

Sarakit wiped her eyes, fought off her husband's arms, and

walked into the hallway without looking back at Beth. Ted stood at the counter, peering out the window. Beth looked past him and saw his hunting bow lying on the patio table, broken in half.

Beth stepped out of the kitchen. She found Sarakit standing by the front door, waving it open.

"Lisa's coming to dinner tonight," Sarakit said. "Think about what she's going through."

"Did you see Lisa in Orient the last few weeks?" Beth asked. "Before the fire?"

Sarakit snorted, as if realizing she'd been entertaining an idiot.

"Lisa's been away at school." Sarakit pulled the band from her hair, releasing a drape of black that reached her elbows. When she looked at Beth again, the harshness had left her face, replaced with the first gentle expression she'd given Beth in six months.

"Look, I'm sorry if I seem callous," she said. "This week hasn't been easy on us. But I can't help wondering why you're so determined to protect a kid from the city at the expense of the neighbors who have known you since you were a child. You need to think about what's right for this community before there's nothing left of it. And if you don't want to, then maybe you'd be better off in the city." Sarakit reached toward the end table and picked up one of her business cards. "I know your mother's been thinking of selling. She won't let the board buy her development rights, but I hope, when the time comes, you'll at least support me in trying to convince the next buyers to join us. It's simple, Beth. If you don't like how we live out here, you don't have to stay." Sarakit pressed the card in her hand.

"Gavril and I are happy in the house," Beth replied. "We're not interested in moving yet."

Sarakit sighed. "Karen Norgen told me that she's seen your husband walking on the street late at night with some friend of his. Strangers walking the streets after midnight isn't exactly comforting after what's gone on. You might want to tell him that."

Beth accepted the cold air of the porch. She was too busy thinking of Gavril to turn around as she said goodbye.

By the time Beth got home—late, at quarter after two—she expected to find Mills waiting at the back door. At 2:25 she called Paul's house, but no one answered.

She leaned on the kitchen table, her head bent and her eyes closed. Today was the day she'd hoped to resolve the fate of the mass inside her. Instead she'd gone into Greenport to photocopy a dead man's journal and buy a birthday cake. The decision to be a mother wasn't something you were supposed to schedule between tasks. Beth knew that what she should do was interrupt Gavril in his studio and have a talk—or *the talk*, since they hadn't really talked for a week. Gavril already thought she was losing her mind—if he even found time to think of her at all, between his tarring and sculpting and all his alleged late-night walks through Orient.

She looked out the window at the garage, just twenty feet from the house—such a small distance between them, but the kitchen door was shut and locked, and it seemed beyond her strength to open it. She was porous, and the wall was solid, and a million distractions blew through her and left her leaning on the table. How could her body possess one brain so scattered and another so willful and concentrated, so sure of its fetal course?

She had always done her clearest thinking while she was painting. Outside her studio in Brooklyn, her mind was a radio of jumbled frequencies, one irritating song exchanged for another, and here in Orient it was the same: a birthday cake, aisle three at Dooley's, the money-troubled Herrigs, Luz and her dinner, all sidetracking her in jumbled succession. She had hoped that her brain would attune itself as her hands and eyes were busy painting Mills, and that the decision would arrive as uncomplicatedly as spring weather: to choose a path and take it, to say yes or no and stick to her choice.

But so many thoughts were coursing through her brain, disrupting any chance of solid focus. What was Gavril doing walking around late at night with a friend when he should have been home in bed? Who had moved the furniture around in her living room? What was the connection between Jeff, Magdalena, and the Muldoons?

Her thoughts were interrupted when Mills knocked on the window and opened the door, bringing the day in with him, wet and cold and reeking of fish. He had two wounds above his lip and a red scratch trailing down his left cheek.

"Jesus," she said, lifting up from the table. "Were you in a fight?"

"I'm fine," he replied, breathing heavily. "I'm sorry I'm late. You probably don't want to paint me. I'm not looking too good."

"You look fine," she said, and for no reason other than that she wanted to, she hugged him. The fish stink emanated from his coat. Mills pressed his forehead against her shoulder, and his words vibrated through her chest.

"They found another one of those Plum mutants. Or I did. Some guys that work for Adam chased me. They were going to beat me up, and I fell onto this pile of fur and bone. Right on the beach by your friends' house, Luz and Nathan."

Beth let go of him. "What do you mean they were going to beat you up?" She couldn't open the door to speak to Gavril, but she had half a mind to confront Adam Pruitt and threaten him into leaving Mills alone.

"You should have seen it," he said. "It might have been on the shore for days. It had a head like a deer and long yellow nails and hooves and two spinal cords twisted together like conjoined twins, except the second head never developed. I've never seen anything so horrible up close. It was all mixed up. How does an animal like that even live? I can't imagine what thing gave birth to it, or what those Plum scientists did."

Her stomach fluttered. She fought the urge to rush to the sink. She tried not to think of the mass inside her, now much larger than a chestnut, growing limbs and eyes—maybe two spinal cords, twisting and forking like a road. Surely the ultrasound would have captured any disfiguration. Surely the doctor would have warned her if it weren't developing right.

"I don't want to hear about it," she said.

Mills tapped his toe on the floor.

"Okay," he said. "It was just horrib—"

"Please." She tried to smile. "Come upstairs. I don't have much time this afternoon. I have to go to"—she steered away from the word *dinner*, repelled by any associations with food—"a party to-night." She assumed the mutant creature on the beach wouldn't cause the Wilson-Crimps to cancel. Nathan probably loved the mutant spectacle, she thought. She turned around at the top of the stairs and by some miracle of trust or obligation she found Mills trailing behind, eyes like diamonds in the coal-darkness between floors.

She sat before the white canvas, legs spread on either side. Her thigh muscles would have to readjust to the position, after all the months she'd stayed away from painting. She had posed Mills in a chair by the door, one shoulder up and one down to stagger his neckline, a painterly trick for irregular lines. He sat impressively still, concentrating on a snag in the window netting, only his eyes moving occasionally from the window to her, in approval or doubt, the rest of him petrified. She dabbed the thin brush into the ocher on her palette, focusing first on the eyes, and from those twin axis points she'd map out the rest of his face and body. It took two points to create the perception of space. One eye could suggest any number of possibilities: up, down, a speck in a void. Two eyes and the image was fixed.

She held the brush an inch from the canvas and for a moment she hesitated, distracted by the familiar doubts: bad reviews, un-sellable show, returned works stacked in her own apartment facing the wall; *no passion, not enough talent, not as defiant as Gavril, not as clever as Luz*; critics like mailmen delivering unwanted news. But then she looked over at Mills, his horse eyes rounding in their sockets, and her wrist bent. She brushed a half circle on the linen, and the pure whiteness, the glacial nothing, was gone.

From the first sentence the next followed. She added crimson and deepened it with Prussian blue. The joints of her fingers steadied. Already, she couldn't start over. Like all paintings, the portrait was ruined at the first stroke of paint; it would never be exactly as she had imagined it, and that failure was what allowed her to continue. The acceptance of failure produced astonishing results. The painting was made of its mistakes, the sum of him and how she saw him and something entirely separate, something more. It wasn't a description or a duplication, it breathed or died on its own. Black dragged across the oval, a slash of the eyelid, a planet half dark. She was trying to get under her own skin, to the blood that moved, to the nerves that jumped, so deep it was the farthest thing from her, just as the fingertip is farthest from the stomach and the toe the farthest from the heart. A flex of muscles brought shade to the iris, an eye staring from the white. She began the second eye with ocher. A person was arriving through a blizzard with news.

Why had she assumed she couldn't do it?

Why had she been so scared?

She looked closely at Mills's right eye, lighter than the left and flecked. She added olive, following the curve, splitting it with a fast horizontal of azure, blue skin encasing a liquid ball. She could do this if she wanted to—paint the portrait, have the baby, bring something different than herself out of herself, and trust that it would find its way. It would have its own flaws entirely separate, a thing to love because it was imperfect. It seemed so obvious to her right now, as her back muscles ached and her thighs fatigued from straddling the easel: the answer to life must be found in the flaws, in mutation, in the discordant, incompatible facts. *Life begins at misconception*, she thought.

Mills had been right, that night in her bedroom during the party.

Art didn't have to provide answers. It only had to ask questions. The mass inside her was asking a question and she was answering yes. The ocean tries to flood a boat, fire wants to eat the wood, the mind wills to regret, and silence shapes a landscape more deftly than sound—all of that was true. But still boats kept out the water, and the wood held, and a voice cut through the quiet, and the mind went forward anyway, swimming through its doubts. A ripe peach with a sliver of blue shine, Mills's cheek, she'd paint the blue of that shine first, more solid than the skin, painting was about decisions, and she'd carry this baby to term, perhaps she knew she would all along, because her decision hadn't arrived as a revelation, it hadn't arrived at all, it was still moving and she was moving with it.

She had painted his eyes, and half a cheek. She dipped her brush in ruby. The scratch on his cheek broke the shine.

It would be an April delivery, in the first warm days after winter. She would turn this room into a nursery. She was saying yes.

Mills noticed the ruby on her brush. "You aren't painting my zits, are you?"

"Not yet."

He huffed. "Well, did you tell Detective Gilburn about Lisa?"

"No," she said. "I will tomorrow. I promise. And I'm going to give him the journal as well. But I still don't understand why Lisa and Adam would have killed Magdalena, even if Jeff had told her that Lisa was back in town."

"Don't you see, Magdalena would have realized what her being here meant after the fire killed her family," Mills reasoned. "That's why they had to get rid of her first."

"But there's no mention of Lisa and Adam in Jeff's book. Why was the book so important? And we still don't know why Jeff Trader warned Magdalena about OHB. None of it makes any sense."

"I still think the police deserve to know," he mumbled, doing his best to hold still. "I talked to Lisa this morning. She stopped by her house again, and I overheard her making plans to meet someone. That's why I went to the beach by Bug Light, only those guys chased me before I could see who it was. Lisa says the *L* pendant doesn't belong to her, because her real name is Elizabeth, but I don't buy it."

Beth told him about her visit at the Herrigs, how she'd tried in vain to defuse their hostility. "And I guess I can't blame them. They don't know you. Of course you seem like a suspect. Don't worry. We'll think of something."

He stretched his neck and returned to his pose. "You don't have to look out for me."

She gave him an exasperated stare. "I want to. And I want you to stay in Orient if you're happy here." He altered the polish of his cheek by smiling. She mixed purple with cobalt to execute the sharp peak of his nose. The confidence sprung from the quickness of the brushstroke. The force of the personality lay in the speed of the line. She could be more hesitant around his lips, which were hesitant themselves, pink speed bumps that held back as many thoughts as they shared.

"Thank you," he said. "You're a good friend." Inside, she was fighting back her last doubts: *not too late to make an appointment, not too late to drive into the city tomorrow, no good, no passion, just dead lines knotted together.*

"I want to tell you something," she said, heard herself saying it. "I haven't told anybody, not even Gavril, so please keep it between us." He half-nodded, unsure whether to break his pose or keep it. "I found out a few weeks ago, but I wasn't sure I wanted it. Or maybe I was always sure but I've been so stuck, like an unwilling participant in my own life. I'm pregnant. I'm three months pregnant, and I'm going to have a baby."

He opened his mouth. She hadn't expected him to congratulate her, but in those seconds after she told him the news—how easy it had been for her to say it, not as a confession but as a simple fact—she couldn't gauge his reaction. His eyelids closed and blood rushed to his cheeks, destroying the blue shine, although it didn't matter, she had already gotten it down. He pulled the cross at his earlobe. His tongue flicked against his gray front tooth. She'd need to paint that tooth, the asphalt gray of a summer sidewalk, hose water drying in the sun. "That's wonderful," he said. "It is good, isn't it? I remember you saying you didn't think you wanted kids."

She closed her left eye and Mills sprung to the left. She closed her right eye and Mills sprung to the right. Every subject was a moving target. Both eyes brought him in between in forced agreement.

"I know. I honestly didn't think I was going to keep it when I told you that. But I am going to keep it. And we're going to stay out here, and this room will be the nursery." It occurred to her that Mills might have personal objections to abortion, that he might think less of her for considering a route his own mother might well have considered. "I'm sorry if that sounds selfish. But it didn't seem that way to me."

"No," he said, lifting from his seat to step toward her. When he realized he couldn't fully reach her, across the easel and the tray of paints, he made the gesture of an older man: he placed his hand against her cheek and held it there, a teenager in dirty jeans and a grass-stained shirt, warming her cheek with his palm. "Don't be sorry. I get it. But you're going to be a great mother. And the kid is going to be so lucky because you're going to love him. I think even Pam Muldoon was probably a great mother, that she loved her children like that."

She took his wrist. "Sit down," she said. "We aren't done yet. And don't look." He ducked his head and returned to the chair. "And I don't know if it's a *him* yet. Maybe if it is a boy, Mills can be his name." She tested it. "Mills."

He broke from his pose, staring at her, his hands rubbing his legs.

"That's not my name," he said slowly. "I took that name when I came to New York. I didn't want my old one anymore and I figured Mills Chevern was good as any to start over."

She dipped her brush in the cobalt to define the sockets below the brows. She would ease the darkness with gypsum, like skin surfacing from ocean water.

"It's Leonard," he said. "My name is Leonard Thorp. Even Paul doesn't know."

Leonard, she said to herself. Mills had always seemed too smooth for him. Leonard fit better, the way a tight school sweater fits, bringing the awkwardness into his shoulders and the deflection into his eyes. A Leonard, not a Mills, stood alone.

"Leonard's a good name. A real name." The eyes on the canvas belonged to a Leonard.

He pursed his lips. Shadows pooled in the indentation of his cheeks.

"I told you I met my mother. Just before I left California. It was the last thing I did. I found out where she worked, at a jewelry store in Sacramento, and I visited her there. Walked in like an ordinary customer." The skin of his neck goose-bumped; she saw a bead of sweat collect above his eyebrow. In the overcast afternoon light of Orient, he made the sound of the bell as the shop door opened.

"Can I help you?" the woman with dark hair said from behind the counter.

She still had her sunglasses on, large black lenses hiding her eyes. He wondered if she might be blind, although she hadn't used a cane, and a blind woman was probably a liability in a jewelry store. The slanting Sacramento light, strong through the window, whitened the glass counter and brought a gleam to the rings and chains inside. Sweat dripped down his neck and his fingers trembled—a novice shoplifter's nerves, she might have thought, if she could see him at all behind her glasses. Her nose was sharp and the dent at the tip deepened as she smiled. Her teeth were white—small, capped, and stained by lipstick. She had no way of knowing that she was speaking to her son.

"I'm just looking," he said, leaning over the counter and pretending to study the merchandise. She fixed the strap of her leopard-print dress, a black bra peeking from the seam below her armpit. Her skin, under her clothes, was as pale as his.

"If you want to see anything, I can take the tray out for you. It's all fourteen, eighteen, or twenty-two karat, we guarantee. Whoever said 'Buy land, they aren't making any more of it' could have said the same about gold." The air-conditioning was refrigerating his sweat, making it impossible not to shiver. In the back of the store, through a bulletproof-glass divider, an old man in a fedora drilled inscriptions with an electric needle. The old man with black teeth looked up at him, distrustfully or out of boredom.

He asked to see a tray of gold chains, thick cables and ropes. When she brought the tray to rest on the counter, he noticed a gold band on her left ring finger. Was she married to his father? Had his parents ever been married? Did she know where the man was, the man she'd been with nineteen years ago?

"I like your ring," he said.

She studied it, spreading her fingers on the counter. "I've had this on for fifteen years," she said. "And it has yet to turn my finger green. Twenty-two karat." Her laugh was deep and spoke of cigarettes, though she smelled of garlic and rosewater. "But you aren't looking for a ring like this, are you? You're too young to get married."

"I'm not that young," he replied, touching a chain and glancing up. "Maybe I look younger through your glasses." He wanted her to take them off so he could see her eyes. Were her eyes brown like his? If he told her he was her son, would she take them off? Or would she call for the old man to remove him from the store?

"I have very sensitive eyes," she said. "I get migraines. It runs in my family." She watched him examine the chains, holding herself up on the counter, as if tired from her lunch break. He did not get migraines. That hadn't been inherited. He wondered if she had other children. When she exhaled, her leopard-print stomach made contact with the glass. "Are you looking for something for yourself or maybe for a girlfriend?" It was a mother's tactic to pry personal details out of a secretive child. He breathed through his mouth and wondered: if he stopped breathing altogether, would she apply her lips to his to induce CPR? When he came around, would she be cushioning his head in her lap?

"Yes, for my girlfriend," he lied. She would be pleased to know that her son had a girlfriend, though he wasn't interested in girls.

"*Oooh*, okay. This is a romantic mission. Those chains are too thick for a young lady. How about earrings? Let me see." She moved along the counter to unlock a case and pulled out a velvet tray. "How about these gold bows," she suggested, tapping her red nail on a pair or earrings. Her nails had grown a millimeter away from the cuticle since she painted them. The bows she was pointing out were for a child, with fake emerald hearts glued to their centers. "Forty-seven dollars."

"I don't know. Do you have a daughter who would like these?" He stared at her with every ounce of force he had; he wasn't sure he had ever looked at another human being so intently. Did all human beings have so many craters and lines across their faces, like satellite elevation maps? She had two moles under her chin, the second sprouting a hair that whitened in the sunlight.

"Um, yeah, I have two little girls." She seemed uncertain of how much she wanted to share with a customer. Or maybe she had worn out her patience on such a small sale. She rubbed the back of her neck and stared out the window, thinking of her two little girls, maybe worrying about some problem—a fight before school, an unpaid orthodontia bill, a father who wasn't around.

"Sure is hot outside," he said dumbly.

"What?"

"Sure is hot outside." He smiled and cocked his head, turning his eyes into sunsets. Could she know how often he had inflicted this look of innocence on other parents just so he could stay in their houses for a few months? Did she ever wonder what happened to the infant she had left with social services, an hour and a half's drive down the I-5 eighteen years ago? When she gave birth to her two difficult daughters, did she ever think to reclaim her son?

"Sacramento is hot," he said. "I'm from Modesto, just up here for the day." She nodded. "Modesto," he said again.

"It's hot there too, I bet."

"Have you ever been?"

She cleared her throat and returned the tray of chains to the case. "Of course I have. I've been all over the valley. In fact I lived there a long time ago. Dirty town." She caught herself. "I mean, I didn't have good luck there. Wasn't the right place for me. *Water, wealth, contentment, health.*" She quoted the lightbulb-studded motto on the arch that curved over Ninth Street, just before the train tracks. He knew those train tracks like his tongue knew the back of his teeth.

"No luck," he said.

She rubbed her neck again and looked at the door, hoping for other customers to enter. "So do you see anything you like?"

"My name's Leonard," he said. He couldn't see her eyes, so he focused all his attention on her lips. They contorted briefly and sunk back into plainness.

"I had an uncle named Leonard, crazy Italian. He drank too much and got into the rodeo. The rodeo, of all things. Never saw him after the age of fifteen." He was Italian, part Italian. He had two half-sisters and he was of partial Italian heritage, and he had a great-uncle in the rodeo. They got headaches. "Well, Leonard, I'm Grace." He already knew her name. "So how about you pick out something for your girlfriend and I'll give you a good price?"

He could say it right now. *I'm your son. I'm the thing you left in Modesto with your bad luck. Maybe I am your bad luck. I've been there my whole life. You never once came looking for me so I came to find you.* He wanted to fill the silence between them with that news. He looked at her and saw himself in the reflection of her twin black lenses, two sons leaning fish-eyed over the counter. He'd been through a dozen houses of Modesto, had made beds in them, found food in them, to grow up and become this man at the Central Gold counter.

"I'll take these," he said, drawing his hand randomly over a pair of earrings.

"Crosses?" She found his choice distasteful. "Well, if she's religious she might like them. I'm not religious myself, not that I'm against those things. Those are eighteen karat, so they're sixty-five, no sixty-seven dollars, and that's ten percent off their sticker price, just because I like you." His mother liked him. His unreligious and unlucky mother liked him. Before he could change his mind, she collected the earrings on their cardboard backing and placed them in a yellow box. "Is it cash or charge? If it's charge I'll need to see some ID."

He didn't have a credit card. He did have ID, but if he showed it to her, she'd see his name and birthdate and know who he was and why he was here. He pulled his wallet from his back pocket, fumbling with it over the glass counter. He was shaking violently by now, and his mother glanced at the old man in the back—was it for help? Or just to make sure he was finishing the engraving he'd been working on?

"Do you like surprises?" he asked.

She turned to him and positioned her sunglasses higher on her nose.

"Do I like surprises," she repeated. "No. Not especially. Actually I hate them. But I'm sure your girlfriend will love a surprise gift of earrings. Who doesn't like good surprises? Expensive, beautiful surprises. Surprises you secretly wish for. It's the bad surprises that don't help my migraines."

He handed her four twenty-dollar bills, almost the last of the money he had saved. She gave him his change. He hoped their hands might touch, but she spread the dollars lengthwise over his palm. She put the yellow box in a yellow paper bag and pushed it across the counter.

"Thank you. Please come again."

"Thank you," he said. On the yellow bag in gold lettering were printed these words: *thank you please come again.* "Thank you for your time and patience with me."

She yawned slightly, bit down on the yawn, and only after completing its warp did she ball her fingers over her lips.

"It's our specialty. Good-bye."

He went outside, into the heat of hot Sacramento, and walked five blocks without thinking of anything but the temperature, and only in the last two blocks was he crying, and when he passed a strip mall with an ear-piercing shop he used the change from the sale to have his ear pierced, and he was crying so much he didn't even feel the puncture, just enough to remind him he had pain receptors, enough to wake him, and he asked the woman to put the cross in, and when he opened the box and unclipped the earring from the cardboard he saw that she'd forgotten to peel off the sticker on the back that read *$45, 14 karat*, and he waited until the woman fit the cross through the hole before throwing the second earring in the trash, and he took a different street to the bus station so he wouldn't pass by the shop window again, and he bought another one-way ticket at full price, and, along the scored, aerosol greens of the central valley, he thought of the city in the east, the one with buildings crowded together like soldiers marshaled against the invading Atlantic, and that's where he headed five days later with his duffel bag.

"I guess my mother ripped me off." Beth dropped her brush on the tray. She didn't try to console him. He wasn't crying. He had told most of the story sitting perfectly still. "But I don't blame her. What did I expect?"

"I think we're done for the day," she said, tucking her lips together. She had no right to pass judgment on his mother. Was she a bad mother for letting go of him, or was she not a mother at all? Some categorizations could only be claimed through time. All Beth could do was listen. But even if Mills said that the memory of his mother was garbage, the gold cross still hung in his ear. "We'll let the oil dry and I'll do more the next time you sit for me." Mills stretched his back.

"Can I see what you've done so far?"

She stood up, and he slid in front of her, the neck of his T-shirt exposing the rise of his collarbone, and she had to stop herself from putting her lips to his neck. He was so thin, and he had come all this way from the desert, and she was sure his mother would have been pleased that he had found people on the other side of the country who cared for him.

"I'm glad you're staying here," she said as he examined the portrait. "I'm glad you've come."

She couldn't tell if he liked what he saw: two eyes and most of a cheek that bled into a circle of chin, the pink hole of a mouth jeweled with a square of wet gray, his forehead swaths of olive that she'd break on his next visit with curls of black. He looked at the canvas as she screwed the caps on the paint tubes. "I'm glad too," he said. "That's why it's important for the police to figure out who killed the Muldoons. I want to be here, with you and Paul, a while longer." He grabbed his chin and pulled it down, as if imitating the face in the painting. "I thought I was lifting my head," he said. Then he put his fingers over his eyes and pushed on his eyelids. "Do my eyes really squint like that?" he asked. "You made me look Asian."

She inspected the eyes on the canvas. "They aren't Asian," she said. "Maybe the lines are a little hard. I can soften them next time. But you do tend to squint."

Beth watched Mills push his eyelids to the sides like the punch line of a racist joke, the kind she and her friends told regularly in grade school—"We're from Orient"—and she thought of the Herrig children, who must suffer that same joke today. "Beth," he said quickly. "Do you remember what Eleanor did when we asked about the other woman Bryan brought there? The one who owned the pendant?"

Beth remembered the Seaview bartender holding her fingers against her eyes to suggest blindness. "She said she couldn't say who it was because she couldn't see."

"No." He turned to face her. "She just went like this," and again he pulled on his eyelids, like a child trying to act Chinese. "Eleanor was racist as hell, so all she'd see was an Asian woman. That's who she meant was sleeping with Bryan Muldoon—Sarakit Herrig. Who's also on the board of OHB. Who happens to be taking over the trust. Who would love nothing more than for me to take the fall." His smile was greedy, the smile of an only child coming down the stairs on Christmas morning.

She tried to picture Sarakit exercising to keep off the fat so that Bryan Muldoon could run his hands along her hips. She tried to picture her lighting a match to gasoline, aware that two children slept in the darkness upstairs.

"But Sarakit doesn't start with an *L*. Neither does *Herrig*. Anyway, she has an alibi for the fire."

"What about her husband, who owed Bryan money? Wouldn't he have been pissed to find out that his best friend was sleeping with his wife?"

She sighed. Mills had blamed Adam Pruitt for the fire after Adam screamed at him for being on his property. Now he was accusing Sarakit because she'd blamed him at the church. He was scrambling to implicate anyone who had crossed him. "Ted is her alibi," she said, "which means she's his. They were together in bed when they heard the alarms."

"One of them could be protecting the other. Or they could have done it as a team. Maybe Jeff Trader knew what they were planning. Maybe Magdalena figured it out. That's why she changed her will. With Bryan dead, her house would have gone to OHB, with Sarakit and Ted making the decisions."

Beth wiped the brushes. "I thought you were so sure it was Lisa and Adam."

"They all had a motive. So did Roe diCorcia. And the Drakes. But what if it's Ted or Sarakit?" He stared out the window, as if he expected to find any one of them standing on the lawn with gasoline-soaked hands. "How can that detective suspect me when all these people had a motive?"

Beth heard something creak in the hallway downstairs and raced to the door. "Who's there?" she called. She felt safer with Mills in the room, but the sound of footsteps passing through the house quickened her fear.

"It's me, and I'm not moving furniture," Gavril yelled. "We have to leave in twenty minutes. Are you ready?" He climbed the steps, and a look of dread crossed his face when he saw Mills standing in her old bedroom, as if he had come upon his wife with an old boyfriend. "We need to go," he said as he stomped down the hall.

"You haven't told him, have you?" Mills whispered, glancing at her stomach. "I hope he'll appreciate you more once he finds out."

She ignored the remark. "I'll call the detective tomorrow. And I have Paul's cake for you in my car. Thanks for sitting for me today." He nodded. "So what do I call you, Leonard or Mills?"

"Mills," he said smiling. "Some decisions you can't take back."

It pleased her to think he was right.

PART 3

Him

Beth decided not to tell Gavril the good news until after the party. He spent the drive over shifting in the passenger seat, yanking the collar of his sport coat, and picking lint off his pants. He had never been comfortable in the constraints of finer clothes. At their wedding, he had complained so much about the starch in his shirt and the knot in his tie that she expected to find him half-unraveled by the time she joined him at the altar. Seeing him there, withstanding the straitjacket of a Brooks Brothers suit, his maroon eyes wild with claustrophobia, she took his commitment to formality as a commitment to her. Gavril was most at home in the relaxed fit of his studio uniform. He liked to think of himself as a worker like his parents, dressing up only to appear before the occasional dictator. She let him have his fantasies, mostly because he let Beth have hers.

She could have told him the good news right then in the car, driving down Main Road, but Gavril was in an insolent mood. He kept carrying on about the Russian collectors traveling from their *huge, new, twenty-seven-million-dollar* house in Sagaponack to slum it for two days in Orient with the young artists they collected—"and like desperate girls in bars we giggle and wink and suffer his bad insights," Gavril groused. He hadn't said a word about the fact that Beth had begun painting again. She wasn't sure he'd noticed.

"They could buy all the sculptures in the garage tomorrow," he said, in awe or disgust. Awe and disgust in the face of wealth—those emotions were entwined as tightly as lust and loathing in the face of sex. "So even before my show opens, they already have the work in their collection. That saves me from being poor, far from poor if they decide to buy all of it. But Yakov Dombrovski began making his fortune in the Soviet army, stealing gasoline from his unit and selling it secretly on the private market. It could be the same strategy with my art. He acts tricky and underpays now, announces he has bought my work, which increases its value, and then sells it off at auction for his own profit." Gavril wiped the sweat from his hairline. "What does that make me? A pawn in making a rich man richer. That is not why I invested my blood and muscle and all my waking hours away from my bed. Why do I even show it in a gallery? I might as well hang a sign on the door: sold to man ranked forty-eight on *Forbes* list of richest in world."

Beth tried to interrupt, reminding him that all art acquisitions were tainted with the financial, that it wasn't any more ethical to sell to a poorer rich collector than to the richest rich collector, and that there were certain advantages in joining a top-tier collection—that Dombrovski could afford to keep the work and that he presumably had plenty of room in Sagaponack to display it. But she eventually gave up against Gavril's gale-force rhetoric. "Consumption is conspicuous. But when an artist is implicated from the start, he is not an outlier but a manufacturer of merchandise. And the worth of that merchandise derives from the man who owns it. It is his name, not mine, that gives it value. He's the real artist of today." Beth stopped listening. A few Orient home owners had already strung their roofs in Christmas lights. Reds and blues and starburst whites blinked cheerfully and out of rhythm. Flakes of snow drifted through the headlight beams. The baby would have to wait until next winter for its first snowfall.

Gavril droned on. "Dombrovski keeps much of his collection on his yacht, hundreds of millions of dollars of art, sailing around the Mediterranean or the Gulf of Aden with his regulation basketball court and three submarine—"

She interrupted him. "I spoke to Sarakit Herrig today. She told me that a neighbor saw you walking around in the middle of the night with somebody. Is that true?"

Gavril glanced at her. His forehead glowed from the dashboard lights. "I haven't been walking. I've been in my studio working."

"That's not what she says. Is that what you've been doing instead of sleeping in the house?" She tried to remember when exactly Gavril had started spending nights in the garage, whether it was before or after the fire.

"I thought you were going to stop with your accusations. Please, Beth, let's have good time tonight. I promise I'll make more of an effort to put you ahead of my work." He reached for her hand, but she needed control of the wheel to make the turn. On the dirt incline she searched for his hand but he had already withdrawn it.

"Promise me one thing," she said. "Don't drink too much. I want to talk to you when we get home."

He grunted. "It's a party. I thought we could enjoy ourselves for once."

For once—there it was, confirmation that he hadn't been happy, that neither of them was. When Gavril started hinting that it was her new young friend, that foster kid, who was putting those ridiculous murder fears into her head, she told him to shut up.

Gavril actually enjoyed being scolded now and then. He whistled and nodded. "Fine. I promise not to drink too much. See, I will be good for you if you promise to be good for me and we can die make-believing for each other." He was joking, and when he offered his hand again she took it, threading her fingers with his.

The old farmhouse was brightly lit. Nathan had built a bonfire on the lawn, and the flames shot in the air, licking and twisting, casting the mud mounds into shadow. There was a thrill in driving up to a party, imagining the drinks and conversations that awaited, the warmth of the interior, the coldness of ice in a glass, the improvised congregations, the temporary solace of retreating to a corner before returning to a conversation that never resolved itself, the wine spilled and the joint passed—even the fragile seconds before climbing out of the car, when, having been so graciously invited, it was still possible to decide against it, to turn around and head home.

"We could call tomorrow and say we had a flat tire," she said. But it was too late. Gavril was opening the car door, and Luz was waving at them from the porch. They both had too much to gain.

There were no walls. Plastic sheets hung in their place on the ground floor, tar-black and shivering in the wind. The rocking of the sea—the high-priced soundtrack of coastal living—was heard between hip-hop tracks shuffling on Nathan's laptop. A wood board with OYSTERPONDS INN written across it served as an oversized cheese plate on the coffee table. Twenty crystal vases with bouquets of yellow lilies were arranged across the living room floor; between them space heaters hummed on full blast, trying to compensate for the lack of insulation. There were warm and cold spots within five feet of each other. The lilies sweetened the air and mixed with the bitter tobacco of Luz's cigarettes, one left burning in an ashtray and another withering between her fingers.

Luz greeted her guests in bare feet, her brown toes scrunched on the marble, her hair dry-brushed back and held at her nape by a simple red band. She wore a body-hugging red silk dress with hook buttons that ascended from her shoulder to her neck. After a minute, she sat down on the sofa, where she told a pretty young woman that she'd had the cheongsam made for her in Hong Kong two years ago, right before the opening of her show there. "You're supposed to have it sewn on every time you wear it, but the dressmaker didn't seem to understand that I wasn't blessed with a servant back in the States." The young woman with brown hair scooted forward, posing in her dress of gray lace, as if she expected Beth to ask not her name but the designer's.

Gavril took a glass of wine from an aproned elderly woman holding a tray by the kitchen. Through a tarp leading to the deck,

Beth saw the blurred shapes of two giants lit by the flicker of cigarettes. She realized that they were Dombrovski's bodyguards. Nathan threaded around the vases in a white suit coat and a pale blue shirt, his cheeks red with liquor. He grabbed a wine from the tray and danced across the Persian carpet as he held it out to Beth.

"Welcome," he said. "Welcome to our construction site with its priceless view of the animal disease center." Beth took the glass. Nathan swung around to his wife. "Luz, how much did we pay for this place so we could have mutant test subjects wash up in our backyard like ship treasure?"

"Don't start on that again," Luz snapped. She took a drag from her cigarette and made eye contact with Beth. "He's been at it all day, taking pictures of the creature and serving coffee to the officers who came in their unmarked vans."

"And news crews," Nathan added. "Two news crews descending on our driveway. It's the end of the world out here. I thought this tip of the east was supposed to be the beginning of the new world, but clearly we're all going to be the first infected citizens. Patient zeroes. You never do know how you'll make your imprint on the world." He lifted his glass.

Luz clasped the knee of the impassive, brown-haired woman, a gesture Beth first took for intimacy until Luz simply used her knee to get to her feet. "Will you please stop scaring our guests? They're already scared enough about the murders." She looked at Beth again, and her pupils rolled behind her eyelids. "Yakov didn't even want to come to Orient because of the arsonist on the loose. We had to promise him it was all just trouble among the locals and no maniac was targeting us." Beth scanned the room for the billionaire Russian for whom all of this had been orchestrated, but she couldn't spot him. She did notice that Nathan and Gavril hadn't said hello to each other. Gavril was standing by one of the plastic tarp walls, already finishing his first drink.

"Don't get the wrong idea," Nathan said. "I really admire its force. It's a social art form, the ability to scare an entire community just by a single fusion of animal parts. I wish my work could be that radioactive. We saw two different families packing suitcases into their cars today. There's a mass exodus happening out here. People are actually evacuating. Where are they going, to the city for safety? It's like the entire island is tilting west and all the people are tumbling into Manhattan."

Only Nathan was tilting west. He was having trouble with his balance.

Luz walked slowly around the vases to hug Beth. "Please shut my husband up," she whispered.

"It had *two backbones*. And claws. Right on our property."

Over Luz's shoulder, Beth stared at the elderly Mexican woman holding the tray of wine. Her face was familiar. It took Beth a minute before she recognized the woman serving drinks as Magdalena's nurse.

A toilet flushed somewhere beyond the kitchen, in one of the many rooms that had accommodated city vacationers decades ago when the farmhouse had served as an inn for summer migrations. A man in his midfifties appeared, short and fit in an unassuming blue sweater with dark hair parted down the center. Yakov Dombrovski was not unattractive for an oligarch who had built his underground smuggling operation at the peak of perestroika and then watched the legitimate government follow his lead. Yakov shook hands with Gavril, the back of his head shaped like a bullet, the front like an understuffed teddy bear. Luz hurried over to formalize their introductions.

"Yakov should just buy the mutant creature and call it a day," Nathan joked. His pupils were glass ashtrays. He brushed invisible lint off his lapel.

"Thanks for the oysters," Beth said. "You didn't have to apologize."

He tipped his head. "What oysters?" He sighed. "That must have been Luz's doing, playing peacekeeper. Well, I am sorry if I ruined your party."

"The note was on your stationery and signed with an N—"

"Oh, the shell? Yeah, Luz and I had that made for the house out here. We chose the oyster because this place used to be called Oysterponds Inn. And you know what? Someone in Orient is furious that we had the audacity to do any renovations on it. That cheese plate"—Nathan pointed to the coffee table—"showed up on our front door like some sort of threat. We should be allowed to do whatever we want to this place, after what we paid."

Beth watched Gavril explaining his new sculptures to the Russian.

"What were you two fighting about, anyway?" she asked quietly.

Nathan's face lost its arrogance. He staggered in place. "He didn't tell you? Well, don't ask me. I was past the point of memory record. I'm sure it was nothing. Professional suspicions. A difference of opinion about what we meant to each other."

Nathan glanced at Gavril and Luz, who were waylaying Yakov with conversation. Luz said something so hilarious that she bent over, clutching her knees in laughter.

"They're really going for it, aren't they? You know, it disgusts me how we all have to act like court jesters the minute a man with a lot of cash starts poking around in galleries. We're like flowers, something for him to pick."

The young woman remained on the sofa, indifferent to the conversation around her. She seemed to be posing for an invisible voyeur, as if some divine entity were staring down at the world the way a reader flips through a lifestyle magazine.

"I almost wish I hadn't invited them," Nathan murmured. "I don't want to make art if it all comes down to a popularity contest. I figure, either I need to make something so explosive that people won't forgive me, or I should just give up."

When Beth looked at Alvara again, the nurse recognized her and dipped her eyes. The wine in the glasses trembled.

"Are the Russians staying with you?" she asked. She couldn't picture Yakov and his wife sleeping in a half-completed plastic-wrapped bedroom.

"They're friends with Arthur Cleaver. They're sleeping on his fancy steamboat for the next two nights. You know what Yakov said to me when he showed up tonight? He took one look at all the acres belonging to that farmer next door and asked me how much he could buy it for. I thought, there goes the neighborhood. We have this beautiful artist community in Orient, and now men like Dombrovski are about to roll in with their billions and turn it into the Hamptons. He should just buy Gardiners Island with Cleaver when it comes up for sale and leave us alone."

Beth smiled at Nathan's latter-day Orient protectionism. Not so long ago, locals were making the same argument against his type.

"I saw the backhoe in the yard," she said. "And all the dirt mounds."

Nathan smirked, a watery twinge of his lips.

"We're building a soundproof, contamination-proof, nuclear-wave-proof bomb shelter."

Luz's ears picked up "bomb shelter," and she spun around.

"We are *not* building a bomb shelter," she shouted. "We're digging a pool. I just keep changing my mind about where I want to put it. Close to the house. Overlooking the sea. Now we have to wait until spring, when the ground softens. I like to keep my options open."

Nathan shrugged. "We'll see if we make it to spring."

Beth took a sip from her glass.

"So what's this explosive new work that no one's going to forgive you for?"

Nathan stared past her as new guests arrived: Isaiah and Vince carrying roses, which paled against the hothouse maze of lilies.

"You won't know it when you see it. It'll be that good."

After Beth was introduced to Yakov and his wife, Klara—she was Polish, not Russian—and Nathan rotated his laptop to exhibit a slide show of mutant-animal parts on the beach, Beth went into the kitchen for a glass of water. A roast was turning in the oven, juice dripping from its skin.

She turned on the faucet. The tap hiccupped, pipes clamored, and brown liquid streamed. She had always drunk the local water, but now that she was committed to the baby, she decided not to risk whatever chemicals had seeped from the soil into the supply. Maybe Adam Pruitt had been right about the need for private testing. Maybe, however foolish the paranoia about the Orient Monsters was, there was reason to be alarmed. She remembered the sick dog on Roe diCorcia's property, the corn reduced to sorghum, the animal parts flashing on the computer screen.

Alvara carried in empty glasses and gathered clean ones from the open kitchen cabinets. Marble tile samples were spread across the counter.

"Alvara," Beth said, touching her shoulder. "It's Beth. Do you remember me?"

Alvara blinked and took Beth's hands.

"I thought it was you, Lizbeth." The nurse's face hadn't brightened in the weeks since Magdalena's death. Her cheeks were leaner, her cracked lips obscured by a layer of Vaseline. Beth felt somehow responsible for her, as if she had conspired to rob Alvara of her nursing duties and had forced her to take the odd catering job that required her not to speak, not to nurse, to stand still and refill wine.

"What are you doing here?" Beth asked.

Alvara scanned the doorway. "My cousin clean house for Crimps. I get this job through her. I need the money."

"But what about the money Magdalena left your son?" Alvara stared at her blankly. "Did her lawyer Cole Drake ever track you down?"

She shook her head and, with money on her mind, filled the glasses with wine.

"No, no one come. And I am thankful. I was so afraid they deport me. I never go back to the house. Even little plastic bag of clothes I keep under the sink I leave."

Beth was furious at Cole for cheating this woman out of her small inheritance. She grabbed a pen from the counter and ripped a corner from a magazine that was stacked by a hive of phone chargers.

"Write down your number. I'll make sure the lawyer contacts you. There's money that's owed to you and your son." Alvara took the pen and wrote ten numbers so reluctantly that Beth knew even before she read the area code—974?—that she had invented them on the spot. The woman was too frightened of lawyers even to allow one promising money to find out where she lived.

"You're a sweet girl," Alvara said. "Magdalena dislike your mother but she always care for you. I miss her so much." She wiped the bases of each glass with her apron and arranged them on the tray.

"One last thing," Beth said. Alvara was begging her to let her get back to work, almost as if she were frightened to be caught speaking to her. "Did Magdalena ever mention to you, just before she died, any doubts she had about OHB?"

Alvara searched her brain for a familiar chord. "No, I never hear her speak badly about the board. She was a proud member. She want to preserve Orient."

"What about Jeff Trader?" Beth asked, pressing two fingers on her arm to keep her from lifting the tray. Why was Alvara acting so nervous? "He visited her about a week before he died. Did you hear what they were talking about?"

"Oh, yes, Meester Trader come all the time, once a week to visit Meesus Kiefer. They were friends. Do hives together. He drank too much."

"But the last time he came, do you remember that visit? He said something that caused her to worry."

Alvara sucked her cheeks and looked up at the overhead lights.

"Yes, that last visit was strange. Meester Trader always visit on Sunday and I let him in. But that last time he come on Monday when I do the shopping. Meesus Kiefer, she was upset about it when I return. She say Meester Trader not act like himself. She says he was scared, scared that someone in Orient was going to hurt him, someone who is bad in Orient, and that the board, OHB, a threat.

And then he die and she talk about murder. She was an old woman. Medicine make her not right in the head."

"The board is a threat? Someone on the board is a threat? Or someone bad in Orient is a threat?"

Alvara shook her head. She didn't know, and her English, when corrected and recited back to her, sounded even more confusing.

"Please, Lizbeth, I must get back to work. I need the money. Mees Wilson is a nice rich lady, good to my cousin. Good to me. I can't say anything against her."

Alvara picked up the tray and walked so carefully she almost knocked into Isaiah, who swooped into the kitchen just in time to help himself to a glass. He swilled white wine around his gums.

"Did your orphan friend tell you that I drove him to the beach?" Isaiah asked.

"You drove him?" Beth replied. "I wish you had waited around. He almost got beaten up by some of those assholes who work for Adam Pruitt."

Isaiah narrowed his eyes in concern. "Is he okay?"

"Barely, but yes."

"Adam Pruitt was scheduled to come by our place this afternoon to do an alarm-system estimate. He never showed. I didn't realize his work crew was too busy trying to kick the shit out of a teenager that I happened to be chauffeuring on his errands. It's too bad too. Ever since the fire, Vince has been scared to death." Isaiah grabbed one of the loose tiles from the counter and waved it. "Want to bet that Luz and Nathan never finish construction on this house? I think they enjoy living in a constant state of chaos. It makes them feel stable by comparison."

Beth returned to the living room. Nathan stood with his foot resting on one of the space heaters, tilting it enough to expose its orange grille. Yakov and Gavril were seated in separate white leather chairs, and Luz had reclaimed her position on the sofa next to Klara. For all of his professed distaste for luring in the Russian collector, Nathan was giving it his all: swiveling his hips and spreading his arms, failed rock star, important artist, swelling like a tick on the fresh blood of his audience. Having upended all other conversations, he was in full command of the room. It was his house, after all. If they got tired of pretending to admire him, they could leave.

"That's what I like about the future," Nathan exclaimed. "No one's gotten their hands on it yet."

Beth could see that Gavril was now on drink number three in a night of sworn moderation, downing each more quickly than the last.

"Maybe boats *are* the future," Nathan said. "Always in transit, like the ocean itself. And most of the time it's the same scenery, a seamless sheet of blue. The water is just information, a reminder that you're nowhere and safe."

"We are always safe," Yakov replied. He wasn't bragging; he had no need to. "I have a private security force on board. No pirate would try, because pirates don't want to die any more than you do. And if anyone does try anything—" Yakov rotated his arms to indicate a body being dumped over the side.

It was not always easy to make small talk with a man who had his own militia. Yakov's pronouncements shed a new light on Klara's affectless silence. She wondered how Klara carried on her daily life while machine gun–strapped bodyguards haunted her periphery. What were the phone calls to her mother like?

Nathan continued his efforts to draw Dombrovski out on the subject of his wealth, like an amateur comedian leaning too hard on his audience for material. "So where do you park that four-hundred-foot yacht of yours?" Everyone shifted uncomfortably.

Luz looked over as Beth crouched against the sofa. "Am I having fun?" she asked wearily, as if worn out by her husband's theatrics. "Come upstairs. I need a break."

Beth followed Luz up the floating redwood steps, their edges licked by candlelight. Luz's hips stretched the silk of her Chinese dress. The walls on the second floor were largely intact, though scarred and chipped. A few of Luz's latest paintings lined the hall.

Beth recognized several of the sitters: Karen Norgen, August and Helen Floyd, a few anemic dockhands with ancestral names. They smiled proudly through the artist's frenzied, rage-filled brushstrokes. They had no idea of Luz's intentions for her series: to prove that she owned them, that she had beaten them on their home turf. The last canvas was still wet, a painting of stitched body parts that looked only vaguely human.

Luz led Beth into the bedroom at the end of the hall, where her books blended with her husband's clothes. A painting with the scrawled tourist-map message YOU ARE HERE took up the entire wall across from the bed. Luz sat down on the stool in front of her vanity table. Its circular mirror reflected her irritation.

"He's making mistakes, being careless," she muttered.

Beth stood behind Luz, watching as she pulled the band from her hair. "You mean Nathan?" she asked. "I think he might be on something."

"Oh, he definitely is. On a few doses of MDMA, I'd guess. He doesn't have the restraint it takes to be a druggie." She wiped her face with a cotton pad. "Still, I was hoping he'd have the decorum not to embarrass himself until after dinner, but Nathan freely admits to having *control issues*," Luz said, with air quotes. "He thinks admitting that frees him of any blame. For Nathan, decorum means not vomiting in public. I'm the only one who gets the privilege of witnessing that. His hangovers are what passes as intimacy between us these days. Oh, marriage." She sighed, as if it were a game she was no longer interested in playing.

Luz took a brush from the table and glided it through her hair. She clicked open a gold compact and rubbed her skin in dark powder. "Do you know what his favorite song is? Do you know what I was forced to dance to at our wedding? 'We Built This City.' *We built this city on rock and roll*," Luz sang. "And every time I hear that stupid song I have to stop myself from saying, 'No, dear, you did not build this city. Eighteenth-century immigrants and slaves built this city.' *On rock and roll?* I really think he might believe that."

She shut the compact. "Did Nathan tell you he wants to buy the property next door from that farmer?"

"No, he said Yakov wanted to."

She laughed. "Yes, and that's one speculator he can't outbid. I think he keeps mentioning the mutant animal just to frighten Yakov away. It's probably working too. Would you want Nathan as your nearest neighbor? Anyway, Nathan only wants it because Yakov does. Yesterday he wanted to move out altogether. That's how desire operates. At least two people need to want something in order for it to have any worth." She licked her lips and noticed Beth's stained hands in the mirror. "Ah! You've started painting again. That makes me happy. You've got a lot of talent. When Yakov comes to Gavril's studio tomorrow, you should show him what you're working on. I think of all of us he might appreciate your stuff the most."

"You're lying, but thanks for the compliment."

"I'm not lying. Now, will you braid the back of my hair and tie it up?" Luz held the band to her shoulder for Beth to take.

One's own hair might be the single matter on which a person can be considered an expert. Everyone has the right of connoisseurship on that matter, earned through decades of battle in the bathroom mirror. Beth reluctantly dug her fingers into Luz's thick, bristling roots, trying to cleave three groupings to form a braid. Luz watched her in the mirror as if she were studying her competence.

"Yakov's wife seems nice," Beth said to break the silence.

"You're kidding, right? Poor girl. You can actually tell what she's thinking. *Can I get pregnant before he loses interest and I become ex-wife number three?* It's a fertility race against time." Luz pursed her lips. "What about you? How far along?"

Beth pulled tightly on Luz's hair. Her head whiplashed back, but she didn't flinch. "How long have you known?" Beth asked.

Luz smiled in the mirror. "I've watched two sisters before me get pregnant, and one after. I can spot the early signs a mile off. First it was Jarissa, when she was sixteen. Then Gaddie at fifteen. Then all eyes went to me, waiting for the first symptoms of the Wilson epidemic. I swear my teenage years were defined by my mother's worried stares. *Is it her turn? When's she going to get sick?* Luckily, I was spared. But my younger sister wasn't. Twins her junior year of high school. And it wasn't liquid-gold Dombrovski semen, I'll tell you that. I've got more nieces and nephews in Trenton than I have friends in New York, but I don't have a single brother-in-law. Anyway, I started thinking you might be pregnant on the night of your party." She picked up an eyeliner pencil and leaned toward the mirror, pulling a twist of the braid from Beth's hands. "You keeping it?"

"Yes," Beth said. "I'm going to tell Gavril tonight, if he isn't too drunk. I've been waiting to make sure it's healthy. I know what you think about babies so—"

Luz lifted the pencil from her eyelid. She watched Beth in the mirror and swiveled around. "Who cares what I think? If this is what you want, that's all that matters. Gavril loves you. And he'll be a terrific disciplinarian. I'm just bitter because I spent too many years changing diapers, and I've seen smart, ambitious girls lose their entire futures the moment some crying, shitting bundle arrives. Arrives and never leaves. It's easy for a white man like Nathan to say that the future is the only thing no one's gotten their hands on. When you're a half-Chinese, half-black girl growing up in the projects, the future looks about as warped as the safety mirror in the West Ward elevator. But here's what I've learned. No one regrets having children. Maybe, in the end, children end up delivering you."

Without asking permission, Luz placed her hand on Beth's stomach. She palmed the slight bowl through her dress. "I've forgotten what it feels like," Luz said, her eyes starting to run. "To be alive on this planet. I keep catching my reflection and thinking to myself, *that's you, right here, alive.* But the next moment I have no clue what that revelation means. It's like a tool you have no use for, so you keep putting it back in a drawer and finding it later all over again."

Luz let go, turned back to the mirror, and applied the pencil to her pink, wet lids.

"Maybe you and Nathan will have a child one day." As soon as

Beth said it, she worried that she'd overstepped. Luz had been generous in her kindness—not cruel or sympathetic, but generous. Why not walk gently across the soft carpet of generosity, rather than risk having it pulled out from under her?

"We haven't been sleeping together much. I think I'd need to look elsewhere if I wanted that. Nathan a father? Can you imagine? But sometimes I think Nathan has the right idea: wait until all the old year-rounders out here sell their houses, and then try to raise a proper community of artists in Orient, the kind that doesn't exist in Manhattan anymore. Aren't we always saying that's what we want? Maybe we'd be better taking over Plum. We could raise two-headed cats and scare off the tourists. We *can* be a kind of plague."

Beth tried to fix the braid, but Luz brought her hands to the back of her head and pulled her hair away. Her eyes were still wet. "I'll do it. It'll be easier that way."

Luz yanked the strands and tied them up. She opened a cedar box on the table and took out an earring, a diamond-studded *L*. She worked at fastening the earring, and her eyes smoothed shut, wide *U*'s emphasized by the black makeup, the kind of heavy lids Beth had inadvertently given Mills in her painting, the kind he said might have belonged to the woman who owned an *L* pendant at the Seaview. Beth turned from the mirror, reaching for the wall. She felt dizzy. A figure stood in the doorway, staring at what must have looked like drunken steps.

"Dinner is on," Alvara said quietly. "Everyone is at the table. They wait for you."

On the drive home, Gavril drifted in and out of consciousness, a casualty of the wine at dinner. They drove along Main Road behind Dombrovski's black-windowed SUV, which would have looked less out of place in Saudi Arabia, until it turned off at the Cleaver estate, and Yakov and all of his power and money diminished into red taillights glowing through the trees. Gavril roused himself long enough to ramble on about Nathan's stupidity. "I respect Yakov. His work cultivates the world economy. Iron ore from Denmark to Russia. Microchips from Taiwan to Pakistan. Oil from Ukraine to Caucasus. His money follows the lines of the globe. And Nathan, what does he do but act like an idiot. He makes us all seem unserious, like what we do is the work of children." And from there, loose-jawed, he returned to sleep.

Who had he been walking with at night on the streets of Orient?

She shook him awake in the driveway. "Come to bed tonight," she said. "Are you sober enough to talk?"

"Yes," he mumbled. "I'll just check the studio before Yakov comes tomorrow. You go in." She unlocked the kitchen door.

Even if Gavril was drunk, she would tell him tonight about her pregnancy. She'd watch his reaction, the happiness that invaded his face or the concern or regret he tried to hide. At the end of the hallway, under the slot, the day's mail spilled out like a puddle of postal sewage. She would no longer have to edit out the baby advertisements, the dispatches from the wrong source arriving to betray her. She picked up the mail, two flyers for cribs and an invitation to visit a day care in Southold. She could throw it all out—the garbage bag in the closet with all of those ecstatic, blue-and-pink mailers—before Gavril came in from the studio, and never have to worry about them again.

Beth opened the closet door and shoved her hand between the winter coats. She felt the bag's bulk, a month's worth of mail, and pulled it over the rain boots. It was heavier than she remembered, and when she tugged on the drawstring, the bag fell into the foyer with a clunk that was louder than any paper would make. That's when she saw it through the plastic, mixed in with the flyers—a canister she didn't recognize. A red canister with a square handle and a black screw cap. The kind used to carry gasoline and spill it through a house. Beth dropped the bag and stumbled back, smelling the odor of leftover fuel. In fright, she almost slipped on the baby announcements that poured like kindling into the hall.

. . . .

At midnight, the officers took pictures of the evidence. They used infrared lasers on the gas can and used plastic gloves to zip it into a vinyl bag. Beth and Gavril waited on the living room couch, both with their foreheads in their hands, not speaking, unwilling to look at each other, two victims in an emergency room assessing their separate injuries.

Gavril had hurried into the house at the sounds of her screams. "It fell out of the closet!" she said in shock. "Don't get near it! It could be the murder weapon!" She blocked the hallway as she dialed 911 so that Gavril couldn't see the clutter of baby mail spilling across the floor. She knew he'd see it eventually, and she knew what he would think. She had briefly considered removing the mail but stopped herself: that would be tampering with evidence.

In the minutes between the call and the arrival of the police, Beth told Gavril the good news. She tried to deliver the message with excitement, with a burst of strumming hope, but tears clotted her eyes—for Gavril, for herself, for the potential murder weapon lying in the foyer, all mixed up now, all part of one picture that didn't make sense.

Gavril stared at her horror-struck. "How the hell did it get in there?" he shouted, stepping into the hall. She tried to stop him, tried to bring him back to her with the news. "Gavril, I'm pregnant, didn't you hear me? That's what I wanted to tell you tonight. Remember I wanted to talk to you? Please remember that."

Gavril pushed her aside, clinging to the walls as he crept toward the front door.

"You think that's what killed that family? And it's in our closet?"

"Please don't go near it," she cried.

It was the other evidence lying in the hall that finally got the message of her pregnancy through to him. A month of stashed mail, a secret cache of babies on paper. Gavril returned to the living room holding an advertisement for cribs. "How long have you known?" he asked, his eyes dazed.

"Just a week or two," she lied. "I was going to tell you, but I wanted to be sure it was healthy." The lie went stale in her mouth, a rationalization that sounded like its own form of madness. *I wanted to see if the blaze spread from the floor to the curtains before I phoned the fire department. I wanted to make sure my daughter was missing for three days before I filed a report.*

"Make sure it was healthy?" His voice cracked. "You didn't think it was important to *tell me* right away?"

"I didn't know—" she wheezed. What she didn't know was what she couldn't say. She reached for him, but he sidestepped her.

"This whole time you've been pregnant? All along while I was in my studio, thinking things were going wrong between us?" he sputtered. "And things *were* going wrong. Why wouldn't you tell me? Isn't that what we moved out here for?"

"We just found a gas can in our house that might be a murder weapon," she shouted. "I don't think *when I told you* is important right now. We're going to be parents. It doesn't matter when—" But of course it mattered. There was no way for her to hide the evidence; the police would be picking through it any minute now, establishing a time line. Their questions would provide his answer: weeks and weeks and weeks of lying, of hiding the truth in the hall. "I was scared, okay? I was scared to have it. I wasn't sure, but now I am."

Gavril's face was a piece of warped metal, his expression distorted around the dent of his mouth.

"Gavril, listen to me. We'll have the child and we'll forget that I had any doubts. Aren't you happy about it?"

He rubbed the back of his neck, his head ducking and turning. "Yes, I'm happy about the baby. It is you that I don't know about. All you've been doing is lying to me, and for how long?"

"I wasn't lying," she screamed. "If you had been here and not locked in your studio, I might have been able to tell you what was going on."

He admired the dodge, laughing inaudibly. "So it's my fault now."

"It's not anyone's fault. It's not a fault. I don't know why I didn't tell you. Because you would have forced me to have it, all right? Even if I decided I didn't want to be a mother."

"Forced you? I shouldn't have to force you."

"You're *not* forcing me, because I've decided to keep it. That's what I wanted to tell you tonight." She grabbed her purse and handed him the printout the doctor had given her. "It's three months along," she said pleadingly, watching him study the blurred shape. "It can still be just like we planned."

He looked over at her, as if his wife had been swapped with a stranger. Maybe she had.

"Things are different. We aren't how we used to be in New York. Neither of us is."

"What are you saying?" As bad as things were, no part of her had expected that this would be the end of their marriage, their union that had begun not at the Swiss embassy but at exactly 2:13 P.M. on a microwave clock. She paced between the chairs, around the coffee table, toward the window, and over to the fireplace, a trapped bird looking for a way out. She became a subscriber to the idea that, if she moved around fast enough, the world couldn't catch up.

"I don't know who you've become," he said, so coldly it didn't sound hysterical. What frightened her about it was that it sounded composed. "Something is wrong with you lately. You haven't been right in the head."

So much had been wrong lately. Maybe if Gavril had been less obsessed with his work, or if she'd never given up painting, or if the Muldoons hadn't been killed in a fire, or if a gas canister hadn't been found in her closet, or if Magdalena had never invited her over that afternoon, or if they'd remained in Manhattan—maybe then it would all be different.

Beth stopped moving. She stood completely still, looking at her husband in his suit and un-knotted tie, at his Hawaiian birthmark and tar-stained fingernails, the defeat in him so palpable he could barely close his mouth. "I'm sorry, Gavril. I truly am. But it was my decision. And I made it on my own."

She sat down on the couch. The world could catch her now.

After thirty minutes of sitting, Mike Gilburn carried the plastic bag of mail into the living room. The detective seemed more awake at night, more efficient and clinical. Perhaps he was simply invigorated to have his hands on some actual evidence.

"So neither one of you is responsible for hiding the canister in this bag?"

"I didn't even know that bag existed," Gavril said. "I don't use that closet."

"Beth, when was the last time you opened this bag?"

She struggled to remember. "Yesterday. I remember I put some mail in it yesterday around eleven, just before the funeral, and the canister wasn't there."

"So it was a bag that you used—"

Gavril didn't look at her. He trained his eyes on his lap.

"I used it to sort out mail about babies. I was storing it in the closet. It's just junk mail. I meant to throw it away."

"And it's been in the closet for how long?" Mike dug his hand deep into the bag, pulling out the oldest flyers. Beth focused her eyes straight ahead.

"About three weeks or so," she said. Mike nodded as he examined the dated postal stamp on an advertisement for diapers. "You see, I'm pregnant, but I was irritated that all of this stuff was being delivered to my house. I felt bombarded by stores when I never signed up to be on their mailing lists."

Mike lifted his eyebrow, expressing honest surprise.

"I thought you told me you couldn't have children. When I visited you last week, you said you two were having trouble conceiving."

Gavril rocked back, wrenching at his hair. "Jesus, Beth." The detective steadied him with a raised hand. She noticed a blue *J* tattooed on his palm, a vestige of his ex-wife, Jill. She wondered if

Mike would transfer his allegiance to Gavril—two husbands who had been deserted by their wives.

"It was a misunderstanding," she said. "But I am expecting. I don't see what that has to do with the canister. Yesterday, I was alone upstairs and I heard someone moving around down here. Someone had broken into the house."

Gavril put his fingers to his eyelids. Mike inched forward on the upholstery and dropped the bag on the floor.

"You heard someone break in and you didn't call the police?"

"When I came down to check, no one was here. The front door was open a crack, which I wouldn't have left unlocked. My purse was moved. It was hanging on the knob of the hall closet. And the chairs"—she pointed to the one that the detective was sitting in— "had been rearranged."

"Rearranged?" Mike scratched his beard.

"Yes. Whoever broke in switched them. They moved the furniture around."

"Couldn't your husband have done that?" He glanced at Gavril.

"No. I was in garage working. I'm the one who told Beth not to call police, because I thought she was confused. She hasn't been acting like herself lately. I figured she was mistaken."

Beth clenched her jaw.

"What kind of work do you do in your studio?"

"Art," Gavril said, grasping his forearms defensively. Gavril had been waiting since he'd become a citizen for a chance to fire back at anyone who questioned his personal freedoms. Beth had to admit he was keeping himself under control. She knew he'd love to defy the detective, to refuse to concede information about his own house where he could do as he pleased. He was just waiting for Mike to mock his profession so he could prove himself a man.

"Do you use any gasoline or accelerant in your work?"

"Yes," Gavril said hoarsely. "I use a torch. But it is butane. And that gas can is not mine."

"Mike," Beth interrupted. Gavril darted his eyes at her, surprised to hear her use his first name. "We don't own that canister. The point is, someone broke in. They moved my purse to the closet doorknob. I thought it was just a threat. I didn't realize they planted that canister in our closet, probably hoping I'd come across it."

Mike nodded, as if the scenario she described couldn't be more normal.

"Now why would someone be threatening you?" he asked.

"Because I've been the one saying Magdalena and Jeff were murdered, and I was saying it long before the fire killed the Muldoons." She looked at the detective, hoping he'd remember. "Whoever killed Jeff Trader also stole the jar of keys he kept in his truck. Those keys open the doors to the houses he took care of, including mine. It probably explains how the killer got hold of the keys to the Muldoons' front door."

"It sounds like you've been doing a lot of thinking," Mike said somberly. "And yet your husband says you've been confused lately." Mike's implication stunned her. She thought they were on the same side. He sensed her anger and tried to offset it. "I know we go way back, Beth, but I have to take your stability into account."

"I *have* been confused," she shouted, "because *you haven't been listening to me.* If you think I'm crazy, I'd like to hear what you've come up with. Honestly, have you found any leads? Because clearly someone is trying to scare us. Why else would they choose my house to hide the canister? Why don't you tell me what you think happened?"

Mike didn't appear bothered by her outburst. He dug his notebook out of his shirt pocket and flipped through pages until he came upon a clean one.

"Everyone is impatient for an arrest," he said calmly. "I understand that. And with that ludicrous creature that washed up onshore today, it's no wonder everyone's nerves are frayed. But I can assure you, we've been making headway in the investigation. I promise I'll look into those missing keys. In the meantime, I need to ask who else visited your house since eleven A.M. yesterday."

"No one," she said. "Just my mother. We went to the funeral together." Beth watched as Mike wrote down Gail's name. "But I saw her when she arrived. She didn't have a gas can."

"She didn't get here by car? And she was never left alone downstairs?"

"Yes, but my mother has nothing to do with the Muldoons."

Mike licked his finger and flicked through pages.

"Actually, your mother's name has come up more than once in respect to a local who had an ongoing grudge against the Muldoons. And she wasn't a particular favorite of your neighbor Ms. Kiefer, was she?"

"My mother is not a murderer," she hissed. "And she doesn't live out here anymore. I think it's safe to say she wouldn't try to implicate her own daughter by hiding the gas can in my closet."

"But it's *her* closet, isn't it? She's the owner of this house. It doesn't seem like a stretch to think she might put it there, unaware that you were regularly hiding mail behind her old winter coats."

Beth smirked. And to think Mike had come to her door only a week ago in the guise of friendship asking for her help. Maybe Roe diCorcia was right—once she moved away, she was no longer a local, no longer someone to be trusted.

"Do we even know if that was the gas can used in the fire?" she asked. "Maybe it's unrelated. It's not like it's covered in blood."

"Who else visited you in the last thirty-seven hours?"

"Luz Wilson," she said. She recalled the black gloves Luz wore to the funeral and the *L* of her diamond earring.

Gavril tapped his finger on the coffee table. "Luz was here two days ago. She wasn't here yesterday or today. But that boy was."

"Which boy?" Mike's eyes brightened.

"No," Beth droned. "He didn't have a gas can either. I saw him when he came in. He'd just come from the beach, and he doesn't drive a car, so there's no way he could have hidden it."

"Which boy?" Mike asked again.

Gavril continued tapping. "That foster kid who's staying in the house next to the Muldoons."

"Would you be quiet?" she snapped. Gavril had never liked Mills, but she couldn't believe he would sacrifice the boy to the police just to spite her. Or could Gavril actually believe that he was saving her? After all, he thought Mills was the one poisoning her mind. Whatever his reasoning, she was stung.

"Mills Chevern was in your home?" It worried her that Mike didn't bother to write down his name.

"I asked him to come over so I could paint him. He was doing me a favor. But he didn't have a gas can. He had nothing to do with the fire, and he was never near that closet."

"He could have hidden it outside and taken the opportunity to stash it there when you left the room," Mike said. "Or, like you said, he might have had Jeff's keys."

It suddenly struck Beth: she was betraying her only friend, had betrayed him already. Without meaning to, she had connected him to the fire. She closed her eyes and clutched the fabric of the couch. There was no way to prevent an entire village from blaming the scapegoat it had already selected. All she could do was watch the evidence mount.

"He was with me the day Magdalena died. And I'm guessing he has an alibi for Jeff Trader's death as well."

"Presuming those are related."

"And wasn't he with Paul Benchley when the fire started? He didn't do it, Mike. Although that would make your job easy, wouldn't it? Blame the one kid that everyone out here can afford to lose."

Mike watched her with an expired smile.

"Why do you defend him?" Gavril snarled. "Even before you defend me."

She ignored her husband, leaning over her knees.

"I found that journal I told you about. Jeff Trader was keeping notes on the secrets of the people he worked for. There's more than enough in there to give one of them a motive. I don't think Jeff was above blackmail. And you should know that Bryan Muldoon had a number of affairs, including one with Holly Drake." She was betraying Holly now too, but she was doing it to save Mills. "They used to meet at the Seaview."

Mike hummed. "I'll take that into consideration. You can produce this journal tonight?"

She nodded. "You should also know that Lisa Muldoon wasn't away at college when her family died. I saw her in Orient two weeks before the fire. She's been here the whole time, not up in Buffalo in her dorm room. I think she might have been seeing Adam Pruitt. Have you even bothered to check her alibi?"

Mike crossed his legs. His cheeks blushed at the oversight. Gavril glared at her in disbelief. She hadn't spent the past weeks deliberating whether to have their child. She'd been snooping through the personal affairs of her neighbors. Confusion was no longer an excuse for the distance between them.

"There are a lot of people out here who had a better motive to kill any of these people than a boy who happened to come to Orient to help out a friend. Why aren't you thinking about that? You asked me to help you because you couldn't figure these things out on your own. So there you go. I'm helping you."

"And you?" Mike asked, his patience with her finally breaking. "Did you have a motive? It seems awfully convenient that you've acquired all this evidence against everyone else in town. I worry about a witness who points in every direction except one."

"Are you serious?" she asked, laughing angrily. "Gavril and I were together in bed on the night of the fire." She was lying. They hadn't been together. They'd been sleeping in separate beds, under separate roofs. Beth opened her hand on the cushion for Gavril to hold. He didn't take it.

"That is right," Gavril said. "We were together all night."

"And you, Mr. Catargi? You don't have any reason for ill will toward the Muldoons? Just out of curiosity."

Gavril glanced at Beth, openmouthed, as if she had brought this accuser to sit across from him in their living room.

"You ask me this in my home?" he balked. "I don't know the people out here. I don't want to know them. I am a peaceful citizen, Detective, and I have as much right to be here as you do. You think because you are born here you have a right to ask me who I like and don't like, and call my wife by her first name but me by my second?"

Mike slipped his notebook in his shirt pocket.

"It's late. Thank you for your cooperation. We've detected fingerprints on the canister, so we're hoping we can trace them to their owner. If, as you say, it was the can used at the fire." Mike stood. "We may need to take both of your prints if we don't get a hit in the system. Of course, that's just procedure. And I might have a few follow-up questions on your theories, Beth. In the meantime, I'll take that journal."

Beth went upstairs and retrieved it from her drawer. She handed it to Mike in the foyer, expecting an apology, but he only thanked her in a distant voice, refusing to meet her eyes. He carried it out along with the bag of mail, as if he were doing her the favor of tossing it in the trash.

She locked the front door and returned to the living room. Wind blew across her arms, and she knew that the draft ran from the back door, which had been left open. Gavril had gone out to the garage and had taken the printout of their baby with him. Beth was left alone with her decisions.

CHAPTER 28

The bullet that killed him was manufactured on his birthday. Not his most recent one, but three years before, in an ammunition factory in Sedalia, Missouri. The bullet was one of five thousand .35 Rem round-nosed slugs to roll off the assembly line that day, at the very moment he was racing to celebrate with a twelve-pack of Miller in his arms and his head stinging in the cold from a fresh haircut. The bullet was lead-bellied and dipped in a coat of polished Utah copper. His friends surprised him with a barbecue even though the temperature neared freezing after sunset, and he danced to the radio just to keep his feet from going numb. The bullet was boxed alongside nineteen other duplicate .35 Rem round-nose slugs and plastic-wrapped on a pallet in a bulk shipment of five hundred boxes. He spent the next two days trying to shake his birthday hangover, or maybe it was the side effects of Toby's special burger recipe. As he was between jobs, he decided to wash his car. The sun camouflaged the day's brutal cold, and his hands practically icicled when he went to scrub the hood with soap. He called his girlfriend to warm his hands on her, and the first thing she told him when she came over was that a bird had taken a giant crap on his car. He told her he was going to save up for a Maserati when he got a decent job. The bullet remained in warehouse storage for ten days, before being placed on a flatbed semi headed for an ammunition wholesaler in Chattanooga. It sat in storage for another ten months, in which time he found a job as an assistant manager at a gas station that doubled as a convenience store. As gas prices rose, his salary kept sinking, like the counter on one of the pumps going in reverse, so he padded his income by taking a second job fixing televisions and stereo equipment at a family-run repair shop. He broke up with his girlfriend, and screwed around with a waitress at Dizmo's Tavern, and if it was late he'd stop by his ex-girlfriend's apartment but was careful to leave before breakfast. The bullet was sent in a shipment to a store in Mobile, Alabama, but by the time the pallet arrived, the store had been taken over by a conglomerate that had its own long-contract vendors, and the entire shipment was returned to the wholesaler in Chattanooga. It lingered in the warehouse for another seven months. He couldn't stand his conversations with the old man. That's what it came down to. He liked the work, liked wiring and troubleshooting and watching a machine that did nothing when you pressed its buttons suddenly come alive and accept DVDs after a few jiggers with a screwdriver. But the old man WOULD NOT SHUT UP about finding Jesus. The old man had already found Jesus, but he kept *refinding* him. He saw Jesus everywhere. In the glass of a television set. In the eyes of children who came into the shop with their VCR-despairing parents. And—this was the clincher—in the marble rye of his sandwich. Not a bad man. He gave him a decent Christmas bonus and Thursday afternoons off, but he just couldn't take another word about Jesus. Those were the unemployed, bowls-of-change months, but they were lively, slow-smoking months, and he came alive in the Orient woods and volunteered for the local fire department and helped his neighbors, especially after one of them had hip-replacement surgery and needed to be carried twice a day down and up her steps. When his father died, he buried him, actually asked the gravedigger if he could help shovel the plot. The shipment was reduced in price, slashed as back stock, but the copper prevented rust. In a managerial barter for a cache of semiautomatics, it was traded to a small regional wholesaler in Wheeling, West Virginia, where it sat for another year and a half in a warehouse. He needed money and sold his father's house and three acres to a neighbor, probably for less than it was worth, but it was cash up front, more than he'd ever touched, and he could use the revenue to start his own business. He had a new girlfriend, whom he might decide to stick with. She pissed him off sometimes with her neediness, but that was just the result of letting someone take up space in your brain. The wholesaler divided up the shipment and sent eighty boxes to a gun store in Riverhead, Long Island. The bullet that killed him sat in a locked cabinet for two weeks under the display case. It seemed to him as if the spaces in his life were finally filling with glue. It had been hard, striking out alone, learning the trade and faking what he hadn't yet learned, drumming up clients, and he had to do a few things that he wasn't proud of, to take and make money by suspect means, but that was the price of getting older. It was worth it to pick up a six-pack of Miller Lite and drink with his friends around their basement pool tables. They sharpened their arrows and greased their crossbows and hunted deer in the woods. Still he did wonder about his luck. If he caught himself on a good day, right after a shave or a haircut, he could seduce himself in the bathroom mirror. And only a few times did he look in the mirror and think he might be evil. Seventeen boxes of .35 Rem bullets had been sold before the box containing the bullet was added to the discount rack at the gun store in Riverhead. It remained on the shelf for two days before the box was purchased for $6.99 and driven in the trunk of a car to Orient. He knew he had to wait out the heat just a bit longer and then he'd be set. Just a little while longer, and then the heat would give way to ice, easy gliding. The glue around the pieces of his life was hardening, becoming a solid wall, and he broke other walls by putting bad things in deliberate spots. He made his way to the time and place of his secret meeting. The waves crashed, and when he heard the sound of feet approaching, he stepped from behind an oak tree and said, "What took you so long?" The rifle blocked the face, and he only had time to lift his hands before the blast, like the entire world was hitting turbulence, his throat a cockpit of pilots trying to radio distress, his life two plane wings breaking off and falling into the ocean. The bullet found him and, as it made its way through his chest, the sound brought gulls to scatter, echoing out until they separated and became part of the reverberation in the sky. This is how easily Adam went.

CHAPTER 29

Mills placed seven candles in the cake around the frosted light-house, one candle for each year after forty. He lit the wicks. Seven reedy streams of smoke rose from the cake, and he hurried to the doorway of the dining room, checking to make sure that Paul was still working on his laptop at the table. They hadn't said a word to each other all morning. He flicked the light switch on the wall, heard Paul mutter "What the?" into the darkness, and returned to the counter, gathering the cake in his hands. He walked slowly through the rooms, allowing the glow to jaundice the wood-work and announce his entrance. He started to sing.

Mills rounded the doorway, his eyes temporarily blinded by the conflation of sugar and fire. *Dear Pa-aul* . . . Paul sprung from his chair, standing behind the table, his face eradicated by the bobbing flames, but Mills imagined a smile there, fingers spread against his chest, a wish forming behind his lips, lungs preparing supplemental storage facilities to blow at their full capacity. He set the cake on the table, one of the candles leaning into the lighthouse and pouring wax on its beacon . . . *to you.* Mills put a fist to his mouth and faked a muffled stadium roar.

Paul looked at him, lips worming, his eyes squinting in the light. It wasn't exactly a stellar reaction, the usual *oohing* at the sight of his own name in cursive icing, emphasized by an exclamation point (that mark seemed so unlike Beth, making "Happy birthday Paul" read like a hysterical demand: *you will be happy!*). Paul missed all his cues: the flurried attempt to hug the deliverer, the disbelief that someone actually remembered the date, the admiration in the choice of the lighthouse as a decorative element on the frosting. Perhaps he was distracted by the sound of bulldozers backing up next door, the pulverized hash of metal and wood being consumed by a shovel and disgorged into a Dumpster. The Muldoon house was being demolished. The county team had been at it all morning.

"But—" Paul started. He took off his glasses and wiped them with his shirt.

"Go on," Mills said. "Make a wish and blow them out."

"But what is this?"

What part of *Happy birthday Paul!* was confusing him?

"Uh . . . it's a cake. For your birthday. November 3, 1966. It's chocolate mud."

Paul leaned over his computer to check the date. "Is that today?" he said. "I thought we were still in October." He laughed at his own confusion. Glassware and china clinked from the reverberation of the backhoe scooping up a nest of iron plumbing next door.

"It became November three days ago. I guess you didn't notice because we had no Halloween." The holiday had been canceled after the fire, postponed until a year when it was safe to allow children dressed as monsters to travel to once-familiar doors.

"Oh, God, you're right. But how did you know it was my birthday?" Paul seemed to turn pale over the throbbing candles, as if the frosting spelled out another year of loneliness and occupational frustration to add to all the others in his life.

"I found your birth certificate."

Paul fit his glasses on his nose. "Ah, the junk in the back ratted me out. I haven't celebrated my birthday in so long. It's something I usually avoid and only remember after it's passed. You didn't have to go to all this trouble. Is that a lighthouse?" Paul examined the red-and-white pole rising from the chocolate. His name swirled under it.

Mills nodded. "I wanted to. I wish I could have gotten you a gift—a case of brushes for your landscapes or a frame for the picture of you and your brother. Maybe even one of those brass desk bells for Seaview." Mills whipped a knife from his back pocket. He held it out, its corrugated blade gathering small spikes of birthday fire.

"Patrick," Paul said quietly. "How did you manage to get one with a lighthouse?" He looked up at him worryingly. Mills knew he must be wondering where he'd gotten the money for the cake.

"Beth picked it up for me, in exchange for posing for her yesterday. The lighthouse is perfect, right? Aren't you going to blow?"

"Thank you," he said, blushing. "That was very kind. I really didn't expect it." He held his sweater against his chest as he bent forward. "Christ, how old does this make me?"

"You're forty-seven."

"That might be the saddest number on earth."

Paul took a last gasp of air, his lips contorted, his eyes wide like a deer's on the road, as if the weight of something awful were speeding toward him. Mills suddenly wondered if he'd done the right thing. As a young person he had assumed birthdays to be universally positive occasions. He hadn't taken into account that older men might prefer to close the windows and let them blow by, checking for damage only in their aftermath.

"I'm sorry. I thought it would make you happy."

Paul's mouth fidgeted. He was not a successful liar. Whatever had been bothering him continued its affliction, and the flames remained on their wicks.

"I am happy," he stammered. "It's just . . . I was going to bring something up, but it doesn't seem like the right time anymore, so—"

"What is it? Just tell me." A lump grew in Mills's throat. Paul pulled the blue winter coat off the back of his chair, the one Mills liked to borrow. Paul shoved his hand in its front pocket and withdrew a rolled-up plastic Baggie, which Mills immediately recognized as the pot he'd removed from Tommy's safe. The pebble in his throat swelled to a tennis ball. In his excitement over finding the journal, he'd forgotten to dispose of Tommy's stash. Paul watched his response with dark eyes.

"Paul," he said, begging, "it isn't mine." The same words every human being since the creation of recreational drugs has uttered whenever illegal substances were found in their possession. The ring of implausibility wasn't diminished by the fact that the pot actually wasn't his, and certainly not by the fact that Mills couldn't reveal how he'd acquired it—stealing it from a broken safe at a crime scene. He queasily felt the guilt of Tommy's drug use slide onto him, like a hitchhiker on a road near a state prison.

"I thought I made it clear that no drugs—"

"Please," Mills said, grabbing Paul's hand. It was warm and hairy and capable of shutting the front door on him. "I'm telling the truth. That belonged to Tommy. I never smoked it. I've been clean." His eyes stung. Five minutes ago he'd been singing "Happy Birthday"; now he was pleading not to be ejected from the house. "I gave you my word, and I'm telling you now I didn't break it. Tommy asked me to hold on to it because his mother was snooping around." It was a small lie in service of the truth. "I shouldn't have agreed, but I did because I liked him. But I didn't touch it, and I didn't even remember it was there. You can search my room. I'll take a drug test. Anything."

Paul watched him as he fumbled between the lookalike states of innocence and deception. He breathed out of his nose, forty-seven years old today, never married, no children, no one else to buy him a cake and light it with candles and remind him that someone else was around to keep track of his years.

"I don't do drugs anymore," Mills swore, almost crying now, Mills, who was nineteen, who wasn't afraid of years. He shoved his fist against his heart. "Listen to me. Please. I'm innocent."

In that moment, Mills might have seen what a young man sees in a father, a decision against all evidence to the contrary to trust the kinder possibility. "Okay," Paul said. "All right. If what you say happened that way."

"You believe me, right? I want to hear you say that you do."

But Paul wasn't staring at him anymore, he was looking past him.

Mills turned around. The police detective stood on the front porch, his hand against the glass. Paul leaned over the table and blew out the candles. Then he quickly shoved the Baggie into his coat pocket.

Detective Gilburn rang the doorbell.

"I want you to stay in the kitchen," Paul said. "I'll handle this."

"It's fine," Mills replied, still trying to pacify him. "Beth talked to him. There are other suspects now."

Paul pointed toward the kitchen. Mills grabbed the cake and carried it to the counter. The lighthouse was covered in wax. He heard the detective's voice over the rumble of the house being torn apart.

"Hi, Paul." Gilburn's tone was professional, edged with concern. "We need to talk."

"Of course, Mike, come in." They moved into the living room. Mills slipped into the hallway, remaining in the shadows, watching Gilburn fill an armchair.

"This isn't going to be easy," Gilburn said. Paul nodded. "I've known you for what, thirty years?"

"Just about. Since you were a little boy."

"So let's cut out the niceties and the hurt feelings. I'm on your side here. But there's a problem."

Gilburn opened a briefcase and dealt five photographs across the coffee table. Paul drew one toward him with the tip of his finger.

"What's that, a gas canister?" Paul asked.

"It was found hidden in the hallway closet of Beth Shepherd's house. She claims someone besides her and her husband put it there."

Paul picked up the photo and pinched the rim of his glasses to study it.

"You think it was the canister the arsonist used next door?"

"Could be," Gilburn replied. "Had trace amounts of gasoline inside. And gasoline was the accelerant used on the Muldoons. It would be quite a coincidence if it weren't, don't you think?" He waited for Paul to finish examining the photograph. Paul placed it back on the coffee table. "Do you own, or have you ever owned, a red plastic gas canister matching the one in the picture?"

Paul flinched as he slumped against the back cushion. "Sure. I think I own more than one. I own a lawn mower, as I'm sure everyone in Orient does, and if you own a lawn mower you own a gas can. I own a snowblower too."

"Do you have all of your gas cans in your possession?"

"Now wait a minute, Mike," Paul said, leaning forward. "I don't exactly keep an inventory. I could check my cellar. Come to think of it, Mills and I threw out a red gas canister just like this when we were cleaning out the junk in the back."

Mills noticed the detective's ears reddening.

"You threw one away recently?"

"We put it out on the curb on garbage day along with a pile of trash. About two weeks ago, maybe three. I can't remember."

"Do you remember if the garbage collectors removed it?"

Paul grunted. "Well, I have no reason to believe they didn't. I do remember that there was a red canister out there in the garbage. What happened after we put it on the curb, I can't say."

Gilburn scratched his cheek.

"We found partial fingerprints on the handle and a complete set on the base."

Paul shifted. His eyes rotated under his lenses. Then, abruptly, he said, "Are you here to take our fingerprints? Before you ask for our prints, especially Mills's prints, I'm going to have to call my lawyer."

"Where is that kid, anyway?"

"He's in the backyard. Why?" Mills retreated a foot into the darkness and waited a minute in case the detective turned around for corroboration.

"You know, Paul, I had a hunch those prints were going to belong to him. I would have bet my house in Southold on it. But we have Millford Chevern's prints in the database. He was something of a juvie thief when he was younger. Racked up detention time in Fort Bragg for stealing hubcaps and car radios and pawning them for cash.

He was even accused of a domestic break-in, but they couldn't get the charges to stick. Did you know about his history of petty theft?"

Mills closed his eyes. He resisted ownership of a record that didn't belong to him. Why couldn't the real Mills Chevern have been a simple teenage truant? He could disown Mills Chevern's rap sheet by submitting his fingerprints now and reclaim the sad, clean file of Leonard Thorp. But how would he explain stealing the identity of someone guiltier than himself?

"No, I didn't know that," Paul admitted. "How old was he?"

"I'll give him credit. Seemed to straighten out by the age of fifteen. We don't have a record of him after that. Not a picture or a crime. Not even a driver's license. But we still have his prints."

"And you're saying they match?" Paul wrung his hands and anchored his chin to his thumbs.

Gilburn straightened his neck. He stopped fondling his beard.

"No, Paul. His prints don't match. The fingerprints on the canister are yours."

There was a second of quiet before the information sunk in. In that second the brain submitted to the words, made peace with their syntax, had not yet jumped into the snare trap of their content. To live entirely in that second was to exist sweetly between the tidal wave and the coast. But no one existed in one second.

Paul jolted from his chair, as if raised by a calling. The floorboards rumbled as a heap of house was tossed in the Dumpster.

"You've got to be kidding me." Paul's laugh was artificial, his smile spiked by spit, a smile of agony and disbelief. He arranged his legs wider so he could smack the coffee table with his hand. "That doesn't make any sense," he screamed. "My fingerprints are on the murder weapon. Is that what you're telling me? You think I killed the Muldoons?"

"I'm not saying you killed—"

"Well, of course my fingerprints are on that can. If it belonged to me, they're going to be all over it."

"We had a set of your prints from your drunk-driving accident last June."

Mills knew about the accident—the tree that got in his way on Main Road coming off the causeway, the injury that still caused him to limp at night or when it rained, the medication he'd been prescribed to help with the pain. He even knew from Tommy that the police had been called to the scene. But Mills didn't know that Paul had been drunk. The accident must have happened right after his mother died.

"I hit a tree in a bad swerve after one too many whiskeys. I was only a point above the legal limit. That doesn't make me a criminal. The judge said as much."

"I'm just telling you the facts of the situation. Have you ever been inside the Shepherd home?"

"No. Not for years. Mike, what reason would I have to kill the Muldoons? They were my neighbors for thirty years." His voice was no longer fighting for Mills's innocence. It was fighting more desperately for his own. "Before I say another word, I want to call my lawyer."

"Easy," Gilburn said, touching Paul's knee. "Now, look, I'm in a predicament. I know you didn't do it. There's no reason you would have hidden a gas can with your own fingerprints in the house of a neighbor who could stumble upon it at any time." Paul's throat made a choking sound, as if he'd just inhaled a small bone. "I realize you could have driven that can to the dump or pitched it in the Sound. But I take this information to my superior, well, it doesn't look so cut-and-dried. You lived next door. You were seen involved in a dispute with Pam Muldoon on the front lawn days before the fire."

"I told you what that was about," he rasped.

"Paul, listen. I'm not arresting you. It hasn't come to that."

"*Hasn't come to that*," he repeated. "Anyone could have taken that can from the curb. Someone must have known my prints would be on it. It's my can!"

Gilburn nodded and collected the photographs on the coffee table. He slowly packed them into his briefcase.

"Mills had been visiting the Shepherd house," Gilburn said. "He had access. Am I correct in saying he also had access to the gas can?"

"Mike, I told you. Mills had nothing to do with that fire."

"Does Mills own a pair of gloves?"

Paul fell back on the cushion, flapping his shoulders, a fish trying to survive in an unforgiving element. "Every single person out here has gloves. Mills also owns shoes. You can try to pin this gas can on me, it's my fingerprints, but I'm not about to let you pin it on an innocent kid."

Gilburn waved his hands. "Okay, I get it. Anyone could have taken that can. It was on the curb next to the Muldoon house for anyone in Orient to pick up. But when I show this to my boss, he's going to look at one thing: your fingerprints on a probable murder weapon that originated in this house. I'm going to tell him that's ridiculous. But if it comes to that, since you and Mills both confirm each other's alibis, my boss is going to wonder if you two did it together."

Gilburn was fishing, and Mills prayed that Paul wouldn't bite. But Paul seemed to have aged during the course of the detective's visit, worn out from the labor of defending himself. When Paul glanced out the window, Mills saw a man losing his pleasure in the view of Orient, in the house he'd grown up in, in the street he'd known since he was a child. If word got out that his fingerprints had been found on the gas canister, he'd be the most hated man on the North Fork. Paul dipped his head and waited for another load of metal to hit the Dumpster before speaking again.

"Mills was asleep on this sofa. He was out like a light when I went upstairs to bed. If there's anyone who doesn't have an alibi, it's me. I was awake in my room by myself. You can tell your superior that I'm the one whose whereabouts can't be confirmed. If Beth Shepherd wants to charge me with breaking into her house, she's welcome to do that. But this is nonsense. You've got a murderer on the loose who could have taken that can from my curb at any time, and you're wasting your time on me."

"We've got other leads," Gilburn said.

"Great," Paul whimpered. "So I'm not your only suspect."

Mills stepped from the shadows, hurrying into the living room. Paul smiled hollowly and the detective turned, closing his briefcase as he watched him advance.

"Paul didn't do it," Mills said. The detective stood up, smoothing a nonexistent tie down his chest. He reached out to shake Mills's hand and, when he was rebuffed, clapped him on the shoulder. "Have you talked to Lisa Muldoon and Adam Pruitt?" he asked. "I saw her out here two weeks before the fire. They're a couple."

Paul tried to silence him with a sharp look.

"In fact we're talking to her about that today," Gilburn confided. "Paul, you haven't seen Adam recently, have you? We've been trying to locate him. He's got some explaining to do, and I don't mean about the Muldoons. You heard about that second creature?"

Still dazed, Paul scarcely bothered to shake his head.

"Seems whoever fabricated the first Orient monster got greedy for a second round of panic. It's a crime to induce public panic. If you do see him—" Detective Gilburn retreated to the foyer. Paul got to his feet and watched the detective open the door. "Just to be clear, we ask that neither one of you leaves Orient without checking in with us." He glanced at Mills. "I know you're only a visitor, but if you decide to run off without warning, it wouldn't look so good for your friend here."

Mills nodded. Paul grumbled, ushered Gilburn onto the porch, and shut the door behind him. He set the security alarm, then took a deep breath and rested his forehead on the wall.

"They think we killed them," Mills said.

"They think I killed them," Paul replied. "Me. Tell me you didn't hide that canister at Beth's house?" His eyes were shut, his wet forehead polishing the wood. "Even if you meant it as a precaution, as a way of trying to protect me, tell me you didn't do that?"

It was the second time that morning Mills had been asked to swear his innocence. Paul was the man who had offered him a family, and his acceptance tied him to Paul. There was no longer any chance of a clean escape. They stood on the ground floor like two trees that had broken through the foundation, their branches growing and twisting together within the four walls. Mills might have clouded Paul's reputation by coming here, but he'd ruin him if he left.

"I hit that tree when I was drunk," Paul confessed, barely intelligible. "It was nothing. Just one drink too many and I was worn-out from how sick my mother had been. It was right after the funeral. The judge gave me a slap on the wrist. I'm careful now. For that to come back with my fingerprints . . ."

"I didn't put the can in Beth's house," Mills promised. "Don't worry. They'll catch who did it."

Orient was his home, more now than Modesto. Maybe, in the end, a home is a place where you have no other choice but to stay.

CHAPTER 30

There were reports that she had gone into custody in handcuffs, that she was crying hysterically and screaming for her boyfriend, "Adam, Adam," as the officer cupped her head when placing her in the backseat of the cruiser. There were further reports from those who happened to be driving by the Seaview that she spat in the face of the arresting officer, that she dragged her feet on the gravel until the officer was forced to carry her, that she threatened a lawsuit against the township for false arrest. None of these reports was verified, and even those who spread them in the days that followed were half-certain of their falsehood. It was gossip that twisted and mutated as it dispersed, through the telephones of Holly Drake and Helen Floyd, on the bitter-cold corners near Poquatuck, in the abbreviated syntax of text messages.

But neighbors on Beach Lane could confirm that police had raided Adam Pruitt's bungalow after receiving an anonymous tip about a foul odor, that they dredged his room and confiscated a box of lime green leaflets along with a rifle for which Adam did not have a permit. They checked his answering machine—a total of twenty-seven messages, mostly from increasingly irate Pruitt Securities customers demanding to know why he had missed his scheduled appointments. The police cut the lock on his backyard shed, and the putrid smell of animal carcasses plagued the air, causing one officer to puke in the bushes. Inside the shed they found a blood-soaked table with a handsaw, a scalpel, and absorbable suture thread. In a sealed garbage bin, they uncovered the dissected remains of various mammals, like replacement parts for the herds and swarms that roamed the eastern fields. It all served as evidence against him. The police questioned Luz and Nathan, the owners of the land where the second creature was found. Yes, Adam Pruitt had visited their house for a consultation; yes, he had cased the property including the beach; yes, Luz had woken a few nights before the creature was discovered to the sound of someone moving in the weeds. Luz giddily texted the details of her police interview to Beth, but Beth didn't respond. Instead, she spoke to Mills on the phone.

"Adam created the monsters himself and put them on the beach," she said. "And he relied on that fear to bolster his security business. Make Plum into the ultimate horror, forcing neighbors to pay for a bunch of expensive environmental tests as well as alarms. Fuck, *I* almost considered having Gail's soil and water tested."

"That means he probably killed the Muldoons too," Mills replied. "He got rid of his only competition, Muldoon Security, so he could have a monopoly on the market out here." Mills's voice full of hope, like hands trying to hold tight to a future nearly lost. "Is that what the police are thinking?"

Beth paused. "Maybe—hopefully. I don't know. I guess they'll know when they find him." She glanced out the kitchen window as if expecting to see Adam Pruitt crouching in the reeds, in camouflage fatigues and black face paint. What she saw, instead, was the same pantsuited Pearl Farms agent unlocking Magdalena's front door. "I'm sorry about the gas can. I never thought they'd find Paul's fingerprints on it. Who would want to frame Paul?"

"But now they know about Lisa. And if Adam is the one, they won't look any further. Either of them could have taken the can from the curb on trash day." Mills sounded so optimistic that Beth wondered if her own doubts were the paranoid mathematics of catastrophe, like a New Year's Eve guest who compares the countdown to the doomsday clock.

"I hope so," she said. "Could you come over today and help me lug some furniture over from Magdalena's? It's the pieces she left me in her will."

"Sure," he said. "I feel like I can go outside again. I feel like I'm finally not the one." He paused before he asked his question. "Did you tell Gavril about the baby?"

Gavril was a light in the garage, a faint yellow smudge in the backyard. The Russians had arrived and departed that morning in their SUV, avoiding the house in their passage to and from the studio, the white shine of their faces as cold and guarded as winter metal. Throughout the forty-minute visit, the bodyguards had stood by the pool, smoking. No one had asked to see the two eyes, a mouth, and a forehead she'd left drying on the canvas in her upstairs bedroom. Beth felt, not for the first time, that she was always gestating, always in between, unfinished. She had phoned her gynecologist that morning to schedule a second appointment.

"Gavril and I are having problems."

"I'm sorry," Mills said. "Maybe you just need time together. When they catch Adam, everything will calm down. Do you think they'll find him soon?"

She thought of Jeff Trader warning Magdalena about OHB, about his fear that something horrible might happen to him. And something horrible *had* happened to him. She remembered his body splayed across the beach by the harbor, and Adam driving his truck to the scene, and the shock on his face as he watched Jeff covered by a police blanket.

"I hope so," she replied. All day she had been saying that—*I hope so*—like an automatic reply to anyone who sent her a message.

The police found Adam's truck parked in the ferry lot. The ferry's grainy surveillance video didn't extend to the edge of the lot where the truck was parked, but the tollbooth operator thought she remembered the truck in the corner for at least a day. Adam could have purchased a passenger ticket to Connecticut, or he could have jumped the fence and scurried onto the restricted ferry to Plum, but further surveillance checks didn't pick up anyone matching his description on either boat. Adam Pruitt was a person of interest. But Orient homeowners who had relied on Pruitt Securities to guard their homes were left to wonder whether those alarms provided protection or were as fraudulent as the man they had led through their homes, pointing out their most vulnerable spots.

Gunshots rang out from the diCorcia farm that morning. Roe diCorcia put a bullet in the brain of four of his six Rottweilers, relieving them of the sickness that had left them paralyzed in the frost. He buried them in his backyard field, and it was rumored that Adam Pruitt might have poisoned them, had put toxic chemicals in the wells he was hoping to test. No one dared to drink from their taps, and many wished they had never supported Bryan Muldoon's outrageous campaign to cut Orient off from the safety of the county water main. The green ice on the road glowed with chemical seepage, and children ran across it into their parents' idling minivans: *Hurry, run, get in.* The sound of house beams resetting in the late afternoon could be Adam, breaking in, waiting behind the sour darkness of a door. A flash in the trees could be Adam, who knew the woods better than anyone. Where was Adam Pruitt to confess to the crimes against his neighbors? They saw him in the deer that ran along the road, their eyes marble-red in the winter sunlight; in the hands plucking Pruitt Securities signs from lawns; in the Dumpsters containing the remains of the Muldoon house, carted across the causeway to the dump. Only Lisa Muldoon could provide clues to the whereabouts of her boyfriend. A few of Adam's hunting buddies stepped forward to confirm that Adam and Lisa had been secretly dating. To some, the question wasn't whether Adam Pruitt was guilty, it was whether Lisa had been complicit in the murder of her family. Many residents felt she should sit in a Southold jail cell until she confessed.

Beth's doorbell rang. An insistent knocking followed. It couldn't be Mills; he would have come around back. Perhaps it was Yakov Dombrovski, deciding to take a tour of her studio after all. Beth turned the locks and opened the door to find Karen Norgen standing on the porch, her lantern-shaped face rising in buttery swells, as if her soft, padded cheeks were protection for the sharpness of her eyes. In her hand was a Ziploc bag of brownies, and from her shoulder hung a shopping bag with more.

"Hello," Karen said meekly. She gazed past Beth, as if inspecting the interior for evidence of recent renovations that hadn't been approved by the historical board. She handed Beth the bag of brownies, her smile frozen, as if by a pause button.

"I wanted to apologize," Karen finally said. "I haven't meant to give you the cold shoulder lately." Beth wasn't aware that Karen had been giving her the cold shoulder. "It's just that with everything that's gone on, with those rumors about Magdalena's death you started, and then with news of that awful fight with Pam just before the fire, not to mention the troubles the village has had with your mother over the years . . . well, I guess I was a bit angry at you." Karen glanced at Beth and mistook her baffled expression for understanding. "And the way you've been carrying on with that young man staying at Paul's place. I'm not too proud to say I might have been wrong about him. I was sure he was responsible, as many of us were. I mean, all the trouble started right when he showed up. How were we to know that Adam was behind it all?" Karen peered across the street, as if to make sure Adam Pruitt wasn't standing in the driveway aiming his crossbow at her. She shivered. "Every time I leave my house I'm frightened I'll see him. Why can't the police just find him, so we can all breathe easier?"

Beth nodded. She thought of Jeff's notes on Karen: bitter about the artists moving into Orient, low on money, passed over for a seat on the board. How would those problems be fixed with Adam's arrest?

"Pam was one of my nearest-and-dearests," Karen said. "She was the one woman in Orient who brought everyone together, with her picnics and volunteer work. Without her, we've all been a bit"— she searched for the word—"*estranged*. But I know the best way to pay tribute to Pam is to bring the community back together. So, these brownies." Karen nodded toward the bag. "A small token from me, to try to heal what's kept everyone apart."

Beth mustered the smile that Karen seemed hungry for. "Thank you," she said.

"I've been taking goodies around to all the houses. Everyone's so shaken up. I was just at the Drakes' and, you know, they had a Pruitt alarm installed and they're terrified that Adam knows the pass code."

Beth thought of Holly and how this new worry might distract her from her sorrow in losing Bryan—or in the fact that neither she nor her husband had an alibi for the fire. There was comfort all around in Adam's guilt.

"Your friend was there," Karen said. "Your pretty black friend, talking to Cole."

"Luz?"

Karen smiled. "Oh, it's none of my business."

"Why would she be at Cole's house?"

"I shouldn't say. They were in the den. I shouldn't have been listening." Karen Norgen was a life-form that survived on gossip. To ask Karen not to repeat what she had heard was like asking a dog not to eat. Her resistance lasted all of twenty seconds. "I might have caught the word *divorce*. But you didn't hear that from me." She blushed, enjoying the fleeting warmth it brought her.

"That can't be right," Beth said. She couldn't imagine Luz and Nathan separating. They depended upon each other. They were happy—selfish and impetuous, but happy. They were the kind of couple who saved each other from incalculable pools of self-doubt. Did Gavril save her that way? Having a partner was supposed to offer some kind of assurance that one met the basest criteria of a human being. To completely undress in front of another person was to expose oneself as a creature not so different from the Orient Monster, a thing of patchy hair and yellowing teeth, asking "Do you love me? Can you look at this animal and see something to love?" Beth felt sorry for Karen Norgen. Maybe she was a closeted lesbian, as Tommy had written. She had no one who would pull the shower curtain aside to watch her bathe and not turn away.

"How sad to move out here and buy such a huge house only to find yourself miserable in it," Karen said gloomily. "The real world outside the city will do that. Out here will make you see what you really are. But that isn't why I've come." She wiped her coat, as if she were wiping away a broken marriage. "It's because of Lisa." Karen stared at her, as if expecting the name to induce facial tics. "I know you and that boy told the police you saw her out here in the weeks before the fire."

"How do you know that?"

Karen shrugged. She had her ways. "And you might be right. But that doesn't mean she had anything to do with the fire. I babysat that girl for fifteen years. I was her confirmation sponsor at UCC. Lisa was loyal to her family. She worshipped Bryan and doted on Tommy. She would never do one thing against them." Karen shook her head. "If Adam is to blame, that's one thing. You remember what he was like as a teenager. But not Lisa. It breaks my heart the way some of our neighbors are ganging up on her. She's got nothing to do with what happened to her family." Karen sounded exactly like Beth defending Mills. How deluded Beth must have seemed to Mike Gilburn, insisting on the boy's innocence, as weepily faithful as Karen was to Lisa Muldoon. "She's in a state of grief, and as a community, I think we've got to be on her side."

Karen spoke as if innocence was purely a matter of consensus, and perhaps it was. Over Karen's shoulder came a figure walking down the street: Mills, in jeans and a flannel shirt, once again feeling safe enough to stroll through the village, now that the collective finger was pointing toward Adam. Karen bowed her head when she saw him approach.

"You're Mills," she said, as if she were naming him. He said hello, looking at Beth for guidance on how to handle her. Karen dug through her shopping bag and produced a bag of brownies.

"How is Paul?" Karen asked him, a pink wash of concern on her face. "He must be suffering. He's had such a hard time. First his mother dying and now his neighbors." Karen tightened the bag strap on her shoulder. "I'll never forget the accident." Beth recognized it as one of Karen's signature tactics: drop a scandalous topic into conversation and wait for others to beg her to continue.

"Last June, Paul hit a tree just off Main Road," she went on. "It was about seven at night. You might not remember, Beth, you had just moved back. We were finishing up our outdoor jumble sale for the historical museum. Pam was there, and Ina Jenkins, and Magdalena and maybe Sarakit. At any rate, he was driving his mother's old Plymouth, and it was such a loud guzzler, the kind that rattles when you take it above twenty. I looked up and there it went, east from the causeway, a white dart directly into a tree." Karen closed her eyes to cull the memory. She placed a cautionary finger on Mills's arm. "Now, don't think badly of him. He had been under so much stress with his mother's cancer. Inoperable. Terminal. We all visited her as much as we could. She had dementia. It couldn't have been easy for Paul to take care of her in those last days. He was so good to her, after all those years she treated him like nothing but a workhorse."

"I remember Mrs. Benchley," Beth said quickly, hoping to change the subject.

"What a tyrant around the village she was," Karen rasped. She broke off a bit of brownie from one of the Ziploc bags and helped herself to it, chewing leisurely. "Something switched in her brain when she couldn't save that foster boy they took in when Paul was a kid. It was like she gave up on humanity. But I tell you, the saddest part about Paul's accident wasn't that he was hurt, or that he'd been drinking. It was that he drove right into that tree without braking. Like he almost meant to hit it, like he wanted to crash. There's a difference between swerving into a tree and driving directly into one. In daylight there is. Who knows what his mind was going through? Paul's always been so lonely. I'm glad you're here to keep him company. Will you give him this little bag for me?"

Mills stiffened, not breathing, then released a white pulse of air and nodded.

Karen turned to Beth. "Did you hear the news? I've been asked to fill one of the empty seats on the historical board. I tried to turn it down, but they wouldn't take no for an answer. Magdalena always called me Orient's most dependable lighthouse because I keep watch for everyone." *For* or *on*? Beth thought. "Oh," she moaned. "I'm not sure Orient will ever be the same. Not what it was—not without the Muldoons." She glanced over at her car and eased off of the porch. "Anyway, I just wanted to say that we have to rally around that poor girl, who's lost her entire life. Who can she count on now, if not her neighbors? It could have been any of us, asleep in our beds." It was as if Karen Norgen wanted to think of herself as a potential murder victim, someone important enough to kill.

They watched her climb into her tan Toyota. The muffler exhaled smoke. Beth rested her forehead on Mills's shoulder.

"That's what life is like when you live out here for too long," she said. "Every birth and separation and death becomes prime-time entertainment."

"I'm just glad they're looking for Adam," Mills said. "I was scared that people like her would decide that Paul did it, just because of those prints on the gas can."

"Come on," she said. "I want to catch the real estate agent before she leaves."

Beth rang the cottage bell. The woman in an ecru pantsuit opened the door. She introduced herself as Donna from Pearl Farms, waving them inside with her clipboard. The Kiefer residence had not yet been cleared of Magdalena Kiefer. Her dusty blue furniture still sat in the front room on her blue carpeting; her beige-framed photographs stood watch on the mantel. "It's not on the market," Donna warned them. "I'm just doing my inventory for our property profile. But no harm in your looking."

"I'm actually here to take the grandfather clock and the armoire," Beth said. "Magdalena left them to me. I live next door. Sarakit knows about it. And you can call Cole Drake, who was Ms. Kiefer's lawyer."

Donna glanced at the clipboard, then reached for her cell phone. She watched Mills tour the living room as if he were not a prospective buyer but a prospective thief. "I'm not from Orient, so I don't know Cole Drake," she insisted. "I live in Mattituck. This is highly unusual."

Beth shrugged. "Call Sarakit."

Now Donna was frowning. "Highly unusual," she repeated, taking her phone into the kitchen for privacy. Beth and Mills exchanged smiles. The grandfather clock stood next to the fireplace, a tall, lean mahogany column with scrolling woodwork and a shiny brass face whose spade-shaped hands had frozen at ten-fifteen. Within the face, a painted circular dial stopped midway between a golden ball and a ship crashing through waves, telling the phases of the moon.

Beth had no idea how time worked, not old time, by pulley and anchor. She stood before the clock and stared at its metallic face. "Do I want this in my house?" she asked.

"I think it's cool," Mills said, eating his second Ziploc brownie. He opened the clock's stomach and pushed the pendulum with his finger. It began to tick.

"We'll have to carry it," Beth said.

Donna peered into the room, pointed her finger as if to say *Not so fast*, and disappeared.

Beth swept her fingers across the rosewood armoire. Its doors were scored with nicks and scratches, and it pitched backward when she pressed against the wood, thanks to a missing leg. It was a cheap piece, stained and polished into the appearance of antiquity. Beth couldn't think of a corner in her house that would accommodate such a bulky item, especially when Gail was on a rampage about tossing out all unnecessary household junk.

"Check this out," Mills said. "I found it in the base of the clock." It was a photo of Magdalena and Jeff Trader in the backyard near her beehives, undated but recent. They were squinting through an unusually bright summer afternoon, but their matching white protective gloves were the only element they shared. Even their smiles were incompatible: Magdalena had the friendly, self-satisfied pride of an elderly woman enjoying the fruits of a spring season. Jeff Trader's grin lurked behind a dark mustache and his eyes looked thirsty. Mills traced his finger over Jeff Trader's face.

"He doesn't look that old, really," he said. "His hair isn't even gray."

"I think he dyed it. You must have seen him that day lying on the beach."

"I tried not to look. But I thought he was older. This guy had muscle left. It might have been hard for a woman to tie him up in the harbor."

"It'd be a lot easier if he had been drunk or passed out."

"So it could have been Adam *or* Lisa."

She turned to him. "But don't you remember, after they pulled Jeff from the water, how surprised Adam looked when he saw the body? It didn't look like he was expecting to find a body there."

Mills didn't respond. Beth got the sense that he was determined to hold Adam and Lisa responsible, no matter what. He placed the photograph on the mantel, against a framed shot of Magdalena in her pudgy middle age. She stood next to a squat, pretty young woman that must have been her girlfriend, Molly. A faint lighthouse drifted behind their shoulders, too faded to identify as either Coffeepot or Bug, though Bug Light wasn't rebuilt until 1990, when she was already deep in age. It was not a particularly complimentary photograph, but perhaps Magdalena had found it later, after Molly died, and seen it as a high water mark. Rarely does a photograph look exactly like a person when it's taken. But, by some law of reverse memory, it becomes more and more accurate as the years pass—it becomes you whether it was right or not.

"If only Magdalena had told me exactly what Jeff said to her on his last visit. He stood there—" Beth pointed toward the sunroom and walked through the kitchen—past Donna, still whispering into her phone—and stood in the sunroom door, where Jeff must have stood on his final visit. Magdalena's wicker throne was still wedged in the corner, newspapers stacked by her footstool. The terrarium on her side table was full of dead male bees, curled into balls. Beth closed her eyes, trying to imagine Jeff at the doorway, frightened, possessed of some secret that would spell his own end within a week, too scared even to sit down. What was it that he had learned? "The historical board is up to something, disguising itself as good," he had told her. What was it about OHB that had frightened him? If only Alvara had been there to eavesdrop. If only Beth had pressed Magdalena for clearer answers.

"Sarakit says okay," Donna said, slapping her clipboard on the counter. "You can take the clock and the armoire but nothing else."

Beth spun around. "I just want the clock. You can keep the armoire." Donna nodded happily and pulled a flyer off the corkboard on the kitchen wall. She handed Beth the glossy Pearl Farms flyer. It bore a photo of Donna, "certified residential and acquisition agent," in the top right corner where a stamp would be. Beth stared at the corkboard. Thumbtacked to it was a piece of familiar stationery, with the drawing of an oyster shell in profile under the name LUZ WILSON, and a handwritten note: "*Please call me. I would like to speak with you before you say anything. –L.*"

Luz had been to Magdalena's house. On the night of Gavril's party, she had pretended that she'd never noticed the cottage before. But she *had* been here, and had left Magdalena a note concerning something urgent. When Donna stepped out of the kitchen, Beth pulled the note off the board and stuffed it in her pocket.

Back in the living room, Beth found Mills hugging the clock, his arms around its tower, slow dancing with an ancient, unwilling grandfather. "Some help," he panted. Beth hurried to tip it upright on its base. They each took an end and carried it sideways, the weights and pendulum clanging as they walked. Donna held the front door open for them. As they crossed the driveway, Mills slipped on a pocket of ice, nearly dropping the clock on the concrete. "Fuck," he said laughing. "It's like a coffin." They made it to Gail's back door, scraping the tower against the frame, but finally got it standing in the kitchen. Mills checked the clock on the microwave, moved the hands to 1:37, and swung the pendulum. It still ticked.

Through the window, she saw Gavril standing at the door of the garage. He must have heard them. His hands were smeared in tar, his clothes rumpled from two days without showering or changing. The dial turned, the golden ball setting and the ship rising. The long hand moved toward the shorter one.

"Where are you going to put it?" Mills asked.

"Upstairs," she said. "In the nursery for now." She smiled at him. "Why don't you go up there and wait for me? We still have a few hours of work to do on the painting if you can spare it. But first I need to talk to Gavril."

Gavril was still standing by the garage as she walked outside, his face frozen, full Hawaii, his eyes staring at the ground. A younger Beth Shepherd would have been nervous, fearful that he had come to some decision that didn't include her. But she wasn't nervous. She was walking toward the man who had moved out to Orient to be with her, and she had given Gavril a place to live and work in peace. How lucky they'd been to have this, for as long as it lasted. A younger Beth might have felt a twinge of pity for both of them, the exhausting situation, the shyness of apologies, the silent opportunism that came between every couple when faced with each other's bad choices. She felt only love.

As she drew closer, Gavril stepped into the studio. It was dark inside, with only scant daylight held captive in the window gratings. A few of the tar walls glimmered with bones and glowing, beelike orbs. Several mounds had been wrapped in black bags and bound in orange nylon cords, as if they were packaged for a cargo ship. The plastic improved the tar sculptures, lent them the mystery of hidden bodies. The less you could see them, the more alive they were, wrapped with wonder in their sleek industrial shells. It looked like a house in transit.

"I sold it all to Dombrovski," Gavril said. "Every piece of my Orient landscape. We did the deal today when he visited."

"Why?" she asked. "I thought you wanted to wait until your show. I thought you didn't want to cave to a billionaire."

"It's not my job to say what happens," he said. "It's not my responsibility to refuse the world we live in. And we need the money. I don't want you to ask later why I made us poor on pride."

"That's your decision." She paused. "You didn't do it for me."

"Yes, I did."

His hand scooped around her waist. She hadn't let him touch her in months. The stink of sage drifted from his arms, and she pushed her nose into his neck to gather as much of it as she could. "I'm sorry," he said, like a man responsible for a small unpleasant act in a larger, more brutal conflict. When she pulled back, he pushed his forehead into her breasts, as if fending off a blow.

They twisted down onto the crinkling tarp. Gavril lifted her sweater and kissed her from bra hook to stomach. "Should I not?" Like a kid asking to go on a ride at a carnival, like the kid who thought his parents had taken him to the carnival to keep him from the rides. Or maybe he was worried about hurting the baby. It was just like Gavril to make the wrong request. On his first flight to America, he later told her, he awoke from a nightmare and screamed toward the cockpit *"Slow down!"*

"Mills is in the house," she said but didn't stop his hands as he unsnapped her pant buttons.

"I don't care," he said. "It's been too long." Too long, but not too late. If this were a search-and-rescue mission, Gavril was whirling above her, having found her in the water. Pant legs were stripped off one by one, underwear pulled down to lace her ankles. Gavril unbuckled his belt. She considered asking if they could redeploy to the cot in the corner, where Gavril had been sleeping, but he was already on top of her. "Should I use a condom?"

"A condom? I'm already pregnant."

They should have spoken about their doubts, traded doubt stories, but there were other means of reparation. Her shoulders rocked against the dry, tar-smeared plastic. Gavril made his customary someone-dying-in-the-next-room moans, like an English word he'd lost control of. The walls of the ruined tar house shook, and the industrial, ninety-watt bulbs in the rafters diamonded her eyes, and his weight was making it hard for her to breathe, pregnant woman dead of erotic asphyxiation in her mother's renovated garage, but the lack of oxygen blended with the red of her eyelids, and she came before he did, which admittedly had been one of her complaints about their entire baby-making process, she came in her fingers, which is how she experienced an orgasm, but Gavril followed closely behind, hand squeezing the tarp, sweat dripping from his nose.

"I love you," he said with struggling breaths as he lay next to her. "I'm sorry. I should have tried to understand you like you have understood me."

She didn't tell him that she hadn't understood him, not for the past month, that leaving him alone in the garage had not been an act of understanding but of not wanting to be understood.

"Let's start over from today," he said. "I've decided, if it's a girl we can name her Gail. And if it's a boy we can name him Yakov. Very American names."

She hated both names. A spear of vomit flared up her windpipe, the sickness of pregnancy, the stomach flutter of resolution. She loved him too.

CHAPTER 31

I t was only five-thirty, but night had fully enveloped the house. Distant lights glowed from the water, and when Mills peered out the back window, he heard animal movements in the weeds. It could be Adam out there, somewhere in the blackness with gasoline and matches, preparing to prey upon another Orient home. Until Adam Pruitt was captured, each house was a lamb marooned in a field, the meat of wood and pink insulation more threatening to its occupants for being so easy to consume.

Paul had the radio tuned to classic rock at low volume, but the music was interrupted by weather forecasts tracking a storm front toward Long Island, promising a 90 percent chance of ice and snow. He and Mills hadn't talked about Adam Pruitt, about the rumors that had saved them both from suspicion. The matter of the gas can had been swept aside by the news of Lisa and her boyfriend. Paul did, however, call the Greenport locksmith to have all the house locks changed. "Thank god we have a Muldoon system," was all Paul said on the matter.

With a dish towel draped on his shoulder, Paul puttered through the back rooms, nudging the remaining boxes with his foot. "Let's take the family heirlooms down to the cellar," he said. "And that will be it. We've done a good job on these rooms. Or you have. I'm not sure these rooms have been this empty since the nineteenth century."

"What are you going to do with all this extra space?" Mills asked, straightening a row of novels against the wall. "Decorate? Maybe turn the big room into a library, and the smaller one could have a flat screen. You can hang some of your landscapes around it."

"Have you been trying to make room for a television all along?" Paul laughed. "That might be good. And a mudroom in the back. A place to put the coats." He hesitated, his eyes scanning the torn wallpaper. "We've never talked about money. I need to pay you something for all the work you've put in."

"I don't need any money," Mills said. "You let me stay here. That's enough." The mention of payment suggested that his services were no longer needed, that Paul's feelings about sharing the house had changed in the last few days. Mills had been sleeping in this house since September. He had claimed his own shelf in the refrigerator, his own Polynesian pillow for lounging on the parlor floor. In his mind, there were household anxieties like Thanksgiving to consider. In his mind, his name was practically on the deed.

Paul caught the jumpiness in his voice.

"Hey," he said. "You can stay as long as you want. I meant what I said. But I still want to pay you. Even if you do decide to stay, you're going to need your own money and maybe also a job. How's a thousand for the work you've done?"

"That sounds right," he replied. He watched as Paul shuffled through the room, his injured knee giving him a graceless limp. "What if those detectives come back? What if they pursue that gas can?"

Paul stopped hobbling and looked at him.

"You didn't do it. You didn't do it, so you have nothing to be afraid of. You're not going to be forced out of this house by a piece of circumstantial evidence. And anyway, it's my prints on the damn thing. If they want to accuse someone, I'm the one with no alibi." Paul spoke so confidently that Mills knew he was trying to convince himself. "In a year, this whole matter will be forgotten. They'll catch who did it and it will be over. It's like Bug Light. They never caught the arsonists, but soon everyone forgot about it, the village just accepted it as gone, and the longer it was gone, the more its loss became a part of the scenery. Every so often you just have to wait out the bad patch and keep your eyes on the road ahead."

Mills tried to imagine Paul last June, a yet-unbroken man with five drinks in him, driving straight into a tree after the last member of his family was buried. Maybe that's why Paul was so insistent on making Mills welcome here. He didn't trust himself alone on the roads, returning to an empty house with so little to show for his days but the junk that filled the rooms. Mills had spent enough time in cars to know how the presence of another passenger could keep a lonely driver from plowing into a tree. He often felt that drivers had picked him up simply to prevent the possibility.

Mills lifted a box of photo albums. Paul balanced another box on top of it, one marked FAMILY, filled with grainy VHS tapes, old letters, and his video camera. Paul grabbed the shoe box of flares but returned it to the floor. "We might need these in case of emergency," he said. "If the storm hits as hard as they're predicting, the power lines could snap and we'll need the flares to mark them."

"There's a gun in that shoe box too," Mills said.

Paul kicked its corner with his toe. "Dad's pistol. You didn't find any bullets, did you? I never found them either. I figured they'd be somewhere in these rooms. Just as well. No bullets, no shooting." Mills didn't tell Paul about the single bullet he'd put in with the flares. Suicide prevention by lack of equipment.

Paul turned the backyard light on and guided him down the steps. Mills's muscles quivered with the heaviness of the load. Paul opened the bulkhead doors, and he sunk into the hole, step by step, a man disappearing into the ground. "Just a second while I get the light," he called. Mills had never been down in the cellar. When a narrow light explained the cement steps, he slowly descended. Cobwebs netted his forehead, and a highway of corroded pipes ran across the low ceiling. The cellar was moist and smelled of chlorine. The ball of a dead mouse contributed a sugary odor. Makeshift shelves displayed jars of paints and the spines of magazines. Paul's landscape paintings leaned against the gray brick, several of them half-completed, with white lighthouses leaking into waves. Mills saw a boxy 1980s television by the floor drain. "You *do* have one," he said. "We could have saved a lot of time getting to know each other by watching that thing."

"Just stack those boxes over by the boiler," Paul said, climbing the steps to haul down the remaining cartons. Mills noticed the antique map of Orient taped across the cellar wall. Now that he knew its geography, he could identify the position of familiar properties: Beth's house next to Magdalena's, Adam Pruitt's by Jeff Trader's, the diCorcia farm next to Arthur Cleaver's mansion and the Wilson-Crimp compound. The bird-shaped land flew toward Plum, home to avian diseases, and toward the lone darting stingray of Gardiners Island. Another map, carbon-purple, showcased Paul's architectural model of Bug Light for its reconstruction in 1990. On a metal desk was scattered the hopeful paperwork of the Seaview: sketched drafts of a seaside hotel, bank statements estimating personal liquid assets, a letter from Arthur Cleaver, solicitor, to Eleanor Ogalvy: "All rights to property will be tendered upon completion of sale . . ." Paul was mortgaging all he had to buy his dream. If Adam hadn't emerged as the prime suspect, the news of Paul's prints on the gas can would have rendered that dream meaningless. And if the police should ever return to renew their investigation into Paul, he would lose what he'd worked so hard to find—and five more drinks might bring him into contact with another tree that had grown for a hundred years just to finish the job of killing him.

Paul dropped the boxes, dusting his hands. "You ready to go back up?"

"That drunk-driving accident last summer," Mills said gently. A giant shadow grew along the brick, which took him a second to recognize as his own. Paul's eyes receded behind their lenses. "It wasn't an accident, was it?"

Paul yanked at his lower lip. He inflated his chest to try to keep his breathing even. Paul had never been willing to talk about himself.

He had smoke-screened himself in kindness, taking on the role of father to refuse the far tougher negotiation of friendship. Only the mention of his brother, Patrick, seemed to shake him, but Patrick had been dead for forty years, and Mills had no idea what shook Paul now. They could go on that way, knowing each other without risking anything deeper, but then Mills would always be a guest in this house. A family wasn't forged out of steel. You dig a hole in a person and then you fill it with yourself.

"It's okay," Mills said. "You can tell me." His voice rose into a question.

"I was drinking," Paul said, almost pleadingly, clinging to the official report. Drunk driving was favorable to vehicular suicide. "I had too much, and I was exhausted. Please don't bring this up now."

Mills thought of the bottle of Vicodin on Paul's bedroom bureau and the pain that had been embedded in him long before the crash.

"I saw Karen Norgen at Beth's house today. She said she witnessed the accident. She said she saw you drive into the tree. There wasn't a swerve."

Paul turned halfway to the steps but stopped. It was uncomfortably quiet, an epilogue's dead page space.

"What do you want me to say?" Paul whispered. "That I've been unhappy? I think I've always been unhappy. That I was lonely? Yes, there's that too. That I watched my mother die and realized, at least she had me to hold her hand and watch her go? That's more than I'll have. I guess it hit me the day of the funeral, like hitting a tree. No, hitting a tree is easier, because it brings you to a halt." His fingers reached for his mustache, but even that was gone, and instead he wiped at his lip with such sorrow it was as if he were mourning the loss of its protective covering. "Yes, I hit that tree. It wasn't an accident. And for a long time the worst part was that I walked away from it. I survived it and came back home."

Mills took a step forward. Paul drew his hand up, either to apologize or to stop him from coming closer.

"You still talk about a family, having kids, the hotel . . ."

"That's not the point of kids, is it? To make you happy? I'm forty-seven. I'm not going to have children. I'm not going to get married. I never was. Can we please not continue—"

"But there must have been someone once." After nearly two months, Mills still didn't know if he should say *a woman* or *a man*. But wasn't there always a *someone once* for everyone? It seemed to Mills as inevitable as the flu, that each member of the human species would eventually bear the loss of a *someone once*. Mills might have been asking for his own peace of mind. He wanted to believe that he wouldn't end up as lonely as Paul.

"A long time ago there might have been, a few. One or two I thought I loved." Paul folded his arms over his chest. *One or two*: gender neutral. Was Paul being vague because he was an expert closet case, or out of some misguided respect for Mills's orientation? "But it didn't work out, and the years added up. Look, that accident, that car crash, whatever you want to call it, was a moment of weakness. A deliberate moment of weakness. But I am happier now." Paul's eyes begged Mills for affirmation, the way a patient begs a doctor for positive test results. "I'm happier. I made a decision to live close to my parents to care for them, to pay their bills. That might have prevented me from other things, but I don't regret it. I owed it to them. They couldn't have other children. I was all they had to depend on."

Mills wondered if not becoming attached—to anyone at all, really—was another sacrifice Paul had made for his domineering parents. If they had treated Paul less like a slave and more like a son, he might have had a chance at happiness. Paul was an architect even in his hobbies, painting landscapes that never included a single human figure. To draw a person was to reduce the scene to scale, to ruin its eternal beauty by fixing it to a time and place. Dead landscape paintings filled the cellar, infinite and impotent in bloodless yellows and blues, a headache of sky and sea. One little dot and they might have taken on life. Paul had brought Mills to his house in Orient to be that dot, the smudge on the doorknobs, the dirty feet on the coffee table, the stains on the bedroom rug. Paul needed to come out, not as gay or straight, but as human.

"I suppose it seems like I don't have very much," Paul said. Mills could have answered yes. Instead, he put his arms around Paul. He hugged him just like he had Magdalena's grandfather clock, savagely, full-bodied, almost lifting him off the ground. "Hey, now," Paul said, but he too was hugging, pressing his weight on him, the stench of their breaths mixing, the scratch of cheek stubble, the dry skin of radiator heat in winter, two men of different ages, not father and son, not lovers, just the tight, grappling hug of two people who had found each other in an underground room. "All right, all right," Paul said, but he was squeezing harder than Mills was. "It's time we went upstairs," he said, as if time were of the essence. As if time were Paul's main problem.

Mills let go. Paul's eyes were as glassy as the lenses that covered them. They climbed the steps, shut the bulkhead doors, and traveled in slow, astronautical strides through the empty Benchley back rooms. These could be Mills's rooms too, and he was so fixated on the possibilities of what these rooms could contain that, as he walked down the hallway toward the front of the house, Mills mistook the red strobes revolving through the windows as a string of Christmas lights, a festive, early twinkle of things to come.

But Paul froze in the hallway, recognizing their source.

"The police are in the driveway," he said. "I want you to go upstairs."

Mills listened from the top of the steps as Detective Gilburn and two officers swept through the front door.

"Where is Mills Chevern?" It was Gilburn's voice, impatient, no longer casual, no longer benign. "We need to take him in for questioning."

"On what grounds?" Paul stammered. "Do you have a warrant?"

"We could get one in a minute. We were hoping to make this easy. If he comes in willingly, it won't be considered an arrest."

"Arrest?" Mills heard the anxiety in Paul's voice. "Arrest for what?"

"We need to question him about the burglary and fire of the Muldoon residence."

Paul again spat the most atrocious word back at the detective. "Burglary?"

Mills heard the rustle of a plastic bag. He stayed in the shadows, not daring to step forward on the landing for fear that they might spot him.

"Does this look familiar to you?"

"No."

"And you can verify that it wasn't in your guest's possession when he came to stay with you?"

"Not that I'm aware of. A flask? Mills doesn't drink."

A blinding memory: Tommy's flask, which he'd given freely to Lisa Muldoon. She had held it between gloved fingers and wrapped it carefully into the empty birdseed bag. His knees wobbled, as if his own blood were sinking him.

"Where is he?"

"He's not here right now." Paul's voice strained, and he mumbled unintelligibly, stalling. "He went out about an hour ago. He won't be back until late tonight."

"Lisa Muldoon submitted this to us as evidence. Paul, it's time you stopped protecting this kid and cooperated in our investigation."

"I *have* cooperated."

"Mills Chevern has a history of theft, and when we get the results back from the lab, I'm guessing we'll find his prints on this flask. It belonged to Tommy Muldoon. It was a family heirloom."

There was a pause. Mills heard a chair being dragged across the floor and doors being opened.

"Mike, I have a hard time imagining Mills burning a house down over a flask. And if he stole it, how did Lisa get her hands on it?"

"That's simple. He gave it to her."

"He what?"

"Handed it to her. In her words, like some sort of mocking restitution. And I'm curious what else Mills Chevern has in his possession that belongs to the Muldoons."

Footsteps traveled along the hallway into the kitchen, right below where Mills stood.

"You can't go back there," Paul called. "Can you please tell your men that they aren't allowed back there? This is private property."

"I'm not arresting him if he comes in on his own volition. I just want to ask him why he had this flask days after the fire."

"Maybe Tommy gave it to him. They were friends, you know."

"That's the version he's been telling. Lisa has a different story."

"Mike, hasn't Lisa already proven herself to be an unreliable source? Hasn't she been in Orient all along, not off at college the way she told everyone? *Of course* she'd like to pin the blame on someone else. I don't want to accuse anyone, but if she was here the day her family was killed—"

"She's copped to that."

"I heard you arrested her."

"She came in voluntarily. I was hoping Mills would do the same."

Mills heard the back door open and boots travel down the cement steps. Gilburn guided Paul closer to the staircase. He lowered his voice. "Did you ever actually see Mills hanging out with Tommy? Was there any moment, any occasion, in which you can swear they actually spent time together as friends?"

"No, but I know they were. Mills told me so. And Pam, that argument out front days before the fire, it was about Mills and her son *being* friends."

"Do you know what I think it was about? I think it was about Mills entering the house and room of her son. Did Pam Muldoon ever once say during the conversation that Mills and Tommy were friends?"

"I can't remember, but why else would he be in his room? That's what friends do."

The two officers reentered the house, weaving through the many, vacant back rooms that Mills had diligently cleared.

"Paul, listen. I know you like this kid, but you really need to accept the fact that you have no idea where he comes from or who he even is. To answer your question, according to Lisa, she *was* staying at the Seaview. She wasn't away at college. And her brother came to visit her there. According to Lisa, Tommy Muldoon was very upset about the young man living next door. He was crying when he went to see her. Tommy told her that Mills kept making passes at him—"

"Passes?"

"Yes, passes. And that he found Mills in his room on more than one occasion, going through his stuff."

"That is bullshit. If he was in Tommy's room he was invited."

"Lisa claims that Tommy was scared. He felt threatened, 'creeped out' was her wording—like the kid wasn't right in the head. This was only a week before the fire. And when Lisa spoke to her mother by phone a few days later, she says that Pam also caught the boy in her son's room. Sarakit Herrig verified that Pam was upset about something of just that sort. And now we have an item—a somewhat valuable family artifact—that Mills is known to have had in his possession."

"I think it's important to remember that Mills *gave* that valuable family artifact back to the one surviving Muldoon, who's now trying to use it against him," Paul said sternly.

"Forget the flask," Gilburn roared. "That's not even the sticking point. I'll tell you what is. The gas can. The more I think about your prints on that canister, the more I'm convinced that the one person who had access to that canister was Mills Chevern. You said it yourself—he carried it out to the curb with work gloves. We found a gas canister that came from this house in the only other house in Orient that Mills had access to—the one belonging to his friend Beth. That flask only bolsters what we already know. If Lisa came in to talk to us, why can't he? We just want to ask him about it."

"I'm sure he has an explanation," Paul said hesitantly. "But I think you're giving Lisa a little too much credit. Jesus, can't you hear how convenient that story is, coming from her? It's obvious she's trying to take suspicion off her boyfriend. She'd do anything to save him. Everyone knows that she's been seeing him secretly for months. Why don't you ask her about that? Ask her where Adam was on the night of the fire. And where was she? Ask her why Adam's been scaring the whole village with those monsters on the beach."

The bag again, crumpling, being returned to wherever Gilburn stored his evidence.

"That did occur to me. And don't think for a second I didn't check. Adam had an alibi. He was with a few of his hunting buddies playing pool in a friend's basement. We have multiple witnesses that could have testified to being with him until the moment he took the fire department call. He was in the clear for arson."

"*Was?* Why do you keep using the past tense? Have you found him?"

"Yeah, we found him. Today, with a bullet in his chest. Do you own a rifle?"

"What?" Paul spit the question out undigested. "Dead? You found his body? Adam Pruitt is dead?"

"That's right."

"And Lisa?"

"Out of her mind with grief, as anyone could expect."

Mills knew that with Adam dead, there was only one other suspect. He had been the main suspect all along, and it was only Adam, alive, who had shielded him.

"Clear," one of the officers said.

"I want it on record that I didn't allow your men to search my house. Mills is not on the *run*." Paul screamed the last word. "He will be back in a few hours."

"And I am asking you, as a man who was born in Orient and cares about his community, if we can at least be authorized to search Mills Chevern's possessions for any additional items that might belong to the Muldoons."

"He wouldn't do that," Paul screeched.

"I have a call in to his family in California."

"He doesn't have a family. He was a foster kid."

"Paul, he was adopted at age thirteen. He has a mother and a father and three sisters in Fort Bragg. We're trying to track them down right now."

"That's not accurate," Paul said quietly, as if to himself. "When he gets back, I'll drive him down to the station myself and this can all be sorted out. He is not on the *run*, and there are no items, no other items, that belong to the Muldoons in this house. It was my fingerprints, not his, on that gas can. Maybe it's my fingerprints on the flask. Why don't you just arrest me for conspiring to steal a bunch of valuables from my neighbors, and then—"

Mills shoved himself deep into the shadows. He moved across the runner on the tips of his toes, fearing at each step that a beam might betray him. He had to walk slowly as the confrontation accelerated downstairs, too slowly, a silent swamp of slowness, as the words got louder, quicker, more abrasive. Paul was trying to buy him time before they climbed the steps to his bedroom.

The hallway was black, and a squeak drove through the runner as his toes made contact. He froze. His room was twenty feet away. He held his hands out to feel the contours of a table midway along the hall, the boards around it the loudest under foot. He hopped over the site of blatant impact, nearly tripping as the runner slipped around his shoes. If he jumped out of his window, he might break his legs. As he passed the hall closet, he opened its door, praying for forgiving hinges, and gathered the rope ladder Paul had stowed there in case of a fire. An officer started ascending the steps, but paused when Paul demanded a warrant. In another second, Mills made it to his room and shut the door behind him.

He grabbed his green duffel bag, quickly packing it with his nearest clothes. He threw the strap over his shoulder, then hurried to the window and opened it. A rinse of cold slid over his face. He threw the rope ladder over the ledge and bolstered its weight bar against the frame. He straddled the sill and found the first flaccid rung. He descended quickly, the rope burning his palms, his eyes falling below the window line as he heard loud steps in the upstairs hallway. His knuckles skidded across the clapboard siding of a house that was supposed to be his, the one he had found amid the millions of homes in America, and he was leaving it like a thief because it didn't belong to him. It never had, and now it never would.

The police lights poured through the trees, across the grass, over his arms and shirt, a wash of red waving and receding. He didn't even have a coat to hide the whiteness of his skin. Eight feet from the ground, he jumped and landed on his side. The metal clamp of his duffel bag struck his cheek; his left arm skinned by a branch. He climbed to his feet and yanked on the ladder, all his muscles fighting the weight that secured it, until it fell from the open window. He gathered it up and headed toward the backyard, realizing as he ran that he'd left Tommy's watch and the *L* pendant in the birthing-room bowl, two more pieces of evidence against him. The watch would be identified as Tommy's, and Lisa could claim the pendant as her own. He was leaving Paul Benchley, who had been his only family, who might also take the watch and pendant as proof of his guilt. Except the fingerprints on the flask didn't belong to Mills Chevern of Fort Bragg, California. They belonged to a young man with no record, who had disappeared almost a year ago over state lines and hadn't been heard from since. His fingers were numb, and his breath trailed white. He saw the bulb flicker on in his bedroom, but he rounded the house before the officers could duck their heads out.

He threw pebbles at the light in the second-floor window. After seven launches and three successful taps, a shape appeared in the glass with unkempt hair and a beefy neck. In the seconds it lingered there, the shape became her husband.

Mills didn't want to plead his case to Gavril. That was the reason he'd decided not to ring the doorbell. He wanted Beth. When the shape evaporated, he panicked at the thought of Gavril scurrying down the steps to shoo him off the property or, worse, calling the police. His body was shivering violently.

A shape cut through the pink, a veil of blond hair and slim shoulders. She raised a finger and disappeared. He rushed to the back door to wait for her. Beth turned down the hallway in sweatpants and a moth-holed T-shirt. She fell back as he entered the kitchen, or he pushed her back, his legs and feet covered in mud, his fingers blue and mooned with dirt, his lips quivering so fast they made even simple words hard to formulate: *"Please help me . . . the police . . . the police think I did it."*

Beth shut the curtains in the kitchen. She made tea in the microwave because it was faster than heating a kettle. He spoke and listened at the same time, pausing only for breath or to check for the Doppler of approaching cars. He rested his forehead against his arm on the table; he could almost fall asleep here, he thought, with Beth across from him, knowing she was there to keep a lookout.

"Adam Pruitt murdered?" Beth had gone away in her head when he told her. She went away and came back and went away again while he continued talking, each time interrupting him again the same way: "Adam murdered? Shot?"

"Yes. And he had an alibi for the fire. The reason they couldn't find him this whole time was because he was dead."

"Do you think he died before or after he met Lisa on the beach that day?" she asked. "If she was the last person to see him, maybe she was the one who shot him. We need to tell the police."

"I'm not going to the police," Mills snarled. Beth still seemed to view them as a source of protection. He didn't. "If Lisa wasn't with Adam on the night of the fire, if he was with his friends like the detective said, maybe she did it alone. She'd have keys to her own house. She'd know where to pour the gasoline. But she's already framed me. And who do you think they're going believe?"

"Okay, okay," Beth murmured, pushing her hair back with her palms as she leaned on the table. Her face was soft and rested. She looked older and calmer than he'd ever seen her. It seemed as if some burden had been taken off her in the last hours, just as the worst burden weighed on him.

"And I left that fucking watch and necklace in my bedroom." He slapped his hand down. "She denied it at the time, but now she'll probably say that pendant was hers. And I took my bag, so they'll think I ran off with the rest of the stuff I stole from the Muldoons."

"I was with you when we took that pendant."

"They'll say I planted it there. I doubt Eleanor will admit she ever had it. They'll say anything, make every piece of evidence fit, because they already think I'm guilty. And I *did* take that watch."

"Okay, okay," she said again. He was sick of her *okay, okays*. He didn't want to imagine what was happening at Paul's right now: the house searched, the beds stripped, all the carefully packed boxes being torn apart. Maybe Mills should have run west as soon as he climbed out of the window.

"This is what I'm going to do," he told her. "I'm going to leave as soon as I can. They don't know my real name. You have to promise not to tell them." He stared at her. "Do you promise?"

Beth nodded. "Of course."

"I'll get warm for a few hours and borrow a coat and I'll get to the train station in Greenport. If I get back to New York, I'll be safe. They won't be able to find me there."

She tapped her finger, slowly and repeatedly, like the ticking of the grandfather clock they'd carried up to the nursery together.

"That's not a good idea," Beth said. He wanted to disagree, but he was grateful to have someone else to think with. "If they're looking for you, they know you're likely to run. They've probably already thought of the train station. They'll have cops waiting there." There went his two-hour ride to safety. "They might even have the causeway blocked off in case you try to walk or get out by car." There went the causeway, a thin passage decorated in siren lights.

"And the ferry won't be any safer. They'll have marshals stationed there and surveillance cameras along the dock." It had never occurred to him that he could be so trapped on dry land. He realized just how remote Orient was, hanging by a single thread to the rest of the country, marooned in a prison of water. If only he could jump over the bay or the Sound and reach the land on the other side. He started to envision a structure that could span impossible barriers. Mills was wanted for murder and he had just spent a minute reinventing the boat.

"I've got to get out," he cried. "They'll arrest me. They'll press charges and keep me in jail until they gather more evidence. They probably think I shot Adam Pruitt."

"Where did they find Adam's body?"

"I don't know." He leaned back, gathering air in his throat. "And this house isn't safe either, because they'll know I'd come running to you. They're probably already on their way here."

Beth took his empty cup from the table. She turned on the faucet and looked out the back window. Her left foot, covered in a wool sock, rubbed the back of her calf. The police were hovering like an eagle on mice, darting for him, and Beth had warm wool socks and running water and a dependable heating system, all the comforts he'd just lost. He couldn't even ask to sleep on her floor. Beth sponged the cup, as if to wipe his fingerprints from the handle, his lip prints from the rim. She opened a drawer, took out the photocopies of Jeff Trader's journal, and slapped them on the kitchen table.

"We've overlooked something. I know there's something in here that Magdalena wanted to find. Something that explains the murders. We've got to think it through from the beginning."

Mills knocked the papers away, several pages falling to the floor.

"I don't care about that anymore," he spat. "I don't care who killed any of them. And I don't have time to start from the beginning. It's over for me here. What I need to do is leave."

A car roared up the street, louder as it advanced. They both froze until the sound peaked and diminished into the quiet of a neighbor's driveway.

Beth turned to him. "You can sleep in Gavril's studio," she said. "There's a cot in there, and we'll keep all the lights off and lock it from the outside. If they come, they won't find you. And even if they beam their flashlights into the windows, they won't see anything but walls of tar. You stay there for a day or two until they open the causeway and then I'll drive you into the city. I'll put you in the trunk if I have to. We can cover you."

Without waiting for him to agree, she went upstairs to retrieve the keys from her husband. Mills washed his hands and face at the sink and picked up the papers from the floor. He heard arguing above him: Beth fighting on his behalf, Gavril resisting on his own behalf and hers. Five minutes later she returned, keys in hand.

"Don't worry," she said, touching his neck. "I promise you it will all be okay."

He almost cried at the risk of believing her.

They crossed the lawn, Beth holding a brown quilt and pillows and a pair of her husband's pants. He had the copy of Jeff's journal in his hands. She unlocked the door. His eyes watered from the fumes. Mills reached for the light switch, but Beth caught his wrist. "Don't turn it on," she warned him. She waved her hand at the cold, prehistoric lumps towering up around them, reeking of tar pits. "It looks like a burned house," she said. "Don't be scared when you wake up tomorrow." She spread the quilt over the cot in the corner, plumping the pillows, laying the pants across the bed like a mother on a child's first day of school. She handed him a small bedside flashlight and kissed his forehead as if steadying him with her lips. "Reread the journal, okay? See if there's anything in there that we missed. Humor me. I'm going to lock the door from the outside, so if you need to pee, use one of the empty buckets." She stopped at the door. "We'll figure it out. Trust me and try to get some sleep." He saw the whites of her teeth before she closed the door behind her. Through a jingle of keys, he heard her lock the dead bolt.

Mills sat on the cot and pointed the flashlight along the sweep of tar and plastic. The beam only glimmered against blackness, a wet surface of damaged and bagged remains. It did look like a house, ravaged, burned, sloppily bundled together on its way to a landfill. He was sleeping in the guts of an incinerated shell, built to appear destroyed, a place not even a homeless man would enter. The flashlight glinted against tools, wire cutters, clippers, wrenches, buckets—like the inside of a bomb-maker's lair. A car pulled into the driveway, and Mills switched off the flashlight. He ripped the quilt from the mattress and climbed on the floor under its wire-netted frame, cocooning himself in the fabric until every inch of him was covered.

After ten long minutes, or sixty short minutes, a thousand breaths, he heard feet moving around the perimeter of the garage, the clink of a flashlight lens on the windows, the wobble of the door-knob testing its lock. And then for the next hour everything was silent. He remained under the bed until he forced himself to sleep as if he were holding his own head underwater, trying to drown.

CHAPTER 32

They found Adam Pruitt's body under an upside-down rowboat on the wingtip of Orient Beach State Park, where a crest of beach beat back toward the mainland like a wave crashing into itself. The boat had been abandoned two decades ago on a grass embankment behind a thicket of trees. Moss had infiltrated its slats, a furred algae hide that ran from bow to rudder, and seasons of teenagers had engraved messages in the boat's knotted hull: "Tyler ❤ Bettina," "no future," "TJ –L–TH 4EVR." Beth could remember sitting on its keel as a high school student on summer nights, sometimes with Adam, often with her friend Alison, drinking and smoking and tossing the cans and butts into the black, sloshy liquid of the bay.

Had it not been for George Morgensen, on a late-morning walk, kneeling down to adjust the Velcro strap on his five-pound leg weight and noticing a boot poking from under the stern, Adam Pruitt's body might have gone undiscovered, might have remained there unnoticed until after the next snowfall. When George flipped the boat from its dirt bed, a blue head with motionless eyes stared up at him. A brown fiddler crab crawled out of the mouth, climbing down the mealy chin with the careful footing of an elderly woman descending a garden ladder. George sprinted half a mile to the vacant ranger shack to call 911, stripping off both leg weights along the way. Word of the body began making its way through Orient even before police cars entered the park grounds.

Everyone was sure Adam Pruitt was The Perpetrator: the supplier of the two gruesome Plum monsters, the instigator of the Muldoon fire. It was he who had set the blaze, to extinguish his rival, and had swept in like a hero with his department to quell it. But George was convinced that the syrupy gunshot wound on his chest wasn't self-inflicted. Adam's hands were empty, George told the police through wheezing breaths; his arms were locked at his sides. In a matter of one phone call, one text, one race between connecting lawns, Adam Pruitt was transformed in death from a person of interest to a hero who had bravely doused the Muldoon fire; who was trying to warn his village with those mutant hybrids (Plum *was* on their horizon, a biohazard waiting to happen); who had been murdered just as the others had been murdered, by someone else, someone still among them.

There was no time to mourn Adam, even if they cared to. Many were busy packing suitcases, packing children, calling relatives to ask for the sudden hospitality of their guest bedrooms or sleeper sofas, getting out of the death trap before it snared them too. Others were looking for the instruction booklets to their Pruitt alarm systems, once distrusted, now the only protection they had. A few took time out to honor Lisa—poor Lisa, not an accomplice but a two-time victim.

After the discovery of Adam Pruitt's body, the shift in blame happened fast. By nightfall, police cruisers had assembled in front of the Benchley mansion, looking for a new person of interest. After two hours, neighbors watched as the police took Paul Benchley away; they didn't bring him back until nearly one in the morning. Even with his glasses, Paul seemed to be suffering unbearable eyestrain as he walked toward his house, leaning forward, stumbling up the steps with two officers. The officers lingered inside for another forty minutes, and everyone knew who they were looking for. It was obvious all along who was responsible. After all, the murders had begun only after he arrived. And it was Paul Benchley who had brought him here. Even if Paul had taken him in out of charity, he had ignored the warnings of concerned neighbors like Pam Muldoon and allowed him to stay on.

Many felt Paul Benchley was getting exactly what he deserved.

At eleven-thirty that night, Beth opened her front door to Mike Gilburn. Gavril had gone to bed, shoving pillows over his head, as if sleep could absolve him of any complicity. Gavril wasn't pleased about hiding Mills in his studio, not even for a night. "I don't trust him," he groused. "Maybe he did do it. Maybe he is guilty. If he gets you into one ounce of trouble, I swear I'll kill him myself." Gavril's ethical stand did not prevent him from lying to the police, which he regarded as the right of a free citizen, but nevertheless Beth relied on emotional blackmail to ensure his cooperation. ("You do this for me. You do this or I'll never forgive you," she said, holding her stomach.)

Beth squinted from the doorway at Mike and his two officers, who stood in the lamplight of the porch. "What's wrong? We were in bed."

"I'm sorry to bother you," Mike said mechanically. "We're looking for your friend, Mills. It's urgent. He's not at Paul's house." He stared past her into the hallway. "I thought he might be here."

She placed her arm over her breasts. "No. He helped me move a piece of furniture this morning, but he left in the afternoon and I haven't seen him since. He mentioned meeting some friend in Greenport. Why? Is he in any trouble?"

She studied Mike's expression with a painter's concentration. At the lie about meeting a friend in Greenport, he scratched his beard and glanced at his partners. One of the officers backed up five feet and spoke into his collar radio.

"He's not in trouble, is he?" she asked again.

"You might say that," Mike replied, tilting his chin knowingly, as if he were calling her out on a lie. "Would you mind if we made a brief search of your house? It will take three minutes."

She held onto the door.

"My husband's asleep," she said. Beth worried if she displayed too much resistance their curiosity would heighten and her performance would fall apart. "But I guess you can. You're wasting your time, though. Mills isn't here. I think he had some sort of date."

Mike grunted. He unleashed his two officers, who were quick to find the light switches in the hall. They moved into the living room, leaving her at the door with Mike.

"You must have heard about Adam," he said slowly. Beth shook her head. "Funny, you and Paul seem to be the only two out here who haven't heard. We found his body earlier today. He was shot in the chest. You wouldn't happen to know if your friend had access to a rifle, would you?"

If Mike's job weren't at stake, if his badge weren't riding on locating this feral foster kid, he might have smiled, knowing in advance how she'd answer. She didn't bother to.

"Is that why you're here? You think Mills shot Adam? That's not possible. Mike," she entreated, "you've been on him since the beginning. You've got to start thinking about a different suspect." She wondered if he had even bothered to read Jeff Trader's journal. Why would he, when he had Mills to wave by the ankles?

"I'm examining all leads. Right now we really need to speak with him."

"If I remember correctly, wasn't Lisa Muldoon going to meet Adam Pruitt out on the beach by the lighthouse on the day that second creature was discovered?"

"How did you hear that?" he asked. Beth just looked at him. "Lisa informed us that she did go there to meet Adam, but she says he never showed up. Apparently he told her over the phone that he was meeting someone else just before. It was right near the beach that we found Adam's body, hidden under the old rowboat. It's the kind of hiding spot a nonlocal might use." Mike glared at her. "But you know who was spotted out there on that same afternoon, running away from the park just about the time that Adam was shot? We got a few of Adam's buddies swearing they saw Mills sprinting like a maniac away from the scene. They even tried to stop him to see what the matter was. We have surveillance footage of him running across the ferry entrances. He looked frightened, like he was fleeing something as fast as he could."

Beth's heart sank. There was no more hope of clearing Mills's name. Even if they did find the real killer, he was tainted by so much circumstantial evidence that he'd never be free of suspicion.

The officers came back to the hallway and started climbing the stairs.

"My husband is in bed," she said, but they ignored her.

"Do you know if Mills has a cell phone?" Mike asked her.

"No, I don't. Paul would know. Did you ask him?"

"Yeah, we currently have Paul down at the station. He's been about as helpful as you're being." Now Mike did smile, coffee-toothed, spit-polished. She pictured Mills in the garage, lying on the cot, thirty feet from where they stood, thirty feet from a pair of handcuffs. "If he had a cell phone we could call him."

"Or track him," she said. "Look, I know you think you've found your answer, but—" She heard the unmistakable sound of a camera shutter upstairs. "What are they doing?" Beth turned and ran up the steps, following the clicking sounds. One of the officers was in the nursery, standing in front of the grandfather clock, using his phone to snap photos of the canvas on the easel.

"You can't take pictures," she screamed. "This is my work."

Mike entered the room. He slipped behind the officer and examined the painting, nodding approvingly at her technique, her impressive skills at rendering their suspect, as it were her unwitting debut as a police sketch artist. She snapped her fingers to deflect their eyes.

"This room is off-limits."

"Go on," Gilburn told the officer, holding his phone up to frame the shot.

"He can't do that," she yelled. "You no longer have my permission."

From their bedroom came a shout of raw Romanian, then a cautionary response in English: "*Relax.*" Gavril's feet boomed down the hall.

"We don't have a photo of your friend," Mike explained. "We need your help on this, Beth." Gavril reached the doorway, took one look at his wife trying to block the phone with her hand, and lurched forward. He yanked the officer's arm, and the other cop came up from behind and restrained him. It was a scramble of black leather and blue nylon, a billy club, a gun handle, a can of pepper spray, leg hair, frayed yellow boxers, a T-shirt of holes exposing breakable ribs. Gavril swung around, his fists balling, and Beth was terrified that a single punch would land him in a holding cell, her husband who had done nothing wrong, who had only complied.

"Please, Gavril, don't," she cried. He glanced at her with drained eyes, all of Hawaii folding on his face, as if she had never taken the time to understand where he came from, how much he had been abused as a boy under a regime that treated his family worse than thieves, a family inside cardboard walls that the police could tear apart whenever they felt like it.

"Okay, enough," Mike said. He tapped the officer on the shoulder. "We've got the shot. No damage was done."

"You cannot come into my home and go through our things," Gavril roared, his mouth open like a mixing bowl. "This does not belong to you. It's *ours*." Ownership had never sounded less selfish or more desperate to her. She pulled at Gavril's arm, hugging his muscle and the artery that strained his heart. "This is Beth's private space, not your evidence room. You have no right to come in here without permission. Do you get that?" He marched forward, craning his neck into Mike's personal breathing space, daring him to push back.

"What about the garage in the backyard?" the officer in the doorway asked.

"What garage?" Mike turned to Beth as he stepped away from the hysterical foreigner she had married.

"No. No way you're going in there," Gavril howled. "That is my studio, a sacred space. My work is not part of your searches, understand? Show me a warrant. Get me your superior on the phone. If you enter my studio, I break your face."

"He's not in there," Beth said softly, sounding reasonable only by comparison. "Gavril locks it behind him every night when he's finished working." She wasn't crying for effect, but the tears seemed to produce a level of credibility.

"I hope you find the kid," Gavril grumbled. "He is trouble for my wife. But he is not here, and you have overstepped."

Mike nodded in defeat, worn out by the Shepherd-Catargi theatrics. He told the officers to do a sweep of the backyard. She followed Mike down the steps and held the door open for him as he retreated onto the porch.

"Did you even bother to read that journal I gave you?" she asked as she leaned against the door. "Did it even occur to you that Jeff Trader might have been the first victim—that this whole thing started with something he found out about and was blackmailing someone over to keep secret?"

"Yes, I did read it," Mike said remorsefully. He seemed genuinely sorry for the episode upstairs. "And it has some damning stuff in it. You're right about the Drakes. Neither of them has an alibi for the fire. I checked into it. And Roe diCorcia claims he doesn't own any rifles. We're getting a warrant to dig up the Rottweilers he put down, just to see if the bullets match the one that killed Adam. There are other suspects. I'm just doing my job, Beth, night and day. Following procedure." He sighed out *procedure*, as if uttering the word depleted him. The two officers returned to the front lawn empty-handed, dragging no resistant teenager between them.

"But, Beth, I need to find Mills Chevern. And I say this because we *are* friends, whether you take me for one or not. You're in danger if you think you're protecting him. You don't have all of the facts about that kid. You're risking your life and the life of your child if you continue to shield someone who might be guilty. You think about that. You think about what you're putting at risk." He backed off the porch, blending into the night.

She shut the door and turned off the lights, climbing up the stairs and ducking into the nursery, where her painting of Mills remained wet and unfinished. It had already been destroyed the moment the officer had photographed it. They had turned the work against her, using it against the young man who had sat for her and trusted her to render him fairly. Beth stared at the eyes on the canvas, two brown pits that didn't breathe like he breathed. The painting didn't record much more than his color and shape. It wasn't him at all.

He wasn't himself: that was what Magdalena had said about Jeff on his last visit. Beth remembered standing where Jeff had stood earlier that day in the doorway of the sunroom, how he had warned Magdalena about OHB and his own death, how he had refused when she asked him to sit down, how the old woman's eyes were so ruined with cataracts that she may not have been able to see him clearly. He had come on a Monday, when Alvara was at the grocery store.

Beth wanted to run out to the garage and wake Mills. She wanted to whisper into his ear: *Maybe he wasn't himself because it wasn't him.* Someone could have impersonated Jeff on that final visit, someone who wanted Magdalena to believe OHB was responsible for his death and that the answer to her own murder could be found in what Jeff Trader knew. But she couldn't go to the garage—the police might still be watching—so instead she went back to her bedroom and crawled into bed. Gavril held the blanket open for her.

"They will always blame the easiest target," he whispered sadly. "And the easiest target is who they don't know."

She kissed his fingers. There were three of them in bed together, she, Gavril, and what they had made. One night, last summer, they had produced the possibility of a child.

She woke early to her cell phone ringing. It was the gynecologist's office confirming her appointment for the following morning. She decided she would tell the doctor that she'd been under extreme stress in the last month, but from here on she would try to breathe lighter, move more slowly, and soften the corners of her body into a welcoming host. She went down to the kitchen, and Gavril came to sit with her. Beth was thankful to see no outward change to his studio through the window. She prepared scrambled eggs, two plates for them and one to carry to the garage.

"He has to go," Gavril said after a few minutes, bringing the fork to his tongue. A housefly landed on his knuckle and he shooed it off. "We can't be normal with him in there. We said we're starting over from here. He cannot be part of our future anymore. You have to let him go."

"I know," she said. She would drive him to the city tomorrow before her appointment. "In the trunk of my car, if I have to. Over the ferry to Connecticut, if the police are doing searches on the causeway."

"I'm going for a walk today," Gavril told her. "I can't work in the studio with him sitting there. I'll check if they have the causeway blocked off. If it's open, you could drive him into Manhattan tonight." He collected his remaining eggs with the side of his fork and looked up at her. "We start over, right? We don't think about before?" She nodded. "I will be done with my landscape soon, and then we can decorate the nursery and build a crib. After you finish your painting in there. We'll need to find you a new room for your work."

She didn't tell him that she wouldn't be finishing the painting, that it was already ruined for her. But this was the first time since they'd moved to Orient that Gavril had put her work before his. She thought of the painting in Luz's bedroom, YOU ARE HERE, and the beauty of those simple self-orienting words.

Beth scraped eggs onto a plate and put on her coat. She pulled a piece of paper from the pocket, the crumbled note from Luz asking to speak with Magdalena.

"I'm going to stop by to see Luz today," she told him. Gavril bent down to lace his boots. "Do you want me to tell them you said hello?"

He eyed her warily, tightening the laces. "You should leave them be. I think starting as a family means losing track of them. They are not good for us."

"Why?"

"Just please. Leave them alone."

His reaction surprised her, but she didn't push him to explain. She wanted to breathe lightly, to adjust her body to the second heartbeat. She opened the door and looked back at her husband, crouching over his knees as he tied a double knot. The fly swam around his head, and Gavril snatched for it, reeling back on the chair. "Damn bugs," he growled. "Nowhere is free of them. Listening things."

Beth scanned the road for any patrol car with a view into their yard. Finding only a stray sprinkling of snow, swept by the wind that carried the cold of a heavier system, she crossed the grass and unlocked the door.

At first she thought he had escaped, maybe after he had heard the officers casing the house last night. The cot was stripped of its blanket, with only the empty mattress dented on its springs. But she noticed the brown, body-shaped cocoon under the frame, with the tips of two sneakers jutting from the seams. He looked like one of the homeless who took shelter under subway benches. When she dropped him off in Manhattan tomorrow, she'd withdraw a thousand dollars from her bank account for him, almost the last of her savings from the *Scientific Frontier*. It was enough for him to get back to California, to reclaim Leonard Thorp with no trace of ever having set foot in Orient.

The quilt moved at the sound of her footsteps, jolting up until his blanketed head hit the springs, and he wiped the fabric from his face. He smiled dejectedly, to be waking up here, in a tar house, on the hard terrazzo, exiled from the warmth of Paul Benchley's home after two months of growing accustomed to its comforts. In a year, would he find a job in Modesto? Would he try again to contact his mother? Would he have a boyfriend or a family of his own? A week ago, she might even have been jealous of his directionlessness, the vacuum of his future, no weight on him but his own body. Mills climbed onto the bed, and she placed the plate of eggs on his knees.

"I had a dream I was saving you from a fire," he said as he ate. "I kept pulling you up a stairwell, but you wouldn't move until I solved a math problem, like the kind from high school. If the fire is spreading at twenty feet per minute and we're running up five flights of stairs per minute, will the fire get to the top before we do?"

She laughed as she sat down next to him. "Did we make it? Who won?"

"I don't know. I woke up before I could find out."

She told him about her revelation, that the Jeff Trader who visited Magdalena might not have been Jeff Trader at all. "'*He wasn't himself*,' she said." Mills chewed his eggs hungrily, and she poured him a glass of water in a dirty mug from Gavril's shelf.

"So if it was someone pretending to be Jeff," Mills said, "it had to be a man."

"Could have been a woman. Magdalena was blind at ten feet. It could have been anyone wearing work clothes and a jacket, just a smudge in the doorway from where she sat. And Magdalena said Jeff was slurring. It's not impossible to imitate an old alcoholic. Magdalena didn't exactly have the best hearing, either."

"So all this time, the whole idea about Jeff Trader's journal was worthless?" Mills picked up the photocopied pages and slapped them on the bed.

"Someone still ransacked his place. Maybe for that book. It just means that whoever killed Jeff wanted to plant the idea that it had something to do with OHB. Whoever it was wanted Magdalena to think that's why he died. Maybe Jeff Trader wasn't blackmailing anyone. Maybe he was just nosy and liked collecting secrets." She pressed her palms against her eyes. "I don't know. He must have known something. Magdalena said he'd been acting strangely for the last few months. But if his death wasn't over blackmail, it turns everything around."

"It doesn't change the fact that I've got to get out of here." Mills stared past the sculptures, toward the streams of daylight cutting through the tar mounds. Beth tried to find the beauty in Gavril's destruction, but the only beauty she saw was that his work was paying for their future. When Dombrovski wrote the check, they would have the money to buy the house from Gail and raise their child here.

She wrapped her arm around Mills's shoulders. "Gavril's walking to the causeway to see if the police are doing searches. And when I drive out to the tip I'll check the ferry. We'll get you out. If they didn't find you last night, chances are good you'll make it out of here tomorrow. They probably think you're already gone. New York might not be safe for too long, either. Go west as soon as you can. You were right. They do think you had something to do with Adam." She decided not to tell him about the video of him running away from the scene of the crime.

"Lisa," he muttered. He finished his eggs, closing his eyes as he swallowed. "Thank you," he said. "I'm going to miss what I had out here. And you. I guess I won't see you for a while." Beth stood up, unwilling to say her good-byes. She would miss him too. People, things, the woman in the mirror—they all moved away, left her hands, entered her world and departed. It all seemed horribly fine. "You said you're driving to the tip?" he asked.

She took out the note on Luz's stationery. "I want to ask her about this. I want to know why she went over to Magdalena's house and what she wanted to talk to her about. What was she trying to stop Magdalena from saying?"

Mills bent forward to read the card. "Luz, *buzz, fuzz*." He blinked and stared up at her, his features rearranged. "I once caught her coming out of Paul's house when no one was home. It was before the fire, on the day that Magdalena died. She said she stopped by to ask Paul if he'd sit for a portrait. Maybe she went inside for something else. Maybe it was your friend who took the gas can."

Beth curled the card around her finger. "I'm going to ask her. There's something not right about Luz and Nathan. I can feel it every time they look at me."

"Don't," he said abruptly. "Don't go looking for more trouble. You should let it alone."

"I'll be back in an hour or two. Do you want me to lock the door or leave the keys here?"

"Leave them," he said. She wondered if Mills had already devised a plan of escape, one that didn't include her. She looked at him sadly. "I'll wait for you. Don't worry," he said. "I just don't want to be trapped inside if someone comes to the house. This place is fucking scary, you know that? Orient, I mean. Have you thought about raising your child in the city?"

"Have you met children raised in the city?" Beth walked across the studio, following the tarp edges. "They know everything by age five. They have their periods by age seven. They're divorced by twelve, and all the spark is gone by eighteen. I refuse to punish this child with early adulthood. I still want it to be naïve enough to like me by the time it learns to talk." She realized she was still saying *it*. She stopped at the door. "God, tomorrow I'll know if it's a boy or a girl. Then it's six months hunting for a name so that, one day, my child can ask me, Why did you limit me with a name like David? Cut my options down by calling me Rachel? Names are cages, places for parents to lock their children into for life." Now she sounded like Luz. "People should be allowed to name themselves."

"It's better that someone does it for them. Otherwise they'd just keep renaming themselves, over and over again." He sat on the bed, bundling himself in the blanket. He was just a smile and eyes, brown irises and a gray tooth.

She dropped the keys on the cart by the door.

"See you soon, Leonard," she said.

Beth drove east on Main Road. Her lane was empty, but more cars than usual were threading west, fleeing to the city and away from the storm clouds already darkening the Sound. She expected heavy snow to fall at any moment across her windshield. Pulling up to a traffic light, she saw a police sketch of Mills—not her own, but a real one—taped to a telephone pole: WANTED FOR QUESTIONING. *"If you have any information on this man's whereabouts, please call the Southold Township Police Dept. Anonymity is guaranteed."* The sign might as well have read GUILTY.

The absence of any name on the poster suggested that Mike Gilburn had already discovered that "Mills Chevern" was an alias. Beth was convinced that the police sketch artist had used her painting as the source: the drawing had the same direct, low-chinned stare, and the artist had mistaken a bubble of paint for a bump along the bridge of his nose. The result converted the soft, liquid lines of her work into the aggressive pencil of an unsmiling, grim-eyed composite. On the wanted posters, Mills looked dangerous, wanted only in one way: to be taken down.

Beth sped up the dirt incline toward the Wilson-Crimp house. Two cars were in the driveway. The farmhouse wavered on the bluff, its tarp walls trembling in the wind. The half-dug trenches for Luz's pool were white with frost. Beth climbed the walk. Indoor lights starred through the plastic; she heard a radio in the living room and one side of a conversation. The wind blew an opening in the tarps, and Beth peered through it. She saw Luz ten feet away, in a purple spandex top and yellow sweats, arm stretched over her head, cell phone pinned between her ear and neck.

"Slick, slick," she said into the receiver. The thin bones of her rib cage protruded through shiny synthetic. "I'm proud of you, Ty. You stick up for yourself, and you listen to your mom. Don't give her trouble." Her torso bent toward the valley between her legs, the notches of her spinal column smoothing flat. "Okay, you tell my sister I called. And tell her I sent it in the mail and not to worry. There's enough for you to get your fish. A big bowl, not a small one. And you got to remember to change its water. All right. I love you. Be good." She tossed the phone on the sofa behind her and turned up the radio. *"Today in history, Nazis looted and burned synagogues and Jewish-owned shops in Germany and Austria on the Night of Broken Glass."*

Luz hummed along to the voice-over, rolling her head and arching her shoulders. Beth watched, slightly mesmerized by her beauty, the tight sinew of her body, the gleam of skin under sweat, the jagged border of her upper teeth, and the elongated cup handles of her closed eyes.

"*Today in history, the Soviet Union solidified plans to drop a hydrogen bomb from an airplane over remote Siberia. Today in history, suicide bombers carried out simultaneous attacks on three U.S.-based hotels in Jordan, killing sixty and wounding hundreds. Today in history . . .*"

If Beth's theory was right—that someone had impersonated Jeff Trader on that last visit—the one person who couldn't have posed as an old white man was Luz. When Beth squinted, Luz became a black shape, the color of her skin the one element unhidden by poor vision or distance. A figure moved across the tarp on the opposite side of the house. It raced and melted into a corner, Caucasian green. The sound of footsteps on brick brought Luz to open her eyes. She scanned the room, stopping on Beth's silhouette behind the plastic. "Hello?"

"*Today in history, astronomer Carl Sagan, actor Lou Ferrigno, and singer Nick Lachey were born.*"

"It's me," Beth said. She stepped through the open seam in the plastic and into the house. Luz drew her legs together and turned the radio off.

"The radio was just reminding me that people have been blowing themselves up since the beginning of time. We're not living in a particularly inventive age." Luz offered a smile, then wiped it dry with a towel.

"How's Gavril?" she asked. "He told me he's nearly finished his work for the show. *An installation of suburban regress.* Isn't it curious that it's always the male artists who try to make The Last Painting, The Last Sculpture, the Last Black Fuck-Off-and-Goodbye? Men always want the last word—they want to take the ball and go home. If you look at women artists, even you and me, we're on the side of life. We're the ones pushing humanity a little farther against the darkness." She glanced at Beth's stomach. "How's the baby?" She reached out and clapped her hands, inviting Beth to step forward and let her touch it. Beth stood still.

"I thought about you this morning when I was clearing a spider nest from the ceiling in the upstairs bathroom," Luz continued, oblivious. "For a week there's been a big spitball hanging in the web, and today there were a dozen little spiders climbing all over it, freshly hatched. They scurried so fast when I tried to squash them. And it struck me, standing on the upside-down trash can, that a spider is a spider when it's born. It knows exactly what it needs to do. But a human has zero instincts at birth. All of its instincts come later. Think of all the work you've got ahead to make that thing inside you into an efficient, functioning being. Please make it a good being. We need more of them."

Beth pulled the crumpled card out of her pocket and held it in front of Luz. "What is this?"

Luz's mouth stiffened. She tipped her head to the side. It took effort for her to return Beth's gaze.

"Oh, that," she said coolly. "Well, you know my project. I've been painting all the old-timers out here. I thought your neighbor would make the perfect subject for my series." She glanced in the direction of her phone, as if it were communicating with her telepathically. "She wasn't interested."

"The note seems more urgent than that. It mentions talking to Magdalena before she could say something. Don't lie to me."

Luz rubbed her lips together to quicken her smile. It was the kind of smile of someone stuck, the kind of expression used to blanket desperation, as if nothing terrible could ever strike Luz Wilson as long as she had that smile on her lips.

"I don't care if you believe me or not. I don't owe you an explanation."

"Tell me the truth. Did you go over there? Talk to her? Maybe fight with her? Were you over there on the day she died? Luz, tell me—"

"Oh my God," Luz wailed, slapping her knuckles on the floor. "You're completely crazy."

"You tried to shut her up about something. Was it to stop her from talking about Jeff Trader's death? Tell me what she was going to say."

Luz was panicking, rotating her head, as if searching for a bystander who was listening to this ludicrous accusation. She tried laughing but it didn't seem to help.

"Tell me," Beth demanded. "Were you involved in any way—"

"You're so fucking blind," Luz shouted, covering her ears. "Can you please for once stop trying to play detective and see what's happening in your own fucking life? Can't you see that I've been protecting you?" Beth took a step back; the paper crumpled in her fist. Luz stared at her, her dark face flushing red. "That we've all been protecting you from the truth? Because the truth doesn't matter now. It stopped mattering to me the minute I knew you were going to keep the baby. And it stopped mattering to Gavril the minute he found out you were pregnant. I could have killed him for taking so long to realize. Men are so slow. But I wasn't going to tell him, in case you decided otherwise." Luz's tongue wrestled in her mouth, purple and tea-stained. The tongue seemed to find her mouth no longer inhabitable, caught with such little room amid her teeth to move. "It doesn't matter now. And it doesn't matter what I was going to explain to Magdalena. Because it's over. You and Gavril are going to have a child."

It's the females you have to be careful about. Beth remembered Magdalena warning her about Gavril, that Alvara had seen him in and out of the garage, bringing in friends, "playing around." Alvara must have spotted Luz going into the garage too often. Maybe she noticed the way they spoke, or interacted, or kissed, behind the garage, hidden from the house but not from the windows of the cottage next door. This beautiful woman sitting on the floor below her, with a philosophy for every situation, had been carrying on an affair with her husband, for weeks or months or maybe longer. They'd been meeting at night for walks through Orient when Beth was asleep in their bed. That must have been the cause of the fight on the night of Gavril's party—even drugged-out Nathan had been able to see what was going on. Even Alvara, slipping nervously in and out of the room serving drinks, had known what was happening. Maybe everyone in Orient knew what was happening. Maybe only Beth was blind.

"So that's what's been going on. You and Gavril." Beth was surprised to find that, at the moment of comprehension, she didn't cry. The tears weren't there to wipe away. She'd been so wrapped up in the murders and the baby that she'd missed the plain facts right in front of her, her marriage burning up like paper in her own backyard. "You were hoping to speak to Magdalena before she could tell me the truth."

Luz took a controlled breath, neither confirming nor denying. On the coffee table, a glass Murano orchid sat on top of the Oysterponds Inn sign. On Luz's feet were black leather slippers handsewn by Italian cobblers. Marble tiles were stacked in a corner, to be installed or returned to their manufacturer upon her whim. The beauty in the room was not fragile. It would survive the lives that rotted around it. It would gain value by biding its time, awaiting new hands for future appraisal. Luz had built such a gorgeous life with her taste and Nathan's money. And yet she'd been willing to risk it all for Gavril, and Gavril had been willing to do the same— risk their life, their house, every part of them except the child. Her anger at Gavril was nuclear, an admixture of love and love erased.

"You were going to get a divorce from Nathan. And you assumed Gavril would divorce me. All of it, so the two of you could be together. Just like that."

Luz balked, tamping back the arrogance that had fueled her entire career.

"I was never going to divorce Nathan. That was never my plan. I love Nathan deeply. And I like it out here. I like what we've found in this place."

"But you went to Cole Drake to ask about a divorce."

Luz shook her head. "No. I was asking him about divorce, but not on my behalf." It was a punch from which Beth took a minute to recover. So Gavril had been considering a split. In his peculiar brand of morality, he felt obliged to end their marriage whether or not he could have Luz. "It was simply to determine who had rights to an artwork made on a property the artist didn't own. But that was weeks ago. You have to know, I went back yesterday and told Cole to forget the whole matter. I didn't want you hearing about it because it doesn't *apply* anymore. Gavril loves you. He wants to make it work."

Luz reached up toward Beth again, not to fondle her stomach but to take her hands. It was as if Luz were trying to catch her. "Beth, it happens. People fall in and out, and they make mistakes. It was an intellectual relationship far more than it was ever sexual." Luz must have thought she would find that distinction comforting. "Don't be a romantic martyr," she hissed. "Don't live by some ossified code of husband and wife from the broom closet of the last century. You don't marry a person just so you can hang a 'no trespassing' sign around their neck. We're artists, not Puritans. We're free. And we've all been protecting you from the truth, like you were a little girl who couldn't handle what real adults actually look like." Luz's eyes glistened, and she battled to keep them open under the weight of the water. "We've earned the right to live however we want. And it doesn't matter anymore, because you're going to have the baby. And one day you're going to forgive me. One day you might even thank me for showing you the truth."

Luz looked ugly when she cried, her face knotted, her eyes bulging, a moment of gracelessness from someone so unpracticed in remorse. She buried her face in the sofa cushion. The tarps bellowed all around them, rattled by sea squalls. "I don't care if you think your life is ruined. You can think whatever the fuck you want. I just don't want to mess up the future for your kid."

Beth turned around, without ever once touching Luz Wilson,

and let herself out through the seam in the plastic. She walked along the concrete path toward the driveway—amazing in such moments that she still respected the twisting path of the walkway—and found Nathan leaning against her car. He wore dirty work clothes and a beaten-up brown leather jacket. He nodded at her as she approached.

"Well," he said in a slurred baritone, freshly stoned. "I guess that makes us the two fools."

"I hope you'll be happy with her," she said as she bypassed him and circled around her car. She felt sorry for Nathan, sorrier for him than she did for herself. Nathan would stay with his wife no matter how many times she changed the rules of their supposed freedom. He would have to play along with her constant shifts until he found himself the last barrier in Luz Wilson's campaign to conquer all restrictions. Until that time, they could hide behind their money and taste. They could disappear into their accomplishments, and drift into Manhattan whenever they were bored of Orient or each other. Beth was certain they would see themselves as happy, and maybe they were. They could break whatever they wanted.

"You know, I blamed you at first," Nathan said, tapping his fingers on the roof of the car. "But then I decided: it's Orient's fault. All this phony peace and quiet, like it can never quite wake itself up. Of course they came together here. They set the trap so they could be caught in it."

"It wasn't your idea to get a house out here, was it?" she said over the roof.

He shook his head. "No, it was Luz's. But I've come to love Orient. No one knows what to do with our kind. But maybe we can wake them up. Maybe we can only make things really new and upsetting if we have a place that still resists us, a place that hasn't already been touched."

"Good luck with that," she said. She opened her door, then paused. "But, Nathan, don't you want anything more?"

"I love her," he swore, stepping back. "She's the only one who's ever called me out on my bullshit. She's the only person who can be honest. That's important, isn't it?"

She drove west on Main Road, passing the neighborhood of her childhood, the brick red slab of her high school and the entrances to summer swimming coves, the cemetery that held her father, the war obelisk, and the church. She kept her arm over her stomach like a second seat belt, driving below the speed limit, with all of Orient pitching and lurching around her wheels. This morning she and Gavril had promised to make a fresh start, the past behind them, the future expanding, a baby waiting on the other side of winter. She loved Gavril, and she forgave him—forgave him his betrayal, forgave him the doubts and uncertainties that had led him to Luz. She loved him for coming out here and for persevering for as long as he could. In his notebook he had written, "Pretend to live the ultimate suburban American dream with wife and child." She loved Gavril for thinking he could live that charade. She would ask for a divorce and not take a single cent from the sale of his work. She would leave tonight, with Mills hidden in the trunk, and then after she'd driven him to the city she would return to the North Fork and stay with her mother in Southold for as long as it took Gavril to realize that she wasn't coming back to him. And when she did come home, maybe by then the locks would be changed. The baby would arrive in April, and she'd let Gavril be the father, on weekends or whenever he was willing to make the drive from the city to Orient.

She parked in her driveway and entered the kitchen, calling for Gavril, thankful to get no response. She climbed the steps to the second floor and pulled a suitcase from the closet. From the window, she saw the garage door, still closed, a single light just visible inside, Mills waiting, with no sign of the police nearby. She packed the bag, watching herself fold clothes in the full-length mirror. The action seemed natural, inevitable, a daily chore to get through, her only incentive being the second after this one, and the second beyond that, and all the other seconds that swum around her like dust in a room.

She heard a car pull in from the street. It was probably Gail—another untimely visit. It was only a minor complication. She wouldn't inform Gail of her pregnancy until she was back at the condo, and surely the news of a grandchild would be enough to convince her not to sell the house. Could Beth afford to buy it from her? She reconsidered taking some of the Russian oligarch's money. Maybe that was the final value of her husband's art: it would provide the security to keep this house in her family for another generation.

She thought she heard the front door open downstairs, but Gail's shoes were still crunching on the gravel. She dropped a shirt in the suitcase. The beam on the second floor squeaked. "Hello?" she called. "Gavril? Mom?" The legs of the easel skidded in the nursery. Beth walked into the hallway. "Mom?" Her foot hit the same squeak in the hall, and when she crossed into the nursery, she was blinded by the glare of the clock's tin face. The painting of Mills had fallen on the floor, and as she moved to pick it up, she caught something out of the corner of her eye, a blurred shape springing toward her. Beth lunged toward the hallway, her hands grabbing the doorframe. An arm swept across her chest, yanking her back into the nursery. She clung to the doorway, her fingers slipping on the wood, until her heart took over, rising up her throat, and she managed to say, "*No, stop, please*" before a voice whispered into her ear, "I'm sorry," and the effort of her heart was released as a knife cut across her throat.

CHAPTER 33

He first saw her on a *vaporetto* in Venice. He was standing on the cobblestones in front of the Accademia as a boat crammed with tourists lurched toward the dock. The afternoon sun was streaming off the water, lightening the hair of passengers until they looked like candles on a wobbly cake. All except for one: a young black woman with iron-straight hair, wearing a black fitted suit. It was the year of the black fitted suit, *le smoking*, but he didn't know that. He had hardly been out of Bucharest before, and at the age of twenty-six, this trip seven hundred miles from home counted as acute international travel. He lost sight of her among the tourists fighting for a foothold on the waterbus, but her face remained with him; she reminded him of the sour, stone-faced Madonnas in the Titians and Tintorettos. He reminded himself of Leonardo's *Vitruvian Man*, a stockier and hairier rendition, but his legs and arms stretching into wide circles.

He saw her again two nights later, leaving a party on a former army-barrack island. The black suit had become her uniform, and her hair was tied back in a bun. Mousse sparkled like snow at her temples. She was worm-limb drunk on the free wine that glowed amid the candles at the bar. That was when he first heard her voice, American, screaming like plucked piano wire as she climbed into a water taxi. Before that, she could have been from anywhere. It was unlikely he'd ever see her again. The art world had brought so many beautiful women to Venice that week, exotic birds collecting on the bridges and squares, stirred easily when he ran across them.

He was in Venice to work at the Biennale, assisting an artist whom no one in his home country respected but who had been chosen to represent Romania with a suite of portraits of Communist leaders made from candy-bar wrappers. The Romanian Pavilion was not so much a pavilion as a two-floor brick hut that shared a wall with a youth hostel run by wrathful hippies. Worse, it was located in Giudecca, a forty-minute boat ride from the art world epicenter. Few bothered to visit. Gavril stacked the brochures on the welcome desk and waited. "After decades of a conciliatory transition toward an 'enlightened' western democracy, the neoliberal paradigm has sprouted an agitated counter-paradigm in Eastern European art that questions the very legitimacy of the project of modernity . . ." He refused to read on, embarrassed by the language of art. When tourists stepped in the doorway to ask where they could catch a boat to the glassblowers in Murano, he deflected his eyes.

On the last day of the show, fifteen minutes before he locked the door, a woman in a black suit entered and took a brochure. "I've seen you before," she said as she squinted at him. She introduced herself as Luz Wilson and fanned herself with the press release. He asked in his best English, "Why have you come?"

"Oh, I never go to the big countries. A bunch of token names who show their better, less pretentious stuff in the galleries in Chelsea." Realizing she was speaking to a humble desk-sitter representing Eastern Europe, she clarified. "New York. That's where I live."

He should have guessed. Her perfume smelled expensive, like New York. She paced languidly through the exhibit, returned to the desk after four minutes, and shrugged. "We have better artists," he swore. "But this is for rich collectors and reporters with no knowledge of the history of my country." She asked if he was an artist. "Yes," he said, but because of the garish litter portraits he didn't mention his own work, the pile of smashed beer-bottle glass he was sweeping into lines and stars.

"I paint," she volunteered. "I was in a few group shows in the spring. Fuck if I know if I'll be painting the next time you see me. The whole thing's got little to do with talent. Sometimes, when collectors want to buy a work, I think they just want to take a picture of me looking desperate to show to their friends. Do you ever come to New York?"

"Sometimes," he lied. "I want to. Soon."

She wrote her number down on the press release. "If you ever get there, call me. I'll show you around." And then Luz Wilson walked out into Giudecca and presumably onto a plane.

He returned to Bucharest, where the cobblestones lacked the golden thread of Italian light. He worked days doing construction on a new block of condominiums. The materials were cheap and black market shoddy and he mixed concrete with sawdust. At night he returned to his tiny apartment off fountain-laced Alexandru Ioan Cuza Park to work on his art in his bedroom. He covered his mattress with a tarp and often fell asleep on the plastic the same way his mother sat for hours on her plastic-wrapped sofa, never once stripping it off for company. He continued his bottle-glass experiments and created abstract sculptures out of metal sheets he stole from the construction site. He showed his glass-bottle lines in small illegal galleries that never sold anything and closed permanently when the electricity was shut off.

That first taste of the art world in Venice had disgusted him. It made him feel complicit in a carnival of fast, expensive merchandise purchased by men who parked their yachts off San Marco like great white whales of pleasure and crude. But he kept the image of the black American girl in his heart the way a drunk keeps a picture of a lost woman in his coat pocket. He thought of her when he fucked his girlfriend on his tarp-covered bed, or when she whined about her job selling ornate wooden clocks at the train station. He dreamed of the black-suited American visiting his first show in New York. It was time for Gavril to up the ante.

One rainy day in April, he hid a crowbar in his jacket and went to

Ceaușescu's House, or the Palace of Parliament as it was known to the rest of the world. When one of the magenta-blazered guards fell asleep on his stool, his mouth a cave of metal deposits and echoes, Gavril popped ten tiles from the mosaic marble floor and loaded them in his pockets. Three weeks later, before a young, inebriated crowd in an abandoned shipment station on the east side of the city, he held his first serious show, smashing the tiles with a sledgehammer and leaving the pulverized marble to collect like stardust on the cement floor.

A reporter from the *Bucharest Herald* wrote an article on the performance, attacking him with typically misplaced nationalist outrage at his vandalism of the palace. The story ran on the back page of the Tuesday paper. Gavril waited to be arrested, waited for the security brigade to break through his walls, behind which he had always imagined them lurking. He was stunned when they failed to appear. Perhaps the surest sign of change in his country was its careless tolerance of petty crimes. Instead of an arrest, he was rewarded with a call from a gallerist in London whose Romanian husband had shown her the article over breakfast. "I love it, I bloody love it," Laura Lucas yelled into the phone, her English so crisp she sounded as if she were having a series of small strokes. "I have a tiny upstairs space for emerging talent. I want you to do the same thing here. We'll call it 'Unquiet on the Eastern Front.'"

London was colder than Bucharest, the faces on the street angrier with less cause. But the interiors were warmer, and the gallerist, a stringy woman high on forty years of an undiagnosed eating disorder, introduced him to artists so celebrated even he recognized their names. He was given a drab, elevator-size room in an East End hotel, but the bed was soft and the room was warm, and from there he wandered around the rolling parks and side streets, fully international, starving but too poor to buy himself lunch. He waited to eat at Laura Lucas's never-ending strategic dinners, her thin arm on the back of his chair, introducing him as her latest "find." When a culture magazine asked to take his picture, he refused. He had witnessed artists in Venice posing for fashion photographers, sucking in their cheeks, channeling their favorite film star, smiling like some misbehaving monkey about to be given an orange, and he swore he'd never play that pathetic game.

Laura Lucas went ballistic. "What you need is exposure!" she screamed. "Exposure is what's going to keep that work from being forgotten in a week." She said the word *exposure* as if it were a virus that would kill him if he didn't contract it. "Do you want to go back to Bucharest and stir cement for the rest of your life? Will you *please* just trust me? I had to call in a favor for that profile." He finally had his picture taken in a headache-lit studio in Islington, where a tipsy woman with silver-plated eyelids handed him a sport coat that happened to be hanging on a clothing rack. Later, reading the magazine caption, he discovered the black sport coat was Givenchy, Spring/ Summer 2006. A journalist conducted an interview by phone, *uh-huh*ing through his explanation of Ceaușescu's slave nation and his fascist desire to build a palatial, first-world empire on the backs of its citizens, and Gavril's own attempts at finding meaning in the fractured remains of that regime. Under his picture—with his birthmark Photoshopped out—ran the title "Dracula Rising," and, in smaller type, "Hot, up-and-coming Romanian artist bites the hand that beat him." The article told a story that must have been spoonfed by Laura herself: "In an art market whizzing with million-dollar surfaces, one rogue artist is literally smashing his way into the gallery scene. Gavril Catargi claims he is 'making gestures of reparation,' but his seriously destructive tendencies are catching all who sift through his rubble. . . ." He was disgusted, enraged, and correctly quoted. Yet he hoped the magazine would find its way into the hands of Luz Wilson in America. The smashed tiles sold for eight thousand pounds to a collector in Geneva. Laura Lucas gave him four thousand, more than he had ever made in his life.

In Bucharest, there were no further shows, no offers of photographs. Most of his friends drifted away from him after hearing of his success in London, as if he had indeed come down with a case of exposure. He couldn't go back to construction. His girlfriend moved to Constanta to work as a nanny for a family of Moldovans. Gavril applied for a paid artist internship at a small contemporary art center located in Chelsea, New York, where Luz Wilson was from, where the less-pretentious big-name stuff was shown, where his career might flourish from the attention of intelligent, black-suited New Yorkers. He received his acceptance by e-mail and waited four months for his student visa to be processed.

Everything in Bucharest was slow—the weather, the bureaucracy, the face of any passerby above the age of fifteen. His mother was furious about his departure. She had suffered for years so that her children could have a better future in Romania, not someplace where things were already better. He brought his four thousand pounds to the bank, where they converted it through the Romanian leu into U.S. dollars, $2,178 to be exact. From there, he went alone to Henri Coandă International Airport and shut the eyelid of the window before takeoff. He didn't call Luz Wilson until he landed.

He punched her number in while he was waiting for his luggage on the Newark carousel. He loved the carousel, the iron plates rotating on a conveyor belt while travelers stared longingly at the gleaming emptiness. Everything in New York could be art. "Yo, this is Luz," *beep.* He left a rambling economy-class, two-connecting-flights, trans-Atlantic, jet-lagged, just-drilled-by-a-homicidal-customs-official message.

Manhattan glittered iridescently, told him dreams of fortune through its arrow-sharp streets as he passed into and then out of the island, to an apartment in Bed-Stuy, Brooklyn. The New York Craigslist section, where he'd found the apartment, was like his childhood idea of New York, a place where all was available: sex, psychics, used stereo equipment, tickets to Carnegie Hall. Unwilling to admit that he knew not a soul in the city, he told his grad-student roommate that he had a girlfriend named Luz Wilson, although his accent was so thick the guy sharing his bedroom hardly understood his declarations of love. He called her again, two days later, and left another message.

The artist internship at the Chelsea museum was a model of indentured servitude. The museum assigned him a broom closet on the top floor to use as his studio, and in return required him to work part-time for $7.99 an hour as a gallery guard and as a barista at its rooftop café. Gavril learned how to make all the drinks he'd never sampled in Venice: latte, espresso, macchiato, decaf iced ristretto with a dollop of whipped cream. Luz never called him back.

He made friends in the internship program, fellow artist aspirants more accustomed to the beat of Manhattan, none of whom had had their picture taken in a glossy magazine. He hated their artwork—ripped covers of Danielle Steel novels with microchips pasted over the heroines' mouths; canvases dipped in latex—but he trusted his own talent and knew by the rules of art world Darwinism that many would end up making their careers standing as still as possible among white gallery walls or preparing caffeinated drinks. The museum cleverly offered apprenticeships in more practical vocations. He accompanied these friends to the Chelsea galleries, white boxes that confirmed Luz Wilson as a liar as well as an unreliable friend. The art was goose-liver pâté, rippling with currencies, the prices of semen-spotted paintings written in bold on the checklists. His new friends were mesmerized, because their own art was reproducible, generic, disposable, and so, in most ways, were they. They were desperate to prostrate themselves in front of anything that was awarded wall space. They had no real politics, although they wore pins to prove they had voted in recent elections. They also wore stickers suggesting they'd sold their blood.

One afternoon, while he was on guarding duty on the third floor of the Dan Flavin exhibition, he finally saw her. Her black suit had given way to a neon orange sweatshirt and tight acid-wash jeans, and her straight hair had fossilized into dreadlocks, which dangled across her shoulders like decaying wind chimes. She eyed him as she stood amid Flavin's fluorescent tubes, and did so again before disappearing into an exhibition room. He was ashamed to be standing there so dumbly, so pointlessly, in such easy reach. At least at the Romanian Pavilion in Venice he had been afforded a desk and chair. She circled back and stared at him, unblinking, moving a gold pendant across a chain on her neck.

"I know you," she said to him without smiling.

"Do you?" He was ashamed of the seven messages he had left on her phone. "I am new to New York. From Bucharest."

She snapped her fingers. "Venice. Am I right? I'm right." Her smile was the jagged line of a heart monitor. "And you called me two months ago." He glanced at the scant foot traffic. The walls were so white in New York, glacier white. He had come to despise that whiteness, its replication of a brain-dead consciousness. In that moment he prayed for anything to happen: a missile strike, the thunder of drones, a rain of fire breaking from the heavens onto West Chelsea. "I'm sorry I didn't call back. I mean, it was two years ago." He felt the blush on his cheeks. "God, two years," she wheezed. "A lot's happened. I was a child then." She couldn't be older than twenty-five now. "But I remember you were an artist."

He was pleased she had at least retained that detail. Before he could stop himself, he told her of his recent show at Laura Lucas, his page in *Wanted* magazine.

"Lucas is such an uptight cow, isn't she?" Luz laughed. "I'm sorry. She's also good at finding talent. Good eyes, bad mouth. But I wouldn't stay with her. She has a reputation for slowly embezzling her artists' money." He nodded, as if he hadn't already assessed the works in his broom closet, three flights above them, for the security deposit on a studio apartment.

"I'm doing a solo next month at Wexler Institute. Please come. No, on second thought—let me take you to lunch, to make up for my rudeness. We can check out some galleries too. Next Wednesday?" Wednesday was his day off. She scribbled something on the

Flavin press release and handed him a series of numbers that were already stored in his phone.

Every morning, before guard duty or the flagellation of the espresso machine, he worked in the broom closet. Every night, after guard duty or the hot-water flush of the espresso machine, he worked more. He took his art so seriously it frightened him. Every day he knelt at his own temple and slit his throat as an offering. He experimented in bulletproof glass, took pliers to steel sheets, deconstructed lightbulbs, and stripped wires from extension cords, trying to achieve an awkward, brutal poetry through the broken industrial equipment. Occasionally he invited friends, curators, and older artists to his closet, subjecting them to the obligatory, mutually misunderstood jargon he had learned in his months in New York. "It's about a paradigmatic shift in value, and, um, working-class labor directed against finished production, and, err, dispersion instead of the authority of closure." His Romanian accent gave the lecture a kind of coarse conviction. He hated, but began to agree with, the words he was speaking. For his sanity, he always said, "But you look, it is what is." He was invited to participate in two group shows, one at a major blue-chip gallery.

Their lunch was awkward. They both kept their knuckles wrapped around their wineglasses, and Luz slapped a credit card over the bill and refused his tissue balls of ones and fives. She wore a Yankees cap through lunch, and when she removed it as they walked west on Twentieth Street toward the galleries, her hair was cut so short he could see the shine of her scalp. It made her eyes huge and her lips a center ring. She was the sexiest organism he had ever walked down a street with. They made out in an abandoned doorway, kissing hungrily after their untouched salads. As he pressed his groin against her, she said, "I have a boyfriend, Gavril. I'm sorry. I can't go further. It wouldn't be right, and you'd only hate me later." "Who?" he asked, like he already knew everyone in New York. She cocked her head. "A-Dep. He's a rapper. His real name is Marcus.

We've been at it five months." Fifteen minutes later, a black limousine slid up to the curb, like in some terrible movie about class defeating love, and she climbed into a backseat he could have sworn was filled with golden retrievers. He had separation anxiety. Then he had plain anxiety. He broke many things in his broom closet.

He didn't see her again for months. She missed the openings of his two group shows and he returned the favor by not attending her solo at Wexler ("a special private reception to honor Luz Wilson at Le Bernardin, formal attire required.") Instead he got wasted and had sex with a few lost strays of the wealthy. He sold three sculptures, quit the internship, moved out of his shared apartment in Bed-Stuy for a studio in Greenpoint, and refused three different solicitations to join fledgling galleries on the Lower East Side. He had enough money to survive and to send one hundred dollars home each month to his family in Bucharest.

Right after that, jackpot. Samuel Veiseler, proprietor of the hallowed, billion-dollar Veiseler Projects, phoned him up on a March afternoon and asked if he could do a studio visit. Gavril expected to hate him, to spit in his face, and planned a career-killing mutinous *no* when asked for a single artwork. But still he straightened his studio and waited for the buzzer. Veiseler, who had satellite galleries cropping up faster than Starbucks across the globe (Veiseler Projects Beijing, Veiseler Projects Dubai, Veiseler Projects Aurora Borealis), appeared in his doorway in ragged chinos and a wrinkled blue oxford. He name-dropped artists that Gavril admired (Beuys, de Maria, Andre, Benglis, Turrell) and never mentioned the artists he sold on the secondary market (Warhol, Johns, Lichtenstein, Koons). He dangled a plastic six-pack ring that held only two beer cans, one for each of them. "I can't drink more than one or I find myself liking everything," he said with his Swiss inflection. "The truth is, I like very little of what people as young as yourself are making these days." Samuel inclined his chin—his chin actually pointed—ready to consider Gavril's work.

Gavril had just started exploring tar and concrete, pulling it in uneven goops across the floor, stretching its limits and textures. He started to explain it to his guest: the shifting paradigms between East and West, the failed dynamics of the Ceaușescu regime, and the haunted residue of a toppled empire undermined by the belief in a democratic utopia of pariahlike self-fulfillment. Gavril rambled on, and Samuel Veiseler sipped his beer and stared out the window at a homeless woman pushing a grocery cart. Gavril sputtered, "And, uh, just the formal elements of material, the stuff." Samuel's eyes redirected, snapping awake. "Yes, yes. Tell me about the material. Don't connect it to Ceaușescu right now." "How tar and steel and concrete bend. They're not rigid. They are soft, pliant, yielding. A flexible form of violence." "Yes," Samuel purred, taking new interest in the work. "I like the formal qualities. Go with that." So he did, and Samuel Veiseler left two hours later offering Gavril twenty-four hours to decide if he'd like to join his gallery.

He texted Luz for advice. He trusted and resented her in equal doses. "YES!" she responded immediately. "He's the best gallerist, way better than mine. You moron, the answer happened the minute he asked you." "I worry I sell out too early." "Huh? Are you flirting with me? Is this because I dumped A-Dep? Stop texting me and call him before he reconsiders." She had broken up with Marcus. "I don't think I want this." "You are only as serious as people take you. Otherwise every talentless drudge on earth is serious. Take it now. Look back later." He took it. The hardest part was telling Laura Lucas that he could no longer exhibit with her in London. First she sent roses to appeal to him, followed by intoxicated voice-mail threats, and she did have a stroke three months later, just as he had predicted, and her gallery didn't survive the impending market crash.

He and Luz had sex the night of the Whitney Biennial. He liked to think he had been chosen for the Whitney because of his talent, but mere news of his signing with Veiseler had brought a tidal wave of curiosity, an apocalyptic welfare line of collectors and editors and museum curators and rich dilettantes outside his studio door, to the point that his sudden fame must have been partly responsible for the Whitney inclusion. He exhibited a tar smear through the third-floor gallery, a formalist's blood vein, and he had also wanted to break through one of the white walls to expose the copper plumbing behind the institutional façade, but the curator wouldn't let him. "Gertrude Vanderbilt Whitney would not have wanted that!" Luz had also been selected for the Biennial, showing five portraits of black Americans she had found working in gas stations along the New Jersey Turnpike: sad, discontent, gas-ravaged faces inside gold frames, like employee-of-the-month snapshots treated as CEO portraits. But her last painting was a secret ode to him. On the canvas, she had written with her middle finger, in black paint: "What GVW would have wanted."

She was single, she was his, the sex was miserable, but they were artists who craved misery, and they kept having it, all night, through the week, into the next, condom by condom, and then both crept away to their studios, and neither phoned for weeks. He was busy. Interviews, studio visits, his photo in a national men's magazine, shirt and pants Yohji Yamamoto Fall/Winter 2009, the cover of *Artforum*, solo shows planned into summer, into fall, all the way to Christmas. He hired two full-time assistants just to keep up with demand. Instead of ransacking the walls of the Whitney, he exposed the copper pipes of a penthouse on Seventy-ninth Street for sixty thousand dollars (forty thousand directly into his bank account).

He kept watch on Luz's career, which was similarly exploding: national women's magazines, the Rome Prize, a conversation at the Public Library with Cornel West on the subject of blues in the arts. Gavril flew to Bern, Switzerland, to disassemble cold war airplane propellers and dip them in concrete at Kunsthalle Veiseler. Luz took the train up from Rome, and they spent an afternoon on the manicured Bern streets, admiring each other's reflections in the windows of clock shops. They had sex in his hotel suite and both of them appreciated that their initial disappointment in each other's performance during intercourse had not abated, a missing frisson for which they tried to compensate by holding each other uncomfortably tight in bed. "I feel like every painting I make is one step closer to my last," she whispered against his chest. "I want to quit before I become a hack." "I know," he said. "I'm just doing what prehistoric cave painters were doing, holding a stick out, applying a mark on the wall. Why do those cave painters seem so earnest while what I do seems so frivolous?" "I don't know." She returned to her apartment overlooking the Spanish Steps; he flew to Oslo, and from there he toured white-walled rooms all over the planet.

By the time they met up in Paris, three months later, two ominous facts were weighing heavily on Gavril's mind: his visa was about to expire, and Luz was dating a fifty-three-year-old music producer who owned a hip-hop label in Brooklyn. He fought with her in her hotel room. He told her he was in love with her, had always been in love with her, that he couldn't keep doing all this traveling and socializing and breaking his back in his studio until five in the morning, if she weren't waiting for him at the end of the line.

"I love you too," she said, chain-rolling and chain-smoking her cigarettes, a one-woman factory, her mouth a purple waste-management vent. "But I don't want to marry you. We're too much alike." He had always presumed that was the reason they *should* marry. "We're undependable," she said, "victims of our moods, too egocentric. What we need are solid, stable, generous, patient partners willing to put up with us." They had miserable sex one last time before he took off for another Kunsthalle in Baden-Baden. She went to Miami for the Basel Art Fair. He stalked her in party pictures on fashion Web sites. They didn't speak for four months.

When Luz reappeared in New York, she was engaged, but not to the music producer. At her side now was Nathan Crimp, the partner she'd been looking for, the one whose trust fund would provide her the stability she craved. Gavril was hurt, put all of his hurt into smashing glass and concrete bricks, and made money doing it, and he drank so much that he began to forget why he smashed glass and concrete bricks in the first place. He smashed like a smash machine. The results were still gorgeous to his eye, even if that eye was freighted with a twitching hangover. At gallery dinners, he and Luz smiled and waved. Worst of all, Gavril liked Nathan—for his humor, mostly, which was rare in the otherwise bumptious activity of the art world. (Nathan's show "that which does not kill you tries again later" consisted of adorable rescue dogs let loose in a gallery—visitors were allowed to pet them but had to promise not to adopt them—while video footage of a euthanasia facility played in the background.)

A crisis was beating its way toward Greenpoint. He couldn't take another studio visit with a self-serious, middle-aged woman in all-black with a pixieish haircut, trying to talk to him about relational aesthetics as if she were testifying on human rights violations at the UN. He was lonely, and the noise of Manhattan that echoed into Brooklyn made him lonelier on a cellular level. He ate his dinners in the pizza parlor on the corner, at the hour when single lonely men ate their single slices, staring into the void of grease and pepperoni. He swallowed down rich chocolate pastries for breakfast. People who ate dessert for breakfast were either reveling in their waistlines or subconsciously contemplating suicide. If Gavril hadn't had his two assistants he might have stopped producing work altogether. Might have sat in his studio with cement bricks tied to his feet and waited for a flood or deportation officers to carry him away.

He met Beth Shepherd at an art opening in the fall, her fine blond hair like a broom sweeping his mess into a tidy pile. He pronounced her name Beff until she patiently taught him the lisping *th*. She was the anti-Luz to all of his five senses: considerate, gentle, calm when an argument exceeded conversational registers, very much a woman out of her clothes. The sex was astounding, addictive to the point of despondency after the fact, a smell that lingered on his sheets and kept him there even after she left in the morning for her copyediting job at a science magazine. She was a painter too—that's what she and his former obsession shared—except that Beth's paintings were careful and affirmative. There was none of the reckless rancorous brushwork that infected Luz's canvases. *Hate, hate, hate*, Luz's brush sang. He celebrated Beth's portraits, but he couldn't convince her that she had to betray her subjects if she wanted them to speak. "Try to hurt them or hang them by their own rope," he advised. "That's not what I'm after," she said.

Gavril and Beth fell into an easy rhythm that he had never shared with another human being: dinners, and bed, and openings, and postopening dinners, and parties, and bed, and occasional phone calls when he worked in his studio until two in the morning. She never complained about how much time he spent away from her, devoted to his art. They moved into an East Village apartment together, and by then he had already confessed his total and unconditional love for her. Luz was right: it never would have worked between them. Their story would have ended in some kind of double homicide worth at least two days of coverage in the *New York Post*. When Beth said, "I'm using the new cutting board" in the kitchen, he didn't have to comb his brain for a clever response. When he bought houseplants the way other residents bought toilet paper, and named each plant in turn, Beth went along without missing a beat: "Diane is dying. Let's move her nearer the sill." Luz would have staged a colloquium on the perils of inter-subjectivity and the capitalist tendency to humanize flora while the poor hid themselves unnamed in the doorways of East Fifth Street.

Beth brought him out to her mother's house on Long Island, and he marveled at the simple, silver-tinted seaside that had given birth to her, a snow globe of humble dreams trembling with giant-winged birds. The people there didn't poop on the beaches, like they did at the Black Sea. By then it had stopped mattering what Luz would have done at every stage of their relationship. He never told Beth about her, never impressed upon the woman he loved the existence of her silent rival. Beth respected him as an artist, and so he started once again to respect himself. He smashed, he leaked. The work sold and sold and sold. Samuel Veiseler could have sold one of his drop cloths. He could have sold a lick on the wall.

At 2:13 one afternoon, he proposed to her. They married. Luz and

Nathan attended. Luz even picked the DJ for the reception. Gavril's marriage to Beth freed him of the restrictions of his visa; he applied for his green card, and strings were pulled to rush the approval. He was building a bank account, clearing about a million dollars after his studio costs and employees were paid. He sent his parents five hundred dollars each month; he offered more, but they refused.

Beth had cured him of loneliness, of his heartbreak for Luz, but over time his drinking increased, spurred by some last voice of self-doubt that murmured nightly in his head. He began, while drunk, to imagine the ghost of his grandfather, who had died in 1982 of pancreatic cancer, tapping on his limbic lobe and saying, "Gavril, you are a joke, where is baby, what is your family but crappy tenement apartment with beautiful fertile wife and all you make is broken garbage." Women aren't the only ones with clocks that tick. The clock in men may be more impervious to environmental conditions, a digital wristwatch instead of a pendulum, but it ticked for Gavril late and drunk, and ticked in the morning mildly hungover and in terrible need of a macchiato. He told Beth an edited version of his dead grandfather's wishes (redacting the ghostly presence of the dead grandfather), and Beth, who had fallen into her own isolation chamber after a disastrous show at a middlebrow gallery, seemed to welcome the prospect of having a baby. Even if time didn't really exist, if it were merely a human invention, Beth's clock seemed synchronized with his.

It was Beth's idea to move to Orient, to her mother's vacant home, to commence work on the Catargi clan. "You're too young in your career to go through a romantic period," Samuel warned him. "I can't have you making watercolors of lighthouses. What you do in the city is really the heart of your work." But the city had deadened his eye, and his eye was the only compass that told him where he was. He didn't want to get stuck spilling tar on rich people's floors, exposing their plumbing like an incompetent handyman paid outrageously for his blunders. For him, Orient was not a dislocation—New York was, a waiting platform surrounded by three international airports. Gavril had stopped referencing Bucharest in his art years ago. He needed a location, a direction, an actual place on a map.

"Orient," Luz said the last time they met in the city. In her Battery Park studio, large framed nudes of her hung on the walls that Nathan had shot (he titled the series "like my wife"). Gavril kept his eyes trained on Luz, uncomfortable about admiring the photographs. "I get it," she said. "Nathan and I have been looking for a place in the country too, somewhere we can reset our brains." She rubbed her foot on her calf. "Nathan has some crazy idea about starting his own artist colony, somewhere away from New York, where we can all live in freedom without ever feeling the slightest need to brush our hair. We've been touring houses out there, on the tip of Long Island." He wanted to beg her not to buy on the North Fork. He could see her nipples underneath her tank top. "Are you happy, with Beth and everything?" she asked.

"I'm very lucky, very happy. I needed someone like her. You were right."

"It's amazing who you fuck in this life, isn't it?" She turned to her view of the Hudson River, as if everyone Luz Wilson had ever slept with formed a human wall along the coast of New Jersey. But if that were the case, he would be across the river, separated from her by a safe ribbon of water. "Who you get to fuck, and who you don't get to fuck. Who you aren't allowed to touch, and who you touched but aren't allowed to anymore." He had no idea where she was going with that thought.

"I want to start making new work," he said to change the topic. "I'm tired of the old tricks. I'm scared my talent's running dry. In Orient, I want to make landscapes, things with life in them, hair and bones and dirt."

Her mouth twitched. She wiped a speck from her eye. "Be careful," she said. "You try to bend your ego, it will break. You try to patch a crack in your character, the hammer makes a hole. I was wrong about us. I mean, I love Nathan. I truly feel moments of joy so pure I could break out of myself. But I was wrong to let you go. Maybe I could have felt those moments with you even faster."

"It was a long time ago, Luz. And who you don't get to fuck anymore, you miss less than you think." She stepped toward him and stopped. She mentioned their first meeting in Venice, at the Romanian Pavilion, recounting details so minute that even he didn't remember: the shirt he wore, the way his birthmark disappeared in the blush of his face. She had never been that woman he first encountered in New York, who pretended to barely remember him. She stood in front of him now in her painting studio, so still it was disorienting, as if she were a perpetual motion machine that had finally stopped moving. She waited in the Hudson River light to be touched, and he didn't dare to, even though his penis pleaded for another dose of miserable sex. He thought of Beth and their future in Orient; he was already out there with her and the baby, somewhere in the vast cosmos of parallel nows, creating landscapes out of water and light.

"I'll see you soon," he told her, opening the door to leave.

She said, and he remembered it, "You'll see."

He waited on a bench near the piers of the Hudson River. He cried cleanly, efficiently, water draining from his eyes without a single gag in his throat. An early summer wind poured off the water, disturbing the plastic in the park's recycle bins and tilting the sailboats in the chop. The sky was a limitless blue, and somewhere on the Long Island Expressway a moving van drove their belongings east. When he heard his name being called, he turned and looked up. It hurt his eyes to look up into the sun and sky, up into the confusion of buildings, into one window where he thought he saw the faint shape of a hand. But he saw her walking toward him, her hair holding the sun, her teeth eating his name. "Gavril," Beth said. "Are you ready? Diane died. The movers dropped her pot out the window. Are you ready? You can sleep in the car as long as you want. We're only an hour behind."

CHAPTER 34

Mills watched Beth's car pull into the driveway. He was surprised when he saw her walk straight into the house without coming to check on him first. When a second car pulled up a few minutes later, a woman climbed out, her face shellacked in makeup, her lips bursting from bee stings. She was ageless and thus must be old. The ageless old woman in a candy-colored dress noticed the light in the garage, and Mills ducked behind one of the tar walls as she came closer. Through the window the woman's hair looked copper, her cheeks flecked from the dirt on the glass. She peered in, looking for signs of life, but retreated when she didn't find any. Mills watched her enter the house through the back door. The stranger worried him. All strangers did now, until he could disappear into the city and join their kind. He hoped Beth would send this strange woman away. He watched the house for five minutes, expecting the woman to return to her car and drive off.

A scream tore through the house, a lethal, lost-hope scream. Fighting the impulse to run toward it, he shoved the photocopies of Jeff's journal into his bag and jammed his feet into his sneakers. The ageless woman bolted from the back door, still screaming, her face now ransacked by age, blood on her fingers as red as paint. She rounded the house and suddenly stopped, screaming as she turned in circles with no direction except upright. The middle of her pink dress bloomed a dark liquid, a Rorschach butterfly, and urine dripped down her leg. Gavril sprinted toward her from the sidewalk. "Gail," Mills heard him cry. She punched his chest until Gavril pushed her aside and ran into the house. The old woman became a zombie and walked into the street.

Mills grabbed his bag and opened the garage door. He fled into the neighboring bushes, snapping branches, his sweater tearing in their grip. He burrowed through the shrubbery and darted across Magdalena's lawn, slamming his body against the scabbed wood of the cottage. He heard a second scream, a mourning roar, fainter by degrees—people went into that house, screamed, and exited changed. He wanted to go back to make sure Beth was okay, but he knew he couldn't. His fingers traced a window screen, finding a hole between the mesh and the frame, then pulled until the screen broke open enough for him to slip through.

He climbed into Magdalena's sunroom, quickly bending the steel mesh back into place. He smelled lemony Pledge and medicinal aerosols, the stink of a house without a resident to neutralize it. He scurried into the living room with his back bent, like a soldier or an ape or an old man, and dropped to his knees in the darkness beside the armoire. In the darkness he could see Beth's house through the window across the room.

It started snowing before the police cars arrived. If the snow had come earlier, he would have left footprints; if it had come later, dogs might have been able to follow his scent. Mills sat in the dark, his attention fixed on Beth's house, praying for her to come outside. He tried to think of things to pray for: an accidental cut, even a miscarriage, anything that would explain the screams and blood and her absence.

Finally, the flashing lights rippled across the exterior, soaking it with emergency. Several officers entered the house. Gilburn arrived in his unmarked sedan.

Mills looked away when they carried out the bagged body on a stretcher. It slid so cleanly into the ambulance, as if the equipment had been invented just to make this one transfer as uncomplicated as possible. Yellow police tape wrapped around the lawn.

He watched Gavril on the driveway, the only man without a coat, bags under his eyes so pronounced they didn't change color in the red-and-blue lights. Gavril led Gilburn into the garage to show him where Mills had slept, a cot-shaped petri dish of fingerprints, hair, and skin. Men in lab coats followed them with tackle boxes and cameras. Gavril left the garage and stood in a corner by the porch, his back to the scene. His shoulders shook. It seemed like he stood there for days.

Mills sat there in Magdalena's living room, on his knees, and cried into his hands. Of all of the victims in Orient, Beth had been the only one he cared about. He had loved her, and his grief was a rat running around the cage of his brain, gnawing the bars, swallowing anything edible, fresh or rotten, chewing past reason, wanting out. News crews arrived as uniformed officers fanned out through the area, one of them passing so close to the window that Mills could make out the squawking voice on his radio: *"Suspect still believed to be in vicinity. Causeway secure."* The wind moaned over the roof, and he heard equipment knocking over on the street, doors slamming, orders yelled. After several hours, Mills risked crawling toward the window. Snow had accumulated, and footprints scattered across the ground, most of them human, a few left by dogs, the falling snow trying to erase them.

He slept that night in the cold house, balled up on the carpeting. No lights were left on in the Shepherd home, but the garage threw fiery reflections around Magdalena's living room, brightening the picture frames on the mantel, and Mills heard the sound of Gavril's sculptures being dismantled, a chainsaw of demolition, a one-man wrecking crew all the way until dawn.

In the morning, starving, he slipped into the kitchen and discovered a chocolate bar in the butter dish. He regretted eating it as soon as he finished because the hunger had diluted his grief. He snaked up the stairs with his bag and sat in Magdalena's bedroom, examining the house next-door from the gabled window. Beth's car was gone from the driveway. The only human presence was an officer stationed at the front door, where a foot of snow had been shoveled into the flower bed. Snow-stained cars slowed in front of the house, paused for thirty seconds, and sped away.

It wasn't safe for him to leave yet. It would never be safe for him to leave. He used an old woman's toilet, stabilizing himself on her grip bars. He took an old woman's vitamins from the bathroom cabinet, gulping them down with handfuls of faucet water. He slept in an old woman's bed, its side gates disengaged in case he needed to run. His mind went from murder to murder and back again. He read the photocopied journal just as Beth had asked him to, page by page.

On the third day, the officers he'd seen stationed in the backyard, or cleaving the coast beds with a bloodhound, seemed to disappear. Gavril came back to the Shepherd home. Luz accompanied him, holding him by the arm and pulling him forward when he hesitated at the door. They left an hour later in her sports coupe, Luz carrying two suitcases, Gavril his notebook and a stack of photographs.

Nothing moved outside except the wind. The trees were locked in ice, their branches low and fractured in painful dislocations, hung with icicles. The deep freeze had stalled the wetlands, and the Sound was burnished and still. Police cars made their rounds, a cruiser passing once every twenty minutes. He read Jeff's journal again, and this time it was what Mills didn't find in its pages that troubled him, that kept him awake as he flipped through its log of Orient secrets.

He crept down the steps and into the living room. He swept his fingers across the armoire, the piece of furniture that Beth had left behind. Opening its doors, he found the cupboard empty except for a thin piece of cardboard wedged in the joint. He pulled it out. It was an old postcard of Bug Lighthouse—not the bland reconstruction sitting a hundred yards into the sea but the original, a herd of waves ringing the crumbling rocks. Bug Light had been destroyed by arsonists decades ago, but Magdalena had stored this faded image of it in the same place where she'd once hid her jewelry. A lighthouse was a *light* and a *house*, two entities that made no sense in the sea. But together they formed a marker, guiding the lost home or warning strangers to keep away.

He noticed a blue pen scribble on the postcard, next to the lighthouse's rocky base. It could have been a stray mark, an accidental curve, but it looked like a question mark. He held the postcard up to the window, trying to find the punctuating dot. He didn't see one, just the shape of a question without a point.

On the third night, hungry, fearful that the next morning would bring a routine visit by a Pearl Farms agent, he put on an old coat he found in Magdalena's closet. It was navy blue and patched with electrical tape, but warm enough to protect him from the cold. He was hungry for word from outside, for any news, so he risked doing what he'd told himself he should never do: he walked into the kitchen and picked up the landline phone. The dial tone hummed like the last living thing, as if he were tapping into a flowing vein. He dialed *67 to hide his location. Then he punched in Paul's cell number. It rang twice before connecting with a scuffling sound.

"Hello?" Paul's voice, familiar, strained but warm.

"It's me," he said. There was no point in whispering, but he did.

"Oh my God. Mills?" Paul whispered too.

"Yes."

"Where are you? What are you doing?" Paul sounded confused, like a man on too many pills, trying to snatch at the tails of reason. "My God, they're looking all over for you. Are you still in Orient?"

He couldn't be certain that Paul was still on his side. The call could be traced, Paul's cell phone tapped. Paul could be at the police station, pointing to the phone and mouthing to Gilburn, *It's him.* Even the temperature of Paul's voice seemed to cool when he heard Mills's voice. Maybe he had come to see him as everyone else had.

"I'm in the city," he lied. "Or pretty near to it."

"So you're not out there." He sighed. "That's good, because

something worse has happened. Much worse. And they're looking for you. Every car on the causeway is being searched."

"I want you to know that I didn't do any of it. I didn't kill anyone." Just saying it brought tears to his eyes.

"I know you didn't," Paul whispered, but the old compassion in his voice was missing. Mills fought the urge to hang up. "Look, I think it may be past the point of straightening this mess out. But if you're in the city, I guess we could try to meet somewhere."

"You're not in Orient?"

"No," he said at a normal volume. "I left today. I'm back at my apartment in Chinatown. I couldn't stay out there any longer. I don't know if I'll ever be able to go back. Not after what happened. They took me in for questioning. They got a warrant to search the house. They found . . . well, I don't know what they found exactly. Proof, I guess. Mills, did you . . ." He dropped the question.

"I'm sorry about that," Mills said. "I'm sorry about everything."

"Me too." A long rasp of dead air followed, a sound like falling snow. "It will never be the place it was for me. I don't think it will ever be like it was for anyone. It was my home."

"I wish I'd never gone out there."

More silence, enough for Paul to supply him with words of comfort, some crumb of fatherly advice that no one would ever live by but that Mills would welcome because of its source. Instead there was only electronic silence.

"Do you want to come around to the apartment?" Paul asked without enthusiasm. He clearly hoped Mills would say no, either because that would mean seeing Mills again or because he would be obliged to notify the police. Perhaps he had already learned that a kid named Mills Chevern had never been inside his home.

"I just wanted to call to hear your voice," he said. "And now I've heard it. I wanted to thank you for everything you've done for me."

"Oh," Paul said. "Okay."

Mills hung up. He stood in the doorway of the sunroom, where someone who claimed to be Jeff Trader had stood, ten feet from the empty chair. He lifted his bag strap to his shoulder. He unlocked the front door.

There were still too many cars on Main Road. Mills tried to stay behind the tree line, but the trees were lean in winter, and unseen ice patches caused him to slip, waving his arms so frantically that a few cars slowed on the road, thinking he was waving for help. He retreated back into the dark. Most of the houses were black, but those still inhabited were as bright as stadiums, lights pouring from every window, spotlights on driveways and walks, lawn lights flooding circles across the snow. He couldn't step onto those lawns without being exposed. He tried to move west, but he kept circling east to hide from cars, pushed ever deeper into backyards. When he finally got back to Main Road, he was farther from the causeway than where he'd begun.

He was climbing through a thicket of evergreens near the road when a vehicle skidded onto the shoulder. The driver's door opened. Mills raced up the hill of a private lawn, his breath trailing behind him. He needed to get back to Magdalena's house. He'd try to leave again at two or three in the morning, which had once seemed a more dangerous time to be a lone figure walking through the snow, but now seemed his only choice.

A second car slowed behind the first, and, twenty feet behind him, flashlights tunneled through the trees. He kept running, hurrying between empty houses, until he came upon a black stream of pavement not far from the Sound. Across the street, an English cottage sparkled, and he recognized the car parked in its driveway, the Saab that had taken him to the beach the day he found the second creature. Behind him, flashlights moved across the backyards. He sprinted across the road and opened the gate.

The doorbell rang throughout the warm interior. When the door opened, it wasn't Isaiah. It was his boyfriend, Vince, wearing a ski sweater and holding two dinner plates. Vince looked out into the night, staggered back at the sight of Mills, and reached to slam the door shut. *"Isaiah!"* he called. *"Help me."*

They had taken him in, or Isaiah had. Perhaps the three days without human contact had increased the desperation in his face. He lifted his chin and swore to the handsome couple in the doorway, "I didn't do anything but they're going to kill me if you don't let me in I'm innocent I loved Beth I would never have done that and if you don't let me in right now they're going to catch me and because I'm not from here they're going to hold me responsible so I came to you for help I'll strip naked you can tie me to a chair I'm innocent please just let me into your house." Whatever was left of Isaiah's rebellion against the social order, or whatever compassion he felt for a young man branded the murderer of Orient, compelled him to pull Mills in by his coat collar.

The warmth of the room prickled his body. A yellow fire swarmed in the hearth. The presence of men he didn't fear overwhelmed him, so much so that he almost collapsed. Vince snatched his cell phone from his pocket, his finger on its button, as if the phone were the handle of a switchblade.

"I can call 911 in a second," Vince threatened, watching suspiciously as Mills took off his coat. "You make so much as one move . . ."

"Stop it," Isaiah snapped. He turned to Mills. "I know what they're saying isn't true. I know because I drove you to the beach that day. You couldn't have murdered Adam Pruitt. I tried to tell the police that. How did a kid get his hands on a rifle when I drove him to the beach in my own car? They wouldn't listen."

"He's already gotten you in enough trouble," Vince muttered, standing protectively behind a green leather sofa. "And even if we do sell, I don't want to be remembered as the idiots who hid the kid everyone knew was—"

"I didn't do it! I didn't kill anyone," Mills wheezed, his shoes forming puddles on their terra-cotta tiles. He slipped out of his sneakers before Vince could protest. In his socks, he left webbed, fire-polished footprints on the tiles.

"Is it true what happened to Beth?" Isaiah asked. He moved toward Vince and took the phone from his hand. Mills suddenly worried that Isaiah was going to call the police, that his tenderness had been a lure to trap him in the house. Isaiah dropped the phone on the sofa and, sitting down, tapped the cushion beside him. Mills stood still. "Is it true that her throat was cut? That she died like that in her childhood bedroom?" Isaiah shivered.

Mills tried to dissolve that image, to leave Beth's throat un-slit. He brought his palms to his eyes, but in the cupped darkness he saw the blood run down her neck, so he opened them, fleeing his brain, scanning the room, the paintings and silver antiques glinting in the fire, the mirror above the hearth with an etching in the shape of a bird—a map of Orient—and the reflection of three different men filling it from beak to claw. Mills struggled out of his sweater and piled it over his duffel bag, leaving it where he could grab it if he needed to run.

"Poor Beth," Isaiah whimpered, massaging his forehead. "I can't stop thinking about her. None of the other deaths out here really hit us. But for that to happen to one of us. I can't imagine what Gavril's going through. What the hell is wrong with this place?"

Mills knew everything was wrong with this place. As if still being chased by flashlights, he quickly crossed the living room and sat on the couch.

"I'd be out for blood if anything like that happened to Vince," Isaiah continued.

"He can't stay here," Vince said. He stared directly at Mills. "I'm sorry, but you can't. We shouldn't have let you in. There are posters of you on every telephone pole. I don't want to get caught up in this." Even infuriated, Vince looked like a catalog model. The perfect symmetry of his face, his dirty-blond bangs rolling over a slightly sun-damaged forehead, made his hands-on-hips posture seem rehearsed, as if he were advertising his ski sweater. Mills turned to the fire, trying to store its warmth.

"Why are you acting like this?" Isaiah yelled. "This poor kid didn't do anything. Just because he's an outsider, everyone's convinced he's guilty."

"You don't know he's not guil—" Vince tried to interject.

"He needs our help. Don't you want to be on the right side of this situation?"

Vince stared at Isaiah like he was in immediate need of a psychologist.

"Isaiah, your neighbors are being murdered. We're talking about an insane person on the loose. People are being killed out here. That's not a *situation.*"

"Fine," Isaiah replied. "But unlike you, I can still decide what's right without consulting my neighbors first. You talk on and on about protecting the oceans and saving the soil, but when you actually have the chance to help a human being . . ." Whatever Isaiah and Vince were going on about, the conversation was thankfully leaving Mills miles behind.

Vince was apoplectic. "Multiple murders," he shouted. "Do you get that? This isn't about you sitting at the front of a bus."

"Isn't it? When *will* it be about that? When it isn't his head but ours?"

Vince gave up. He stormed into the kitchen, which was clearly his ninth-inning, two-strike dugout.

Isaiah sighed, rubbing his temples. "He's right," he whispered wearily. "You probably can't stay for more than a few hours. I can't hold Vince off from his good-citizen mentality for long. But I know you didn't do it." His palm gently stroked Mills's knee. Even the slightest shared body contact reminded him that he wasn't alone. "What are you going to do?"

"I'll get past the causeway and back to New York. I figure from there I can go west where they won't find me."

"That's good," Isaiah said, nodding. "As far away as you can. Rest here for a few hours and then take off."

Vince returned from the kitchen, carrying a bottle of whiskey topped with three shot glasses and a plate of half-eaten chicken, its wings tied to its ankles. Mills moved his knee away from Isaiah's hand. He didn't want to give Vince another reason to demand his ejection from the house.

Isaiah stacked the papers on the coffee table: Pearl Farms flyers, Pruitt Securities brochures, a handful of clippings on the Orient monster. Vince set the plate down. "Eat," he said, less harshly than before. "You must be hungry." He poured three shots. "This should help you get warm."

The sight of the chicken carcass made him queasy, but out of politeness he picked off a piece and ate it. He helped it down with gulps of whiskey. The alcohol burned his gums and warmed his blood. He placed the empty glass on the table, and when Isaiah poured him another shot he drank it fast.

His panic receded with the whiskey, then returned heavier and abstract, like a wave at high tide pulling away softly before racing back to shore.

"I talked to Luz today," Isaiah said. Vince sat stonily in the arm-chair, staring at Mills as if he was still trying to picture him as the killer, as the face on the telephone poles. Mills listened through the gaps in Isaiah's conversation for the sound of approaching feet or unfamiliar cars. "Gavril is staying at their place for the next few days. They'll wait until the funeral before going back to the city, maybe forever. We are too. But from what I hear, Gavril wants to go back to Europe. I guess even New York is bound to remind him of her."

"I don't want to wait for the funeral," Vince grumbled.

Isaiah ignored him. "It's awful to say this, but I keep hoping Beth's murder had something to do with her being from Orient. I need for this to be about the year-rounders, not just a random killer who'd murder anyone he happened to come across. Murder like that, the insanity of it . . . oh, Christ, but what else could it be?"

"Well, everyone's going to want out of Orient now," Vince replied. "There's no way it's going to be the sweet community we all thought it was, with Karen Norgen and her brownies showing up on our doorstep. That's gone. Instead it's him on our doorstep." Mills remembered what Isaiah had told him—that Vince had taken out loans to buy the cottage, not because he thought Orient was a sweet community, but because it had resisted him.

"After all the work we put into this place." Isaiah's eyes swam. "All those months scraping wallpaper." Even the memory of his exertion exhausted him, and he leaned against Mills for support, clasping his shoulder and groping his knee. "You know, Beth really cared about you," he said. "She asked me to look out for you. I think she was training for her own kid one day."

Mills didn't tell them that Beth was already pregnant. He didn't have the heart to say that out loud. He slipped out of Isaiah's embrace.

Isaiah stretched his arms. "We should get some sleep," he said. "Maybe before dawn, if the roads are clear, I can try to drive you over the causeway."

Vince shook his head.

"You can take the couch. I'll get you a blanket." Isaiah disappeared into the darkness of the bedroom. Vince stiffened, left by his boyfriend to keep company with a fugitive.

"Isaiah's drunk," Vince murmured. "He was drunk before you arrived, which is probably why he let you in. I'm sorry if it seems like he's hitting on you. He has zero tact, no sense of what's appropriate. None of the artists out here do. They live like nothing ever fazes them."

"It didn't bother me," Mills assured him. "I wouldn't do anything to come between you." Vince grunted, as if that was never a concern. The alcohol was blurring the lamp shades now, dragging solid objects around in soft circles. It had been months since he'd had a drink and he remembered its warm dissolution. If he stood up, his feet would track a curving world.

"Isaiah sees people as trees to climb," Vince said, taking a sip of whiskey. "When he gets to the top, he jumps. I guess he's stayed with me because I went higher than he expected, and he worried if he jumped he'd hurt himself."

Mills thought of the postcard of the lighthouse at Magdalena's place and the question mark floating near its base. "Can I ask you something?" Mills said. Vince nodded distrustfully, as if waiting for him to demand money or his car. He glanced at his phone on the sofa, as if to reassure himself that it was still within reach. "Isaiah told me you planted a maple seed in the soil at Bug Light." Vince smirked at the distant memory. "He said you buried something else there too. I wondered what."

Vince paled, his suntan sickly. He leaned forward in the chair. "A picture of us. I put in a picture of us from when we first met. I wanted the tree to grow over it. I wanted it stored in the roots."

"Is that all it was?" Isaiah asked, emerging with a blanket slung over his shoulder. "Why didn't you tell me?" Vince got up from the chair. He walked toward the bedroom, pulling his sweater over his head. He had a strong swimmer's back, with deep crenulated folds. There were so many words to describe the front of a person, but too few for the back, which seemed to Mills at that moment a particular injustice to Vince Donnelly.

Isaiah threw the blanket on the couch and sat down next to him. "I heard what you said before," Isaiah whispered. "But you should know that nothing you can do could come between me and Vince. When no one tells you how to live, you get to invent the rules for yourself." Isaiah touched his knee again, not flirtatiously, but as if he were trying to ground it. "I hope you remember that. The world can be any way you want. You're one of the free ones, freer than you think."

"I'm not free at all right now," Mills groused. Isaiah nodded in drunken apology, and Mills tried to lighten his tone. "Are you going to stay out here? I mean, after all the murders."

Isaiah inhaled tightly. "I don't know. Vince really liked it here.

I guess I was getting to like it too. I was beginning to think he was right about this house being a good investment and that we'd be sitting on our retirement fund when Plum and Gardiners Island got bought up by billionaires. Only right now, with all the murders, we'd be lucky to get half of what we paid. I wish we'd let those other bidders buy it. I wish we'd never come out here."

Isaiah grabbed the Pearl Farms flyer from the coffee table. He flicked it in defeat and traced his finger over the logo. Mills watched Isaiah's finger follow the outline of the oyster shell, a line curving down, rotating in a circle, and running out in a liquid line. Isaiah repeated it, and the sight took Mills's breath away.

"It's not an *L*," he said, choking. "It's an oyster shell."

"It's a hate sign is what it is," Isaiah said with a smile. "That stupid pearl logo hanging on every real estate marker."

"Pearl Farms," Mills said. "They were the ones that sold you this house."

"Sold us?" Isaiah laughed. "No. They were the ones bidding against us. They were the group I told you about who was trying to buy this place from the owner at a bargain rate. They tried to buy Nathan and Luz's farmhouse too but couldn't match Nathan's endless family money. That horrible woman who runs Pearl Farms, she's the reason we had to clean out our savings and go so high. And she's on the historical board, so Vince has no chance of getting his precious seat. Don't the locals realize, the more we fix up these moldy old homes, the more their own properties are going to be worth? I don't blame Luz and Nathan for trying to figure out a way to buy more land out here behind her back."

"I need a glass of water," Mills said, standing up. Isaiah got up too, smiling sadly.

"I'm going to get some sleep. If you need that ride before dawn, just wake me. And if you don't, well, I'm wishing you luck."

After Isaiah went into the bedroom, Mills unhooked the mirrored map of Orient from the wall above the hearth. He found a marker in the kitchen and unzipped his duffel bag to remove the photocopies of Jeff Trader's journal. In the dying firelight, he drew an X over every property that appeared with a "no" or a "maybe" at the bottom of each page. Then he put an X on the yeses. The bird was feathered up its back, crosshatched in a line along the Sound from tail to crown, until there was only one empty space.

The clock by the phone read 12:04. He called information. He had the information. He saw so clearly why and how it was done.

"Hello?" a voice drenched in sleep mumbled through the receiver.

"This is Mills Chevern. I know what happened and how you did it. I'll be at Paul Benchley's house in forty minutes. I have the proof with me. If you aren't there, I'll take it to the police."

CHAPTER 35

The Benchley mansion glowed palely in the moonlight. No lights shined inside. When the storm clouds covered the moon, the house disappeared into darkness, and all Mills heard was the shifting of ice. Paul's Mercedes was absent from the driveway. The frosted tire tracks traced his departure into the street, reverse, forward, and gone. Mills hurried to the back of the house, passing the empty lot where the Muldoons had lived.

He expected to find the back door locked, but it wasn't. No alarm, either. In the back room, a collection of junk piled in a corner: fishing rods, canoe paddles, items not yet dragged to the curb for garbage day. Mills dropped his duffel bag and walked through the rooms leading to the parlor. He unlocked the front door for the visitor and gathered a few logs in the fireplace, lighting them with a match. The fire glinted the marble of the dining room table and silvered the whitewashed floor. What a home this could have been, what a laboratory for age and distortions. He returned to the back rooms and found the box of flares, jamming one in his back pocket. He pulled out the old service revolver and loaded the single bullet in its rusted chamber. The front door clicked in its latch, ten minutes early, and the fire welcomed the visitor. Footsteps traveled through the rooms Mills had cleared. It was all navigable now. He had been brought to Orient to make things navigable.

A figure appeared in the doorway, a black shape vibrating in the shadows, a bulky coat and cap, and only when she unwound her scarf did the bones of her face converge into a frame for almond eyes and sharp, moist lips, a hothouse flower wilted by too many winters in the West. She had come farther than Mills had to make her home on the North Fork. He had come east, she west.

"You shouldn't be here," Sarakit Herrig said, keeping her distance by the door. "You aren't *supposed* to be here anymore. It was my understanding you'd be gone."

"That's not—" he began to say as he stepped forward.

"Don't move," she shouted. "You move another foot and the phone I hold in my pocket calls the police. *I'm* not the one who should be worried about the police. I'm not the one they're looking for." He remained in place, ten feet from her. "So what is this about? Extortion? You think you can get some money from me? If that's what you're after, I want to know what *proof* you claim to have."

"You really believe you can just give me money and walk away? After you murdered my friend?"

Sarakit's laugh was harsh with sickness, the hacking of a winter cough. But it was still confident, mocking the naïveté of the young man in front of her.

"I don't think you're in a position to make demands. As far as everyone knows, you're guilty. You should count your blessings that you aren't already rotting in a prison cell. That will be my gift to you, that I don't turn you over to the police."

"They might want to know what I think."

"They don't *care* what you think. You're just a body they can lock away. And I could have made sure you were caught earlier, but I didn't." He heard the thud of metal striking the floor by her feet.

"No," Mills said, "because it's better for you that I don't get caught. But that was a nice performance you gave outside the church at the Muldoons' funeral, accusing me in front of everyone, breaking down as you pointed the blame."

"I didn't kill anyone," Sarakit said sharply. "I didn't kill a single person, so as far as I see it there's no blood on my hands. You forget, Mills Chevern or whatever your real name is, that I have an alibi for every death. So stop wasting my time. What proof do you have? Tell me now, or I call the police and we'll see how fast you can run."

Mills let a moment of silence pass. He controlled the time now between them. He could make this moment last an hour or a night. The fire in the parlor could die and dawn could eat into the room and still she would wait to hear the evidence against her.

"I have Jeff Trader's journal, with all the notes he made."

Her eyes disappeared in the darkness.

"That's all?" She seemed almost joyous in her disappointment, rolling her head back. She had left her home and sleeping children in the middle of the night over nothing.

"He was keeping a record of every house Pearl Farms is hoping to buy, one by one, so that they can be consolidated into larger tracts of land. That's what you've been promised, isn't it? That's what you're getting out of the deal you made."

She blinked. "You think that holds up as evidence? Pearl Farms is a legitimate real estate agency. We have every right to purchase any property we choose and repurpose it—" but Sarakit flagged halfway through her speech, exhaling a slow, phlegmy breath. Her voice rose, the coppery tang of her Thai inflection slapping against her Long Island vowels. "Do you know what it's like to come from where I came from? Can you possibly understand the poverty I grew up in?" She waited two breaths for him to answer. "The whole family is sick, no doctor. The whole village starves, no food. Oh, there's a world of opportunity, but it's over there in the West, and all we can do is watch it on TV. Sometimes we even see ourselves on your news, but only for a minute."

She paused. The Long Island was coming back into her tone, angry, demanding, the grind of boats on a dock. "Of all the people in Orient, you might understand the squalor I came from. But I wasn't lucky like you to be born here. I had to fight just to get to this country, had to marry a Peace Corps volunteer passing through Bangkok so I could get to this side of the world. All that fight and sacrifice just to move to this hateful little town, because Ted insisted on it." The whites of her eyes shrunk. "And what do I find when I get here but looks? Decades of looks, like I didn't work harder to be here than any of them. But I put up with it, and we made a comfortable life, surviving on what money we earned, clipping coupons, getting by. Then what happens? The rich suddenly decide to move out to Orient in droves, to this nothing of seaside, to this place where I've built a life and a safe nest for my children. Am I supposed to sit by and watch as these artists and bankers glide in on their money and steal the land out from under me? Oh, no. I fought for my piece of it. I got here first. I'm owed something for that." She balled her hand to her mouth as her cough returned, her eyes closing and brightening with each blink.

"This deal you talk about," she said. "It is only what I deserve. I promised myself a long time ago that I was not going to be poor again, squeezed out, forgotten. I haven't killed *one person*. Do you hear me? All I did was let it happen. How does that make me guilty? I've never blamed anyone for watching when bad things happened to me."

Sarakit absolved herself in the darkness, just as she must have absolved herself after every death. "Five hundred dollars for the journal," she said. "Five hundred dollars and I don't call the police."

"But Bryan's murder—that was personal," he said.

"Bryan," she whispered in disgust.

"You two were having an affair."

"Nonsense."

"You left your necklace in the Seaview, room thirty-one. A silver pendant of an oyster shell." Almost involuntarily, Sarakit grabbed at her chest. "I got it from the old woman who runs the place. She must have pried out the pearl and left the silver clasp." Mills remembered Eleanor swearing she'd once returned a ruby ring, or at least the setting, and the piano player singing, *sure you did.*

She dropped her hand from her neck.

"Maybe," she said. Her voice softened, folding in on its grief. "Maybe Bryan was going to be another way out for a while. But he lied to me and took up with Holly Drake. Maybe I didn't mind what he was going to get. But it was only supposed to be him." She began to choke on an obstruction far more obstinate than phlegm. "It wasn't supposed to be the whole family."

"Just enough to destroy the board. Just enough to break the conservancy trust before the development rights were sold, because that would have ruined the value of the land you were hoping to develop." Orient's real threat was its trust, or the one person left to oversee it.

Sarakit stepped forward. She cleared her throat. Absolution took only a few seconds. "You have the necklace?"

"Yeah."

"Five hundred dollars. And I get the journal and the necklace and I'll even drive you over the causeway. You're right. It would be better if you aren't caught."

"Okay."

"Come here," she said. "The money's in my hand." It was too dark to see what she was holding. He moved toward her. Her skin was purple and wet, her eyelids the soft undersides of beetles. As he stepped closer, he saw her gritted teeth, and as she raised the metal poker above her head, he pulled the trigger. A spark of yellow and a boom that swept like moths around his ears. The bullet entered her chest and bit into the wall behind her. Her body dropped. Sarakit tried to speak, but whatever she was trying to say, through spit and blood, he didn't bother to hear. He bent over to search her pockets, pulling out a roll of hundreds. Black liquid flowed around his feet. He tucked the gun in the waistline of his pants and tracked the liquid behind him. Lifting his bag onto his shoulder, he went out the back door.

The wind blew in circles off the Sound. He worried that a neighbor might have heard the shot, although few neighbors were still around to hear anything. He sprinted to the bulkhead doors, wrenched them open, and climbed into the hole. His last task was down there.

In the cellar was Paul's museum of landscapes, his private shrine of seas and yellow autumn bluffs. Orient's rustic, lighthouse-dotted coast hung there, dry and cracked as old mosquito bites. On the wall was the ancient map of the village, and on the desk the silver slab of his laptop. Next to it sat the box of heirlooms marked FAMILY. Mills could smell the earth through the walls.

When Mills climbed out of the cellar, he heard the motor in the water. He walked into the darkness and looked over the silver-tipped grasses at the scaly, ice-white surface of the Sound. A motorboat lumbered through the ice into the rocky shallows. The engine died, and a man crawled onto the beach. He climbed through the weeds that sloped up toward the lawn, using his hands as he ascended. Mills pulled the flare from his pocket and twisted the cap. It sparked like a summer firework. Through the fizzy, red halo of light he watched the man scuttle through the tall grass and find the open trail. The man walked toward him, the killer, his friend, wearing a yellow boating jacket, his hands empty at his sides.

"I figured you might come," Mills said.

Paul stopped a few feet from him in the backyard. The flare light flushed his face. His smile looked pained. Mills yanked the gun from his waist and pointed it.

"You've gotten to know me pretty well," Paul replied. "After all, we've been living side by side, like any family."

"Should I call you Patrick?" Mills asked.

Paul's tongue moved behind his cheek. "If you want. But what do I call you?"

"Mills is fine."

"Okay, then," Paul said. He squinted at Mills like they shared a similar burden. Everything about Paul was a lie.

Mills knew why he had done it. He'd seen the motive firsthand. Ten minutes ago, in the cellar, he had turned on Paul's laptop. As he stood at the desk waiting for the machine to power on, his fingers fumbled across the spines of magazines on the shelf. At his touch, they toppled limply to the ground. Shaved vaginas, hairy bushes, headless women spread-eagled with seed-bag breasts: a glossy oil slick of flesh leaking across the floor. Paul Benchley's orientation was a secret no more.

While the laptop was booting up, Mills took the digital camera from the box marked FAMILY and pressed play on the last video recorded. A dying old bald woman appeared in the arsenic sunlight of what was now the guest bedroom, Mills's room. At the edges of the frame he could see the poster of Bug Light and the indent of the birthing bowl. Her tongue licked through crusted lips.

Mills placed the camera where he could see the screen, then sat down at the laptop. It asked for a password. Below it was an unchecked box marked REMEMBER ME.

"Patrick," the dying old bald woman wheezed as she stared into the camera. Her face was a china plate of hairline cracks. "Patrick, turn that damn thing off. I don't want you filming me."

Patrick he typed into the password box. The laptop brightened. He found the file marked "OrientReal." Real for real estate. Real for reality in the making.

"Patrick, stop it, you little shit," the dead woman argued. Her arms swung helplessly. There was nothing else her arms could do. "Shut off that camera. We need to talk about what we're going to do when I get better. You gotten the inn back yet? And I don't mean that whorehouse that Eleanor runs. Don't you dare think you're buying that place as a consolation. I want my inn, where I can sit and watch the birds and greet the guests on the porch."

The voice that answered was loud in the microphone, warm and familiar.

"Mom, what if you don't get better? The doctor says it's likely you won't."

The old woman lay back on her pillow, as if rehearsing for her coffin. She was cremated, Mills remembered. No DNA left to test against Paul's own. "Then you get it done without me," she said.

"Because it's our land, the family that saved you. Without us, you'd be nothing. It's sacred land, you hear me?" She smiled skeptically, as if she didn't trust him to carry out her wishes. "And if you don't, you're in a world of trouble. Because they'll find him, *they'll find him*, and what are you going to do then? How will you explain? You owe us that. Now get that thing out of my face."

"Mom, you aren't thinking straight. Will you tell me some stories of your early days in Orient."

"Don't Mom me, you little shit."

On the laptop screen, the OrientReal file opened into a series of gridded renderings: golf-green swaths of land with warbler-blue views of the Sound. Imperial condominiums multiplied along the shore, hotels shooting skyward, all of it crawling with the tiny black ants of future Orient settlers. The architecture was global, interchangeable, and accommodating. These were the buildings that Paul had been designing all those weeks he sat at his computer: a new Orient landscape, reset with soulless fitness centers and parking lots. Each building was emblazoned with an oyster shell. Paul was an architect. He dreamed as he was trained.

Now, in the cold, 2:00-a.m. backyard, Paul stood glazed in torchlight. His boot toyed with a rock in the mud.

"Why don't you drop the gun?" Paul said calmly. He still had the voice of a father in him. "You can still make it out."

"You brought me here to be your scapegoat," Mills shouted. If the gun contained a bullet, just one inch of copper, he might have fired it. A part of him would have enjoyed watching Paul's body accept the bullet and the ground accept him, one orphan killing another. "You found a homeless kid in the city who no one would miss and everyone could blame."

"Come on," Paul rasped, pushing his glasses up the bridge of his nose. "It isn't like that. You're confused. Why don't I take you out on the boat and get you past the causeway—" The last person who trusted Paul on a boat was Jeff Trader. Mills shook the gun to shut him up.

"It's too late. I saw the plans for Orient on your computer. But I knew it was you even before that. I figured it out from Jeff's journal."

Paul's mouth tightened. Mills could see his teeth moving behind his lips.

"There's something about me in there?"

"No," Mills said. "There's no listing for you in that book. But Jeff Trader was your caretaker, wasn't he? Jesus, Paul, you're an ideal candidate for what Jeff was recording in those pages with all of his *yes*es and *maybe*s and *no*s. It was speculation on who in Orient was likely to sell their homes because of personal or financial problems. You're the only one who lives on the Sound who isn't in his book. And yet you've got so many problems. Everyone saw you crash your car in that phony suicide attempt." Paul flinched, drawing his hands into his coat pockets. "Why wasn't that in the book? Or the fact that this is only your summer home. Or that you have no love life."

"Mills, I—" Paul said, struggling. He kicked the rock across the yard.

"You're not in that book because you were paying Jeff Trader to find out who was likely to sell. That's what those notes about money were on the last page. He wasn't blackmailing anyone. Jeff was gathering information, snooping through houses for signs of divorce or debt or unhappiness, so that you and Sarakit could swoop in and buy them before they hit the market. They would never get on the market because Pearl Farms had already found an interested buyer. Pearl Farms was the buyer. You and Sarakit, your own secret land trust."

"I really wish you'd made it to the city," Paul said. His eyes were no longer sympathetic. His hair whipped in the wind; his hands balled in his coat pockets. Paul hardly seemed to notice the gun trained on him. It was empty, but holding it between them made Mills feel like he had some last hope of remaining alive. The possibility of one bullet in its chamber, one he'd found amid the boxes and junk, was the one thing Paul hadn't counted on.

He had planned everything else so carefully. The day he shaved his mustache, Mills should have realized that he'd only grown it to pass for Jeff Trader. If Mills squinted, he could see the man in front of him standing in the doorway of Magdalena's sunroom, ranting about a wrongdoer on the board, frightening Magdalena into changing her will. He and Beth had gotten it wrong. They'd assumed that Magdalena was murdered for what she knew about Jeff, but it was the other way around: Paul had to kill Jeff so he could get away with murdering Magdalena. As soon as Pearl Farms bought Magdalena's property, Jeff Trader would have known that Paul was behind her death—would have known it because of the information he was paying him to collect.

"It must have taken courage for you to drown Jeff in the harbor," Mills said. Paul shivered, from the cold or the memory. "Just like it takes courage to drive into a tree."

"I was depressed," Paul snapped, clinging to his broken story.

"You weren't trying to kill yourself. You needed to get your fingerprints on record. You had to do something just on the wrong side of the law so they'd book you. That way the police could identify your prints on the gas can right away. You couldn't run the risk of relying on my prints, because you didn't know if they were on record, or if I might leave before they got to me. You knew that any detective would be able to link your gas can to the delinquent staying in your home, especially after you hid the can in Beth's closet. You already had Jeff's jar of keys. You had access to every house."

Paul stood there unmoving, blinking behind his glasses. Mills had been duped just as all of Paul's neighbors had been duped, convinced he was a sad, lonely man, lost without his family, the kind of person who might take in an orphan against all reason and complaint.

Mills raised the gun. "Did you see Tommy on the landing after you started the fire?"

"You can't blame me for your mistakes with Tommy," Paul said. "You got mixed up with the Muldoons on your own."

"Can I blame you for Beth? She was pregnant, you know."

"That's horrible," Paul said somberly. "Look, Mills, I don't know why you think—" He took a step back.

"Don't move," he yelled. "And don't lie to me. I've already spoken to Sarakit. I know you did it. I see you now."

Paul smiled thinly. He didn't look caught. He looked like a man who had destroyed a house and was left with a splinter to pry from his thumb. He took a long breath, which whitened before the wind swept it away.

"What do you want? Want me to tell you that I'm greedy?" His hands moved in his coat pockets. "You were greedy too. I could see the greed brewing in you each day, right behind those sad little eyes. You were practically redecorating the house, waiting for me to write you into my will. We're not that different. I grew up here. Orient's my home. All this land was ours for a century along the Sound before my grandfather broke it up."

"We're different, Paul. We're nothing alike."

"I want you to know that none of this was personal," Paul said. He spoke like he was still trying to teach Mills a lesson, like it was another fireside talk on the meaning of land and local values. Maybe it was. "There's nothing personal about it except for you. Believe me, I tried to figure out another way. I spent nights going over it, undoing the plans so you could stay. But it all came together against you too well. I was stuck with my original blueprint. You can't change the footprint after the foundation is laid."

Mills had wanted a confession, but once it arrived, smoothly and without regret, it frightened him.

"You could have stopped."

"Stopped?" Paul repeated caustically. "There was no stopping. Time mattered. Even with dementia, my mother understood that. The board was already forming their conservancy trust, and all those rich artists were snapping up the waterfront houses. I knew they'd sell their rights and more would come. It was now or never. Any later would have been too late."

"First Magdalena, then Bryan," Mills said. "With them out of the way and Sarakit on your side, you knew the conservancy trust was as good as dead."

Paul smiled, like just hearing someone else explain it confirmed its demise.

"It makes me sick to think about that trust. How can you buy a piece of land one day, land that's been here forever, and decide that no one can ever build anything on it for all of eternity? Why should some outsider who just got here dictate what happens decades after they're gone? The Sound was our property. And it's my family, not the Muldoons, that should decide what happens here. I was just following my family's wishes. I owed it to them."

"So you murdered your way along the Sound, consolidating properties with each death. Sarakit said that Bryan was the only one who was supposed to die, but you knew the whole family had to go to be sure that Lisa would sell."

Paul shook his head, as if the complication didn't belong to him but to the world.

"Mills, it wasn't personal. It pained me to have to do that. But that kind of fire was the only way to bring fear to Orient. Don't you see? Fear was the motive. That was the whole point of funding Adam Pruitt's mutants on the beach. It got people frightened of the place. Who's going to buy in Orient when biological waste from Plum Island is washing up in their backyards? Who's going to live in a village where people are being murdered? I would have loved to pin the blame on Adam, but he had an alibi for the fire. And if word got out that Pearl Farms had already bought his father's property from him, those fingerprints on the gas can would have taken on a different light. You see? Even in death Adam did what he was good at. He put the fear in people."

"Patrick," Mills screamed. "This isn't your land. Those parents weren't your parents. You're a foster kid that some misguided family decided to take in. I should have realized you weren't their son when you didn't remember your own fucking birthday."

Paul removed his glasses and wiped his face. The flare was dying, sputtering out its chalky remainder, and Paul squinted through the shine, blinded like an animal caught by flashlight.

"I *am* their son," he shouted, for the first time losing his composure. "The Benchleys took me in as an infant because they couldn't have more children after Paul. I was only a few months younger than he was, except I wasn't sickly and deformed." Paul shrugged. "Who knows, maybe Plum did mess him up. I was the healthy one, the one they could count on to do their work. Paul was hidden in the house most of the time. The neighbors confused us, and my parents were proud people, maybe too proud to admit that their own child was so broken and sick. When Paul died, I replaced him. I was all they had left to depend on."

"That's why your mother was so broken up when he died," Mills said. "Because he was her natural son."

"Natural," Paul said, grimacing. "You must hate that word as much as I do. They loved me enough to send me off to boarding school, and they kept me out of sight working on the boats at sea in the summer. After a few years, I was Paul. And I never took for granted the world that came to be mine. I loved it more deeply because I knew it was hard work and not birth that had brought me this inheritance." He waved his arm as if the whole seascape belonged to him. "The Benchleys could have been given any foster kid, but they got me. I was the one."

Mills remembered the day that Paul found him on the floor of his apartment building, how kindly he had taken him in. He imagined Paul walking the streets of Lower Manhattan, cruising the fugitive teenage bodies huddled under blankets, their smells and accents mixing in the late summer lagoon of trash and smog, searching for the weakest and easiest. Paul had so many candidates to choose from, and he found one right outside his door.

"Just like if I hadn't been the one, you would have found another kid in New York to frame." Mills hoped Paul could see the hatred in his eyes.

Paul fidgeted with the cuff of his yellow slicker. "Mills, you are special. You work hard, and I respect that. You're self-made too, although I had to reinvent you a little bit. I like to think we've developed a special bond. Why don't you put the gun down? I can still get you out of here on the boat. I'm giving you a choice. If we trust each other one last time, it doesn't have to end in the worst way."

Paul's talk of the future unsettled him, as if he assumed they could both leave the backyard alive. A different fear braced Mills, colder and less concrete, the fear that this wasn't an ending but a bridge.

Paul held out his hand, his fingers mimicking the shape of the gun. The flare died, its last sparks shooting onto the snow. The darkness diluted Paul, made him limitless, part of the air and the beating grass. The gun was almost invisible between them.

"There's no bond between us," Mills spit, lifting the gun higher. "You used me, and you killed Beth."

A faint yellow motion. Paul dropped his hand in his pocket.

"You're not listening," Paul snarled. His glasses silvered liked the leaves, like the flecks of cresting water driven over the ice. "You ask for the truth, but you don't listen. Killing Beth wasn't just about getting my hands on her mother's property. Her death was necessary because it spread the fear beyond the year-rounders. I need the rich artists and trust-fund brats to be scared. I need the city people so frightened that they'll leave Orient, or never come here at all—at least for the next few years, while I buy up as much property as I can. Christ, Mills, don't be stupid. I told you the murders weren't *personal*." Paul kept repeating that word, as if an impersonal murder cleared him of blame.

"You can save your confession for the police," Mills said. He dropped the flare and wiped his mouth. The wind lashed his outstretched arm as he steadied the gun.

Paul's face crumpled in disappointment. "Do you think this is a confession? I'm trying to get you to understand your part in it. I told you, fear is the gas that runs the whole operation. I'm happy you haven't been caught. I did everything I could so you wouldn't be arrested. I begged and stammered and wrung my heart out in front of the police for one reason: because you being out here, on the loose indefinitely, fuels the fear that the land is still unsafe. Mills, I need you to do what you're good at. I need your face out there on the wanted posters. I need the fear of you circulating in everyone's mind until they decide it's better to sell than risk exposure. I need you to run."

Mills's stomach fluttered. The wind off the Sound rocked him. His mind scrambled for some way to unravel Paul's plan. He had been woven into it so tightly, even disappearing couldn't free him. Disappearing would only complete Paul's picture of Orient.

Paul eyed the weapon. He did what a man faced with a gun was not supposed to do. He smiled.

"There's nothing so dangerous as an unloaded gun," Paul said. "I know about the bullet. And I heard the shot from the Sound. Sarakit called me to say you were demanding to meet her. I've been staying at the Seaview in case you turned up. I told her you were harmless—just greedy, like she was. But I figured either you or Sarakit was going to end up dead. I had to come, in case Sarakit needed help hiding your body. I couldn't be seen driving anywhere near my house, but Eleanor was kind enough to lend me her boat. Now put the gun down."

The gun lost its power, turning into a hunk of metal. Mills gripped it by the barrel and extended it, offering it to Paul in resignation.

"You're right," Mills said tiredly. "It's empty. It belongs to you."

Paul retracted his hands.

"Nice try," he said. "But I won't get my prints on it. Your fingerprints are where they should be, and they prove you killed her. Which is fine, because Pearl Farms is a shared enterprise. And another murder only increases the fear. Another body just licks the seal on the envelope." He rubbed his arms through his coat and exhaled. "Aren't you cold? I'm cold. I can't go inside, though, and enjoy the fire you set. Mills, it's time for you to go. Come with me on the boat and I'll make sure you get to the other side."

Mills stammered, caught—worse than caught. He could run, but that was precisely what Paul wanted him to do. He stood three feet from the man he had treated as a father, unwilling to leave with him, because leaving with him was helping him.

"I could go to the police," Mills stuttered.

Patient white contrails drifted from Paul's nostrils.

"And tell them what? Where's your proof? You don't have any, except for the gun you used to shoot Sarakit. Do you think they'll believe you? Mills, I only told you all this so you'd see you have no option but to run. If you're caught, you're the one they'll blame. You need to leave, and it's in my interest that you make it. Get in the boat. I promise I'll get you across."

"I'll say we were in it together," Mills sputtered. "I'll tell them I was just following orders from you. I'll say we were lovers." Mills could reinvent him, too.

Paul stared at him, dimples denting his cheeks. "So you could go to jail forever? When I deny it, you'll still be caught. There's one thing I know about you. You don't have the discipline for permanent confinement. It was sad to watch you trying to make this place your home. It never would have been, even if things had been different. I don't think that restlessness will serve you well in prison." Paul's eyes blinked behind his glasses. "I offered you a ladder once. I'm offering you that again. Like I said, I've really come to be fond of you. So let's make this a painless good-bye. You still have a chance at a future. Either you get on the boat, or I'm going to have to kill you with the knife in my pocket and dump you out at sea. I'd rather not think of you out there in the water. I'd rather think of you some-place warm."

Mills dropped the gun. Paul started to walk toward the Sound but turned to find Mills standing in place. Paul's grin faded by de-grees, and when his lips finally leveled, he sighed and grabbed the switchblade from his coat pocket.

Mills glanced at the houses behind him, none of which would take him in. They'd call the police as soon as he appeared at their door. In all of Orient, Beth was the only one he had loved. The rest of the village had put their faith in their own. Paul flipped the blade, a three-inch razor. He shook it as if it were wet. He actually looked saddened by his need to use it. "Damn it, Mills, now you're going to make me bury you too."

"Bury me too?"

Mills thought of the Bug Light poster above the birthing-room bowl and the question mark at the base of the lighthouse on Magdalena's postcard. Paul had taken him to his mother's farmhouse inn, to the bluff where Paul and his father had built their miniature model of Bug Light. His mother missed her favorite lighthouse, so they built a scale model for her, so she could look out and see it on the horizon—the first building he ever made. His dead mother on the video: *And if you don't, you're in a world of trouble. . . . Because they'll find him, and how will you explain?* Magdalena must have paid a visit to Paul's mother during a dementia spell, raving on about a secret buried long ago below Bug Light.

"That's where your brother is buried, isn't it? " Mills said. "At your mother's farmhouse, under that slab where your model of Bug Light was. It *is* personal, Paul. You've been killing since you were a kid."

Paul didn't stumble. He tightened his foothold in the snow. But his eyes stumbled, shot with light, trying to steady themselves behind his glasses."You murdered your brother," Mills said. "He never died of that sickness—you never gave him the chance. You killed him first, so you'd be all your parents had left. I bet they were never going to adopt you. They wanted you to be their workhorse while they took care of their son."

"You don't know what you're talking about," he stammered. "It was an accident. There's no—" Silence blocked his throat.

"That's what you owed your mother—not the whole coast, but the property on the tip where her real son is buried. All of the rest is greed. Your mother didn't want his grave disturbed. Only Pearl Farms couldn't outbid Nathan and Luz to buy it back. Now, if Luz Wilson decides to dig her pool under that slab in the spring, they'll find the skeleton of a boy. And if the police learn the identity of that boy, even the Benchley house won't belong to you."

Paul let out a tuneless wail, which the wind stripped into quiet. He stood shaking with his eyes on his target. "You think you have all the answers?" Paul murmured, his strength broken and voice trembling. "It was an accident." He stepped forward and reached a hand out to clasp Mills's shoulder for support. "They would have taken me away. My parents understood that, and they needed me, so we dug—" Paul was trying to lull him with this sad confession, but Mills saw the glint of the switchblade coming alive in his other hand. Before he could thrust it, Mills lunged, knocking his arm aside, and buried his fingernails into Paul's dark face.

Paul stumbled back, pitching the knife skyward. They dropped together onto the snow, Mills's stomach pressed against Paul's chest, his knees scrambling on the island Paul's body made. The air left their lungs. Mills gouged his fingers into fat and tissue until he felt warm liquid. Paul was stronger, writhing under him with compact arms and legs. From a distance, for a millisecond, they could have looked like two creatures mating on ice.

Paul groaned in pain, his teeth stained in blood. He gathered his fist. Mills took a blow to the jaw that sent him rolling. Blue amoebas filled his vision, and when he opened his eyes they dissolved into clouds, the moon searching through them like a flashlight. His breath was short, and his jaw throbbed. Paul launched another fist, but Mills continued to roll, and snow scattered in the cold. Mills found his legs, wobbly, and held onto the ground to steady them. Paul crawled away in search of the knife, his feet trailing through blood-spotted white. His glasses had fallen off behind him in the snow. Mills rushed toward the frames and broke them in his fist. He tossed them as far as he could. Paul pivoted on a knee and rose. He had the knife in his hand, but blood poured from his forehead and cheeks. His eyes were potholed, empty craters he was struggling to see out of. Paul sliced the air with the blade, stepping forward, slashing at the blurry figure in front of him. Neither of them cried for help, each for his own reasons. Each had his own need to escape unseen and alone.

Mills drifted back to the log pile and picked up a split of wood. Paul must have heard him, because he started running toward the water. He disappeared through the grasses, which sucked him up like food. Mills followed, fighting through the blades. He heard Paul's heavy breath hurtling down the slope, releasing a trail of weeds that slapped Mills's chest and face. He would kill him if he could, he would drag Paul's body into the backyard and shove the pages from Jeff Trader's journal in his mouth, one by one, till he choked. Paul clamored on the rocks, swatting the frost winds as if they too needed killing, and Mills swung, cracking the log on Paul's shoulder. Mills grabbed for him but pulled his arm back to avoid the gashing motion of the knife.

Paul dropped into the Sound, breaking through the thin ice, and climbed frantically onto his wooden boat. The skiff strained in the water under his weight. Mills tried to grab the mooring hook, but Paul thrust a pole against the rocks, leaking the boat backward between the ice sheets.

"You little shit," he called, wiping the blood from his eyes. *You little shit*, a Benchley pet name. Mills heard him whimper followed by the whipping of the engine cord. Paul fell twice before he got the motor started. It hacked sickly diesel; then, ten feet out, the bow light came on, yellowing the ice and half the shore. "Where are you? I can't see. How am I supposed to explain?" The shore didn't answer. Nothing in the landscape did.

Mills stood just beyond the light. By the time Sarakit's body was found, he knew Paul would find his explanation. Paul might even accuse Mills Chevern of attacking him, but by then Mills Chevern would cease to exist.

Paul's light grew small as the boat reversed into the Sound. When it was safely out of range, Mills raced into the backyard to retrieve his duffel bag. Even if the truth about Paul's identity came out, Mills knew that he would still be blamed for the murders. Paul would see to that. And if they did find that murdered boy on the tip, how could they prove who he was? Paul had already cremated his mother and father. The boy would probably be left unclaimed, a nameless victim of an unknown crime. Mills knew he had no choice.

He returned to the rocks, following the shoreline west. The coast swerved past the black, defeated houses of weekenders and year-rounders, asleep or exiled to safer ground. As he ran, he stared out at the water and found the frail yellow light of Paul's boat. It was zipping the wrong way across the Sound, east instead of west, its captain disoriented without his glasses, his eyelids drowsy with blood. The marsh waters thickened with ice as the coast arced toward the causeway. Stalks of phragmites trembled through the water's surface. The invasive weeds survived in the worst conditions.

In front of him, the causeway was lit by red-and-blue strobes, but few cars passed through the police barricade so late. The officers dozed in their heated cabs, boots crossed on their dashboards. Far off, the light on Paul's boat pinpricked, blinked, and grew stronger. He must have realized he was headed the wrong way, toward ocean instead of land, that where he wanted to go had been behind him. The tiny molecule of light shot west across the Sound before suddenly its drone went quiet. The boat light froze in the center of the water. When Mills concentrated, he heard a pull cord thrashing a choking motor, but the hum didn't return and the bright molecule remained in place.

Mills couldn't walk on the land that led to Long Island and the city beyond. The shore snaked too near to the patrol cars. He'd have to try his weight on the ice. He pressed his foot on the shallow, frozen inlet. It cracked delicately, and veins grew from his shoe, but it held. He trusted his other foot one step beyond his first. The ice crumpled but didn't split. He slid over the water, skating without blades, and when he looked behind him the boat was still stuck out at sea. He pictured Paul there, marooned in the Sound, too far from dry land to swim, his adopted home so close that, if he still had his glasses, he could make out his distant roof and the dying fire in his windows. He was a man trapped on a boat half a mile from his house, and Mills was running across the water toward nowhere as fast as he could. The western lights flickered, the trees reached out from shore, his homeland beckoned somewhere in front of him, alive in the darkness beyond his arms. It had no choice but to take him back.

He ran.

Acknowledgments

While this novel is entirely fictional and I've made a beautiful village on the North Fork far darker than its reality, I want to thank the residents of Orient—weekenders and year-rounders alike—for their kindness and patience during my years of research and writing. Any adverse reaction to the license I've taken in re-inventing Orient should not be directed toward those who helped along the way (they are innocent, I swear). I also want to thank the following for their time, generosity, question fielding, or occasional use of a spare bedroom: Wade Guyton, Thomas Alexander, Joseph Logan, T. J. Wilcox, Todd Huckleberry, Kelley Walker, Elizabeth Peyton, Rob Pruitt, Jonathan Horowitz, Ted Webb, A. M. Homes, Jill Dunbar, Steven Shareshian, Leo Bersani, James Oakley, Cathryn Summerhayes, and the Orient Country Store for their egg sandwiches.

My writing doesn't always feel like much until I get it into the hands of my friend and agent Bill Clegg, who guided me through every tangle and dead end. I'm forever grateful for his support. I want to thank the team at Harper for their enthusiasm and eagle eyes, particularly my editor Calvert Morgan who basically played co-detective in smoothing out the tosses and turns of the mystery and the prose. Also thanks to Kathleen Baumer for her crucial input. The team at Simon & Schuster U.K., Jo Dickinson, Rowan Cope, and Jessica Leeke, were essential flashlights in helping this book find its footing. Thanks again to Thomas Alexander for his notes along the way.

Finally, thanks to my mother and sister, George Miscamble, Ana and Danko Steiner, David Armstrong, *Interview* magazine, my grandmother, to whom I trace the familial interest in mysteries, and everyone who had to listen to me talk endlessly about Orient over the years.

Insights,
Interviews
& More . . .

Christopher Bollen

Original credit to Jefferson Hack and AnOther Magazine. *Used with permission.*

CHRISTOPHER BOLLEN is a Manhattan-based novelist, writer, and Editor at Large of *Interview,* the legendary pop magazine founded by Andy Warhol in 1969. Originally from Cincinnati, Ohio, Bollen moved to New York to study English and American Literature at Columbia University, from which he graduated Summa Cum Laude in 1998. Along with working at *Interview,* he's also contributed to some of the most respected publications, including the *New York Times, Artforum,* and *The Believer.* Following the success of his debut novel, *Lightning People,* in 2011, the forty-year-old fiction author presents his new book, *Orient.* To mark the long-awaited release, here Bollen answers Jefferson Hack's personal version of the famous Proust Questionnaire, discussing life achievements, the greatness of spontaneity and childhood memories.

What are you thinking of right now?

Greece. I'm trying to figure out my next novel set on an island in Greece, and as I tend to do in the early stages of writing, my mind races and u-turns and nearly topples over cliff edges in the attempt to assemble a workable story. It's really a full-time obsession—and sadly, even though it's set in Greece, not much of a mental vacation.

What makes you laugh?

I laugh too much. I've actually been told this as if it were some sort of character flaw. But so much makes me laugh: strange looks from people passing by, awkward incidents related by friends in the course of their day, dogs pooping on the sidewalk, Graham Greene novels, Fran Lebowitz, texts from my friend Tom.

What makes you cry?

I don't do this activity as often. On average, I cry maybe once every six months. A few weeks ago I cried while reading a memoir and I couldn't remember the last time a book brought me to tears. In the past few years, I tend to cry if I think about my father, who died in November 2012.

What do you consider to be the greatest invention?

I'm going to say the coffee maker. I still can't figure out how it boils and filters hot coffee so quickly. It's the veritable printing press around my apartment in the mornings.

Do you have a mentor or inspirational figure that has guided or influenced you?

It's always saddened me that I had no particular mentor in my early years— ▶

3

perhaps an older New York writer who would take me under their wing and steer me down certain paths. I've always blamed that on AIDS and all of the creative spirits who died so young in the generations before mine. We really lost more than we can ever measure by that disease.

Where do you feel most at home?

New York City. It's really the only place that will have me. I've lived here for nineteen years now (in about fifteen different apartments). Your home is not supposed to surprise you, but New York does every single day.

Where are you right now?

Seat 17A, economy window, on an American Airlines Boeing twinjet two-thirds of the way over the Atlantic Ocean from London to New York. Altitude: 34,000 feet. Dinner: Beef or pasta?

What is your proudest achievement in work?

Switching gears. As much as I've loved working as an editor in magazines—and I continue to do so, usually joyfully—I really always wanted to write fiction, and I'm glad I stopped, leaned against a wall, took a breath, and at age thirty, said, "What happened to that novel you were always promising yourself you'd write?" So I wrote it. And then I wrote another one. I'm proud of being able to move in different directions. It's never too late.

What is your proudest achievement in life?

To be filled in later in pen when I either A) have a child or B) find homes for every abandoned dog. In the meantime, I'm going to write this answer in pencil: staying relatively sane, trying to be an empathetic person who cares about and listens to others, not always needing to be in the center, and also that I still read one novel a week.

4

What do you most dislike about contemporary culture?

The acceleration of constant distraction and the loss of distance: both hinder the imagination.

What do you most like about the age we live in?

Online chess. I would never have learned this highly addictive, brilliant game without it. Now please someone delete it from my phone. I can't stop playing it. Actually, the real answer is also found in the answer to the last question: the loss of distance due to the Internet has also created supportive communities for those who have no outlet in their own towns and neighborhoods. And that's a wonderful thing: finding others like you.

At what points do life and work intersect?

I used to spend sleepless nights wondering if my entire life was eclipsed by work, even down to my friendships. I don't worry about that anymore. If you're very lucky, work and life move fluidly together and they build constantly off each other. It's part of my job to grab the scraps of the world that interest me and mine it.

What's the best advice you've been given?

"Hurry up." Because you have to do as much as you can with what you're given and time is the most democratic institution there is. We all, hopefully, get roughly the same amount and you better utilize it. Hurry. Don't wait.

What is the biggest risk you've ever taken?

After college I moved to Venice, Italy. I didn't want to leave the warm pocket of New York I had found, but I went alone and I stayed for several months and that single decision at the age of twenty-three transformed me. It made me fall in love with the world. ▶

Christopher Bollen *(continued)*

Recommend a book or poem that has changed your perspective on life?

It's an obvious one, but I still find myself quoting lines from
T. S. Elliot's "The Wasteland." It holds inside of it so many raw
truths. "These fragments I have shored against my ruins. . . .
Shantih, shantih, shantih"—peace passeth understanding.

What is your earliest childhood memory?

No one believes me, and I'm not sure if I believe me anymore,
or if this memory is merely some very early induction based on
the story someone told me, but I swear I remember lying under
a bright light on a surgical table at about six months old while
doctors are crowded around me: I had pyloric stenosis and I was
having an operation to remove the blockage in my intestines.
I remember my father coming into the unit. And that's it. Just
that memory, the light, the doctors, my father, then darkness.
But I do have the scar across my stomach.

What's the most important relationship in your life?

This seems like a dodge, because I have so many people in my
life that I love so much it almost frightens me, but, as I'm just
releasing a novel into the world, I'm going to say the reader, the
one I don't know, who takes a chance and follows my story. It's
really a miraculous relationship between writer and reader, and
I think it's generous in both ways: I always find it very generous
that someone has taken five or eight or ten hours out of their busy
lives to read something I wrote.

What's the most romantic action you've taken?

I did buy someone I love plant-cultivation classes at the New York
Botanical Gardens. Why give flowers when you can give the gift
of growing them? A very edifying romantic action, I think,
although I didn't have to wake up early every Saturday morning
and take the subway to the Bronx for the lessons.

What's the most spiritual action you've taken?

A writer friend once said to me that she struggles every day *not* to find God. And I agree. I was raised Catholic and I feel like I spent my teens and early twenties stripping religion from my life. Now that I'm older, I do see the beauty and community and the drowning of the ego in it too. Occasionally, I will creep into a church and sit in the back pews or line up on Ash Wednesday and get ashes on my forehead. But really the most spiritual action for me lies in travel. I'm a humanist and there is something approaching God in seeing how others on the opposite side of the planet live and work and take care of their families.

If you could wish for one change in the world what would it be?

Better, less expensive health care for everyone. And while I'm at it, I'm willing to reconsider the invention of a microchip placed in the brain that instantly allows you to speak foreign languages. I used to be opposed to that idea, but I've yet again just stopped Italian classes. I am never going to learn this damn language on my own. ❧

Writing *Orient*

A version of this essay was originally published on literarysofa.com.

I HAVE COME TO REALIZE I suffer a rare condition: perfect contentment in writing in Manhattan. I've never understood the age-old lament that it's impossible to get decent writing done in the city due to all of its distractions and noise—as if we're rhythmic gymnasts whose routines keep getting interrupted by traffic jams. I've written both of my novels—*Lightning People* and now *Orient*—in the cramped bedrooms of rented downtown apartments, at a tiny walnut desk, more often than not, five feet from my mattress. That being said, the idea for my second novel actually sprung from a trip out of town. I was finishing the edits on my first book, and some friends had recently bought a country house in Orient. Orient is a quiet fishing village on the far North Fork of Long Island—located at the tip and connected to the rest of the island by a long, narrow causeway between the Long Island Sound and Gardiners Bay.

I had already been to Orient for summer weekends several times, freeloading at the rentals of artist friends who had refused the usual city migration to the South Fork (with its crowded, obscenely expensive Hamptons beach communities) and who had staked out the tranquil, under-the-radar North Fork as a potential art haven. For a few years, my friend, the artist Wade Guyton, had rented the converted stables of the former Bird's Eye (as in frozen vegetables) estate. The ramshackle house overlooked a settlers' graveyard, and while we were all convinced the place was haunted, I'm afraid I was usually so drowsy with wine by the end of the night that I felt no otherworldly visitations even if the ghosts did come calling.

But for this trip, I was going to a different house alone. I drove my rental car east on the Long Island Expressway, crossed the causeway, and found the tiny, two-story clapboard on the edge of the tiny historic village that would be mine for an entire week. It felt like the perfect place to work. Maybe the city and my slowly perishing air-condition unit were conspiring to keep me from great reservoirs of literary flow after all. The house's interior had already been stripped of its past—the trim and wallpaper gone—and had yet to be renovated into its next life. But I liked the emptiness of the rooms, with the yellow sunlight pouring through the hand-blown glass panes, and out the back was a view of long sword grass blowing in the fields and the blue ribbon of the Bay studded with sailboats. I set a wicker table on the back porch, and there I got to work, often glancing up from my Word document to marvel at the beauty and silence of the landscape: birds and deer and the hypnotic, fluttering branches of a maple tree. I couldn't believe how close I was to the city, but a million miles from its chaos. I felt lucky and envious at the same time. This is what I had been missing, not just as a writer but as a ▶

Writing *Orient* *(continued)*

human being—the nature, the animal air, the ability to walk on grass without a subway rumbling twenty feet below it. A passing neighbor waved to me. I waved back as if it were a normal activity: waving at neighbors, smiling, going about one's day in a yard by the sea.

Then the night crept in. Darkness swallowed the house, not little by little but snakelike, entirely. I turned on the few lamps there were, and the walls, which had looked so provincially charming by day, were slashed with marks as if some previous captive had tried to claw his way through them. The stairs to the upstairs bedrooms were broken and slanted. Most of the light switches didn't work, and the ones that did involved chains hanging mid-way into rooms, forcing me to swat for them in the dark. And the sounds—out the window was total blackness, but strange noises broke, squeaks and invisible bodies moving through bushes. The house had stood empty, and now it wasn't, evident by the light in the windows, and I suddenly—and irrationally—felt vulnerable for my absolute unfamiliarity with the village or its ways of escape. I knew I was being ridiculous—me, who had lived in some of the worst crime-ridden neighborhoods in New York and occasionally forgot to lock my apartment door at night. I simultaneously wanted to burst out laughing and sleep with a knife under my pillow. The thing is, I had never spent a night alone in the country before; the sounds of a house settling or raccoons digging through the garden were entirely foreign to me.

It was an awful night, I barely shut my eyes, and simply going to the bathroom stirred up all of the horror-movie conventions I had unknowingly memorized since childhood. When morning came, there it all was again: the peaceful, beautiful, benign Orient, neighbors waving, the water sparkling, a child riding a bike. I had always wanted to write a murder mystery, being something of an Agatha Christie fanatic in my pre-teen years. It dawned on me on that weeklong visit that Orient was a perfect place to set a series of disturbing crimes—a village connected to the mainland by a slender thread of road, and a community undergoing a strange gentrification of rich, city artists buying up weekend houses from families that had lived there for generations. I was struck by my own embarrassing experience: a dream by day, and a nightmare after the sun went down. That trip was really the impetus for the novel that became *Orient*.

In my mind, the book had all the proper ingredients for both a thriller and a piece of literary fiction—all the discordant lives intertwining on this rather unexpected shelf off of the Long Island Sound. I used Christie as a sort of model—in terms of structure but not in terms of writing style. Many research trips to Orient ensued, many long stays, many notes and wanderings, many conversations with locals and new arrivals.

What I attempted to do in *Orient* was to make a cross-pollination of so many stories and genres that it would be relevant and readable on so many different levels. It's relevant because it refuses to stick to one section of the bookstore or library—it's a thriller or mystery but it's literary fiction at its core. It's a city book, but it's also set in the country. There are relevant themes to today's society—art, homosexuality, abortion, divorce, marriage, wealth, the environment, land, gentrification, and greed. I tried to play off all connotations and denotations of the word "orient"— the east, the exotic, but also how you physically locate yourself in space and time, sexual orientation, orientation as in arrival, disorientation of the mind. And, for me, it was especially exciting to write about America outside of the bubble of Manhattan. I visited Orient continually for research. But I wrote most of it in the safety of my East Village bedroom. ◠

Eight Books That Influenced the Writing of *Orient*

No BOOK EXISTS alone on a shelf. While one of our leading literary critics famously found influence to be a source of anxiety, I tend to see it as a welcoming guide. After all, what is the prompt for becoming a writer? Being pinned to the floor by the intensity of a book and the little wish to do the same to others. What is true for me, re anxiety, is that I put myself on a reading diet when working on a novel. I can't read anything too similar in subject or form to the book I'm writing—i.e., I try not to read novels that are set in the exact location I've chosen, or, in the case of *Orient*, I steered clear of ones that focused on orphans or the art world. But there were moments when I was stuck on a scene and scurried to my library (or to the clumps of paperbacks around my desk) for inspiration—or simply the distraction of beautiful prose. On a list of research for this novel, you would find regional history and maritime books, a cache of news articles on Orient Point, mostly from the *Suffolk Times*, a film documentary on the reconstruction of Bug Lighthouse, years of visits to art galleries and friends' studios, and a huge stack of rental-car receipts for all my trips along the Long Island Expressway. The list below, however, is reserved for the works of literature that sunk their teeth into me and wouldn't let go. They helped me understand how to build my *Orient* ecosystem.

My Ántonia by Willa Cather

This is the only novel I actually name-check in *Orient*. What blows me away about the book is how Cather manages to evoke the sights, smells, customs, and conflicts of the Nebraska prairie so richly and convincingly it's as if the reader is pioneering right alongside the characters. Her descriptions of weather and seasons, especially, are breath stopping. I can't think of another writer who nails her setting so exquisitely—to the point that even the more vicious moments of the book bleed perfectly into the environment. I also happen to love this novel because I picked it up quite randomly in a tiny bookstore in Montana, and my gut told me this was the right read for the trip. Always trust that spooky instinct.

In Cold Blood by Truman Capote

Wait, I can think of another author who's an ace at painting the mood of a place. My god, *In Cold Blood* is a masterpiece. It's built like a cuckoo clock, an innocent, pastoral shell that hides a ruthless, ticking instrument. What particularly floors me about Capote's crime story is how he juggles so many competing narratives—the horrified locals of Holcomb, Kansas; the police on their desperate hunt for the assailants; Perry and Dick on their terrifying road-to-nowhere odyssey. But Capote never belittles or cheapens ▶

any of his characters. He shows that you can sympathize with the victims and still have empathy for and a strange fascination with the killers.

Murder on the Orient Express by Agatha Christie

I would be remiss if I didn't mention a Christie. When I set to work writing a literary murder mystery, I didn't want the literary aspect to outshine the pleasure of a well-orchestrated whodunit. And no one could put a puzzle together like the Queen of Crime. It's astonishing that she penned some seventy-eight mystery novels and always found a new twist, an unlikely villain, or a means of misdirection with which to throw her reader off balance. While *Murder on the Orient Express* isn't my absolute favorite Christie (that would be *And Then There Were None*), I kept thinking of *Orient Express* as a kind of forebear while writing *Orient*—almost as a way of saying to myself when handling the plot: be clever, be clever, be clever. And, of course, my novel is called *Orient*, so there's a little bit of Christie built into it. I hope I'm not giving too much away by confessing that, no, everyone isn't guilty in my book. At least, not of murder.

The Swimming Pool Library by Alan Hollinghurst

Every writer faces a challenge when introducing a new character—not just what do they look like, but how do I describe this person with authenticity? Finding interesting ways to depict humans could be a full-time job unto itself. But if you want an author who is a genius at portraying bodies—the shadow and sweat and weight and movement of them—Hollinghurst is your man. He renders each human form like a painter, stroke by careful stroke. He's also pretty damn exceptional at minds. *The Swimming Pool Library* is flush with wit and sex and various sizes and shapes of gay men throughout history and their loves and struggles. It's an addictive, passionate read.

The Great Gatsby by F. Scott Fitzgerald

I know what you're thinking: too obvious. But hear me out. Everyone perceives *The Great Gatsby* as the ultimate New York

City novel. I happen to believe it is, in fact, the ultimate Long Island novel. Since I, too, was tackling Long Island—granted, the North Fork instead of the North Shore—I had to face the brilliant, glittery specter of Gatsby. It's one of my favorite novels, filled with that perfect mix of glamour and dirt under the fingernails. It's pure literature of the American East, but I will point out, it's also a murder mystery that resolves with the framing of the wrong man.

After Henry by Joan Didion

For all of the much-deserved love Joan Didion receives, this collection of essays from 1992 seems perpetually overlooked, maybe because it homes in on culture and politics more than it does on intimacy. Like so many writers of my generation, I've learned a lot from Didion, and *After Henry* has all of her tough, moody prose but also a set of x-ray eyes that sees through all of the performances and false fronts of the American psyche. Didion is thought of as a California writer, but fearsome things happen when she moves east.

Leaving the Atocha Station by Ben Lerner

In so many novels, meeting a character is like going on a first date. You get the impression that the author really, really wants you to like every quality—even the quirky ones, especially the quirky ones—of the protagonist. So I was impressed by Lerner's willingness in this excellent travel novel to construct a main character that isn't all that loveable. He lies, he's confused, he's selfish, and he's not apologetic about it. And because of those glitches, Lerner's character truly lives on the page.

Unnatural Causes by P. D. James

This inclusion is a bit of a cheat, because I read it after I finished the first draft of *Orient*. But I was so taken with it, I feel it makes a rather nice companion. James is a mystery writer who also pens gorgeous prose. She sets her murder thriller in a seaside hamlet where life imitates art, but the real treasure is her detective, Adam Dalgliesh. In the annals of mystery fiction, detectives are far too cool and composed; they're generally impassive players in the ▶

Eight Books That Influenced the Writing of
Orient (continued)

plot who care little about the emotional toll of the case they're solving. Here, Dalgliesh gets dumped by his girlfriend in the opening chapters. Now that's a detective I want to follow. ∾

Discover great authors, exclusive offers, and more at hc.com.